The Expansion Team

LISA SUZANNE

VEGAS HEAT: THE EXPANSION TEAM
THE COMPLETE SERIES
© Lisa Suzanne 2025

This book is a work of fiction. Any similarities to real people, living or dead, is purely coincidental. All characters and events in this work are figments of the author's imagination.

Cover Design: Najla Qamber Designs
Content Editing: It's Your Story Content Editing

Books by Lisa Suzanne

VEGAS HEAT: BASES LOADED
Scoring Position (Book 1)
Caught Looking (Book 2)
On Deck (Book 3)
Bases Loaded (Book 4)
Grand Slam (Book 5)

VEGAS ACES
Home Game (Book 1)
Long Game (Book 2)
Fair Game (Book 3)
Waiting Game (Book 4)
End Game (Book 5)

Click the QR Code below to visit
Lisa on Amazon for more titles:

Dedication

As always, for Team M.

Curveball

Chapter 1
Cooper

"**T**hanks for inviting me to the club tonight, man," I say to my buddy Troy as we wait near the bar to order another round.

I don't really want to be here, but when Troy Bodine calls with an offer to hang out at the club he owns in Vegas, it's a hard offer to turn down.

And so here I am.

"This floor is great, but the third floor isn't really my thing." It's not a sex club, per se, but more of a place for the rich and famous to hang out where sex happens to take place on level three.

"I had ulterior motives," Troy admits.

Color me shocked. Troy *always* has ulterior motives. "You always do." I offer an easy laugh to dispel the accusation in my voice.

"I'm sure you've heard by now the expansion team was approved," he tells me. "Las Vegas is getting a new baseball team, and they've given me an offer to be the manager. I want you to come play for me."

I shake my head, maintaining my cool despite the tightness in my chest at his words. Of course I've heard, but I haven't really been following the news about it. It affected my former life, I suppose, but it doesn't affect what I'm doing now in San Diego. "Nah, man. I've been out of the game for years. You don't want me."

"Is the elbow healed?" he asks.

I nod. "Yeah. Surgery pieced me back together, but I'm far from being ready to play." I've been enjoying my fair share of pizza and beer in between my work for StrongFitKids, an organization designed to offer affordable fitness to kids, and I haven't tried tossing a ball twenty feet since my surgery, let alone the hundred twenty feet or more it takes to get the ball from third to first base.

Troy laughs. "Then it's a good thing we've got five months of off-season training before we need to head into pre-season training."

He's not wrong. If I put in the work, I'll see quick results. It's like riding a bike, right? Baseball was my life from the time I was seven until I dislocated my elbow at thirty. You don't just lose your love for the game even though you've been out of it a few years. "You really want me to unretire? I don't know. I mean, I miss the game, of course. I loved every second of playing. But I've got some good shit going on now, too."

"Listen, Coop. You know how these expansion drafts go. Everyone holds tight to their best players, and we get our pick from the leftovers. We need you. We need a born leader. We need someone to be the face of the Vegas Heat, and I want that someone to be you.""The Vegas Heat?" I repeat, a chill running up my spine as the words leave my mouth for the first time. Vegas isn't really in my blood the way it is for some people, and I've been out of the game three years now. But the Vegas Heat? "That's a kickass name."

The couple in front of us turns around, and I recognize Tristan Higgins, a wide receiver for the Vegas Aces. "Hey man," he says to me.

I nod a friendly greeting to the kid, and I turn back to Troy. "Let me think about it."

I can't just throw out a yes the second he asks when I'm half-drunk in the middle of the desert. I need to analyze it from every angle, but I also need to make him sweat it out.

"If it's a yes, I need you here by September first," he says.

I nod. "You'll have an answer by then."

We each order another drink—a beer for me, some whiskey for him—and as we're waiting, a woman sidles up to Troy and whispers in his ear.

He glances at me. "If you'll excuse me, I have something I need to tend to. Enjoy yourself."

The bartender sets our drinks in front of us, and I nod my thanks.

"Thanks, man," I say to Troy. I take my beer, drink down half of it, and bolt.

He got his words in, and as nice as the exclusivity of this club is, it's just not the place for me.

Troy offered me his personal driver, so I have him take me back to Caesars Palace, the hotel where I'm staying on the Strip. It's early, and I'm in Vegas. I'm not just going to head up and go to bed, so on the way back, I send out a few texts to see what my buddies in town are up to.

And I come up empty.

Baseball is in season, so my friends that still play the game are busy tonight. I know a few local football players, but they're in preseason now and nobody's available tonight—and a handful of them were at Troy's club. I check in with a few other friends, but everyone's busy.

I stare out the window at the flashing lights of Las Vegas Boulevard as we get closer to my hotel.

Could I really live here?

I was raised a Cubs fan in the suburbs of Chicago but chose to play for UCLA and eventually worked my way up from the minors to the Dodgers, where I played my entire seven-year career.

My mom is still back in the Chicago suburb where she raised me, but my life is in California now. I love San Diego even though it's a little too close to my ex up in Los Angeles. I love what I'm doing now with StrongFitKids. I feel like I'm making an impact, and I'm working with kids—exactly what I wanted to do after I stopped playing the game.

But if I'm being honest, I'm also a little bored. I need something new and exciting to focus on.

There are certain things I wanted out of life by my age, and it feels like the decisions I've made along the way have prevented those things from happening.

I thought by nearly thirty-three I'd be married and have a few kids running around. Instead, I have zero prospects on the horizon. After a brutal end to a five-year relationship, I'm more than a little reticent to get back in the game. I just want to have a little fun.

I guess I'm reticent to get back into more than one game.

I wasn't ready to be done playing ball, but when I dislocated my elbow and tore my UCL, I knew I had a long recovery ahead. The Tommy John surgery following my injury two years ago was a success, but it was only recently that I started to feel back to my old self again.

I'm nervous to pick up a ball, though.

My life is different now than it was then.

What if I reinjure it? What if I injure something else?

7

On the other hand, I could just ease myself back into both games. Maybe I need to look at it as a way to get a little fun and excitement back into what has become a rather monotonous existence.

It's a risk, but everything in life is a risk. You either sit on the sidelines or play in the game.

And I think I want to play in the game again.

Talking with Troy tonight felt very much like I was in the right place at the right time.

Well, metaphorically. Coax isn't really the right place for me, but Vegas very well could be.

I thank the driver and get out of the car. As I walk through the casino toward the bank of elevators, not sure what comes next now that I know I want to jump into not one but two games again, my eyes fall onto the blackjack tables. I glance ahead toward the high-limit area. I'm sure I could get a private table if I wanted one, but tonight…well, since I'm into playing games, I park my ass in the first chair I see and toss a few bills onto the table.

Game on.

Chapter 2
Gabby

"Happy Birthday!" my group of girls yells at me as we clink our glasses together. I chug down the champagne faster than I should, but I'm fine.

It's not like it's the first time I've had champagne despite the fact that it's my twenty-first birthday.

We just came from a club and took a quick detour at the casino bar for a glass of champagne before we head to the next club. "Let's play blackjack," I suggest, wanting to try everything I can now that it's legal.

"I want to try the slots," Cassie says, and a few of the other girls opt for the slots, too.

"I'll come with you," my best friend Mia says.

"Meet back here in a half hour?" I suggest, and everyone nods.

Mia and I head toward the first blackjack table with two open chairs we see, and there's a super hot guy sitting there playing by himself.

"Mind if we join?" I ask the table in general since I don't really know the etiquette. The man on the other side of the table doesn't look up from his chips, and the dealer eyes Mia and me.

"IDs please," the dealer says as we sit, and I reach into my wallet and proudly hand it over as Mia does the same.

"Happy birthday," she says, and I thank her as I slide the card back into my wallet and toss a hundred-dollar bill onto the table like I know what I'm doing.

"It's your birthday?" the man on the other side of the table asks.

When I glance up at him, our eyes connect across the small table. My jaw falls open as a beam of heat seems to pass between the two of us, as if our eyes have powered some electrical connection the likes of which this planet has never seen before.

The room goes silent and it's as if we're the only two people in it, in the casino, in Vegas...in the entire world. It's surreal, some out of body experience as I feel like I'm looking into my future, like I already know this man even though I've never met him before.

He's a little older than me, but it's hard to tell how much older. His blue eyes light with surprise as they focus on mine, like he feels the same thing I'm feeling, this weird feeling like my life's about to change.

He runs a hand through his dark hair and then along his jaw peppered with the sexiest scruff I think I've ever seen in my life. It's not quite a beard, but it's almost a beard that covers a chiseled, strong jawline.

Even just sitting at a blackjack table, he looks like he could command the attention of every single person in this room.

Mia elbows me, pulling me out of my trance, and the volume in the room turns back up as I realize I'm staring.

My cheeks flush as my voice seems to return to me, but I have to clear my throat before any words squeak out. "Yes, it is."

"Happy birthday," he says, and he shoots me a smile.

But it's not *just* a smile.

It's absolutely devastating. It's the kind of smile that burrows into your soul, the kind of smile that makes me want to take him upstairs to my hotel room.

My eyes flick down to his lips.

It's the kind of smile that makes me dream of what those lips taste like. What they'd feel like on mine, on my body.

Damn.

"Have you ever played blackjack before?" he asks.

I shake my head. "Want to teach me?" I'm flirting, but I can't help it. How do you *not* flirt with Hottie McHotFace? It's my body's natural response.

He laughs, his lips tipping up into a warm smile, and a tingle runs from my chest all the way down to my toes.

"Sure. Come here," he says, patting the chair beside him, and I practically fall off my chair to get to him.

The dealer pushes chips over toward Mia first and then toward me in my new seat next to Hottie McCuteGuy. I glance at his hands, and good gravy even *they* are hot. They're all strong and lean, like the rest of him, and the sudden image of those hands on my body flashes through my brain.

Welp, I know that's an image that'll stay with me a while.

I blow out a breath.

It's just blackjack, Gabby. Focus on the cards. He's just being nice. Plus he's like...older. There's no way he'd be interested. Slow your roll.

"Put two chips on the circle," he says, and his voice is all gruff and deep and even *that* is sexy.

Geez, this dude.

"Two chips?" I ask.

"Oh, man, you really are a newbie. It's a ten-dollar table, so yeah, two chips equals ten bucks." He nods toward the little sign that tells us it's a ten-dollar table, and I nod...and then I watch as he takes a few chips off the top of his pile in the circle.

"Why'd you do that?" I ask.

"I'm not betting a hundred bucks a hand with a total newb playing next to me."

I giggle. "I know the basics. I've played at home with my dad before, just never in a real casino."

"Prove it."

The dealer, whose nametag reads Kelly, deals the hand, setting a card each in front of Mia, me, and Hottie McHotStuff, face up, and then she deals one to herself face down.

"What about you?" he asks Mia, and the slightest twinge of jealousy bolts through me that he's talking to her rather than me.

I brush it off.

He's just a guy at a table being friendly to the birthday girl.

Scratch that. He's just a *hot* guy at a table being friendly to the birthday girl.

"I've played a couple times," she says.

The dealer gives us each another card before placing one face-up on top of her other one that's face down.

The dealer is showing a seven. I glance at Mia's cards. She has a ten and an eight, and she waves her hand to stay.

I look down at my own cards. I have a three and a six.

"The object is to beat the dealer, and a nine doesn't beat a seventeen, assuming she's got a ten under there. So tap the table if you want another card," the hot guy tells me.

"I thought the object was to get to twenty-one," I say, narrowing my eyes at him.

He shakes his head. "You want to get closer to twenty-one than the dealer without going over. If she has a sixteen or less, she has to take another card."

I tap the table, and she gives me a queen.

"Nineteen," he says. "Wave your hand if you want to stand at nineteen."

"What if I want another card?" I ask.

"Then I'm going to another table," he mutters.

I giggle and wave my hand.

He has a twenty, so he stays, and the dealer flips over a ten, giving her a seventeen, which means we all win.

He holds up a fist, and I bump his with mine.

And then I freaking die right there on the spot as his hand touches mine for the first time. It's a simple, friendly gesture, but in my semi-champagne-tipsy state, it feels like something else entirely.

My face flames as heat seems to engulf me, and a waitress comes by just then.

"A glass of champagne, please," I order, and Mia gets one, too.

"Miller Lite." He throws another poker chip on top of his pile.

"Do I need to do that, too?" I ask.

He shrugs. "Up to you. I don't know your budget, but when I win, I stack one winning chip on top of the pile."

I do the same, and Mia does, too. My budget went out the window when I sat next to Hottie McSexyPants.

Yeah, another glass of champagne is a great idea right about now.

We all win another round, and on our third hand, the dealer deals me an Ace. She sets my other card face down. "Why'd she do that?" I whisper.

"She's teasing you," he whispers back.

I don't really know what that means, so I wait my turn. She flips my card over when it gets to me, and sure enough, it's a jack.

"Twenty-one," he says, and I let out a little whoop. "Hold your cheer until she shows her cards. If she's got twenty-one, you tie."

My brows dip. "What?" I nearly screech. "I might not win with twenty-one?"

He shrugs. "That's the way the cookie crumbles, babe."

Babe.

Oh my God.

Did he really just call me *babe?*

Hottie McGorgeous just called me *babe?*

I die again. Right there on the spot.

The dealer flips her card, and she has a six. She pays me my money with a little extra for the blackjack on top, and she finishes the hand with Mia and the hottie. He wins, she loses, and we go again.

And again and again.

I've doubled my money after a half hour, and not only do I still not know this guy's name, but I'm also supposed to be meeting my friends.

Mia, who has *not* doubled her money, cashes in her chips. "It's time to go meet everyone."

"I think I want to play here a little longer," I say. It's my birthday, and I'm winning and having fun laughing and drinking with this sexy stranger at my table.

Maybe I want to get a little crazy tonight. Would that be so bad?

I'm in freaking Vegas. I'm twenty-one now. I want to live a little, and what better way to celebrate my birthday than flirting a little longer with Hottie McHandsome?

"I'll tell them," she says.

"Thanks, Mia." I shoot her a furtive grin on her way by, and she lets out a little laugh.

"Your friend's name is Mia?" the hot guy asks, and that little pang of jealousy darts through me again. Is he interested in her? "Should I call you Mia's friend, birthday girl, babe…or something else?"

I laugh. "Birthday girl or babe would be fine, but my name's Gabby."

"Nice to meet you, Gabby," he says, and the way my name rolls off his tongue sends a shiver right down my spine. "I'm Cooper."

"Nice to meet you, Cooper." And then, because I'm a huge dork apparently, I stick out my hand for him to shake. He chuckles and grabs it in his, and damn if I don't feel the launching of a million butterflies flapping way down low in my belly as they ascend all the way into my chest.

"Thanks for teaching me how to play blackjack."

"My pleasure." He leans in close. "I can think of a few other things I could teach you."

My eyes widen as I catch his innuendo, or maybe the champagne is playing tricks on me.

"You know, like roulette or craps," he amends, and my cheeks flush at the gutter where I find my mind. I keep my eyes down on the table as I feel his gaze on my profile. "Wait a second. Were you thinking I was implying something else?"

I laugh a little nervously. "Baccarat?" I suggest, and he laughs.

"Yeah, that's what I was thinking, too." He winks at me, and I giggle. He really *is* flirting with me. It's not just my imagination.

I spot the girls across the way as they all stare at Cooper, and he notices them, too.

"Are those your girls?" he asks.

"Yeah," I say.

He waves at them, and they all squeal to my total and complete mortification.

"You want me to give them a show?" he asks.

My brows dip. "What does that even mean?"

He laughs, and before I realize what's happening, his hand finds the back of my head and he pulls me in until his lips crash down to mine.

A million different sensations hit me all at once as his lips move over mine. His are firm and commanding at the same time as they're gentle and tender. He smells like beer mixed with some sort of woodsy aftershave, and he intensifies the kiss as he opens his mouth and his tongue brushes mine. It's not tentative or nervous like the boys who've kissed me in the past. No, this is all man. He is one-hundred percent confident in what he's doing, and I have no issue sitting here allowing him to do it to me for the rest of the night.

Allowing him to do *whatever he wants* to me for the rest of the night.

I don't even know him, but I know feelings. I know attraction. This is it.

The room goes silent again as the only thing I hear is the rushing of blood through my body as it seems to come completely alive with his mouth covering mine.

He pulls back, and his eyes are hazy when they focus in on mine again.

"Whoa," I breathe, and he chuckles. The volume comes on again in the room, and I hear my friends squealing across the way.

He seems wholly unaffected while I'm just glad I'm sitting because my knees would've given out after that. He leans in toward me. "I've wanted to do that since you first sat down," he murmurs, and maybe we're both a little drunk…and maybe that's the recipe for the kind of twenty-first birthday I'll never forget.

Chapter 3
Cooper

Holy *fuck*.

I can't remember the last time I felt this sort of magnetic connection with another person. She's younger than me, but age is just a number, right? She looks like she's in her mid-twenties, eight or so years younger than me at most.

Maybe I felt it with Stacy back when we first met seven or eight years ago, back before she cheated on me and everything went to hell...but I don't remember ever feeling it with her.

And it's not just that.

She has no idea who I am.

There's something insanely hot about that.

And she's not just hot—though, to be fair, she *is* hot with her almost black hair falling in soft waves down to the middle of her back and the black dress she's wearing that showcases her mouthwatering tits and perfect little ass. She's also adorable and wide green eyes that make her look like she stepped out of a movie about princesses and the way she looks at me with curiosity like I'm a tiger who could pounce at any second.

Is it any wonder I had to know what she tasted like?

I wasn't disappointed.

Champagne mixed with cherries. Sweet with just the slightest edge of spice.

She's piqued my interest, that's for sure.

But I'm only in town for another thirty-six hours, and she's here celebrating her birthday. It's not like we're two people destined to end up together.

That doesn't mean we can't have a little fun over the next thirty-six hours, though. Except for the dinner date I have planned for tomorrow night.

"Feel free to do that again any time," she says, and her cheeks fill with color again.

I chuckle. "How long you in town for?"

"I live here," she says.

"I thought locals stayed off the Strip."

She shrugs. "We do, but we make exceptions for birthdays."

I laugh. "You staying here tonight?"

She nods. "The seven of us are sharing a suite upstairs. You?"

"I'm staying here, too. Just tonight and tomorrow night."

"Where are you heading to after that?" she asks.

"Home in San Diego."

She presses her lips together and nods, and I can't help but think I detect a little disappointment there. Maybe I'm projecting. Maybe I want her to be disappointed I'm not sticking around longer.

"Are you in town on vacation?" she asks.

I shake my head, wondering how to word the complicated situation that brought me to town. "A buddy invited me to town to talk about a job offer," I say, minimizing the extent of what really went down tonight.

Her wide eyes flutter up toward mine. "Are you going to take it?"

I shrug. "I don't know. What do you think I should do?" I don't know why I ask her. She doesn't know anything about my situation or what the job even is.

She chuckles. "Do you like what you're doing now?"

I nod.

"Then ask yourself whether you'd like the new job more." She shrugs. "Do whatever will bring you the most joy."

The way she says it so simply makes me think this is a conversation I'll revisit time and time again over the rest of my life. Honestly, it's solid advice for *any* major decision. *Do whatever will bring you the most joy.*

I think tonight…this girl is what will bring me the most joy.

"What about you?" I ask. "What do you do?"

"I'm in marketing," she says. "I also occasionally substitute teach dance classes for a friend whose sister owns a studio." She glances up and waves to her friends across the way, and it's clear they're waiting for her to join them.

"Stay with me." I'm not sure why I'm not quite ready to let her go yet. She should go celebrate with her friends. She should make memories with them…not with me, a dude passing through town.

Her brows dip. "Where?"

I lift a shoulder, not sure whether I mean in my hotel room with me or here at this blackjack table, but I just came from a sex club owned by a good friend of mine who offered me a job playing ball again, and I'm still a little fired up from that, if I'm being honest. Add in some beer and the high of winning at the blackjack tables plus a gorgeous woman who has definitely caught my attention, and I feel more than a little out of sorts at the moment.

I just told myself I want to jump back into both games, right?

It's been too long since I've had sex, an even longer time since I've spent the night with a stranger, and it might be just what I need to kickstart my dating life back into gear.

I lean in a little closer to her. "With me," I say, and I press a soft kiss just below her ear.

She shivers, and I know she feels it too. How can she not? It's too powerful to be one-sided, and she's been giving me the nonverbal cues since the second she sat down.

The way she scrambled to sit beside me when I told her I'd teach her how to play.

The way her nostrils flared when I addressed her friend.

The way she leans in a little closer to me with every glass of champagne she finishes.

The way she sticks her chest out when I glance over at her, like she's trying to make those tits look even more appealing than they already do.

The way her knee keeps bumping mine, and I'm pretty sure it's on purpose.

The way she gasps softy every time I find some excuse to touch her.

I want to make her gasp like that when I have her writhing naked on my bed as I drive into her.

I blow out a breath as I try to get Indiana Bones, the pocket rocket under control…an impossible feat with Gorgeous Gabby beside me.

These are inappropriate thoughts…but like I said, it's been a while.

Stacy and I broke things off a year and a half ago. She stayed in the house I still own in Los Angeles, and I moved to San Diego, where I took a job working as the co-programming director for

StrongFitKids, an organization that promotes active and healthy lifestyles to kids through a series of health and fitness programs. The hot chick who was my partner at work, Kaylee, became my close friend when we worked and lived together in San Diego, but she was from Vegas and ultimately moved back. She was never a real option anyway since she was hung up on another dude.

Incidentally, she's my dinner plans for tomorrow—along with her husband, who plays football for the Vegas Aces. We still work together, but we're no longer co-programming directors out of the same office. Instead, she and her husband took the content Kaylee and I created and repurposed the StrongFitKids program to fit into the chain of fitness clubs her husband owns.

I had a friends with benefits situation with another woman in San Diego, but we broke that off nearly six months ago.

Jesus, has it really been that long since I've had sex?

The pocket rocket says yes. It's been a long and lonely six months, but I've been busy with work.

Or so I've said. It's an easy excuse to avoid the complications that come with relationships, but diving into work rather than trying to meet somebody just pushes the goals I always wanted for my future further and further away.

It's complicated and complex, and I know one night with a girl like Gabby won't solve anything, but maybe it doesn't have to be just one night.

Not if I'm coming back to Vegas to play for the Heat.

Not if she's from here.

If it's meant to be, it'll be.

Or maybe I rock her world for a few hours and we both leave in the morning with smiles on our faces. Right now, I'm enjoying drinking beer, playing blackjack, and laughing with the gorgeous woman by my side. I guess we'll see where the night takes us.

Chapter 4
Gabby

When he asked me to stay here with him, I assumed he meant the blackjack table. But the longer we sit and play, the more I think he means something else entirely.

And the longer I sit beside him, the more I want whatever he's implying.

"What did the dealer say to the deck of cards?" he asks me when the dealer starts to shuffle the six decks we've been playing with.

I glance over at him in confusion. Did the dealer say something and I missed it? "What?" I ask.

"I can't deal with you anymore." He laughs at his own joke, and I roll my eyes. "What?" he says, holding up his hands. "It's funny!"

I twist my lips as I narrow my eyes at him. "It's the cheesiest joke I've heard in a long time, my friend."

"You got something better?"

"How's a casino like a woman?" I ask. I know this one's raunchy, but he's been flirting with me all night, so I have a pretty good feeling he won't be offended.

He squints at me a beat before asking, "How?"

"Liquor up front, poker in the back."

He laughs. "Yeah, that was better than mine but I didn't know we were on dirty joke terms just yet."

"Dirty jokes are always fine by me," I say.

He nods. "Okay, then how about this one? How do you make a pool table laugh?"

"How?"

"Tickle its balls," he deadpans, and I giggle.

"That's still pretty cheesy," I say. "What's the difference between a G spot and a golf ball?"

"What?"

"Men will actually search for a golf ball."

Even our straight-faced dealer Kelly chuckles at that one.

"What's the difference between a genealogist and a gynecologist?" he asks.

I shrug.

"A genealogist looks up your tree. A gynecologist looks up your bush."

I giggle. "You're getting better. I may have to teach you a thing or two."

His eyes seem to heat over at the prospect of that.

My friends are watching from across the way, and they seem to be waiting on me. I'm not the girl who ditches my friends for some random dude no matter how hot he is, but I'm torn because just for tonight…I want to be that girl.

It's strange, this connection I feel with Cooper. It's the first time a guy has ever made me feel this way literally seconds after meeting him, but maybe that's what twenty-one is. Legal to drink, gamble, and have one crazy night with a stranger.

"They're waiting for you," he murmurs.

"I know," I admit. "But I don't really want to go." I glance sideways at him, and he grins with exactly zero modesty, so I decide to take him down a peg as I nod toward my cards. "It's a hot table. I can't quit now, not when I've nearly tripled my investment."

He chuckles. "Is that the only reason?"

I shrug. "You got more than that?"

He leans in and presses his lips to mine again, and I'm immediately convinced.

"Does that count?" he asks when he pulls back.

Oh *God* yes, it counts.

An ache of need pulses between my legs, and I nod. "That's uh…quite a convincing argument."

He chuckles and leans back in his chair as we play the round of blackjack mindlessly, not focusing on the cards or the dealer but instead on each other. "The birthday girl should get what she wants on her birthday. So what do you want?"

You. The birthday girl wants YOU.

I bite my lip to keep from saying those words aloud as I scramble for a solution. "What are your plans tonight?"

He shakes his head. "I don't actually have any."

"Come with us to the club."

He wrinkles his nose. "Nah, that's not really my scene."

20

I raise my brows pointedly. "It's what the birthday girl wants."

He chuckles and pushes his chips toward the dealer. "Touché." He nods toward my chips as if to tell me to do the same. He stands then holds out a hand to me, and he doesn't let go of it as he leads me toward the cashier. We cash in our chips, and then we walk over toward my group of friends.

"Ready for the club?" I ask, and I'm met with whoops and cheers. "This is Cooper. He's coming with us."

My friends are all pretty tipsy at this point—in fact, I think I'm most sober in the group of girls, and two bow out, heading up to the suite my dad booked for my group of friends here at this hotel tonight while the rest of us walk toward the other nightclub.

We're carded before we go inside, and Cooper stops to say something to the hostess. She leads us to a table, and a minute later a waitress brings over a few bottles of champagne along with champagne flutes and a bottle of beer for Cooper.

He wiggles his eyebrows at me as the waitress hands me a glass of the champagne, and I can't help but laugh—and at the same time, I can't help but wonder why he'd do this for me. It's not exactly cheap to get last-minute bottle service at a club, and he doesn't even know me.

I head out to the dance floor with my girls, and he hangs back at the table, sipping his beer. I spot a woman approach him, and she walks away a few beats later. A man approaches him, and they get to talking for a minute.

Admittedly my eyes keep edging over toward the table to see what he's up to.

He's talking to another guy, and they fist bump.

Does he know these people? Who exactly is this handsome mystery McHottie who's taken an interest in me tonight?

And why me?

Because I happened to sit down at the table beside him?

I finish my glass of champagne and realize it doesn't matter why it's me.

I'm just going to count myself lucky that it is.

I head back for a refill, and two of my friends, Kelly and Becky, follow. "We're going to head upstairs," they say. Mia and Chelsea are next, and Mia makes sure I'm okay before she heads upstairs. And that's it. That leaves Cooper and me all alone in a club filled with people.

"Dance with me," I demand, and he chuckles and nods.

He follows me out to the floor, and suddenly our bodies are pressed up against each other as the mass of people out here moves and sways with the beat. His hands find my hips, and I link my arms around his neck. His eyes burn down into mine, and I get the strangest sensation like I already know him. I know I'm safe with him even though I just met him tonight, and my gut instinct about people is usually spot on.

He seems like a good guy, and even though I'm slightly champagne-drunk, I've got enough wits about me to know I can trust him.

Our dancing starts playful but quickly turns sexy as he shoves his hips toward mine. I feel his erection against my side, only confirming how much want and desire pulls between the two of us. Someone bumps into him, sending him careening a little closer into me, and then no space separates our bodies as his leg comes between both of mine. I grind down on his leg, a side effect of the champagne that I'd normally be way too reserved to do with a virtual stranger, but tonight all bets are off.

He wants this.

I want this.

Heat consumes the space between us, and tingles light up my spine as my tummy flips. His lips collide with mine again, and this kiss is hot and desperate in the middle of a crowded dance floor. It's sexy and nearly illicit as his tongue batters mine, his fingertips digging into my hips as we continue to sway to the beat of the song. I feel so much more than just attraction coming through this kiss, like attraction is just the spark that's going to light this inferno between us...like it's leading us somewhere bigger than just tonight.

I still know nothing about him. He's staying here at this hotel, so I don't have high hopes for more than one night together.

But it still feels like the type of opportunity I can't let slip by. If my dad has taught me anything over the last three years, it's that we can't live life with regrets. We can only take what's right in front of us.

He drags his lips from mine, across my cheek and toward my ear. "Spend the night with me." His voice is raspy and filled with some unspoken promise, like he can somehow see into my thoughts and he feels the same way...he doesn't want to let this chance slip by, either.

I nod, and he grabs my hand. He weaves through the throng of people and leads me back out to the hallway.

"Hey, that's Cooper Noah!" some guy yells at him, and Cooper simply nods at the guy, tightens his grip on my hand, and leads me through the hotel.

I hear other people say his name, too, and maybe this was happening earlier and I was too tipsy to notice, but all the dancing has sobered me up a little.

We arrive at a bank of elevators, and I think about that name. Cooper Noah. It's vaguely familiar, like I've heard it before, but I have no idea who he is.

"How do all those people know you?" I ask softly.

He twists his lips. "You really don't know?"

I shake my head, and the doors open in front of us. A couple gets off, and we step on. The doors seal us into isolation, and he walks toward me, backing me up against the mirrored wall. His blue eyes focus down on my green ones. "God, you're gorgeous," he murmurs. "And you don't even know who I am." His mouth crashes down to mine, and as much as I want to ask more questions, it seems his kiss offers the exact sort of distraction he's going for.

Chapter 5
Cooper

They say dancing is like foreplay, and if that's true, we're both in for a treat tonight.

I can't stop thinking about the way her eyes lit up with laughter when we were telling each other jokes, or the way her body moved on that dance floor, and when my leg moved in between her thighs and she rubbed her pussy on me...

Fuck.

I haven't been this attracted to a woman in a long, long time.

Hell, I haven't been this *horny* for a woman in a long time, either.

I can't keep my mouth off hers. I can't stop kissing her. I don't want to stop unless it's to taste more of her, and it's a brand-new phenomenon for me to feel this connected to a woman. It certainly started as physical, but I already like *her*, too. I like her dirty jokes. She's funny and smart, and she isn't afraid to tell me my jokes are cheesy.

Women rarely tell me like it is. They usually want me because of what I used to do for a living, because of my bank account, because of my connections. They tell me what I want to hear. They don't challenge me. They laugh at my cheesy jokes, or they ditch their friends to spend time with me. They tell me to do whatever will most benefit themselves instead of telling me to choose joy.

This girl isn't like that, and it's a fucking breath of fresh air.

It's the kind of fresh air I want to spend more time around, and I'm not sure I'll be able to let her go when morning comes.

The elevator doors open to let us off on our floor, and I hold her hand as we stroll down the hallway toward my room. I open the door, and I let her into a suite.

At first I think she'll be impressed by the suite until I remember that she was planning to stay in one herself—with six of her closest friends, by the way.

"What do you need all this space for by yourself?" she asks.

I shrug. The truth is that Troy flew me out here and got the room for me. He probably figured I'd spend more time exploring his club, but I wasn't really feeling it.

I'm glad I didn't. If I would've stayed there, fate might not have intervened by putting Gabby at the same blackjack table as mine tonight, and she might not be walking over toward my windows to look down at the view.

"This place is ridiculous," she mutters, and I move in beside her to look down at the traffic.

"Did you grow up in Vegas?" I ask.

She shakes her head. "I've only been here about three years. I grew up near Denver."

"What brought you to Vegas?"

"A combination of things," she says vaguely. "What about you? Did you grow up in San Diego?"

I shake my head. "I grew up in the suburbs of Chicago, but I moved to California when I was eighteen and that's home now."

"How long has it been home?"

"Almost fifteen years," I say, and her eyes widen a little as she does the math. "How long was Colorado home for you?"

She clears her throat. "Eighteen years."

I raise my brows. "Today's your twenty-first birthday?"

Twenty-one.

The same number you need to score a blackjack.

The same number I've worn on the back of my uniform since little league.

The number that's been my lucky number my entire life.

She giggles a little cautiously and nods.

I wouldn't have guessed that. I don't hang with a lot of women in their early twenties, but she strikes me as much more mature than her twenty-one years, like maybe she's lived through some things but came out the other side with that same sunny disposition.

"Twelve years between us," she murmurs, turning toward me. "Is this crazy?"

"I don't think the age thing is what makes this crazy." I reach over and pull her into my arms, and I drop a kiss to her forehead as she links her arms around my waist. "I don't know what this is,

Gabby, but I like you. A lot. I could throw out the cliché about age just being a number, but somehow I don't think it would matter. It doesn't bother me. Does it bother you?"

She shakes her head, and she tips her chin up. I drop my lips to hers for a quick kiss.

She pulls back but not out of my arms. "Have you done this before?"

"What?" I ask cautiously.

"One night with a stranger," she clarifies.

I duck my head a little, averting my eyes behind her for a beat before bringing them back to hers. "I've had a one-night stand before, yes. But it wasn't like this. It was just attraction, no substance. But with you…" I shake my head as I trail off, grappling for the right words. "I don't know. There's substance. There's something between us I can't explain."

"Why does it feel like I've known you my whole life?" she asks.

I shake my head. "I don't know. It feels like the start of something, though, doesn't it?"

She nods. "It feels important, Cooper. It's a little scary."

"I keep thinking about your words from earlier, about doing what brings you joy. I've been in such a goddamn rut for the last year, but tonight…it's been full of joy." I can't help but wonder if it's because of her age. There's a certain naivety that comes with being over a decade younger than me. Shit, if she's twenty-one, she's probably not even out of college yet.

Disappointment looms over me at the thought. I can't go back into the big league holding onto a girl that's still in college. It wouldn't be fair to her, and the press would have a fucking field day with that.

But that doesn't mean I can't bask in her joy for tonight. Besides, we've made no promises to each other going forward. We didn't agree to anything beyond tonight.

But without anything more than a kiss, I know beyond a shadow of a doubt that whatever this is will take us beyond tonight. It has to. A connection this magnetic feels like a once in a lifetime experience.

Her eyes seem to sparkle at my words, and then she leans in and rests her head on my chest. I tighten my arms around her, and as much as I feel the heat radiating between us, as much as I want to strip her naked and slam into her for the rest of the night, I'm also content right here, just talking and getting to know her on a different level in private without prying eyes wondering what we're up to. Up here in my room, I can just be Cooper and she can just be Gabby and the rest of the world ceases to exist. There's something magical about that. Something I'm not going to be ready to let go when the time creeps in on us.

"I feel the same way," she whispers, and her eyes flick to my lips for a beat.

"Is this okay?" I ask. "I mean...are you drunk?"

She nods then shakes her head. "Yes, it's okay. And no...I'm not drunk. But I do want this. I want *you*."

And then because I can't wait another second without tasting her again, my mouth crashes back down to hers.

Chapter 6
Gabby

I've never been with a man like Cooper before. I don't know what life experiences he carries or what baggage he has because of them, but I find myself thinking less about the fact that he was twelve when I was born, that he was seventeen when I started kindergarten, or that I was six when he started college.

Instead, I'm thinking about what he knows as an experienced, confident man compared to the unsure boys I've been with before.

I'm thinking about all the ways he knows how to pleasure a woman—because he certainly knows how to kiss one.

And I'm thinking that I'm pretty damn lucky that I sat down at that blackjack table tonight...and not just because I walked away two hundred dollars richer than I was when I sat down at it.

His hands start to move, dragging along my back and up into my hair, and then they trail down to my ass. He squeezes it then slides one hand along my thigh and beneath the hem of my dress. I moan into his mouth, never wanting this to stop, and then he grabs the backs of my thighs and tugs, lifting me. I link my legs around his waist and my arms around his neck, straddling him as we shift so I'm situated above him now. Our tongues continue to tangle as he carries us over to the bed, and then he gently leans down as if I weigh nothing, setting me on my back on the bed. He thrusts his hips toward me, hovering over me as he still stands on the floor, and I haven't let go of the way I'm clinging to him. He drives his hips again and again, and I feel his hard length as it pummels against me through his jeans and through my dress and panties.

I finally loosen my grip on him, and he doesn't stop kissing me as he reaches under my dress for my panties. He slides them to the side as if he can't get to me fast enough, and he dips a finger right inside me.

"Oh!" I cry out, arching my back and accidentally disconnecting our kiss. He uses the opportunity to dip his face down into my cleavage, and then he reaches down and pulls one of my breasts out of the cup of my dress. He sucks my nipple into his mouth as he drives that finger into me then lets it go to swirl his tongue around the tip. He groans as if it's the best meal he's ever eaten, the sound landing straight in my core and pulsing a needy ache between my legs.

He moves down the bed then pulls his finger out of me. He uses both hands to yank my panties down my legs, and he tosses my shoes to the side, too. He pushes the hem of my dress up then dives face-first into my pussy.

That joke I told back there about the G spot?

Yeah…it doesn't apply to Cooper Noah.

He's the type of guy who doesn't need to search for his golf balls *or* the G spot. He already knows just where to find it.

He sucks on my clit as he shoves a finger into me, and then he adds another one, curling them in a way that also makes my toes curl. I grip onto the sheets as my legs start to thrash, and then my body seems to lose all control as my legs clamp around his ears and violent contractions of pleasure careen through my entire system.

I'm not sure what animal noises come out of my mouth, but growls and moans seem to burst forth out of me the likes of which I've never heard before. When the spasms start to slow, this heady sense of euphoria takes over for a few precious beats, a blissful sort of paradise I would live in forever if I could.

But these things aren't meant to last forever, and even if I wanted to, I wouldn't.

Because Cooper straightens, and then he unbuckles his belt. He flicks the button of his jeans and lowers his zipper.

Since I want a front row seat to this show, I sit up. Wooziness overtakes me, but I fight through it. I'm not about to miss a single second of this.

He yanks his black shirt over his head and tosses it to the side. Oh. My. God.

I've never seen an actual six-pack in person before.

Wait…is that six? Or eight?

It's unreal.

I think for the briefest second he's wearing one of those t-shirts with a picture of hot abs on it…but nope, it's real. I know because

I can't help when I reach out and touch them. I run my fingertips along every cut ridge, and my mouth waters.

He pulls his jeans down along with black boxer briefs, exposing a thick erection pointed straight up at the ceiling.

My mouth waters again.

I have never had a male form in front of me that I've wanted to taste so badly in my entire life. The ache between my legs is back in full force even though he just satisfied it, but I have a feeling that with someone like him, I'll *always* want more. It'll *never* be enough.

It's animal and primal and not meant to last. I push away the sadness that seems to blanket me at the thought, and I reach forward, taking his cock in my hand. He hisses when I fist him and pump my hand up and down, the tip of his cock glistening with his arousal. I scoot forward to the edge of the bed and take him in my mouth.

He grips my hair with a throaty growl, and I already know that sound will be the soundtrack of my dreams for the foreseeable future.

I take him all the way to the back of my throat, and he groans. "Fuck, Gabby," he mutters. "Your mouth is magic." He pushes his hips toward me then pulls them back, his head tipped back in pleasure and his neck corded as he fucks my mouth.

It's hot.

Like…*really* hot.

Hot enough that I have the sudden urge to let my fingers drift down to touch myself, and I can't say that's something I've ever done in the middle of the action. I always let the guy take over.

Just another thing that feels different with Cooper. I can just be myself, I guess, even in the heat of the moment. Something about him allows me to just let go, to take what I need.

I glance up, and our eyes connect. He's watching me as I suck him down.

"You're so gorgeous taking me all the way like that," he mutters. "Do you like how my cock tastes?"

I moan my affirmation to that question. God, yes, I fucking *love* how it tastes.

He shoves into my mouth again, and I swallow as he hits the back of my throat. "Good girl," he murmurs, and I rub the circles over my clit with one hand a little faster as I fist the base of his cock with my other hand at his sexy words of praise.

He moans through his pleasure, and then he pulls back abruptly. His eyes are ferocious when they meet mine.

I let go of his cock, and he pulls my hand away from where I'm touching myself. "That orgasm belongs to my cock," he says, his voice raspy with a needy desperation that I feel, too.

I'm not sure I've ever heard anything hotter in my entire life.

He's possessing me, possessing my pleasure. He wants to give it to me, and I want to take it, and I don't know how I'll walk away from this hotel room after knowing this guy all of a few hours with just the memories. I don't think I can do it.

Maybe that's my age showing. My naivety.

It's just one night, I remind myself. *Just enjoy it. Get out of your own head.*

I decide to listen to that inner thought.

"Fuck," he mutters.

My brows dip. "What?"

"There is nothing I want more than to be inside you right now...but I didn't bring any condoms with me."

"Oh." I snag my bottom lip between my teeth. "I, uh...I have a few. Over in my purse."

He looks surprised. "Were you expecting to get laid tonight?"

I giggle and nod. "Oh, yeah. I just found the first guy who looked desperate and sat at the same blackjack table as him."

He chuckles as he shakes his head. "Well, mission accomplished."

"Do we need to have the talk before we have the sex?" I'm pretty sure I wouldn't have said that if I hadn't had a handful of glasses of champagne tonight, but it felt like something that merited mentioning.

He wrinkles his nose. "Do we have to? I'd rather just get to the sex."

I laugh. "Do you do this with a lot of women?"

He shakes his head. "I got out of a serious relationship about a year ago. I had a few...uh, *encounters* since then, but it's been a few months since the last one."

I raise a brow, and then I think better of it. It's not really my business to question what he means by that. "It's been a few months for me as well," I say, not going into detail about my recent dry spell.

"Are you on birth control?" he asks.

I shake my head. It doesn't merit mentioning why, but suffice it to say I had an IUD that was less convenient than advertised, so I had it taken out after my last relationship ended, and I haven't really had much reason to get back on anything.

"Condom it is, then," he says, and I stand and walk across the room. We're both naked, and as I walk by, he says, "God damn, you're fucking hot." And then he proceeds to grab my ass.

I squeal with a giggle. "Back at you, Handsome." I grab my purse and pull out a condom. I hold it up between my fingers. "Your love glove, sir."

He chuckles as he snatches it out of my hands. "I prefer the term *cock sock*, if I'm being honest."

I can't help a laugh at that, and I also can't help but think how much *fun* I'm having. Is sex supposed to be fun? It's always been serious for me. Pleasurable, sure, and most often with a boyfriend or with someone I knew more than a few hours, but I can't recall cracking a smile in the midst of it.

But with Cooper, it's different. It's fun and it's easy. It's lighthearted and uncomplicated.

I can't help but wonder whether he's like this in everyday life, too—outside of this bubble where we find ourselves. He seems laidback and easygoing. I wonder what he's like when he's fired up. I wonder what he's passionate about. I wonder what makes him angry, what makes him happy, what drives him and what challenges him.

I can't think like that, though. I can't allow my naïve expectations to creep in on our good time. Whatever happens tonight happens, and either I walk away with a memory or I walk away with a phone number.

I'm hoping for the latter, especially after the way he licked my pussy, but I guess time will tell.

Chapter 7
Cooper

How will I ever leave this place with just that little taste?

I tear open the condom and roll it on while she settles back onto the bed. She's on her back, and I wonder how many guys she's been with. It's not a fair question to ask, and it's not like I want to give her my total, but I get the strong inclination she's never been with somebody who knows what he's doing.

And I know what I'm doing. I enjoy doing it.

I've learned a thing or two over the years, and I want to show her all the ways I can make her come.

One night won't be enough.

And furthermore, how do I leave this place with a girl like her, one who's so eager to please, who can take my cock all the way down her throat the way she did?

I don't want morning to come.

I don't want our time to end.

It's why I pulled out of her mouth. She was sucking me so good, I was going to lose it. I couldn't lose it in her mouth when I haven't had the chance to fuck her yet.

This isn't me, this dirty talking guy. I've never once asked a woman if she liked how my cock tasted, but I wanted to know. And when she nodded her head while my cock was still in her mouth, well…it was nearly enough to end our night too early.

And so I'll tease her.

I'll tease myself, too.

I'll drive us both to the edge of explosion before I pull it back and slow it down.

I climb over her and hover for a beat, and I drop my lips to hers. It's a way to prolong the night, to kiss her as I try to get my cock back under control, but I can't.

And so I fist myself and slide my dick through her slit, stopping to pump myself over her clit for a beat before I slide it in.

Her body clamps onto me, tight and hot and wet as we both moan at how good it feels to be connected this way. I slide out and push in again, and her eyes lift to mine. Hers are filled with wonder and need as everything about this feels so right.

I drive into her again, slowly, luxuriously, as if we have all the time in the world when the truth is that we don't. We might only have tonight…and that's why we both have to take advantage of the time we have together.

She wraps her arms and legs around me as I pump into her, and I hold onto her, buried inside her as I flip us so she's on top of me. I perch on the edge of the bed with my feet on the floor, and she buries her face in my neck as she settles into her new position. I lift her ass and pump into her from beneath her, her body still clinging to mine and wrapped around me like a vine. I bury my face in her hair, and it smells like warm vanilla. It's not overpowering, but it's deeply sensual and gives me an odd sense of comfort.

I wrap my arms around her, too, holding her close to me, and she lifts her face from my neck. I gaze into her eyes, and I'm not sure if I've ever had a more intimate moment during the act of sex before.

It's like some ethereal connection bonds us, something totally out of our control. I could easily see myself becoming addicted to her, and I'm afraid I'm already halfway there.

It's intense, these feelings.

Strong.

Powerful.

But she's twenty-one. We're in different places in our lives, and I'm not sure how they can intersect beyond tonight. But I have to try. This feels like the type of thing that only happens once in a lifetime, and I'm not stupid enough to let that go without a fight.

I lift her ass and slam her back down over me as her tits brush against my chest, and I feel my balls tighten as the need to come pulses through me.

I lift her off me and set her on the bed.

"Why'd you stop?" she pants.

"I'm not ready for it to end."

Her brows dip. "Why's it going to end?"

"Because you feel so damn good that I'm going to blow my load way too soon, and I'm nowhere near done with you."

Her eyes glaze over with lust at my words, and I stand, pulling her legs up so they're resting on my shoulders. I slide my cock back inside her, and it oddly feels like I'm home, like this woman's body was made for mine, like we're two souls put on this planet to find one another.

I drive into her like this, my eyes down on her tits as they sway with every thrust I make into her.

"Oh my God, Cooper," she gasps. "Right there! Oh God, oh God, oh God!" Her words are paired with shrieks as she starts to come, her pussy contracting over my cock. The vicelike grip she has on me is too much, and as much as I wanted to make this last longer…I can't.

I start to come, some ferocious growl ripping from my chest as I do, some sound I've never heard myself make before to match the symphony of her gorgeous shrieks. I usually close my eyes when I come, but I find I can't take my eyes off her gorgeous face as it twists with pleasure while she works through her own climax.

Her release wanes first as my cock continues to pulse and twitch inside her, and when it finally comes to an end, I lay down over her. I don't slip out of her, not yet, because I'm not ready to break the physical connection we just shared.

But it's so much more than physical.

How can I have an emotional connection with somebody I don't even know?

I don't have the answer to that, but I already know one hit won't be enough.

Chapter 8
Gabby

I stare at myself in the mirror a beat as I wonder whether that was real or if I'm dreaming.

I'm pretty sure I'm dreaming, but I'm naked and I'm starting to wonder if it's one of those dreams where you're naked and when I open that door to my left, an audience is going to be there waiting for me to give an important presentation on stage.

Except when I open the door, I'm still in Cooper's hotel room, and he's pulling on a pair of athletic shorts near his suitcase. I realize too late that the only item of clothing I have is the dress I wore tonight, and I don't really want to slip back into that to cuddle. So my options are walk around naked, or put the dress on and leave to get my own suitcase on another floor where my friends are. That also doesn't sound overly appealing, so I stare awkwardly at Cooper for a beat, and then he tosses me a blue Dodgers t-shirt and a pair of shorts.

"You're a Dodgers fan?" I ask.

He chuckles and shakes his head, and I feel like I'm missing the joke as I pull his shirt over my head.

It smells like him, that same woodsy scent I picked up on earlier.

It's *hot*, and I want to smell like him, too. I want to roll in the scent and remember it forever.

I wonder what comes next and whether it's about to get awkward as I pull my panties on and skip the shorts. He lays on the bed and waves me over, skipping right over the awkward conversation about what comes next. Instead, I snuggle into the nook between his shoulder and his chest like we've done this a million times. His fingertips flutter in little circles on my bicep.

"I usually ask this *before* I have sex with somebody, but tell me about yourself," he says.

I giggle and press a kiss to his jaw. "Well, it's my twenty-first birthday, as you know. I moved to Vegas to attend UNLV, where I'm majoring in marketing, and I'm about to start my senior year." I leave out the complicated part about finding my dad when I turned eighteen and my toxic mother who made me think my dad wanted nothing to do with me. Instead, I keep it simple.

"Jesus," he mutters. "You're still in college and I'm already on my second career."

"Your second career?" I echo.

"I currently work as the programming director for an organization in San Diego that promotes active and healthy lifestyles to kids through a series of health and fitness programs," he says, and it feels like he's leaving stuff out of the conversation, too.

"But you're here in town for another job offer, right?" I ask.

He nods. "Sort of. It's complicated, but basically an old buddy wants me to work with him. I could probably do both jobs to a very modified degree, but I'm not sure I want to."

"What's holding you back?" I tilt my head up so I can look at him, and he tilts his head down to look at me. When our eyes connect, I feel like I see some clarity in his.

"Fear," he answers, and the honesty in his tone is unnerving.

"What's there to be afraid of?"

"Giving up the stability and freedom I have now for the type of career that's totally and completely consuming," he says.

"But one which you think might bring you some degree of joy?"

He nods and twists his lips before running a hand through his hair. "I know it will."

"And will it mean you'll be in Vegas more?" I ask, the ulterior motive for my question clear in my suggestive tone as I toss a thigh over his leg with the unintended effect of my vagina rubbing on his leg.

"Fuck," he groans. "Hell, if it means I'll get to see you again, I'll quit my job tomorrow."

I let out a little gasp at his words. "Do you really mean that?"

He clears his throat, and I lean up on my arm and gaze down at him. He blows out a breath. "I don't know what the fuck is happening, but I'm not walking out that door tomorrow morning without knowing how to get in touch with you again."

I can't help the wide smile that stretches across my lips. "Thank God," I murmur, and I lower my lips to his.

"It's crazy, right?" he asks against my mouth.

"Definitely," I say against his.

"Insane."

"Totally," I agree, and we kiss for a beat before he pulls back.

"This doesn't happen to me," he says. "I want you to know that. I want you to know this is different. I don't take twenty-one-year-olds back to my hotel room just to give them a birthday present."

I giggle. "Well, it was my favorite of all the gifts I received today." And my dad got me a new truck…something I fail to mention.

I don't want him to know about my dad.

I don't want to feel like he only wants to be with me because of my connections.

Maybe that's what makes this even more special. Our connection developed first, and now we can get to know one another. First impressions mean a lot, and, well…he's made a good one.

"It was pretty damn good," he says, pressing a kiss into my hair. "God, you smell good." He tightens his grip around me. "You *feel* good."

I run my hands along the cut ridges of those abs. "You're all right, too."

He bursts out a laugh, and it's contagious. I laugh, too.

"So when *was* the last time you were with somebody?" he asks.

"Going there already, huh?" I ask. He shrugs, and I plow forward. "That would be my ex, Jace. He was a year older than me, and when he graduated in May, he moved to Nashville for a job. I didn't go with. It was as simple as that." We'd only been together eight months, and while I did have feelings of love for him, I knew neither of us was willing to put in the work to make a long-distance relationship last.

Before him, there were a total of two other guys.

"You?" I ask.

He clears his throat. "My ex and I broke up about a year ago. A friend and I hooked up a few times, and I had some Tinder dates that went exactly as advertised."

I make a face at the Tinder dates. "So you're thirty-two?" I ask.

"Yep. Thirty-three next month." His tone is flat, and I can't get a read on how he feels about that.

"Damn, you're old."

He laughs. "Thanks."

"How are you still single?"

"I always feel like that question is a backhanded compliment," he says.

"I don't mean for it to be. I just mean that you seem like you're the total package. I don't know how some little filly hasn't snatched you up yet."

His brows dip. "Some little filly?" I giggle, and he shrugs. "Some fillies have tried, I guess. I played the field a long time, and then I was with Stacy for five years. It took me a while to move on from what happened between us, and I guess I haven't met the right person."

Yet.

Until now.

Until me.

I force the thought out of my brain. It's dangerous. And yet, the longer we sit here talking about ourselves and getting to know each other beyond a physical attraction, the more that thought keeps sneaking back in.

Chapter 9
Gabby

At some point, we both fell asleep, and I wake when the sun starts to peek into the windows we never bothered to cover last night in our haste to have sex.

We talked late into the night, and even though we just met last night, it feels like I've known him my entire life. I know his favorite singer is Dave Matthews, he's obsessed with Slim Jims, he likes to eat mangoes, he's six feet, four inches tall, he loves sports, he wants at least three kids by the time he's forty, he's a total mama's boy, and he's a Dodgers fan.

He learned that my favorite singer is Taylor Swift, I've never eaten a mango before in my entire life, I clock in at five-seven, I'm more of a movie buff than a sports fan, I don't know if I want kids ever, I'm not close with my mom, and if I *had* to pick a team to root for, I guess I'd say I'm a Vegas Aces fan…a Ben Olson fan, in particular, but I wouldn't kick Jack Dalton out of bed for eating cookies if you know what I mean.

We laughed together, and he held me in his arms as he traced patterns on my skin, and there was zero pressure on either of us. We just lived in the moment, and I'm not sure I've ever done that before with a guy. I prefer living in my head, overanalyzing every word, every smile, every tick of an eyebrow.

Cooper's just about the easiest-going guy I've ever met, and I'm not exactly uptight, but sometimes I suppose I can be. I was once described by my high school math teacher as the sunshiniest Type A personality he'd ever met, and he was right. I'm positive and sometimes I can be way too nice, which can often make me a doormat, but I'm also competitive and have a strong aptitude for achieving whatever I set out to do. I just do it with a smile on my face, I guess.

He wakes with a bit of a jolt when I move out of his arms, and he grabs onto me and tightens his grip, not letting me go.

"Where the fuck do you think you're going?" he says, his tone gruff.

I can't help a soft giggle. "I really have to pee."

"I need a kiss first." He puckers his lips, and good gravy, I'm not sure I've ever seen a man who was both so dang hot and also adorable at the same time. I drop my lips to his, and he grabs onto me, hoisting me over his lap and gripping onto my butt cheeks with both hands. He moves my body over his, letting me know he's raring to go even at this early hour.

I let out a soft moan, and then I climb off him because I really do need to go use the restroom. He grunts as I leave.

"Be right back," I promise on my way.

When I get out of the bathroom, I expect things to be awkward. Despite the unfamiliar feelings streaming through me, he's still a virtual stranger, and I've never really done the one-night stand thing, so I'm expecting one of us to make it weird.

But that doesn't happen.

Instead, he's pulling on a shirt, much to my disappointment. "Wanna grab some breakfast fuel then come back here and have sex all day long?"

I laugh. "Uh, yeah. I do."

He grabs my hand and pulls me into him, wrapping his arms around me so I'm crushed against his body, and his lips tip up as he gazes down at me. He drops a soft kiss to my lips before letting me go. He looks me up and down a beat. "You're gonna need some pants, Sunshine."

"Sunshine?" I ask.

He shrugs. "It's your sunny personality, I guess. Or the fact that the sun coming up is casting you in this spot of gold right now and it's fucking ethereal, like you're some angel dropped down into my hotel room."

I step out of the spot of light. "What about now? Am I whatever the opposite of sunshine is?"

He chuckles. "Moonshine?" He shakes his head. "Nah, I don't think so. Still Sunshine."

"What about you?" I ask.

His brows furrow in confusion. "What about me?"

"If you're going to call me Sunshine, what should I call you?"

He tosses an arm around my shoulder. "Stud Muffin? Captain Orgasm? The best sex of your life?"

I twist my lips. "I'm thinking Snuggle Bunny."

He tosses me the same pair of shorts I didn't bother to wear last night. "We'll work on it over breakfast."

"Hottie McHotFace?" I suggest as I pull them on.

He narrows his eyes at me. "It's a little better, but I'm kind of partial to Captain Orgasm."

"You were definitely captain of my orgasms last night," I murmur, and I grab a hair band out of my purse to pull my hair up.

"I will be again this morning after a balanced breakfast with a lot of protein." He grabs a black baseball hat with a simple black UA for Under Armour on the front out of his suitcase, and he turns it backward when he puts it on.

Good God, as if he wasn't hot enough before.

I'm pretty sure my ovaries explode. Something is definitely happening down there, and I'm not sure I've ever gotten horny before just from *looking* at a man the way I feel around Cooper. I'm at a point where the disbelief is hitting me so frequently that I'm *almost* starting to get used to the idea that this is reality.

I follow him out to the hallway, and he tosses an arm around my shoulders. I slide my arm around his waist, and we navigate down the hall and toward the elevators as if we're a real couple and we've been together forever.

He turns his hat forward and tugs the bill down lower once we're on the elevator. Still hot, still captain of my orgasms, but the backwards thing was more *king of the world* material than captain of one single entity.

It's half after six as we're seated toward the back of the restaurant in a booth. He faces the kitchen from the seat he chooses, while I can see the entire restaurant from where I sit.

It's as we're perusing the menu that I ask, "So Snuggle Bunny is a hard no?"

He laughs, and it's that same hearty laugh I've heard out of him before. It lights me up from the inside, and the wide smile that accompanies it is nearly enough for me to strip naked so he can take me right on top of the laminate tabletop between us.

"At least make it something cooler than *bunny* if you're going that route. Snuggle Fucking Tiger or something."

"Snuggle T-Rex?" I suggest.

"Snuggle Wolf," he throws out.

"Snuggle Jellyfish?"

His brows dip. "Jellyfish? You want to nickname the best sex of your life fucking *jellyfish*?"

42

I shrug. "I read somewhere that there's this one jellyfish that has a sting a hundred times more potent than a cobra. That's pretty freaking ferocious, right?"

"Oooh, Snuggle Cobra. Now that's kick ass."

"Maybe we drop the snuggle all together," I say, squinting at him as I twist my lips.

"Back to square one, then. Captain Orgasm?"

I giggle. "You're not letting that one go, are you?"

He shrugs.

"Okay, Captain."

He smirks at me, and a waitress comes by to take our orders a few beats later. He orders a protein-filled breakfast skillet, while I opt for the pumpkin-walnut pancakes with a side of bacon.

He wrinkles his nose after the waitress walks away. "Damn, just when I thought you were the perfect woman, you go and order pumpkin pancakes."

"What's wrong with pumpkin pancakes?" I demand.

"Just the thought of what it's made out of…pumpkin guts." He shakes his head. "Disgusting."

"You're trying them, and you'll like it, Captain."

He laughs again.

"When do you head back to San Diego?" I ask.

"My flight is tomorrow morning," he says.

"What's your plan for the rest of your trip?"

His eyes seem to glaze over with lust, and he leans in a little closer toward me across the table. "You."

I raise a brow. "What if I have plans?"

"You'll cancel them. After all, it's not often you get full access to the captain."

"So modest," I say, rolling my eyes.

He chuckles. "In all seriousness, I'm meeting some friends for dinner tonight, but otherwise I'm free. Unless I decide to meet up with the buddy who offered me a job."

"What are you going to tell him?" I ask softly.

He thinks about it for a beat before he answers. "I'm not sure yet. But if I'm deciding based on what brings me joy, then I think I want to spend more time in Vegas." He raises his brows as his eyes focus in on mine, and I melt into a pile of lust right there in the booth.

I hope he decides to take the job—whatever it is.

I hope I get to see him again.

I hope we get the chance to explore whatever this is outside of this fantasy weekend.

But one thing's for sure.

I didn't stay together with Jace because neither of us wanted to bother putting in the work that would be required of a long-distance relationship.

I haven't even known Cooper twelve hours yet, but I can already tell he's someone worth putting in the work for.

I can't help my curiosity over who he's meeting for dinner or what the job offer here in Vegas is, but he's been pretty open with me, all things considered. He'll tell me when he's ready.

Just like I'll tell him more about my parents when I'm ready, too.

"What do you want to do all day?" I ask.

"Sex," he says.

I laugh. "*All* day?"

"Well, yeah. Have you seen yourself? I could get lost in that body for the rest of the month. One day won't be nearly enough time."

My cheeks flush, and he chuckles at my reaction.

"You shine brighter when you're embarrassed," he says. "So I'm going to do it as often as I can."

I purse my lips. "Great."

He laughs, but he reaches over and squeezes my hand. "Since you live here, I want you to show me a side of Vegas I've never seen in all the times I've been here."

I raise both brows. "Way to put pressure on a girl."

He shrugs. "You want to plan a day date or something after my dinner tonight?"

An idea comes to mind, so I opt for tonight.

He nods. "It's a date."

"So what about the rest of the day?" I ask.

"Want to be tourists in between all the sex?" he suggests.

I nod. "Absolutely. I want one of those yard drinks with a strawberry daiquiri, and I want to play slot machines, and I want to watch the fountains at Bellagio."

"I want to ride the giant Ferris Wheel and I want to go to the top of the Eiffel Tower. Can we fit all that into one day?"

I shake my head. "Nope, but we've got today plus part of tomorrow, and then..." I trail off as I realize I don't know the answer to that.

His face falls a little, too, and his voice is low when he says. "And then I have a good reason to come back."

I press my lips together and nod, and then the waitress delivers our food.

And, incidentally, he *loves* my pumpkin pancakes.

Chapter 10
Gabby

After breakfast, I head up to the suite I was supposed to sleep in last night with my friends while Cooper heads to his room to make a phone call.

When I open the door, my six closest friends are all awake and lounging around, and they all look a little hungover. I, on the other hand, have a wide smile gracing my lips.

"Where have you been?" Mia asks, leaping to her feet with an accusatory finger pointed in my direction, anger all over her face.

"I was with Cooper," I say, my voice all dreamy even to my own ears.

"Haven't you checked your messages?" she asks.

"I was with Cooper," I repeat. "Sorry, allow me to amend that. I was getting banged like a drum at a marching band parade by Cooper."

Mia's jaw drops open. "You had sex with him?" she whisper yells.

"Yes. And I'm just here to grab my suitcase so I can get back to his room and have some more sex with him. Have I mentioned how good he is at the sex? He's got this tongue that's, like, unreal, and he—"

"Gabby!" Mia says, fisting my biceps. "Do you know who he is?"

My brows draw together. "He's Cooper," I say. I think back to the semi-fuzzy walk last night when people seemed to recognize him as they called him by his full name.

"He looked familiar to Chelsea, so we looked him up. He's Cooper Noah. He played third base for the Dodgers for seven years before an elbow injury took him out of the game."

My eyes widen as my palm moves toward my forehead. "A baseball player? For the Dodgers?" I think I might be in shock as her words hit me. Why would a megastar baseball player have any interest at all in someone like me?

The t-shirt I'm still sporting makes a hell of a lot more sense now.

I don't follow baseball. My mother hated the game, so we never watched it when I was growing up, and it wasn't until much more recently that I took an interest in it at all.

I still don't know much about the game, but I'm learning.

Maybe Cooper can teach me a thing or two. And if he's been out of the game a few years, I guess it makes sense that I wouldn't know who he is since my interest in the sport is very recent. Our timelines just didn't overlap, I guess.

I wonder why he didn't mention it, but I don't want to be the one to bring it up. Maybe he prefers it this way, and I think I do, too. If we see each other beyond this weekend, I'm sure it's something that will come up at some point, but I don't want him to think I'm just after him because of who he is.

And I really don't want him to find out who I am, either. I don't want what we're starting to be tainted by things completely out of our control. Not when our dynamic together is so good.

"I don't even know what to say," I admit. "I'm supposed to just come up and grab my bag so we can spend the day together."

"Well...how was it?" Becky asks.

I sigh dramatically as I drop down into a vacant chair. "I can't even come up with the words, to be honest. It was..." I shake my head. "It was like I've known him my entire life. It was like we were destined to sit next to each other at that blackjack table, like our paths were meant to cross."

"But he's like, in his thirties, isn't he?" Kelly asks, scrunching up her nose. "Doesn't he have wrinkly old balls?"

I nod. "When the connection is this strong, age is just a number," I say, citing the same words he used as a cliché. Maybe it's a cliché, but it's also the truth. "And there's nothing wrong with his balls. They're quite firm, as a matter of fact, and they seemed to be working just fine as they slapped against me last night."

Mia's still narrowing her eyes at me like I'm a child who needs scolding, but Chelsea lets out a loud laugh. Chelsea's the resident perv, so I know she'll be on my side. She probably wishes she was the one in my shoes right about now.

Proving my point, she sighs. "You're so lucky. He's hot, even if he does have wrinkly old balls."

"Yeah," I murmur. "He is pretty fucking hot. His abs are just…" I lick my lips as I think about those abs. Damn, I want to run my tongue along every ridge.

I miss him.

I already fucking miss him and we've been apart all of four minutes.

This isn't good.

I'm in deep. Way too deep for how little we know about each other. He didn't even tell me he used to play baseball, but he *did* shake his head with silent laughter when I asked him if he was a Dodgers fan. I guess that makes a little more sense, too.

It's fine. I'll let him keep his secret.

That way I can keep mine, too.

I bid my friends goodbye, grab my suitcase, and head back to Cooper's room. He throws the door open and basically attacks. "Shower with me," he demands once we come up for air.

"Can I brush my teeth first?"

He laughs. "Be my guest."

"I'll go fast. Promise." I brush my teeth in record time, and as a fun surprise, I decide to strip naked. I open the door and step out into the living area of our hotel room, and his jaw falls open.

"I think I want to marry you," he says, and heat floods my core at his words.

We're nowhere near that yet, and it was obviously a joke, but now it's in my head, and I'm not sure I'll ever be able to move on from the former professional baseball player who just told me he wants to marry me.

He stalks toward me, the hunter as I wait quietly as his prey, and when he gets to me, he runs his palms along the sides of my torso, grazing the sides of my breasts before sliding them around to cup my ass. He squeezes as he pulls me against him, the fabric of his t-shirt rough against my nipples as his mouth crashes down to mine.

We stand there kissing a few beats, our tongues dancing in a hot, intense battle, and then he pulls back suddenly. He rips his shirt off and slides his shorts down his athletic legs, and then he grabs my hand and pulls me into the bathroom. He starts the shower water and peppers kisses along my neck while we wait for it to warm up, and I pull the tie out of my hair. He steps in first and pulls me with him, and then he wraps his arms around me and kisses me in that deep, intense way he has as we stand under the spray of water together.

I'll be honest. I've never taken a shower with a guy before.

It's not that I'm totally inexperienced, but my most serious relationship was Jace, and college dorm showers aren't exactly built for romance.

But this shower clearly was. It's all encased in glass, and it has two showerheads—one which happens to be detachable. There's plenty of room for two people, and there's even a bench that's probably designed for towels or shower gel but also would work as a seat.

He lets me go and spins me around. I turn to watch as he pumps some shampoo onto his hand then massages it into my hair, and I lean back as I let his fingers work his magic. I moan at the feel of his hands on me anywhere—even my hair—and he thrusts his very hard dick against my ass.

I grab the bar of soap and lather up my hands while he works his magic, and then I reach behind me, fisting his dick with my slippery hands.

"Jesus," he grunts, and I grin. I can't help it. Hearing him make sounds like that because of what I'm doing to him might be the biggest turn on of my life.

He pulls his hips back out of my reach then grabs the detachable shower head to help me rinse the shampoo out of my hair. I shampoo his hair next, and even though I ran my hands through it last night, I love the feel of the thick strands between my fingers. He's quite a bit taller than me, so he bends down as I reach up to scrub, and he moves in to latch his mouth onto my nipple.

Have you ever tried shampooing someone's hair while they're sucking on your nipple?

It's quite the distraction.

I manage to finish the job, and then we wash each other with the bar of soap. Our bodies slide together in a sensual way as we work, and once we've rinsed each other, he orders me to sit on the little bench.

He pulls the detachable showerhead down. "Spread your legs for me, baby," he says, and I do as requested. "Now lean back and enjoy."

I lean back and watch as he sinks to his knees, and then I close my eyes as I wait for the sensations to hit me.

He doesn't disappoint. He aims a burst of water right at my clit as he grabs a nipple between his fingertips with his other hand, tweaking and pulling in painful pleasure. He pulls the water away and licks his way through my entire pussy, stopping to suck on my clit before dipping his tongue back in, and then he pulls his finger from my nipple to thrust it into me. He aims the water at my clit again as he drives his finger in and out, taking a nipple in his mouth again.

It's too many sensations. Pleasure on top of pleasure on top of pleasure.

I spiral out of control as wave after wave of bliss career through my entire body.

And as the pulses start to slow, he doesn't stop what he's doing. I'm writhing on the bench, need and desire pummeling through me even though he literally just sated that ache, and he *keeps going*.

Jace would always stop as soon as I hit my peak.

Cooper wants to do it again. He makes me feel like he could spend the entire day in here with the sole purpose of making me come.

But I want to make him come, too.

I shift, and he gets the hint as he pulls his fingers out of me.

"I want to see you come again," he murmurs. "It's the most gorgeous vision I think I've ever witnessed."

"Your turn first," I pant. "Stand up."

He does, and he places the showerhead back in its cradle. When he turns around, I don't get up, but I do grab onto his thighs to pull him closer to me. I fist his cock and pump it a few times before I suck it into my mouth, and he reaches onto the wall over my head to brace himself as I suck and pump and lick.

He groans through his pleasure, and I pick up speed, wanting to give him the same type of bliss he gave me. "I'm close," he warns, but I don't care. I keep sucking, pulling him as far back as I can, and his thighs tremble as he starts to lose control.

The hot jet hits the back of my throat, and my automatic reflex is to swallow. A few more pulses hit the back of my throat, and I keep sucking, keep doing what I'm doing as he fights his way through an intense, brutal orgasm.

When the pulses slow, he pulls out of my mouth and collapses on the bench beside me. He tosses an arm around me, and I settle into his side, the perfect placement as our bodies just seem to fit together, like we were each missing a piece of ourselves until we found each other. We both sit in quiet bliss as the water streams down in front of us, and eventually he stands and shuts off the water.

He silently exits the shower and grabs a towel, wrapping it around his waist, and he steps back in with a second towel. Instead of handing it to me, he starts to dry me off. Something about it is intimate and sweet. We're both quietly lost in our thoughts, quietly lost in the afterglow, quietly lost in each other.

He pulls me to a stand and wraps the towel around me, and I grab another one to towel dry my hair while he finishes drying himself, too.

We comb our hair together in the bathroom, me fighting through the tangles while he makes quick work of his hair. I put a little make-up on, and we each get dressed, both of us comfortably quiet as we work through our individual routines together.

Once we're ready, his gaze lifts to mine. His eyes look a little tormented—something I haven't seen from him in the short time I've known him, a reminder that we have a long way to go. "When can I see you again?" His voice is low, and I'm not sure how to lighten the sudden somber mood in here.

My chest warms as I think about the fact that he wants to see me again, and it tightens at the same time as I think about how this blissful time with him will inevitably come to an end. "Depends on when you're back in town."

He presses his lips together, slinging one arm around me as he crushes my body to his. "That's not good enough."

I'm not sure what to say. My instinct is to tell him to stay, but I worry that'll just show my age. He has responsibilities. I'm not even sure if he has the ability to just pack up and move to Vegas with the snap of a finger.

But I want him to.

"Then stay," I finally say because it's the only choice I have. Fuck naivety. Fuck my age. All that matters is how we're both feeling right now, and the desperation in his tone is the exact same thing I'm feeling down to my core. "Take the job, whatever it is, so we can see if this powerful thing between us is as big as we feel like it is."

He drops a soft kiss to my lips rather than responding, and when he pulls back, he heaves out a heavy sigh. "Let's go get you a daiquiri."

I blow out a breath, too, and then I slide my hand into his and follow him down to the Strip.

Chapter 11
Cooper

I order her a strawberry daiquiri and I get myself a half-pina colada, half-strawberry daiquiri mix. It's quite a delight, if I'm being honest, and I keep my ballcap pulled down low over my eyes. Between that and the sunglasses mixed with the amount of day drinkers here on the Strip, nobody notices that Cooper Noah is strolling down the sidewalk hand-in-hand with a gorgeous woman twelve years his junior.

I was hit with a blast of reality when I asked her when I could see her again.

This is real, but we're providing an awful lot of fodder for the media—particularly if I take the offer on the table from Troy. I'll be thrust front and center back into the tabloids, and if we take this thing beyond this weekend, she'll be thrust there, too.

At some point I have to tell her who I am…but I sort of like the dynamic between us just the way it is. Once people find out, they change—and I don't want this to change.

We walk with our drinks down to the Bellagio, where we watch the fountains. We step inside to play some slots. We even manage a romantic trip to the top of the Eiffel Tower, where we kiss as we look down over Vegas and I tell her how I want to take her to the real one in Paris someday.

We ride the giant Ferris Wheel, which is neat during the day but would be spectacular at night, and I note how she attacks every new activity with excitement and a positive attitude. The line for the Ferris Wheel was longer than we'd been expecting, and she spent the time waiting by grilling me with *this* or *that*, allowing us to get to know one another on another new level.

I discover she prefers pizza over pasta, tacos over spaghetti, and pancakes over waffles. She learns that I like trucks over sports cars, outdoor activities over indoor—sex included, and bars over nightclubs.

We wind up back at the hotel a little before it's time for me to meet Kaylee and Ben.

I think about asking if she wants to tag along as my date, but I realize I could use the opportunity away from her to talk to some of the people who know me well and to see if it's all just the illusion of sex or if there are real feelings taking root after barely knowing her a full day.

And so we have to say goodbye.

I kiss her in my hotel room once more. I'm already running late for dinner, so we didn't have time for sex, but at least we fit in all the touristy things we'd planned for the day.

"You'll be back at ten?" she asks.

I nod. "I'm anxious to find out what sort of inside look at Vegas you have planned. Give me your phone," I say. She pulls it out of her purse and hands it over, and I send a text to myself with one word.

Sunshine.

"You've got my number now, and I have yours." I hand her phone back to her. "I'll text you if I'm done early."

She drops it back into her purse then links her arms around my waist. Her head tips back and her green eyes gaze up into mine in that way where she has the ability to completely strip me raw. I want to give her every single part of myself when she looks up at me like that. I want the world to stand still so we can be with each other in it in this way just a little longer.

But time marches on no matter how much we want to freeze the perfect moments.

"Tell me this was real," she murmurs.

I drop a kiss to her lips, and then I pinch her ass. "It was real."

She yelps and giggles as she swats at my hand, and it's that giggle that I could spend the rest of my life listening to.

She leaves, and the second the door closes behind her, I feel the loss. It's a strange sense where I feel like she walked out with a piece of myself I've never been without before.

The only time I've ever felt that way before was when she left earlier to grab her suitcase from her suite.

A strange feeling of restlessness pervades even though I have things to do.

I change my clothes ahead of meeting my friends. Dinner is at a restaurant inside my hotel, so I don't have far to travel to get to

53

them, and when I walk into the private room in the back Kaylee booked for us, I spot Ben Olson, the tight end for the Vegas Aces—Kaylee's husband—first. Of course I do. He's a big dude, and he's just a *presence*. No matter what room he's in, he fills it with loud and gregarious laughter. He glances up and nudges Kaylee, who's staring down at her menu.

She grins and leaps up to tackle hug me before she sits back down, and Ben stands and gives me a bro-hug, too. "Good to see you, man," he says.

He hated me when we first met since he thought I was stealing his girl from him when they were on a break, but eventually he came around when he realized Kaylee and I were nothing more than good friends.

"You too," I say. I slide into the chair across from the two of them, not bothering with the menu. "How's everything?"

They both stare at me with tilted heads for a beat, and then Ben speaks up first. "Why do you look different?"

"I *look* different?" I ask.

Kaylee nods, the crease between her brows deepening as she studies me. "You're right," she says to Ben. "He *does* look different."

"Different how?" I ask, my brows knitting together.

Kaylee studies me with narrowed eyes. "Your smile is wider." She squints at me a little. "You're...I don't know. Lighter, maybe, like your shoulders aren't pressed down by a weight."

"Dopamine," Ben says to her, and then he turns toward me. "Did you...did you get laid?"

Jesus. One fucking night with the girl and even my closest friends can see the difference.

"In fact, I did," I admit.

"Are you dating somebody and you didn't tell me?" Kaylee asks, her voice full of both accusation and bewilderment.

I chuckle. "I'm telling you now, aren't I?"

"How long has this been going on?" Kaylee demands.

I clear my throat. "I just met the girl last night."

"Wait a second. You met her *last night?*" Ben asks. He lets out a low whistle. "Was it a one-night thing?"

I shake my head. "We didn't go into it with any expectations. We spent the night together, and then we spent the day together."

"And you let her go to come meet us for dinner?" Kaylee screeches.

"What can I say? I'm a good friend." I offer an arrogant shrug. "Besides, the Captain down low needed a recharge and she's meeting me back at my room after dinner for another round."

Ben bursts out a laugh as he shakes his head. "Man, are you fucked or what?"

I twist my lips then let out a heavy sigh. "Yeah, I am. Totally fucked."

Kaylee giggles. "And you *got* fucked, which, good for you, Coop. We all know how bad you needed that after your recent dry spell." I shoot her a glare, and she laughs. "Tell us about her."

I don't even know where to start. "She's fucking hilarious for one. We laughed all night together. She's honest and tells it like it is. Plus she's so hot it's unreal, and she's smart, too. She doesn't know who I am, which is an obvious bonus."

"You best believe that girl is Googling the fuck out of you right now, sir," Ben says.

I purse my lips with an easy shrug. "Probably. And it's fine. She got plowed by the Captain first, so she knows what she's getting into." I wink at Kaylee, who giggles as Ben offers a hearty laugh.

"Good for you, man," Ben says.

"What does she do?" Kaylee asks.

I run a hand through my hair and along my jawline, and then I clear my throat before I give it to them straight even though I *know* they're going to tease the shit out of me for it. "She's, uh…studying marketing at UNLV. Last night was her twenty-first birthday."

"Fuck yeah," Ben says, fist pumping. "Wreck that shit, man." He tosses an arm around Kaylee. "You gotta get 'em young these days. Chicks our age just aren't as fun."

Kaylee's lips tighten into a flat line as she gives her husband a look. "I guess I'll let the *chicks* comment slide since you're somehow complementing me. I think?"

Ben laughs, and Kaylee looks at me.

"So that puts, what…about twelve years between the two of you?" she asks.

I nod.

"Ben and I are a decade apart and it works for us. People talk, but we ignore it. With that said, though, she's still in college. Twenty-one is *young*."

"Weren't you twenty-three when you and Ben got together?" I point out.

"Right, but Ben and I had known each other for years and years, and I was out of school," she argues. "We both knew what we were getting into. He was getting a mature, capable woman, and I was getting a big old oaf."

"Hey!" Ben grumbles, and I laugh at the two of them.

The waitress comes by for our order, and I scramble to find something since I haven't bothered with the menu yet.

I change the subject once our orders have been placed.

"How's Tight Fit doing?" I ask Ben, referring to his fitness club. He started with one in Montana, and between Kaylee and him plus the StrongFitKids program, they have six incredibly successful locations with more in the works.

"Doing great," Ben says. He nods toward his wife. "She's more well-versed in what's going on in particular with SFK since I'm in pre-season now."

Kaylee's eyes light up at the chance to talk about StrongFitKids. "SFK's exponential growth has been totally overwhelming. I have all these ideas about running Jumpathons or other types of -athons and charity events in the different Tight Fit locations, probably starting here at one of the locations in Vegas, but I don't have time to put any of it together and all our employees are already overworked. Between the Montana location, the three Vegas locations, and the two in San Diego plus the one we're building in Los Angeles on top of taking care of the twins..." She glances over at Ben as she trails off, and his eyes meet hers tenderly.

It's beautiful to witness the love between these two. They have the whole package—the love, a marriage, jobs they love, a couple of kids. It's what I want, too. It's what I've always wanted, but it's the thing that's always escaped me, the thing that's always been just out of my reach.

"She's doing great," Ben says. "Amazing. She's the best mom in the world. She's the best *partner* in the world, and I don't know how she does all she does."

"I need help," she admits.

I clear my throat. "Would it help if I moved to Vegas?"

They break their gaze as both their heads whip in my direction.

"What?" Kaylee asks.

"This is on the down low, and I haven't made a decision yet, but there's a reason I'm in Vegas," I begin.

"What is it?" Kaylee presses.

"Troy Bodine has been tapped to manage the expansion team the MLB is bringing to Vegas. He wants me back in the game."

Ben lets out another low whistle.

"Oh jeez," Kaylee murmurs. "And then you met the girl last night. All signs point to Vegas. What are you going to do?" She bounces a little excitedly in her seat.

"I think I'm gonna do it," I admit. I blow out a breath. "Not because of her, to be clear, though I'm definitely interested in seeing where it can go with her. But before I even met her last night, I thought it through and knew it was time to get back into the game. Well, both games. Baseball and dating."

Kaylee claps her hands together with excitement as she squeals. "Oh my God, you're moving here?"

"Hey, Peaches," Ben teases his wife. "Calm your tits. You're married."

She rolls her eyes. "I know I am. And so does he," she says, jerking her thumb in my direction.

I nod. "The only romance between the two of us was for your benefit," I say, referring to the brief time we teased the media when we first met.

Ben chuckles. "I'm just teasing you both. It'll be great to have you in town, man. Another dude for golf and poker nights, another face for Tight Fit. Shit, the Daltons will want you at every Monday night family dinner." He glances at Kaylee. "We're all gonna need bigger dining tables." He turns back to me. "But you won't have time to help with SFK if you're playing ball in between wrecking that chick's pussy," he points out.

"I've got five months of offseason," I counter. "Plenty of time for both pussy-wrecking and helping out at SFK."

"So this is really happening?" she asks.

I press my lips together and nod. "Yep. It's really happening."

Kaylee squeals as realization dawns.

It's really happening.

Chapter 12
Cooper

A woman stands near the window when I open the door and walk into my hotel room, and the tightness I felt in my chest on the walk back to my room seems to dissipate at her presence.

I wondered whether she'd really show up.

She did.

"Hey," I say when I walk in, and she blows out a breath when she spots me. I twist the ballcap I'm wearing down low over my eyes so the bill is in the back since I know I'm going to want to kiss her and the bill tends to get in the way of that.

She studies me a beat. "Did you get hotter in the time we were apart?"

I chuckle as I make my way across the room. "Yes. I worked hard on that."

We stare at each other a beat, neither of us touching as we both take in the fact that we're here in this place again and the fantasy we started twenty-four hours ago can continue.

I lean in and press a soft kiss to her neck just below her ear. "I missed you." My voice is low and gravelly, and it forces a soft moan from her.

"I missed you, too," she says, and then she loops her arms around me and my lips find hers.

Just like with everything between the two of us, the kiss intensifies to fire rather quickly, but she forces the end first. "My truck is down at valet if you're ready for the thing I planned, but if you'd rather get naked, I'm down with that."

"Back up a second," I say. "You have a truck?"

She laughs. "I do. A Ford Ranger."

"I drive an F-150," I admit. "And can I just say it makes you even hotter that you drive a truck?"

"Yes, you can say that," she deadpans. "And it's true. I always wanted one, and I find guys who drive trucks hot, too. Now answer the question. Date or sex?"

I laugh at her impatience. "Let's go on a proper date. Then I'll get you naked afterward."

"Deal. Unless *I* get you naked *during* our date." She grabs my hand, and heads toward the door, pulling me behind her.

"Where are we going?" I ask.

"It's a surprise."

"Is it another nightclub?"

She narrows her eyes at me. "A, you don't like nightclubs, and B, the challenge was to show you a side of Vegas you haven't seen before. I assume you've been to your fair share of Vegas clubs, so no, that's not what it is."

I turn my hat forward again to duck beneath the bill as we approach the elevator. "Thank God." I sling my arm around her shoulders as we take the trip down to the first floor, and I follow her out to the valet stand.

As expected, a black Ranger pulls up a minute later. She hops into the driver's seat, and I settle into the passenger one. I pull my hat off and run my hand through my hair, and she navigates out of the busy valet area and onto the even busier Strip. Taylor Swift plays in the background, the *Red* album, and I'm quiet as I let her focus on getting out of traffic.

She heads toward the highway and merges on. We travel north for a few minutes before she merges onto another highway to head west. As the car carries us further away from the bright lights of Las Vegas Boulevard, I start to see stars in the sky and I'm even more curious as to where the hell she's taking me.

Eventually she gets off the highway and turns toward Red Rock Canyon. I spot the hours of the driving loop, and it's closed, so I still have no idea where we're going. She follows the signs toward a campground but then drives right past it, dust kicking up in our wake toward the nearly deserted campground. She drives another couple minutes, and eventually she pulls off the road to a stop in total darkness except for the lights of her truck.

"We're here," she announces proudly, and she gets out of the truck. She opens the door to the backseat while I jump out of the passenger seat and walk around toward her, and when she emerges, she holds a huge basket.

"We're...here?" I ask.

"Yep!" She nods toward the tailgate. "Can you open that?"

I pull the handle, and she sets the basket down. She pulls out a camping pad with pillows built in, and she spreads it out along the bed of the truck. She grabs a blanket, too, and a bottle of wine— no glasses.

"Are you a camper?" I ask.

"I've gone a few times, but I got this pad for my birthday and figured it was time to break it in."

I hop onto the tailgate easily, and I hold out a hand to help her up. She sets the bottle of wine on the side, and we both take off our shoes to get comfy before we lay back on the camping pad.

I draw in a deep breath. It's still hot and dry in the middle of August here in Vegas at eighty-five degrees at nearly ten at night, but without the sun beating down on us, it's not so bad.

"You asked for a side of Vegas you've never seen before, and I assume you've never driven out to the middle of the desert to look at the stars," she says as she settles into a comfortable position.

I reach over and grab her hand, linking my fingers through hers. "This is incredible." My voice is low even though it's just the two of us out here. The closest people are probably a mile away at that campground, and it was pretty quiet back there.

We stare up at the night sky as it glitters with stars. It's a clear night, so clear that I can even see the milky haze of the Milky Way from here.

It's peaceful and quiet—the opposite of the loud exuberance the Strip offers, and it's hard to believe all that excitement is just a half hour away from this tranquil paradise.

"The pad's comfy," she muses as we both stare up at the sky, baffled by its complexity and its beauty from this angle.

"I want to take you camping someday," I say. "We can sit around a bonfire drinking beer and roasting marshmallows, and then I can wreck you in the best way inside our tent."

She laughs, and it's that heartwarming sound that's already so familiar to me. "I'm in." She clears her throat. "But that assumes we're taking this beyond this weekend."

"I'd like to," I say quietly. Earnestly.

"I'd like to, too. But you'll be in San Diego, and I'll be here...it'll get complicated, don't you think?"

"Most definitely. But it'll be easier once I move here," I say carefully.

She sucks in a breath. "You're taking the job?"

"I was seventy-five percent sure I was going to take it anyway, and then I met you. You put up a pretty convincing argument to cover that last quarter, and then I talked to my friends tonight at dinner…it just feels like this is where I'm supposed to be."

Her fingers tighten in mine. "This?"

"Right here. Beside you. We'll have challenges, but I want to figure out how to make this work in the real world. You're in college, and I'm…not. You're young and have so much life to experience." Meanwhile, I'm almost thirty-three and I'm at a point in my life where I'm ready to start a family.

Could it be with her?

Crazier things have happened.

My parents were only together a few weeks when they got engaged.

"But if you want to see where it goes, well…so do I," I finish.

"I want that more than anything," she breathes.

"My parents only knew each other three weeks before they knew they were going to spend their lives together," I admit.

"Tell me about your parents," she says.

"I grew up in Chicago. My mom is a first-grade teacher, and she's my best friend. My dad was an electrician."

"Was?" she asks softly.

"He passed away when I was nine."

"Oh, God, Cooper. I'm so sorry," she murmurs.

I squeeze her hand. "Thanks. He lost his father when he was a teenager. It made me feel like the men in my family don't get much time with their kids, and that's part of why I always wanted to have kids at a young age."

"Do you have kids?" she asks.

"No. I have two nephews, my brother's kids. He's four years older than me and his kids are nine and eleven. It just…hasn't worked out for me yet, and now I'm beyond what I'd consider *young* to have kids. But I still want three or four," I admit. "What about you? Do you want kids?"

"Yes and no. I don't think about it much. I figure I have plenty of time, and it's not a pressing priority at the moment. I've never been one of those people who felt like I was born to be a mother. I want to establish myself in a career first before I'm ready to go down that path."

I think about that for a beat. It's the first red flag of our short time together. I'm at a point in my life where I want to settle down, where I want to start a family. She's not ready for those things, and that's fine. She's young, and she shouldn't have to make those types of decisions yet.

But what the hell am I doing here?

Am I just prolonging the inevitable?

Or is this worth exploring?

I don't know the answer to that, but I do know one thing.

I'm not quite ready to let go yet.

Chapter 13
Gabby

He's quiet, and I wish I knew what he was thinking. It's a reminder that we're still virtual strangers.

I want to know everything about him. I don't want to be strangers.

But the thought of having kids right now is pretty low on my radar. He wants them, and soon. That feels big—like it's something that could eventually spell the end of whatever it is we're starting. It's a reminder that the twelve years that span between us actually *could* get in the way of making this work outside of this fantasy weekend.

"What about your parents?" he asks.

"I didn't know who my father was until about three years ago. My whole life, my mother lied to me and told me she didn't know who he was. Just before my eighteenth birthday, I took one of those ancestry tests. I tracked down a first cousin, and I ended up meeting my dad through her. He lived in Vegas, so I decided to switch from UC Denver, where I'd already committed to attending, to UNLV, where my best friend had already committed to attending anyway and I'd already been accepted. I've spent the last three years getting to know my father and learning all the ways my mother was totally and completely toxic through my entire childhood."

"That must've been really tough," he says.

I press my lips together as the hot sting of tears threatens behind my eyes. "It was. She lied to me my entire life. My dad knew she'd had me, and he sent her checks every month, but she threatened him in a lot of different ways to stay out of my life." I sigh. "It's complicated. I had a good childhood, for the most part, but every time I asked about him, she lied."

"Why?" he asks. "Did she do it to protect you or something?"

"I haven't asked, to be honest. I'm still too angry with her."

"She's still your mom, Gabby. She must have had some reason," he points out.

"Maybe. And maybe someday I'll ask, but I'm happy living with my dad and getting to know him better," I say. "I don't want to cloud that with whatever my mom says about him now. I won't know if it's truth or lies anyway, so I've taken the last three years to form my own opinion."

"What was it like when you met him?" he asks.

I shake my head as I swipe away a tear that tips over. "It felt like I'd found a missing piece of myself, you know? I'm so much like him and I never had the chance to know him growing up. I don't know if I can ever forgive my mother for that."

"Well if losing my dad at a young age taught me anything, it's that we're not guaranteed anything. If you want to make amends with your mom, do it before you lose your chance," he says.

"Yeah," I murmur. "You sound like a wise old man spouting platitudes."

"I'll show you old, Sunshine."

I giggle, but then he shifts so he's suddenly hovering over me, and the giggling ceases as pure lust drives into its place. He thrusts his hips against mine, his hard cock ready to come out and play.

He presses soft kisses to my neck. "We need to get you on birth control so I can have my way with you any time I want," he mutters against my skin.

"I'll get on it tomorrow," I moan as I roll my hips against his.

He chuckles, the sound humming through me as my tummy does a little flip.

His lips move along my neck to my jawline and eventually to my own lips, and we kiss luxuriously there in the bed of my truck, the stars gleaming above us as the feelings I've been feeling since the moment I met him take root deep in my chest, burrowing in as they vow to stay a while.

I reach down and pull a condom from my pocket, and I hold it between the two of us. "I came prepared," I say, and he nips another soft kiss to my lips as he snatches it from between my fingers.

We both glance around. There's nobody out here, and even if someone *was* coming, we'd hear them from plenty of space away to cover ourselves with the blanket.

With that in mind, I push on his chest. I pull my shirt over my head and unhook my bra, and then I shimmy out of my jeans and panties. I push on his chest until he's lying all the way back. He's still fully clothed, but I'm completely naked. I climb over the top of him, spreading my legs so they're on either side of him as I feel the rough fabric of his jeans right against my most sensitive parts. He reaches up to run his hands along my torso, stopping to feel my breasts, and I gyrate over the top of him, my movements picking up speed as he tweaks my nipples. He pumps up into me, managing to hit my clit through his jeans, and I cry out into the quiet stillness of the night.

"Fuck yeah," he murmurs. "Get it, baby. Come for me." My eyes meet his as he brushes his thumbs across my nipples, and the sight of his lust-glazed eyes in the darkness out here is overwhelming.

I reach down to tease my own clit as I keep gyrating over him, and he continues to thrust toward me.

The sensations are enough to push me over the edge, and I tip my head back and push my tits into his hands as a fierce orgasm rips through me. My legs shake as the contractions ripping through me start to slow, and he drops his hands from my breasts to run them along my thighs.

I collapse down on top of him, and his palms move to my back. He rubs my back gently as I live in the bliss for a few beats, and then he says, "Fuck, that was hot."

I'm inexperienced. I'm not a virgin, but he makes me want to do things I've never done before. He makes me feel confident and sexy…something the boys I've been with before never managed to make me do.

Eventually my heartbeat starts to return to normal, and I sit up again. His dick is still hard against my body, and I reach down and tug on his shirt. He wrestles out of it, and I move off him long enough to tug on the button of his jeans. He helps pull them down and kick them off along with his boxer briefs, and then he rips open the condom and rolls it on.

"Do you need a minute?" he asks.

I shake my head slowly as I climb over him again. "I want you inside me."

"Your wish is my command," he says, and he fists his cock as I line up over the top of him.

I slam down, and we both grunt at the feel.

"God, you're so tight after that orgasm. I fucking love how you feel," he says.

I don't know what to say to that. *You're so big and hard* sounds stupid, but I force the self-conscious thoughts away and live in the moment. "Your cock feels so good inside me." My voice is tentative, but the lust in his eyes seems to intensify at my words, so he must like it.

"Get used to it, Sunshine," he says, and then his hands move to my ass, and he directs our movements from the bottom as he starts to move his cock in and out of me.

Emotions course through me as we each fill the air with our moans, a beautiful soundtrack to the quiet night. I never want it to end, but I feel it building toward another orgasm. I never want to let him go, but he has to. He's catching a flight back home tomorrow and who knows what will come next? Even if he moves here, there's no guarantee it'll feel the way it has over this weekend.

It's unnatural for feelings to be this intense this soon…or maybe that's just what we're taught either by society or through personal experience as we allow feelings to grow and develop over time.

It's not love yet…but at the same time, what I feel for Cooper after the last twenty-four hours is even stronger than what I felt for Jace, who I dated for eight months.

It might be love. And if it's not, if it's just passion and lust, I know that with enough time and nurturing, it could turn into love.

We don't need to define it for now. We just need to live in the moment, to live in the feelings, to live in each other as inhibitions are tossed aside and we allow this to happen.

"Fuck," he growls, and my eyes fly open to watch the show as he starts to come. His face is beautiful as it contorts with pleasure, pleasure he's taking from *me*, from my body, and I memorize every beautiful freckle, every gorgeous line, every masculine detail as he pumps into me. When his pleasure slows, he lets go of my ass and grabs one of my breasts in one hand and he thumbs my clit with the other. I ride out the wave, and then the pleasure slams into me all at once.

I cry out as the brutal climax takes over. I writhe over the top of Cooper while I wait it out, and when it slows, I collapse over him once again.

He doesn't pull out of me. Instead, we lie together for a long time in silence as he strokes my back and our panting slows. I think

I fall asleep for a beat, because eventually he shifts and slips out of me, and it's the loss of our connection that seems to wake me.

I move off him and reach into the basket, and then I hand him a little package of tissue I brought along in case that happened. He chuckles as he takes care of the condom, and I put my clothes back on. He does the same, and then we gaze up at the stars together a little longer.

Soft conversation flows between us as we continue to get to know one another on a deeper level...as we continue to inexplicably fall for each other, the end in sight as time marches on later and later into the night, both of us dreading daybreak when it'll be time for this weekend together to end.

Chapter 14
Cooper

W̲e drive up the hill a little and gaze down at the view of the Strip as we pass the bottle of wine back and forth.

I'm really doing it.

This will be home.

I have a lot to do before that can become my reality, though, and only a few weeks to do it in. Troy wants me back here September one to start training, which means I have less than three weeks to train someone to take over my position at SFK, pack up my apartment, find a place in Vegas, and make the move.

And I don't really want to tell Gabby the truth about the job yet—not when things are so new between us. Not when things are so *easy* between us. My career will complicate things, but it won't affect what's happening between us until spring training, and that's still months away. I'll tell her before then. In fact, it might be fun to take her to the stadium once I've signed my contract and tell her there in person.

Despite our easy conversation as we learn more about each other, I've left baseball out of the discussion entirely. Surely she knows by now. Surely like Ben suggested she's looked me up. But if she has, she hasn't mentioned it. I love just being regular guy Cooper who works for a health organization for kids, not being the five-time All-Star and World Series MVP known for keeping calm under pressure.

It's a huge part of who I am, but I like that I'm not defined by it in her eyes. It makes me want to leave it out of the conversation a little longer, especially after what happened with Stacy.

She didn't just cheat on me. She cheated on me after I got hurt and had to stop playing. She cheated on me with a teammate.

She said it was because she felt alone and sad, that I was lashing out at her because I was depressed I had to stop playing.

I wasn't depressed. I was a little down, sure. A little out of character considering I'm the kind of guy who's always in good spirits. Maybe not the party animal Ben Olson is, but still generally friendly and sociable, even when I was hurt and taken out of the game.

She blamed *me* for her cheating on me. That's the thing that hurt the most, I think. That was the part that made me question things about myself…like how I could be with someone like her in the first place. I don't mention much of that to Gabby, though over the course of this weekend, we managed to touch on a lot of it.

"What time's your flight?" she asks.

"Nine," I say. I glance at my watch. "Less than nine hours from now."

"Can you stay a little longer?"

I blow out a breath. "I wish I could. My mom is coming to visit me, and her flight gets in close to the same time as mine so I can just drive us both home from the airport. This was just supposed to be a quick trip to town to meet with my buddy about a job opportunity, and I booked an extra night to meet my friends for dinner."

"Your mom is coming to visit you?" she asks.

"Yeah. She's going to love you." The words are out before I can stop them, but they feel as natural as breathing. Of course she'll meet my mom someday. Just as I'll meet her dad, and maybe her mom down the line when she's ready to forgive her. "She always hated my ex, and I guess I should've listened. She's a great judge of character."

"How long's she staying?"

"Tomorrow through Friday, so all week." I take a sip from the bottle of wine and hand it back to Gabby.

"Don't you have to work?"

I nod. "And give my notice. And pack up my place."

"What will she do while she's in town?"

"Spend her days either shopping or reading at the beach under a giant umbrella, and spend her evenings cooking me all my favorite meals."

"She sounds amazing," she says.

I smile as I think about my mom. She's my biggest cheerleader, and she's also candid and honest with me even when the conversations are difficult, and I'm very interested to hear what she has to say about me playing again before I confirm with Troy. Even though I've already made up my mind, I'm still curious to get her take on it. "She is."

We finish the bottle of wine between the two of us, and we fall asleep on the mat in the back of her truck for a while. I wake first just as the first dawn of light starts to paint the horizon.

When I shift, she jolts awake, too, and we both sit up and lean our backs on the rear panel. I toss an arm around her shoulder and she leans into me as we stare silently together at the landscape. Dawn turns toward the sunrise. It's gorgeous here, and I look around at the red rocks where this canyon derives its name.

As I glance around, I can't help but think that we'll be back here together someday.

Of course we'll be back. This is where we fell in love.

That *has* to be what's coursing through me right now.

One of the things my previous relationships always lacked was the ease in which I find myself with Gabby. She's lighthearted and fun, my perfect match in a lot of ways despite the differences looming between us. I want to make this work. If I can wake up with this same feeling one more day, that would make it all worth it.

I think back to my time with Stacy. Not once in the five years we were together did we drive out to the middle of the desert and fall asleep in the back of my truck after staying up too late talking and stargazing.

Not once.

She wasn't right for me, but I suspect Gabby just might be.

I hear a quiet sniffle, and when I glance over at her, I see her brushing away her silent tears.

"What's wrong?" I whisper.

She lifts a shoulder. "Sunrises always make me a little emotional. I'm not sure why. The beauty of the Earth, the gratitude for another day."

"Oh, Sunshine," I murmur, thinking how appropriate that nickname is for her even though it just sort of spilled out of me when I first said it.

"It's something else today. Today it signifies the end of our time together. I don't want it to end. I don't want the sun to rise."

I pull her in closer to me, squeezing her shoulders. "This isn't the end," I say softly, pressing my lips to the top of her head. "It can't be."

I feel emotion clogging my throat, too, an unfamiliar and strange feeling that tells me just how deep I already am into this thing with her.

It's a little terrifying, if I'm being honest, but we're jumping in together.

That makes it feel like we're both going to be okay.

We don't have time for one last bang once we're back at my hotel. I have enough time to toss my clothes in my suitcase and grab her into my arms as that same emotion closes up my throat.

I don't know what to say, and I'm the kind of person who is never at a loss for words.

But even if I *had* the words…I'm not sure I could get them out at the moment.

"Well," she says. "You've got my number. Ball's in your court, I guess."

I chuckle. "Ball's in both our courts, Sunshine. We're not playing games here. If you want to text me the second the car door closes behind me, do it."

"It won't scare you off?" She snags her bottom lip between her teeth.

I drop a soft kiss to her lips to get her to stop biting them with worry. "Would it scare you off if I did it first?"

She shakes her head. "Point taken. Have a safe trip."

"You too."

"Why is this so hard?" she asks.

I press my lips together then offer her a sad smile. "Because it's real, and reality hurts sometimes. Come home with me."

My mom will flip if I bring a girl home to meet her, but I'll deal with that storm when the time is right.

Her shoulders drop a little, and I think it might be from relief that I invited her. "I can't. I'm going out with friends tomorrow and I'm meeting with my advisor on Monday. And I'm helping substitute a dance class for kids this week while the regular teacher is out of town."

"Next weekend, then. Come to San Diego."

She nods a little as she thinks it over. "Okay. Yeah, I think I can do that."

I can't help the wide smile that breaks across my lips. I knew I'd be coming back here eventually, but having solid plans in the works to see each other again lifts a weight that was heavier than I realized.

I press my lips to hers. "I need to go, but I can't wait to see you again."

"Back at you, Captain."

I chuckle and kiss her once more, and then she walks me out. I get into the car, close the door behind me, and pull out my phone to send her a text.

There's already one waiting for me.

Gabby: *Boo. I'm first. Hope I didn't scare you. [kiss emoji]*

Me: *Boo back at you. Miss you already.*

I turn toward the window to wave, and I spot her as she brushes away the tears falling from her eyes.

My heart cracks as I wave until she's out of sight, and then I exhale a long breath as the car carries me away from her and toward the airport.

Chapter 15
Cooper

I head down to baggage claim even though I carried on so I can meet my mother. I spent the whole flight thinking about my weekend in Vegas, and the second I landed, Gabby was the first person I texted, and she replied with a selfie she took of us on the top of the Eiffel Tower and a line about how she wishes I was there with her.

It felt right for her to be the first person I contacted with news. My mom was the second.

I spot her standing by the carousel waiting for her suitcase. She's never been a light packer, and she's only gotten worse with age.

She's in her own little world when I sneak up behind her with a bear hug, and she whirls around to face me, her face breaking into a huge smile when her eyes land on mine. "Cooper Michael Noah, don't you ever scare me like that!"

I chuckle.

"Good timing." She nods toward the belt. "That purple suitcase is mine."

I grab it off when it comes near us. "Ready?"

"No, I've got one more."

"One more what?" I ask stupidly.

"Suitcase."

"You brought *two* suitcases for a six-day trip?"

"Honey, yes, of course I did. One of them is filled with stuff for you, though. I did some spring cleaning and found a few things I thought you might want now that you're settling into San Diego," she says.

Oh boy.

She pauses as she studies me for a beat. "Oh my God, you met a girl."

"What?" I ask, the second time in the last five seconds I've sounded like a dumbass.

"You met someone!" She claps her hands together and squeals a little. "When can I meet her?"

"Not anytime soon." I don't mention that I actually invited her to come home with me and if she hadn't had plans tomorrow, she'd be meeting my mom right now.

"So there *is* someone? That was a test! You failed!" She grabs onto my arm and hugs it. "Tell me everything about her and leave out not one single detail."

I laugh. This is going to be a long six days. "I have a lot to tell you, but let's save *something* for the car ride home."

"Ahh, I'm so excited, my baby boy!" she says, clapping again.

So I get my sunny disposition from her. But she's more Type A, while my dad was more laid back—I get that from him. My older brother is my opposite. He's Type A like my mom, but he takes it to the extreme as a successful attorney in Chicago. He's married to his high school sweetheart and they have two very active boys. He seems like he's got it all.

"How's Connor?" I ask.

"Busy busy. He's got some big case he's been prepping for, and he's been in and out of town a lot. I went to Ethan's summer league baseball game a few days ago, and gosh, every time I watch him play it reminds me of you at that age. And Jacob's still doing swim. He had a meet a few weeks ago and got second place," she says, catching me up on the latest news with my nephews.

"And Marissa?" I ask, referring to my sister-in-law.

"Did I tell you she decided not to return this year?" she asks. She and my mom teach at the same school—my mom teaches first grade, and Marissa teaches fourth. Or she did until this year, I guess.

I shake my head. "Why?"

"Those little journals she makes went viral on the clock app and she can barely keep up with orders. Between that and the kids, something had to give."

"The clock app?"

"TikTok," she clarifies, and I laugh.

"Right. And you?" I ask.

"I go back next Monday for teacher meetings, but I'm all ready for the year. My team and I met over the summer to plan and we

74

even made all our copies for first quarter. We've got it down pat, which is why I get to enjoy the last week of summer with my baby boy." She squeezes my cheeks, and she's pretty much the only person in the world who could get away with squeezing Cooper Noah's cheeks in public.

I laugh. It might be a long week, but it's also going to be a fun week.

The second we're sealed into the quiet privacy of my truck, the relentless grilling begins. "So this girl…"

"I have other items to discuss first, but I will get to the girl." I navigate out of the parking lot and pay the exorbitant fee for leaving my truck at the airport, and then I head toward the highway.

"Go for it," she says, holding her hands out.

"When we get home. Maybe over a glass of wine."

"Uh oh," she says. "He's already breaking out the wine. This must be big."

"It's huge."

She sits quietly, her mind working I'm sure on the thirty minute drive from the airport to the three bed, two bath luxury apartment I've been renting. When I first moved out here, my boss, Carla, put me up in corporate housing close to the office. I opted for a place with a view of the water despite the convenience of literally walking across the street to get to work. This way I can relax with a view when I get home, but I'm also not far from downtown where I can find the action if I want it.

So far I've not really found myself wanting it, though. I've been enjoying my quiet existence here in San Diego.

I'm in East Village, literally a three minute walk from Petco Park, where the Padres play. I've attended more than a few games since I've lived here, and I still keep in touch with a lot of the men I played ball with over the years.

Once we're home, I lug my mom's suitcases plus my own up to the eleventh-floor suite I rent. She gets settled in while I open a bottle of merlot, her favorite, plus a bottle of beer for myself.

"Chinese okay for dinner?" I yell across the apartment, and I hear a *yes* from her bedroom.

She appears a few minutes later, and I hand her the glass of wine while I grab a second beer since the first one's already gone.

"Balcony?" I suggest, and she nods. "The food will be here in a half hour or so."

She follows me out, and we each take a seat in the chairs out there. This place came fully furnished, a definite bonus considering all the furniture I own is currently in the house where my ex lives.

I don't know why I let her stay there. I just wanted to get out of town. I should sell the place, but it's a lot of work to sell a house and I haven't had the motivation to put the work into it.

And so it sits there, my ex who cheated on me living there because I'm too goddamn nice to kick her out.

"What's going on, Coop?" my mom asks after a long sip of wine.

I rub my palms together up and down as I draw in a deep breath. In my head, I recite the little poem my dad used to say when he was teaching my brother and me to remain calm in any situation. *Up palm, down palm, time to get calm. Breathe real deep and take the leap.*

She glances at my hands. She knows what I'm doing.

"Troy Bodine asked me to fly to Vegas with a job offer. The Vegas expansion team was approved, and he'll be its manager." I pause, and then I rush the final sentence. "He wants me to play."

She spits out her wine, the red liquid flying everywhere. "What?"

I suppress a laugh. It's so her personality to have an over the top reaction to the news. "He said with expansion teams, he'll end up with leftovers, so he wants someone who can be the face of the team."

"You do have a cute face," she says, grabbing my jaw to cup it and squeeze. "But do you even *want* to play again?"

I clear my throat then kick my feet up, balancing them on the handrail in front of me as I stare out at the view.

"I think it's time to get back in the game." I chug some more of my beer as I think that through.

"Is your elbow back to a hundred?"

"Yeah. And the stats don't lie. Remember what my doctor said? Around eighty-five percent of patients who get the Tommy John surgery are back in the game after a year of recovery. The pain is gone." I straighten and bend my arm at the elbow to demonstrate my bionic elbow after the orthopedic surgeon reconstructed my elbow with ligaments from my hamstring tendon.

"How are you feeling about it?" she asks cautiously.

"I'm thinking honestly I'm a little bored. I like working with Carla, but I can still do work for StrongFitKids off-season, and Kaylee and Ben are up in Vegas, so I can work more closely with them on that side of the program. When I left Troy's place," I say, leaving out what Troy's place actually was, "I made a vow to myself that it was time to get back into both games—baseball and dating. And wouldn't you know it? A gorgeous woman sat down at my blackjack table not ten minutes later."

"Oh!" she says, clapping her hands again. "This is it! The meet cute!"

I roll my eyes. "We spent the entire weekend together," I admit.

"And?"

"And…" I shrug, and I take another swig of my beer before I answer. "And I think I might have fallen in love with her."

"What?" she screeches again, and thank God she didn't have a mouthful or merlot this time.

I nod. "She's incredible, Mom. She's beautiful. Long dark hair that's almost black, and these big green eyes that just look into my soul. She's smart, and she's hilarious."

She looks a little skeptical, and I answer the question before she even asks it.

"She has no idea who I am," I say.

"You're sure?"

I shrug. "Maybe she looked me up, maybe not. But she never mentioned it, and neither did I."

"You can't fall in love with someone when you're not being honest about yourself," she says.

"I *was* honest about who I am." I lift a shoulder. "I just left out baseball."

"But that's a huge part of who you are, Coop! You can't just leave it out of the conversation," she points out.

"I'll tell her at some point. I keep thinking it might be good to take her to the stadium and confess it all there. Once I've signed the contract and it's been made official, of course. But for now, I really like being Cooper, the guy who works with kids, instead of Cooper, former baseball player."

"I suppose I can't fault you for that, but you have to be honest with her. She needs to know what she's getting into before she falls for you, too." She follows up that statement with a sip of wine.

"Too late. We both felt it, Mom. We toured Vegas, and she took me out to the middle of the desert where we watched the stars when it was dark and we stayed out there long enough to watch the sun lift over the horizon while we drank wine and talked about everything."

"Except baseball," she reminds me.

"Except baseball," I confirm.

"So she's the one?" she asks.

"It's way too early to decide that, but if the next time I see her feels anything like this past weekend did…then yeah, I think she might be the one."

"I want to meet her."

I laugh. "No." I don't tell her I invited her home with me.

"Oh, come on! You *know* I'll know within ten seconds whether she's right for you. Like with Stacy, remember?"

"Exactly why it's a negative, Mother. I'm not letting anyone get inside this yet." I drain the rest of my beer.

She blows out a loud and dramatic sigh. "Fine. But if I don't like her and you want me to say I do, I'd do that for you."

I laugh. "Like you did with Stacy?"

She rolls her eyes. "Point taken."

Stacy first met my mom when she came into town from Chicago to visit during the offseason. We'd only been together a few months, and she wasn't living with me yet, but she was staying over most nights. She headed up to bed first, and my mom let me know how she felt the minute she was out of the room.

"I don't like her," she'd whispered to me.

She hasn't liked anyone I dated. Ever. Mostly, I always suspected, because even though she wanted me to settle down and have kids, nobody would ever be good enough for her baby boy.

She loves Marissa, but it's different with my mom and Connor. He's always kept to himself, while I've probably overshared with her. He was thirteen when we lost my dad, and he turned inward while I clung onto my mom. He bolted from her house the second he turned eighteen, and that left us time to grow closer and closer as her life became my baseball games.

"Do you at least have a picture so I can have the mental image of you with her?" she asks.

With a bit of reluctance, I pull out my phone. I flip to the message she sent me with the photo of the two of us, and I stare at her for a beat. Her smile is wide, and her green eyes are expressive. God, she's beautiful.

I hand over the phone, nerves pinging my chest as my mom studies the photo.

"She's gorgeous," she says. "Those eyes…wow. So pretty." She looks over at me. "And your smile, Coop. It's genuine. It's the first genuine smile I've seen out of you with a girl…maybe ever." She studies the picture again, and then she looks back at me. "I like her with you. You complement each other really well." She hands the phone back and clears her throat. "How old did you say she was?"

I let out a long, deep sigh. "Twenty-one."

"Twenty-one?" she shrieks.

"Twenty-one," I confirm.

"Cooper Michael Noah! You're robbing the cradle!"

"Oh my God, Mother. Stop it. I am not." Keeping true to character, my tone is even rather than defensive. "She's legal."

"Barely," she mutters. "What does she want with an old man like you? Money? She wants a sugar daddy?"

"Mom!" Okay, maybe I'm getting a *little* defensive. "It's not like that. I taught her how to play blackjack, and it was her birthday, so she invited me to the club. We danced, and then we talked, and then we spent the night together. We ate breakfast, we went up the Eiffel Tower, we got to know one another. It was a perfect weekend, and I won't let you sit here slandering it and vilifying me."

"Is she still in school?" she asks quietly.

I nod. "She's studying marketing."

"And you're getting back in the game?"

I know where she's going with this. "Yes."

"You don't think the press is going to have a field day with you dating someone half your age?"

"Half my age would be sixteen," I say dryly.

"Almost sixteen and a half," she points out. "Meanwhile, she's only five years beyond that."

"Half plus seven is the old saying, isn't it?"

Her brow crinkles. "Yes, exactly. Half plus *seven*. Not half plus *five*."

I blow out a breath. "I don't care about her age. You shouldn't, either."

"She's almost twelve years younger than you, darling. When Dad died, she wasn't even born yet. When you went into high school, she was *two*. When you went into college, she was starting first grade. When you hit the minors, she was in fifth grade. It's a wide gap, baby boy." Her tone is gentle even though her words are harsh.

"You don't think I've thought of that? And I keep coming back to the same thing. It. Doesn't. Matter. All that matters is how she makes me feel, and I've never felt like this with anybody else." The passion in my voice surprises even myself.

"Okay, then, honey. I'll give this a chance." She takes a quick sip of her merlot. "But only because you really do seem a little different to me. You really do seem like you made some connection, and I just want you to be happy. But I want you to be happy while you've ensured you've fully thought this through."

"Thanks, Mom. I will make sure to do that." I say the words to brush her off, but the truth is clear. I've already thought it through, and I can't wait until the moment Gabby is back in my arms.

Chapter 16
Gabby

"**H**ave you thought about an internship for your senior year?" Dr. Foley, my academic advisor at UNLV, asks.

I shake my head. "Not yet. When do I need to have that lined up?"

She glances at the calendar in front of her. "By February first, so you have lots of time, but some students have already started finding them and they've started working." She lifts a shoulder. "Something to think about. You'll just have the internship and your Marketing Policies course remaining."

"I'll find something." Now that I think about it, I bet I could work with my dad. I'll have to ask him, but he's been gone a lot the last few weeks.

My meeting lasts all of five minutes, but it's the kickoff to school starting in just two short weeks. My advisor reviewed my schedule for this semester, which is intense but not horrible as I finally get to focus on the courses I've always been interested in taking: Marketing Planning and Analysis, Global Consumer Behavior, Leadership and Management Skills, and Business Marketing. It should be both a challenging and interesting semester of classes, and I overloaded my previous semesters so I could take a slightly lighter schedule my senior year.

That way I can enjoy it, too.

And I'm hoping I get to enjoy it with Cooper around.

Speaking of Cooper, we talked last night for an hour before we both reluctantly called it a night, and we've already texted a little this morning.

I decide to try calling him on my way home from my meeting.

"Good morning," his warm voice answers, and it sends a little thrill up my spine. "How was your meeting?"

"Good," I say. "My advisor told me I need to figure out an internship next semester."

"Have you thought about it?"

"A little. I have some ideas, but nothing set in stone yet."

"Let me know how I can help," he says.

I hear someone in the background yelling from what sounds like another room. "Cooper Michael Noah! You have to come see this!"

"Just a second!" he yells back.

"Is that your mom?" I ask.

He chuckles. "Yeah."

"Cooper Michael?" I tease.

"What's your full name?"

"Why do you want to know?" I narrow my eyes even though he can't see me.

"So I can yell it out when I come inside you."

I gasp. "Gabriella Rose Grant."

"Well, Gabriella Rose, I told her about you."

"You did? What did you say?"

He lowers his voice. "That you're so goddamn hot it's not right. That when I slide my dick into your tight pussy, it's the best feeling I've ever experienced in my life."

"Shut up," I say, my cheeks flaming as I merge onto the highway, his voice filling my truck with his dirty words over the Bluetooth. "You did *not* tell her that."

"No, I didn't." He laughs. "I said you're funny and beautiful and honest and smart, you light up the room with your sunshine, and you make me feel things I've never felt before."

"Back at you, Captain." Warmth spreads through my chest at his words.

The depth of emotion I feel with him already is frightening. I can't imagine the exponential growth that might occur if we nurture this and give it time to grow.

"I better go before she asks to talk to you," he says.

I giggle. "Tell her I said hi."

"And stoke those flames? Not a chance in hell. I'll call you later, okay?"

"Okay. Miss you."

"Not as much as I miss you, Sunshine. Bye."

We hang up, and I can't help the dreamy and breathless little sigh that falls from my mouth.

Instead of heading home to my dad's place, I head to the apartment Mia and Chelsea share to pick Mia up for lunch. Chelsea headed to California for a trip with her family for a few days, and Mia and I made lunch plans.

"How was the meeting with Dr. Foley?" she asks once she opens the passenger door and slides into the seat. She's working toward her bachelor's in business management, so we've taken a lot of the same classes together over the last three years and we share the same advisor.

"Fine. She told me I need to start looking for an internship for next semester."

"Any ideas?" she asks as she buckles her seatbelt.

"I want to find somewhere that might hire me on after I finish my degree," I say. I pull out of the parking lot and head toward her favorite Thai restaurant. "I've thought about asking my dad if he might have something for me."

"Ooh, that's a great idea. Ask him if there's anything for me, too," she says. "Wouldn't it be fun to do an internship together?"

"It would be *so* fun!" I say, but the truth is I'm not sure I'd really want that. We've done everything together since we met our freshman year of high school. I love her dearly. She's the sister I never had. But I also sort of want something that's just for me. I feel selfish telling her that, though, so I exaggerate my excitement over the idea.

"It probably wouldn't work out, though, since I'd need something on the business side and you'd more be looking at the marketing angle. Maybe he can get me in the front offices and you in the marketing department," she suggests.

"I'll ask," I say.

If it was anybody else, I'd assume she's using me for my connections. But this is Mia. She'd never do that.

Still, it feels…weird. We've never had issues regarding my family, but for most of our friendship, we didn't know who my dad was.

And then we did, and now I'm a little territorial over him.

I shouldn't be. I trust Mia more than anybody else in the entire world.

But that doesn't mean I want her getting close to my dad. He's been like a father to both of us since we moved here, and just like when Cooper asked Mia her name at the blackjack table that first night we met, a bit of jealousy tears through me any time my dad gives Mia fatherly attention or advice.

It's not just that.

My dad...he's a complicated man.

As it turns out, he has a lot of money. He has his hands in a lot of different business ventures in Las Vegas, and he recently accepted a new position that will take him away from me a lot more. I'm so excited for him—thrilled, actually, since he told me it's everything he ever wanted out of his career, but I'm sad I won't get to spend as much time with him. So maybe if I can snag an internship with him, I'll get to have more time with him.

And it's not just all that. Sure, he's successful. Sure, he's rich. He's even pretty famous, which is why I don't want to mention him to Cooper.

But he's also devastatingly good looking. Women flock to him, and I see the way my best friend looks at him.

She literally swoons when he pays her the tiniest bit of attention, and he never does it in any type of sexual way. But he's young at only forty-one. He got my mom pregnant when he was nineteen, long before he became a household name, and when I tracked him down through a cousin, of course her first instinct was to believe I showed up out of the woodwork to claim something that didn't belong to me.

But my uncle was there at that first meeting, and he saw the resemblance immediately. He knew my dad had gotten a girl pregnant. He knew my dad sent monthly checks to help with the expenses of raising a child. He believed me, and a DNA test proved the rest of the truth.

It was weird at first, and I didn't live with my dad when I first moved to town, instead opting to live in a dorm my freshman year. But I found myself driving over to his place for dinner or meeting him in between classes, so when the school year was over and I needed to find housing for the summer, I opted to stay with him. And he convinced me not to leave when my sophomore year started.

My close group of friends know who my father is, but for the most part, I've kept it quiet at school. We don't share the same last name since my mother put her last name on my birth certificate, and sometimes I wonder what he did to her to make her hate him as much as she does.

And then I think about how narcissistic she is, and I truly believe it had more to do with her than him. He's a good man, passionate about the things he loves, smart and business-minded, talented and athletic. I admire so many things about him, and I often wonder what it would've been like to grow up with him rather than with her.

But I can't change the past. I can only react to the present and plan for the future.

Such an optimistic life view, and I find it adorable how Cooper immediately picked up on that part of my personality so easily that he nicknamed me Sunshine.

I love when he calls me Sunshine. I love when he calls me Gabby. I love when he calls me babe.

That feeling of missing him claws at me in a way I've never felt before.

"Are you okay?" Mia asks.

"Fine," I murmur, still lost in thought about Cooper as I pull into the parking lot.

"You're just…quiet."

"If I say what I'm thinking, you're going to think I'm crazy."

"Say it anyway," she says.

"I miss Cooper."

Her brows rise. "That's not what I was expecting you to say."

"What were you expecting?"

"I don't know. Something about the internship maybe. How'd we get from A to B? Or C, for Cooper, I guess."

I shrug. "I feel like I'm always thinking about him. I don't know what took up my brain space before I met him, because he's starring solely in my thoughts at the moment."

"You're in deep, huh?" she asks.

"I'm in deep," I confirm.

"But you just met him," she points out. "How can it be more than just sex?"

A prickle of defensiveness races up my spine. "I don't know. It just *is*. We had amazing sex, sure. But we had amazing conversation, too."

"Do you love him?" she asks softly.

I stare out the windshield at the restaurant in front of us. "I think I do," I murmur, and she lets out a soft gasp. I glance over at her. "I've never felt this before, Mia."

She reaches over and squeezes my arm. "I'm happy for you, girl."

"I'm happy for me, too."

"Just be careful. You hardly know him."

I feel like now would be a terrible time to bring up the fact that I'm going to San Diego this weekend, but I tell her anyway.

I trust him implicitly, but I'm not dumb enough to go out of town without telling someone where I'll be.

"He invited me to San Diego this weekend," I admit.

Her eyes widen. "Are you going?"

I nod. "I want to see where he lives. I want to see what his life is like. And despite the fact that he's a celebrity and he still hasn't told me, I trust him. I refuse to look him up, but Chelsea said everything she's read about him has been positive. He's not going to do anything I don't one hundred percent want to do, too."

She purses her lips. "How about this…if you have sex in the first hour after you get to his place, it's just sex. If you have a conversation first, then maybe it's more."

I roll my eyes. I know she's just looking out for me, but now she put that in my head and I sort of hate her a little for it.

We head inside, and we spend our lunch talking all things internships and our senior year of college as I avoid the topic of Cooper. He's all I want to talk about, but I don't want more warnings about him. I know what I'm getting into.

I just hope I can make it all work together. If our one weekend together taught me anything, it's that I'm not going to be able to focus on much of anything except him once he moves to town.

And I can't wait for the distraction.

Chapter 17
Cooper

I stare at the mess in front of me.

My mom literally brought every paper she saved of mine starting from preschool and going all the way through high school.

It's cute, but…what the fuck am I going to do with all this?

She holds up a paper that must be from preschool. There are raw noodles glued to it in the shape of a baseball, and a few have fallen off.

"Look! You were even into the game when you were in third grade!"

"Third grade?" I repeat. "I made that in *third grade*? I thought I was *three* when I did it based on the terrible artwork."

"Yeah, you weren't very artistic back then." She shrugs. "Not everyone's a Picasso, honey."

"Clearly. What do you want me to do with all that?"

"I don't know, but it was just sitting in a bin at the house and I don't really need it, so I thought maybe you'd want it," she says. She flips through more papers, and it seems like she kept virtually every single thing I ever did. It's all a disorganized mess, but at least she wrote the grade and year on the back.

"I guess I'll go through it and keep what I want for the memory book," I lie to make her feel better. The second she's on a plane back to Chicago, it's going in the dumpster.

"At least keep the noodle baseball. Oh! And this paper on Jane Eyre. Your insight was incredible for a high school junior." She holds up the paper.

"Correction. Sparknotes had incredible insight on the book, not Cooper Noah."

She purses her lips and rolls her eyes. "Don't tell me. I don't even want to know."

"I made it to the big leagues, so I guess I did something right along the way, right?"

She sighs. "You just don't tell a teacher these things."

"You teach first grade, Mother. I hardly think your first graders are looking up plot summaries for Dr. Seuss."

She purses her lips again, clearly annoyed at the direction of this conversation. "You just never know. My job is to keep those kiddos honest."

"Your job is to teach them *how* to read, not to worry about whether they're looking at Sparknotes."

"Touché." She sets down the Jane Eyre paper with a clear look of disapproval, and my phone buzzes with a notification that tells me I have a delivery down in the lobby.

"I'll be right back," I tell her, and I head down to grab my package. Or my *packages*, I suppose.

It's a big load, so the doorman grabs a cart to help me out. I take it all upstairs, and my mom's brows dip when she spots me and my big load.

"What's all that?" she asks.

I open the box and pull out packing tape, unprinted newspaper, and two tape guns. I open the other rather large box and pull out an assortment of brand new boxes that aren't even taped together yet.

"I'm putting you to work, ma'am," I say. "I need to pack up this place so I'm ready to move to Vegas." I gloss over the fact that Gabby's coming next weekend and I don't want any baseball shit out. I don't have much since it's an apartment that came furnished, but I do have a closetful of clothes, a kitchen full of dishes, and a pantry full of beer.

And a few priceless items of memorabilia that dear ole Mom can help me pack while she's here in town.

Plus, of course, the assortment of schoolwork from my tenure in education.

I tape up a huge box and set it beside her, and then I start heaving the papers she brought me into it. This'll fit nicely in the dumpster once she's gone.

She snatches the noodle paper out of the box and hangs it on my fridge as I continue shoveling the stuff she brought right into the box.

"You're not even going to look?" she whines. "Maybe I should just take it all back home."

"What are you going to do with it? It sat in your basement for the last fourteen years."

She presses her lips together and nods. "That's right. Fourteen years since you graduated high school. Remind me how long your girlfriend has been out of high school?"

I blow out a grunt of frustration. "I thought we were letting that go," I say.

"We are, we are. But it felt like it merited mentioning again."

"You're not okay with it," I say.

"And I don't have to be. As long as *you* are good with it, how I feel doesn't matter. But I do want you to think about one thing. If you're getting annoyed at *me* for bringing it up a second time today, imagine how you'll feel when it's *all* the media talks about once they get wind you're not only playing again, but you're dating someone half plus five."

I press my lips together.

I guess I don't have a response to that.

It's something I'll face when the time comes. Until then…I'm not going to worry about it.

After lunch, we drive to the beach and sit in the sand for a bit, and I think about the things I want to do when Gabby gets here this weekend.

If we even leave my apartment, of course.

I want to take her to all the places I love here in town, and I feel like we'd have a lot of fun together at a place like Sea World. We can ride the roller coasters and admire the fish, walk around hand-in-hand as we laugh and buy cotton candy and ice cream to share.

I want to take her to the beach, and to my favorite pizza place. I want to show her SFK and all I do there. I want to introduce her to Carla and my friends at work.

But I also don't want to do any of that. I want to spend the entire weekend naked.

"When are you going to officially accept Troy's offer?" my mom asks, breaking into my thoughts as I stare out at the waves.

I glance over at her. "It's kind of fun to make him sweat it out. He wants my answer by September first, so…August thirty-first?"

She smacks me in the arm in jest. "Be nice. If your answer is yes, call him now. Nail it down. Get the contract, and make sure he shows you the money."

"He will. He's a good friend, and he's been in this business a long time. He wouldn't fuck me over that way."

She raises a brow.

"Sorry. He wouldn't *screw* me over that way."

"Better," she says, and I chuckle.

"I'll do it when we get home," I say.

We spend another hour or so at the beach, and once we arrive back at the apartment, I make good on my word to my mom. I sit at the kitchen table and pull up Troy's contact information, and my heart starts to race.

I'm really doing this.

He really wants me to play even though he hasn't seen me pick up a ball in three years.

And I really want to do it. I'm scared I'll fail, but that's a fear in anything in life, not just in being a professional athlete. What if I don't fail? What if I soar? What if it's even better than the first time I did this?

It's a new team, and it'll be a new dynamic—one that he wants me to lead. I love the idea of mentoring young players, of building a team with Troy and creating our own destiny.

I click the call button.

"You got an answer for me, Noah?" he answers.

"I do. Pending contract negotiations, of course, it's a yes."

"Fuck *yeah!*" he yells, and I laugh. "We're really fucking doing this, man. This is *our time.*"

We never played on the same team. Troy played shortstop fourteen years for the Rockies, and I played my seven years with the Dodgers. The difference between us is that he retired a few years ago, while I was forced from the game due to an injury, and I decided to turn it into an early retirement.

Despite never having played together, we found a friendly rivalry on the field and we became close friends off it. He started taking more and more interest in charity events, and he invited me to many of them over the years. We lost touch for a bit when I stopped playing, mostly because of me. I isolated myself from my friends because I didn't want to hear about how they got to play when I didn't.

But Troy continued to reach out despite my silence. He's a good friend, and even though we don't talk as much as we once did, I'm excited to get back on the field with someone I know will support me one hundred percent in the dugout.

And I'm even more excited to make the move to Vegas...to start my life there and see where Sin City takes me.

Chapter 18
Cooper

I took Monday off to spend the day with my mom, but when Tuesday rolls around, I have no choice but to head into the office. I'm not sure what my mom does all day when I'm at work, but she said she'll find things to entertain herself. I'm pretty sure she means walking downtown to find a store to shop in. That's enough to fill her day, I guess.

I'm dreading going to work today. I texted Carla after I spoke with Troy last night. I told her I needed to talk to her in the morning, and I'm sure she's expecting anything but my two weeks' notice.

I knock on her doorframe when I get into the office, and she waves me in.

I shut the door and slide into the chair across from her desk. She tips her glasses down her nose and glances at me over the frames, and she looks a bit like a stereotypical librarian about to scold a loud child.

"What's this about, Cooper?" She presses her palms together in silent prayer. "Please tell me you're not leaving me."

"I'm not leaving you," I say, and she lets out a loud sigh of relief. "But I do need to modify my schedule." I clear my throat. "And location."

"What?"

"This is confidential." I squeeze my eyes shut and rip off the bandage. "Troy Bodine is managing a new expansion team in Vegas. He wants me to play third and I sort of already agreed to it."

Her eyes widen. "You're going back to the game?"

I nod. "I know. The reality of it hasn't quite hit me yet. And I'm not quitting. I'll be in Vegas, so I can work on things there with

Kaylee. She's totally overwhelmed right now and could use some extra hands. And I promise you, Carla, I will shout about this program from the rooftops every chance I get. Think of it as free advertising."

She huffs out a chuckle. "Free advertising, huh?"

I lift a shoulder as I try to lighten the weight of my words. "I need to be back in Vegas September first to start offseason workouts, but I'm happy to train my replacement here."

"Ugh, your replacement. Don't you know yet that Cooper Noah is irreplaceable?"

I laugh. "Obviously," I say sarcastically. "Do you still *need* professional athletes with celebrity status for this position? Or do you think Jamie could take on the whole thing?"

When Kaylee left, the idea was to find a replacement for her, but Carla ended up not really doing that since Kaylee and Ben were taking the program into his fitness clubs. She restructured how we run the office here, but she still uses me as the face of her company. And I can continue to do that from anywhere—I just won't be able to attend as many in-person events as I do now.

Since I knew I wanted to work with kids after the game, I worked hard to earn a degree in elementary education.

I had several reasons for selecting that as my major. On the one hand, I did it since the classes were filled with hot girls. On the other hand, my mom's a teacher, and she's the strongest, bravest person I know. I wanted to be like her.

And then the farm system came calling. I was drafted into the minor leagues my sophomore year of college, and I had to work hard in the off-season over several years to complete my degree. Players around me were working on degrees in business management, but I knew I wanted to work with kids. Maybe not as a teacher, but the degree set a base for my career here at StrongFitKids.

"Jamie could probably do it, especially if you, Kaylee, and Ben would consider splitting duties as our spokespeople," she says.

"Ben?" I ask, narrowing my eyes at her.

She shrugs and raises her brows. "What? He's a hot commodity right now, and he's supportive of his wife. You think I'm not going to capitalize on that?"

"Touché." I nod.

"But if I move Jamie there, she'll need help with her current position. You're not quitting, exactly, but I'd still like you to stay two weeks—until you need to be in Vegas, if that's okay with you.

That way you can go over everything with Jamie and we can work on finding someone to help her out," she says. "I'll put up the application today, and if you know of anybody you can recommend, let me know."

"Will do," I say. "Thanks, Carla. For everything."

"I hate to lose you, but these opportunities are once in a lifetime. Just know one of your biggest fans will be watching every gameday and cheering for a W." She offers a sad smile, and then she says, "Now get out of here. I have a job posting to create and you have work to do." She sighs. "I can't believe I'm losing another perfectly good employee to Las Freaking Vegas."

I laugh, and then she follows me out of her office to announce to the rest of the staff that I'm going to be relocating...but she doesn't say where or why just yet.

They'll all find out soon enough.

I call Troy later in the evening after my mom has called it a night. I can tell he's at the club since I can hear music playing in the background, and I swear that guy practically lives at that place. I'm not sure how he's going to handle it once he's back in the game and managing a team. He won't have the time to do whatever it is he does on the third floor—a place I still haven't seen. A place I'm not sure I'll *ever* see.

"Hey, it's Twenty-One!" he answers. "What's going on, man?"

I kick my feet up on the handrail on my patio as I let out a chuckle. "I gave my notice at my job today. My boss would like me to hang around a bit to help train my replacement, but I'll be there September first as promised."

"September first. Great. I'll throw a party here at the club," he says, indicating he's there right now.

"Maybe just at your place," I suggest. "I need a few things from you first, though."

"Name it," he says.

"A real estate agent, for one. I'm booking a flight out for next weekend to look at places."

"Done. I'll text you my strongest recommendation. What else?" he asks.

"Well, if I can't find a place in time, I'll need somewhere to live," I say.

"You're welcome to stay with me until you figure out where you want to settle."

I pull my feet off the handrail and push to a stand. "You sure?"

"Of course. What else do you need?"

94

"Well, since you're asking, my boss could use some extra hands at StrongFitKids. You know anybody who can help her out?" I ask. "She needs someone who knows something about athletics in San Diego, and my friend working out of Vegas could use some local help there, too."

"I have a few buddies who retired to the area that might be able to help in San Diego, and I have a daughter who might be interested in helping in Vegas," he says.

My brows dip. "You have a daughter?" I had no idea, and we've been friends for years. But he does seem like the kind of guy who keeps his personal life close to the vest.

Except for sex, of course, which he possibly performs in public on the third floor of his club.

I'm not here to judge anybody who likes to partake in that particular brand of fruit punch, but it's not my beverage of choice.

He chuckles. "Yeah, I do. She's smart, too. So much smarter than me."

"She'd have to be if I'd even consider passing her name along to my boss."

He barks out a laugh. "Fuck off. I'll talk to her and see if she's interested. Any other requests, Twenty-One?"

"That's all I got for now, boss, but I'm sure I can come up with more soon."

"Great. Now get your ass to Vegas. We have a team to build at the draft mid-November after the World Series, and we have workouts to start."

I grin. "Yes sir." I hang up as excitement permeates my chest that he wants me to be a part of the team build. It'll be as much my team as it is his, and there's already a sense of pride in that.

I dial up Gabby next for our nightly chat.

"Hey there Hottie McCuteStuff," she answers, and I laugh.

"Hottie McCuteStuff?" I repeat.

"You should've heard all the names that raced through my head when I first saw you at that blackjack table," she admits.

"I only had one thought in my head when you sat down," I say, sitting back down and kicking my feet back up on the railing.

"Oh? What was that?"

I mimic a robotic voice when I answer. "Hot girl alert! Hot girl alert! Need to get inside her now."

"The voice in your head sounds like a robot?"

"When I see someone as hot as you, yeah. My brain turns to mush and the robots take over."

She giggles. "Well glad I could help bang the robots out of there."

"You think that's what happened? Pfft," I say. "Nah, it's all mush up there since the moment I met you." I turn the robot voice back on. "Call hot girl. Get hot girl to San Diego. Let hot girl know how much you miss her."

"I miss you, too. I've honestly been a little bored this week, but Mia and I have gone to lunch a few times, and I've been enjoying that toddler dance class. Oh, and Mia is seeing this dude who rented a boat on Lake Mead tomorrow, so she invited me to that."

"Sounds dangerous. You shouldn't go," I tease, mostly because I don't want some college kids ogling my girl when I'm not there to ogle her myself.

"Yes, Father," she mocks.

"That's Daddy to you," I say, my voice low and gravelly.

She lets out a soft gasp that might be part laughter, part surprise at my words. Honestly, I'm surprised, too. I always thought the *daddy* thing was a little weird, and maybe even weirder since she's twelve years younger than me. But it slipped out, and she gasped, and maybe it's a thing now.

She clears her throat. "Whoa."

"Yeah. Saturday needs to get here faster," I groan.

"Agreed," she says. "But you know, we *could* do stuff, um…over the phone."

I wish we were on a video call right now so I could see the color lighting up her cheeks at her own suggestion.

"Now there's an idea I like," I say. "I'm hanging up now."

"What? You hated my suggestion?"

I laugh. "Fuck no. I'm hanging up so I can call you back on video."

"Oh sweet Jesus, what can of worms have I opened," she mutters, and then I disconnect the call.

Chapter 19
Gabby

"Hi," I say a little tentatively as I look at the handsome face filling my screen. My chest races and my tummy flips.

"Hey."

We just stare at each other a few beats, and I wonder why we haven't done more video chatting since he's been gone.

With his mom there, though, I don't want to bother him.

"Are you outside?" I ask.

"On my patio." He flips his phone around, and it's mostly dark but I can see lights in some buildings and a view of total darkness. "That's the water." He flips it back around so I can see him again.

"I like this view better," I admit.

"I like this one, too."

"So...when I said that, I really thought we'd just, you know, do whatever to ourselves and listen to each other breathe heavily through the phone."

He laughs. "I want to see your face when you come." His voice is low and sexy with a little growl behind it. "Are you wet?"

I lift a shoulder. "I'm always wet when I'm with you. Or talking to you. Or thinking of you." My cheeks burn with the admission.

He chuckles, and his eyes seem to glaze over with lust.

"Are you sure you want to do this outside?" I ask.

"I'm on the top floor of my building. Nobody can see me, and nobody's out tonight. It's silent out here, and I'd rather do this out here in the dark than risk my mom hearing when I come all over my hand in my bedroom."

"Yeah, let's not do that," I say. "So...now what?"

"I assume you're alone?" he asks.

I nod, and then I get up and lock my bedroom door just to be safe.

"Show me your tits," he demands quietly. "I miss your gorgeous tits."

I lift my shirt and flash him.

He chuckles. "Take off your bra and your shirt, and then show me."

"You first," I demand, and he lifts his shirt over his head and tosses it somewhere out of the frame. He pans down to those gorgeous abs, and my mouth waters as I think about how good it felt when his weight hovered over me.

I set my phone down, pull my shirt off, and unhook my bra. I toss it to the floor before I pick my phone back up. I pan down to show him my breasts, and he groans audibly through the chat.

"God, those look perfect. Touch one of your nipples for me," he says, and I do. I pinch it between my fingers, and he moans. "Flick it with your thumb." I do what he says. "Now reach down into your panties and touch your clit, but keep the phone on your face so I can see how good it feels."

"First you have to get your dick out," I say.

He does it, and he shows me the evidence a second later.

"Stroke it," I demand.

"It's real fucking hot when you tell me what to do," he murmurs, and I hear the slide of his hand over the thick, tight skin he just showed me. "Now finger yourself while I jerk off."

I dip a finger in and close my eyes at the feel of it, his groans in my ear, his face in my sight, and the feel of my own touch making me hot and needy.

"Just like that, baby," he murmurs, and I drive my finger in and out a few times.

I pull it out to rub my clit, and the feel is almost too good as I listen to him touch himself. I watch the phone as he tips his neck back, closing his eyes for a beat while he pumps his fist up and down his shaft.

"Oh God," I whisper, rubbing myself faster as the ache starts to build. I wish it was him here doing this to me, but this will work for tonight.

His eyes open as he hears my whisper, and he starts to move his hand a little faster, something I can only tell by the way the phone starts to move.

"Fuck, even in a different state you make me come undone," he mutters.

"Right back at you," I moan, and it's too much, way too much as the pleasure edges in on me. "I'm going to come."

"So am I. Come with me," he demands. "Fuck yes, baby. Oh God, yes."

I let out a loud gasp as the pleasure hits a peak, and we come together, my legs trembling with the brutal force of it, and as soon as the contractions start to wane, the ache is back. It felt good to give myself an orgasm, but it feels far better when it's him giving them to me.

He grabs his shirt and uses it to clean up his mess, and I grab my shirt, too, pulling it back over my head.

"That was unexpected," I say.

"It was your idea," he points out.

I laugh. "Maybe I should have that idea tomorrow, too."

"Or again in, say, forty-five minutes?" He grins, and it's so sweet and sexy at the same time.

It didn't bring us that much closer to Saturday, but it was still a fun way to pass the time.

It's the only time we do that, in fact, before I head to the airport to board a plane a few days later. The week dragged for me, including the boat ride where Mia hung out with the boy who invited us and I hung out by myself in a corner wishing Cooper was with me. A few college boys flirted with me, but I had zero interest in flirting back. I let them down gently by telling them I was seeing someone, and we left it at that.

Cooper was busy between training his replacement at work and entertaining his mom while she cooked meals for him. I'm only staying the weekend since I promised the dance studio I'd sub again this week, and then school starts.

I don't know how much time I'll have to spend with him once I have the weight of four senior-level classes in front of me, but school has always come easily for me. If anything, I'll have tons of time on my hands. Maybe I should look for a job, but that might interfere with my internship next semester.

It's why I started helping out at the dance studio. I always loved to dance, and I took ballet all the way through my sophomore year of high school. That was when my mom started pressuring me to look at colleges for ballet, and I didn't want it to be my career. I wanted it to be my hobby.

I taught one class last semester on Thursday mornings when I had an opening in my schedule, but I opted out of that this semester so I could focus on finding an internship to benefit my major.

I'm sure Cooper will find other ways to fill my hours anyway, depending what his new job is.

The flight is only about an hour long, and when I land, I practically race through the airport to get to him. I know he's here somewhere, and it's on the other side of security when I spot him.

He's standing there, black Under Armour baseball cap on his head, jeans and a black t-shirt…and my memory betrayed me. He's even hotter than I remember.

I run across the airport to get to him, and he laughs with an *oof* when I plow into him. He turns his hat backward to lean down to kiss me, and he *really* kisses me good, even dipping me at the end. I'm pretty sure some audience standing nearby is clapping for us, but I can't be positive since the only thing I'm positive about right now is that I'm back in his arms, exactly where I belong.

The dynamic between us is exactly the same. His kiss is even more intense, his arms hold me even more tightly—everything is kicked up a notch between us including the feelings. Last weekend was about getting to know each other. This weekend is about seeing if the magic we both found last time we were together was an anomaly or if it's still there.

And in the first five seconds he holds me in his arms, I already know the truth.

It's still there, and it's even better than it was before.

"You smell good," he says, pulling back and pressing a wet kiss to my neck as he breathes me in.

"You do, too," I say, pressing a kiss to his cheek where I take in the woodsy scent that's all man and all him.

"Let's get home and get naked," he suggests. He turns his hat back around and nods at my suitcase. "What's in there?"

"Clothes."

"Pfft. Won't be needing those," he says, and I laugh as I smack him in the arm.

We head out to his silver Ford F-150, and he helps me into the passenger seat, lugging my suitcase into his backseat while I buckle in. He drives us toward his apartment, and he's cool and easy behind the wheel, just like he seems to be in every other aspect of his life.

"Welcome to San Diego," he says once we arrive, and I'm curious to see where he lives. It's like I'm getting an inside look at who this guy is after we skimmed the surface last weekend, and I feel like by the end of this weekend, we'll know each other on an even deeper, more intimate level.

I'm not sure what that means or where we take it from there, but I can't wait to find out.

Chapter 20
Cooper

I open the door and usher her in first with my hand on the small of her back, and she glances around with a bit of awe. If she still doesn't know who I am, that's fine by me. But surely she'll have questions given the fact that I live in a luxury apartment with a killer view in downtown San Diego…and, at least as far as she knows, I work with an organization focused on kids' fitness.

She doesn't know about the eighty-four-million-dollar contract over three years I was guaranteed the year before I got hurt. She doesn't know about the money I made before that, either.

This place costs a pretty penny in monthly rent, but it's a drop in the bucket. It feels strange even thinking that considering I'm not really a guy who cares about *things* so much, but I do care about a nice view and comfort. This place offers both, and it's a monthly lease so I can move out whenever I want.

And that appears to be the end of this month.

Everything's already packed thanks to mommy dearest and her Type A organization skills, and the boxes are stacked neatly in the third bedroom. The essentials are all I have left to pack, and I have plenty of time to get the rest before it's time to head to Vegas.

So this weekend is about relaxing with my girl.

My girl.

The girl I didn't even know a week ago.

While the snake trouser is telling me to get her naked, my brain is telling me she'd probably like a little romance before I fuck her until she can't walk straight.

I give her a quick tour of the place, and when we stop in the kitchen, she moves toward the refrigerator to check out the artwork displayed there.

"A noodle baseball?" she asks, and I laugh.

"My mom brought all my papers she saved from when I was in school. The noodle art I made in third grade, a paper on *Jane Eyre* I wrote in high school..."

"Wait a minute. You did this in *third grade*?" she asks, her eyes widening as she looks between me and the noodle baseball.

I clear my throat. "I didn't exactly win any awards for my stellar artwork as a kid."

She laughs, but it fades as she stares at it. "Your mom kept stuff like this?"

I nod. "Yeah. Doesn't everybody's mom do that?"

She shakes her head, and my chest squeezes for a beat. I take for granted that my mom is thoughtful, kind, and an all-around incredible mom. Gabby didn't have that, and it makes me sad.

I wrap my arms around her.

"I wish my mom would've done stuff like that," she says quietly.

A pang of guilt stabs me in the ribs. I was planning to take that box filled with all the shit my mom brought me straight to the dumpster, and it took one conversation with Gabby to realize how priceless all that shit actually is. I took it for granted, and I should know better. After losing my dad at such a young age, I should know how fleeting life is, how lucky I am to have the mom I have. And yet, even after spoiling her here with me for the last week, I was less than grateful that she kept all those papers when Gabby would love to have just one ridiculous piece of noodle art from her own childhood.

I hold her in my kitchen for a beat, and then we head out to the balcony. She looks out over my view with a bit of awe. "This is beautiful."

"Have you been to San Diego before?"

She shakes her head. "I didn't go on vacations with my mom when I was growing up. She was busy either working or dating. We did some local things, and my junior year we took a class trip to New York City. That was my first time on a plane, and my mom made me raise the money for the trip myself." She blows out a breath, and I sling an arm around her shoulder as she shares the memory. She slides her hand around my waist, squeezing me closer to her. "By the end of my senior year, I knew the best option for me was to get out of Denver, away from her, and then I found my dad. It was perfect timing. What about you? Did you travel much?"

"We'd drive up to Wisconsin Dells every spring break when I was a kid. My parents love to travel, so they had something planned for every summer break and every winter break. We were almost never home on New Year's Eve since we'd be on an adventure somewhere in the days after Christmas." I smile fondly at the memories of my childhood. My mom did her best after Dad died, but money was a little tighter as she raised two boys on her teacher salary, so mostly we went to the Dells, oftentimes with her parents tagging along.

"What's Wisconsin Dells?"

"It's a place known for water parks and all sorts of different entertainment. It's changed a lot since I was a kid, but we used to go to Noah's Ark and race down waterslides all day, then we'd go next door and battle it out on the mini golf courses as our sunburns started to peek through. We'd stay at some seedy old hotel that always smelled like smoke and mildew, but it was walking distance to the park, and we'd go across the street to Pizza Pub for a late night dinner." I stare out over my view of the water. This is sure a long way from Wisconsin, but there aren't any places quite like the Dells out here.

"Oh wow! We didn't have anything like that by us in Denver. You and your brother would battle over mini golf?"

I chuckle. "All four of us would battle. I was the youngest, and I never won, but I always spent the entire time with a stomachache from laughing so hard. Time with my family always meant a great ab workout."

"Must be how they got to be the way they are today," she muses, and I chuckle. "So where else did your family go on vacations?" she asks.

"Oh, we went anywhere and everywhere. Before my dad passed, the trips that stick out the most in my memory besides the Dells were to Disney World, Disneyland, Hawaii, South Carolina, and Nashville."

"Do you like to travel?"

I nod. "I love it." And I do it—a lot, and I will even more once I'm playing again. But my time to actually tour the cities I'm traveling to is limited. We get a decent amount of free time if we're not warming up, working out, sleeping, or rehabbing, and I made it a personal goal a long time ago to visit at least one landmark or museum and to try a new restaurant in every city I travel to.

I get that wanderlust from my dad. He loved museums, and when I was a kid, I found them boring as hell. I wish I could get those years back.

"You're quiet," she murmurs. "What are you thinking?"

I pull her a little more tightly into my side. "I'm thinking it's a little scary how well you already know me."

She wraps her other arm around me to hug me from the side. "You're thinking about your dad, aren't you?" Her voice is soft, and I lean over and press a kiss to the top of her head.

"Yeah. He's been gone twenty-three years, and I miss him every day."

"He'd be proud of the man you've become," she says.

"I like to think so." I press my lips together as emotion plows into me.

Stacy never once brought up my father, and Gabby is bringing him up a week after knowing me. She's asking about him…asking about *me*. She cares about *me*, the guy who works with kids and might move to Vegas to accept a job offer. She wants to be with *me*, not the All-Star MVP third baseman.

It's a breath of fresh air.

She is a breath of fresh air.

And I don't want to stop breathing her in.

Chapter 21
Gabby

This place is pretty sweet for a guy who works with a kids' fitness organization for a living.

I know that's not what he does, exactly, but I can't imagine he's making big bucks from his current place of employment. At least not enough to finance this fancy apartment—and he knows I'm smart enough to figure that out.

I decide not to ask. He'll tell me when he's ready. I'll tell him I already knew, and then we'll just move forward from there.

I have to admit, though, I'm curious as to *when* he's going to admit what he used to do.

I get the sense he likes keeping it in his past, though I'm not exactly sure why. From what I gather about his ex-girlfriend based on snippets here and there, I can't help but wonder whether she was with him because of his job, not because she actually loved him.

I imagine that happens far more often than it should in his former industry, and my heart breaks for him that someone would treat him the way she did. He's such a good guy. He didn't deserve that.

He ordered up lunch from the restaurant inside his apartment complex, and we eat out on the balcony. I've been here at his place for an entire hour already, and neither of us has even brought up sex yet since we've been so busy talking.

The snarky voice inside my head reminds me to tell Mia that we made it past the first hour without sex, but even if we didn't, it wouldn't have made a difference to me.

That flame burns bright, and each passing second we spend together, it gets more and more dazzling.

Once we finish lunch, we take a walk and end up at a cute little area with restaurants, shops, and bars that Cooper refers to as the Gaslamp Quarter. It's only about a ten-minute walk from his place, and we find ourselves strolling along, hand-in-hand as we duck in and out of shops. He wears his hat pulled down low as usual, we steal kisses on the sidewalk, and we stop in one dive bar for a drink before we head back to his place.

On the walk back, he nods in the direction we just came from. "Another few miles that way is my office."

"Have you talked to your boss yet?" I ask.

"Oh, Jesus. I forgot to tell you." He snaps his fingers—the ones on the hand that isn't holding mine. "It was that day we had phone sex, and then the week just got away from me. But yes, I talked to her. I told her I'm moving to Vegas, but I'll still be able to help out from there."

"How will you be able to help from Vegas?" I ask. He hasn't told me much about what he does, just that it's some organization and he gets to work with kids and help them become stronger and more athletic.

"It's a long story."

"I'm here all weekend," I joke.

"When I first started working at StrongFitKids, the company partnered with the San Diego school district to promote healthy and active lifestyles for kids. I had a co-programming director, but she relocated to Vegas. When she moved, she proposed this idea to rework the program we were using in schools to get it into fitness clubs—so kids could go there while their parents worked out in the adult area. Her husband owns a chain of fitness clubs in Vegas, and she started it there. It's been really successful so far, but Kaylee's gotten really overwhelmed with all the work. Plus she just had twins in January, so she could use some help in Vegas since it's growing so quickly. And Carla could use some help here in San Diego, too."

"I'm looking for an internship for next semester," I say. "I might be able to help out with your Vegas friend if there's any sort of marketing angle to it."

He considers that for a beat. "I'll talk to her. I have a buddy whose daughter might be interested in helping out, too, but I'm still waiting to hear back from him."

"Let me know. My advisor told me on Monday it's never too early to start looking for opportunities. I think my dad might have something for me, but it doesn't hurt to come up with a few options to make Dr. Foley happy."

We arrive back at the building and head upstairs after a quick stop to a corner market so he can pick up some Slim Jims because, according to him, the four he has left feels like a really small supply, and as soon as we get inside, he kicks the door shut behind me and backs me up into it, his eyes dark with lust as he stalks his prey.

His lips slam down to mine, and we kiss in his foyer until I'm completely breathless. He is, too, and we both pant as his lips drag from mine down to my neck. His scruff is rough against my skin, a reminder that this isn't just some dream but I'm really here with him.

His hips drive against mine, and I feel his erection against my side.

"I need you," he says, his voice low and gritty and full of longing. "I love every second I get to spend with you," he says, kissing my neck some more as I lean my head back to give him more space to work with. "Clothed or naked. Talking or silence. Laughing or not. But you've been here six hours, and right now, I need to fuck you like I need to take my next breath."

Whoa.

I gasp at his words, and my only response is to jump up, wrap my legs around his waist, tighten my arms around his neck, and press my lips to his as this kiss in the front hall turns from hot to intense. "Fuck me, Cooper," I say, my voice breathless and hoarse and needy.

He lets out a little growl at my words then grabs on under my thighs. He carries me toward his bedroom, his mouth connected to mine the entire way. He sets me down on the bed, reluctant to let me go but doing it simply so he can start stripping off his clothes. I do the same from where I perch on the bed, tossing my shirt and bra in a pile on the floor as I kick off my shoes then shimmying out of my jeans and panties.

I lie back naked on the bed, and he pauses in his movements, his jeans unbuttoned but not pushed down yet, those gorgeous abs of his smiling over at me.

"Christ. Am I the luckiest guy in the world or what?" He stalks over toward me again, and he settles in between my thighs, his jeans still on. I wrap my legs around him as he presses a soft kiss to my lips, and my clit rubs right against the rough fabric of his jeans.

I moan at the sensation, and he rocks his hips toward mine, brushing against my clit again.

I cry out this time, and he breaks our kiss to offer a salacious smile down at me. "My girl likes that," he murmurs, and he does it again as I tilt my neck back and push out my breasts, a clear invitation for him to do what he wants to them.

And does he ever.

He sucks a nipple between his lips then laps at it with his tongue, driving his hips toward me and hitting that magic spot over and over again.

I'm so close, so damn close to coming, when he stops. He moves off me, finally stripping off his jeans, and I pant as I impatiently wait for him to return. He grabs a condom and rolls it on, and then he moves back toward me, settling in between my legs again.

"We'll take our time later, okay?" he asks softly, and I nod.

He lines up his cock and slides into me.

"Fuck, that's so tight," he mutters, and his lips find mine. He pulls back and looks at me, his eyes connecting with mine as he stills inside me.

A hot beat of intimacy passes between us, his blue eyes focused on my green ones, nothing between us except a condom, both of us here and present in this moment as emotions course through me in the stillness.

How can I possibly love somebody I just met?

It doesn't make any sense.

It defies logic.

And yet...I feel it.

My pussy seems to contract all on its own, goading him into movement as his eyes stay on mine. I close mine as he pulls back and pushes in.

"Eyes on me," he demands, and why is that so freaking hot?

My eyes open and focus on him again.

"I'm going to go hard and fast now, okay?" he murmurs, and I nod.

And then he delivers.

Hard. And. Fast.

And holy fuck, it's unlike anything I've ever experienced in my life.

My chest tingles with butterflies and my stomach flips as he rocks my body thoroughly and vividly, the heat between us palpable and the intimacy thick all around us.

He hammers into me, long, strong drives, pushing himself all the way to the hilt before pulling out, over and over, his eyes on mine as I start to see his cloud over with the need to come. Watching it all unfold as I hang on for dear life at the intensity of his body slamming into mine is something I'll commit to memory and dream about for the rest of my life.

I lose my mind as everything around me starts to fade away except Cooper and the way he makes me feel—not just physically, though that's certainly topping the list at the moment, but also emotionally, and spiritually and mentally and every other pillar of health that exists. I force my eyes to stay on his as my climax slams into me with brute force, my body quaking as it hits the peak. With anyone else, it might feel awkward…but this is Cooper, and nothing has *ever* felt awkward with him. It's been natural since the moment he patted the chair next to him and told me he'd teach me how to play blackjack.

And it's as I'm coming in that state of numbness, my mind and body lost to the pleasure, lost to *Cooper* himself, that the words come out of my mouth before I can stop them.

"I love you."

His face contorts as he loses his mind, too, and as he comes, my cheeks flame with the juvenile words that escaped my mouth. I study his face, his beautiful face with the sexy, masculine scruff, the blue eyes that are so pure, so kind, so beautiful, the straight nose and the perfect jawline, the light smattering of lines that prove more than a decade stands between us. I study those lines and admire them for every laugh he's laughed, every smile he's cracked, every frown he's made, every emotion he's ever felt, and when his thrusts start to slow and his cock stops twitching inside me, he drops a kiss to my lips, and then he buries his face in my neck.

"I love you, too," he whispers, his breath warm near my ear, and tears fall from my eyes as I feel like this is the type of love people wait their whole lives for. The type of love people dream about and pray for and long for.

I only hope we can carry this feeling well past these first two weeks and hold onto each other through whatever the future may bring.

Chapter 22
Cooper

It was a blissful weekend that was far too short, and she cried when I dropped her at the airport.

I'll be honest. My own eyes burned when I had to pull away knowing she was flying out of my reach.

Carla tracked down a replacement for me through Troy's recommendation, and she tapped former outfielder for the Padres and homerun hitter Tim Williams. I've met him at several different events, and I have no doubt he'll be a great spokesperson for local events. Plus he has four kids, and they're all in the San Diego district, so he's already somewhat familiar with the mission.

So now I just have to see if I can work something out between Gabby and Kaylee, and then Gabby and I might have opportunities to work together.

Maybe it's a little crazy to even be considering that, but I know what I feel, and this is way more than just some fling.

When she said the words, I felt them in my chest.

We didn't say them again over the weekend apart from that one time, and her words came out in the blissful moment when her body was racked with pleasure, but it didn't matter. There they were, and she couldn't take them back.

I wouldn't let her even if she tried.

It was the most beautiful thing anyone has ever said to me.

With my ex, she said the words so often they lost their meaning.

When Gabby said them, it was because she *felt* them. She was in the moment, living and breathing that feeling, and the words just fell out of her. It was pure and beautiful, and that's how I knew it was genuine.

And when I leaned down and buried my face in her neck, it was so she wouldn't see the emotion in my eyes. I'm not an emotional man. I tend to be incredibly even-keel off the field. On the field…that's a different story. I'm passionate, and I feel things, but there are only two times I can remember feeling enough emotions to cause me to cry: at my father's funeral and when the doctor told me I'd need surgery that would take a year to recover from and I might never play baseball again.

The first was tears of sadness. The second was tears of frustration.

And when Gabby said those words, this strange sense of relief filled my chest that I wasn't alone.

She made me feel like I'll *never* be alone again because I'll always have her by my side.

We've known each other a sum total of eleven days. It's too early to be thinking that way.

But I'm also a firm believer that people are put in our paths for a reason.

It took me a long time to see why Stacy was put in my path. In fact, I'm not sure I fully realized it until this moment.

I wasted five years on her.

I knew she was wrong for me from the start, yet I continued to chip away and try to make it work.

I should've listened to my gut.

And that's the reason she was in my life. To learn that lesson.

To listen to my gut.

To not waste any more time.

I want to be with Gabby. She wants to be with me.

We can take it fast, or we can take it slow, but the end result will be the same either way. There's no other choice.

The week drags as I get busy training Tim and spending my post-work hours at the apartment complex gym. I'm not out of shape, exactly, but I'm also not in playing shape, but I remember the rebuilding process from my playing days. I'm in the phase that comes before training to train, a place I refer to as Phase Zero. My goal is to start running five times a week and to do a total body workout three times per week. Then I'll take the weekends off to rest…or, better yet, to work on my endurance in other areas.

Wink, wink.

I drive to Coronado Island to run on the beach since the scenery is nicer than the workout room at my complex. I see Gabby everywhere I go, including on the small island where we went out to dinner Saturday night before driving to Torrey Pines State Park to stargaze in the back of *my* truck this time.

I start to change my diet, opting to only eat pizza once per week and getting back on the lean meats and veggies I used to eat.

I'm feeling a difference already, and even though I'm exhausted by the end of each day, I still call Gabby before I head to bed.

"I hate to cut this short, but I need to go to bed," I say with a yawn on Thursday night.

"Can I ask you something?" she asks, and she sounds a little nervous.

"Anything," I say.

"Are you…avoiding me?"

"*Avoiding* you? Why would you think that?" My brows dip as I rack my brain to figure out some reason she'd ask that.

"Well, we said *The Big Thing* last weekend, and this week it just feels like you're rushing through our calls and you're not texting me throughout the day…I don't want to sound juvenile or needy, but you set the expectation early and I feel like you're fading away."

My chest tightens.

I feel like shit that I've made her feel this way.

"No!" I say, vehemence in my voice. "No, that's not it at all. I'm training a new guy at work to take my place, and I've been spending time away from work, uh…prepping for my new job. I'm wearing myself out, that's all. My feelings for you haven't changed, Gabby."

"I just keep thinking how I'm going to start school and you're going to start a new job, a job you still haven't told me about, by the way, and I don't know…I guess I'm just feeling insecure. The distance is hard when you're still getting to know someone, but the feelings don't go away, you know?" she asks softly, baring her very soul to me with her words.

I wish I could hold her in my arms right now. I wish I could kiss her and show her that nothing has changed. "I have never felt like this in my life, and your ass better be at the airport waiting for me tomorrow at exactly seven twenty-six so I can take you back to my hotel room or to your place or just to the back of your truck and fuck you until you can't walk straight."

A soft laugh falls from her lips. "I'm still sore from last weekend," she admits, and I chuckle.

"I'm sorry, Sunshine," I murmur. "I'm sorry I made you feel like I'm fading. I promise, that's not what this is, and I appreciate you being honest with me."

"Okay. And let's go with your hotel, by the way. My dad will flip out when he finds out I'm dating someone twelve years older than me."

"Oh great," I mutter. "Something to look forward to."

"You have no idea," she says. "So listen, when do I get to hear about this new job?"

I've been thinking a lot about when to spring it on her, and I still think the best time to do it is to just take her to the stadium and show her in person like I told my mom. "I haven't officially signed the contract yet, but I'm supposed to meet with my new boss September first to make it official."

"So you're telling me you quit your job, you're coming to Vegas this weekend to look at places to live…and you haven't even signed a contract yet?" I hear the disapproval in her tone, and it's just one more thing to love about her. The way she asks the hard questions will prove challenging in the future, I'm sure, but it'll also keep our relationship strong and healthy. "Cooper Michael, that's a terrible idea."

I laugh. "Normally I'd agree with you, but the contract and salary negotiations are purely a formality at this point. My boss and I used to be really tight. He's a good friend, someone I could see becoming my best friend in Vegas, and it's a done deal."

She clears her throat. "Um…what now? *Who* is going to be your best friend?"

I laugh at her teasing. "You, of course, but what am I going to do when you have a big project due and you want me out of your hair so you tell me to just go have a boys' night out? This way I know who to call."

"I guess I can let that slide."

Our conversation returns to lighthearted teasing, and it's the dynamic where I find my cheeks hurting from smiling so widely.

I love how this girl makes me feel, and I can't wait to get her back in my arms—and my bed—tomorrow.

Chapter 23
Gabby

School starts Monday, and traditionally the weekend before it starts is filled with on-campus parties and shenanigans. It's something we've looked forward to every year…something my friends will participate in this year.

But I just can't muster up the enthusiasm to go to college parties when Cooper Freaking Noah is in town.

I don't give a shit about the shenanigans taking place on campus when Coop and I can get into some private trouble of our own.

And so when I pick him up from the airport, the group text chat with my closest friends is going bananas. They're setting up where and when to meet, and meanwhile I ate dinner an hour ago and sat around twiddling my thumbs until an appropriate time to leave for the airport to pick him up.

I glance at my watch. It's seven twenty-five, and a text comes through.

Cooper: *Landed! [airplane emoji]*

Me: *I can't wait to see you. [kiss emoji]*

Cooper: *I can't wait to get you naked. [eggplant emoji] [waterdrops emoji]*

Me: *I really like how you don't beat around the bush. [eyeroll emoji]*

He writes back with a laughing emoji, and then I wait as patiently as I can until I see the familiar black Under Armour baseball cap pulled forward and low over his eyes.

My tummy flips as thrills start to dance along my spine.

My body seems to have the same reaction every time I see him, but it gets more and more intense each time. The feelings of love are starting to edge out the lust, but both are fierce.

If you didn't know you were looking for him, he'd be just another hot guy walking through the airport. But I know who he is. Intimately. And even though there are still parts of himself he hasn't shared with me—and I him—I still feel like I know him in a way nobody else in this airport ever will.

I mean…assuming he's never banged a flight attendant.

We haven't really gotten into our histories where that's concerned, and I still haven't Googled him to learn more, but Mia has informed me that he was a player in more ways than one back in the day. It sounds like it was before his time with his ex. And he wears that ballcap all the time in public, so I assume people know who he is. I just don't want to know his past since I'm enjoying who he is now.

We all have histories, and he can share his with me whenever he's ready. And maybe that'll be the same time I'll be ready to share mine with him, too. My recent history, anyway. I've been pretty open about the other stuff.

His eyes lift to mine across the airport, and I can't help it. I spring into a sprint and launch myself into his arms, and he laughs as he catches me this time, prepared for the impact. His lips immediately collide down to mine as everything seems to tilt back to the way it's meant to be.

"God, I missed you," he says, his voice raspy and low against my mouth. He pulls his lips from mine and buries his face in my neck like he's trying to get as close as he possibly can to me, and I simply wrap myself around him and hang on for the ride as much as I decently can in public, still unsure how it's possible to feel so completely whole again with him when we're still at the early stages of this.

But that's the thing. I'm here to hang on for the ride, whether it lasts one more week or one more lifetime.

"Let's get to my hotel," he suggests, and I nod. We walk out of the airport hand-in-hand toward my truck, and I weave through traffic, racing to get to Caesars Palace where Cooper's staying again.

After all, it's where we first met when we were playing blackjack together, and it's a place I will forever associate with him regardless of what happens between us.

I have a feeling I'll always look at this landmark with hearts in my eyes and the fondest memories.

I leave my keys in the car, collect my valet ticket, and head with Cooper toward his room, bypassing the check-in counter since he already took care of that whole process digitally while I drove.

He waves his phone in front of his door, and it magically unlocks. We walk in, and he abandons his suitcase in the middle of the entry, instead stalking toward me. Thrills shoot up my spine. I am so ready for this, ready for *him*.

Last time we spent half the day together before we got naked. This time, it's about half a second after we enter the privacy of his hotel room. To be honest, I'm a little surprised we made it this long and didn't just get naked in the back of my truck.

It's with lightning speed we both shed our clothes, and we stand naked together making out in the middle of the room. He booked a suite with a view, and the bed is located in a room to the left. I don't care if we do it on the bed. Hell, I'll opt for doing it up against the hotel window if that's what he wants.

He must read my mind.

"Go put your palms up against the window and bend over for me," he orders, his lips inches from mine, and I love the needy edge to his demand. He kisses me once more before he lets me go to submit to what he just requested, and I stand with my ass up in the air, my palms against the glass, and my tits on display for everyone outside to see.

We're on the twenty-fifth floor in the land of hotel rooms and blinking lights, so it's not like anyone can actually *see* us, at least not without binoculars. But the thrill of it is ever-present anyway, the thought that someone could be watching as Cooper slams into me in our most private, intimate moments, and something about that makes this even hotter.

The ache between my legs becomes unbearable as I wait for his touch, and it's featherlight at first, his fingertips tracing down my spine and along the curve of my ass.

My pussy aches for him, and I'm certain I'm wetter and more ready for him than I've ever been for anybody in my life.

He leans down and peppers soft kisses along my spine, and then he sits on the floor and leans up against the window. I look down at him, and he's looking up at me, lust in his eyes along with a gleam.

"Sit on my face," he says.

"What?" I ask.

"Lower yourself down, use the window for balance, and *sit on my face.*"

Dear. Lord.

I've never had a man ask me to sit on his face. I don't even know what he means by that, but I lower down all the same.

My thighs tremble as I'm basically doing a squat over him, and I feel his tongue as it swipes through me before sinking inside me for a beat. He moves it up to suck on my clit, and then he inserts two fingers.

And then my thighs *really* start to tremble.

"Oh God!" I cry out, bracing my arm against the window and bracing my head on my forearm. I look down at him.

He pulls back to peek up at my face, his fingers still driving into me, and he grins. "My name's Cooper, but you can call me whatever you want."

It's cheesy, it's adorable, and it's so freaking sexy all at the same time.

He pulls his fingers out and dips his tongue into me again, and then he really goes to town, licking and sucking and doing something magical that I've never experienced before. "Fuck, you taste good," he says, and he continues doing what he's doing, but my legs can't handle it.

"Cooper!" I gasp. "I can't—I can't—I can't—"

I can't form a sentence, apparently.

He chuckles as he pulls away, and then he moves out from under me, and I straighten then collapse on the couch beside us. I watch him as he pads across the room toward his suitcase, and he opens it, locates a condom, and rolls it on as he walks back across the room toward me. "I'll take you up against the window before this weekend is over, but I don't want your legs giving out on you," he says once he's hovering over me.

I don't have time to form actual words since he chooses that moment to slam into me. My eyes roll back at the feel of him again, of *this* again, and I was seconds from tipping over the edge while he ate my pussy, so my climax is nearly immediate once he's back inside me again.

He keeps going, riding out my orgasm with me, and then he slows his pace, luxuriating in the feel as the pulses over him start to wane. He keeps thrusting, making love to me, and I swear I see fireworks as he goes.

Once I've come back down, he starts to pick up speed again. He leans down to suck one of my nipples into his mouth, and I feel the crescendo start to build all over again.

This has never happened to me before.

Usually I'm a one-orgasm-per-night kind of girl, not multiple in the same few minutes.

But Cooper Noah has experience that trained him well. He knows what he's doing when it comes to my body. I'll gladly let him lead me into my second orgasm of the night. Hell, I'll gladly let him lead me pretty much anywhere when he has me in his clutches this way.

"Fuck," he hisses, drawing out the word, and just the sound of his voice and knowing that he's deriving that pleasure from my body is enough to kick me into my second one.

"Wait for me," he murmurs. "I'm almost there." He picks up the pace, slamming into me, and I can't hold it off. I'm desperate to come, greedy to soothe the brand new ache pulsing inside me, and then he growls, "Now."

We both moan through the intensity, the two of us in sync as our bodies vibrate and throb with racking pulse after pulse of pleasure. And when it's all over, when our bodies start to calm, he pulls out and collapses beside me, the two of us panting and sweating after the workout that just wrung us both out.

The *best* kind of workout.

"Let's just stay here all weekend," he suggests sleepily.

I giggle. "Didn't you come to town to look at houses?"

"I'll just stay with my boss."

"Is he cool with you bringing women over?" I ask.

"Well, he's part owner of a sex club, so yeah, I think he'd be okay with it," he says. He shifts so he's leaning up on his elbow, his eyes moving toward mine. "And let me clarify. Not women. Woman. One. Singular. I'm almost thirty-three. I'm allowed to bang my girl."

"The one singular woman thing is cute, but back the truck up a sec," I say, my brows knitting together. "What's this now about a *sex club?*"

He chuckles. "That's what you picked up out of all that?"

"I said the other thing was cute," I protest. "Sex club. Explain yourself."

"I have nothing to explain," he says, his hand moving to his chest in defense. "The dude invited me to this club he owns. The first floor is part nightclub, part..." He trails off as he searches for the words. "I don't know. Part lounge with pool tables and these leather wingback chairs where big men can talk business." As he says the last part, he lowers the pitch of his voice to mock the very men he's talking about. "The second floor is basically a high-rent strip club, according to my buddy. I stuck to the first floor when I went. But the third floor…" He trails off again, and this time he shakes his head.

"The third floor?" I press.

"From what he said, it's six private rooms that are basically suites with big beds and plenty of sex toys, and then there are four rooms that aren't so private with either windows or two-way mirrors and little viewing areas where voyeurs can sit and watch." He lifts a shoulder. "To each their own, and I won't be a killjoy, but I feel like sex should be a private thing between two people."

"Two things here. One, let me just say that I agree completely and I'm so glad we're on the same page. I'm also glad to hear you didn't actually go on the third floor. Or the second, for that matter. And second, just so you know, *killjoy* is an old man word. Now we say either *buzzkill* or *don't yuck someone else's yum*," I tease.

He laughs, and then he tackles me, peppering kisses on my naked body as I laugh right along with him. "Maybe I should take *you* to the sex club."

"If it means I get to have sex with you…I'm in."

Chapter 24
Cooper

T his one's gorgeous, Cooper," Gabby says as she twirls around in the kitchen.

It's spacious, I'll give it that, but the location isn't exactly what I'm looking for…and neither are all the nail holes in the walls from the previous owners. Honestly, I think I'm after a new build at this point.

The realtor, a dude named Paul that Troy recommended, gave me the addresses and had his assistant unlock them for me ahead of time to give me privacy to look around. I appreciate not having someone hovering over us, and even more, I appreciate not having someone talking baseball stats with me the entire time we're looking around.

Gabby drives while I navigate from the passenger seat to the next one and the next, and I text Kaylee to see if she knows of any new builds in the area.

Kaylee: *Yes! My brother is in real estate development in the off-season, and I can check with my sister-in-law to see what spec homes are currently available.*

I thank her profusely for the help, and she texts me a handful of addresses shortly after that, telling me her sister-in-law, Kate, happened to be on site and unlocked a back door for us to check them out as long as we promised to turn the handle lock on our way out.

Done and done, I texted back, and we drive toward the first address.

On the way there, she pops a question completely out of the blue. "Are you excited to start your new job?"

I press my lips together and nod. The more I've thought about it, the more excited I've become. I'm at a point where I've finally wrapped my head around the fact that this is real. It's actually happening.

"Are you excited for your senior year to start?" I ask.

She sighs and stares out the windshield. "I am."

"What's wrong?"

"I'm just a little scared, I guess," she says.

"Of what?"

"Of things changing between us. I'll get busy with classes, and you'll get busy with your new job. Then I'll be working an internship that hopefully leads to something full time, and who knows if I'll even find something here in town? What if we lose this dynamic between us?" she asks.

I glance over at her, and then I reach over and grab her hand. I squeeze it in mine. "We won't lose the dynamic, Gabby. We can't. When it's this strong, it's impossible for it to be any other way."

She nods, but she's quiet the rest of the trip.

The community Kaylee sent over is gated, so I read the gate code to Gabby once we arrive. A large iron gate swings open, and she drives slowly through the neighborhood as we look at the mansions in here. They're spaced apart so every lot is enormous—perfect so I can put up some batting cages in the backyard—and they're situated on a hilltop with a view of the Strip not so far away in the distance.

We pull into the driveway of the first address Kaylee sent, and Gabby squeals. "Oh my God, Cooper, this is freaking incredible!" Gone is the melancholy mood that fell over us for a beat, a reminder that we can talk about the fears, but ultimately that's all they are. Fears. We just have to hold hands and conquer them together as they plow across our paths.

I have to admit…the curb appeal of the first house is pretty fucking sharp. The driveway and sidewalk leading to the front door are white travertine, and the entire house is a pristine white. Desert landscaping is already planted, and it looks like it's close to being finished and nearly move-in ready. I click the link Kaylee sent me and read the features aloud.

"This one is six bed, eight bath, and fifty-five hundred square feet. All the bedrooms have ensuite bathrooms. They're putting in a pool out back along with an outdoor kitchen and a full basketball court, and inside there's a gourmet kitchen, upstairs and downstairs wet bars, dedicated office spaces with custom built-ins and bookshelves, an exercise room, and a huge two-story fireplace in the living room."

"Isn't that a little…big for you?" she asks.

"It's ridiculously huge for one person, but I'd like to have space for when my mom comes to visit or my brother and his family," I say. "And, you know…I'd like this to be a permanent move, so I want space to grow into should the right time come." I chance a glance over at her, and her eyes are sparkling as she catches my drift.

I can see us in this place just from staring at the imposing black security door, and as we get out of my truck and walk around the house to the door Kaylee said would be unlocked, I get the sudden feeling like I'm already home.

Maybe it's the Gabby effect, of listening to her oohs and ahhs with each new feature we discover, or maybe it's because I really can see myself moving into a place like this with her.

As we walk through the house, that feeling only intensifies. Everything in the place is black, white, and gray, a perfect balance of monochrome that just somehow works. Despite the cold, raw colors, the place is filled with warmth.

And then we step out onto the balcony off the primary bedroom upstairs.

Holy shit.

I stare out over the hills and into the distance, where I have a perfect view of the entire Strip from Mandalay Bay on one end all the way to the tall tower of the Stratosphere at the other end. It's fucking magical in the daylight. I can only imagine what this view would look like at night.

Included in that view is the House, the nickname for the brand-new stadium built for the brand-new team.

I guess this one will be close to work.

"Wow," Gabby breathes beside me.

"What do you think?" I ask.

"I think it's too much, but I think it's absolute and total perfection." She glances inside at the primary suite. "I can see myself spending a lot of time here." She winks over at me, and I chuckle.

"Sold."

"And bonus, it's close to my dad's place, too, and not too far from campus," she says.

I pull her into my arms. "Total bonus." I drop my lips to hers. "And there's a market within walking distance in case it's three in the morning and I've had a few drinks and I'm running low on Slim Jims."

She giggles.

I glance around again. "I'll just text Kaylee and let her know I want this one."

"Don't you want to look at the others?" she asks.

I shake my head. "Not really, but I did promise I'd lock the doors, so we can go check them out."

The other two she sent me are beautiful homes, but my gut instinct was right. The first one is *the one*, and I let Kaylee know that immediately while Gabby drives us back toward the Strip.

Me: *I want the first one. I locked up the other two, though.*

Kaylee: *Your decisiveness is out of character. [wink emoji] Glad you'll be close. I'll let Kate know.*

Another one comes through before I get the chance to reply.

Kaylee: *She said it'll be ready to close by September 30. Does that work?*

Me: *I need to be back in town the first of September, but Troy said I can stay with him.*

Kaylee: *You can stay with us, too. If you don't mind twin girls who don't give a shit if you're in the bathroom.*

Me: *Thanks for the tempting offer, but I'll stick with Troy.*

Kaylee lets me know that Kate will be in touch with the paperwork. I text Troy next to let him know I found a place but that it won't be ready until the end of September, and his reply comes quickly.

Troy: *The offer to stay with me is still on the table. I have plenty of space.*

I thank him, and he tells me that a draft of my contract is waiting in my email.

My chest tingles with anticipation as I quickly open it and scroll to the number on the bottom line.

My eyes widen. It's more than I thought...and yep, I can definitely afford this place.

Ninety million over three years.

The next three years of my life, I'll be playing baseball again.

I'll be thirty-six when the contract is up.

Three years is enough time to build a brotherhood. To lead a team. To give this everything I've got.

I forward it to my agent for a quick review.

"The contract for my new job is in my email," I say nonchalantly even though excitement courses through my veins.

"And?" Gabby asks.

"And I think I'm about to start the adventure of a lifetime." She glances over at me with her sunshine smile, and that pretty much seals the deal.

Chapter 25
Gabby

I t's another weekend come and gone way too soon, and I find myself leaving the airport as Cooper boards a plane Sunday evening after yet another tearful goodbye.

My dad isn't home when I get there, but his cook left some dinners in the fridge. I settle on a salad and add some chicken to it, and I stare out the window as I eat by myself.

I'm my dad's only child—that we know about, at least—and he tells me how I'm the puzzle piece that's always been missing from his life. He regrets not being there in my childhood, and he's been good to me since we found each other. We've gotten very close in a very short amount of time, but he's busy with tons of different business ventures.

And now he'll be embarking on the busiest one of all. He's excited, and I'm excited for him, but I already miss having him around. It gets lonely in this big old mansion, but as I stare out at the view that's similar to the one in the house Cooper's going to purchase, I can't help but think maybe I won't be living here much longer.

It's a little early to think I'll be moving in with Cooper once he's in town, but he hinted at it, and I did, too. It's the path we're traveling, and I think we both see it coming sooner rather than later. My only reservation still is that he wants kids—and soon. I'm not there yet. I'm not even out of school, and I always imagined I'd work a few years to establish myself in a career before I settle down with kids.

Cooper texts me when he gets home, and I know it's time to focus on school. I open my class schedule and start reading through the materials in preparation of classes tomorrow.

When I set up my class schedule for this semester, I created an ideal schedule. I have no classes Thursday or Friday, I don't start on Monday or Wednesday until ten, and I'm done by early afternoon every day. It's a great schedule in terms of having a long weekend and having plenty of time to get my classwork done throughout the week, and it's also a great set-up for snagging either a job or that internship I'll need for next semester.

Or, you know…plenty of time for Cooper Noah.

Mia and I chose two classes to take together, so I'll see her on Mondays and Wednesdays in Global Consumer Behavior and on Tuesdays in Leadership and Management Skills.

My first class on Monday morning is a marketing one, and it meets for seventy-five minutes. It's a tedious first class where we go over the syllabus and play icebreaker games that are pointless given that I know the majority of my classmates since we've been in the same cohort for our major for years. We get our first writing assignment, one I'm confident I'll be able to knock out in a few hours, and then I have a fifteen minute break before heading to my second class of the day—the one I have with Mia.

She's already waiting for me, and I slide into the open seat beside her.

"How was your morning?" I ask.

"Eh," she says with a shrug. "First day means the same old shit in every class."

"Same," I admit. And then Dylan walks in, and he sits on Mia's other side. Her attention moves to him. Mine moves to my phone, which I pull out to text Cooper, and I find one from him already waiting for me.

Cooper: *Good luck on your first day. Miss you.*

Me: *Thanks! Just about to start my second class.*

Cooper: *How was the first one?*

Me: *Boring. Syllabus and icebreakers, just like every other first day of every other college class.*

Cooper: *I've got syllabus and an icebreaker for you.*

Me: *Why does it sound sexual when you say it?*

Cooper: *Because it IS sexual when I say it. [wink emoji]*

The professor starts talking, so I reluctantly put my phone away.

But I want to hear more about that icebreaker Cooper has in mind.

I'm having a hard time focusing on much of anything this week as Cooper's move-in date looms closer and closer. I run home from classes, eat, and immediately get my work done so my weekend will be clear.

We talk every night, but his daytime texts have been limited as he finishes training his replacement and starts working on the new role he'll take on with his company once he's in Vegas.

It's on our Tuesday night call after my second day of classes when he says, "I talked to Kaylee, and she said she'd love to have you come help out. But I think she's more interested in actually meeting you than in having you work for her."

I wrinkle my nose even though he can't see me. "I'm nervous to meet your friends."

"Don't be. They're pretty awesome."

I let out a nervous giggle. "I'm sure they are if you chose them to be friends with, but they're going to judge the years between us."

"So? We've already determined it doesn't matter to us. Besides, Kaylee's only like twenty-four, and she's already married with two kids. Her husband is a decade older. If anyone will understand, it's the two of them."

"Okay, okay," I grumble. "Still, it's scary to meet the friends, you know?"

"Yeah, I know. I lucked out that I met yours the night we met."

"Truth," I say with a giggle. "So when can I meet her?"

"My boss invited me to his place Thursday night, but maybe we can plan a dinner Friday if they're not busy."

"I'd love to," I say. "What time is your thing with your boss?"

"I'm not sure. I'll talk to him, and I'll be staying at his place, too, but let me get there and make a good impression before I start inviting you to stay the night."

I laugh. "Deal. But make your good impression fast because it's either your boss's place or my dad's house, and neither really sound like a good option."

"Maybe I'll rent a room for the month at Caesars so we can stop by whenever we need some private time," he suggests, and there's a sexy, desperate edge to his tone.

"I think that's a great idea for the month of September. Or we can just, you know, put that camping mattress to good use in the bed of my truck," I suggest, and I hear the desperation in my own voice, too.

He chuckles, and it's a raspy sound that sends an ache pulsing between my thighs. "I better go or this is going to turn into another night of phone sex and I need to finish packing up my kitchen since my storage pod is arriving tomorrow, and you need to finish writing your paper due tomorrow."

"All right, buddy. But be warned. I'll be ready to put that camping pad to good use once you're back in Vegas."

"So will I," he promises, and we say our goodbyes.

Only a few more days until he moves here. I'm not sure how I'm supposed to concentrate on which global consumer behavior I want to change about myself when all I can think about is Cooper.

Chapter 26
Cooper

The drive from San Diego to Vegas is a little over five hours, and I pull up to the address Troy gave me a little after six at night. I took a half day for my final day at StrongFitKids' San Diego location, and we spent most of it eating celebratory cake and talking about what I'll be doing with Kaylee in Vegas. I'm excited to work closely with her again, excited to be close to Ben, too, excited to get back into the game, and most of all, I'm excited to live in the same town as Gabby.

So when I passed over a hill and the famed Las Vegas Strip came into my view, my heart started beating faster. That view is home now—especially given that it's a similar view to what I'll see when I sit on my balcony at my new house in another month.

The same view is in sight from Troy's place, which is only about a mile from my new place—he's a mile closer to the stadium than me. We're both close enough that it won't be much of a commute, convenient given that the field is where we'll spend most of our time once we're in season and not traveling.

And that convenience store that's within walking distance of my place is the mid-point between our houses. I stop just to grab a few Slim Jims, and sure enough, there's a big display of them right beside the register.

I tell the cashier to keep them fully stocked since I'll be in quite often.

I suck in a breath.

This is it.

I'm really doing this.

I talked to my mom for an hour on the way here.

I blasted Dave Matthews Band for the other four hours.

I allowed a few Taylor Swift songs in the mix, too, and I thought about Gabby the entire time, imagining her dancing across the room as she belts out the words to the songs.

My life is about to change. There's no way around that. I'm finding myself suddenly in a committed relationship with a girl twelve years younger than me. I'm getting back into the game. I'm moving over three hundred miles from what's been home for the last few years.

There will be highs and lows with these changes, of course. That's just part of life. But right now, everything's looking pretty damn rosy.

I ring Troy's bell, and the door opens a few beats later. Troy stands there, a glass of whiskey held out in greeting. "Welcome to Vegas, man," he says, and I take the offering from his outstretched hand.

"Thanks, boss."

"Come on in," he says. He glances down at my suitcase beside me and the duffel bag slung over my arm. "You got more in the car?"

I shake my head. "All my shit is packed up on a pod that's being parked in the next day or two in some storage facility a few miles away. I'll be living out of my suitcase until my house is ready."

"Well, mi casa, su casa. Make yourself at home, and help yourself to anything you'd like." He opens the door wider to allow me in. "Let me show you your room."

He takes me through the mansion, and I recall him mentioning a daughter, but apart from her, nobody else appears to live here. Nobody else is home, either.

"A few others who will be working with us are coming over in a bit," he says as he shows me the bedroom where I'll be staying. It has a king size bed with nightstands on either side, a desk and dresser, an ensuite bathroom, and a balcony with a great view—all I need, really. "My daughter's room is right next door, so try to keep your bachelor shenanigans to a dull roar when she's home."

I laugh as I think about Gabby, and sometimes we just can't help it…we're not quiet when we're in the heat of the moment.

"I'm not so much the bachelor anymore," I admit as I roll my suitcase to one corner and set my duffel down on the bed.

"Oh?" he asks.

"I met a girl when I was in town for our initial meeting. It's been a fucking whirlwind, but…yeah, I think it's safe to say I'm officially off the market."

"Good for you, man. I'm off the market myself. My better half, Joanie—at the club, she goes by her last name, Sapphire—and I have been in a relationship for a while now. It's probably about time to introduce her to my daughter, but it's complicated," he says.

I offer a wry smile. "Aren't they all?"

"Doesn't sound like it was for you," he points out.

I shake my head. "Nah. It came really naturally, actually. There's just something about her…it's like I've known her my whole life and we were both just spinning our wheels until fate brought us into each other's orbits."

"Good for you, man. I know you had it rough with Stacy."

I close my eyes and shake my head. "You have no idea. This girl's a breath of fresh air. She's warm and kind, and…" I trail off, and then I glance over at him.

He fills in the rest. "And she's a fucking animal where it counts?"

"Top notch." I make a circle with my thumb and forefinger.

He raises a brow. "You sure you don't want to bring her to the third floor of my club?"

I chuckle. "Thanks for the offer, but we'll pass."

"It's on the table if you change your mind. Let me show you around the place," he says, and I follow him around his house. He shows me the kitchen, the family room, the workout room, a game room, and the massage room. It appears to be a totally normal house—something I questioned in my mind after learning about Coax, but since his daughter lives here, I imagine he keeps his extracurricular activities limited to the club.

He takes me outside last, and he shows me the killer batting cages he has set up out there along with a gorgeous, luxury pool that I could spend hours relaxing in.

"I think this'll do for the next month," I admit, and he laughs.

A catering service arrives shortly after that, and while they set up for the party tonight, I set to unpacking in the room where I'll be staying for the next few weeks.

I text Gabby, too.

Me: *Just got to town. Wish you were here and wish I could see you tonight but I have no idea how late this party's going to go.*

Gabby: *I wish I could see you, too. I'm planning to just stay at Mia's until late, but let's meet for breakfast in the morning. Work for you?*

Me: *If by "breakfast" you mean your body, yep, that works for me.*

Gabby: *Did you figure out a hotel room situation yet or are you cool with bringing me over to your boss's place yet?*

Me: *Camping pad, back of your car. I'm sure we can find a dirt lot somewhere. Or we can sneak into my house if there aren't any workers there.*

Gabby: *Lol YES. I keep thinking about that balcony off your bedroom and how you could just bend me right over it...*

Me: *If this party's over early, I'm calling you for phone sex. No way I'm waiting until morning to rub one out.*

Gabby: *I'm down for phone sex, but if I'm still at Mia's, I'll have to go out to my truck to do it.*

Me: *Works for me. Then I can picture you doing that to yourself every time we get into your truck. That's hot as fuck, Sunshine.*

Gabby: *I'm cool with allowing you to let that live rent free in your head.*

I laugh out loud, and then we say our goodbyes. I head down to see if Troy needs my help with anything, but it's already done, and a few guys have already shown up.

The party celebrating my contract is underway, and it feels like the kickoff event for many, many more fun evenings to come.

Chapter 27
Cooper

I haven't been this drunk in a long time.

We've been drinking straight whiskey all night while I've been on a beer kick the last couple years, and we've eaten our weight in finger foods and appetizers. We've moved onto playing poker, the other guys are smoking cigars, something that never appealed to me, and we're laughing. Loudly and heartily.

I'd estimate there are around fifteen or twenty guys here, some who I've met before and others who I haven't, and we're already building the sort of brotherhood that comes with working together for a common goal.

Most of the men here are from either the coaching staff or the front office staff. While our team draft isn't for another two months, Troy has already managed to sign a bunch of free agents, a couple who showed up tonight. I know most of the coaches here from when I played, so the majority of the night has been spent really just catching up with old friends.

It feels good. It feels *right*, like I've landed in the place where I'm supposed to be…like it doesn't matter that I haven't played in the last three years. It'll all come back exactly as it's meant to, and that's been a big theme of my night here.

Guys head in and out as they go outside to smoke cigars, the heat of Vegas swooping in every time the door opens or closes. I'm facing away from the door, too wrapped up in my poker game to worry about who's walking in or out, but by midnight most of the guys have left and the last of the poker tournament is down to Troy, Aaron Jacobs, Holden Thatcher, and Jeremy Bardot, three of the free agents Troy already signed.

Holden goes all in, and that's when my cockiness rears its head. I feel good about my pair of queens, so I call him even though it'll wipe me out if I lose.

He flips his cards, and he's got a full house.

My queens look weak in comparison, but I laugh it off, pay the man the money I owe him, and call it a night.

I have phone sex to get to, after all.

I stumble up to my room, trying to remember which one's mine, and I set my hand on a doorknob before I remember that was the daughter's room. I move to the next door, open it, and I'm elated to find I chose the right door.

I leap onto my bed and grab my phone.

She answers on the first ring. "Hey, Captain."

"God, you sound sexy. You should come over right now."

She giggles. "Are you drunk right now?"

"Maybe a little."

"Ooh, this'll be fun." She giggles. "I've never had phone sex with a drunk Cooper before."

"Are *you* drunk?" I demand.

"No. Mia had a boy over so I ducked out early and snuck back home even though my dad's got some friends over. I snatched a seltzer from a big tub of alcohol and snuck up to my room, but I'm definitely not drunk."

"Was it boat boy?" I ask, and she giggles.

"It *was* boat boy. I felt like a third wheel, so I bolted early. My dad's old friends are still downstairs, so I put on my earbuds to drown them out and now I have you in stereo in my head."

"That's hot. But now you're home, so my fantasies of you fingering yourself in the front of your truck will have to live on in my imagination."

"Correct. But I'm open to doing it in person for you if it's really a fantasy." Her tone is sly and sexy and Jesus Christ, when did I get in so deep with her? Oh, right. The moment I met her.

"You'd do that?"

"I'd do anything for you," she breathes.

Her words speak directly to my cock once again.

"Where are you now?" I ask.

"My bed."

"What are you wearing?"

"You want the truth or the fantasy?"

I laugh. "Whatever story you want to tell."

"Black lingerie with a garter belt and straps holding up my thigh-highs. But I'm not wearing any panties under the garter belt."

My cock strains painfully against my jeans as I close my eyes and picture it in my mind.

"What are you wearing?" she asks.

I glance down at my faded jeans and plain Under Armour shirt. "No shirt, just for you, and gray sweatpants you can definitely see the Captain through."

"Oh, God," she whimpers as she pictures it. I love that I do to her the same thing she does to me.

"Since you're not wearing any panties, slide your finger through your pussy for me, baby," I murmur.

She must do it, because I hear her soft moan over the line. "Reach into your gray sweatpants and play with your balls," she demands, and she's no longer tentative when she issues instructions over the phone.

Fuck, that's hot.

I touch my nuts, and then I stroke myself. "I can't help it," I say. "I'm fisting my cock now as I imagine your hot little mouth."

"Mm," she groans.

I hear a knock on the wall beside me. I guess Troy's daughter's back home. It takes me out of the moment for a beat, and I move away from the wall and over to the desk chair just in case someone's in the room next door.

"Take off your bra and touch your nipple," I demand. "Pretend it's my hands on your body."

I hear some rustling through the line, and then a soft moan.

I love the sound of her moans. I love knowing that she can touch herself and imagine me doing it. I love that she can be so completely herself with me. I love *her*. "Now finger yourself while I jerk off, and let me know how good it feels."

"Oh, God, Cooper," she moans. "I wish it was you. God, I wish you were here."

"So do I, baby." I fist my cock and squeeze the head before pumping the shaft. "So do I." I pick up speed, listening to her soft sighs and moans as she does the same thing to herself, as we listen to each other move toward the brink of climax.

"Faster," I say, and we both pick up the speed even more. "I'm close. Rub your clit for me."

"Oh God!" she practically yells, the sound forcing my orgasm to wash over me way too soon. The white jets stream onto my hand as I think about her touching herself and picturing me.

135

I grunt through my climax as I listen for her moans through the line, and when we're both finished and panting slightly, neither of us says anything for a few beats.

"Damn," I eventually say, breaking the silence.

"Yeah," she agrees. "I can't wait to do that in person."

"Neither can I. Are we still on for breakfast?"

"Absolutely. Let's meet at Kings Diner at nine, okay?" she asks.

"I'll see you then. Sweet dreams."

"Same to you," she says, and we end the call.

I sag back into the chair for a beat. The hangover that hits me in the morning is accompanied by regret, but I'm seeing Gabby for breakfast, and that's enough of a motivator to get me out of bed.

Damn. I can't drink like I used to.

I fumble my way over to the shower, and I feel a little better after breathing in the steam. If I don't get a move on, I'm going to be late for breakfast.

I run a hand through my wet hair after my shower, grab a pair of athletic shorts and another Under Armour tee, and head down to the kitchen to grab a cup of coffee before I run out the door to meet my girl.

When I get down to the kitchen, a young woman is bending down as she looks in the bottom drawer of the fridge, which I assume is the freezer. Her ass is sticking up in the air, and I assume this is Troy's daughter. Out of respect for both my girlfriend who I'm meeting shortly and Troy, I glance away.

"Dad? Is that you?" she yells from its depths.

"No," I say tentatively, my mouth dry from the hangover. "It's your dad's houseguest."

She straightens and whirls around to look at the stranger in her kitchen, and when she does, she gasps as a hand moves to her chest. I suck in a sharp breath as a shot of disbelief darts through my chest.

My wide eyes meet her even wider eyes.

"What are you doing here?" we say at the exact same time.

"Oh good, you two have met," Troy says as he saunters into the room. "Cooper, this is my daughter, Gabriella."

Oh fuck. This has to be some sort of joke...or some sort of nightmare.

It can't be true.

Gabby is Troy's daughter?

To be continued in Book 2, FASTBALL

Chapter 1
Gabby

"Oh good, you two have met," my dad says, his voice shocking me from my frozen state of seeing Cooper standing in my kitchen. What the hell is going on? "Cooper, this is my daughter, Gabriella."

My eyes feel like they're going to fall out of their sockets, they're bugged out so wide.

"Cooper's the guy who's staying with us for the next few weeks until his house is ready," my dad explains. "He's going to be playing third base for the Heat."

He...he's *what?*

He's going to be playing third base for the Heat.

Of course he is.

I blow out a breath. "Nice to meet you," I say, pressing my lips together and hoping he plays along. I dig my fingernails into my palms, hoping I don't feel the pain so I can wake up from this nightmare.

But nope...the pain slices fresh.

Shit.

So that's the new job that brought him from San Diego to Vegas.

He's going back to the game, and my dad is going to be his *manager.*

That's a pretty big detail to leave out of the story, but he's *still* never told me he played baseball. Or *plays* baseball, as in present tense. And on the exact same hand, I've never told him I'm the daughter of a baseball legend.

My dad isn't going to react well to Cooper and me. We need to talk. We need to touch base and figure out how to best handle this.

Troy Bodine is a passionate man to begin with, but a flip switched in him when he met me and when the two of us started getting close. He's protective of me—maybe *more* protective than most fathers would be over their twenty-one-year-old daughters since he missed out on the first eighteen years of my life. It's like he's making up for lost time now, and there's no way he's going to take kindly to the fact that one of his players is fucking his daughter.

Particularly not one who's twelve years her senior.

"Nice to meet you, too," Cooper says, his brows pinched together like he's trying to piece all this together, too.

Is our breakfast still on?

Where do we even go from here?

"I was just heading out to meet a friend for breakfast," I say, going for nonchalance but epically failing as my voice comes out all high-pitched and weird.

"Have a great time, sweetheart," my dad says, clearly missing my total internal battle, and my cheeks flame as I pass by Cooper to head upstairs and grab my purse.

I hear my dad behind me as I pass by. "She's a good kid. Great head on her shoulders."

"She seems lovely," Cooper says softly, and tears pinch behind my eyes as I think about what this is going to mean for us.

I never in a million years imagined he was the new player my dad invited to stay at our house. My dad's been gone so much lately that most of our communication has happened over text message. Between school starting and falling for Cooper, I haven't been around much myself.

I thought he retired. I thought he had an injury that took him out of the game.

I guess I thought a lot of things I was wrong about.

Oh God.

He told me the buddy who invited him here to play owns a sex club.

Is his *buddy* my *father?*

Is that where dear old Dad is always running off to?

I think I'm going to be sick.

I grab my keys and purse before I head out to the truck my very rich father purchased me for my birthday, where I draw in a deep breath and take a moment to regroup. This all seemed so easy yesterday, so natural, and now…it's not.

I arrive at the restaurant first, and I ask for a private table in the back. I face the door so I can watch for him to walk in and so he as the *celebrity* here can face the wall, my heart thundering in my chest as I wait.

I chug down an entire glass of water in about six seconds flat.

It feels like a lifetime passes before he finally walks in. He glances around the room, and when his eyes land on mine, they don't warm over like they have in the past.

I can't quite read what's there, but it's hard to tell anyway with the bill of his black baseball hat pulled down low over his eyes.

Nerves rattle me, but this is Cooper. This is *us*. Whatever happens, we'll make it through. What we've built in a short amount of time is solid.

Or maybe that's just my naivety showing again.

He slides into the booth across from me, his eyes down on the table.

"Hi," I begin tentatively.

His eyes finally flick up to mine, and his are positively tormented. "Hey."

"So, uh…you play baseball?"

He offers a sad, wry smile. "So, uh…you're the daughter of Troy Bodine?"

I nod. "Just found out a few years ago."

He presses his lips together. "I played in the majors for the Dodgers for seven years and retired early after an injury." He holds up his elbow. "Surgery pieced me back together, and then Troy— uh, your father…" he trails off and clears his throat. "He called me with an offer to come back to the game, to be the face of the new Vegas Heat expansion team." He blows out a breath.

"I knew you played for the Dodgers. My friends looked you up the night we hooked up, but I figured you'd tell me when you were ready," I say.

His brows draw together. "You didn't think it was important to tell me who your father was knowing I used to play?"

"I had no idea you knew him," I say, defensiveness jumping into my tone even though I have nothing to be defensive over. "I don't like telling people who my dad is, particularly people who might benefit from that knowledge." My words feel like heavy weights leaving my mouth.

He glances away from me and out the window. "I get it. I really liked how I could just be Cooper, the guy who works for a kids' fitness organization, around you. I liked not being Cooper Noah, All-Star MVP. I liked that we built something based on the me deep down rather than the me everyone sees in the media."

Tears continue to burn behind my eyes as he uses past tense in his speech.

"We both had our reasons for keeping things close to the vest, I guess," I say softly.

"Can I get y'all something to drink?" a perky waitress asks as she appears at our table.

"Coffee and orange juice, please," I say, forcing a smile for her benefit.

"Same," Cooper says, not looking up from the spot where he's staring at the table.

"Do y'all need more time to decide what you want to eat?" she asks.

I glance at him, and he doesn't look up or reply. "Sure, that'd be great," I tell her. I stare at the bill of his hat, my eyes memorizing the UA on it as I wonder whether I'll ever get to see it in an intimate setting again or if this is all going to disappear as quickly as it began.

I don't know what to say.

I've never been at a loss for words around Cooper, but right now…I've got nothing but a wish and a prayer.

He doesn't say anything, either.

"Talk to me," I finally say softly.

He blows out a breath, and when his eyes meet mine, that same torture is there, only it seems worse than before.

"This changes everything," he says.

He's right. He's a megastar baseball player, and I'm his coach's daughter.

But I don't want it to change a thing.

"It doesn't have to," I protest. We can do this—we can hide it from my dad if we have to, but this can't be the end.

It can't be.

"It does. It's straight up disrespecting one of my best friends—my *boss*. The man who pulled a lot of fucking strings to get me here. We can't be together, Gabby. I'm so sorry." His voice breaks as he says the words. "I need to get out of here."

He gets up and strides out of the restaurant, and I'm left with the two glasses of orange juice and two cups of coffee the waitress delivers along with a whole host of questions…and worst of all, a broken heart.

Chapter 2
Cooper

I shouldn't have walked out, but what the fuck else was there to do?

All I could think about were the ways we could try to make this work, but my stupid, logical brain kept showing me all the different reasons why it can *never* work.

I can't play for a manager I'm lying to, and he'd never be okay with me dating his daughter.

It's his *daughter*.

He's a good friend of mine. One of the very few friends I feel like I can count on right now, at least in this town since he offered me a place to live along with the incredible opportunity to get back in the game.

I owe him a lot, and that has to start with my respect.

The man knows how I used to live my life before I got serious with Stacy, and for fuck's sake, I know how he lives his, too.

It's too messy, too complicated. Too ugly.

But the love I feel for her is the opposite of all that. It's beautiful and simple and easy.

It's the greatest thing I have in my life, maybe the greatest thing I've *ever* had in my life, and I'm making the decision to let it go.

I knew if I stayed in that restaurant one second longer, I'd break down in front of her, in front of the waitress, in front of every other patron in that place, and then you can bet your ass I'd end up as a fucking headline in the media with her sitting across from me. And you can bet your ass my boss would see it, and then we'd be in an even bigger mess than we are now.

We're lucky that shit hasn't happened already. We're lucky we're in Vegas where the people sitting beside us are too drunk or high or wrapped up in their vacations to realize Cooper Fucking Noah is in the house.

I want to be angry she never told me who her dad was, but it's hard to be angry when I left a pretty big puzzle piece out of the conversation myself.

I guess I just want someone to blame, but other than myself...I keep coming up empty.

And so I allow myself to break down once I'm in the privacy of my truck. It feels like a death as the loss of what could have been starts to wash over me. I think I'm still in that state of shock.

When I took the hit that took me out of the game, I didn't cry. The pain was too intense and I went into shock.

This pain feels worse.

At least with the injury, I knew what I was dealing with. I could take painkillers if I needed to, and they would help ease the pain.

I'm not sure anything could ease what I'm feeling right now.

I pull myself together, and then I take a drive. I can't go back to Troy's house like this, especially not given the fact that I'm *living* with Gabby now, so I drive up some hills and into the mountains. I find myself driving and driving, and a little under an hour later I wind up at Hoover Dam.

I pull off the road and get out of the car, staring at the magnificence of the dam, wishing she was here tucked into my side as I press a kiss to her temple and we take in the view together.

I don't know how to deal with this.

I don't know how to get through this.

I don't know how to come out on the other side and live my life without her in it.

I stare out over one of the places I always wanted to visit. While it is fascinating, it's not the magic I was expecting. How can it be after I walked out on Gabby?

I read a sign letting me know how the dam does something with the water from the Colorado River, but I can't concentrate on the details when it feels like my chest cavity is being shredded in two.

How could I not have pieced this together?

I felt like we knew each other so well, so intimately, and now it feels like we never knew each other at all.

How did I not know she was leaving something out of the story just as I was? How could she have not wondered whether her father and I knew each other given our career history? We ran in the same circles, and she had to have puzzled that out.

I guess it's easy to blame her naivety or her inexperience. From everything she's told me about her mom, she wasn't allowed to show any interest in anything that her father might've been interested in, so I guess it makes sense she wouldn't know much about baseball, particularly baseball that took place three years ago before she moved in with him, back when I was still in the game.

It would be the easier choice to give into what I want, but that would mean either disrespecting my boss in lying to him or it would mean telling him the truth...that I've been disrespecting him for weeks by wrecking his daughter.

But my brain keeps returning to the entire reason I'm here.

Troy Bodine wants to build a team that I lead.

While I believe in what Gabby and I shared in the few weeks we've known each other, there are hard and fast rules in both the game and in friendships. You don't fuck a friend's mom. You don't fuck a friend's ex. And you certainly don't fuck your friend's daughter.

Another sign tells me how the dam provides water to millions of people. What the hell am I doing here?

I shouldn't have run away from her, but I couldn't see any other option. My choice was to sit at that table and bleed out in the booth across from her, baiting somebody to get a picture of us...or fucking bolt. And so I fucking bolted.

The media paints me as the unemotional third baseman whose feathers are never ruffled. The guy who's never bothered. I'm painted that way because that's what I allow others to see, so that's what I allow others to believe.

Gabby might've been the first person I ever really let in apart from my mother—and even dear sweet Mommy doesn't know me in many of the ways Gabby does. She's the first person I ever really let see all my different sides even though it was terrifying to let her in.

I told her things I never told Stacy.

I felt different ways about her that I never felt for Stacy, too.

I can sit here trying to convince myself that it was meaningless or that we didn't know each other long enough for it to have mattered—or any one of another million lies swirling around my mind, but I know the truth.

Now that she's part of my life, I'm not sure how to exist without her. And even worse, I don't know how I'm supposed to live with her for the next month when I won't be able to touch her or kiss her or look at her or fall further in love with her.

Because one thing's for sure. I either lose a friendship that's over a decade old with the kind of guy who offered to pay me more than I'm worth and who is depending on me to start a new legacy here in Vegas…or I lose Gabby.

Which would be less destructive? To put the entire Vegas Heat organization in jeopardy after I committed to building a brotherhood? Or to take that shot for myself and bury it deep and deal with the pain?

I can't let the entire organization down. There's Troy, but there's also the entire team. The staff. The crew.

I have no choice but to take the hit this time.

Chapter 3
Gabby

Right about now I'm really regretting not scheduling any classes on Friday.

It seemed like a good idea at the time, but now it just feels a little masochistic.

I couldn't bring myself to stay at that restaurant and eat breakfast when everything is hanging in the balance, so I chugged both orange juices, left some cash on the table, and bolted for home. Cooper isn't there, of course, but my dad is.

"What did you want to talk to me about?" he asks, referring to the text message I sent him a few days ago.

I blow out a breath as I wonder whether this is a good time to bring this up or not. I think Cooper just got scared, and we both know this is worth fighting for. But obviously I need to talk to him before I bring it up to anyone else…particularly my dad.

I'm not sure asking about an internship at my dad's new baseball stadium is the best idea given the fact that it'll push me into closer proximity to Cooper.

Or maybe that's exactly what we need.

"I met with my advisor a few weeks ago and she told me I need to start looking for an internship. Do you happen to have anything at the stadium?" I ask. The question is out before I can stop it. In truth, that's always what I'd planned to ask. But it feels even more important now that I know who one of his star players is going to be.

His brows shoot up. "Really? You're interested in coming to work with me?" He sounds excited at the prospect of having me close at the stadium.

I nod. "I think it would be really neat to learn about the front office responsibilities of a professional baseball team even though

I don't know that much about the game. But I am excited to learn, and I've learned a good deal about marketing and social media."

"I can put you in touch with our marketing department since they run the internship program. We will definitely find a spot for you. I'm thinking you might be a great fit as an intern since the program touches on a lot of marketing and social media as you just mentioned, but you'll also get all kinds of experience with all different levels of office staff, the crew, and the clubhouse."

"Clubhouse?" I ask.

"The locker room," he clarifies.

"That sounds really interesting," I say. "When would it start?"

"I'm heading into the stadium later today if you'd like to come with me and get a feel for things to see if you think it would be a good fit. You could start as early as Monday if you want. That would just be paperwork and training, and of course it would be a paid position," he says.

I force a laugh even though I can't feel much joy knowing where the hell Cooper ran off to. "I don't need to see the stadium today to accept your generous offer, but I'd love to see it anyway."

It's the first time he's invited me to go with him, but I suppose it's also the first time I've shown an interest in seeing it. It's currently closed to the public, but the clubhouse and weight room recently opened to players as the team started signing free agents. I think. I hear my dad tossing around words like that but I don't really know what any of it means. It's a brand-new, state of the art facility, and as soon as it's ready for the public, the crowds will swarm to check out Vegas's newest attraction.

"Great. I'm just waiting for Coop to get back from his meeting, and then we can go," he says.

"Cooper's going?" I ask, and I know my voice sounds hopeful, but dammit, I need to see him. I need to talk to him.

He nods. "Yes. He texted me a little while ago and said he'd be back in an hour or so."

I can't help but wonder where the hell he went and why he's going to be gone another hour, but I don't ask questions. I'll save them for the man himself.

"I'll be ready," I say, and then I head upstairs to take care of some work I was assigned yesterday.

Except I can't focus on a damn thing, so I call up Mia.

"Hey girl hey," she answers. "How's it going?"

I can't help it. I burst into tears.

"Whoa, Gabs. What's going on?"

"Cooper's going to be playing for my dad's new team and I don't know how I could have been so stupid to not piece that together but he told me this morning he can't be with me," I ramble and sob at the same time.

"Oh, Jesus. I knew he was too old for you, girl. Older guys, they just don't give a fuck. They do whatever serves them. Hell...*all* men do that," she says, and I know she's trying to make me feel better, but I still jump to his defense. I'm not sure *why* I do that after he walked out on me at breakfast, but it's my gut reaction.

"He's not like that, Mia. We just need to talk, I think, but he left and I don't know where he is," I say.

"Have you tried calling him?"

"No," I admit. "We met for breakfast but he told me he couldn't do this and walked out before we even ordered, and I figured I should give him space."

"Well go call him, girl. If you really think it's not like that, then you two will figure it out, right?"

"I hope so," I whisper...but after the way he reacted to this new twist, I'm not so confident in that right now.

I hang up with her and try his phone, and it makes that funny beeping sound where I can tell he's on the phone with someone else.

Eventually it goes to voicemail, and I lie on my bed staring up at the ceiling as tears leak from the sides of my eyes, dripping down my temples and onto my pillow.

He's talking to someone. Is he talking about what just happened? Did he call a friend to get advice the way I did? Or, knowing him the way I think I do...did he call his mom to get her take on it?

If I can get him to talk to me, maybe I'll learn the answers to these questions.

But if he's going to ignore my calls and refuse to talk to me...I'm not sure how we move forward.

Getting over the boy I dated for eight months was a walk in the park compared to even the thought of trying to forge ahead without Cooper Noah.

Chapter 4
Cooper

"He's her *father*?" my mother asks, and her voice is all high and screechy and definitely judgmental.

"Yep," I confirm as I merge back onto the highway to head toward Troy's house.

"Oh, God, Coop. What are you going to do?"

"I told her this changes everything and we can't be together. And then I ran like a fucking coward."

She clears her throat, but I can't be bothered to care that the *F* word isn't her favorite word. "Why does it change everything?"

"It just does," I mutter.

"But why? Are you scared of telling Troy?"

"Scared?" I say, my tone more mocking than I mean for it to be. "I'm not scared of anything." It's a lie. There's plenty I'm scared of, and right now I feel like I'm living a nightmare.

"Right," she says. "And I'm the Pope. But listen, honey, only you can decide how this is going to play out."

"I know, and that's the whole problem. I can't stop thinking about how my choice here is to potentially screw over the entire Heat organization or to screw over myself. Don't you think I need to take one for the team…literally?" I ask.

She huffs out a laugh. "Stop making yourself out to be some martyr."

"I'm not," I protest. "I'm just trying to do what's right."

My phone beeps to let me know another caller is trying to get through, but I'm driving and focusing on the road, so I ignore it, opting to continue my conversation with my mom hands-free.

"You weren't concerned whether or not it was right before. Why do you care now?" she asks.

"Because it's more than just her and me now," I say. I signal a lane change to get around a semi, and I pick up the pace to get back a little faster since I promised Troy I'd be back soon to go to the stadium with him. It's the one thing I'm holding onto right now—seeing my new home, the place where I'll spend more time than anywhere else as a new season is on the horizon. "It's a friendship that spans more than a decade. It's my *boss*, Mom. It's the entire team dynamic when I made a commitment to lead that team."

"Where did you see it going before you found out about Troy?"

I suck in a sharp breath, and my voice is soft when it finally comes out to answer. "I saw it going all the way. I saw us in the long haul. She's young, sure, but it just felt right between us."

"Then why does Troy being her father have to be the end of it? Why can't you just be honest with him?"

It's a valid question. "I know Troy, and I know how he'll react."

"Maybe he'll surprise you," she suggests.

"Right. How kindly would you take to me telling you I had an affair with Janice Roberts?" I ask, naming her best friend.

She's quiet a beat, and then she exhales loudly. "Okay, fine, point taken. It would be weird. But Janice Roberts is fifty-eight, which puts her at twenty-five years older than you, so it's a little different."

"Is it, though? Is it the age gap that makes it weird, or is it the fact that she's your best friend?"

"I get it, honey, but I also saw you with her, and I don't mean *with* her, with her, but I saw how you were on your own when she was part of your life the weekend after you met her. You were different. You were the Cooper you used to be before your injury, before that damn Stacy dragged you down. You were light and free. And now everything's heavy again. I can feel it in your voice."

"It *is* heavy, Mom. I feel like my heart is breaking." My voice breaks at the end just to really drive that point home, and I'd be mortified if I was talking to anyone other than my mother.

"I'm so sorry, baby. I wish I could make it all better for you."

"Then make it better," I whisper.

"I love you," she says. "I'm here no matter what you decide, but that's the thing. Only *you* can decide."

"I know. I'm almost back and I need to call Kaylee, so I better go. I'll talk to you soon."

"Take care of yourself, okay?" she says. "Your mom worries about you."

"I will. I love you."

We hang up, and I instruct my truck to call Kaylee Olson next.

"Cooper Fucking Noah," she answers, venom in her voice.

"Shit. What did I do now?"

She giggles. "I'm teasing. What's up bestie?"

I let out a heavy sigh. "It's been a day."

"It's barely noon and you're already having a day?" she asks.

"Yeah," I mutter.

"What happened and whose ass do I need to kick?"

"I don't really want to talk about it, and I guess if there's anyone who deserves a kick in the ass, it's me," I admit.

"How can I help make it better?" she presses.

"I'm not sure. Distract me with work?"

"You got it. Is your girl still interested in coming to work with us?" she asks. Her tone is careful, as if she senses that the girl is at the root of my issues.

I clear my throat. "I'm pulling that particular offer."

"Oh, Coop," she says, and the sympathy in her voice is exactly why I didn't want to talk about it. I don't want anyone's sympathy. I'll get over it. I'll move on. "What happened?"

"Her dad is Troy Bodine." My tone is flat, and I hear her gasp. "Can we just…" I trail off and sigh. "Can we not talk about it right now?"

"Ben will be home a little later. Do you want to talk to him about it instead of me?"

"No," I say with a frustrated sigh. "I don't want to talk to *anyone* about it. I just found out this morning, I told her we couldn't move forward from it, and that's it. End of story. On a separate note, I have an idea for SFK and a huge local sponsorship opportunity if you're interested in setting a time to chat."

"I'd love to. Name the time and the place, and I'll be there," she says.

"I'll text over the details once I have them. Thanks, Kay."

She pauses. "I'm here for you, you know. You don't have to go through this alone."

"Thanks," I murmur, and then I say goodbye and end the call just as I pull up in front of Troy's house. I stare at the house a beat. Her truck is in the circular driveway. It wasn't there last night. Maybe things would be different if it had been—if I knew who she was before I even got to town.

Maybe things would've been different if I would've known before we even had our first night together. Then I wouldn't have allowed myself to fall for her and I wouldn't be in this situation now.

I keep trying to figure out the lesson here, and I think it's that I should always lead with who I am, and I should expect others to do the same. I can't escape Cooper Noah the All Star, and maybe it was wrong to ever have tried.

I put my hat back on, backwards this time since I'm not trying to hide from anybody, and I glance at my phone and discover the call I missed was from Gabby. She didn't leave a message, and she's probably wondering where the hell I ran off to.

But I have an appointment scheduled with her dad, so the big talk that I'm already dreading will have to wait a little longer.

Chapter 5
Cooper

I let myself in since Troy told me to, and the house is quiet. Everyone's surely home, but in a mansion of this size, I suppose it's easy to find a quiet corner to hide in.

I think about what that could have meant for Gabby and me if I wasn't being a martyr, as my mother suggested. Is that what I'm doing?

No.

If the situation was reversed and I had a twenty-one-year-old daughter, well, I would've been quite the young father…but I wouldn't want a teammate screwing around with her, much less a player in a position subordinate to my own. And certainly not someone I opened my house to, someone I paid big money to get to town, someone I'm building an entire team around.

It's a lot of responsibility, and rule one in any situation where a teammate or manager is concerned is respect.

It's that damn sense of responsibility rearing its ugly and unwanted head, and I'm powerless to prevent it from forcing me to do the right thing. Even if it doesn't *feel* like the right thing.

I swing by the kitchen to grab some ice water and I spot Troy at the counter tapping away on his laptop.

"Question for you," I say without preamble as I help myself to some water from the refrigerator dispenser.

"Fire away," Troy says, closing his laptop lid.

I like how he gives me his undivided attention. Everything the man does is important, but he has a knack for making whoever he's talking to feel like they're deserving of his time.

"Do you have a sponsorship for any kids' play areas yet?"

He shrugs. "That would fall under community relations and marketing. I can introduce you to Joanie, the head of marketing, at the stadium today and she can offer you more information, but from what I know, she's still searching for the right fit for a kids' sponsorship."

Joanie. Why is that name familiar? I feel like he mentioned his better half once and that was her name. Does his girlfriend work for the Heat?

I lean against the counter. "What do you think about a play area with a circuit for kids sponsored by StrongFitKids?"

"Sponsored by StrongFitKids? Or sponsored by Cooper Noah?" he asks.

I lift a shoulder. "Does it matter?"

He presses his lips together. "Not at all. I think it's a fantastic idea and I'm sure Joanie would love to hear more. Let me text her to let her know we'll be stopping by."

"Great. And I know these sponsorships are generally handled by the corporate world, but I'd love to be as involved as I can be in everything from design through launch, barring the times when I need to be down on the field, obviously. This organization has meant a lot to me in my retirement, so I want to give back as much as I can."

"Noted, and I'll be sure to let Joanie know you have final approval at every level," he says.

"Thanks, man. Can I have my colleague Kaylee meet us there as well?"

He nods. "Send me her information and I'll be sure to get credentials to security."

I tap around on my phone and send him the details.

"Joanie is free at two o'clock," he says as my text to him comes through with Kaylee's information.

"Great. I'll text Kaylee and let her know."

"I'll be ready to leave in about ten minutes," he says.

I nod and bolt from the kitchen—mainly because ten minutes is plenty of time for Gabby to make an appearance and fuck more with my brain, but also because I want to change my shirt before we head out.

A heavy weight settles onto my chest as I walk the stairs up to my room. Gabby's door is open when I walk past it, and I can't help when my eyes move in her direction. Naturally she's sitting on her bed with her laptop propped on her legs, and she glances up when she sees me paused in the hallway outside her room.

"Hey," she says softly.

"Hi."

She closes her laptop and sets it beside her. "Can we talk?"

I blow out a breath. "Now's not a good time." I glance down the hallway even though Troy is on the other side of the house right now.

"Well when can I make an appointment to get on your busy schedule?" she asks, her tone both full of impatience and annoyance with a side of brat.

I lean on her doorway and close my eyes for a beat, trying to keep calm. When she talks to me like that...hell, when she *looks* at me like that, I want nothing more than to turn that frown upside down, so to speak. By shoving my cock in her, of course.

But clearly that's off the table, so I think the better call here is avoidance.

I rub my palms together up and down as I try to figure out what to say.

Up palm, down palm, time to get calm. Breathe real deep and take the leap.

"I don't know what we have left to talk about, Gabby," I finally say, trying my hardest to keep my tone neutral despite the waves of emotion plowing into me. I don't want to have this conversation. I don't want this to be the end. I don't want to look at her and know that I can't have her again.

"Oh, okay. So that's how old people do this, then?" she asks, the side of brattiness taking the lead in her tone. "They just bow out at the first sign of a problem?"

I know what she's doing. She's forcing this conversation now even though I said it's not a good time. And it's not. I'm meeting Troy in a few minutes to head to the stadium. But maybe she's right. Maybe if I just get this over with, I can focus on baseball.

And it's not just that. She's pitting our ages against us, and I don't like it. But I guess it's what I'm doing, too, in forcing this thing to end. Our ages are, after all, a big part of the reason why we can't be together. If Troy was a little older, and she was a lot older, then maybe he'd understand. Or maybe if I was closer to her age, he'd be okay with it.

But this is different. Troy and I have a previous relationship. We're friends. Good friends, and he's depending on me. I can't fuck this up.

"A, I'm not old. Don't use our ages against me when we both agreed it didn't matter. And B, that's not what I'm doing. It's complicated, and I'm just trying to do the right thing," I say. I rub my palms up and down a little more, trying to create some sort of warmth and friction to force a calmness that isn't coming.

"It didn't matter." She leaps to her feet and shoves an angry finger in my direction. "You're the one making it matter now. You're the one who thinks it suddenly can't work."

"It can't, and it has nothing to do with our ages. It's because your dad is a good friend of mine, and I made a commitment to him."

"That's harsh," she says, hurt in her tone. "So he wins since you and me never made any sort of commitment?"

"That's not what I meant." I blow out a frustrated breath as I run a hand along my jaw. "Nobody wins here. I was brought in because your father trusts me to create a brotherhood. How can I do that when I'm lying to him?"

"Why do we have to lie, then? Why can't we just be honest?" she asks.

"Because we can't. You've told me how protective he is of you. You're the one who said he's making up for missing your entire life. You know how he is. He will not understand this no matter how we present it to him."

She glances away from me, and I can see in her eyes that she knows exactly what I mean. "So where do we go from here?"

"I'm sorry, but I just don't see that there's *anywhere* we can go from here." My voice is low and apologetic, and she closes her eyes as if I physically struck her. And it *feels* like I physically struck her even though I'd never actually hit anybody. The words coming out of my mouth feel all wrong and jacked up.

"What about the job we talked about with your San Diego company?" she finally asks, clamoring to find a final link between the two of us.

"We never had anything official set up, so I guess Kaylee will just have to find someone else."

She presses her lips together and nods. "Fine. I need to go." She heads toward her closet, and I take that as my signal.

"I'm sorry," I whisper to her back, and then I head to my room, not sure how I'm going to get through the next month living in the room next door when fighting this is the very last thing I want to do.

Chapter 6
Cooper

"Ready?" I ask Troy when I walk into the kitchen. He's waiting at the table for me, tapping away on his phone, and I try to force enthusiasm into my voice that I just don't feel.

This should be everything I dreamed of since the day I dislocated my elbow and thought I was out of the game forever, and instead of excitement, the shock has worn off and I'm just feeling that heavy weight on my chest, like it's too difficult to draw in a deep breath.

It was short-lived, but it was fucking *everything*.

I really thought somehow we'd end up together. I really thought that despite all odds, somehow we were destined to be together.

With the snap of a finger, it all came to a skidding halt.

And then it gets infinitely worse. Infinitely heavier.

"Just a minute. My daughter will be joining us," he says.

Oh.

Why?

I want to ask. I want it just to be Troy and me. I don't want her clouding this moment for me, and instead of going to the stadium for the very first time, breathing in the air that always just somehow smells different, and feeling all the old familiar feelings that come with stepping onto the diamond, but this time for the very first time as it signals a new beginning...I'll be feeling the grief that accompanies the end.

I'm not ready for it to be the end, but since we don't have a choice, the least I can do is stay away from her.

But I don't have a choice there, either.

I press my lips together and offer a nod, and then I slide into the chair across from him.

"Ready, Daddy?"

I hear her voice from around the corner before I see her.

Daddy. I remember one time when I jokingly told her to call me daddy…

I shake it out of my head.

She stops short when she sees me. "Oh, right, you mentioned Cooper's coming along."

Am *I* coming along?

Am I coming along? Of fucking course I'm coming along. *She* is the one *coming along* on this excursion.

I'm not sure why my blood boils at her question, other than the fact that she shouldn't be coming at all. This is a trip for a manager and his player, not for his sexy as fuck daughter.

Dammit.

I'm in real trouble here.

Nothing about what she just said should incite such anger within me, but it's only because I have no idea how to deal with these feelings racing through me. These emotions are unfamiliar. It shouldn't be so hard. We don't even know each other.

Except she knows me better than anyone ever has in my entire life, and I suspect she could say the same about me…so these weak justifications are doing nothing to quiet the torrent inside me.

Up palm, down palm, time to get calm. Breathe real deep and take the leap.

"Right," Troy says flippantly to her, completely unaware that the two of us have unfinished business. Unaware that we have any business at all between us, I suppose. "I'm taking Coop for a tour, so I figured this way I can kill two birds with one stone." He glances over at me as he stands. "I offered Gabriella an internship at the stadium for part of her senior coursework, so we'll walk around and I'll introduce you both to the staff."

"Congratulations," I mutter in Gabby's general direction without looking at her.

"Thanks," she mutters back.

Surely Troy can feel the tension in the air, but if he does, he's good at acting like he doesn't.

I was planning to ride with Troy to the stadium, but I can't sit in a car with the two of them and act like this is normal. "I'm meeting a friend a little later, so I'll just take off from the ballpark if that's okay," I say to Troy.

He nods. "Just follow me in and I'll tip off security that you're with me."

We head outside, and I slip into my truck, muttering curses to myself once I'm alone. He and Gabby get into his Bentley, and I follow at a safe distance because the thought of rear-ending his precious luxury vehicle makes me nervous the entire way there.

It's only an eight-minute drive. Ten from my new place.

And when we pull into the player lot, I feel an odd sense of peace. I realize Gabby's in the car in front of me. I park far away from the two of them, draw in a deep breath, and tell myself that I'll get some time alone in this stadium today. I'll get some time to soak it in away from her. It's a promise I have to make to myself.

I head toward Troy's car as they get out, and we walk together into the front offices.

Well…sort of.

I let her walk with her father, and I walk a few paces behind as I try to take it all in and enjoy it separate from them.

Troy introduces us to the receptionist in the lobby, and then he leads us through the offices, pointing out various team members on the way. Eventually I'll learn all their names. I used to pride myself on knowing every member of the grounds crew and security all the way up to the executives by first name. I'll get there.

The first wing houses the executive offices, where Troy introduces us to the people who are in today. We meet some employees in ballpark operations, player operations, finance, community affairs, and administration.

We get to the General Manager's office, and it's more of an introduction for Gabby than for me considering I've met the man tapped as GM for this team several times.

"Mike Perry," he says by way of introduction, shaking Gabby's hand, and then he zeroes in on me. "Welcome to the team, Noah." He gives me the kind of hug where he pounds me on the back, and I slap his back, too. He's another guy in this business I'd consider an old friend, and I realize in that moment how much baseball has become a family to me.

He played for the Rockies a number of years with Troy, and while most GMs manage the roster and front office personnel while team managers manage the players, I can already tell the two of them will be making a lot of decisions as a unit. That can only mean good news for the team.

I'm introduced to the scouting director, Pete Holt, the man who will officially draft our new team members when November rolls around.

The owners' offices are empty, except for one. "The owners are a three man team. Dave Shapiro, a local businessman, owns forty percent. Actor Victor Bancroft, a good buddy of mine, owns another forty percent."

"And the final twenty?" I ask.

Troy grins broadly and pounds a fist on his chest. "You're looking at him."

I raise a brow. "Good for you, man." It's rare, but it has happened before where the team manager is also part owner of the team. I suppose that gives them an entirely different sort of stake in wanting to win.

We head back through the huge loop of wings and offices, and we take a detour into the marketing department.

"Joanie," Troy says as he knocks on the office door.

She glances up from her computer and when she looks at Troy, I have the sneaking suspicion she is, in fact, the woman in his life.

"Mr. Bodine," she practically purrs. "Lovely to see you again."

"And you," he says, his voice husky. "This is my daughter, Gabriella." He puts his arm around Gabby and pulls her close to his side. "And this is Cooper Noah." He nods to me, and I stride over and reach across her desk to shake her hand. "He's our man on third."

"Nice to meet you," I say.

"He's also the one who wanted to talk with you about a sponsorship, and I have a few ideas on that," Troy says.

"Come on in," Joanie says, motioning for the three of us to step into her office. Her phone rings, and she moves to answer it as she nods at a round table with six chairs around it. "Send her over," she says to whoever is on the other end of the line. "And can you send up Justin Larson as well?"

Troy and Gabby sit, and I take a seat across the table from Gabby so I don't have to worry about bumping my knee against hers or smelling her warm vanilla or in general being distracted by her at this meeting.

Joanie walks over with a pad of paper and a pen, and she sits beside Troy. "Justin is one of our interns, and he's a really smart and creative young man. I think he'd be great on a project like this."

"While I'm here, I'd like to chat about finding a spot for Gabriella here as an intern. I like the idea of the general internship program for her. She's a marketing major at UNLV, and I think there are plenty of opportunities in marketing and community affairs," Troy says, and my heart drops down into my stomach as I

160

can fucking predict exactly where this is going. "Cooper wants to run a sponsorship for the kids' program in conjunction with StrongFitKids, and I think Gabriella would be a great fit to work on that project. I love the idea of having her work closely with Cooper. He's a stand-up kind of man, someone I trust to be a great mentor to her."

Jesus. This guy can really lay it on thick.

"Oh, Dad, I—" Gabby begins, her eyes as wide with horror as mine certainly must be, and a knock at the door interrupts her sputtering.

We all swing our eyes toward the knocker, and sure enough, there stands Kaylee Olson...one of my best friends in the whole world. My chest warms despite the cold breeze that's been blowing in there all morning.

I stand and stride across the room, taking her in my arms and squeezing her tight.

"Whoa, Coop," she says when I swing her around, and then she laughs when I set her down. "Chill, dude."

I chuckle along with her, and I spot Gabby at the table shooting eye daggers at Kaylee. It's only then I realize Gabby must not know Kaylee is happily married and we're nothing more than friends, but somehow my heart lifts a little knowing that she's jealous.

It's wrong to feel that way, but I can't help how I feel.

"This is Kaylee," I say by way of introduction to everyone gathered. I toss my arm around her shoulders, and it feels like a little piece of home having her here with me. "Kaylee, this is Troy Bodine, his daughter Gabriella, and Joanie, the head of marketing here at the stadium." I nod toward Kaylee. "Kaylee is local and she's been incorporating StrongFitKids into the Tight Fit fitness clubs," I explain. "She's overworked and overwhelmed, so I thought we could add a little more to her plate." That gets a rousing round of laughter out of everyone in the room barring Gabby, but I'm sure in my conversations with Gabby since we met, I've talked about what a good friend Kaylee is to me.

Another knock at the door interrupts us again, and a punk-ass twenty-something kid with his jeans sagging down too low stands there wearing a Spongebob t-shirt like he couldn't be bothered to dress up for work today. What a dick.

"Justin," Joanie says. "Great timing."

This is the really smart intern? He looks like a douche. He doesn't even have any facial hair. He's probably too damn young to grow any. Hasn't hit puberty yet.

Okay, fine. I'm a little cranky today.

But then his eyes fall over to Gabby. His brows arch a little in surprise that a sexy woman like Gabby is in the room with the rest of us, but he maintains his cool. Still, I saw it. I saw his interest piqued. And I want to fucking rage on the kid.

I stare at Gabby as I await her reaction, and her eyes are down on the table. They dart to mine before moving to Justin, and she offers him a warm smile.

The kind of warm smile she used to reserve for me.

Is she…is she *interested* in this guy?

Or is she trying to make me jealous?

"Everyone, this is Justin," Joanie says, and then she moves around the table introducing us as Kaylee takes a seat beside me.

She gives me wide eyes like she's trying to communicate something with me, but I'm too distracted to pick up on her message. We'll talk later.

"So where were we?" Joanie asks.

Troy jumps in on that one. "Cooper is interested in organizing a StrongFitKids sponsored kids' section at the stadium. Coop, would you like to expand on that?"

"StrongFitKids is an organization whose focus is to provide health, fitness, and athletic information to assist kids in building active and healthy lifestyles," I say, reciting the script I've committed to memory over the last year. "My idea in conjunction here with the Heat is to sponsor a kids' play area. I'm envisioning some sort of play structure with slides and climbing walls, a circuit with different kid-friendly exercises, some batting cages, maybe some tees or a catching station, things like that."

Kaylee's eyes light up. "We have the program in place at Tight Fit, the fitness clubs run by Ben Olson of the Vegas Aces, and we would absolutely love to partner with the Vegas Heat to create a fun and engaging area for children who come to the games."

"Don't we want the attention on the game?" Justin asks.

God, this kid. What a fucking asshole. Yes, Justin, we want attention on the fucking game. I barely refrain from rolling my eyes.

"Well, what about those antsy kids who were dragged to the game by their parents?" Kaylee points out. "Kids can't sit through a three-hour ballgame, and trust me, anyone old enough to have children would understand that." God, I could kiss Kaylee for putting this kid in his place. She moves her gaze from Justin over to Joanie. "We could provide additional resources for parents who want to watch the game, and the focus would be there while they are assured their kids are safely having a good time in another section of the same ballpark."

"I love it," Troy says first, nodding at me before waiting for Joanie's thoughts.

"I think it's a great idea, too," Joanie says, and I can't help but wonder if she really does or if she's doing what Troy tells her to do.

It doesn't matter. Either way, punk-ass jackass has been put in his place, and I'm getting what I want out of this, too. Except for one thing…

"So here's what we'll do," Joanie says. "I'll draw up some paperwork and we'll enter negotiations. I'll arrange a meeting between Cooper and Kaylee with my team as well as ballpark operations to work on the physical design of the space, and we'll have Justin and Gabriella as our main interns on the project. Sound good?" She raises her brows at Troy, which is interesting to me given that he's the team manager.

And you know what else is interesting? The fact that Gabby automatically gets the internship. Joanie just said she'll be one of the main interns on the project. No interview process. No paperwork. Boom. She's in.

He nods at her. "Sounds perfect. Anyone have anything else?"

Silence moves around the table.

I don't want to work with Gabby on this.

We're already too close in proximity with me living with her. Now she'll be at the one place I had planned to use as my escape, and I'm not sure how to feel about that.

But I can't think of a single reason to object that wouldn't raise about a million red flags with my boss, so I keep my mouth shut.

Chapter 7
Gabby

I can't stop picturing him leaning against my doorframe earlier.

He was tormented—that much is clear. And I wasn't making it easy on him. But why should I? He's bowing out of what could be the most important relationship of our lives because of my dad?

It's bullshit.

But I also don't know how to fix the problem. I found my dad later in life, but I didn't choose him, just as I didn't choose my mother. I was made to believe my father never wanted me only to learn it was my mother who never did. I was raised believing nothing I ever did was quite good enough.

And now I'm questioning whether *I* am good enough for someone like Cooper.

Yet…in the time we were together, he made me feel like I was. Like we were compatible. Like we were meant to be.

But the tables have turned. We're no longer Cooper the guy who works for a kids' organization and Gabby the girl who's still in college.

Now he's the bigshot baseball player and I'm nothing more than his manager's daughter.

Still, the question remains. Would I give up what I've built with my father in the last three years for someone I've barely known three weeks?

That's hard to say.

My gut leans toward no. It doesn't make sense, but God…what we have—what we *had*—was intense.

He leaned on that doorframe with his hat backwards and the scruff on his jaw and I've never seen a more beautiful man in my entire life. His blue eyes were dark and stormy, and even now as he sits across the table from me, I can't help but study his hands. He's rubbing them together like he's trying to stay calm, and then he lifts one of those hands and runs it along his jawline.

Long fingers that know every inch of my body move slowly along, and I know I'm staring, but I can't help study those fingers. Strong and lean, muscular and athletic. Skilled.

Ropes of muscle ripple along his forearm with his movement...a forearm that held me as little as a few days ago. A forearm that should be holding me again, and instead, maybe it never will.

My chest aches, but I put on the act like everything's fine. Justin slipped into the open seat beside me, and I wish it was Cooper instead. I wish I could smell that clean, woodsy scent of his. I wish our knees could bump together and we'd both leave them there, touching beneath the table where nobody could see.

Instead, I've got someone who's probably more appropriately aged for me wearing a Spongebob tee. Is it any wonder I found someone a decade out of my zone when Spongebob over here is my option?

Justin doesn't smell like fresh wood, and he's going to be my partner for the next few months as we work together on a project...with Cooper as our lead.

Complicated doesn't even begin to describe it.

When the meeting starts to wrap up, my dad offers to show me off—I mean to *introduce* me—to more people, but Joanie jumps in to save me from that particular torture.

"I can have her start filling out paperwork in here if that's okay with you." Her gaze connects with my dad's, and I can't help but wonder if there's something more to their relationship than colleagues. In fact, the way his gaze burns at her tells me there's *definitely* something more there, but I've never seen her before in the three years I've been living with my dad.

He nods once at her then turns to me. "Is that okay with you, honey?"

I nod. "I'd actually love to hang here for a bit." I avoid Cooper's gaze even though I feel it on me.

"Fine," my father says. He glances at Cooper. "Then let's continue our tour." He looks over at me. "We'll be in the clubhouse. Text me if you need anything."

"Thank you all so much," Kaylee says. "This has been great and I'm so excited to get started."

She seems sweet, although when Cooper tackle hugged her when she walked in, I felt my hackles rise as my claws started to emerge...until I realized I have no ownership over him. He's free to hug whomever he wants. He made that pretty damn clear.

And I also caught the way he stiffened when Justin walked into the room and sat beside me. I'm not saying I'm going to take advantage of that, but I'm not saying I'm not going to, either.

"Let me just check in with HR, and they'll send a copy of our intern contract so you can get started," Joanie says, and she heads to her desk and taps around.

I glance over at Justin, who looks a little bored. He's probably early-twenties like me, and if nothing else, maybe I can make a friend.

"Are you at UNLV?" I ask while Joanie gets my paperwork together.

He shakes his head. "I was. I graduated last year."

My brows dip. "So what are you doing interning here?"

"I took a sabbatical, and my dad told me I had to get a job when I got back." He shrugs, and I laugh.

"A sabbatical? Do you mean a gap year?"

He offers a wry smile. "Sabbatical sounds better. But very few employers are excited about hiring someone with zero experience who took a year off from the real world, so my dad hooked me up with this gig."

"Where'd you go on your sabbatical?" I ask, suddenly full of questions.

"Europe for a while, and then I headed to Australia and worked in a bar there for a few months to make dear old Dad happy." He rolls his eyes, and he seems like the kind of boy who gives his dad a ton of trouble but has the sort of winning smile that gets him out of it most of the time.

"And how was it?"

He shakes his head and closes his eyes. "I didn't want to come back. It fulfilled that dream of freedom and independence and it was just the fucking best."

"But your dad made you?"

He nods. "He's one of the executives I'm sure your dad introduced you to up in the front office. Dean Larson, Executive Vice President and Business Manager of the Vegas Heat." He rolls his eyes and leans in, lowering his voice to a whisper. "I don't even *like* baseball."

"I totally heard that," Joanie calls from her desk. "I promise I won't tell." We both laugh.

"So what do you want to do for your career, then?" I ask Justin.

He shrugs. "Something that will allow me freedom, independence, creativity, and travel."

"Sounds like you need to figure out something where you can work for yourself."

He glances up so his eyes meet mine. "Or find something where I can partner up with pretty girls." He raises a brow, and I feel my cheeks heat.

Joanie walks over with a tablet, and she sets it in front of me. "Fill out these forms and let me know if you have any questions. Justin, you can head back to Caitlin's office. I think she has some graphic design work for you."

He nods, and then he reaches into his pocket and pulls out his phone. He hands it to me. "Text yourself."

My brows dip in confusion.

"Text yourself so you have my number," he clarifies. "You know…in case we need to get in touch about our project."

"Oh," I say dumbly. Is he asking me for my number? Well, no. He's demanding my number, but it seems innocent enough. "Sure." I tap in the number, send myself a text that says Gabby Grant, and hand it back.

"Nice to meet you, Gabby Grant," he says, and his fingers brush mine when he takes his phone.

"You too, Justin Larson."

He grins, and then he walks out of Joanie's office, and I'm left wondering whether the cute boy who just gave me his number is interested in friendship or something else.

Chapter 8
Cooper

S tepping into the clubhouse feels almost like an out of body experience.

I didn't think I'd be back in one of these again, certainly not as a player. My contract was up two years after I got hurt, and since it was going to take more than a year to recover, I figured my playing days were over. I figured nobody would want a recovering thirty-year-old on their team, so I bowed out early.

I like the little life I've built for myself out of the spotlight, but in hindsight, I wish I would've fought harder to stay in the game.

I took the early retirement so I could focus on giving back. I used my name to help StrongFitKids catapult to success, and I'll continue to do so. Carla and I are old friends—never in any sort of romantic capacity, but we attended the same high school. She was in my brother's class, and they kept in touch over the years. When he told me she'd started up a kids' organization in San Diego and was looking for a programming director, I jumped at the chance.

I always thought about returning to the game, but it was in a more abstract sort of way—a *what if* sort of way. Not in a realistic sort of way.

But when that call from Troy came through, it seemed like a pretty easy decision. Things are rarely handed to us in this life, but Troy was handing me the chance to play the game that saved me more than once in my life.

And here it is, saving me again.

I realize it's also *because of* the game that I can't be with the girl I love—hell, it's *because of* the game that I met her in the first place...but if I didn't have baseball to fall back on when the inevitable end with Gabby came, I'm not sure how I'd get through it.

The logical side of my brain is trying to force me to believe that the end *was* inevitable. How could it have ever worked? Finding out her father was Troy just saved us weeks or months or even years of added pain and suffering after we fell harder and harder for one another.

I blow out a breath as Troy takes me to my locker.

My name is already listed on the plaque above it.

Noah 21.

A jersey hangs on the side. *Noah 21.*

This is really happening, and my breath catches in my throat as reality slams into me.

I sit on the bench that will be my new home for at least the next three years, and my chest tightens with emotion. I grab a Vegas Heat towel sitting on the bench beside me, and I study the logo for a beat. A baseball with flames coming off it, representing our team.

My eyes heat, and I grab the towel and hold it up against my face as I draw in a deep breath to try to ward off the unfamiliar threat of tears that seems to be getting more and more familiar lately.

"Congratulations, Noah," Troy says quietly beside me. If anyone understands the sort of emotions that are plowing into me right now, it's him. I pull the towel away from my face as he talks. "I felt the same way when I first walked into this clubhouse. It's fucking magic, man. Together, we're going to be magic. We're going to obliterate history when it comes to expansion teams, and we're going to win out of the gate. We're going to be a fucking force. You and me and the rest of this team we're building. This is something special, Coop. Let's fucking go."

"Let's fucking go," I repeat, my voice hoarse but still full of fire.

"I'll give you some time in here. I'll be in the weight room when you're ready." He nods to a set of doors that lead directly to the weight room, and then he takes off through them.

I lean back into my locker and suck in a few deep breaths. I rub my palms up and down. It's time to take the leap.

I look around the quiet clubhouse. Soon enough, it'll be filled with players. We'll all arrive around two on game days, and we'll play video games or poker or waste time until it's time for team stretching and batting practice. It'll be relaxed until thirty minutes before game time, and then we'll all move into focus mode as the inevitable nerves will start to kick in.

Will Gabby be in here then? If she's interning for the team, she might be. Team and manager family members aren't allowed in, but it's different if she's working for the team. She's in marketing, so if she gets put on social media assignment, she might have to come into the clubhouse when I'm trying to focus on game mode.

I can't have that.

I can't be distracted by her in those important moments before game time.

I realize I have six months before I need to worry about it. I realize how different things may be in six months, but I can't seem to push her out of my brain in *this* moment.

I just want to skip over the rest of this offseason and fucking *get there*. I want to play. But time's a real steadfast bitch. When we want it to slow down, it doesn't. When we want it to speed up, it doesn't. It's one of life's most frustrating constants.

The door opens, and I recognize the man who walks through it.

"Danny Motherfuckin' Brewer," I say, and he grins as he walks up to me and grabs my hand in a bro shake that turns into a pound on the back.

"Cooper Motherfuckin' Noah," he says. "What are you doing here, man?"

"Playing third. You?"

His brows shoot up. "The elbow?"

"Surgically repaired," I say dryly.

"They tapped me for first." He shrugs. "Looks like we're gonna be teammates."

I make a face at him to indicate it's my worst nightmare, and he laughs.

"Guess I'd rather play on the same team as you than against you," I admit. Danny Brewer was the reason I fucking hated playing the Rockies. He's a master of first base, and between him on first and me across the infield on third, we're going to be a fucking force right out of the gate—just like Troy said. But the thing about Danny Brewer is that even though we were enemies on the field, we were friends off it. He's a hell of a fun guy, and we went out more than once after a game and got fucked up together. "Troy hasn't mentioned anything to me. How'd you end up here?"

"I wanted out of Colorado and you know Mr. Bodine. He made it happen."

"How?" I ask, feeling a little stupid that I haven't taken the time to research more about this team. In my defense, I've been preoccupied...but the team must already be filled with players considering the draft was back in July and the trade deadline was in August. We've got the expansion draft coming in November, too.

Jesus, I've really had my head in the sand.

"A few hours ahead of the trade deadline, he struck a deal with the Rockies back in August. They're taking the first two picks from the expansion and Troy traded two picks for the regular draft next season." He rubs his knuckles on his chest. "You know, four good players for me. No big deal."

I laugh. "So modest. It's good to see you, man. You still have my number?"

He nods. "I'll use it sometime this weekend. I'm putting together a poker crew and we need a fourth."

"Count me in," I say. "I'll talk to you soon."

I head to the weight room, excitement coursing through me now that I've met my first teammate, and my breath is stolen by the sight in front of me. I feast my eyes on state of the art equipment, the types of machines that will get me into game mode the right way.

Troy stands talking to a man sitting at a desk near the back of the room, and I saunter over in that direction.

"Cooper, this is Nick Lynch, our head athletic trainer here at the Heat. We've spoken at length about you and he has some ideas," Troy says.

I nod at Nick, a guy who appears to be around the same age as me with a much bushier beard than me. "Nice to meet you, man. I only have one request."

Nick raises his brows, and he looks like the kind of person I could grab a drink with after he puts me through the wringer. "What's that?"

"Be gentle."

Nick laughs, and it's a hearty laugh. "Have you done anything recently or are you in what we in the business like to call *active rest?*"

"A better description might be *inactive* rest." I twist my lips, and Nick laughs again. "I've hit the treadmill a few times since Troy gave me the offer, and I ran on the beach back in San Diego before I moved here. I've started changing my diet. But I could use a program to guide me from rest back into anything at all."

"Can I take a look at your arm?" he asks, and I nod. He stands and moves around the desk, and he bends and flexes it at the elbow for me, nodding and muttering as he works. "It looks good, man. Looks to be in working order, and I think we'll start you off light as you come off active rest and transition into rebuilding. In six weeks or so, we'll shift into phase one, and you'll be season-ready by February. I've worked out a diet plan, too, and I just ask you do your best in sticking to it."

"Do pizza and-or beer appear anywhere on the menu?" I ask.

He doesn't laugh this time. "There's always a spot for pizza and beer. You know how to distribute your calories, man, so do what you need to do."

He holds up a hand, and I grab onto it as we bro-shake. I love this dude already.

I chat with Nick a few more minutes, and he tells me he'll send me everything I need. "You can call me any time if you don't feel like reading it and want me to walk you through it."

"Thanks, Nick," I say, and Troy flicks his head toward the door.

"Ready for the next part of the tour?" he asks.

I draw in a deep breath as I *think* I know what's coming shortly.

I follow him through the tunnel underground, and he points out the batting cages, the place where we'll warm up prior to entering the game and the place where we'll practice before games.

I follow him up a short ramp, and we're in the dugout. I stare down at the bench before I turn around and look up, and when I finally do, my breath is stolen once again.

The stadium is before me. It's empty, but I can already hear the volume of the crowd gathered to root for the home team rushing between my ears.

I look out at the seats that'll hold over forty thousand fans at one time, and my eyes shift around the place to the scoreboard that I'll look up at thousands of times in the future.

Finally, my eyes skim the green grass over to the dirt. I focus on the place where third will be once the field is ready…the place that will be my true home away from home.

A feeling of restlessness runs through my legs, and I fucking take off. I run out onto the field with my arms spread wide open, sucking in gulps of fresh air since the retractable roof is open. I run all the way to the outfield before I realize I never asked if it was okay for me to step on the grass, but I don't care.

This is where I need to be.

This is where I'm *meant* to be.

It's where I feel most myself. It's where I feel closest to my father. It's where I feel like I'm home and accepted no matter what else is going on in my life.

I sink down into the grass, and then I lie on my back and stare up at the sky. It's cloudless, the norm for Vegas, and I pant as I try to catch my breath.

"Good form, kid," Troy says over me a few beats later.

"Kid? I'm only eight years younger than you." I chuckle, and then I sit up and draw in a deep breath.

"Everything okay with you?" he asks. He sinks down beside me, and this right here…this is what's going to make him an incredible manager. Connecting one-on-one with a player. Mental check-ins. All of it.

I huff out something resembling a laugh, though it's not very funny. "I'm all right." I stare ahead at third base. I'll *be* all right, anyway. Eventually.

This all feels so goddamn dramatic for something that barely got off the ground, and all that does is tell me how very much she came to mean to me.

"What's going on?"

I clear my throat. "The girl I told you about…it's over with her."

"The one you talked about just yesterday when you said fate caused you to crash into each other?" he asks.

I nod. "Yeah."

"Want to talk about what happened?"

She's your daughter, Troy. "Nah. It's complicated."

He sputters a short laugh. "Aren't they all?"

"Is Joanie…" I trail off, not sure how to finish the question, and he nods so I don't have to.

"Yeah," he says. "Nobody here knows, so if you could keep that quiet, I'd appreciate it."

I hold out a fist for him to bump as a signal of my silence.

"Look, Coop. I need you at your best, and I felt like I had that for a night when you pulled in, but something's different today."

"A lot is different today." I draw my knees up and wrap my arms around them. "I guess I just realized where my focus needs to be."

"Can it be here if you're thinking about her?" he asks.

"Isn't it better to end it now, six months before we take this field, than to hold out for the inevitable anyway?" I shoot back.

"You do realize what you're doing, don't you?" His eyes are on my profile.

"What am I doing?" I ask, keeping my gaze ahead on the dugout.

"Sabotaging whatever it is before it even begins. You were always like that. It's why you quit playing after the elbow injury. But when you said so proudly that you were off the market yesterday, I saw a new fire in you. One I hadn't seen before, especially not with that ex of yours."

I glance over at him, not sure what to say. I felt the fire he's talking about, and I think he might be right about sabotaging myself. I end things before they get too complicated. The one time I didn't, I got cheated on.

But his words in the meeting earlier only confirm my suspicions. He trusts me to be a mentor to his daughter. He sees me in an authoritative position over her. What he does *not* see is me fucking her.

Could I tell him? Could I break it to him gently?

Could Gabby and I find a way to be together?

"You know, shortly after you broke up with her, she called me," he says quietly.

My brows dip. "Stacy did?"

He nods. "She knew we were old friends from your playing days. This was before I met Joanie, and I was single. Playing around, you know how it is. Anyway, she asked if I wanted to grab a drink, and I declined. You just don't do that to a friend, you know? You don't fuck around with exes or family. And I know we're in different positions now with you playing and me coaching, and that comes first in season always. But out of season, I always saw you as a friend, and I'm glad you're here and we're on the same team for once. I have a good feeling about teaming up with someone I trust the way I trust you, and I think we're going to own this fucking town."

Yep. That's a big fat negative on going for the truth.

It's only been a few hours. Time will heal whatever this is.

I hope.

Chapter 9
Gabby

Cooper must've stayed at the stadium, or maybe he went out afterward. I guess it's not my right to know anymore. I texted Mia that I needed to get out, so she invited me over for dinner.

I'm not very hungry, though.

And Dylan's here, which means Mia is distracted and trying to impress him, and I'd rather be curled up in my bed by myself.

"Ugh!" I grumble as I collapse on her couch after she orders the food.

"So let me get this straight," Dylan says. "You were banging Cooper Noah and you didn't know your dad invited him to play for the Heat?"

I blow out a breath. "He knows?" I whine to Mia.

She shrugs. "We can trust him."

Right. Noted. Don't tell Mia secrets anymore unless I want Dylan to know them.

"Fine. Yes, that's the gist of it. He said he can't be with me knowing who my dad is, so it's over."

"And now he's living with you," Dylan says.

"We literally share a wall," I confirm.

He makes a low whistle noise. "That's some messed up shit."

"Thanks for the reminder," I mutter.

"How was the stadium?" Mia asks brightly. Too brightly. She's trying to change the subject, trying to take my mind off Cooper, but nothing on God's green Earth has the actual ability to do that.

"Fine. My dad assigned me an internship working with Cooper, naturally. He trusts Coop to mentor me," I say, throwing air quotes around the end of my sentence.

Mia wrinkles her nose, and Dylan's brows knit together.

"Wait a minute. Your dad *assigned you an internship?*" he asks.

"Yeah. Why?"

"I've been in the application process for an internship with the Heat for *months* now. It's incredibly competitive and they're only taking six interns this year. I'm vying for the final spot with hundreds of other applicants, and you walk in and your dad just hands it to you?" He sounds angry, and I feel bad that he sees it that way.

"I'm sure I didn't take the final spot," I say. "I think my dad sort of created a new position for me to slide into." Shit. I'm not sure that makes it any better.

My phone dings with a new text. I pull it out just in case it's Cooper.

It isn't. Surprisingly…it's Justin.

Justin: *A couple of the other interns and I are heading out for beer. Want to join?*

I stare down at the text.

"What's that?" Mia asks me first.

I clear my throat. "One of the other interns asked if I want to join a group of them for a drink."

"One of the other *male* interns?" she presses, and Dylan simply huffs.

I roll my eyes. "Yes, Justin is male, but it's not like that."

"Sure it isn't," she says, a wide grin on her lips like her teasing is going to distract me from the real issue at hand here.

"It isn't," I say flatly.

Mia's brows knit together as she raises a shoulder. "Maybe it isn't, but Cooper doesn't have to know that."

I flatten my lips. "You think I should use my new friend?"

"I didn't say that, exactly," Mia says a little defensively. "But I didn't not say that, either."

"I'm not going to use someone I just met to make Cooper jealous. It's juvenile."

Dylan is surprisingly quiet during this exchange. He always seems to have an opinion.

"You're right. Sorry for mentioning it. I just know that if I saw Dylan hanging out with some other girl…I'd be jealous. I'd do something about it." She settles into Dylan's side and he draws her in a little closer.

I've been so wrapped up in Cooper that I didn't even realize Mia and Dylan had gotten as serious as they have.

I suddenly feel like a third wheel here. I decide to text Justin back—not because of what Mia is suggesting, but because it can't hurt to get to know some of the other interns.

Me: *Name the time and the place.*

He writes back with the details nearly immediately, and I punch in the location to maps. It's only a ten-minute drive, and it's on the way home to my dad's house, which makes sense given its proximity to the ballpark. I let him know I'll be on my way shortly.

"I'm going to meet them so you two can have your date night," I say.

"Yeah!" Mia says, punching a fist into the air. "She's going for it!"

"I'm not going for it." I purse my lips together. "I'm just making friends with the other interns so I don't feel so alone."

"You're not alone, Gabs. You always have me," Mia says, and she gives me a hug.

I appreciate her words, but she's got Dylan now, and he's commanding her attention just as Cooper commanded mine for the few weeks I knew him. And it's fine. It's as it should be, so I'm just doing what I have to in order to find my place in this new routine.

And if making Cooper a little jealous is a byproduct of that…well, that's on him.

When I get to the bar, I spot Justin right away. He's hanging out of a booth, and he waves me over with a wide smile. I slip into the booth beside him, and he introduces me to the other interns. "This is Gabby," he says, and then he points to his left. "This is Chase." He points across the booth at the three on the other side. "Brian, Mackenzie, and Chloe."

I wave as all four names go in one ear and out the other. They all have drinks in front of them at various levels, and there are a few empty glasses in the middle of the table. I wonder how long they've been here.

A server comes over, and I order a vodka soda—a much faster route to the tipsiness I'm currently craving.

I just really hope I don't spill anything once the truth serum kicks in. I tend to be a loud and happy drunk, and that's what I need right now to help fill up the hole in my chest where my heart used to be before Cooper ripped it out and took it with him.

"You go to UNLV?" the girl across from me asks.

I nod. "You?"

She nods, too, and two of the others also go to UNLV, and they look familiar, like we've passed each other on campus or maybe had a class together at some point. We get to chatting about all the professors we have in common, and parties and events and dorm rooms and people…and laughter, so much laughter as the vodka starts to slide down faster and faster.

I love this group of people already. They're fun. They're my age. They're silly, and the boys get into a pissing match of chugging and dares while the three of us girls giggle at their antics. I find a quick bond with Chloe, though Mackenzie doesn't seem quite as friendly, and after my first couple drinks, I feel Justin's leg pressing against mine. During my third drink, he tosses an arm around my shoulders. It's friendly, though. It's non-threatening. It's fun and light.

I stack my third empty in front of me after only an hour.

I haven't eaten anything, but the pressure on my chest has started to ease up.

The pressure in my bladder, however, has not.

"Need to pee!" I announce, and I practically fall out of the booth before I beeline for the restroom.

I pull my phone out of my pocket.

There's nothing there from Cooper.

I'm not drunk enough just yet to think texting him is a good idea, so I skip over that particular cliché.

I finish my business and head back to the table, where a fresh vodka drink awaits.

I'm slightly tipsy, and four will push me over the tipsy line, but I don't care.

I force a smile as I force Cooper out of my head. I'm here to have a good time, and I focus on that thought as I pick up my drink and get started on number four.

Chapter 10
Cooper

It's more crowded here than I'd like, but I pull my ballcap down low over my eyes and manage to score a booth in the corner facing the wall. A server takes my order, and contrary to Nick's advice, I go with a beer. As a compromise, I get a Michelob Ultra. Fewer calories and all that.

Kaylee slides into the booth across from me. "What's up, Coopster?"

I laugh. "Coopster?"

"I'm trying it out. You like it?"

I shake my head. "No, I don't."

She shrugs. "I'll keep working on it. You doing okay?"

I shake my head. "Not even a little. But good news about SFK and the sponsorship, right?"

She nods. "Great news. I take it that was your Gabby in the meeting?"

"Of course it was."

She presses her lips together. "I'm so sorry. What are you going to do?"

"What *can* I do?" I chug down the rest of my beer before the server comes over to take Kaylee's order, and I ask for a second one along with some nachos. Fuck the diet. It can start tomorrow.

"You can be honest with her father," she points out.

"Right. Her father, the guy who confessed earlier today that my ex hit on him but he declined since you don't fuck a buddy's ex or family members."

"Oh shit," she says. "He said that?"

I nod. "He said that."

She shakes her head. "Do you *want* to stay away?"

"Fuck no," I say. "But what choice do I have? He's paying me ninety million over three years to build a legacy, Kay. I can't just fuck that over because I think his daughter's hot."

She tilts her head and shoots me a look of disappointment. "We both know it's more than thinking she's hot."

"Yeah, yeah. But it doesn't change anything, so it doesn't matter."

The server drops off her drink plus mine, and she holds her glass up to mine. "To figuring this out," she says.

I huff out a chuckle as I tap my glass to hers. I can't figure out the un-figure-able, but I can drink beer and eat nachos with a good friend.

"So how's mom life?" I ask as a way to get the heat off my problems.

And it works. It *always* works with new moms. Any mom, really. Ask about her kids, and she'll launch into enough stories to fill the rest of the evening.

"Oh my gosh," she starts, and she launches into some story about the twins. I'm only half-listening as I glance around the bar. Some loud assholes across the way are laughing noisily, and the merriment is over the top for me considering where my head's at. I squint a little as I think how one of the loud drunk kids looks a lot like that douche intern I met earlier today, but I'm looking across a rather large, crowded bar, so it's hard to tell if it's him— not that it would really matter if it was.

I force my gaze to Kaylee to make it look like I'm listening, but the laughter across the way gets loud again.

And that's when I see her.

Gabby walks to the table, a little unsteady on her feet, and she slides in beside the douchey kid.

It *is* him, and he tosses his arm around her shoulders as she picks up a drink.

Even from this distance, I can tell she's a little drunk. I can also tell by the way she moves that she's not interested in him as more than a friend. She's not leaning into him the way she'd do with me. She's not resting her head on his shoulder, and it almost seems like she's more interested in her drink and conversation with the girl across from her than she is in the Spongebob douche.

I could fuck that kid up with a fist, that's for damn sure.

"Cooper? Cooper!"

Kaylee snaps her fingers in front of my face.

"Huh? What?"

"Are you even listening to a word I'm saying?" she demands.

"I'm sorry. It's just…" I trail off and incline my head toward the other side of the bar.

She follows my gaze. "Oh," she says knowingly with a nod as she draws out the word. "Go get her, Coopsey."

"Coopsey is far worse than Coopster."

She shrugs. "It was worth a shot."

"And I'm not *getting* her. She's sitting with an intern from the Heat. She's laughing and having a good time. I can't just walk over and claim her," I say.

"But she's laughing and having a good time *without you*," she points out.

It's a clear shot to my heart, and I can't help when my hand moves up to cover it in defense. "Ouch."

"Truth hurts, right? Fucking *do something* about it, then."

"You're meaner than I remember," I say, my hand not moving from my heart.

"You're less of a fighter than I remember," she says, pursing her lips.

"Nah, you just never knew me that well," I tease, and she laughs.

"Go get her, Coop. It's obvious you're in love with her."

I shake my head and drain the rest of my second beer. "Doesn't matter. It's over."

"Coward."

I shrug. "Fine. If disrespecting my friend and boss makes me a coward, then I'm a coward."

"You disappoint me, Cooper Noah."

"Thanks, Kaylee Olson. Way to kick a guy when he's down."

She laughs, and she kicks me lightly under the table to drive her point home. "I'm rooting for you. If anyone can find a way to make it work, it's you."

I glance over at Gabby. She's laughing. She's having fun. She's with people her age, not some old man who's ready to settle down and have kids when they shouldn't even be on her radar at this age. "Thanks," I finally say.

And I leave it at that.

Kaylee takes off shortly after that since Ben is done with practice and she wants to soak up every minute she can with him while he's in season, so I'm sitting alone in a corner booth sneaking glances across the bar pretending to eat the plate of nachos that has long grown cold.

She's had at least two drinks since I spotted her, and I have no idea how many she had before that.

She's drunk, and she's out with people she doesn't know.

I'm worried about her.

I'm not leaving here until I'm sure she has a way to get home safely—no matter how long that might be.

Spongebob tosses his arm around my girl and leaves it there while she drains another drink.

I can't take it anymore. I have no rights over her, no claim to her when I'm the one who told her it's over, but I can't sit here and watch her with another guy. I send her a text.

Me: *Are you having fun or are you looking for a way out?*

She slides her phone out of her pocket, reads my text, and glances around. She doesn't see me, but she also doesn't reply to me.

She slips her phone back into her pocket, purposely ignoring my text. She has to know I'm here. She has to know I'm looking out for her. She has to know she's safe, that I'd never let anything happen to her regardless of where we stand.

But knowing all that and ignoring my message tells me she wants to play games.

The only game I'm into playing is baseball.

My blood boils as I watch the girl across the table from her stand and pull Gabby up with her when the song changes. They start dancing and giggling with each other right there at the end of their table, and douchenozzle stands and moves in behind Gabby, grabbing her hips and swaying behind her.

That's when things take a turn. I know she's doing it because she knows I'm here somewhere watching her, but she starts sticking her ass back toward him. She's dancing with him while she dances with the girl across from her.

They're still laughing, still having a good time, and I'm sure the kid is fine—smart, according to Joanie, though I have yet to see any evidence at all of that—but the fact that she's dancing with him when she's drunk just to play games with me pisses me all the way the fuck off.

I'm seething as I sit watching her. Steam pours out of my ears as I glare across the bar at her, and I don't even realize my fists are tight balls until I glance down and force myself to unclench them.

The girl Gabby's dancing with points toward the restroom, and Gabby nods. This is my shot, and I'm not fucking missing it.

I leave some money on the table and bolt toward the hallway where the restrooms are.

It's dark here in this hallway. There are no overhead lights, and the only light comes from the flashing lights over in the bar or the occasional swinging of the restroom doors as they open and close.

I bide my time, rubbing my palms up and down as I force a calm I don't really feel. When she exits the bathroom, she's following behind the other girl. She doesn't see me, but she does stumble when she walks by me. She nearly falls before I reach out an arm to grab her, and I help her back up. The other girl doesn't notice as she skips back toward their table.

When she finally tilts her head up to get a look at her savior, the blood seems to drain from her cheeks. Her eyes are dilated, but I spot the fear in them as she must spot the anger in mine.

She's never seen me angry before. Not like this.

I can't even remember the last time I was moved by enough emotion to be quite this angry.

When Stacy cheated on me, I guess I saw it coming.

She never moved me to the sort of feeling Gabby incites in me. It's dangerous and scary and thrilling all at once.

She straightens, and I take the opportunity to pin her to the wall with my hips.

"What the fuck are you doing?" I ask, angling my head down toward hers. Our lips are inches away from each other, and my *God* do I have the strong urge to kiss her.

To fucking obliterate her with my tongue.

To hear those moans the way I was privileged enough to before we learned the truth this morning.

How was that only this morning? It feels like a fucking lifetime has passed since then.

"Having fun with my friends," she slurs, her alcohol breath hot on my jawline as she tips her chin up with a bit of defiance.

"You're drunk," I accuse.

"Am not." She purses her lips.

I raise a brow. "Prove it."

"I don't have to prove anything to you." She places both hands on my chest and pushes, but I don't budge. The door to the bathroom swings open, illuminating her face, and it's hard to tell back here, but I think she looks a little green, like she's seconds away from losing her lunch.

"I'm taking you home."

"You are not!" she practically yells. "You've already ruined my life once today. Fuck you if you think you're going to do it again." She clenches her fists into balls and starts beating them against my chest, and then she freezes a beat later.

Her eyes grow wide, and she slaps a hand over her mouth, ducks under my arm, and bolts for the bathroom.

I think for a beat that I should follow her in, but it's a women's room in a busy bar. I head toward her friends to let them know, but the girl she was with appears in the hallway as if she just discovered her friend was missing.

"She's in the bathroom getting sick," I tell her, and she glances up at me in confusion. I'm not sure if she's confused how I know or if she recognizes me and she's confused why I'm here. I point toward the bathroom and issue a command. "She needs help."

She nods and takes off into the bathroom. Despite the loud music in the bar, I still hear the retching when the door opens.

And then I wait.

It feels eternal as I stand in the hallway wondering whether she's okay, but in reality only a few minutes pass before both girls emerge from the restroom.

Gabby looks exhausted, but she's as gorgeous as always.

"Rally time!" the friend shouts with glee, and I shake my head.

"You're coming home with me," I say, grabbing Gabby's elbow.

"Who the fuck are you?" the friend asks.

"Cooper Noah. I'm staying with Gabby and her father."

Her eyes grow wide as recognition dawns. I don't wear the low baseball cap practically covering my eyes for nothing. "Coop...Coop...Cooper Noah?"

"Thanks for helping Gabby. I'll take it from here," I say.

"You will not," Gabby says, poking me in the arm. "I wanna stay." She attempts to pull her elbow out of my grip, but it's a weak effort since her bones are the equivalent of jelly after the amount of alcohol she's consumed.

"Yeah, I will. Let's go." I grab her hand to pull her along, and she stumbles behind me—not because she's trying to escape my grip, but because she's so drunk.

So that's how it's going to be.

I lace an arm around her waist and help her walk toward the table where her friends are. I pull my wallet out and toss a hundred dollar bill on the table. "For her drinks," I say. "I'm taking her home." I zone in on the Spongebob jackass and lean in with a low hiss. "And if you ever treat her like this again, you'll answer to me."

He looks like he might be shitting himself as I straighten and help Gabby out of the bar toward my truck.

Chapter 11
Cooper

Maybe she would've been fine to rally, but I wasn't about to let her sit back down with that idiot kid. I realize they were just having a good time. It was innocent enough, and if it was any other girl aside from Gabby, I wouldn't have cared much at all.

But it wasn't.

It was *my* girl he was touching. Nobody touches my girl.

Except…she's not mine. Because of me and my decisions.

That doesn't mean I want her any less than I've always wanted her.

A stab of guilt plows into me. Did I just make her leave a good time with her friends to get her away from the douchecanoe?

I keep telling myself I did it because she barfed in the bathroom of a bar. Nobody wants to get sick on a night out with friends, and once the vomit comes, that's always a sure signal the night's over.

"You're an asshole," Gabby says as I navigate toward home. Her eyes are closed and she's leaning her head on the cool glass of the front passenger window. She didn't exactly fight me when I put her in the front seat of my truck. I grabbed an old blanket I keep in the back in case she has to puke again. It's better than puking all over my leather seats, I guess.

"That's fine," I mutter. She can beat me up all she wants. It's not worse than what I'm doing to myself.

"I hate you. I hate that your truck smells just like you." She's grumbling, and she's nearly passed out.

"I love you," I whisper when I know she won't hear me.

My chest aches with regret.

It's a short drive, and she's out by the time I pull into Troy's circular drive. I walk over to the passenger side and open the door slowly since she's passed out against it. I lean in and unbuckle her seatbelt, and then I heave her into my arms and carry her into the house.

Troy is in the living room, the first room off the entry, when he sees me carrying his daughter through the house.

"What the fuck?" he demands when he spots us. He jumps to his feet and tosses the tablet he was working on to the side.

"She was out with the intern kid in the Spongebob shirt and some other kids," I explain. "I ran into her at the bar. She drank too much, so I brought her home."

"Jesus, Coop. Thanks for looking out for her. Is she okay?"

I nod and don't say anything, and then I carry her up the stairs to her room. I lay her on the bed, and Troy is right behind me. I want to stay with her, to pull off her shoes, to watch her sleep, to make sure she's okay, but her father's here now.

It's not my job anymore.

"You're a good man," Troy says as he starts pulling her shoes off. "The best. Thanks for what you did tonight. I won't forget it."

"It was nothing," I say softly, gazing down at the girl I somehow have come to love more than anything in the world. My heart squeezes. Can this really be it for us? "Just saw a girl in trouble and handled it." The words feel thick around the lump in my throat.

"Are you in for the night?" he asks.

I nod.

"I was just getting ready to leave for the club. I have some work to take care of there, and then I was planning to head to Joanie's afterward. Can you keep an eye on her, make sure she's doing okay?" he asks. "I wasn't planning to be home until after noon tomorrow, but I can change my plans if it's asking too much of you."

"Of course," I say. "I'll be around. Don't change your plans."

"Text me if you need anything. I'll have my phone on me." I nod, and he reaches over to squeeze my shoulder. He presses his lips together. "They sure don't make them like you anymore."

"Thanks, Troy. I'll make sure she's okay."

He nods and leaves. I head to my room, take a quick shower, throw on some basketball shorts, and check in on her. She's in the exact same position we left her in.

I head downstairs and find some water and ibuprofen for both of us. The house is quiet, so Troy must be gone. I climb back up the stairs and set the pills and water on Gabby's nightstand, and I stare down at her as she sleeps peacefully. She's going to be hurting in the morning.

I shift her a little so she's resting more comfortably on her pillow, and then I glance around her bedroom.

There's a textbook open on her desk. I walk over and glance at what it is. Something about consumer behavior that looks boring as fuck.

I spot a t-shirt and pair of short shorts I've seen her sleep in, and I'm sure they'd be more comfortable than the jeans and tight shirt she's currently wearing, but I feel like I lost the right to undress her when I told her we couldn't be together.

I finally settle onto the chair at her desk and turn it so I can prop my feet up on her bed. I pull my phone out and start doing a little research on the Vegas Heat.

I learn who's already publicly signed with the team. Aside from myself and Danny, I spot former White Sox pitcher Rush Ross along with former Braves right fielder Duke Owens. Troy's building a team of superstars, and I'm not mad about it.

Her phone starts ringing—loudly, and it interrupts my research. I spot the brick outline in her jeans pocket. I slip out her phone and glance at the screen as I click the side button to silence the call.

Justin Larson.

I'm pretty sure that's the Spongebob jackass.

I think about answering, but it's not my right to. I shouldn't even have looked at the screen, but the fact that they exchanged numbers already and he's calling her when she disappeared from the bar speaks volumes.

I decline the call and click the volume off so the loud ringing doesn't wake her should she get another call, and then I pace around her room a bit as I try to figure out what to do. She's fine. She could sleep in here alone. I should go back to my own room.

But I promised Troy I'd look after her.

She's already tossed up most of the alcohol, so now it's just about sleeping it off and curing an epic hangover in the morning.

And maybe when morning comes, we can have that talk we need to have…if she's up to it.

Chapter 12
Gabby

I 'm hot.

Too hot.

It takes me a minute to realize it's because I'm sleeping in my jeans.

Why the hell am I sleeping in my jeans?

I'm in my bed...I think. The room is dark, so at least I was coherent enough to close the room darkening shades my dad had custom-installed, which normally I'm grateful for but today they're just confusing me. There's enough light peeking in around the sides that I know the sun's up.

What the hell time is it?

And how the hell did I get home?

I pry my eyes open and glance over at the clock, and the numbers haven't quite registered when my bed shifts beside me.

"Ahhh!" I scream, and I push the offending figure clean off the bed, using both my hands and my feet before I realize maybe I'm overreacting just a smidge.

Cooper Noah's head pops up from the floor, and his eyes are sleepy and confused. If I wasn't the most hungover I've ever been in my entire life, I might find this amusing.

Instead, I feel like I'm going to barf.

Did I barf last night?

It's a blur.

"What the hell are you doing in here?" I yell at him as I hold my head between my palms and press—like if I press hard enough, the pain will subside.

It doesn't.

"There are three ibuprofen tablets on your nightstand," he mutters as he stands, and he's not wearing a shirt.

He's not. Wearing. A. Shirt.

His abs shimmer in the darkness, and my dry mouth miraculously starts to salivate.

God, do I want him.

He rubs his hip and winces. "And a bottle of water. Take the pills and drink the bottle and maybe don't kick and push someone out of your bed for taking care of your drunk ass all night."

A tiny pang of guilt stabs into me. "You took care of me all night?"

"You got sick at the bar, and I took you home. I looked after you. I didn't want to leave you alone, so I slept beside you." He holds up both hands. "Nothing happened." His hand returns to his hip again to rub it.

"Did you hurt your hip or is that just your old age showing?"

He glares at me. "I landed on it when you literally kicked me out of bed for taking care of you."

"What about my dad?" I ask, and I realize my tone is both sassy and bratty, but I'm out of fucks to give.

"He had some business to take care of and said he wouldn't be home until after noon today. Can we talk over breakfast?"

I blow out a long, frustrated breath. "*Now* you want to talk?" I demand. "When I feel like I got hit by a truck?"

"Finding out your dad is Troy Bodine had much the same effect on me, and you wanted to talk yesterday," he says, holding up both hands.

I roll my eyes. "You weren't this big of a dick when we were together, were you?"

He chuckles and leans down, palms on my bed as he gets a little closer to me. His voice is low and husky when it comes out. "You seemed to have quite the affinity for my dick when we were together, darling."

His words steal my breath, and I hate that I'm still this attracted to him even though he's made it clear that what we had is over.

I can't do this. I can't live with him, I can't wake up with him next to me in my bed. I can't pretend like I'm not head over fucking heels in love with him when he's all I've ever dreamed of.

But I have to.

Love and hate ride a thin line, so I guess my only choice is to opt for hate.

"Fuck you."

He presses his lips together and raises both brows. "I'm going to turn on the coffee pot then head to the workout room for a quick workout. If you want me to make you breakfast, meet me in the kitchen in forty-five minutes for scrambled eggs and a chat."

He stalks out of my room and disappears, and I collapse back onto my pillows as I try to ward off the emotions plowing into me.

But one feeling swoops in to trump everything else, and I run to the bathroom where I dry heave for a few minutes before giving up.

I take the pills Cooper so thoughtfully left for me, and I start to cry as I think about how fucked up all this is. We're so damn right together, and I can't help but wonder if it would be different if I'd told him who my dad was up front.

The only thing that might've changed is that he never would've agreed to be with me in the first place.

I head to the shower where I let the water mingle with my tears, and I feel marginally better once I'm clean. I brush my teeth and check the time. I still have another fifteen minutes before Cooper told me to meet him, but I head down to the kitchen anyway and grab a cup of coffee. I check my phone as I slide into a chair at the table, and I see a missed call from Justin. He left a voicemail.

"Hey girl. Just wanted to check on you to make sure you got home all right. Call me."

I decide to ring him back even though he left the voicemail nearly ten hours ago.

"Hey," he answers. "You're alive."

"I'm alive," I say, my voice a little hoarse. "Barely."

He laughs. "I figured you were fine with Noah since he was in our meeting yesterday."

"Yeah," I say. "He's a good friend of my father's." I leave it at that since apparently it's nothing more than that. Not anymore.

"I had fun with you last night." His tone has a hint of suggestion to it, and I know where he's going with it. "I'd like to see you again. Maybe grab another drink but just the two of us this time."

"It's a nice offer, Justin, but I'm, uh…it's complicated." I'm fumbling for an excuse when the truth is that I can't tell him the truth. I think about what Mia suggested yesterday—that I go out with Justin to make Cooper jealous. It's a terrible idea. Right?

"I didn't ask you to marry me, Gab. I asked you out for a drink. Just friends if that's all you want. We have to work together for the next few months, and I like to be friends with my coworkers," he says lightly. He's not offended that I basically declined his invitation, and I like that about him. He's confident. Maybe more than he should be…but he's right. I want to have fun at work, too, and I've got enough heaviness surrounding me. I need something light. Maybe Justin can be a friend to help combat the darkness.

"Okay," I say. "Sure. I can do the friends thing. But just coffee this time. I can't even think about alcohol without dry heaving right now."

He laughs. "Coffee it is. Today at three, Starbucks near the bar last night?"

Cooper walks in as we end our conversation.

"That works," I say. "I'll see you then. And Justin?" My eyes are on Cooper's as I say another man's name.

I'm not doing what Mia said.

I'm not.

"Yeah?"

"Thanks for a fun time last night. I'm excited to hang out with you again."

I see the physical change on Cooper's face when I say the words to another man. Cooper doesn't know that I just told Justin that I'm not looking for anything other than friendship, so it's not *quite* Mia's plan, but it still has the same effect.

His brows are pinched and his nostrils are flared. His cheeks are an angry red and a vein makes itself visible in his neck, and I'm pretty sure it's from what I just said to Justin but it's possible it's from his workout.

"You too, girl," Justin says. "See you at three."

We hang up, and Cooper draws in a deep breath as he walks past me.

He's a little sweaty from whatever he just did in the workout room, and he runs a hand through his hair before grabbing a coffee mug and filling it to the brim with hot, black coffee.

"Black coffee?" I ask.

"The trainer gave me a plan to get ready for the season," he mutters. "I'm making cuts where I can." He grabs a Slim Jim out of the pantry and starts to peel open the packaging.

"What were you doing at the bar last night?" I demand.

"I met Kaylee for a drink. I saw that Spongebob douche putting his arm around you and I didn't like it. You were drinking a lot and I wanted to make sure you were okay."

My heart clenches and my chest tightens. "I was fine," I grit out.

"How were you planning to get home?"

"It's not your business. You gave up that right when you decided this was over." I wave a hand between the two of us.

"Do you want scrambled eggs, toast, and bacon?" he asks as he chews his beef stick.

I blow out a breath. "God, you're frustrating."

"Right back at you. Answer the question."

"Yes," I say, my tone full of petulance. I slide into the chair without bothering to offer to help. I don't want to help. I want to sulk and feel sorry for myself first for the hangover and second for the broken heart.

"So you're meeting him again today?" he asks casually as he starts grabbing what he needs to make breakfast.

"It's none of your business."

He presses his lips together and nods, and then he drops the loaf of bread and a pound of bacon onto the counter before turning around to lock eyes with me.

"Look, Gabby. Last night when I walked in with you passed out in my arms, your father told me what a good guy I was for taking care of you. He trusts me to treat you a certain way, and wrecking your tight little pussy with my nine-inch cock while I suck on your tits is not that way."

Butterflies take flight in my stomach at his words. God, could he wreck me good.

But that's not what I'm upset about.

Sure, I'll miss the sex. But it's so much more than that.

"We have no choice but to live beside one another for the next month, and I can't lose focus now," he continues. "Your father is trusting me not just to treat you right, but to mentor you. To honor the commitment I made to the Vegas Heat. I can't fuck this up. It's my one shot after being out of the game for three fucking years."

I suck my bottom lip between my teeth and bite hard to try to ward off the tears heating behind my eyes. I should be all cried out by now, but apparently I am not.

I nod a little. "It's not about the sex, Cooper. We had something that's once in a lifetime, and I know you felt it, too. I know you did. I may be young, but I know what love is, and I know I've never felt even an ounce of what we shared with anybody else. If you're choosing to put an end to this even though it's not what I want, then you have to let me all the way go. You can't steal me away from my friends to protect me. If you're out, you're out, and you have to let me live my life. You have to let me dance on tables and fuck up and learn from my mistakes on my own, or else you're just acting like another parent and I've already got enough of those."

He clenches his jaw at my rant, and he looks like he's about to go one way with his words, but then he pauses, rubs his hands up and down, and blows out a breath. "You're right. I'm sorry. If you like that jackass, it's your right to go for it."

He turns back to his work at the counter, pulling two slices of bread out of the bag and setting them in the toaster, cracking eggs, sprinkling salt and a little bit of garlic powder.

I watch him work, thinking about how to respond to his words. He's plating our food when I finally offer a reply, my voice quiet and full of regret. "For the record, it'll be a long, long time before I'm ready to *go for it* with anybody."

He sets a plate in front of me, and I quietly thank him. He sets the other plate in front of the seat beside me, and he slides into the chair. I dig into my eggs, and they're delicious.

I glance up when my plate's almost empty, and I see him watching me. He hasn't even started his food yet, and my tummy does a little flip at the realization.

He leans his elbows on the table and closes his eyes, resting his head in his palms for a beat. "I love you, Gabby. So fucking much. This is the hardest thing I've ever had to do."

I run my tongue over my back teeth and point my fork in his direction. "Then why are you doing it?"

The front door opens on cue, and he blows out a heavy breath. "You know why," he mutters.

"There's my girl!" my father says, striding into the room. He's wearing a suit, which seems odd for ten forty-five in the morning, but who am I to judge? "How are you feeling, sweetheart?"

"I'm fine. Cooper made me some breakfast and it's really helping cure the old hangover," I say.

"Good man, that Cooper Noah. Good, good man," he says. He strides over and claps Cooper on the shoulder. "Thanks for taking care of her."

"Not a problem," Cooper says flippantly. "You're back early."

"I was worried about Gabriella, so I cut my endeavors short," my dad says.

"Was Joanie your endeavor?" I tease.

His eyes widen a little as if he's been caught, and he turns accusatory eyes onto Cooper, who holds up his hands innocently.

"Wait a minute. Is there something I don't know?" I ask.

"Joanie and I have been seeing each other a while now," my dad admits. "I confessed it to Coop yesterday, but I wasn't ready for people to find out."

Cooper holds up both hands in defense. "I didn't say a word."

I raise a brow at him, noting that he's apparently good at keeping secrets, and then I turn toward my father. "The way you two looked at each other when we stepped into her office yesterday sort of gave you away."

He chuckles. "Did it, now? We'll have to work on that." He shoots me a wink. "Glad to see you're feeling better. Do you have plans for the day?"

"I'm meeting Justin the intern for coffee a little later." I finish what's left in my cup of coffee, and I glance at Cooper, who has finally started eating.

My dad slips into the chair beside me. "Isn't he the boy who got you drunk last night?"

I roll my eyes. "I made my own decisions last night. Admittedly they weren't the brightest, but I felt safe knowing both he and his father work for the Heat. I was out with an entire group of interns, so it's not like I was ever in danger. And Justin's nice."

"Nobody's nice enough for my little girl," he growls, narrowing his eyes at me.

I glance at Cooper again, who gives me a pointed look as if my dad's words are proving his point that this is the right decision for us.

I pick up my plate and rinse it in the sink before setting it in the dishwasher. "I have an essay to write and a few chapters to read for my Global Consumer Behavior class, so I'll be upstairs."

Cooper presses his lips together and offers a friendly nod, and my dad stands and pulls me into a hug before he lets me go. I hear his voice behind me piling on the compliments as I trail up the stairs.

"She's such a good kid. Hard worker, smart as a whip."

I'm not as smart as he thinks I am.

I did, after all, fall for a man twelve years older than me...and then I allowed him to break my heart.

Chapter 13
Cooper

One week from today I turn thirty-three and I'm feeling all sorts of ways about that.

The life I imagined for myself at thirty-three is nothing like the life I'm living.

I thought I'd be in my tenth year playing ball, for one thing. I figured I'd be cresting toward the end of my career, deciding what comes next...not getting back into the game after a three-year hiatus and feeling like a freshman all over again. But I won't have the chance to *act* like a freshman since I've been tapped to lead this team. Fake it 'til I make it, I guess.

I thought I'd be married by now. Instead, I'm grieving the loss of something that might have been the most powerful thing I've ever come across.

I thought I'd have two or three kids, and I'd be torn between wanting to be on that ballfield and wanting to be home with my family. Family would be edging out the game because you only get one life. None of that matters now since I made a three-year commitment.

My dad was forty-one when he died. Us Noah men, we don't get long lives to spend with our kids, and the longer I put off having them, the shorter that window gets. I've always felt the ticking of the clock, but lately it's started to sound more like a timer for a bomb that's getting ready to detonate.

I realize I already did a run this morning and I'm supposed to be slowly moving out of active rest into pre-season training, but I'm restless. I need to move.

I grab my keys and head toward the stadium. Troy worked out my credentials yesterday, so I breeze past security and head toward the weight room.

Nick's in there, and so are a few other players—including Danny and Rush, and two other guys as well.

"Rush Ross," I say, and I always thought he was a cool dude. Plus, it's fun to say his name since it sounds like one word.

He's younger than me—in his mid-twenties, and I wonder if Troy would be receptive to a younger player dating his daughter as opposed to someone like me.

I hate myself for the thought.

"Noah!" he says genially, and he claps me on the back. "How's the elbow?"

It's amazing to me what a community this game is. Everyone knows Cooper Noah retired early from an elbow injury. Everyone knows Rush Ross came close to breaking Randy Johnson's thirteen strikeout record last season when he had eleven in a single game. Everyone knows that Danny Brewer is a triple threat since he can run, field, and hit.

And now the three of us are in the same room together.

"Cooper Noah," one of the men across the room says. He looks vaguely familiar, and as he approaches, I place him. He was an assistant coach for the Rockies a few years ago. "Joe Buchanan, the third base coach."

"Great to see you, man," I say, slapping him on the back. I glance over at the other coach standing near him. "And Chris Jarrett." I reach out a hand to shake his. "Former first baseman for the Astros and now…"

"First base coach," he announces proudly.

"Great to have you here," I say.

"Likewise." He nods, and I get another excited feeling that Troy and the brass upstairs have assembled a kickass team here.

Nick saunters up behind us. "The big three," he says to Danny, Rush, and me, and he nods toward the treadmills. "You want me to put you through it today?"

"I already went for a run this morning," I admit. I glance at Danny and Rush, who are looking at me with challenge in their eyes. I'm not one to back down from a challenge. "But I'm in for a second one."

And then Nick hands us our asses.

Danny emerges the victor, Rush comes in second, and my slow ass learns real quick what it's going to mean to get back into season shape. More black coffee, less nachos. And my hip hurts…not because I'm old as fuck, but because I was literally kicked out of someone's bed this morning.

"Anyone want to head out to the field and toss some balls?" I ask.

"I need to shower and head to a meeting," Rush says, wiping his face with a towel.

"I'm in," Danny says with a nod. "Does this foursome work for poker?" he asks, nodding around to the three of us. He's met with three enthusiastic confirmations. I know Danny fairly well already, but I'm interested in getting to know both Rush and Nick moving forward.

I need a brotherhood. I need the bond. I need the distraction from the constant ache in my chest knowing that Gabby is so close yet so far. Knowing that she's meeting that jackass for coffee today. Knowing that I can't have her.

I blow out a breath.

Focus, Noah, I tell myself.

It's not like I can unload my woes on any of these guys. They're too close to the picture—too close to Troy.

But at least I've got a group of guys I can play poker with. That's something, anyway.

"Are you all free tonight around eight?" Danny asks before Rush leaves.

"I can't," Rush says. "Sorry. Next weekend maybe."

"I can't, either," Nick says.

"I guess I'm the only loser without plans," I admit to Danny, who laughs.

"Then let's fuck up this town together. Or let it fuck us up." He shrugs, and I nod with a laugh, glad to have plans for the night to distract me from Gabby and her new *friend*.

Nick tosses me a glove since I don't have mine here, and it'll do. Danny grabs a bag of balls, and we head out to the infield.

I draw in a deep breath as I walk over toward third base. There's no bag here, just the dirt, but it still feels like home.

Danny moves into position at first, and it feels like a long fucking way away considering I haven't done this in three years.

We both do a few warm-ups to get the muscles moving, but I'm still pretty warm from what Nick just did to us in the weight room.

I pull a ball out of the bag, and I grip it in my palm for a beat as I stare down at the cowhide stitched together by the red laces.

How many thousands of baseballs have I held in my hands over the years?

And how have I gone this long without holding one?

God, I love this game.

"You gonna make out with it or are you gonna toss it?" Danny yells from first, and I brush off the feeling as I pull my arm into position and launch it toward first base.

It falls right into Danny's glove.

Like riding a fucking bike, and goddamn does it feel good.

We play catch for maybe a half hour before we call it good, and I know my arm will be sore tomorrow, but my elbow feels fine— good, even, and I have plenty of recovery time to build the muscles back up to where they need to be.

It felt right being back out on the field, and I shower and spend a little time fucking around at the stadium before I leave with a renewed sense of hope.

I stop to pick up an early dinner, and I call my mom on the way home.

"Hey, it's my favorite baseball player," she answers, her voice filling my truck.

I chuckle. "Hello Mother."

"What are you up to? Feeling any better?"

"It's only been like a day, and no, I'm not. But I did go to the stadium twice now, and I worked out. I picked up a baseball, Mom."

"You did? How'd it feel?"

"Like I had my purpose back," I admit.

"I'm so happy for you, honey. The diamond always seemed to be the place where you felt most at home."

"It always was, and I'm glad to be back on it. Have you looked anything up on the Heat?" I ask.

"Nope. I wanted to hear it all from the source," she says.

"Rush Ross and Danny Brewer are the first two I've met. I guess Duke Owens is joining us, too. Danny and I tossed a ball around and he invited me to be part of their poker group." I stop at a red light.

"That's great! Building that team atmosphere already. I'm happy you're finding people. I worry about you, you know."

"I know you do. But you don't have to. I've got this," I lie. I don't *got this* at all, and my heart starts to hammer loudly in my chest as I turn into Troy's subdivision.

Her truck is in the circular drive. A Jeep is parked behind her truck, and it's got one of those bumper stickers with Calvin peeing on the Ford logo.

Fuck this kid.

Is he purposely doing this shit just to piss me off?

I park as close as I can to his bumper so he'll have a hell of a time getting out of his spot. A little dent in my bumper is worth it if it comes to that.

The house is quiet when I let myself in, but I know they're around here somewhere.

I head to the kitchen, where I set my food on the table and start eating. I hear some loud laughter as it carries through the house, and my chest tightens a little at the sound. She's having a good time with another guy.

Good. She should. She should move on from me and laugh and smile since those are things I can no longer give her.

But not with a douchebag like that kid.

I hear footsteps and voices approaching as I finish the meal that meets Nick's calorie guidelines, and I think about running out of the room, but intimidation tactics might be more fun.

They're laughing again when they turn the corner, and Gabby freezes when she spots me sitting at the table.

Her eyes connect with mine, and I swear I spot some guilt there before she glances away. "Oh, didn't know you were here," she mutters.

"Feeling better after that epic hangover?" I ask.

She offers a glare at me, and the douche is silent beside her. He's wearing a hat today, and it's backwards, and it just makes him look like he's trying too hard. Guys like me, we can wear our ballcaps backwards because we actually play the game. This skinny bitch looks like he's never even picked up a baseball, let alone learned how to throw one.

But whatever. To each his own.

"I feel fine," she says.

"I'm sure the afternoon coffee helped," I say, a little more suggestiveness in my voice than I'd planned for.

She clears her throat and moves toward the fridge, where she grabs a couple cans of soda, and then she turns to her little friend.

"You ready for a ping pong tournament?" she asks him, her tone taunting. "I'm gonna kick your ass."

Some mocking sound escapes my chest, and she shoots me a dirty look before he puts his hand on the small of her back.

All the hairs on the back of my neck stand at attention when he touches her.

I nearly leap out of my seat to physically pull him off her when I realize…it's not my right to.

He can touch her if he wants.

I've chosen not to. Instead, I've chosen to mock her hangover when she walks into the room like an immature child.

They walk out of the room together without a backwards glance, and I toss the plastic fork down into my salad, suddenly not very hungry.

What the fuck am I doing?

I don't want it to be like this. I don't want to fight with her, or to nitpick or argue every time we see each other. I don't want it to be awkward.

But if I can't have her, I don't know how else to be around her.

Chapter 14
Cooper

I've already had too much to drink.

I've already thrown Nick's dietary advice in the trash.

Maybe it's not that I've drank too much, but it's that I didn't have enough food as a base in my stomach after checking his caloric suggestions.

I opted for whiskey tonight instead of beer, which is a faster train to Drunktown, and we're at a strip club. It's not my usual choice in entertainment, but fuck it. I'm a sad and lonely old man at this point, so I may as well play into all the cliches.

Apparently Danny has buddied up with Ben Olson, who highly recommended Honeys for top-notch Vegas dancing entertainment, and so here we are.

"You been to Bodine's club yet?" Danny asks.

"It's where he brought me to schmooze the deal," I admit. "But I avoided the third floor."

"Yeah, I haven't been up there, either. I feel like he's riding a line there, and I'm not sure it's one I want to cross." He takes a swig of his whiskey.

Yeah, I don't want to cross it, either. Particularly not now that I've been intimate with his daughter.

"You wanna get out of here and blow some money on blackjack?" he asks after we've been drinking an hour or so.

I nod, and we both chug what's left in our glasses and head out. He grabs us a ride share, and we head toward a casino nearby.

"Heard you're single," he says. "Any prospects?"

I think about telling Danny about Gabby, but ultimately I keep my mouth shut. Enough people know. I don't need to widen that circle, and I don't need Troy finding out now that it's over.

I shake my head. "After Stacy I sort of played the field a while. Met a girl and fell for her fast, but it didn't work out." I leave it at that. "You?"

He makes a *pfft* sound. "Fuck no. Take a look in the mirror if you want to know why."

My brows dip. "What does that mean?"

"The sagging shoulders. The general cynical demeanor. The Cooper Noah I knew a few years ago wasn't like that, and I'd put up a pretty hefty sum on the fact that it was a woman who did this to you."

I press my lips together. He's not wrong.

He nods. "That's what I thought. You know the best way to get over someone, don't you?"

I raise my brows.

"Get on top of someone else, dude."

Is that what she's doing? Is she getting on top of Spongebob? The thought of it makes me want to throw up. It makes me want to put my fist through something, probably not the smartest move given my future at the Heat.

Still, though, the thought of her with someone else fills me with rage. I think back to those headlines about Cooper Noah, the guy who never loses his cool—except that time when I clearly tagged Pete Mitchell out and the ump called him safe…the one time I was ejected from a game for unloading on the asshole who clearly got it wrong.

All the replays were on my side, but I may have gotten a little mouthy with the umpire.

"Yeah," I finally admit on a deep sigh. "A girl fucked me up and I get it. I get why you wouldn't want to subject yourself to that. I don't really want to subject myself to it anymore, either."

"Stacy?" he asks. "Wasn't that her name?"

I'm about to reply in the negative—that it wasn't Stacy this time, even though she fucked me up pretty good herself, but then the car arrives at the casino and we both stumble out of the backseat.

I start to think this was probably a bad idea. I have a nagging suspicion this is going to be an expensive evening out with a friend.

We head toward the high limit area in the back, mostly because it tends to offer privacy than the main tables. Plus the fact that we're two fairly well-known professional baseball players wearing hats. They help protect our identity, but they don't make us invisible, and it's mere moments after entering that Danny is noticed by a group of women. He grins over at me, and they follow his gaze to his friend. I'm recognized pretty quickly by association after that since apparently our names have been paired in the local media as fans anticipate the new expansion team.

"Now this is what I was just talking about," he says, and I can't help but laugh.

Maybe he's right. Maybe the best way to get over Gabby is to get on top of somebody else. But I'm not sure I have it in me to just pick up a random girl and spend the night with her, not when what I shared with Gabby was so unique, not knowing a woman has it in her to make me feel the way she did. Nobody here tonight is even going to come close to that. Maybe no woman ever will again.

We head toward the tables, where I blow way too much money, drink way too much whiskey, and laugh until my stomach hurts with my buddy, and I'm hurting on Sunday when I wake up.

Nobody's in bed with me to make sure I didn't choke on my own vomit while I slept…though I'm old enough to know my limits and to stop before it gets to that point.

That fact doesn't dull the headache or help with the loud rumbling of my stomach. A shower doesn't really help much, either, and I get back in bed after my shower hoping to catch a little more sleep.

And that's when I hear it.

My bed is up against the same wall as hers, and I hear voices.

I can't make out what they're saying, but she's not alone in her room.

And the other voice?

It's decidedly male.

If that little fucker spent the night, I might just lose my shit.

Chapter 15
Gabby

Maybe it's wrong. Maybe it's immature. Maybe I don't care.

Justin and I drank a little bit last night during our epic ping pong battle, and I told him to stay the night. He didn't stay in my room. He stayed in one of the guest rooms in my dad's wing, so he wasn't even in the same part of the house as me while we slept.

I heard Cooper come in late last night—or rather, I heard him stumble in. My door was shut and my light was off. I was in the middle of tossing and turning for the seven thousandth time when he not-so-quietly headed to his room.

I thought about going out to the hall to check on him, but I stayed where I was. He's making his feelings pretty damn clear, and nothing good would've come from me confronting him when he was drunk.

Even though I was incredibly curious what a drunk Cooper looks like.

I learned a lot about Justin as we bonded over coffee at Starbucks yesterday, and I learned even more once I invited him back to my dad's game room.

And perhaps one important fact I learned is that…well, we both find Cooper Noah incredibly attractive.

I didn't tell him that Cooper has been inside me. I didn't tell him how I fell in love with him. I did, however, tell him I have a monster crush on the guy. I told him how he acts all protective over me but won't give me the time of day. I told him my friend thinks I should flaunt another guy in his face, and Justin was all too happy to volunteer for the job.

His exact words, in fact, were, "Maybe he'll notice you, or maybe he'll notice me. Either way, one of us wins."

I laughed and laughed as I realized Justin was never interested in anything more than friendship with me, and we bonded over the fact that our fathers put baseball first, though we had incredibly different paths that led to our internships.

Justin hasn't come out to his family. His parents don't know he's gay, and his father has spent his entire life pushing for him to play ball.

He never wanted to play ball.

He did it anyway, and he was good at it. He's also quite the actor. He puts on the front like he's interested in every pretty girl who walks across his path when the truth is that he'd rather cozy up with Chase or Brian than Chloe or Mackenzie.

So he's a twenty-two-year-old man living a total lie.

None of the other interns know the truth.

I asked him why he told *me*, and he said he knew he could trust me with his secret nearly immediately after meeting me. My heart melted, and just like that, I have a new gay best friend...one I'm rooting for in every way I can.

He's dated a few guys in secret, but all his meaningful relationships have ended because he refuses to be honest with his parents. He told me he'd tell them someday, and that was good enough for me. It's not my place to push him, but as his new friend, it *is* my place to support and encourage him however I can.

When he popped into my room this morning, I flipped the covers back and patted the mattress, and he snuggled in beside me.

"How'd you sleep?" I ask.

"So good. Can I get a permanent reservation at Hotel Bodine?"

I laugh. "You'd have to ask Troy himself about that, and I'm guessing it'll be a hard no if he thinks you and me are a thing."

"How would he react to that? If we're faking it for his benefit," he says, jutting his thumb toward the wall I share with Cooper, "doesn't that mean we have to fake it for your dad's, too? And everybody else?"

"We can lay it on thick in front of..." I nod my head toward the wall to indicate Cooper, too. "With everyone else, we can be vague."

"You think it'll work?" he asks.

I shrug. "Probably not, but it's worth a shot to see if he notices either of us, right?"

He grins and nods. "How do you think he'll react to the two of us in your bed together in the morning?"

I laugh loud enough to try to wake up the man next door. "Not well."

Justin leaps out of bed and opens the door. "Let him take a peek at this, then." We both giggle, and then he slides back into bed beside me. He wiggles his arm behind me so I'm forced to rest my head on the nook at his shoulder.

"So what are you thinking about this kids thing we have to work on together?" he asks.

"Tomorrow is my first official day, so I imagine we'll learn more then." I lift my shoulder a little to shrug, a difficult feat since I'm smashed up against Justin.

"How awkward will it be working with Hottie McThirdBaseman over there with the huge crush you have on him?"

"The most awkwardest ever," I admit, and he laughs.

His laugh is infectious, and I start laughing, too.

And it's that moment Hottie McThirdBaseman decides to exit his bedroom. We both watch as he walks by, jaw clenched as he peeks into my room. He sees us on the bed snuggling together, and I swear I see fire come out of his ears before he disappears from our view. I hear him as he stomps down the stairs, and for a second, I feel pretty damn good about what we've accomplished here this morning.

Until I realize I don't want to hurt Cooper. Sure, I want to make him jealous. Sure, I want him back, and a part of me hopes seeing me with somebody else will be enough to spur him to action.

But I don't want to make him miserable. I know him pretty well, and I have a feeling he's working pretty damn hard to make himself miserable all on his own.

Chapter 16
Cooper

I'm seething as I pour a cup of coffee, and fuck this. I'm not hanging around the house all day watching her get closer and closer with some other guy as she flaunts it in my face. Close the goddamn door. At least have some respect and close the door so people walking by don't have to see.

But no, she's lying there on his chest all cozy, and it should be *me* holding her in my arms, and I'm completely out of sorts after the shit I witnessed.

I can't do this.

I can't live here, I can't watch her move on, I can't fucking even enjoy this new adventure in my life because she's right fucking there marring all of it.

I text Kaylee.

Me: *Are you going to the game today or are you watching at home?*

It's Ben's last preseason game before the regular season begins, and last I checked, the Aces were going to Los Angeles for the game.

She writes back nearly immediately.

Kaylee: *Home with the girls. Come hang out, everyone else went to California but I wanted to get a jump start on the SFK ideas. We can watch the game and talk ahead of your meetings tomorrow.*

She texts her address, and I chug my cup of coffee before racing out the door to get away from Gabby and her new lover before they come down for breakfast.

Did she really move on so quickly? Did I ever mean anything at all to her?

Those are the questions that plague me on the drive over to Kaylee's house.

Two baby girls are crawling around on the floor when I arrive. One is using the coffee table to help her stand, and the other is attempting to pull herself up onto the couch.

"Holly, no!" she says, and clearly the rambunctious one trying to climb the couch is Holly. Holly jumps at her mother's tone, and she falls to the floor in a heap of tears. "God, I'm really dreading the teenage years with the dramatics of nine months."

I laugh. "May I?" I ask, and Kaylee nods while she picks up Hailey. I reach down to quiet the now screaming Holly. "Hey, baby girl," I say quietly, soothingly. "You're okay. Take a deep breath with me." I suck in a dramatic breath of air and let it go, breathing my dragon coffee breath right in her face.

Tears turn to giggles.

"Jesus, how are you still single?" Kaylee mutters.

I shoot her a look. "You really want to get into that right now?"

"If I wasn't married to the hottest tight end in the universe, I swear to God my ovaries would've just exploded. That whole *baby girl* line in that sexy gravel tone? Good Lord, Coopsey."

"I thought we nixed Coopsey."

She shakes her head. "You thought wrong."

We play with the babies as a twinge of something pulls at my chest.

This is what I want. Maybe not with Kay—definitely not with Kay—but with the right woman. Kaylee and I were a non-starter. I found her attractive, and it was mutual, but she was pregnant when we met, and I was still reeling from my break-up with Stacy. We fell into a brother-sister type relationship, and over the last few months, we've gotten closer and closer.

It never would've worked between us, anyway. She's from a football family. They never would've let her get with a ballplayer like me.

Although athletes are athletes, and while our games are different, our dedication is not.

Somehow Kaylee tamed the wild Ben Olson, and they're living their happily ever after. He went on record hundreds of times spouting how he never wanted kids...and now he's blessed with not one but two perfect girls, and he's gone on record twice as many times proving what a family man he's turned into.

I'm happy for Kaylee. I'm glad they worked it out. I'm not jealous, exactly. I'm just wondering when my time will come.

We watch the game, and we chat about SFK during commercials while the girls nap. It isn't until the fourth quarter when the starters are benched and the Aces are ahead by three touchdowns when Kaylee mutes the television and turns toward me.

"The girls will be up soon, and we need to talk."

My brows dip. "About what?"

"About *you*, Cooper Noah. You're acting like your best friend just died, but I'm right here."

I laugh. "While you *are* my best friend, Kaylee Olson, you're wrong. I'm fine."

"You are not, you big dumb idiot. You're clearly broken up over Gabby, and I need to know what you're going to do about it," she says.

I blow out a breath and keep my eyes on the screen. "My hands are tied. What choice do I have?"

"You choose love. You *always* choose love," she says, reaching over and squeezing my forearm.

"Like you did when you ran away from Ben?" I mutter petulantly.

"Hey," she says sharply enough that my head whips in her direction. "That was different." Her tone gentles.

"It's fine, Kay. I don't need the distraction right now anyway. It's just…that dopey intern kid that walked in, he's been hanging around her. He spent the night last night."

"Oh, God. You don't think…"

"I don't know what to think. I think she's playing games. I think she's flaunting something in my face but I know her, and I know she's not the type to just jump into something new when she's hurting over the end of us. I fucking hate it, but what can I do?"

"You can fight, Cooper. You fight for her. You fight for what you know is right."

"But what if it isn't right? What if it was exciting and thrilling and steamy for a few weeks, and it was going to sputter out anyway? What if there's too wide a gap and the fact that I want kids yesterday scares her off because she's not even out of college? What if she doesn't want to be with a ballplayer who just signed a three-year contract and will be gone half the year when he was the one who wanted to start a family in the first place?" I blow out a breath at the end of my rant, collapsing back on the couch as the confession drains me of everything I have left in me.

"Hey, Coop," Kaylee says gently. "It's all going to be okay. It's all going to work out."

I press my lips together and nod as I keep my eyes trained on the television and push down the emotions welling up. I won't let them spill over, but I'm also not sure I can trust what Kaylee's telling me.

I want to believe her, but I just don't know how it *can* work out…unless I allow feelings to overrule logic, something I've never done before in my life.

Chapter 17
Cooper

These are great ideas," Joanie says in our Monday afternoon meeting. Gabby's here—we waited to hold this meeting until she was done with class for the day, and I spent the morning working out with Danny and Nick. "I'll get my team on it to start drafting some models, and we'll get your approval before moving it to the ballpark operations department."

"Thanks, Joanie." I nod my thanks. "I'm going to walk the Spade Level again and see if it sparks up any other ideas." The first floor everyone enters the stadium on is the Heart Level, the second level is the Diamond Level with the Club Boxes, and the third level is the Spade Level, all catchy little titles that reflect the city we're in. They picked hearts for the first level since we're playing with our fans' *hearts* or some silly jingle that makes me want to roll my eyes every time I hear it, but the Spade Level is where the kids' area is planned.

"Great," Troy says. "Gabriella, why don't you go with him? I think if the two of you put your heads together, you'll be unstoppable."

Gabby clears her throat uncomfortably as a vision of us putting our *heads* together pops uninvited into my mind. Or, you know, not so much *heads* as her pussy and my cock.

I purse my lips and offer a short nod. "Sure."

"You know, Mr. Bodine," Joanie says. "I was thinking it would be a good idea for Gabby to shadow Cooper for all things SFK to take a deeper look at the marketing angle, and maybe Justin could shadow me to get a look at the business operations side of things. Thoughts on that?"

"Perfect," Troy says with a sharp nod. "I think it's an excellent idea. When Cooper isn't working on SFK, what would you like Gabby working on that's still related to marketing?"

"We need social footage. This TikTok thing is all the rage, but to be honest I'm lost. I'm seeing all sorts of insiders post things at ballparks and they're going viral. Imagine the clout we'd get with this brand-new stadium," Joanie says.

"Can you handle that?" Troy asks Gabby.

She nods a little weakly. "Socials are part of my area of study."

"Great. Then shadow Coop everywhere when you aren't working on anything else for Joanie," Troy says, and my heart drops somewhere near my nuts. "He can introduce you to the other players, show you the clubhouse, the weight room. Just run everything by Joanie before you post anything anywhere."

Fuck. My. Life.

Is he fucking serious right now? *Shadow Coop everywhere.* Not your best idea, Mr. Bodine.

As if she wasn't already ruining this experience for me, now I can't even come here to the stadium to avoid her.

"Right. And I'll be sure to check the clubhouse for any nudity before I allow your young daughter in there," I say a little more snidely than I mean to.

Troy misses my tone, and I'm pretty sure it's because he's been playing footsie with *Sapphire* under the table for the last forty-five minutes. More and more I'm getting the image of him being a dominant over her on the third floor over at his nightclub that decidedly *isn't* a sex club. "Excellent," he says, and I scrape my chair against the floor more aggressively than is necessary, stand, and thank everyone for their time before stalking out, my shadow following close behind me.

"I don't like this any more than you do," she grits out once we're out of earshot of anyone in there.

"Really?" I ask snidely. "Because it sure as fuck feels like you put him up to this."

"Are you kidding me right now?" she practically screeches as we enter the Heart Level concourse.

"I'm not kidding you. Did you ask him to shadow me?" I hiss.

She's so taken aback by my accusation that she sputters out a laugh. "Hell no! I haven't said a damn word to him about any of this! I can't believe you think so little of me."

I blow out a breath. "Sorry," I mutter. "I don't think little of you." And that's the whole goddamn problem, isn't it?

We walk silently side-by-side toward the escalator that will take us up to the third level, and the entire way, I fight every natural instinct to grab her hand in mine.

I also fight every natural instinct telling me to ask her what the hell is going on with that punk-ass kid she's seeing.

Once we get up to the empty area that will soon be filled with structures and kids and their parents, I walk around a few beats while Gabby watches me carefully.

"What are you thinking?" she finally asks.

I don't know how to answer that. I'm sure as fuck not focused on my purpose for being here, but telling her that feels out of left field.

"I think a large contained structure over here," I say, pointing. "One of the ones where kids climb up all the levels and there are huge slides up at the top. Maybe a ball pit they can slide down into and play."

She follows my finger to where I'm pointing. "Are ball pits a good idea? Won't someone just have to constantly pick them up? And if they're at the bottom of the slide, won't kids just stay there and not move and then the next kid coming down the slide will crash into them?"

I refuse to admit I hadn't thought about that. "They'll be fine. Over here I was thinking a batting cage kids can play in, one of the kinds with an automatic pitch. And over there, a catching station." I walk around the area until I'm standing near the wall, and she follows me, standing far enough away that I can't reach out and touch her. A safe distance. "Then a circuit with different stations for activity around it. Jumping jacks at one, squats at another, you get the idea. And in between each exercise platform will be a spot to march in place."

"What about trampolines instead of marching?" she asks.

I lean back against the wall and harden my gaze at her. I don't want her to be so goddamn beautiful and smart on top of it.

My nephews go bananas for those trampoline parks, and in my thoughts about the circuit, I was thinking about how adults would navigate it, not how *kids* would. But this is for kids. Kids don't want to fucking march in place. They want to bounce. They want to get their energy out.

They want trampolines.

I blow out a breath. "Yeah. Trampolines might work."

She flattens her lips. "It's not against the rules to tell me it's a good idea, you know. A compliment wouldn't hurt you."

"You don't think so?" I ask. I shake my head, and then I mutter a curse under my breath as I stare down at the floor.

"It would hurt me more than you, but that's sort of the theme of our relationship, isn't it?"

I lift my gaze to hers, and she's studying me. The way she's staring so intently at me, like she can see right through me…it's unnerving.

"You think it's hurting you more than it's hurting me?" I ask quietly.

She lifts a shoulder and gives me a pointed gaze.

I harden my gaze on her, and then I push off the wall and stalk toward her. She backs up until she hits the wall behind her, and I pin her there with my hips. I grab her wrists between my hands, and I yank them up above her head, locking them in one of my hands while I use my other arm to haul her closer to me.

I have to lock her hands up there.

I can't allow her to touch me. I won't be able to resist her if she does.

Our bodies are pressed close, and I can feel the pounding of her heart against my chest, hers hammering as loudly and as rapidly as mine.

I drop my lips to her neck because I can't go another second without tasting her skin. I breathe her in, memorizing every scent that's not mine to have any longer.

It sure as fuck doesn't belong to Spongebob, either, but that's her choice to make.

"I don't want to fight against this, Gabby. Believe me. But I have to," I murmur against her skin.

She lets out a soft cry, and then she twists out of my hold. I let her go even though I have the strength to easily hold her there if I wanted to.

"I can't do this," she rasps, looking wildly around before she bolts away from me.

Chapter 18
Gabby

I don't know what the hell that was, but it can't happen again.

It can't.

I happen to run into Justin as I get off the escalator at the second level and turn into the concourse.

Literally.

"Oof," he grunts when I spin around the corner. He pulls back and grabs my biceps to steady me. "Whoa, girl. Are you okay?"

I shake my head, and he links his arm through mine and walks me through the concourse and over to one of the Club Level suites.

We collapse into two of the chairs there.

"What's going on?" he asks quietly.

"I lied," I say as I stare down at the field. I study the place where Cooper will stand for all the home games, all the practices, all the events. Third base.

Maybe telling Justin the truth is a mistake, or maybe I can finally unload some of this and have someone to lean on when I'm here at the ballpark.

I wonder if Cooper has told anyone.

"About what?" he finally asks after waiting for me to go on.

I draw in a deep breath and exhale it loudly before I answer. "Cooper."

He presses his lips together. "What about him?"

"My friends took me out for my twenty-first birthday." It feels like ages ago even though it was literally less than a month ago. "I sat at a blackjack table next to a hot guy who offered to teach me how to play. I spent the whole weekend with him, and we decided to start seeing each other despite the almost twelve-year age gap between us."

"You spent the *weekend* with Cooper Noah?" he asks, his tone absolutely incredulous.

"That I did. And then he invited me to his place in San Diego, so I went there for the weekend," I admit.

"You went to his place in San Diego? Wait a minute…and you didn't know who he was?"

I shake my head, my eyes still focused on third base. "My friends looked him up, but he'd been long retired and I never paid attention to baseball anyway. How am I supposed to know every player who ever retired? And how was I supposed to know he was planning to *un*-retire?"

"Because he's Cooper Fucking Noah, Gabriella. He's one of the most gorgeous men who has ever played the game. *That* is how you know," he says, and I roll my eyes.

"Right. Anyway, we spent some blissful time together, I fell in love with him, and then he showed up as my dad's houseguest and told me he couldn't be with me because he's friends with my dad and blah blah blah."

"Oh, sweet baby Jesus," he mutters. "And now Joanie's making you shadow him."

"He broke my heart," I admit quietly.

"I'm so sorry, Gabs." He reaches over and grabs my hand in his, and he squeezes tightly. "All the more reason to fake it until we make it, right?"

I share some more details about the time Cooper and I spent together. We talk quietly in case someone was to walk up behind us.

"Please don't tell anyone," I beg.

"You have my word," he says. He reaches around my shoulder and draws me in a little closer, and I rest my head on his shoulder, glad I seem to have found a new friend.

He leans down and presses a soft kiss to my temple. It's nothing more than a friendly gesture—one friend comforting another—but to the man clearing his throat behind us, it must have looked like more.

"I'm sorry to interrupt, but I'm going to walk the one hundred level to see if there are any places where mini centers might fit in to try to get people up to the Spade Level." Cooper's voice is flat, emotionless, and if I didn't know him better, I'd even venture to say it's a little uncaring. But I know him, and I know that's not the case.

He just admitted to me when he had me tied up, when his lips were on my throat, that he's hurting, too. That this is hard on him, too. I've been so wrapped up in my own broken heart that I haven't really stopped to consider that this might be painful for him, too.

And the reason why?

Because he's the one doing this to us.

If it were up to me, we'd sneak around a while and we'd figure out how to handle my father. I'd find some way to make this work. Instead, he'd rather give up at the first sign of trouble.

I lean over toward Justin and plant a kiss right on his cheek. He gives me a little bit of a warning look that goes undetected by Cooper behind us.

"I'll talk to you later," I say to Justin, and then I stand and turn around to face Cooper.

His clenched jaw works back and forth as anger vibrates off him.

"Ready?" I ask as sweetly as I possibly can.

He spins and takes off, and I practically have to run to keep up with him.

"Will you slow down?" I ask, but he ignores my plea as he keeps going, maybe even picking up speed a little.

We make it down to the one hundred level, and since I'm his shadow, I trail a little bit behind him. He doesn't talk to me at all, doesn't indicate what he's thinking or what ideas he has as we walk the entire loop of the Heart Level.

I look around to try to see what he's seeing. I spot the Vegas Heat logo everywhere. I spot restaurants that have already started building out their booths with their own logos and customizations. I see some empty booths not yet filled by sponsors, and I see other areas where I could imagine a mini circuit or even just one or two of the platforms we were talking about upstairs—a trampoline, maybe, with an attendant or a sign letting people know there's more stuff like this up on the third floor.

We head down to the field and walk through to the weight room, and I pull my phone out of my pocket to film some footage for the social channels as requested by Joanie. Cooper stops to chat with some guy sitting at a desk in the weight room, still completely ignoring my presence until the guy nods at me and asks who I am.

If not for the question, Cooper would have been completely silent, his jaw still clenched, still working back and forth the whole time. Clearly whatever has gone down between the two of us has struck a nerve with him, and you know what? It struck a nerve with me, too.

Now if I could just get him to talk about it instead of running around ignoring me, maybe we could actually get somewhere.

Chapter 19
Cooper

I'm seething as I chat with Nick. I'm trying to steady my emotions, but it's impossible.

I can't seem to keep my goddamn hands off her, and then I see her run right to the other kid.

She shouldn't be with him.

But she can't be with me.

And that's the crux of the problem, isn't it? I offer a breadcrumb, and she runs with it toward Spongebob Dickface.

This situation is impossible, and it's only made worse when Troy walks into the weight room. I glance around and see Gabby over by some equipment taking video footage on her phone. At least that's what I think she's doing.

"I have a surprise for you, Noah," Troy says when he sees me, interrupting my conversation with Nick. His grin is wide and honestly it makes me a little nervous.

"What is it?"

"We're heading to the media suite on the Heart Level. News of your contract broke last night and they were knocking down the door this morning to be the first to get an interview."

An interview?

Right now?

My heart is still pumping from seeing another dude wrapped around my girl, and now I'm supposed to just walk into the media room with a fucking smile while they film me and my answers to all the questions they're going to fire at me?

"Let's go," I say.

I follow Troy there, practicing breathing exercises as I focus on my palms. *Up palm, down palm, time to get calm. Breathe real deep and take the leap.*

I can do this.

We walk into the room from the back so we're entering on a small platform holding a table and two chairs. The Vegas Heat logo repeats to infinity on a backdrop behind us as I slide into one of the chairs in front of a huge group of microphones perched on the other side of the table. I can hardly see over them to the crowd of reporters gathered here.

"I'm pleased to introduce you to our third baseman, Cooper Noah," Troy begins.

"Good morning, everyone," I say with a wave and a smile.

It's like riding a bike, that old skill of acting in front of reporters, and I climb on and grip the handlebars for dear life.

"Jerry Garner, Vegas Times. How did Troy manage to lure you out of retirement?" the first reporter asks.

Images of my mouth on Gabby's pussy as I wrestled with the idea of moving to Vegas seem to flash before my eyes. I clear my throat as I force them away. Now is not the time, and certainly not when I'm sitting next to her father. "He gave me an offer I couldn't refuse."

"So it was all about the money?"

"The money's nice, but the love of the game is ultimately what brought me back. The chance to play for Mr. Bodine after we've been friends for years, the chance to build a team, the chance to go for the Commissioner's trophy with a new expansion team…it all appealed to me."

"When did you know you were coming to Vegas?"

The moment I slid my cock into Gabriella Grant.

Fuck.

That's not true. I had a feeling I was going to say yes when I took that ride from Troy's club back to Caesars Palace, and that was before I met Gabby.

But my weekend with her solidified my feelings that Vegas was the place I wanted to be. I was hopeful it would be with her, but things don't always work out the way we hope.

I glance over at Troy, who's showing no emotion on his face. I had to sign a nondisclosure agreement when I stepped foot into his club, so I can't exactly mention that he proposed this idea there.

"He presented the idea to me, and it was in the car on the way home when I knew I couldn't pass it up," I say.

Troy pushes my shoulder teasingly. "You made me wait over two weeks for my answer and you knew five minutes after you left?"

I laugh. "I knew three minutes after I left."

The reporters gathered crack up at that, and the rest of the conference goes as well as it can. They ask me about what I did in my retirement, and I plug SFK. They ask me about my elbow, and I mention my surgeon by name.

But when they ask me about my personal life…that's when I trip.

"Mr. Noah, is there a special woman in your life making the move to Vegas with you?"

The sports reporters here don't give a fuck about my personal life, but this is Vegas. I'm not surprised an entertainment reporter is in the mix. Between the Vegas Aces football team and the different rock bands based out of this city plus the fact that it's Las Vegas, this is a city ripe with entertainment.

No. There's not a special woman making the move to Vegas with me.

But there *is* a special woman, and she happens to be the daughter of the man sitting next to me, and I can't have her and it's fucking with me so badly that I'm nearly reconsidering the move here at all.

I wouldn't do that.

I wouldn't pull out, and I wouldn't say those things to the reporters.

But imagine if I did. Imagine if I just let the truth out.

It's not just the nature of the question throwing me for a loop, though.

It's the fact that less than a minute before this reporter asked this particular question, the door to the media suite swung open, and Gabriella Grant walked in. She took a seat in the back of the room, and despite the spotlights on me and the microphones blocking my view, I still saw her walk in with an angelic glow surrounding her, and I haven't been able to tear my eyes off her since.

And now I have to answer a question about a special woman when I can't have the only woman I want.

We're all keeping secrets, and there are even more we need to keep from the people interviewing me today.

I keep my eyes trained on Gabby, and I can feel their heat on me even from across the room.

After a pause that's far too long, I finally say, "No. No special woman."

Gabby closes her eyes as if the words physically plow into her, and I feel it, too.

The wind is knocked out of me at my bald-faced lie to the media, and I watch as she gets up and walks out of the room, taking what's left of my broken heart with her.

Chapter 20
Cooper

I should have chosen a different bar. Any other bar in the entire universe, really.

But no. I chose the same place where I have the pleasure of sitting across the bar watching Gabby get shitfaced for the second time in less than a week.

I have the absolute privilege of watching what's-his-nuts pull her in close with his arm around her shoulder.

I don't know if they know I'm here. I was here before they got here, sitting in a corner booth across the way with Danny, who's already on his fourth glass of whiskey and chatting up some woman who just slid into the booth with him.

I've been spending a lot of time with him outside of my time at the stadium, mostly as a distraction to get out of Troy's house, but I'm not sure I can keep up with him. The guy has a different woman on his arm every night, and that's not my style anymore.

I wonder for a beat if I should go back to the club. Troy gave me an open invitation, and my attendance would help me bond with Troy. Maybe it would help me see whether I'm making the right choice or the wrong one.

But I already know the truth. I'm doing what's best for my career.

It's why I'm sitting in a booth with Danny Brewer when I'd rather be the one slinging my arm around Gabby's shoulder across the bar as she laughs with the other interns.

I signal to the waitress that I'd like another whiskey, and when she brings it over, she slides onto the booth beside me. She nods over at Danny and the blonde.

"Feeling like a third wheel?" she asks.

I laugh. "Yeah, a little. He told me it was going to be a fun night out, and then he ditched me for her." I glance down at her nametag, talking softly enough so just Kelly can hear me.

She rolls her eyes dramatically. "Men."

"Right?"

She giggles, and this is the moment when she's waiting for me to ask her what time she gets off so I can take her somewhere to ravage her.

But I don't want to ravage her.

She's not Gabby.

"Well, uh," she says a little awkwardly. "I guess I better get back to it."

I press my lips together and nod. "Thanks for the laugh."

She gives me a sympathetic look, and if it were another time and my chest wasn't hollow right now, maybe I'd find it in me to at least get her number.

But that's not where I'm at.

A reminder comes through on my phone.

Stay at Caesars Palace on Saturday.

Right.

Two days from now is my thirty-third birthday, and sometime back when Gabby and I were together and we weren't sure where we were going to be able to meet up for sex, I reserved a room for the night for us.

I figured she celebrated her birthday there, so I should, too.

It was going to be a romantic night just for the two of us—where I didn't have to worry about my boss overhearing my antics and she didn't have to worry about her father overhearing hers.

Little did we know the man was one and the same.

I move my finger to cancel the reservation, but I pause over it.

Surely I could round up a few buddies to hang with me this weekend, and I could collapse onto a bed at Caesars rather than running back to Troy's place drunk.

I can take the night away from both Gabby and her father to try to get my head on straight.

I move my finger away from the cancelation button, and I suck down my whiskey, pulling an ice cube into my mouth to suck on it.

The girl Danny's been chatting with gets up, and he wiggles his eyebrows at me across the table. I laugh.

"She has a friend that's meeting her here in a bit," he says suggestively.

"I'm not in the place," I say around the ice cube, and then I chew it.

"So what place are you in?" he asks.

I can't help it. My eyes move across the bar toward Gabby, and when they flick back to Danny as I realize my mistake, his eyes widen a little as he's looking where I just was.

"Wait a minute. Aren't those the interns?" he asks.

I flatten my lips and nod.

"You've got a thing for an intern?" he practically roars.

"A, shut the fuck up, and B, no. It's not a *thing for an intern.*" I stare down at a spot on the table. If there's anyone I could trust with this secret, it's Danny Brewer. He's a good guy who'll take it to the grave, and it might help to have someone on the field who understands what I'm going through.

When I finally glance up at him, he's staring at me with concern.

"Then...what is it?"

"I met Troy's daughter before I knew she was Troy's daughter," I admit, and his jaw drops open a little. "We had a thing, and now it's over."

"Ah, so that's the girl who fucked you up. I thought it was your ex," he says.

"I know. I let you think that because I can't have this getting back to Troy." I offer a pointed look, and he nods.

"It won't." He pretends to zip his lips, but then he downs half a glass of whiskey, so I'm not sure how trustworthy the promise is.

The girl he was talking to slides back in beside him.

"Did you ask him about Leila?" she asks him, pointing toward me.

"I mentioned you had a friend, but Coop's going through some things," he says.

"I bet Leila could make you forget," she offers.

"I'm sure she could. I'm so sorry, but I'm going to have to politely decline," I say.

I glance over at Gabby just like I've been doing all night, and see the two of them with their bodies basically all over each other.

I shouldn't decline Leila before I've even met her. I should take the offer on the table.

But I won't stoop to her level. I won't flaunt some new thing in front of her on purpose.

Though at the stadium today, when I found her in the Club Level...it didn't seem like she was doing it on purpose.

I can't help but wonder whether what we had was so meaningless to her that she could just move on so easily. I'm not like that.

I need some time. Time to heal. Time to move on. Time to focus on baseball.

Fuck it, maybe I'll just play my three years before I even look at another woman.

That thought is confirmed as I hear Gabby's loud laughter carry all the way across the bar.

"I'm going to head out," I announce once I finish my whiskey. I've had four, which means I shouldn't drive.

I decide to head out front and call up a car because I just need to get the fuck out of the bar where I can hear her having fun and laughing while I feel like a constant weight is pressing against my chest.

I bid goodbye to Danny and the girl whose name I never learned. I don't know where to go besides home, so I open the Lyft app and order up a car back to Troy's place.

One week down, three more to go until I have my own place and won't have to head back to the same house where Gabby lives. Although from the way things look between her and her new boyfriend, maybe she'll start spending more time at his place.

I'm leaning against the building, head down as I try to remain incognito, when the door of the bar bursts open and I spot Gabby rushing out. She looks wildly around, and I get the sense she's drunk.

I am a little bit, too.

She spins on her heel then spots me standing against the wall. "Did you follow me here?" she hisses at me. "Watching me, making sure I'm not drinking too much? Or were you going to force me to go home again?"

I clear my throat. "I could ask you the same considering I was there with my buddy before you even showed up." I force all emotion from my tone.

She points a finger at me. "I want you to leave me alone."

"I'm trying. Believe me, I'm trying."

"Justin and I are very happy together." She juts her chin out, and I get the sense she's lying.

"Great. Happy for you." I avert my gaze to the ground at my own lie.

"Good. Now leave." She glares at me.

"I'm waiting for a Lyft. Why did you come out here, exactly?" I glare back.

She huffs out a sigh, but the way her eyes widen just slightly, the way they flick down to my chest like she's thinking about rushing into me so I can wrap my arms around her...the actions speak louder than the words. *Justin and I are very happy together.*

Sure you are, Gabby. Sure you are.

She spins on her heel and heads back inside without answering me, and she just made one thing very clear.

Whatever is going on between her and Justin doesn't matter. Because when it comes to the two of us...it's not over.

Chapter 21
Gabby

I can't focus on having fun after that exchange. When I saw him walking through the bar toward the doors, it set my blood on fire.

This thing between us...it's passionate, that's for damn sure. Whether it's love or hate remains to be seen. It started as love, but now I think I hate him. The fact that he's dangling himself in front of me constantly when I can't have him just solidifies that feeling.

He passed right by my table like I wouldn't see him. Everyone else at the table was laughing at the chugging contest between Brian and Chase, but I glanced away long enough to spot him.

Under Armour hat pulled down low. Tanned, strong arms. The chest I could lose myself in. The long legs covered in jeans. The firm torso covered by a black shirt with abs of marble underneath.

I didn't need to see his face to know it was him, and I was propelled by a vodka-induced rage to confront him.

And that confrontation didn't go so well. I wasn't sure why I was even out there other than the fact that I was a little drunk and I wanted to see him.

He's still so beautiful.

Too beautiful.

It's not fair.

He was mine for such a short time, and I just want to go back to the way things were. I just want a weekend at a hotel where we're two strangers who are falling in love.

I just want him back.

Is that too much to ask for?

I guess it is.

"You okay?" Justin asks when I get back to the table.

I close my eyes real tight as I try to ward off the tears, but it's futile.

"Let's get you home," he says.

I blow out a breath and shake my head. "That's where *he* will be," I whisper to him. I catch Chloe looking at us from across the table, and I'm sure she's wondering what we're whispering about as I look to be on the verge of tears. She's nice enough not to ask, but I'm getting to know everyone here at this table.

It won't be long before our friendship forces me to either confess or lie, and I don't want to lie to these people. But I can't exactly confess the truth, either.

"All the more reason for me to take you there," he says.

"Okay," I murmur. He picked me up and drove me here, and he's only had one drink the entire time we've been here. "Let's head out then."

"I'm gonna take Gabs home," he tells the rest of the group.

"You two are getting awfully cozy," Mackenzie says, and there's a clear accusation in her tone.

They don't know he's not into me.

Justin tosses an arm around me and pulls me in close. "Yeah we are." He gives an exaggerated wink to everyone at the table, and uproarious laughter follows us out the door toward his car.

I glance at the spot where Cooper stood a few minutes ago, and he's gone. I grab Justin's arm and squeeze it as we head toward his Jeep. "You don't have to lie to them for me."

"I didn't lie. We *are* cozy. They can interpret that however they want." He shrugs as he unlocks the doors and walks me to the passenger side. I hop in, and then he moves around to the driver's side and slides in behind the wheel.

"You're a good friend to me," I say softly.

"I feel like we have a lot in common. We're both lying to our parents. We're both unhappy. We're both at a crossroads. It's natural we'd gravitate toward each other." He pulls up some rap song for the ride home, and I wrinkle my nose.

"What is this?" I ask.

"Bad Bunny," he says.

"I've never heard of him."

"He's a Puerto Rican rapper."

"I'm not into rap music," I admit.

His hand flies to his chest. "What?" he asks, clearly horrified by my admission. "I'm not sure we can still be friends. What do you listen to?"

"Taylor Swift." I shrug.

"Like…exclusively?" he asks, surprised.

I nod.

He laughs, and then he changes the song to something off her newest album. "Me too. I just put the rap on to make myself seem cool since it's the thing."

"Taylor makes you way cooler." I lean over to bump his shoulder with mine, and we head toward home.

I let us in through the front door once we're home, and it's quiet. Dad's car wasn't out front, so he might not be home, and neither was Cooper's—but he was waiting for a ride from the bar. I'm not sure where he was headed.

We collapse together on the couch and put on some Netflix, and I must fall asleep on Justin's shoulder because some loud banging in the kitchen startles me awake.

"What the hell is that?" I ask.

"I think it's Cooper," Justin whispers. "He passed by a few minutes ago. Didn't say a word to me when he walked by but I'm thinking he's making something for dinner."

I listen a little more closely and recognize the sound of pots and pans banging together—the kind of noise like he's trying to get to the pan on the bottom of the drawer and everything else is stacked on top of it. And then the loud clatter of a plate being set onto the counter with a bit of aggression, along with some silverware.

The fridge door slamming shut.

The pantry door opening and closing.

The icemaker dispensing ice. And more ice. And still more— one of the loudest sounds in the entire kitchen.

The sound of liquid being poured into a glass and a glass bottle slamming down beside it onto the countertop.

He's stomping around the kitchen in a huff, and I feel a little guilty that he's probably extra huffy because he spotted me with my head on Justin's shoulder as I lay sleeping and my friend watched a movie.

It's complicated, this whole thing. I don't want him to feel hurt, and yet…he's the one causing the hurt. I guess I don't need to mislead him where Justin is concerned, but part of me feels good, like I'm getting revenge for him ending it when it's not what I want at all.

The other part of me feels like I should be honest with him, but every time we try to talk we just start yelling. Or he grabs me and pulls me into his arms, and I think he might change his mind, and then he doesn't.

The movie ends, and Justin heads out. I stand by the door for a beat as I debate going into the kitchen where I know he is or going upstairs to my room.

Upstairs is safer. Besides, I don't know if my dad's somewhere here at home, and I don't want him walking into the kitchen when we're inevitably yelling at each other.

I'm about to walk into my bedroom when I feel a hand on my arm pulling me back out into the hallway. I'm slammed up against the wall, pinned there by his hips, and a thrill rushes up my spine.

Adrenaline courses through me. I want this. I want *him*. I want him in a way I don't quite understand…in a way I've never wanted anyone before him, in a way I'll never want anyone after him.

His eyes lock onto mine, and the stormy blue depths is all I see. I stare into them, his full of anger and fear and hopelessness, and I'm frozen to the spot as I take a breath.

I smell him. I'm close enough to breathe in that woodsy scent, the smell that became so comforting to me so quickly. I'm close enough to see the hitch of his breath, the flapping of his pulse in his neck.

"What the fuck are you doing with that jackass?" he demands.

"It's not your business," I grit out thickly.

"You can do better."

I jut my chin upward a beat. "You mean like you?"

"You know it can't work between us."

"Why are you pushing so hard against it?" I ask him for the millionth time. There's a begging desperation to my tone, but he stands firm for a beat.

And then his mouth crashes down to mine.

Now this…*this* is a kiss.

It's hot and angsty and dramatic as his mouth opens and the urgency kicks in. His tongue moves against mine, one of his arms slinging around my waist as he hauls me closer to him, the other hand still perched on my arm. I kiss back with everything I have, wrapping my arms around his body, my fingertips reaching under his shirt so I can feel the warm, smooth skin of his back. I moan into him as he kisses me, pressing my body to him as closely as I can.

It's messy and wet, hot and sultry.

No space separates our bodies, and he shifts his hips so I can feel how hard he is for me, how ready he is. His mouth brutalizes mine with his kiss, teeth clashing together and tongues battering in some sort of epic battle that we're both winning.

Except we can't. Neither of us will win, not when he keeps building a stronger, taller wall between us.

And that's when we both hear it. The front door opens and closes. My father's voice rings loud and clear through the house as Cooper kisses me. "Gabriella?"

He pulls back, his eyes hazy as he drops his hand from my arm and unlaces his other arm from around me.

He takes a large step back, nearly bumping into the wall behind him. "I...I can't. I can't do this."

He's stuttering—unusually for the always cool and poised Cooper Noah, and I take a little pride in the fact that I'm the one who caused him to lose his cool.

"I can't resist you, but I have to fight this. I *have* to. Too many people are depending on me. I can't fuck it up." His voice is low and resigned. He doesn't want to walk away from me, from this, from *us*, but he has to. He's convinced himself of that, and even though he's having a hard time fighting against it, he's trying to make good on the commitments he made, and I'm throwing something that's nothing more than a friendship with a boy who's more interested in *him* than he is in *me* right in his face.

He steps away, down the hall, down the stairs, back to whatever food he was making in the kitchen, back to start a conversation with my father, and I stare after him until he's long gone, the scent of him still in my nostrils and the feel of his lips imprinted firmly on mine forever.

Chapter 22
Cooper

Maybe I should just live in a hotel until my house is ready.

Or maybe I could stay with Kaylee.

But moving out now would just look suspicious, and that's the opposite of what I'm trying to do here.

I've never felt more stuck in my life.

I could stay away—could hang out somewhere else, but I'm new to town. There's always action in Vegas, but the people I trust around these parts consist of Kaylee and Ben, who are busy with babies and the start of a football season; Danny, who I spend most of my time with except when he's busy banging somebody; and Troy, who I can't exactly confess my most recent heartbreak to given the fact that he's the one person I'm trying to hide it from.

I could go out, sure. I could meet people. I could make new friends pretty easily.

But it's hard when you're almost thirty-three and you own a status as a celebrity. I guess I could head to Troy's club to meet people in situations similar to mine, but I don't really want to. There's a stigma with a place like that, and even if I want to stay on the first floor, that doesn't mean everyone else will want to.

The season will start soon enough, and since Troy has unofficially named me team captain, I've started spending time sketching out details for building brotherhood through teamwork. He gave me an office near his where I can work, and I've gone in early every morning this week to work out and then to sit in my office watching film, strategizing, and getting to know the strengths of the players already assembled on the team as I do some research onto the short list of players Troy thinks we'll be acquiring in the expansion draft in a couple months.

Gabby doesn't have classes Thursday or Friday, so she's at the stadium bright and early, and I just finished my workout and a quick shower on Friday morning when Troy told me to pay a visit to Joanie's office.

The interns are all sitting at the round table, and Gabby is talking. I watch for a beat while she finishes what she says.

"I think StrongFitKids would best fit under Fan Experience if you'd like me to focus on that department next week." Her eyes drift to me at the conclusion of her sentence. Joanie turns around to see who Gabby is looking at, too.

"Sorry to interrupt," I say, stepping into the office, "but Troy said your team got back to you with the blueprints?"

"Right," she says. She turns to the interns. "I love that idea, Gabby. I'd like to put you and Chloe on that for next week along with Corporate Sponsorships because I think SFK really fits both. Justin and Brian in Broadcast, Chase and Mackenzie in…" She pauses as she runs down a list. "How about Game Operations? Excuse me for one minute." She turns back to me as I wonder what other departments the interns work in, but then I realize it doesn't matter. The fact is that she'll be working with Chloe on something and not Spongebob, so that's something.

Joanie pats Gabby's shoulder as she stands, and I see a bond between the two. Troy has confirmed that he's dating Joanie, and from over here, it looks like Gabby approves and accepts that relationship.

I'm happy for her. I know how her relationship is with her mother based on the things she confessed to me, so to see her have a positive female authority in her life can only be a good thing. I think of my own mother and what an impact she's had on my life, and I can't imagine not talking to her nearly every day. But Gabby seemed almost happy not to be talking to her mom—like the very thought of it stresses her out.

There's still a lot of mystery where all that is concerned, I guess.

"Come on over," Joanie says to me, and I meet her at her desk. She hands me a portfolio, and I take a look at the preliminary sketches of the kids' play area. "No ball pit, as requested, and an entire trampoline area with bouncy platforms between each station of the circuit."

I'm sure Gabby is gloating from her chair over at the round table with the other interns, but I force my focus on the paper in Joanie's hands. "This is incredible, Joanie. Thank you." I study it for a few beats.

"Can I see?" Gabby asks, standing from her chair.

Joanie nods. "I think it's important to get your feedback, too."

Gabby moves in beside me, and I can smell the vanilla in her hair.

My dick wakes up this close to her. He strains against my zipper. Goddamn, I miss her.

"Looks good to me," she says softly. "I love the trampolines."

She walks away and sits beside that jackass once again, and I suck in a breath and snap a photo of the blueprints. "I'll send these to Kaylee and Carla for any last-minute feedback but I think it's going to be a green light from SFK."

"Excellent," she says with a nod. "I'll wait to hear from you before sending it up to the next level. Is there anything else?"

I glance over at Gabby, and she's got her head bent toward Spongebob in conversation.

I clear my throat. "No, that's all. Thanks again." I'm not sure if Gabby is supposed to shadow me for the rest of the day, but I take the opportunity while she's busy in a meeting to head back to my office to get a little more work done.

And then I bolt the fuck out of the stadium before she gets the chance to come find me.

Troy was still at the stadium when I left, working away at all things baseball management, and I'm sure he would've liked me to stop in and touch base regarding teambuilding, but we have time.

It may be a big stadium, but today it felt like it wasn't quite big enough for both Gabby and me.

Troy wasn't home this morning when I woke up, and I've started to notice he rarely spends the night at the house. He's around here and there, but he must either be sleeping at Joanie's place or at the club—either that or he's out late, comes home for a few hours, and leaves again before the rest of the house is awake.

I talk to my mom once I'm back in the car. I keep it quick and leave out the details about how I'm feeling, but it always helps to hear her voice even if it's just for a quick check in.

I call Kaylee next.

"Did you look at the blueprints?" I ask when she answers. My ulterior motive is to get her to invite me over. I'd invite myself, but that's not really my style.

"I glanced real quick but Ellie's nanny is sick today so we're all just winging it and Hailey won't stop climbing the goddamn couch and I just got them down for naps and I'm about to take one myself."

"Sorry for bothering you," I say.

"Why would this be different than any other time? You're always bothering me," she teases, and I laugh.

"Right back at you, kid."

"You doing okay, Coopster?" she asks.

"I'm okay," I lie. She's got enough going on. She doesn't need me droning on about how heartsick I am over Gabby.

"You call me if you need anything," she says.

"I will," I assure her, but the truth is I *did* call her because I needed something but she's busy with twin babies and caught up in her own shit and I'm not going to burden her with my shit, too.

I swing by my house to check the progress, and there are two trucks in the street in front of the place, signaling that somebody's there working. I hang out in my car for a while as I dream up all the things I can do once I'm not fighting against myself every goddamn day.

I feel like I don't have anywhere else to go, so eventually I head back to Troy's place.

And when I pull into the driveway, I spot a car I haven't seen before…but the woman leaning up against it sure looks familiar.

"Stacy," I mutter as I pull in behind the white Lexus and put my car in park.

What the fuck is she doing here?

Chapter 23
Gabby

Joanie had interviews today for the final intern position, which means my spot was added in thanks to my father. I'm not sure how to feel about that.

She said she felt like she needed better organization with the intern program, so I suggested a focus department each week for us. This broadens our knowledge and it gives the different departments access to our skills, and apparently the idea never occurred to her. She's smart and great at what she does, but the interns were sort of thrust in her lap last-minute, so she's been struggling with where to place us.

The way she praised my idea felt wonderful.

My father has barely acknowledged that he's been seeing her, and I've certainly never seen them *together*, but the fact that someone in a semi-maternal position over me had something nice to say to me felt surprisingly good.

Any time I did something worthy of praise before, my narcissistic mother would either claim responsibility for it or she'd find something about it to nitpick.

This wasn't like that. It was a simple *I love that idea* followed by a hand on my shoulder.

Admittedly my normally sunny disposition has had a bit of a cloud over it since Cooper Noah broke up with me, but her words helped lighten those clouds just a little.

I felt something good pull at me again—a feeling I haven't felt since I turned around after digging around in the refrigerator and Cooper was standing in my dad's kitchen.

He was there to witness the moment, though, and that seemed to steal something from it. The clouds darkened a little again, and when he left, they seemed to settle in for the long haul.

"I've made a short list of all our departments here," she says, handing out slips of paper with all the departments listed. "Write your name on the top and rank the top five you think would most benefit you. I can't guarantee you'll get all of them, and this is still a general internship program, so you'll deal with every department at some point, but I'd like to place you a little better based on your strengths."

I'm not sure if this applies to me, too, or not since I've already been tapped to shadow Cooper and work on social media. Still, I glance over the list. Business development and analytics, baseball operations, marketing and social media, broadcasting, fan experience, guest services, community relations, corporate sponsorships, public relations, ticket operations, finance, planning and development, HR, IT and video…the list goes on. There are way more departments than I ever realized that are involved with a baseball team, and I look over my options.

I have no idea what I want out of my future. Working at a ballpark would be fun, sure, but I'm not sure how good a fit it is if it means I'm going to be around Cooper more often. I like the idea of working with my dad, but he'll be busy on the game side, not on the front office side.

And I don't really know all that much about baseball. I'm learning, and I'm a fairly quick study, but that doesn't mean this is a good fit for me.

I mark marketing and social media as my top choice, followed by community relations and business analytics. I like the fan experience and corporate sponsorships, too, so I add those on as my fourth and fifth choices, though most of the options listed sound interesting to me in some capacity.

I glance over at Justin's list. He has numbers listed next to business, marketing, corporate sponsorships, finance, and IT. I almost erase my choices and choose the same as him so we can work together, but I don't. I want to learn from this internship, and picking the same things as my friend doesn't seem like the best way to do that. Besides, finance and IT sound boring.

I guess I'm just finding myself clinging onto him, and it's as I stare down at my paper that I realize that. My entire life, I've had difficulty choosing direction. I defer to other people when I don't want to make a decision, and I become clingy when someone shows me positive attention.

Maybe that's what I'm doing with Cooper. Maybe it was never about love at all between the two of us, but someone stepped in, made me feel good, and I clung to that.

Maybe it's time for me to let him go.

It's what he wants, and I've been stuck in neutral the past week as I've tried to deal with the loss.

I've also spent my whole life believing that in order to matter, you need to be the best. It's why I'm a perfectionist, and it means a lot to me to be recognized for the things I work hard at.

It's why I found my father. I wanted him to be proud of me since I never felt like I was good enough for my mother.

It was terrifying when I started the search. My mother convinced me he abandoned me, and I spent my life believing that. I spent my life nurturing huge abandonment issues all because of my mother's lies.

Instead of giving me that praise I always craved, my mother was the best at finding something wrong. At prom, the night I felt most beautiful in my entire life…she didn't like the way I did my hair.

When I was named salutatorian at my high school graduation, she asked who valedictorian was instead of congratulating me. I'd never felt like more of a failure even though salutatorian was something that should have been celebrated.

That's how it went my entire life.

Is it any wonder I wanted to get away from her the moment I found my father?

Is it any wonder I fell so hard and so fast for the wrong person? And now that I think about it, does the fact that Cooper is twelve years older than me play into it, too? I never *looked* at him as a father figure. He wasn't…but the fact that someone older in an authoritative position made me feel so damn good about myself might speak to my issues.

Or maybe it speaks more loudly to how I should *face* those issues. Maybe my relationships will *always* fail until I can resolve the problems that I cover with a sunny disposition.

But I have no idea how to resolve any of it. The fear of rejection and abandonment. The fear of trusting the wrong person or being taken advantage of. The fear of being punished for my mistakes. The fear of falling short, or of coming in second, or of being a failure.

Maybe it starts with choosing a path instead of being indecisive about what I want out of my future.

I like marketing, and I like social media. I put a big circle around that department on the list, and I write a little note beside it. *Very interested in pursuing this in my future.*

I realize that will force Joanie and me to spend more time together since she's the head of the marketing department...but maybe that's not such a bad thing. We've started to bond even though neither of us has acknowledged her relationship with my father, and maybe we can sit down and have a good, honest talk.

Or not. The thought of doing that and being rejected creeps in. The thought of growing close to Joanie only to see my father end things with her makes me nearly physically feel the abandonment before it even happens.

Maybe I should start with an honest talk with my father first. He's been busy, and I've been busy, and we haven't connected as much lately as we did the first couple years I lived with him.

I send him a text while the others finish filling out their preferences.

Me: *Can we do dinner soon? I miss seeing you.*
His reply comes quick.
Dad: *Of course. Tonight, five o'clock, Desmonds?*
Me: *It's a date.*

Chapter 24
Cooper

I step down from my truck, and I can't help but wonder what I ever saw in Stacy aside from a pretty face.

Now all I see is the ugliness. I know what she did while we were together, and it was enough to make me want to leave Los Angeles and never look back.

It's with that realization that something connects in my brain.

She is the reason why I didn't want to keep playing.

I found out she was cheating on me a few months after my injury. Rather than being there to help me through it, she bolted into someone else's arms.

Los Angeles felt too small for the two of us, so I trekked down to San Diego to rehab my arm after the surgery, and I stayed there.

I didn't want to go back even if it meant I wouldn't get to play any longer, and the woman standing in Troy's driveaway was the cause of that.

I blow out a breath as I walk up beside her. "What are you doing here?"

Our eyes meet as she slides her phone into the back pocket of her leggings. "I came to win you back."

I let out a grunt that I can't even bother to fill with any sort of merriment. "Fat chance, Stace. You lost that game when you slept with Hamilton."

She sighs, her eyes turned down to the ground and a forlorn look across her face. I keep my distance because I will *not* get wrapped up in her tangled web ever again.

"You just…you wanted all these things I wasn't ready for back then," she says. Her tone has an edge of begging to it, but she can beg all she wants. It'll never happen. "You were talking kids, and back then, I was scared to be a mom. I didn't think I could do it.

But I've changed, baby. I want those things, too. And I want them with you."

It strikes me as I listen to her beg that she's the polar opposite of Gabby when it comes to certain physical attributes. She has short blonde hair and brown eyes to Gabby's nearly black hair and green eyes, but she's tall and thin like Gabby. She doesn't walk in like a ray of sunshine the way Gabby does. Instead, it feels like the skies opened and a cloud settled over her white Lexus the way Olaf's snow flurries follow him around in the second *Frozen* movie.

Yeah, so I watched it with my nephews a few years ago.

And I liked it.

I got a little choked up at the end, and I will fight anybody who has a goddamn word to say to me about it.

"That's nice, but I no longer want them with you, and the more time we've spent apart, the more I've come to realize that I *never* wanted them with you." I shrug.

She looks momentarily shocked at my words, but she takes a step forward toward me rather than my words having the effect of pushing her back.

"You don't mean that, Cooper. You're just upset, but we can get through it." She runs her fingertips along my chest, and in my periphery, I hear a vehicle moving along the street behind me. It stops for a second, and I'm tempted to turn around. I'm tempted to start screaming for help.

But I don't. Instead, I fist her wrist in my hand. The vehicle behind me peels off, and I keep my eyes trained on my ex-girlfriend's face.

I shake my head. "No, that's not it." I let out a heavy sigh as I drop her wrist. "You hurt me, Stacy, but I'm not sure it mattered. There's a reason we were together five years and I never once actually considered proposing to you. It was a waste of time, and I actually think I should be *thanking* you for cheating on me. It helped drive us to the end, and I'm much happier here on the other side."

"The bags under your eyes tell a different story," she retorts.

"I'm sure they do, but they have nothing to do with you. They're not your business anymore. Now if you'll excuse me, I have shit to do that doesn't involve you."

"I drove all the way from LA and you won't even invite me in?" she whines.

God, what did I ever see in her?

I nod and twist my lips. "Yep. That pretty much sums it up." I move to walk past her, and she grabs onto my arm.

"Coop, wait."

I turn and look at her. "For what, Stace? You stole five years of my life, cheated on me, and now you come crawling back because you heard I'm back in the game?" I shake my head. "I see right through you. It's over. I've moved on. I fell in love with someone who made me feel valued."

"I always made you feel valued," she says, her tone suggestive.

I shake my head and offer her a sad smile. "You valued what I did for a living. You never valued *me*. If you did, you wouldn't have run to Alex Hamilton's bed right after we broke up, and you wouldn't have snuck into it before we did, either." I turn to head back inside, and her voice halts me.

She sighs. "I'm pregnant."

I stand for a beat and stare at the door in front of me. So close. So goddamn close to getting inside without her confession.

She says the words as if they'll be the thing that changes my mind.

"Congratulations," I say, turning back toward her. "Whose is it?"

She presses her lips together, and that tells me a whole lot. She used to do that every time she didn't want to tell me something, and in this case...I think she doesn't want to admit she doesn't know who the baby belongs to.

But it's not my circus, not my monkeys, and no longer my problem. "I hope you figure it out," I say gently. "I do wish you all the best, but a future with me is absolutely out of the question. Go back to LA. Go back to Alex. Take care of yourself, but please, Stacy...leave me alone."

With those words, I head into Troy's house without inviting her in and close the door behind me.

Chapter 25
Gabby

Cooper was holding that woman's hands when I drove by. I went slowly and blinked a few times as if it would clear the image out of my vision, but it didn't go away. It didn't change. He was holding her hands, and they were talking, and I idled for a beat as I debated whether to step in and blow that up as I claimed Cooper as mine or if I should just stay out of it.

Tears burned behind my eyes as I opted to stay out of it.

I can't claim Cooper as mine because *he isn't mine* to claim.

I peeled off to meet my dad rather than stopping home first for a quick change of clothes before dinner like I'd planned.

Once I was off my dad's street, I pulled off to the side of the road and cried.

I get it. I'm throwing another man in his face, making him think Justin and I are a thing, and he's taking that as his signal to move on.

But I don't *want* him to move on. I want him to be with me.

He didn't throw this woman in my face. Instead, he's meeting her when he thinks I won't be around. I ducked out of the office a little early to stop home, and I caught them when I wasn't meant to.

My chest feels heavy as I drive toward the restaurant, but what can I do?

He's made it clear we can't be together. How do I keep fighting for him and playing these games when I'm just going to lose? It takes two people to *want* a relationship, and I'm flying solo here. I can't force him to be with me.

I arrive a little early, and I don't see my dad's car just yet.

I take the opportunity to finally run a search on Cooper Noah.

And sure enough, a few pictures in, I spot her. The woman he was talking to just now was his ex.

Did he invite her here to get back together with her? He said he never would, but he also made me feel like he'd never break my heart, so clearly he's a man who changes his tune on a whim.

I nearly drop my phone when I hear a knock at the window, and I spot my dad standing on the other side.

I cut the engine and open the door, praying he didn't see what I was just looking at. "You scared me!" I say, clutching my heart not because of the fear but because it hurts from seeing Cooper with another woman.

He chuckles a little. "Sorry. That wasn't my intent." He wraps an arm around my shoulders and squeezes me in a side hug, and we walk together into the restaurant.

It's not crowded yet at this early hour, but my dad is a busy man, and if an early dinner is when I can have his undivided attention, then so be it.

We're seated, and he orders a tumbler of gin. I make a face as I order a glass of wine, and he chuckles.

We glance through the menu and place our orders before he cuts to the chase. "What's been going on with you, Gabriella?" he asks by way of starting the conversation.

As I'd rather not discuss my current heartbreak with his star player, I throw the question back to him. "Not much. How about you, Father?"

He chuckles. "Just running businesses and assembling an all-star baseball team."

Running businesses.

Does he mean that sex club?

Is now the time to ask? Or does that fall under the category of *things we don't want to know about our parents?*

"And spending time with your girlfriend?" I ask.

His lips thin into a flat line. "Not my best kept secret, is it?"

I laugh as I shake my head, and then I reach over and squeeze his forearm. "I'm happy for you, Dad. I want you to be happy. I want you to find love, and if it's Joanie, then that's great. I love her, and I love her for you. But I'm finding myself growing closer to her because of this job, and I don't want to get caught in the middle if it isn't what I think it is. Do you know what I mean?"

He nods and blinks, his eyes moving down to the table. "It's going to last." His eyes move back to mine. "We have an unusual relationship, but one thing is for certain. It will last. We're not ready to take it public in large part because of our work situation, but there are other factors at play."

"What are they?" I press.

He glances around. "I'd rather not discuss them here."

I can't help but wonder if it has to do with the club Cooper insinuated he owns. I don't know how to research that since it seems like the kind of place that would be off the grid, and I also don't really want to ask him about it.

I let him leave it at that.

"So this thing between you and Joanie…it's pretty serious?" I ask.

He nods. "We've been together almost a year, and I've never met anyone like her. She's a hard worker, the kind that goes above and beyond for her job, and so she gets that I need to be that way, too. We just have an understanding between us that I've never found with another woman."

"Are you going to marry her?"

He presses his lips together again. "I plan to someday," he answers honestly. "But it's complicated."

"All relationships are," I murmur.

"Ain't that the damn truth?"

I laugh, and we clink our glasses together in a toast of understanding.

While I feel like I got some answers about my dad's love life, I'm left with even more questions after his vague responses. At least he confirmed they're together, and he loves her, and it's long-term. Beyond that, I'm not sure if it's necessary for me to know more.

But that doesn't mean I'm not as curious as a cat to find out the answers.

He clears his throat. "What's complicated about yours?"

My cheeks flush, and he smirks.

"You think you can get away with asking about me and not get the same sort of grilling?"

I wrinkle my nose. "I was kind of hoping I could."

He shakes his head. "No such luck, my girl. Is it Justin?"

I narrow my eyes at him. "What if it was? How would you feel about me dating someone I'm working with?" It's my way of fishing for whether he'd be okay with a Gabriella-Cooper connection…because if he *is* okay with it and green lights it, then maybe we actually could be together. Maybe we wouldn't have to lie about it the way Cooper seems convinced we would.

He lifts a shoulder. "It'd be a little hypocritical of me to say you couldn't when I just admitted I'm doing that very thing, don't you think?"

"Good point. But we're both interns. What if I wanted to date a player?"

His eyes dart to mine, and there's a little something close to anger there. "Terrible idea. Ballplayers are assholes, and they're gone eight months out of the year. You deserve better."

My face must fall because he adds more.

"Why? You got a crush on Danny Brewer or something?"

I grunt out a laugh. Not exactly.

"What if I did?" I tinker with the stem on my wineglass.

He shakes his head as he palms his tumbler of gin. "That would be a hard no. I've seen the way Brewer gets around. Besides, he's way too old for you."

"How old is he?" It's a test that has way more to do with Cooper than with Danny Brewer.

"Twenty-six."

Noted. Twenty-six is *way too old* for me.

I wonder how he'd feel about almost thirty-three.

Which reminds me…Cooper's birthday is tomorrow. And that's when it hits me.

That's why his ex is here. She's giving him a birthday treat—the kind I was planning to give him for his birthday.

"You look positively despondent I said no to Brewer."

I obviously can't say it has nothing to do with Danny Brewer and everything to do with whatever Cooper is doing with his ex, so I just shrug.

This entire conversation gave me plenty of insight about how my father really feels about me potentially dating one of his players. It's a hard no from him, which means maybe Cooper was right all along.

With the combination of this conversation with my dad and what I saw in front of the house earlier, what little hope I was holding onto that somehow we'd fix this evaporates. The hope we'd figure it out and make it right and end up together is blown to bits all in a matter of a half hour.

I don't really know where to go after dinner, but I know I can't go back home. Not with this new realization. Not with knowing he's in the room right beside me…maybe with another woman.

It's too much to bear.

I get in the truck and call Mia.

248

"What's up girl?" she answers, and I very nearly burst into tears but somehow manage to hold them off.

"Can we have a girls' night?" I beg.

"I'm getting ready for a night out with Dylan," she says. "I'm so sorry. Tomorrow night?"

And that's when *very nearly* turns into the ugly cries I've managed to keep at bay all night.

"Oh shit," she murmurs. "Come over right now."

I heave in a few deep breaths before I make my way over to Mia's apartment.

She pulls me into a hug the minute I'm in her doorway, and I notice immediately that she's definitely date night ready.

"Oh, God. I'm so sorry," I say as I look her up and down. "You look gorgeous. I'll just go. I'm okay."

"Don't be silly. Hoes before bros, right?" She slings an arm around my neck and forces me into her apartment.

I let out a soft giggle.

"What happened?"

"A variety of events crashed together in a way that forced me to realize it's really over with Cooper. I was holding out hope this whole time that there was still a chance for us, and then I saw him with another woman. Right after that, I met my dad for dinner, and he made it clear he'd never be okay with me dating a baseball player, and add those two things together and it just feels like a shitty night." I'm rambling, and she sets a hand on my arm.

"I'm sorry," she says. "How can I make it better?"

"Alcohol?" I pad over to her couch and collapse. "I don't really know. I don't think I'll *ever* feel better about losing the best thing that ever happened to me. We came so close, and we had a good run. My only option now is to move on, but I don't know how to do that."

"Alcohol," she says.

"I might be able to help," Dylan says, appearing as if from out of nowhere.

I glance over at him then cover my eyes in mortification. "I didn't know you were here. Sorry for ruining your date night."

"You didn't. You just made it a double date instead."

I move my hands from my eyes, which I narrow at Dylan. "What are you talking about?"

Mia laughs. "He invited Hansen over."

I let out a sound that sort of resembles a strangled grunt. "Hansen? Are you serious? Is this because of the internship? Are you punishing me?"

Dylan chuckles. "No. It has nothing to do with that, but by the way, I'm a finalist for the final spot. Hanson has always had a thing for you." His words are flippant, as if we all already knew this fact.

"He has not!" I practically screech.

"Oh yes, he has," Mia says.

Dylan sits on the loveseat and Mia perches on his lap as if there's nowhere else to sit in the room. Mia and Dylan met when she went to a party at his off-campus house. One of his roommates is Greg Hansen, and while he's nice enough and decidedly cute, he's not my type. For one thing, he's a year younger than me, and I think I've established pretty clearly that I prefer older guys.

Aside from that, though…since age supposedly doesn't matter to me, he's super into gaming and wants to find a girl who will game with him twenty-four-seven.

That girl is not me.

"I'm happy to inform you he's on his way over right now," Dylan says with a little too much triumph in his tone.

"He's gonna make me play Minecraft, isn't he?"

Dylan laughs. "No, he's not gonna do that. At least I told him not to."

"I'm going to need some tequila for this," I tell Mia.

She gets up and moves over toward the kitchen, returning a moment later with my wish granted.

Shortly thereafter, the rest of the night gets a little blurry.

Chapter 26
Cooper

I can't help when my eyes automatically turn to her bedroom as I pass by it. The room is empty and the bed is made.

I glance at my watch. It's early, and I know Gabby. She wouldn't be up this early on a Saturday.

I don't even know why *I* am up. I'm guessing it has something to do with the fact that I listened all night for her to come home. I fell asleep at some point, but I never did hear her come in when I was awake.

Her truck isn't in the driveway, another signal that she never came home.

Did she spend the night with Spongebob?

The thought fills me with rage. I head toward Troy's workout room and attempt to get some of the anger out on the punching bag. It doesn't help.

I work my ass off until I'm an exhausted, sweaty mess, and I guess this is thirty-three.

It feels empty and cold.

I have a few messages from friends and women and family. My brother sent me a video text of his entire family singing "Happy Birthday" to their favorite uncle. They're the perfect fucking family, and he has the perfect fucking life, and it's just another reminder that I'm now officially edging toward my mid-thirties and I'm still alone.

I'm a little worried I'm turning into a cranky old man. I take a quick shower and make myself a screwdriver for breakfast.

It's my birthday. I can do what I want.

I shouldn't feel broken over the fact that she moved on when I'm the idiot who pushed her to do it, but seeing Stacy yesterday was a real wake-up call.

You sort of expect feelings to come rushing back when you run into your ex, whether they're feelings of love or hate or something in between. But when I saw Stacy, I just felt…resigned. I didn't care. I didn't have the fire to stand there and fight with her. I just wanted her to leave. She's caused me enough pain and enough trouble, including giving up the future I wanted for myself while I wasted so much time with her.

When I think of Gabby, though, I don't feel resigned. I feel fire. I feel heat. I feel need. I feel *love*, and every time I see her, those feelings only get stronger.

I don't know what to do.

I need to stay away, but I don't know if I can.

And now…knowing that maybe she has moved on, maybe she's spending the night in another man's bed—and I use the term *man* loosely for someone who's barely out of his teen years—the thought causes a pain in my chest the likes of which I've never felt before.

I didn't feel it when I found out Stacy was cheating on me, and I'm starting to think maybe it's because I knew the end with Stacy was inevitable.

But I never truly saw the end coming with Gabby.

I've only been in Vegas a week. It feels like a fucking decade.

I just want time to pass so I can get back on the field and get over all this and get my mind right again.

But time is a cruel bitch that steals so much from us, and my only choice is to wait it out.

The doorbell rings as I'm finishing up breakfast, and I set my dishes in the sink before I head over to answer. I peek through the peephole in case it's a salesman, though in this gated neighborhood that would be fairly unusual.

And when I peek through that peephole, I spot someone I'm utterly shocked to see standing there.

Maybe even more shocked than seeing Stacy standing in Troy's driveway yesterday.

I open the door, and I glance at his shirt. I force myself not to roll my eyes. "Spongebob," I say in greeting. "What are you doing here?"

"Hey, uh, I'm here to see Gabby. Is she around?"

My brows shoot up in confusion as a pulse of relief seems to shoot through my spine. "She didn't spend the night with you?"

His brows dip and a shock of something seems to flash in his eyes, like he's supposed to play the part and he's not…but then he glances away from me as he shakes his head. "Uh, no. I guess I'll just talk to her later."

He scampers away, and I'll admit I'm just the tiniest bit worried about her since she didn't come home last night and she wasn't with the number one suspect. But I also know she has a lot of friends here. Hell, the night I met her, she was out with friends. My best guess is she spent the night at one of their places, and she'll be back soon.

I'm not wrong.

I do the dishes and set them in the dishwasher, and then I make a plan for my day. I grab my laptop to study some more film, but first I send out a few texts to friends seeing if anyone wants to meet for some high stakes gambling tonight at Caesars. I get hits back from a few friends.

And it's as I'm texting with Danny on the couch in the family room when I hear her truck pull up.

Troy isn't home, and my best guess is that he spent the night at the club with Joanie again.

It'll be just the two of us, and I'm not sure what to do with that.

The door opens, and she walks in. She's wearing the same clothes she wore yesterday, and she looks exhausted…like she drank way too much last night and is suffering the consequences this morning because of it. The usual sunshine that surrounds her seems to be missing today.

"Good morning," I mutter, unable to muster up any sort of sunshine myself.

"Hey," she grunts.

"You need some ibuprofen?" I ask, a little teasing in my tone.

"I can get them." She pads over to the cabinet where Troy keeps medicine in the kitchen and helps herself to a few pills. She disappears up the stairs, and I hear the shower running.

I open my laptop and watch some footage from games with Rush Ross as I figure out where we'd want him in our line-up. He's not a closer, but depending who we pick up from the draft, he'll probably fill either our number one or number two spot with his fastball.

I'm pausing and zooming in on one of his pitches when Gabby walks back into the room over an hour later.

"Feeling better?" I ask, closing my laptop lid and setting it beside me.

"A little," she says absently. "I laid down for a bit after my shower, and now I'm just hungry."

"Want me to make you something?" I ask, getting up from the couch and walking toward the kitchen behind her.

"Why are you being so nice to me?" she asks, narrowing her eyes at me.

I shrug. "You seem like you might've had a rough night."

"Yeah, lots of drinking with Justin."

I raise a brow. "Yeah?"

She nods. "We had a really fun night."

"You stayed over there with him?" I press.

She presses her lips together and nods, her eyes defiant as they move toward mine.

I move in a little closer to her, and she backs up until her backside bumps into the counter. I keep moving closer until I've got her boxed in. I set my arms on the counter and lean down, getting in her face as I smell her fresh vanilla after her shower.

I breathe her in deeply for a beat, and then I say, "Oh did you? Then why did he come by here asking for you this morning?"

Her eyes widen as she looks caught, but before she can come up with any sort of defense, I plow forward.

"Don't fucking play games with me, Gabby. Where were you last night?" I move so my face is right in front of hers.

"None of your business."

"Where were you?" I demand again.

"At Mia's." Her voice has an edge of fear in it, and something about her showing vulnerability pushes me to take her and make her mine, to mark her and protect her. To hell with the commitments and what Troy might think. I fucking need her like I need to breathe, and I will not stop until I get the truth out of her.

"Are you sleeping with Justin?" I demand, my lips centimeters from hers.

"No," she says softly.

"What's going on with the two of you?"

Her eyes flick to my lips. "We're just friends."

My lips crash down to hers, and she moans as she gives in, her lips parting to mine and our tongues languidly brushing against each other's.

We both hear a key slide into the front door. We don't have much time, and I don't know what to do. I told her not to play games, and two seconds later I kissed her after I told her time and again that I couldn't do this.

She pulls back first, resting her palms gently on my chest for a beat before she pushes me away. "I never meant anything to you, so why do you care who I'm sleeping with?"

"Goddammit, Gabby, you know that's a lie," I say, frustration stabbing into me like a million tiny knives all at once. I hear the door open, and I lower my voice to a whisper as I fight to finish this conversation. "I don't know what to do. I fucking love you so much, but we can't be together."

"I don't think we have a choice," she says, and her eyes are still hot on mine when her father walks into the kitchen.

To be continued in Book 3, FLYBALL

Chapter 1
Gabby

He's kissing me, and I never want it to stop, but the key sliding into the front door lock fills the silence in the kitchen.

I pull back and rest my hands on his chest. Confusion swirls all around me. He tells me one thing then does another, and I'm getting freaking whiplash from the constant change in direction. I push him back out of my orbit because I can't think straight when he's this close to me, but one thing rings true. "I never meant anything to you, so why do you care who I'm sleeping with?"

If I *did* mean something to him, if this wasn't just a fling to him…wouldn't he fight?

But he won't. He's just laying down and dying, and my only choice here is to lay it all on the line.

"Goddammit, Gabby, you know that's a lie." His tone is fierce, and I see some exasperation there at my words. Maybe he *does* have some fight left in him, or maybe he's back together with his ex.

We both hear the front door open.

He gets a few more whispered words in. "I don't know what to do. I fucking love you so much, but we can't be together."

I don't know what to do.

I fucking love you so much.

A piece of my broken heart latches onto those words.

If there's still love there between us, then that means we still have a chance.

"I don't think we have a choice," I say, our eyes locked when my dad walks into the kitchen.

My dad turns the corner and pauses as he sees us standing there facing off. He freezes a beat, and I swear he eyes me with a bit of suspicion.

Does he know?

Does he suspect something?

My heart races.

Cooper turns away first, breaking the connection, and I have no idea where we stand right now.

"Good morning," my dad says as if he didn't just interrupt one of the most intense moments of my life. He whistles a little to himself as he moves toward the refrigerator and grabs the carton of orange juice, and maybe that look of suspicion was all in my imagination.

Enough space must span between the two of us not to clue my father into what's really happening between us, but I just went from hopeless to hopeful in a matter of seconds.

"Isn't today a big day for you, Cooper?" my dad asks.

Oh, shit. It's his birthday, and I haven't even wished him a happy one yet. I keep my mouth shut, though, since I'm probably not supposed to know details like that about our houseguest.

Cooper nods, his eyes bouncing over to my dad.

"Any big plans?" my dad asks, and I grab two glasses from the cabinet so my dad can pour me some juice, too. I nod toward Cooper as if to ask if he'd like one as well, and he shakes his head.

"I'm meeting some buddies at Caesars Palace tonight."

My dad is facing the refrigerator, and Cooper's eyes fall to me again. He raises his brows, and I'm not sure if he's inviting me or if he's making some other sort of comment with those brows.

Either way, I know we need to talk. *Happy birthday*, I mouth to him without making a sound.

One side of his mouth lifts. *Thanks*, he mouths back.

"What's the big day?" I ask for my father's benefit.

"Old man Noah over here is another year closer to his midlife crisis," my dad says.

"Old man?" Cooper repeats, raising his eyebrows at my dad. "Last I checked, you're nearly a decade older than me."

My dad laughs. "I never claimed I wasn't in the middle of my own midlife crisis. What do you think that little red Corvette in the garage is?"

"A tribute to the late, great Prince?" I suggest.

Cooper barks out a laugh, and I can't help my own giggle that he got a kick out of my joke.

My dad's phone starts to ring, and he glances at his watch to see who's calling. "Excuse me. I need to take this." He heads out of the kitchen and down the hall toward the office, and we both hear his office door click shut.

Cooper's eyes fall to mine. They're so blue, and they have all this hope in them when before all seemed so lost.

"We should talk," Cooper murmurs.

I nod, pressing my lips together.

"Stay with me tonight at Caesars."

My brows dip as my eyes dart toward the hallway my dad just disappeared down. "To talk?"

He clears his throat, and my eyes slide back to his. When our gazes lock, fire burns between us. "To figure this out."

It's the place where we first met, and maybe it'll be the place where we reconnect.

I nod. "Okay."

I try not to allow too much hope into my heart, but I can't help it. It balloons inside me in anticipation of tonight.

"I'll text you my room details once I check in, and I'll leave a key for you at concierge."

I snag my bottom lip between my teeth as my thighs clench together. I know what this means...or at least I *think* I do.

He takes a step toward me and his gaze moves to my lips. "Stop biting it. I need it soft and ready for what I have planned."

A soft gasp escapes me, and he chuckles.

"I thought we were getting together tonight to *figure it out*." I put air quotes around the words he literally just said to me.

"Oh, we are. But I estimate it'll take all of ten seconds to come to an agreement, and then we'll have the rest of the night ahead of us." His words are a flash of the old Cooper—the one I fell in love with. The one who made me feel like together, anything is possible. The one who didn't know I was Troy's daughter.

He drops his lips to mine for a soft kiss, one that only serves to drive the need between us to even more intense levels, and then he backs away just when I was about to open my mouth.

My dad is right down the hall.

It would be wrong to brush my tongue against his here in the kitchen.

But maybe I don't care. If being wrong feels this good, then I don't want to be right.

He chuckles at the look on my face. "Save that feeling for tonight, and maybe do a little hydrating since I'm planning a fairly intense workout this evening."

My jaw slackens. I have an idea of what he has planned, and I'm ready for it. Whatever it is.

Chapter 2
Gabby

The text came through a little while ago, and I've been pacing around my bedroom ever since.

Cooper left to go to his birthday shindig with his buddies, and I stayed behind to pack an overnight bag and try to come to terms that this is in fact reality and not some crazy dream I'm having.

Cooper: *Booked penthouse, Augustus tower. Key waiting for you at concierge. I'll be up at eleven.*

He'll be up at eleven.

That gives me way too much time to kill.

It gives my brain time to overanalyze every potential detail about this night.

Is this really about making up? Or is it a chance for us to talk to each other without the risk of my dad walking in on us—to have a real and honest conversation about why we can't be together, or about why he was with his ex yesterday?

Does he want me there naked and waiting?

Or is he bringing friends back with him?

I opt not to be naked and waiting just in case, but even if we *were* to somehow get back together, which is what it felt like was going to happen, certainly he wouldn't flaunt it in front of his friends before we get the chance to talk to my dad.

Maybe I've gone nuts and I read something into it that I shouldn't have.

Either way, in four long hours, I'll find out the answers.

I pace.

I pack my bag.

I pace some more.

I dance around my room as I try to burn the nervous energy.

I hydrate.

I eat a light meal.

I hydrate some more, dance some more, try to watch a movie but can't.

Mia texts me.

Mia: *Greg wants to see you again.*

Me: *He's really sweet but I'm just not quite ready to get into something.*

I don't mention anything about tonight in fear of jinxing it.

Mia: *You're going to break his heart.*

I'm not sure why she's pushing me onto Greg, but I don't want to be his girl-gamer. She's just trying to help, I'm sure, and maybe she wants another couple to hang out with, but it's not going to be Greg and me. It's *never* going to be Greg and me, and it wasn't even a possibility *before* I met Cooper. Now, though? Even less of a possibility.

Me: *I'm sorry.*

I leave it at that, and I'm sure she's mad at me, but I have bigger things on the horizon and she'll get over it.

And then it's finally ten-fifteen, the time I told myself would be appropriate to head out.

It'll give me time to get there, valet my car, and grab the key from concierge before heading up. It'll give me a minute to check the place out, a minute to take a deep breath and compose myself, a minute to overanalyze just a little more as if I haven't done that enough over the last four hours.

When I finally arrive and get a valet ticket for my car, I head inside and spot the concierge. I give the man standing there my name, and he hands me an envelope. Inside is a keycard and the room number along with a map to help me find the right tower.

It's only ten-forty when I step off the elevator and head down the fancy hallway, and when I flash my key in front of the panel on the door, it opens before I even hear it unlock.

For a second, I jump back, a little startled that I have the wrong room.

But then my eyes meet his.

Nope. This is definitely the right one.

"I was hoping you'd get here early," Cooper says, opening the door wider to allow me to step in. He's wearing jeans and a black shirt, and his arms stretch the fabric at his biceps as if he's gained muscle since the last time we were lucky enough to be this close.

It was only a little over two weeks ago when he came back to town to look at houses and we spent the weekend together.

It feels like a lifetime ago.

He closes the door behind me, and I'm suddenly nervous. He pulls my overnight bag from my shoulder and sets it in the entryway, and I walk into the room and look around.

It's not a room.

It's a freaking condo.

It's bigger than Mia and Chelsea's apartment, and from where I stand, I see at least three different sitting areas and a doorway that must lead into a bedroom. In front of me is Vegas at night.

Lights flash before my eyes, and I spot everything across the street from the Eiffel Tower to my right over to the High Roller Ferris Wheel to the left.

But I can't focus on the view for long as Cooper moves in behind me. He doesn't touch me, but I spot his reflection in the window beside me.

I turn to face him. "Did you have fun with your friends?"

He shrugs. "It was fine."

"Just fine?"

"I was thinking about you. This." He waves a hand in the air, and then he moves toward the couch that faces this gorgeous view and he sits. "I was restless and anxious."

"What about now?" I ask. I move to perch beside him.

"I told you earlier, Gabby. I love you. Deeply. In a way that didn't quite hit me until something happened yesterday. I keep trying to do the right thing. I keep trying to fight against this, but maybe I've been wrong all along and the right thing isn't what I think it is." He sighs, obviously still tormented.

"What happened yesterday?" I ask. There's a certain desperation in my voice, something I don't try to hide, but I'm hoping he can explain away what I saw.

He clears his throat. "My ex showed up uninvited. She must've seen the press release that I'm playing again, and suddenly she was interested in getting back together."

"And?" I ask.

"And I told her she could take the next broom back to LA where she came from."

I can't help my giggle at that, but the sobering reality is that I was affected when I saw him with her. Knowing that it wasn't what I thought it was seems to quell a bit of the fears that plowed into me yesterday.

"I saw you with her on my way to dinner with my dad last night," I say. I'm not sure why I'm leading with that fact, but I want to get it off my chest before we move forward.

"How did it make you feel?" he asks.

Maybe he's fishing, and it might mark the first time I realize that it's not just women who need reassurance in relationships. Cooper walks around with all the confidence of a guy who knows he'll get what he wants, but that doesn't mean he doesn't clamor for me to express those things to him the same way I want him to express it to me.

"It looked like you were holding her hands, and it made me rage. It made me hurt. It made me lose all hope. And then I had to go to dinner with my dad."

"I'm sorry," he says softly. "I never want you to feel that way, even less so because of fucking Stacy." He slings an arm around my shoulder and pulls me in for a side hug. "What did your dad have to say?"

I take a step back to hit him with the truth. "Essentially what I got from our conversation is that he wouldn't be okay with me dating one of his players, and he thinks Danny Brewer is too old for me."

"Brewer? You asked him about *Brewer*?"

I shake my head. "I asked him what he'd think about me dating a baseball player, and he told me he'd want better for me. That players were assholes who were gone eight months out of the year."

He lifts his shoulder, conceding. "He isn't wrong about that."

I nod. "I know. But then he asked if I had a crush on Danny, to which he said he's too old for me anyway."

"He's seven years younger than me," Cooper says flatly.

"I know. So whatever we decide here tonight, I need you to be aware that my father can't know about it."

"We're on the same page there." He sighs again. "This sucks. I don't want to keep the best thing that's ever happened in my life from anybody, let alone one of my good friends...one of the guys who's the reason I came out here in the first place."

I point to my chest. "Me?"

His brows knit together in confusion.

"I'm the best thing that's ever happened in your life?" My heart races as I think I understood his meaning, but maybe I'm wrong. Of course I'm wrong. This guy has played professional baseball. Surely he doesn't mean *me*.

He looks surprised by my question for a beat, but then his eyes flick to my mouth. He nods, and he leans in to press a soft kiss to my lips that's far too short. "Yeah. You are."

Tears pinch behind my eyes. "Then we have to be together, even if it means we don't tell my father."

When it gets serious, and it *will* get serious—if we're not already there—we'll be strong enough as a united front to find a way to tell him. And until then, sneaking around might be kind of fun.

He sighs. "Then that's what we have to do."

"Can you just quickly tell me if this is real or a dream?" I ask.

His eyes dart to mine. "What do you mean?"

"I mean this whole time I've been hoping and praying we'd figure out a way, and it looks like it's actually happening."

"It's real," he says softly. His eyes move toward the window and he sighs. "I told you earlier in the kitchen, and I meant every word. I fucking love you so goddamn much and I don't know how to move forward without you. It's too short. We hardly know each other. It doesn't make any sense, and yet..." His eyes return to mine, and even though I can tell he's tormented, he seems more settled than he's been since we've been apart.

"I can't live without you." We say the words at the same time, and my heart twists in my chest in a way that feels unfamiliar and thrilling and terrifying and perfect.

His eyes burn into mine as a new understanding dawns between us.

He takes my hand in his and pulls us both to a stand.

"Happy birthday," I murmur.

"It's the cheesiest thing I've ever even thought, but you are the greatest gift I've ever received," he says.

I giggle. "Yeah, that's cheesy as fuck."

"My apologies," he says. "Would my dick inside you erase the memory?"

"God yes," I breathe. "I want you all over me. I want your tongue against mine and your hands on my body and your voice in my ears. I want you surrounding me everywhere so all I breathe in is your scent. And I don't want to wait another second."

He takes my words to heart, and his mouth crashes down to mine again.

We're back where we belong.

Chapter 3
Cooper

I could stand here with the Strip out the window and my girl in my arms forever as I kiss her with all the pent-up emotion I've been holding back for the last couple weeks.

It's fair to say this might be the best birthday of my life, and I've had some good ones.

But I've never had one where I fixed the biggest mistake I ever made, and there's some personal satisfaction in that. And even better? Gabby is back in my life, and not just as the girl I have to avoid.

The way we're going to have to go about this isn't ideal, but it's where we are, and we'll fight to make it work. I tried laying down to do what I thought was the right thing.

But as I hold Gabby in my arms and kiss her like this, I know that *this* is the right thing.

Nothing in my life has ever been as right as this.

And I will fight to be with her. Whatever it takes.

Because I can't live without her.

I tried. I failed.

And now, we celebrate.

My cock begs for release as it strains against my jeans, like it's trying to spring free and get to her, and I can't help but thrust my hips toward her. A soft groan escapes her at the feel, only causing my already throbbing cock to ache and beg for her even more.

I lower my lips from hers, trailing them down her neck. I want to take my time with her. I want to luxuriate in the feel of her soft skin, to smell her warm vanilla, to worship at the altar of her body.

But the captain in my pants is leading this ship, and I'm powerless to take it slow when she's begging for me.

I have this hotel room all night. We can take our time later.

For now, animal instincts kick in.

I reach for the hem of her shirt and pull it over her head, and she unhooks her bra as soon as I toss her shirt beside us. Her gorgeous tits are out, and my mouth waters for them. She reaches for my shirt before I get a chance to put my mouth on her, and her eyes are hooded with lust as they fall upon the abdomen that's gotten a bit more cut in the last two weeks since working out has become my only solace.

Before I can stop her, she's down on her knees and she's palming my cock with one hand while she kisses my abs and trails her fingertips over each ridge there.

She unbuckles my belt and scrambles to pull my cock out, and her mouth is on me with an incredible birthday treat before I even get the chance to stop her.

I don't want to stop her.

Fire blasts up my spine as the pleasure mounts, and I don't want to lose it in her mouth or on her tits even though the thought of marking my territory literally almost makes me come.

I need to be inside her. I need that connection. I need to feel our bodies moving as one as we find our rhythm together, to feel the intimacy with her, to show her how much I love her through the words our bodies can speak so well.

And so I pull back. She looks up at me with a little confusion, and as I gaze down at her, an overwhelming wave of love pulses through my chest.

Her lips are swollen and red, her tits are perky with her nipples two tight, pink buds, and her hair surrounds her like a fucking angel.

"If I don't stop you right now, I'm going to come," I murmur.

"Isn't that sort of the point?" she asks, sassy as always.

I laugh. "It's the end game, yeah. But I'm not ready for the end just yet." I reach out a hand, and her eyes soften as she takes it. I help her to a stand, and then I tuck my cock back into my boxer briefs before I lead her over toward the couch in front of the giant window overlooking the Strip in front of us. I set her down on the couch and remove her shoes, taking my time to try to give the big guy some breathing room.

Eventually she lies naked on the couch in my hotel room, and I couldn't have imagined a better end to this evening.

I couldn't have dreamed this up.

I didn't even allow myself the hope that we'd find a way until I literally couldn't take another second away from her. And the fact that she waited for me, that she held out even though I was the one fighting it...it tells me everything.

It tells me she doesn't give a shit that I play baseball. She only cares about *me*. That's all I ever wanted...someone who loves me for me, someone who will fight for me, someone who will wait for me.

Someone who is perfect for me.

I dive into her pussy, licking all the way through it before pausing to suck on her clit, and then I dip my tongue inside her. Her hips jerk up at the feel of my tongue, and I move back to her clit to suck some more as I push a finger into her, driving in and out as I tongue her clit.

She moans as her body jerks. Her fingers thread into my hair and she yanks as I hit a particularly good spot, and I chuckle as I pull back. I grab a condom out of my back pocket and rip the top off and roll it on. I move her so she's lying across the couch, and I climb over her to hover for a beat.

My eyes are hot on hers as I line my cock up with her gorgeous pussy, moving my cock through her folds and using all my willpower not to push into her. I spread her legs a little wider as I take my place between them, and her head falls back as she closes her eyes.

"Eyes on me," I say softly, and she obeys the quiet command. I slide into her warmth, that overwhelming feeling like I've come home again pulsing everywhere within me.

"Oh God," she cries as I push all the way in. I slide back out slowly then move in again, both of us relishing the feel, her tight pussy a vice on my throbbing cock as I start to drive into her. I balance my arms on either side of her, surrounding her as requested, and I lower my lips to hers. She takes my jaw between her palms, her mouth opening and her tongue immediately moving against mine as our bodies rock together. Pleasure pulses everywhere around me as I finally know once and for all that this is the only woman I will ever want, will ever *need*, for the rest of my life.

I'm in the place where I'm meant to be.

I could fight it as much as I want, but when the right thing comes along, fate finds a way of making it happen. When she heard the desperation in my voice as I tried to fight it one last time, we both knew it was futile. We both knew this is where we'd land. It was destiny.

"I'm coming," she shrieks, her words somehow evolving into a sexy moan that will play on repeat in my mind.

I drive in a little faster, a little harder, as I carry her through her orgasm, the feel of her body overwhelming me with sensations that cause my own body to tip over the precipice into the sort of brutally hard climax that causes me to shudder afterward.

She wraps her arms around me, holding me as I stay inside her long after we've both found our release, as our panting calms into a quiet afterglow and my trembling recedes.

"I love you," she murmurs against my neck, and I wrap my arms around her and squeeze her to me. I'm sure I'm crushing her, but she isn't complaining and I'm not ready to move from this spot where we're physically one as much as we're emotionally one.

"I love you too," I whisper back, so overcome with emotion that I can't force any volume into my voice.

I've never felt a love like this.

And I will do everything in my power to keep us where we belong.

Chapter 4
Gabby

I don't want to fall asleep. I don't want to miss a second of this time we have together, but fatigue creeps up on me and I wake with a jolt when I feel myself moving.

Or, rather, when I feel myself being moved. His weight is no longer pressing down on me. His warm comfort is no longer surrounding me just as I asked him to do, and I feel cold in the absence of how I fell asleep.

I shiver in his arms.

"Shh," Cooper soothes. "I didn't mean to wake you." It takes me a moment to realize he's carrying me through the hotel suite. My eyes focus out the window, where the bright lights of the resorts flash in the dark night sky.

"Where are you taking me?" I ask.

"To bed."

"I don't want to sleep," I say, and I yawn as I completely contradict my own words.

He chuckles. "Neither do I. I don't want this night to end, but I thought we'd be more comfortable in the bed."

I'm sure he's right, but now that I got a short nap in, I feel ready for more.

I've never been in a relationship like this before—one where I'm constantly raring to go, but also one where we can have a conversation and we can laugh together and we can feel ourselves falling further and further down into a place neither of us will ever be able to climb out of.

He sets me down gently on the bed, and I climb under the covers. I'm still naked, and he takes his jeans off before he slides into bed beside me.

We lie facing each other, staring at each other wordlessly, as if we're both in awe that this is actual reality right now and not some dream we're about to wake up from. Maybe that's why I don't want to be in the bed. Maybe I'm afraid I really will wake up and he won't be here and I'll feel that same sense of heartbreak when I realize it was all just a figment of my imagination.

I reach out and run my fingertips along his jawline, the rough scruff there scratching my fingertips, and I know it's real. The delicious ache of my body after being thoroughly fucked on the couch is another sign that this is real.

And the love I feel for him, that overwhelming sense that I've never felt before…that makes it feel awfully real, too.

His eyes study me as I touch him, my fingertips dropping from his jaw down to his neck, along his collarbone, around his shoulder, and down to his bicep, where my palm settles for a beat. I watch my fingertips, and he watches me.

"What are you thinking about?" he murmurs.

My eyes move to his as I go for honesty. "Just trying to figure out whether this is real or a dream."

One side of his lips curls up into a partial smile.

"You?" I ask.

He blinks, and then his eyes flick to my lips for a beat. "All night I've been thinking about how stupid I've been."

My brows knit together. "Why?"

"For pushing you away. For thinking I could give this up. For acting like what we started a few weeks ago isn't the best thing I've ever had in my life." He shakes his head a little as if he can't quite grasp all we've been through, and when he speaks again, his voice is a little lower. "I'm also thinking I don't know how long we'll be able to hide it. These feelings, this thing between us…it's big, and it shines. It's bright and bold, Gabby, and your father is a smart man."

"I know he is," I say with a little nod. "And I don't want to deceive him, but I also think it's okay for the two of us to revel in our secret a while before we need to tell anyone anything. I think when the time is right, when we're both ready…that's when we tell him. But for now, he needs to know what's going on between the two of us as much as I need to know about the club he runs."

He freezes a beat, surprised that I brought it up. "The club," he finally repeats.

I nod. "My father's a smart man, and maybe that's where I get it." I lift a shoulder. "You told me once that the friend who offered you a job owns a sex club."

"It's not a sex club, per se. It's a place where celebrities and athletes can congregate without the general public looking in. The first floor is pretty rad, if I'm being honest, but I didn't go beyond that. From what I gathered, the second floor is a high-rent strip club, and the third is where optional extracurricular activities happen."

"Sex?"

He lifts a shoulder and nods at the same time, and I wrinkle my nose. He takes the opportunity to press a kiss to the tip of it while it's still wrinkled. "We never have to go there."

I make a face like I just ate something rotten. "We never *will* go there. My father owns it?"

"He's part owner along with Victor Bancroft, James McKinney, and some silent business partner from Vegas," he says.

So an actor, a famous rock star, and a businessman along with an athlete. Interesting combination of people.

"It's not my thing," he says. "Your father, he does a lot of business there on the first floor. What he or anybody else does on the other floors is none of my business. Your father is also the manager of the Vegas Heat, and that's pretty fucking kickass."

"And your boss," I remind him.

"And one of my closest friends," he finishes. "I won't be able to hide this smile for long, and when you're with somebody for an entire season, plus the pre-season…let's just say men chat in the locker room."

"Are you okay with this?" I ask.

His eyes flick to my lips again before moving back to mine, and they're a little cloudy when he finally answers. "I have to be. We tried the alternative, and it just isn't an option."

He drops his lips to mine and kisses me softly, sensually, luxuriously…as if we have all the time in the world.

And maybe we do—just as long as we can keep it a secret.

Chapter 5
Cooper

S he fell asleep as we talked late into the night holding each other. Neither of us wanted to let go for fear the other would be gone when morning came, but as I awake to a brand-new day, she's in my arms.

I'm a whole year older.

She's twelve years younger than me.

She's my best friend's daughter.

This is all wrong...but as I hold her in my arms at dawn, nothing has ever felt so right to me in all my life.

I breathe her in, and she shifts a little, waking as the sunlight starts to stream through the sides of our heavy drapes.

"Good morning," she says, peeking through one eye to see I'm already awake.

"Good morning," I murmur. I press my lips to her forehead, and she offers a soft moan. It's similar to the sound she makes when I'm fucking her, and the Captain down below is wide awake and ready for more Gabby action.

I push my hips toward hers, and she tosses one leg over mine so I'm lined up with her. We're both naked. We're both ready. I have the overwhelming urge to slip inside her, and I grab my cock and lazily run it along her slit. She groans as I feel how slick she is for me already, and she pushes her hips down just as I line up with her hole. I dip inside, and the feel of her with nothing between us is fucking magic.

I don't move for a beat, my cock twitching and begging for friction, but being inside her like this is so perfect that I don't want to move. I don't want to break the connection. Instead, I want to memorize this feeling, this moment, this overwhelming love that rushes through me as I feel her without anything between us for the very first time.

She slides her hips down because she needs the movement, too, and then we make love. It's slow and lazy and luxurious, and as I feel her body start to stiffen over mine, that feeling like I'm going to come tears down my spine. I pull out of her and replace my cock with my fingers, which she rides as she fights her way through her climax, and I fist my shaft as my balls tighten and I start to come. I spill it all over her stomach just as she starts to come down from her release, and as my own climax starts to wane, I slide my cock through the mess I just made on her, spreading it around and marking her with my come.

"Why is that so hot?" she murmurs.

"Because you did that," I say softly. "We did something intimate and sexy and sensual, and that's the final product of our pleasure."

"That's both sweet and disgusting at the same time."

I laugh. "Then let me clean it off you in the shower."

"Deal."

After our shower, I order room service. We lie together on the couch in front of the windows overlooking the view of the Strip while we wait for our food.

"What are your plans for the day?" she asks.

"I'm actually heading to the Vegas Aces game this afternoon. Want to come?"

"Of course I do, but what if there are cameras there showing all the celebrities? What if my dad sees us together?"

"Then we tell him it's all part of you shadowing me," I say with a shrug. "He's the one forcing us to work together."

She nods and presses her lips together as she squints at me if to say *yeah, that could work.* "In that case, I'd love to go. I just need to go home and get a change of clothes first."

"I don't want you to go," I murmur, reaching out to grasp her foot between my fingertips.

"I don't want to go, either," she admits. "Good thing you live with me."

I chuckle. "And good thing your dad is rarely home."

"Even better that he hardly ever makes an appearance in our wing of the house," she adds.

We both laugh at that a little, but the laughter fades as we start to realize exactly what all this means. Sure, it's great that I'm living at her dad's place until my house is ready in a few weeks. Sure, we'll have time together.

But we'll also have to hide the most important thing to ever happen to either one of us. We'll be sneaking around, jumping apart at the sound of cars pulling into the driveway or doors opening, acting like we're nothing more than acquaintances when she might know me better after a few weeks than people who've known me my entire life.

It's a little disheartening, but it's what we have to do right now. Maybe we'll test the waters and see how Troy will react, or maybe it'll get easier once I'm living at my own place.

For now, we'll make the best of it.

After breakfast, she heads home to change, and I follow her to the door.

It feels strange telling her goodbye considering we live together, but there's just something special about this hotel. It's a meaningful place for us, I suppose. It's where we first met, where we first had sex, where we first fell in love, and it's also where we first reconnected after I acted like an idiot.

Thank God she took me back. Thank God she waited for me.

She believed in us, and she stuck around. She knew eventually I'd figure it out.

Jesus, she's smart.

Too smart for a dummy like me, but I will take what I can get.

I grab her bag from her shoulder and set it on the ground beside her, and then I pull her into my arms. I drop my lips to hers for a slow and sensual kiss, and her eyes are clouded with lust when she pulls back.

"You keep doing that and we're going to miss the game," she murmurs.

"Worth it," I say, and I kiss her again. I back her up until her ass hits the wall, and this kiss is different. It's urgent and it's hot and it's intense.

It's overwhelming.

I grab her wrists in one of my hands and hold them above her head, dropping my lips to her neck, tasting her with my tongue, and moving my mouth back to hers as I hold her in place, my hips pinning her to the wall and my hands still tight around her wrists. She thrusts against me, not scared that I have the strength to do whatever I want to her as I have her literally within my grasp. Instead she relishes it. She *wants* it, and I want to give it to her. Again and again and again.

Heat fires through my body, but I know we don't have time. I also know we both need to recover. We're both exhausted, our bodies wrung out but never fully sated unless we're in the midst of an orgasm together, always wanting more, needing more, craving more.

Eventually I let her go.

Not because I want to, but because I know I need to. I need to check out. I need to call Kaylee to let her know I'm bringing a guest. I need to stop back at Troy's place to change. Maybe I even need to warn Troy that I invited his daughter to shadow me at the Aces game.

I rest my forehead against hers for a beat as I drop her wrists and lace my arm around her, hauling her into me. The emotions racing through me are unfamiliar and terrifying, yet I know that I'm safe with her. "I love you."

"I love you, too," she says. Her palm finds my cheek, and she cradles me there for a beat, her eyes tender on mine when I pull back. She presses one final soft kiss to my lips, and then I release my hips from hers.

She doesn't move for a beat, instead drawing in a deep breath like she has to compose herself before she can force one foot in front of the other to walk out the door.

The time in this room is over—for now, at least.

But what happened last night, well…it was the start of the rest of forever.

Chapter 6
Gabby

We walk into the Vegas Aces stadium, and I can't help when a thrill of excitement races through me. I follow Cooper up to the owner's suite, which is apparently where a lot of the family members of players sit, and while we're not family, Kaylee is and she's the one who invited Cooper.

It's strange walking through the concourse not holding his hand, but we agreed we're attending as friends—if that, even.

It's strange pretending to be friends with someone who made love to me this morning the way Cooper did to me. I can't stop thinking about how good it felt when he slid into me with nothing between us.

I'm still not on birth control—I didn't see much point when he ended things and I wasn't jumping in the sack with someone new—but I'm far enough away from my period that I'm not worried. Besides, he pulled out.

But I do need to get on something as soon as possible. Sex with Cooper is incredible, but sex with Cooper without a condom is about ten levels above incredible. It's the kind of sex I didn't know actually existed outside of romance novels and porn where you're not sure if they're acting or legitimately that enthralled with what's happening.

I shake sex with Cooper Noah, Captain Orgasm, out of my head as we walk into the owner's suite. Buffets are set up on either side of the room with large televisions hanging on the walls showing pregame coverage, and there are rows of seats for anyone who wants to watch the game live on the far side of the suite. Kaylee spots us when we walk in, and she beelines for Cooper in her Olson jersey. She tackle-hugs him, and he laughs as an *oof* spills out of him.

She glances at me over his shoulder and narrows her eyes as she smiles. "I see your shadow is here," she says loud enough for me to hear, and I get the sense Cooper already filled her in on what happened last night. And again this morning. "Happy birthday, Coopster," she says, and she presses a kiss to his cheek.

"Thanks, Kayster," he says, and he mock-punches her in the shoulder.

She giggles, and then she pushes him aside to give me a hug, too. "I'm so glad you're here," she says warmly. "He's smiling again, so that's something."

"He wasn't smiling?" I ask.

She pulls back and shakes her head as she wraps her hands around my biceps for a beat, studying me. "He was lost without his shadow."

I twist my lips as the burn of tears threatens behind my eyes, and she offers a smile before she drops her hands and takes a step back to include both Cooper and me in the conversation.

"Is this your first Aces game?" she asks.

We both nod.

"Help yourself to food and drinks. It's all on the house…or, rather, it's all on the owner, and he's got plenty of cash to throw around." She lowers her voice for the last part as she glances around to make sure nobody's in hearing distance, and both Cooper and I laugh.

She skips down toward the seats, where she's sitting with a few other women. One wears a Dalton jersey with the number five on it, and I'm pretty sure that's the quarterback. The other wears a black Aces t-shirt, and by the end of our time, I learn that the woman in the t-shirt is Ellie Dalton, wife of former Aces Wide Receiver Luke Dalton, who has recently taken on an assisting role with the coaching staff, and the Dalton jersey woman is Kate, wife of Jack Dalton, the legendary Aces' quarterback.

So basically…I'm in a suite with the wives and girlfriends of football players I've watched play on television for years, and it's all a little surreal.

I suppose this could've happened courtesy of my father, who's fairly well-known in the sports world, but instead, it happened because of Cooper. Either way, three years ago—before I knew who my father was—this would've been nothing more than a dream.

Yet it's my reality.

The Aces jump to an early lead against the Rams in the home opener, and by halftime, it's a clear blowout. We eat, and we drink, and we cheer. We laugh and we high-five and we fist-bump as we get to know the other people in our suite. Kaylee is a sweetheart, but she's also got a tough side to her that I already love. She'd have to considering she's married to the former party king of the NFL.

And the best part? Everyone in this suite makes me feel like I belong. I never feel like I'm just Cooper's shadow, and I don't know if Kaylee told them we're something more or not, but either way, it's a fun group and a great atmosphere.

It's just after halftime when Cooper asks if I want to take a quick walk. We're on the suite level, and we pass by a bunch of doors that appear to be other suites or possibly offices.

He tries the handle on one, and it's locked. He tries the next one, and it opens.

He pulls me into a dark office, and he locks the door.

"What are you doing?" I ask.

His mouth collides with mine, and he kisses me like he needs my mouth for his very survival…and I'm starting to think I need his for mine, too.

"Jesus, I can't stay away. I can't keep my hands off you." He tugs at my shirt, and suddenly he tears it over my head and tosses it to the ground. He works my bra next, pulling it off, and then he buries his face between my breasts before he moves his lips over to suck a nipple into his mouth.

"Ah!" I cry out, my entire body arching toward him. He reaches down into my jeans and skips the foreplay, bypassing my panties and shoving his fingers right into me. I cry out again as I grab onto his shoulders, digging my nails into the cotton of his t-shirt and wishing I'd been coherent enough to pull his shirt off, too.

He works my nipple with his mouth, and he works my clit with his fingers, and before I know it, I'm falling apart in some stranger's office as my body pulses and throbs its way through a fierce orgasm.

I sigh as I sag back against the door, and his lips immediately find my neck.

"I love when you fall apart like that," he murmurs close to my ear. "I've never seen anything sexier."

"I love it when you make me fall apart like that," I whisper. "Nobody's ever done it as easily as you."

He crushes my body against his as he pulls me in close. "That's a damn shame. Good thing you ran into me."

I giggle, and he lets me go. He bends down to collect my clothes and he hands them to me.

I pull my bra back on first. "What about you?" I ask.

"What about me?"

"Um, don't you want me to get you off, too?" I rush through the words, embarrassed as I pull my shirt over my head.

He gets close, his fingertips touching my chin. "It's not some eye for an eye thing, babe. I wanted to hear your moans as I made you come, and I found a place to do that." He shrugs.

"But what if I want to hear you come, too?" I protest.

He grabs the door handle when he's sure I'm decent again. "You will." He tosses a wink over his shoulder, and I guess I'm just supposed to follow him back out into the hallway and act like everything is normal after that brutal orgasm he just gave me.

I have to admit, finding a place to do that in secret was sort of fun.

I can't wait to see what sorts of places we can find around the House for more secret fun.

Chapter 7
Cooper

We spot Troy's car in the circular drive, so we know he's home. I squeeze her hand. "Ready to put on the act again?"

She sighs, and I feel it deep in my own chest. "Nope."

"Me either." I lean my head back on the headrest then slide to the side to face her.

She stares out the windshield. "I keep thinking what if we just tell him? Why do we need to be so scared?"

"We're not scared, Sunshine. We're just playing it smart while we take our time developing whatever this is between us."

"How do you think a conversation with him would even go?" she asks.

"I think he'd ground you for life and he'd bench me," I say.

"He can't *ground* me for life. I'm twenty-one." She rolls her eyes.

"I know, but my point is he'd find ways to punish us both. He already said he doesn't want you with a ballplayer."

"A ballplayer seven years younger than you who is too old for me," she adds.

I let out a little snort. "Exactly. He'll have a fucking heart attack if he thinks I'm taking advantage of the baby girl who just came into his life when he's the one who brought me here."

She nods and presses her lips together. "Yeah. I know why we have to. It just sucks."

"I'll give you something to suck."

Her head whips toward me, and I can't help my laugh.

She purses her lips as if to scold me, and then I squeeze her leg.

"We can do this," I say softly. "He's probably going to head out soon anyway."

She wrinkles her nose. "To his club?"

I lift a shoulder, and she shakes her head with a little disgust. "Gross," she murmurs.

We get out of the car and head inside, and Troy stands in the kitchen making himself a ham sandwich. He freezes when he sees us walking in together, and he narrows his eyes suspiciously at us as he holds a bottle of mustard in one hand. "Where have you two been?"

"Kaylee invited me to the Aces game, and I invited your daughter to shadow me," I say smoothly.

"All part of the job," Gabby adds, her voice just a little higher than it should be.

Troy studies her for a beat, and I can practically see her heart beating out of her chest. "You okay?"

She nods a little too quickly, and it's not like I'm some great actor over here, but I'm going to have to coach her on how to school her behavior. "Just hungry. Can you make me a sandwich, too?"

"Ham okay?"

"Ham's great. Be right back!" She practically runs upstairs, and I force myself not to laugh.

"You need one, too?" Troy asks me.

"Thanks, but I'm okay. Big buffet at the game and my boss is forcing me to get into shape." I pat my stomach, and he nods knowingly.

"That boss of yours is a real tyrant."

"Tell me about it." I head toward the fridge and grab a beer, and I hold it up toward Troy. "Want one?"

He shakes his head. "No, and you shouldn't, either, considering you need to get in shape." He gives me a warning glance before he turns back to his sandwich. "I've got some business at the club tonight before my...free time." He raises his brows which basically tells me he'll be fucking Joanie in one of the rooms, and for a beat I wonder if he does it in the type of room where others can watch him.

Is he into that?

It doesn't matter, but my curiosity is piqued. He's just sitting there making a ham sandwich like he isn't one of the richest men in baseball, like he isn't about to get his freak on at a sex club, like he's not the manager of a hot new expansion team.

My curiosity shouldn't be piqued considering he's my girlfriend's father, but he's also a good friend of mine—the kind of friend I would talk to about those types of things. The kind of friend I'd brag to about that little office I found not far from the owner's suite this afternoon.

But I can't, and it feels…strange.

"You got any plans for the night?" he asks.

I shrug. "I might take a look at some more film for the team prospects, but I'll probably turn in early so I can get up for a nice early morning workout tomorrow at the stadium." I slide into a chair at the table and chug down half my beer.

"Good plan." He finishes making his sandwich along with Gabby's, and he sets her plate on the table between him and me before he takes his seat across from me and starts to dig in. "Joanie said all the plans have been approved, so next week they're working on finding the contractors who will make your kids fitness thing happen."

"That's great news," I say.

"What's great news?" Gabby asks as she reappears in the kitchen.

"Your sandwich is ready," Troy says, and Gabby glances at it then sits in front of it. Her knee bumps mine when she sits, and neither of us moves.

What would Troy say if he could see our legs touching under the table? Would he think anything of it?

How long can we expect him to be oblivious to this when the connection between us is smoking hot?

"Troy was just telling me the plans for StrongFitKids have been approved," I say. *Come on, Noah. Think of a way to throw him off.*

She takes a bite of her sandwich as she nods. "Oh, that is great. What's the next step?"

"Finding contractors to start construction," Troy says.

"What will our roles be once that starts?" Gabby asks.

"That's a better question for Joanie, but she was telling me how impressed she is with your social media skills. This is on the down low for now, but our current social media manager, Zelda, wants to take on a smaller role since she's having her first baby in a few months. It'll be tough to keep up her current schedule with a newborn, so she wants to move out of management and into an assistant role. Joanie suggested a sort of contest between the interns if any of you are interested in the position."

Gabby's brows rise. "As in…one of us would have a full-time job as a social media manager for an MLB team right out of college?"

Troy nods. "Joanie and I are very impressed with the crop of interns this year, and there's still that final spot she's going to fill in the next few days. We both feel that giving the position to someone younger who understands all the different social networks would be beneficial to growing our brand."

She raises her hand. "I want it."

Troy chuckles. "Then prove you deserve it, baby girl. From what I hear, the other interns might be interested, too."

Certainly she would have an edge given who her father is, but on the other hand...how would the other interns treat her if she got the job over them? How would they treat her if it was a competition the way Troy just presented it?

"Oh, and that final intern spot?" Gabby says. "I know one of the applicants. I can vouch he's a good guy."

I keep my gaze down on the table as I push down the feelings of envy that she's vouching for some other guy. I don't like it.

The complications keep swinging toward us, but I'm confident enough in what we have that we can overcome them.

I just hope I'm not *overly* confident the way I was three years ago when my cockiness took me out of the game.

Chapter 8
Gabby

My dad takes off for the night, bidding us both goodnight before he goes, and we head up to my bedroom. I think about snuggling on the couch with him, but I don't know if my dad has some secret cameras set up here that might catch us in the act. I say as much to Cooper once we're in my room.

"I feel like this is our only safe place," I say, sitting on the edge of the bed. "What if there are cameras down in the family room and the kitchen."

"I thought you were inviting me in for sex," he admits, and I giggle.

"I mean, of course. But I also thought it might be nice to just lay together and do normal things you'd do with your boyfriend." My eyes widen as the word leaves my mouth.

"Did you just call me your boyfriend?" he asks.

I slap a hand over my mouth as my entire face flushes a bright red, and he starts to laugh.

"I just meant—" I begin, but he cuts me off when he bends over so I'm forced to lie back, and he drops his lips to mine as he hovers over me.

He drops his lips to my neck. "I know what you meant, and I can't tell you how good it feels to hear you call me that." He says the words softly against my skin, and I shiver a little as his words register.

"I'm embarrassed I said it first," I admit, my heart still racing that the word slipped out.

He pulls back and his eyes lock on mine. "Don't be. I think it's cute."

"Puppies are cute, Cooper. I'm a woman."

He thrusts his hips to mine, and my chest races with anticipation. "Oh, I know you're a woman. You're *my* woman. You're my *girlfriend*. You're the only woman I want to be with."

His lips move to mine. We kiss there on the bed like that for a minute or for an hour, I don't know, but I feel lost in him like this. He pulls back and rolls to the side of me as our kiss starts to intensify from that languid luxurious kind into a more urgent one.

"Baseball, apple pie, baseball, apple pie," he chants softly to himself, and I giggle. "What movie did you want to watch?" he asks, sitting up and glancing down at me. His eyes are a little hazy.

"Um, the one where you stick your dick in me?"

His eyes widen and he coughs a little as if I just made him choke on something. "You want to watch porn?"

"Homemade," I say.

"Are you serious right now?"

I shrug. "I've never filmed myself. Have you?"

"Well, I mean...yeah, I have."

I was hoping he'd say no, that this adventure could be special between the two of us, but I also know he's been around the block a few times. He's twelve years older than me. Surely there's very little he has left to experience for the first time, and something in that makes me a little sad. I want to be special for him. I want to be a first for him the way he will be for me in so many ways.

He leans up on his elbow and looks over at me. "You seem upset by that." His tone is cautious, and his brows are knitted together.

I lift a shoulder, surprised that he can read me so well. I shouldn't be surprised. I think that's what's supposed to happen when you're with the person you're meant to be with.

"I just feel like I'll never be your first for anything," I admit.

His face softens, and he leans over to press his lips to my cheek before he lies back and stares up at the ceiling. "You're the first woman I've been with who's twelve years younger than me."

I can't help a little laugh at that.

"You're the first woman I met at a blackjack table on her twenty-first birthday. You're the first woman I've been with who's the daughter of one of my friends. You're the first woman I've been with in probably fifteen years who didn't immediately associate me with baseball."

He pauses, and then he turns and props himself up on his elbow again as he stares down at me. "And you're the first woman who has ever stolen my heart the way you have. I swear to God, Gabby,

I have *never* felt like this before. I've never felt like I would put everything on the line for a woman. I've never felt like I could see into my future with a woman before, and definitely not this fast. I've never felt like a piece of me was missing until I found you and you held that piece in your hands." He leans down and presses a kiss to my cheek, and my heart races. "And maybe most importantly, I've never met a woman who I wanted to be with more than I wanted to be out on the field. So don't you dare say you won't be my first anything because you're my first *everything*."

My eyes fill with tears at his words, and one falls down the side of my temple, splashing down onto the blanket underneath me. Another follows in its wake, and he brushes it away with his fingertip.

I don't know what to say to that. I don't know how to take those beautiful words in and give him a response that's worthy of what he just said to me. I don't know how to make him feel half of what he made me feel simply with his words.

"Thank you," I whisper.

He presses his lips together and shakes his head a little. "Thank *you*. Thank you for waiting for me. You knew we'd find our way back to each other. You kept the faith while I was a fucking idiot."

"Stop," I say sharply. "You were not an idiot. You were being cautious, and I don't fault you for that. It's something we still need to hold onto."

He nods. "But right now, the house is empty…" He trails off suggestively, and I take the hint, tossing my leg over his and shifting us both so I'm straddling him.

And then there's no more talking…just lots of moaning as waves of pleasure pulse through us.

Chapter 9
Gabby

H e slept in my room with me but snuck out sometime before dawn, and as my alarm wakes me to a new day, I feel like everything has changed.

I dreaded getting up to go to work last week. It meant I might have to shadow Cooper while pretending like I wasn't totally head over heels in love with him, but today I'm hopeful I'll get to shadow him since it means more time we get to spend together.

I find a text from him when I turn on my phone.

Cooper: *Thank you for one of the best nights of my life. Really enjoyed the movie. [wink emoji] Hoping to make one with you soon. Leaving for early workouts, hope to see you at the stadium. Also might want to change my contact name in your phone just in case.*

Me: *You're now Captain in my phone, and I enjoyed the movie, too.*

Captain: *You're Sunshine in mine. And you just let the captain know any time he needs to deliver the goods.*

I melt a little at the fact that he calls me Sunshine. I think about his words about me being his first for so many things, and he is so many firsts for me, too. First secret relationship, first guy who has ever managed to give me multiple orgasms in one night, first guy who I've ever really felt connected to. First guy I've ever really loved. I feel a little giddy as I think he'll be my last, too.

My morning classes seem to drag on even though I'm done before one, and I head straight for Joanie's office once I get to the stadium for our Monday post-lunch meeting.

Once all the interns arrive, she starts the meeting. "We're switching things up, and I'm really excited about the new plan. And our newest intern has been with HR filling out paperwork all morning."

"Who is it?" Justin asks.

"He'll be here any minute," she says.

I can't help but wonder if it's Dylan, and then he walks in a minute later.

"Here he is," she says. "Dylan Fisher, meet the interns."

I wave, excited to work with Mia's boyfriend. If he's good enough for her, he's good enough to be a friend here with me…even if I'm a little concerned since he knows about the history between Cooper and me.

She eyes us each individually. "Is anyone here interested in a full-time job here with the Heat after graduation?"

A few hands go up while others nod their heads. The only one who doesn't seem overly enthusiastic about it is Justin, and Dylan looks a little shell-shocked considering he was just hired for this internship and has no idea what's going on.

"The woman we hired to be our social media manager isn't going to pan out, so we're looking to fill that position. Zelda will still be here to train her successor, but as she's pregnant, she won't be able to be at the stadium as much as she thought she would be. We'll be keeping her on as a content creator, but we need someone dedicated to the team, someone who's willing to travel to away games to take footage and post to different social networks. After speaking with some of the department heads here in the office, we agreed that grabbing someone with a little experience with the team might be a great start, and with Zelda by your side, we all know one of you will excel in this position. We may be interested in hiring on more content creators as well, and so in that vein, we've decided to institute a competition between our interns."

"A competition?" Chloe asks.

Joanie nods. "You'll earn points over the next few months for different challenges, and we'll be keeping tally of all the points. We'll take our top three interns with the most points earned at the end and you'll each interview for the position. If the rest of you score high enough, you might be in contention for additional content creator positions. Any questions so far?"

She glances around the table at each of us, and we're all shaking our heads. Excitement blooms within me. I may not be the athlete Cooper is, but I still love a good competition…and I'm more and more interested in working here at the stadium with my dad and my *boyfriend* full-time once I graduate this spring.

"For our first challenge, I'll be pairing you up and giving you a general topic. You'll film a ten second video to be uploaded to social media, and I have a handful of judges who will decide which of the three videos will be posted. The winning team will receive one point each."

She looks around the room, and we're all listening.

"The topic for the first challenge is an inside look at the stadium. Take that however you want, and you have until lunch today to work with your partner on this challenge. In three hours, we'll view all three videos together and choose a winner to post." She pulls a slip of paper from a little bowl in front of her. "Justin," she begins, and she grabs another slip of paper. "Your partner is Mackenzie."

They look at each other and smile slyly as if they're already conspiring how they're going to win.

"Chloe," she says after grabbing the next slip of paper. She takes another one out. "You'll be with Gabby. That leaves Brian, Chase, and Dylan, and you three will work together." She offers Dylan a smile. "Nothing like jumping right in, am I right?"

The boys first bump while Chloe and I lock pinkies.

"If you finish before the time is up, come see me. Now get to it, teams, and good luck!" Joanie says, and we all stand and head in separate directions.

"An inside look at the stadium," Chloe says, tapping her chin once we find a seat in the back row of some seats in a section of the Heart Level.

We brainstorm what we think fans would most want to see, and we take some raw footage of the dugout, the stadium seats, and the view of the field.

And then I get an idea. "Follow me," I say, and we head down to the weight room.

We find a very hot and sexy Cooper as he works on the rowing machine. Danny Brewer is on a squat machine nearby, and Rush Ross is lifting what looks like a fairly heavy weight on the bench press with Nick, the trainer, spotting him from above. We take some footage of the guys doing their thing since it is, after all, part of what happens in this stadium.

And as I take a video of Cooper on the rowing machine, I can't help but think part of me is taking it for my own personal use.

He wears a hat backward on his head, and he glances up at me as I take the video. His eyes flick from my chest up to my lips before landing on my eyes, and a salacious smile lifts his lips as he narrows his eyes at me a little. The sheen of sweat makes him somehow glow even hotter than usual. He isn't wearing a shirt, and

I don't think our female judges are going to complain about the view.

In fact, I think the way he just looked at me and shot me that sexy little smile—as caught on camera…that's what's going to help us win the challenge.

I make sure to get a little footage of Rush and Danny, too, and then we head back toward the offices to find a quiet place to share footage and edit it into one amazing video.

We meet back in Joanie's office at the end of our time limit. "I'd like to introduce you to the judges," she says as we all wait patiently to showcase our videos. "First is me, of course. And then we have Zelda," she pauses dramatically as Zelda walks in the room, waving to us all. "Caitlin," she calls, and Caitlin from marketing walks in with a wide smile. "Trainer Nick," she says, and the man from the weight room comes in. "And finally, third baseman Mr. Cooper Noah."

My chest races at the mention of his name, and his eyes find mine when he walks in. He glances away quickly, but after we made him the star of our video, I feel like we've got a pretty good shot to win.

We watch Justin and Mackenzie's video first, though Joanie doesn't say which video belongs to which team. It's pretty obvious by the way Justin preens thinking how great it is. Theirs is mostly shots of the stadium from the outside, and they tell a story of what it would be like to walk through the doors on game day as a fan.

Brian, Chase, and Dylan's video is next, and they show snippets of different parts of the stadium, focusing on the dugout and the locker room.

Our video is last.

We start with the outside of the stadium, and then we have a few shots inside, too—the seats, the field, the dugout. We head into the locker room for a few sweeping shots, and then we show the batting cages and finally, the weight room. We end with shots of the players. Rush first, then Danny, and then that gorgeous look Cooper gave me, the smile lifting his lips the final image on the screen.

The image that will stick in my mind for days.

Cooper chuckles a little at the end, but he *has* to know how freaking sexy he is.

"Wow," Caitlin says, clearing her throat as our video wraps.

Nobody said anything like that after the other two videos.

"The judges will now write down a one, two, or three to indicate which video they think is the best." The judges hide their papers as they write, and then Joanie collects the papers and reads them.

I catch Cooper's eye, and he nods a little as if to tell me he voted for mine.

Joanie clears her throat. "Well, it's unanimous. All five judges chose video three, so congratulations to Chloe and Gabby for earning a point for this first challenge."

I hear Mackenzie scoff a little, but that's the only reaction from the group other than Chloe and me high fiving.

The judges head out, and when Cooper passes by me, he says, "Congratulations."

I melt.

I don't even know why, but hearing that single word that feels like praise coming from him means everything to me.

I can't wait to do more things to earn his praise.

Chapter 10
Gabby

Before I left, Mackenzie told me it wasn't fair I was in contention for the job since my dad's the manager," I tell Cooper later that night as we sit down to dinner at my dad's kitchen table. He's not home, and we're feasting on some chicken Cooper ordered in from some restaurant nearby.

"Did she say anything about Justin?" he asks.

I shake my head. "Apparently it's different since Justin's dad is a business manager, not the *team* manager." I shrug.

"Nepotism is nepotism, right?"

I shrug. "I think only when it's me."

He points his fork at me. "My guess is she knows you're hotter than her and she's jealous." He winks, and I laugh.

"I'm certain that's it. Or, you know…the fact that Joanie put me on shadowing you and not her."

"I like having you as my shadow. I don't even know which one Mackenzie is."

I hold up a hand. "See? My point exactly. She's jealous I get to spend time with you, and you don't even know who she is."

He wiggles his eyebrows. "She'd be *really* jealous if she knew exactly *how much* time you get to spend with me."

I giggle, and I'm about to lean in to kiss him when we both hear the front door open. My dad walks into the kitchen a few beats later.

"You two together again," he says. "What's going on here?"

My eyes widen as I feel very caught, but Cooper jumps in.

"We both got back from the stadium at the same time, so I ordered in."

He studies us a beat as if he's piecing things together, and then he grins. "What are we having?"

Relief rushes up my spine.

"Lemon chicken and veggies from Desmonds," Cooper says.

"My favorite," he says, and he grabs a plate and a fork without asking whether there's enough for him. It's a tiny bit of insight into how close Cooper and my dad actually are. You don't do that with people who are nothing more than houseguests.

"It is pretty delicious," I say as I take another bite. I moan a little at the taste as I close my eyes and lean my head back, and then I feel Cooper's foot as it connects lightly with my shin.

I open my eyes and Cooper shoots me a look before he shifts in his chair.

I can't help my small giggle, which thankfully goes unnoticed by my father.

"Coop, Mike and I are heading to Boston to talk with management there about AJ Winters and I'd like you to come along. We leave next Monday morning."

I'm pretty sure the Mike he's referring to is the team's general manager.

He nods. "Of course. Let me know how many nights to pack for."

"I'll have Joanie send you the details," he says.

"Joanie?" I ask, interjecting myself into their conversation.

My dad nods. "She's not just the head of marketing, you know. She started out as my assistant and earned her newer title all on her own, but I wasn't about to give her up as the best assistant I ever had. She still helps out, but she splits the title with Heather."

Is he banging Heather, too?

I feel like that question would be grosser even in my own head if he'd raised me from birth rather than coming into my life when I was already an adult.

"Anyway, we'll be gone two nights, maybe three," he says.

My chest tightens a little as I think about three nights away from Cooper. We just got back together, and he's already leaving.

I suppose that's a feeling I'm going to have to get used to. My dad wasn't lying when he said he doesn't want me to be with a baseball player since they're gone so much. The travel must be insane, and I'd imagine most guys don't bring their girlfriends along for every single away game.

All the more reason to win the competition so I can interview for the social media manager job. Then I'd get to travel with the team because of my job in what I can only describe as the best-case scenario.

I can't imagine an entire season of being away from him, but that could very well be our reality.

They chatter about AJ Winters and I'm clueless as to who he is, but I decide then and there to get to know more about the game.

And what better person to teach me than Cooper Noah?

"Who's AJ Winters?" I ask.

They both stare at me like I have three heads.

I hold both palms face up. "What?"

"He's only one of the best shortstops to ever play the game," Cooper says. He glances at my father. "Are you sure you two are related?"

My dad laughs. "I'm sure. She has the DNA results to prove that."

"I blame my evil mother. She was so hell bent on keeping me from anything baseball that I never learned a thing about it. So why would this guy leave his team to come play for you?" I ask.

Cooper fields the question even though I directed it at my dad. "Right place, right time," he says. "Your father is a baseball legend, and his name alone will get players to the team. He's the kind of guy who's been around this game a long time, and from where I sit, I feel like we're assembling a championship team right out of the gate."

"Is that usual for these expansion teams?" I ask.

My dad shakes his head. "Typically expansion teams take a few years to get off the ground. But with Cooper on third and Brewer on first, we've already secured big names other guys will want to play with, and being in Vegas is a huge draw for a lot of these younger, single guys. Right, Coop?" my dad asks, elbowing Cooper in the ribs.

He clears his throat. "Damn straight. Between the women, the tables, the booze, and the fact that there's no state income tax in Nevada, we've got a hell of a set up here."

I raise a brow and purse my lips, carefully treading the line of showing my *boyfriend* I'm disappointed in his words while keeping my dad from sniffing around us. "Is that all Vegas is to you single guys?" I ask, clear disappointment in my tone.

"Well, no," Cooper says. There's a clear twinkle in his eye that tells me he's just kidding around, but I think I can also tell he's about to say something for my father's benefit. And I'm not wrong. "There's also the strip clubs, the horny bachelorettes, and the first-class entertainment."

My dad barks out a laugh, and I want to smack Cooper for his words. I shake my head. "Freaking men," I mutter.

My dad gives me a pointed glance. "See? Just like I was telling you the other day. Ballplayers are assholes, so you should stay far, far away."

"You got that right." I shoot Cooper a look.

"We're not *all* assholes," Cooper mumbles, but he keeps his eyes focused down on his plate.

My dad lets out a snort. "Yeah we are."

"Speak for yourself, man," Cooper shoots back.

"Look, any guy on the team will tell you ball comes first in our lives in season. Even out of season, look how much time we're spending at the stadium. Even if you're not an asshole, that still doesn't mean you have time to focus on a relationship," my dad points out. He digs into his chicken, grabbing a huge forkful and shoving it into his mouth.

"What about you and Joanie?" I ask.

"That's different," my dad says around the chicken in his mouth, and I narrow my eyes as if to ask how it's different for them. "For one, she puts up with a lot of shit from me. And for another, I wasn't in season when we got together. I started as an assistant coach when I retired, but then I moved into the front office with the Rockies. I did a lot of that remotely from here in Vegas as I started investing both time and money in other ventures. We grew close *because* I was out of the game, not in spite of it."

"So you're telling me not one single baseball player has ever had a successful relationship during the season?" I ask. That simply can't be true.

My dad shakes his head. "No, I'm not saying that. I'm saying it's hard. It's a lot of time away, and it's difficult to build a relationship with someone you never get to see. Which is why Coop here is swearing off women for the next three years, right, man?"

It's Cooper's turn to offer a snort, and I can't help a small giggle at that.

"I was just telling Gabriella the other day that she deserves so much better than what a ballplayer could offer her. Don't you think?" he asks Cooper.

Cooper nods. "Absolutely," he says a little absently, avoiding eye contact with me.

What my dad doesn't know won't hurt him, but it's clear he really believes in the things he's trying to sell us. I'm just starting to worry he's selling Cooper on the idea, too…and that's a little concerning given how strongly I feel for him.

Chapter 77
Cooper

It's Monday morning and Gabby's at class, so I put in some extra time in the weight room. Joanie's been talking about the next challenge in the intern competition, and she wants players judging this time. I already know where my vote is going, so I'm trying to find a way to opt out of it so I'm not making it obvious that I'm in love with the woman I keep voting for.

It's just after noon when Gabby walks into the weight room and spots me near the squat machine. Her eyes seem to land on the muscles in my legs, and I offer a raised brow as I glance around and realize we're alone in here. Nick and Rush just headed out for lunch, and Danny's probably still at his place in bed with his conquest from last night, whoever that may be.

She glances around then makes her way over toward me, her phone out and perched in my direction as she takes video.

"Is that for the intern comp?" I ask.

She laughs as she makes her way over toward me. "No. It's for my spank bank."

I chuckle as I finish my set of squats, and then I lunge for her. She drops her phone as I grab her up into my arms and plant a hot, fiery kiss on her mouth.

She pushes on my chest, hot from the workout but not slick with sweat since I've got fans pointed right on me.

"My dad could walk in here at any time," she whispers as she breaks away from my mouth.

I press one more soft kiss to her lips. "I'm not sure I care." She shoots me a look, and I hold up both hands in surrender. "Okay, okay. How was class?"

"Fine. The professor let us out early, so no complaints. But Mia is acting weird. She arrived late and bolted early and we didn't get a chance to talk."

"Have you tried calling her to ask what's up?" I link an arm around her waist and pull her back into me. I can't help it. I need to touch her. I need to feel her. We'll hear the door if someone walks in, and we can move apart then.

"No. I haven't told her we're back together, and I think she's being weird with me either because her boyfriend scored the final internship spot or because she's been trying to hook me up with one of Dylan's friends forever and I've been a little...preoccupied with you."

I lean down and press my lips to her neck. "Is that all I am to you? A preoccupation?"

She snickers. "You know what you are to me."

"Do I? Maybe you should remind me." I nibble the skin along her neck again, and she shivers.

"You're my boyfriend, remember?"

"Ah, yes," I murmur in a low, gravelly voice close to her ear. "And you're my girlfriend." I practically growl the words, and they serve their intended effect.

Her hand finds the back of my neck and her lips catch mine, and then we're making out in the weight room like we will never get our fill of each other.

I let her go and pull her back toward one of the training rooms—the room where players will be taped up and tended to before and after games, but empty for now—and I lift her by her hips and set her on the exam table. I lock the door behind us, opting to keep the light turned off, and then I move back toward her. I drop my mouth to hers, and she wraps her arms around my shoulders.

Jesus, I could kiss her forever, but the Captain down below has other plans. I pull her to the edge of the table and thrust my hips to hers to give her the hint, and she lets out a soft moan.

"Fuck me, Cooper," she murmurs.

"Okay," I say, trying to keep the glee out of my tone. "Shit. I don't have a condom."

"I do," she says, and she does *not* keep the glee out of her tone. She produces one from her back pocket.

"You're just carrying condoms around now?"

She lifts a shoulder. "You never know when you'll have a minute for secret sex at the House."

I drop my mouth to her shoulder. "I swear to God, you were put on this Earth for me to find you."

Her eyes are a little misty as they connect with mine, and she holds up the condom. "Right back at you, Captain."

I snatch the condom from her fingertips, yank my cock out of my shorts, and roll it on while she unbuttons her jeans and leans back awkwardly to pull them down her legs, and then I take over, pulling them off her and tossing them to the ground.

I line my cock up with her glistening, gorgeous cunt, and then I slide my way into her wet heat.

I pull her in a little closer with one arm around her waist so she's seated right at the edge of the table, and she wraps her arms around me as I really start to move. I want to suck her tits, to taste every inch of her as I take my time, but this has to be quick.

And it is.

It's way too quick.

"Oh God, Cooper, oh my God!" she nearly yells, and I cover her mouth with mine to keep her screams at bay as I plow into her tight little body. She holds on for the wild ride, and I feel her starting to contract over me to the symphony of her moans, and that's when my body can't take it anymore. I let go, too, falling into the ocean of bliss far below right along with her, pumping into her as I grunt through my climax, my neck corded as I tip my head back through the release.

She clings tightly to me as we both make our way out of the haze, and I press my lips to hers once more, my body trembling from a hard and fast climax it wasn't expecting less than five minutes ago.

"Jeez, Noah. Where'd you learn to bang like that?" she asks.

I laugh as I pull out of her. I grab a tissue from the counter and head over toward the bathroom to take care of the condom. "You really want to know?" I ask as I tuck my dick back into my shorts and return to her.

She wrinkles her nose as she hops down from the table to gather her clothes. "No, not really. I wish we were each other's firsts."

It's my turn to wrinkle my nose. "You wouldn't have wanted to be my first. It wasn't pretty. But I do wish I was your first. The thought of you with somebody else makes me want to rage."

She giggles. "You should've seen your face every time Justin came over."

I narrow my eyes at her. "You were trying to make me jealous."

She shakes her head. "I was trying to get you to see how stupid you were being." She reaches over and taps me on the nose, and I can't help a laugh.

"Well, you won."

She reaches over and lightly runs her fingertips along the outside of my shorts, feeling her way along my cock. "I think we both won." She offers a sassy little wink, and I can't help my laugh.

She turns toward the door, and I grab her ass before I haul her back into my arms. I kiss her good and hard, leaving her with a memory that will help get us both through the rest of the day, and then I open the door, peek around to see the weight room is still empty, and let her out first.

We both hear the door to the weight room open a beat later. "Oh, hey Dad!" she says way too brightly as I'm walking out of the training room.

"What are you two doing in here?" he asks a little gruffly.

I glance over at her, and her cheeks are turning red as she keeps her eyes firmly planted on Troy.

"I, uh, was just using the restroom in the training room," I say, my voice hitching a little with my lie. "I didn't know Gabby was in here."

She clears her throat. "I got out of class early and came down here looking for you," she says to her father, and she moves toward him and away from me.

They head out of the weight room, and I collapse down on a bench as I think how close a call that was.

I really need to become better at lying, especially if what we're doing is going to continue to be our little secret.

Chapter 12
Cooper

I n the last week, we've managed to find time alone together every day. It helps tremendously that Troy has been spending the night away from the house, but he doesn't exactly fill us in on his plans, so while we find places to kiss and touch and be together, I've been heading back to my own bedroom just in case he happens to come home looking for his daughter.

It all feels so…immature.

This is an adult relationship, but I'm in it with someone who isn't ready to tell her father.

Hell, I'm not ready to tell him, either. Mostly because I know he isn't going to like it, and I want to live in this bliss just a little while longer.

It's Sunday night, and I don't want to leave her, but tomorrow morning we fly to Boston to try to talk AJ Winters into playing ball with us.

We're laying in her bed in that post-sex afterglow, her head on my chest and my arms around her, when I say, "You should hang with Kaylee while I'm gone."

"I would love to, but is she looking for new friends?" she asks.

"She loved spending time with you at the game. You two are close to the same age and I think she likes having someone to bond with in a similar situation."

"Being the young filly taming the party boy athlete?"

I grunt out a chuckle. "Something like that. Is that really how you see yourself? How you see *me*?"

"I mean…you were with Stacy a long time and admitted you never thought about the future with her the way you thought about it with me." We're both quiet as we let that simmer between us, and then she says, "Can I ask you a question about her?"

I nod, my chin bumping the top of her head with the movement.

She shifts so her head is on my shoulder and her eyes meet mine. "Why'd you stay with her as long as you did?"

I twist my lips in contemplation. It's a good question, and I think after all this time I've finally arrived at the right answer. "You know how sometimes it's easier to just leave things the way they are?"

She nods.

"It was that. When you're with someone for as long as we were together, your lives are so entwined that you forget where you stop and the other person starts. She made sure of that, anyway, while I was gone for eight months, as your father likes to remind you." My words are laden with regret, but the feeling has nothing to do with Stacy and everything to do with Troy's words over dinner.

They've been weighing me down ever since.

"You seemed kind of down when he mentioned it." She runs a fingertip along my jawline.

"I was. I *am*. It's a constant reminder that I'm not good enough for you, and he will never think I'm good enough for you. He'll never think *anyone* is good enough for you, least of all a thirty-three-year-old third baseman." My eyes cloud over as I gaze up at the ceiling, and I tighten my arm around her.

She leans up, her face in my line of sight.

"Good enough?" she murmurs softly. She presses a soft kiss to my mouth. "*Good enough* implies that you're just adequate, but nothing could be further than the truth. You aren't good *enough*." She shakes her head. "Saying that is a total insult to what an incredible man you actually are. You're a catch, and I don't deserve you, yet you're somehow perfect for me. Somehow we landed in each other's arms, and I'm not letting you go."

My chest warms at her words. "I hope I can live up to the expectations you have of me," I say. "Things are going to change once the season starts."

She presses her lips together. "I know they will. And I also know we have several months before we need to worry about it. So from now until then, we build. We strengthen. Just like those workouts you're doing in the weight room to prep for the season, we nurture our relationship. We'll be prepared, and we'll cherish what moments we do get to spend together, and when you're gone, we'll do whatever it takes."

One of the things I love so much about her is her ability to quell my fears, and somehow she just did it without even realizing it.

When Troy was talking at dinner, I felt his words settle over me like a dark cloud. But she comes in with her sunshine and manages to obliterate the clouds so all I see is bright, blue sky again with her at the center of it.

It's incredible, really, how she does that, and it's another signal to me that she was put on this planet to find me.

"Thank you," I murmur, and I pull her face down to mine for a kiss. This is one of the slow, languid ones that I could live in for days, but I know I need to get up and pack a bag so I'm ready to go for my eight AM flight. I pull back and run the back of my knuckles against her cheek, staring at her as emotion flows through me. "Thank you for being everything I need."

She offers a soft smile, and then she falls beside me.

"I need to go pack a bag."

"Can I watch?" she asks.

I chuckle. "Whatever floats your boat, my love." We both get up and head over to my room. She sits on my bed while I grab everything I need for up to three days away on a business trip, and then I climb into bed beside her, set an alarm to make sure we're up before Troy might come bang on my door to wake me, and I wrap her in my arms.

My eyes fly open what feels like a few hours later as I hear banging on my door.

"Cooper?" Bang, bang, bang.

Is that Troy?

"Cooper!" Bang, bang, bang.

That *is* Troy, and his gorgeous daughter is asleep in my bed beside me.

"Fuck," I hiss as I glance at my phone.

I set my alarm for PM instead of AM. Rookie fucking mistake, Noah.

God dammit.

I gently shake Gabby awake, and she startles as she hears the banging.

"We need to go!" Troy yells from the other side of the door.

"Quick, hide in my bathroom," I whisper to Gabby. We both leap out of bed, and if this was some scene I was watching rather than living, I'd be laughing hysterically at the two clowns half-asleep as they stumble around.

"Fuck!" I yell as I bang my leg on the nightstand.

I make sure Gabby is out of sight, but I'm pretty sure she tripped her way into my bathroom and she *may* have fallen and I hope she's okay.

I open the door, trying to remain calm.

"Oh, hey there, Troy," I say, leaning casually on the doorframe, and I'm certain I fail at that whole remaining calm thing.

"Our plane leaves in ninety minutes and we need to get to the airport. What the fuck have you been doing?" he demands.

"Uh…sleeping?"

"Have you seen Gabby? Her car's here but she's not in her room. I was hoping to say goodbye to her before we left."

"Oh, nope, haven't seen her anywhere, sorry. Just been sleeping here in my bed. Alone." I'm lying, and I'm a bad liar, and he must see right through me because he narrows his eyes at me.

"Why are you acting so strange?" he asks.

"Who, me?" I ask, a little too overly dramatically.

He squints a little, and *come on, Noah, fucking THINK!*

"I need to jump in the shower before we head out. Give me ten minutes and I'll be ready to go," I promise, and then he finally nods and turns.

I practically slam the door behind him and run to the bathroom. "I'm so sorry!" I whisper-yell.

She giggles. Fucking Sunshine giggles, and those giggles turn into cackles. Quiet cackles, but cackles nonetheless. "Oh my God, Cooper, you are the absolute *worst* liar I have ever seen in my life!" She's laying on the floor of my bathroom laughing so hard at me right now that literal tears are falling from her eyes, and I can't help my wry smile.

She isn't wrong, and this is our first close call with her father…and I have no idea how I'm going to continue this charade. She sucks in a few deep breaths as she tries to calm the laughter, and I reach out a hand to help her up.

"I need to get ready to go," I say.

She nods, and the laughter subsides as we both know what this means. Two to three days away from each other. I'm traveling with her father and the general manager of the Heat, and I really don't know whether I'll even get a chance to call her and talk to her since this is a business trip.

I pull her into me, and we stand in my small en suite bathroom simply clinging to one another for a few beats. I lean down and touch my lips to her forehead, and she squeezes her arms around my torso.

"Travel safe and keep in touch," she says.

"I'll try to call but I have no idea what this trip will look like. I don't even know if I have my own room," I admit.

She nods, and she tips her chin up so I can lean down to press a kiss to her lips.

"I love you," I murmur. An intimate beat passes between us, and then I swat her ass. "Now scram. I gotta get in the shower before your dad comes back up here."

She giggles and kisses me once more, and then she heads out while I cross my fingers that Troy isn't waiting in the hallway to catch her coming out of my room.

True to my word, I leap down the stairs ten minutes later so we can head out. Gabby's sitting rather calmly at the kitchen table with a bowl of Cheerios, and her father is leaning against the counter sipping a cup of coffee. He sees me and dumps the rest of the liquid in his cup into the sink, and then he sets the mug in the dishwasher.

"Ready?" he asks.

"Let's go. I can grab coffee and breakfast at the airport."

He nods once, and he passes by Gabby, pressing a kiss to the top of her head. I wish I could kiss her goodbye once more, but I settle instead for waiting for him to pass by, and then I offer her a wink and blow her a silent kiss while his back is turned. She smiles at me—a smile that doesn't quite reach her eyes as we both face the reality that this is our first time apart, that we're doing this in secret, that I might not even get to talk to her for the next few days while I bond with her father.

What a mess.

It's only three days.

It's going to be worse during the season.

I remind myself of these things, but it doesn't make it feel any better in the moment.

And then I get in the car with Troy and we head toward the airport as I try to push the image of his daughter's naked body out of my head.

Chapter 13
Gabby

I finish my bowl of cereal before I grab my phone and draft a text to Kaylee. I feel like a loser, but after my last conversation with Mia that happened via text message a few days ago, I also feel like Kaylee might understand me more than Mia would.

It's only now I realize I haven't spoken with Mia since Cooper and I reconnected. I've seen her boyfriend more than I've seen her.

I want to tell her about Cooper and me, but I also feel like she'd rather see me with Greg than with Cooper...and it's not her decision to make. She slipped into class late yesterday, so we weren't sitting by one another, and I had to run out to get to the stadium for the Monday intern meeting, so we didn't talk after class. I'll see her in class today, so maybe we can chat then.

It's not even a contest for me when it comes to the great Cooper versus Greg debate, though. It's between the man who feels very much like he might be my soul mate versus a guy I've known a couple years and have never once been interested in. If Mia can't understand that, maybe she isn't the friend I thought she was.

I finally shoot off the text to Kaylee before I lose my nerve even though she's married to the hottest tight end in the NFL and I'm freaking out a little as I click the *send* button.

Me: *Hi Kaylee! It's Gabby. Cooper told me to text you to see if I can help you with StrongFitKids while he's out of town, and I'd love to grab coffee and chat if you have time! I have class and then need to swing by the stadium, but I'm free after five today and tomorrow.*

Her response doesn't come right away, but I don't really expect it to since I know she's busy between her job coordinating the SFK program in her husband's fitness clubs and raising twin baby girls.

I take a shower and head to school, and I'm ten minutes early for class since I'm hoping I'll run into Mia. It's while I'm sitting waiting for class to start that I get a return text from Kaylee.

Kaylee: *I would love that! I'm so swamped. Would you mind coming over to my place? Tonight works better since Ben has tomorrow off. We can chat SFK and see if you still want to do some work for me. BTW I'm absolutely thrilled Coop pulled his head out of his ass and got back together with you. I love you for him.*

My heart melts as I read her words. She's one of his best friends, and she approves. Her words seem to push me up onto the kind of floating cloud I can ride for weeks.

And then a text comes through from Mia.

Mia: *I'm going to miss class today. Can you take notes for me?*

Me: *Is everything okay?*

Mia: *Just an epic hangover. Dylan and I went to a concert last night. He'll be at the stadium for the internship though.*

I guess I won't see her today...and I swear I'm not judging her reason for missing class.

Except I'm totally judging.

I'm a Type A, straight A student. Mia used to be, too, before she got tangled up with Dylan. I'm starting to wonder how good he is for her, but given how I feel like she's judging my relationship with Cooper, I also think it's not my place to judge hers with Dylan.

Me: *I'll send you my notes after class.*

I text Kaylee back, too, letting her know I can swing by after work and bring dinner with me, and then I ignore my phone a while so I can take meticulous notes for Mia.

I hit my second class of the day with enough time to eat a granola bar in between and to catch up on my messages, and I'm happy to spot one from Cooper.

Or rather, from *Captain.*

Captain: *Landed and missing you.*

Me: *Still here and missing you. I made plans with Kaylee for dinner.*

He doesn't respond by the time my next class starts, and I hate the distance already.

After class, I head to the stadium to work a few hours, and I learn we don't have another challenge until Thursday, but it's going to be a big one. My mind races with all the possibilities, but we'll find out soon enough. The interns are split up into different departments, so I don't get a chance to chat with Dylan at all. And then I order dinner and grab it on my way to Kaylee's house.

I'm immediately impressed by the gorgeous mansion I pull up to after following my GPS to her address, and when I ring the bell, I hear a baby crying through the closed front door.

Kaylee looks stressed as she opens the door, bouncing a girl on her hip. The girl has tears streaming down her cheeks. "This entire freaking house is tile, and these little girls are racing to see who's going to walk first, and it's impossible to keep two babies from crawling and standing and falling backward right onto the tile." She shakes her head and blows out a breath. "Come on in."

I giggle a little as I walk in with the bags of food I picked up on my way. "Can I help with anything?"

"You brought me dinner. You're a freaking lifesaver."

I giggle, and then I realize there was nothing to be nervous about. Kaylee is a new mom doing the best she can, and she's flustered and stressed and I'm the girl stepping in to make things just a little easier for her today.

I set the food on the table and spot the other twin playing on the floor with a stuffed animal. I walk over and talk in a baby voice with her for a minute, and she coos happily.

Her sister is in her mama's arms, and she's calming down, too.

I get a weird feeling in my chest...like this is something I want. I've never been sure if I wanted kids given how I was raised, but I feel like in the right circumstances and with the right person, it could be a really magical thing.

Is Cooper the right guy? Am I in the right circumstance?

Time will tell.

And then the one Kaylee is holding must remember what just happened because she lets out a loud wail of a scream.

Then the one on the floor cooing happily starts up with screams as loud as her sister's.

Kaylee sighs as she makes her way over to the one on the floor. "I'm going to go feed these two and tuck them in. Go ahead and start dinner while it's hot. I'll be down in a half hour or so. I'm so sorry." She scoops the one on the floor into her free arm. She carries both babies up the stairs, both screaming their heads off, and I stare after her in horror for a beat as that warm feeling in my chest evaporates like the wind, and I'm left wondering whether or not this is something I might ever want.

Chapter 14
Cooper

I glance at my phone for the hundredth time today, and I'm disappointed there's nothing new from Gabby…or rather, from *Sunshine.*

I shouldn't be. We talked about this and we both were on the same page. We knew it would be difficult to communicate given the fact that I'm traveling with Troy.

I mentally calculate the time difference, and it should be around dinnertime in Vegas. As for me, I find myself at a bar with my two bosses and a potential new addition to our team. We're just a few blocks away from the local strip joints, and given what I know about Troy's club, I'm one hundred percent positive that a gentleman's club will be on the agenda at some point while we're here in Boston.

I wonder how Joanie feels about that.

The Red Sox are in town for the next week, and there was no game tonight, so we met AJ and his agent a few hours ago. Mike is putting the hard sell on the agent, and on the plane ride over, I was informed that my job is to sell AJ on Vegas.

The problem?

I don't really feel like I've gotten to know Vegas all that well. I've been…preoccupied, as my girlfriend would say.

"I hear Troy owns a club," AJ says to me, and I'm not sure how much I'm allowed to say about that.

Troy's busy chatting up the agent, so I just nod.

"You been there?" He tips his bottle of beer to his lips, and I nod again.

"I only toured the first floor, so I can't really speak to much more than that," I say.

He leans in close so the conversation is just for the two of us. "Give it to me straight, man. You think Vegas is the place for me?"

I glance across the table at Troy, Mike, and Doug before I turn back to AJ. I study him for a beat, and then I nod. "What Troy is putting together here is going to be fucking legendary, man. He's got Rush Ross, Danny Brewer, and Duke Owens already committed, already starting workouts at the stadium."

"And you," AJ points out.

"And me," I repeat. "I don't know. Every time I step into the stadium, I get this strange feeling that I'm in the right place at the right time. You know? That feeling you can't quite explain but that just feels right. There are very few people who could've talked me into unretiring, and you know Troy. This is as good as it fucking gets, man." I shake my head. "It's a once in a lifetime sort of thing, and my honest opinion is that anyone who gets the offer to come play for him would be stupid to pass it by."

The strangest thought bounces into my brain at that moment.

Could Troy be my father-in-law someday?

I never thought about marrying Stacy despite how many hints she dropped that she wanted to. But Gabby?

I think about it all the time.

I think about a future with her all the time, and I want our future to start now. I want her to work for the team so she can travel with us. I want her by my side through every victory, through every loss, through every thing that happens in season and out of it.

I want our future to start now...but I also know I can't rush her. She's still in college, for fuck's sake.

He ponders my words a while as he chugs down the rest of his beer. "Hey Doug," AJ yells over the bar noise to his agent across the table, interrupting the conversation between the three men. Doug turns toward AJ, who says, "Make it happen."

Doug nods once and resumes his conversation with the Heat brass, and I chuckle as I shake my head. "Just that simple?"

He nods. "He knows what to do. We've been together a number of years, and he knows if I ain't happy, he ain't gonna be happy, either."

There's a lot of truth in that statement, I suppose.

"You seeing anybody?" he asks, and he flags our waitress down to order another beer. I hold up my bottle, too, to indicate I'd also like another.

"Can I plead the fifth on that one?" I laugh, but it comes out hollow. For as much as I was just thinking about a future with her,

I know I can't exactly blurt out the fact that we're together. I like AJ, but I don't know him all that well. I'm not ready to trust him with something as huge as the fact that I'm currently banging the manager's daughter.

He laughs. "Is this one of those complicated situations?"

"Something like that," I mutter. Complicated doesn't really even begin to describe it. "You?"

He shakes his head. "Nah, man. Tried it and failed, and I made the decision a long time ago that I will only fail at something one time in my life."

"So the next one will be a success?" I guess.

He lets out a laugh. "Nope. There won't be a next one to fail. I live out of a suitcase, anyway. It's just easier this way."

I'll be living out of a suitcase again shortly, too, and I can't help but feel a little melancholy over the whole idea. I like having a place to call my own...especially if Gabby is there. There's no better place to sleep than home. But I'll be out of town for at least eighty-one away games a season, and the thought of that much time away from her causes my chest to ache.

I don't even like tonight.

The thought that AJ just told his agent to make it happen gives me hope that we can head back to Vegas as early as tomorrow, but the logical side of my brain knows it won't happen that way.

Which is why I chug down another beer.

And another, and another.

Troy suggests a strip club, likely as a bargaining tool to get the very single AJ even more amped about the idea of moving to Vegas, where the strippers are of an elite class, and even though I have no interest in looking at tits that belong to anyone other than Gabby, I'm simply along for the ride. It's not like I can stay back in the car while the rest of the guys in my group are getting lap dances and tucking twenties into G-strings.

So I go along.

I should tell Gabby. I should be honest with her. I know this, but I'm also stuck in beside her father. My only chance is to escape to the bathroom and send a text on the down low...but as I make my way toward the restroom, guess who accompanies me?

Troy.

Guess who sits beside me at our table?

Troy.

Guess who orders me another beer?

Troy.

And guess who is pictured beside me as we stumble out of the club and head back to our car, drunk women from inside following us and hanging on us despite our continued gentle rejections?

You got it...Troy.

Chapter 15
Gabby

"What the hell?" I murmur as I zoom in on the photo.

Maybe he's trying to push her away. It's fuzzy and far away and hard to tell, but I definitely spot Cooper and my father with a bevy of women hanging around them. They look to be outside a building with a logo emblazoned on top.

I zoom in on that, too.

The Bare Kitty Gentleman's Club.

I roll my eyes. Real classy, Dad. Extra classy, Cooper.

I blow out a breath.

I haven't heard from him all damn day, and it looks like it's because he's been out looking at boobies while I've been engaging in a clinic regarding all the reasons I may never want to have sex again.

Or rather…all the reasons why I may never want children.

Kaylee swore up and down this was just an off night, but those two girls never fell asleep the entire two hours I was there. We tried to chat about SFK, but she ran up and down the stairs so many times that *my* legs started to hurt.

She ate a cold dinner while she explained that both girls are currently teething, and when I confessed I didn't really know what that meant, I got a long explanation about how teeth erupt from the gums and it's actually such a painful process that adults wouldn't be able to handle it.

I left unsure if I was the kind of adult who could handle other sorts of pains associated with babies, too. Like childbirth and emotional trauma from a nine-month-old smacking me in the face.

She has twins, I remind myself. It's way harder with twins. One starts crying and the other tries to one-up her by being louder and then the first one tries getting even louder and I'm not sure how Kaylee does it.

The odds of me having twins someday are like one in a million. Or…I search that stat. One in two hundred fifty. Still a longshot.

She told me she loves being a mom. She said she gets a ton of help, but tonight was one of those weird nights where Ben was at the practice facility late and her mom was busy with her brother Jack's kids and she was flying solo.

I asked her what it was like with Ben constantly gone, but as it turns out, football teams only have about ten away games per season, and they're only gone a few nights when they travel. So Ben *isn't* constantly gone—not the way Cooper would be with a baseball schedule.

Could I do that alone?

Sure, she's had nine months of practice, and she handled it with grace. But I don't know if I'm built for that sort of thing. Cooper, on the other hand, is ready to be with somebody who wants to start popping out babies immediately, and meanwhile, I'm vying for a position that someone is leaving because she's pregnant and won't have the time to dedicate with a newborn.

Am I holding Cooper back?

It's something that merits discussion, for sure.

I'm not at the age where I feel my biological clock ticking, but he is…and maybe that's the biggest detriment to our age gap situation.

One of us is going to have to give in on that, and I'm not ready for it to be me.

That's not to say I'm not open to the discussion *someday*, but after spending a couple hours at Kaylee's…that discussion feels even further down the road.

The house is quiet—too quiet as I stare at the pictures posted moments ago by some gossip site, and I decide to call Justin, who I haven't had a chance to hang with in a few days.

He picks up just when I think it's about to go to voicemail. "Hey baby girl, what's good?" He's sort of whispering but also not whispering and it's weird.

"Hey. Did I catch you at a bad time?" I hear some rustling.

"No, I uh…" he trails off as he seemingly searches for an excuse.

And then I hear it. A decidedly male grunt that doesn't belong to Justin.

"Oh, God. You're busy. I'll let you go."

"No, no, it's fine." I hear more rustling, and then his voice gets a little louder. "What's going on?"

"We just haven't talked in a few days so I was calling to see if you want to hang out."

He clears his throat, and then I hear a door click shut. "I have someone over," he says, and this time he is definitely whispering.

"Who?" I whisper back.

"Fucking Brian! He's interested and he totally made the first move. We were just kissing a little and it was maybe going to heat up to another level and then my phone rang."

Brian? Brian…like intern Brian?

"Oh my God, why did you answer?" I screech.

"He told me to!"

"Get back in there! We'll talk tomorrow!"

He laughs. "Okay, okay. Bye!"

"Good luck!" I yell at him, but the call has already dropped.

I wander around the house by myself a while as I suddenly feel really lonely. Mia's been acting strange, and Justin doesn't even know I'm back together with Cooper. I haven't talked to Chelsea, Kelly, or Becky since my birthday party a month ago. Between getting caught up with Cooper and school starting at the same time as my internship, it's been a busy month.

It's times like these I wish I lived on campus. There's always someone around to talk to, somewhere to go, something to do.

Instead I'm dating a thirty-three-year-old who's hanging out at a strip club thousands of miles away while I'm sitting in my dad's mansion by myself.

I glance at the clock on my phone. It's after midnight in Boston, and I haven't heard from Cooper all day. I decide to send a text.

Me: *Hope you're having fun with the strippers.*

God dammit. I regret it the second I hit send, but I can't change it now.

I don't hear back from him, which only tells me he's having a blast with the strippers.

I really need to get a hobby because sitting here sending passive aggressive texts can't be healthy.

My phone rings an hour after I sent the text, and it's him calling.

"Hi," I answer.

"I told you once not to play games." His voice is low and gravelly, a little demanding, and it's freaking hot.

"I'm not playing games. I really did hope you were having fun looking at boobs. Maybe some vaginas, too."

He barks out a laugh. "Have you ever even been to a strip club?"

"No," I admit.

"They don't show cunts, babe."

Something about hearing what feels like the dirtiest dirty word out of his mouth presses a wild ache between my thighs.

"Well, that's comforting," I mutter.

"I'm sorry I haven't been able to get in touch all day. And I'm sorry I went to the club." His words have just the slightest edge of a slur to them. "I had to sneak out of the room just to call you. Your father rented some suite so we could all stay together."

"Any idea when you're coming back?" I ask.

"No. We're going to the Red Sox game tomorrow night and I have a feeling both Troy and Mike will want to stay for the Wednesday night game, too."

"Do you want to?"

"Look, I love baseball. Of course. It's my fucking life's work," he says, and I hear the crunch of gravel beneath his feet like he's taking a walk outside. "But there are other things I'd rather be doing than be stuck here right now."

"What would you rather be doing?" I don't even realize my voice has dropped an entire octave until it comes out all gritty and hoarse.

"You."

"I miss you."

"I miss you too. We just got back together, and I'm stuck here, and all day long I've been looking for some window to try to get in touch. I'm not really a strip club guy, Gabby. You know me. I'm laid back. I'm pretty simple. I just want to lie on the couch with my girl watching a movie. I just want to take you to bed and make you come so I can see that look on your face when your eyes roll back because of the pleasure I'm giving you. I just want to kiss you, to hold you, to laugh with you."

"Do you really mean that?" I ask softly.

"With all my heart."

Tears spring to my eyes.

"How was your night?" he asks.

I laugh softly. "Interesting. I brought dinner over to Kaylee's, and let me tell you…it was chaotic."

He chuckles. "How?"

"Both twins are teething at the same time, whatever that means, and it just made me realize I'm not ready for that anytime soon."

The words just sort of slip out with a little giggle before I realize this is probably part of a much larger conversation, and certainly not one I should be giggling through.

He clears his throat. "Oh. Uh…" I hear someone yell his name in the background. "Shit. I need to go. I'll talk to you soon."

He ends the call with my truth bomb just sitting in the middle of the road.

I have no idea what the debris following the detonation is going to look like…and I have no idea when I'll find out.

Chapter 16
Cooper

"**N**oah!" AJ yells again, and I quickly cut the call as I turn around to face him despite the thing she just said.

The thing that feels like a heavy weight pressing on my chest.

The thing I fear has the power to spell the eventual end for us.

Fuck.

But this is why I'm here, after all, and if AJ showed up at the hotel to talk some more, well, it's part of my job to listen. It's part of being the leader Troy tapped me to be.

"What's going on, man?" I ask. We parted ways an hour ago, and I thought he was heading home. Apparently I thought wrong.

"Sorry, I didn't mean to interrupt your call. Was that your girl?"

I laugh. "I thought I pled the fifth on that."

"You did, but the way your face lit up when I brought it up told a different story. Who is she?"

"It's new and I'm not ready to talk about it yet." I leave it at that and opt for a swift subject change. "So what brought you back here?"

"I got home and realized it's not every day a guy gets the chance to really pick Cooper Noah's brain." He looks so genuine, so earnest...so confused. "I don't know what I'm doing. I told Doug to make it happen, but is it a jackass move to leave what I've got going on here?"

"Well, what've you got going on here?" I ask. We head toward the lobby bar and slide into an empty booth.

A waitress approaches our table before he can even answer that question. "What can I get y'all?" She glances up from her notepad at the man across the table from me, and her jaw drops clean down to the floor. "Oh my God, you're AJ Winters." Her head twists toward me, and her eyes widen. "And you're Cooper Noah!"

"Ball fan, I take it?" I ask. AJ looks a little too preoccupied to answer her with charm, so I take over.

"Only the daughter of like the *hugest* Red Sox fan alive," she confirms. She looks like she's around Gabby's age, maybe a couple years older. "And I'm also secretly a Dodgers fan," she whispers in my direction with a huge smile.

I chuckle. "But not them damn Yankees, right?"

"Right." She nods resolutely.

"Can I borrow your pen and a sheet of paper?" I ask her.

Her brows dip, but she rips a sheet off her notepad and hands me her pen. I glance at her nametag and write on the paper.

Hannah — thanks for all the drinks. Cooper Noah

I pass the paper over to AJ, and he signs it, too.

Hannah squeals.

"Two Miller Lites," I order, and she grins.

"Coming right up."

She spins and scampers away to get our drinks, and I turn back to AJ.

"What've you got going on here?" I repeat.

He sighs as he settles back into the booth, and he lifts a shoulder. "I've been here a long time, you know? It's like leaving family, and it's not usually in the player's court like it is with this situation. If Jim knew I was even considering it..." He trails off as he mentions his general manager.

"I know. It was different with me since an injury took me out," I admit, my eyes down on the table. I tug on the bill of my black Under Armour hat.

"But did it?"

I glance up and see him studying me, and I blow out a breath. "I mean, yeah. I could've gone back to finish out my contract, but things felt too fucked up for me by that point. My girl cheated on me with another player, and I guess it all just came together in the perfect storm. I'd started working a job I liked, and I just didn't want to go back to the life I had before. I didn't want to go back to LA."

He glances up at me. "Baseball has been my entire life since I was six." He shakes his head a little. "I don't know how to be any other way. Was that what brought you back?"

"Honestly? It was Troy that brought me back. He gave me this offer at a time when I was starting to feel a little restless, a little ready for change. Right place, right time." I remember making that choice in the car on the way back to Caesars Palace just moments before I met Gabby, and somehow that weekend with her sealed the deal. Turning what might have been a one-night stand into what could be the most important relationship of my life just confirmed the fact that I made the right decision.

I don't tell AJ any of that, obviously. He's not here to listen to my love life woes, anyway.

He's here so I can convince him that Vegas is the place where he needs to be.

"I signed on for three years," I say. "You can do just about anything for three years, right?"

Hannah swings by with our drinks, and thankfully she drops them and runs so we can continue our private conversation.

"What'll it be like playing somewhere else? I've spent eight years here." He's clearly torn, the buzz from drinking earlier worn off as reality sets in.

I take a long drag from my glass. "I can't answer that yet since I spent my entire career in Los Angeles, but what I can tell you is that Vegas is ready for this, and the members of the first Vegas Heat team will be creating a legacy that will live on forever. That's the vibe I get every time I walk into The House."

"The House?" he repeats.

"The nickname for the stadium. You know—Vegas, gambling. The House always wins, right?"

He chuckles. "So if I don't join 'em, I'm gonna get beat by 'em?"

"You're gonna get your ass handed to you by 'em, man. You've seen what Troy is capable of."

"I have." He nods and chugs down half his beer. "And he got you to agree not only to make a comeback, but to lead this team. How the fuck can I say no to that?"

I grin as I reach a hand out across the table, and he shakes it.

"Teammates, brother," he says, and I nod.

"To the Vegas Heat." I hold up my glass, and he laughs as he holds his up, too.

"To the Vegas Heat."

We both finish our beers and order another while conversation moves to the fact that we'll be standing as close as two bros can on the field since he's in the position beside third.

It's a little after two in the morning here in Boston when my phone starts to ring. I figure it's Gabby calling on the off chance

I'm able to pick up and say goodnight, but when I glance at my screen, I find it's not Sunshine at all.

It's my mother.

And calls after midnight never mean good news.

Chapter 17
Cooper

"**M**om?" I answer.

AJ's brows are knitted together across the table from me as he looks at me in alarm.

"Baby, sorry it's so late but Marissa just called and said Connor was having symptoms of a heart attack. There's an ambulance on the way for him and she asked if I could come stay with the kids."

"Shit. Is he okay?"

"I don't know." Her voice wavers, and if it's hard for *me* to hear this, I can't imagine how hard it is for *her* to hear this given the fact that she lost her husband to heart disease nearly twenty-five years ago. "I'm on my way over there now."

My heart races. "Mom, just focus on driving. We can talk later."

"No, no. Keep talking. You always know what to say."

My chest tightens as I try to think of the right thing to say. I fail. My mother is the one who comforts me in times like this...not the other way around.

"It's going to be okay," I say softly. "What were his symptoms?"

"I'm not sure," she says. I hear her turn signal clicking in the background.

"Are you close to their house?"

"Mm-hm," she murmurs. "Two minutes away."

"I'm getting on the first plane I can so I can be there with you, okay?"

My mom needs me. I've needed her plenty of times in my life. It's my turn to be there for her.

I thought she'd put up a fight. I thought she'd tell me not to come because it feels too scary to have me there. Instead, she says, "Okay."

Fear plagues me that it's serious.

This is my older brother. I was born when he was four, and I spent my entire childhood idolizing him. I was three and he was seven when he taught me how to climb the rock wall at the park near our house. I was five and he was nine when he broke his arm because we were jumping on a trampoline and he fell off. I was nine and he was thirteen when we went through losing our father to heart disease. I was twelve and he was sixteen when he first snuck porn into the house. I was thirteen and he was seventeen when I caught him having sex in the backseat of our mom's minivan after his homecoming dance. I was fourteen and he was eighteen when he moved out of my mom's house and went to college, but we talked every single day. I was twenty-one and he was twenty-five when he married Marissa.

We haven't talked every single day like we used to, but life happens. He's married with two kids and has the kind of career that keeps him incredibly busy all the time, and I have my own shit I'm dealing with that keeps us from being able to talk as often as we once did.

And maybe I don't idolize him the way I once did, but he's still my brother. He's still one of my best friends. We can get together at Christmas and pick on each other and laugh and wrestle like we did when we were kids...although he *did* throw his back out two years ago when I pinned him against the wall. I've gained athleticism in the last decade, while he's gained grays and a receding hairline.

I will not be thirty-three when I lose him.

"I'm here," she says. She blows out a breath, and I can tell she's nervous to go inside.

"Mom, it's okay. You've got this. Call me anytime, no matter what it is. I'll text my flight details when I have them. Okay?"

"Yeah. Thanks, baby. I love you."

"I love you, too."

She ends the call, and I stare at my phone a beat while silence passes between AJ and me.

"Everything okay?" he finally asks.

I shake my head. "My older brother might be having a heart attack."

"Oh, Jesus. Where is he?"

"Chicago suburbs."

"What can I do to help?"

I shake my head as my eyes meet his, and it's in that moment I remember exactly why I wanted to play again. It's not just the love

324

of the game. It's the brotherhood. The atmosphere. The respect and the teamwork and the dedication to doing everything we can for each other. "Nothing, but thanks. I need to let Troy know what's going on then catch a flight out of here." I stand and throw some cash down on the table. "But you're joining me in Vegas, right?"

He nods as he stands, too, and he reaches out to shake my hand, pulling me in for a quick hug where he slaps my back. "Yeah, man. You need anything, you call. And let me know how he's doing, all right?"

I nod. "Thanks, brother. I'll see you soon."

I head up to the suite I'm sharing with Troy and Mike, searching for flights as I go, already knowing they'll understand that I need to get to Chicago as soon as possible.

And I'm not wrong.

"Family first." Those are Troy's exact words, and part of me wonders whether those words would've been different before he found out he had a daughter.

The daughter I'm banging on the sly.

What the fuck am I doing?

Chapter 18
Gabby

When my phone rings a little after one in the morning, I'm still awake even though I know I need to go to bed. I've been catching up on some trash TV I've missed out on over the last few weeks, and my chest tightens when I see Cooper's name on the screen.

Is he calling to talk about what I said earlier?

A dart of nervousness pings my stomach.

"Hey you," I answer, trying not to sound guarded.

I hear a sniffle on the other end of the line, but no words accompany it.

"Cooper?" I ask, sitting up in bed.

He clears his throat.

"What's going on?" A sense of alarm pinches my heart. Is this it for us? He can't take being with someone who doesn't want kids tomorrow, and he's calling to break it off with me over the phone?

He wouldn't do it over the phone. He's not that kind of guy.

He doesn't answer, and the sense of alarm turns from a pinch into a cold, icy grip.

"Cooper, baby, talk to me," I beg.

He lets out a shaky breath before he says, "My mom just called to let me know my brother was having symptoms of a heart attack tonight."

"Oh my God, Cooper. I'm so sorry. How's he doing?" The relief that pings through me that this isn't about me or us is replaced by a different sort of panic.

"I, uh, I don't know yet. I'm not sure. My mom was on her way to his house to watch my nephews so Marissa could be with him. I haven't heard anything from her in the last hour."

"Where are you now?" I ask.

"On my way to the airport in Boston. I guess I've been in action mode since I heard from her and when I heard your voice pick up the call, I got a little emotional." His voice is quiet, like he's trying not to let whoever's driving him listen in on his conversation.

"Oh, baby," I murmur, my heart breaking for him at the same time his words fill my bucket all the way to the top that we're close enough that he can trust me to hold onto his emotions. "What can I do? Do you want me to come meet you in Chicago?"

"Fuck," he mutters. "Of course that's what I want, but we're keeping up this fucking charade so that's not an option."

"If you need me there, we blow our cover. I don't care. Nothing matters right now except you."

"Christ, Gabby." He sounds like he's getting choked up again. "That means so much to me." He inhales a long breath before he exhales. "It's okay. I'm okay. I just keep thinking about this time we were kids and I fell off my bike and scraped my leg. My knee was bleeding and we were a few blocks from home. My brother legit picked me up and carried me on his back the entire way home. Like how did we get to the point where he's old enough to have a heart attack after that's what we lost our dad to? I can't lose him, Gabby. I'm not ready to lose him."

He unloads everything he's been carrying onto me, and I take all the weight I can to help lighten his load. "You're not losing him, Cooper," I say firmly. "You're not."

"Okay," he whispers, and my heart breaks at the pure fear in his tone. "I'll be a better brother, I swear. If he just makes it…" He trails off, and I know he's in the bargaining phase. I don't know what it's like to have a sibling, but I do know what it's like to lose people I'm close to. I was never all that close with my mother, but my grandmother was a saint. She got sick when I was eleven, and I remember the bargaining phase. The quiet prayers where we tell God that we'll do whatever it takes to keep the person we love around.

It didn't work for my grandma, but that doesn't mean it won't work for Cooper.

"You're a good brother," I say softly. "You're leaving a business trip to be with him. You're dropping everything to support him and his family."

"It's not enough," he says, and I can hear the way he's beating himself up. "I haven't talked to him in over a month."

"So you'll call him more. You'll send funny memes to make him laugh."

"Yeah, for the first few weeks, and then what? We'll slip back into old habits. Life moves on, but I can't watch life move on without him. He's only four years younger than my dad was when he died. What if I'm next, Gabby?" In his last question, his voice is barely above a whisper.

"You take care of yourself. You're an athlete. You work out. You're in shape. Was your dad that way? Is your brother that way?" I ask.

"I don't know about Connor. He's got a high-pressure career and he's been traveling a lot, which makes me wonder whether he's been hitting fast food and not taking care of himself. That was my dad's downfall. He was an electrician, and he ate garbage food for lunch every day, and eventually it clogged enough arteries that it took him from us way too early."

"I'm so sorry, Cooper. Maybe this is the wake-up call your brother needs to take better care of himself," I suggest.

"Maybe. Or maybe it's the wake-up call I need." He leaves his sentence at that, and it feels ominous.

I don't like it.

"I'm almost at the airport, so I need to go." His tone is flat. Emotionless after all the emotion he's shared with me during this call, and I don't know what to do to get him back. To hold him close. To keep him in my arms where he belongs.

"Call me any time you need me, okay?"

"Yeah." His single, grunt-like word comes out flat.

"I love you," I say.

"You too." He ends the call, and even though he expressed the feeling, I'm worried what this could mean for the two of us.

He called me and unleashed his emotions on me. That has to be a good thing...right?

Except then he clammed up, and he's miles and miles away, and I have no way of making sure we're still on the same page.

I look up flights. I don't even know where he is, but I could be in Chicago in a few hours.

I think about just showing up, but he's the one who said I shouldn't. I don't want to step on any toes. I don't want to walk on the wrong side of the imaginary line we've drawn.

But I want to be with him.

I want to hold his hand through this—and not just this, but through everything.

Chapter 19
Cooper

My own heart has been thundering since the plane landed. Is this it? Is it happening to me, too?

I realize it's just nerves, but that doesn't make it any less stressful as I get off the plane and find a ride to take me to Connor's place.

The last time I was here was last Christmas. Santa came, and in with him apparently flew Uncle Coop.

I texted my mom as soon as the plane touched down to let her know I was here, and she said she was at the hospital. Marissa went home to get the kids off to school, and their dad has been traveling so much lately that neither of them even knows he's at the hospital. I guess they wanted to keep it quiet until they knew what they were dealing with, and it's one of those odd situations where I wonder how I would've handled it with my own kids.

Would I have woken them and hugged them before I let the ambulance take me away, or would that have just traumatized them?

I think back to when my own dad passed. I was the same age my nephew Jacob is now.

He had a heart attack while he was at work. He was inspecting a circuit breaker one minute and unconscious the next. The ambulance didn't even make it on time to try to revive him.

When we said goodbye that morning before I left for school, I had no way of knowing it would be the last time.

But that's life, isn't it? We never know when we're doing anything for the last time until we look back and can say it was the last time. It's fleeting and it's ever-changing and it's indiscriminate.

I didn't know when I busted my elbow that it would be my last time playing ball, but it was—or at least I *thought* it was until a month ago when Troy gave me the opportunity to come back. But it's rare to get a second chance at the big things.

He's only thirty-seven.

That's the thought I keep circling back to.

He's only thirty-seven.

My dad was only forty-one.

I'm thirty-three. Four years away from thirty-seven. Eight years away from forty-one.

I don't feel like I'm on the way out. I feel young most days, but I'm afraid growing old just doesn't run in the genes of the Noah men, and the whole reason I'm here today proves that.

Troy was beyond understanding, and he surprised me when he admitted heart disease runs in his family, too. He told me he lost his father to a heart attack a decade ago, and if he wasn't so stubborn and he would've just gone to the hospital, he might've survived it.

That's what I'm clinging to—that Marissa called the ambulance in time. That she got my brother help in time.

My sister-in-law opens the door when I knock. She suggested I swing by the house first to drop my bags. She's going back to the hospital anyway, so she showered and waited for me so we could go see my brother together.

"How's he doing?" I ask as I step in and wrap my sister-in-law into a hug. Marissa and Connor have been together for nearly as long as I can remember. They met in junior high and have been inseparable ever since. She was there when Dad died, and she's been like a sister to me for just as long.

"They put in a stent last night to release the blockage, and now he's in the CCU," she says.

"The CCU?" I ask.

"Cardiac Care Unit. They're running labs to see how he's responding, and he's resting in between. He has to stay flat for a while since he's on blood thinners and has an open entry point, but we're hopeful they'll move him to the regular telemetry floor later today. You ready to go see him?"

I nod, setting my suitcase to the side of the door, and I follow her through the house to the garage, where I slide into the passenger seat of her SUV.

"How are the boys?" I ask, trying to make conversation as we head toward the hospital, and I guess that's the question that breaks the camel's back, because Marissa starts to cry. I think about trying to backtrack, but I'm not even sure how at this point.

She blows out a breath. "I just feel so guilty that they're at school totally oblivious to what's going on with their dad."

I reach over and squeeze her arm. "It's okay. You're just protecting them."

"But what if he doesn't make it and we kept them from him in his last moments?" Her voice barely comes out above a whisper.

"We can't think like that, okay? He's going to make it. He's strong. He's young. He's got a lot to live for."

So was my dad. He was strong, and young, and he had a lot to live for. That didn't keep him here.

I don't say that, obviously.

She nods and draws in a deep breath. "Okay." She sniffs. "You're right. This is all just scary." She reaches over to grab my hand, and I squeeze hers back.

"Of course it is. I'm scared, too. But we'll rally around Connor. He's stubborn, and he's not giving up without one hell of a fight."

She nods. "He's *so* stubborn. God, he didn't even want to go to the hospital last night! He was clammy and shaking and could barely breathe and I had to call for the ambulance when I left the room because he wouldn't let me do it."

I squeeze her hand, which I'm still holding. "You might've saved his life, Marissa."

She glances at me as she pulls up to a stoplight, pressing her lips together. "I hope so."

We arrive at the hospital a few minutes later, and we walk toward the Cardiac Care Unit after we're screened at the front desk. I text my mom to let her know we're here, and she's waiting by the elevators when we step off them. She practically leaps into my arms for a hug, and I hold her tightly. "It's okay, Mom." I try to soothe her and fight off my own emotions at the same time.

"I'm scared," she whispers.

"I know. Me too." I squeeze her again, and she pulls back and leads us down the hall to his room.

When she opens the door, I find my brother lying on a bed looking rather pale and weak, a whole bunch of white stickers with wires sticking out of them attached to his chest. A nurse stands by reading a screen, and my brother's brows rise as he turns his head and sees me walk in.

"Hey, Pooper's here!" he says a little weakly, using the nickname he gave me when I was two and in diapers and he thought he was a hilarious six-year-old.

"He's on morphine," the nurse says as if that explains his nickname for me. It doesn't. He'd call me that whether or not he was hopped up on drugs.

I force a laugh even though it doesn't feel like there's much to laugh at right now. "How are you feeling, Con-man?" I ask cautiously, throwing one of the nicknames I dubbed him with when he started law school back at him.

"I'm fine. These nurses don't believe me when I say I'm fine." He shoots a glare at the nurse. "I told them I need to get the hell out of here. I'm losing time on an important case. I'm up for partner, you know." He says it proudly.

"We know, we know, Mr. Noah. We're still running tests, and I already told you that every time you talk about making partner, your heart rate picks up speed," the nurse says.

Connor draws in a deep breath and blows it out slowly as if that'll slow his numbers.

"Honey, maybe partner isn't the best thing right now," Mom starts to say, and the nurse shoots her a dirty look as we all watch the lines on the screen jump. She holds up her hands in surrender. "Sorry, sorry."

A doctor steps into the room, and the nurse shoos us out so he can examine my brother. We head out to the hall to get out of the way.

"He looks good," I lie. I shouldn't lie. Everyone who knows me knows I can't lie, but the truth is that while he looked pale and weak, he also looked *okay*. He didn't look like he was banging down death's door, anyway. But I don't really know what heart disease looks like on the outside.

Marissa presses her lips together. "Just don't bring up partner," she says. "It's a point of contention between the two of us anyway. He hasn't been to a single one of Jacob's swim meets this season, and don't even get me started on the last time he was at one of Ethan's baseball games."

She shakes her head, and I get the feeling it's not just Ethan and Jacob's events her husband has been missing out on. In fact, I wonder if she quit her job teaching so the boys would feel like at least one parent was focused on them.

It's a terrible thought to have, but the fast-paced, stressful job could potentially be what led Connor exactly where he is right now. Well, that combined with the fast food, the genetics, and the blocked arteries.

Doctors and nurses are in and out, and I'm confident my brother is getting the best care possible. We head down to lunch, and it's as we're finishing that Marissa looks at her watch and promptly breaks down crying.

My mom tosses an arm around her shoulder. "What's the matter?"

"The boys get out of school in two hours and I don't know how I'm going to tell them," she wails.

"Let me tell them, then," I say quietly.

Her brows dip.

"You stay here with Connor," I say. "Mom and I will go pick them up from the bus stop and take them home. We'll let them know what's going on, and we'll answer their questions. We'll make sure they're safe and taken care of."

Marissa cries a little harder for a second before she sucks in a deep breath. "How are you still single?"

My mom laughs, and I roll my eyes.

"What?" she says. "You're just so…" she trails off as she searches for the right word. "Good. Wholesome. Kind. And if you weren't like a little brother to me, I might even say good looking."

"Good looking?" I repeat, wrinkling my nose. It's a far cry from Hottie McCuteStuff, as Gabby once referred to me.

Gabby.

My chest tightens. She's never far from my thoughts, yet in this moment, her appearance front and center feels somehow gut wrenching.

It's gut wrenching that she isn't here with me…that she *can't* be here with me.

It's gut wrenching that she's twelve years my junior and my best friend's daughter.

It's gut wrenching that she doesn't want the same future at the same time I want it.

Are our worlds and our lives just too far apart, or can we really find a way to make this work?

That's the question on my mind as we finish up lunch and return our trays. It's the question that plagues me as I make small talk with my mom on the way to pick up the boys. It stays with me as we feed them dinner and as they video chat with their dad and as I settle into bed in the guest room.

And once I'm there, settled in under the sheets and blankets that are already making me way too hot, exhausted from getting no sleep last night but knowing I need to have this conversation anyway or I'll be in for a restless night…it's time to finally ask the question to maybe the only other person who can help me answer it.

Chapter 20
Gabby

I haven't heard from him since this morning. He sent one text shortly after he arrived to let me know he landed, but otherwise I guess he's been occupied today.

A two-hour time difference separates us, and it's a little after eight when my phone finally rings.

I answer immediately. "Cooper?"

"Hey," he says. He sounds exhausted.

"How's your brother?"

"He'll be okay," he says. "He's got to change the way he does things, but he'll be all right. They're moving him from the cardiac unit to a step-down unit where the care isn't quite as intensive. They think another day or two before they'll spring him."

"That's great news. And how are you?"

"I've been better," he admits.

"Did you sleep at all last night?" I settle back into the couch, getting comfortable for our chat.

"No. I tried to close my eyes on the plane, but it was useless."

"Go to bed, babe. We can talk tomorrow," I say.

"Nah, I won't be able to sleep anyway."

"How come?" I press, and as soon as the answer comes—in the form of another question—I immediately wish I hadn't pressed.

"Are our lives just too far apart, or do you really think we can find a way to make this work?" he asks. His voice is soft and full of regret.

I gasp at the question. I guess it wasn't what I was expecting. I'd be stupid to ask what's bringing this on since I can guess, but I ask it anyway. "What makes you think our lives are too far apart?"

He's quiet a beat while he thinks over the best way to answer. "I've never made it a secret that I want a wife I can build a family with in the near future. I guess this whole thing with Connor is making me feel the pressure to get started on that. What are we doing, Gab?"

He's never called me Gab, and part of me wonders if it's the emotion in his voice causing him to cut my name short. A fresh pain slices across my chest as I fumble for words to answer that question after I literally told him yesterday I'm not sure I want kids anytime soon. "I, uh…we—we're trying to figure that out. Together."

"Yeah," he murmurs. "I guess I just don't want to waste your time."

I fear his hidden message in those words is that he doesn't want to waste his own time, either. What if we're a dead end?

"You're not," I say, fighting back tears. "You're the best thing that's ever happened to me."

"And I feel the same way about you. But what if it isn't enough?" His voice trembles, and I give up on the fight to stop my own emotions.

Tears start to trickle from my eyes. I don't have the answer to that.

What if he's right?

I need to see him. I need to be with him, consequences be damned.

I need to hold his hand through this, whatever it takes.

I need to kiss him and to love him and to be there by his side as he deals with this.

"What if it *is* enough? Isn't it worth fighting for to find out?"

"Yeah," he murmurs, and I'm not sure I buy it from his tone. He's still questioning things, and this can't be it. This can't be the end of the line for us.

Not when I already see our entire future mapped out in front of us.

"I'm getting a call on the other line from your father," he mutters. "I better take it."

"I love you," I say, not sure what else to say or do.

"Love you." He cuts the call, and my first instinct is to look up flights to Chicago. Fuck tomorrow's classes. Cooper needs me, and not just to prove to him that we belong together, but he needs me holding his hand through whatever this is.

My phone rings a few minutes later, and it's my dad.

"Hey Dad," I answer, realizing too late my voice is still chock full of emotion.

"Hey. You okay?"

"I'm fine. Just watching one of those rom coms on Netflix and I'm all choked up," I lie.

He laughs. "Women and their rom coms, I swear. Listen, can you do me a huge favor?"

"Of course."

"This is really huge," he warns.

"Okay, then I retract my of course and raise a question. What's the favor?"

"I'm tied up all day tomorrow in meetings with upper management here at the Red Sox. It's going to be a fight to get Winters to Vegas, but I'm confident Mike and I can do it even without Cooper, who had to duck out. His brother had a heart attack in Chicago, and I know this is a big ask, but do you think you could check on him?"

"Check on him?" I ask, my heart racing at what he's asking.

"I just talked to him, and I'm worried about him. He's not handling this well. He's with his family, but you know how that goes—he's trying to be strong for them, but sometimes you can't talk to family about family the way you can a friend. I've seen you and him becoming friendly, making jokes, that kind of thing since you've been shadowing him. Like you're the younger sister he never had, and I'm the older brother he never had…if our family was really fucked up, I guess. Anyway, what I'm trying to say is that I can't be there with him right now because of these damn meetings, but maybe you could?"

"Like you want me to call him and check on him?" I ask, confusion clear in my voice.

"No. Like I want to book a flight for you and get you out to Chicago so you can talk to him for me and make sure he's doing all right."

"Oh, uh…um—" Of course the answer is yes, but I'm struggling with how to answer my dad without giving anything away. "I, uh, I have class tomorrow," I finish lamely.

"I know, and I told you it was a big ask. And you're right. You shouldn't miss class. I just felt after talking to him that he could use a friend, and you've been spending so much time with him at the stadium that I thought maybe you could be that steady presence he could use right now, or maybe you could distract him with updates on the fit kids center. I know I've personally used work as a distraction lots of times."

"We're not really all that close, but I guess I can do it if you think it'll help." My heart races as I close my eyes and cross my fingers that I didn't go *too* far in the wrong direction. I need to see Cooper with everything inside me, and it's like I wished so hard for it that I manifested this exact phone call.

"Thanks, baby girl. You're truly the best and I don't know how to repay you, but I'll think of something. I'll have Joanie get you a flight and she'll be in touch with the details."

"You don't need to repay me, Dad," I say. "Cooper's a good guy and if he's having a hard time, I'm happy to go be a friend." And whatever else he needs me to be.

"Thanks. I'll get the ball rolling and be in touch."

"Good luck at your meetings tomorrow. Go get that Winters guy."

He chuckles. "Will do. Love you."

"Love you too."

We hang up, and I click off the television, run upstairs, and start packing a small suitcase. I don't know how many days I'll be there, so I pack for five. I can do laundry if I need to. I think about texting Cooper to ask if he needs anything, but I think I'd rather make this a surprise.

I head into his room and glance around. I've been in here plenty of times, but it still feels strange being in here without him—like I'm snooping even though that's not my intention. I pick up his pillow and pull it to my chest, breathing it in. It smells like him, that woodsy, fresh scent that causes a fresh ache right between my thighs every time I breathe it in.

I set it down and move toward his closet, where I find a few suits on hangers and a few nicer shirts. I grab one with a collar. I head to his dresser next, and I find a stack of Vegas Heat t-shirts. I grab two of those, and then I open the drawer with the socks and underwear.

I grab a couple pairs of each, and I spot a box of condoms. It's not why I'm going, but I grab a couple anyway. You never know, and I'd rather be prepared than not.

It's as I'm closing the drawer that something in the corner of it catches my eye. It looks like it's supposed to be hidden beneath the socks, but it's sticking out because the drawer is almost empty and clearly he needs to do laundry.

My brows knit together as I stare at it for a few beats, not sure I'm really seeing what I think I'm seeing.

A red box with the word *Cartier* emblazoned across the top in gold lettering.

I stare at it for a beat, and then curiosity and nosiness get the better of me. It's not my finest moment.

I should close the drawer and walk out of the room and pretend I never saw a thing.

It could be a necklace.

It could be a bracelet.

But necklaces and bracelets come in bigger boxes.

Maybe it's just a promise ring.

But I know if I don't look, I'll forever wonder.

I take the box in my hands, guilt creeping through me for being so nosy. I shake the bottom from the top of the box and find a smaller red box inside.

I pull it out and open it to reveal a rather large pear-shaped diamond set in a platinum band.

My eyes nearly pop out of their sockets. Is this…for *me*?

He never wanted to marry Stacy, and while I don't know *for sure*, based on what he's told me, I doubt he ever bought her a ring. And even if he did, wouldn't it be packed away with the rest of his belongings where they're stored until he moves into his place in a few weeks?

Maybe not. This looks expensive.

I flip the lid closed and put it back into the box, replacing it in the drawer exactly where I found it.

And then I slam the drawer shut, carry the few items of clothes I grabbed with me back to my room, and finish packing for my trip to Chicago while thoughts of what this might mean swirl all around me.

Chapter 21
Gabby

I don't sleep.

My flight is early in the morning anyway, and the plane ride is three hours and twenty-five minutes from Vegas to Chicago.

The entire way, I stare out the window and think about that ring.

The ring hidden away in a sock drawer.

The ring I'm not supposed to know about.

The ring I'm obsessing over.

I'm young, sure. But I've also had to grow up quickly in my life. Once my grandmother died, I was basically on my own at the age of eleven. My mom showed up when it was an absolute necessity, but never without detailing to me why she was making a sacrifice to be there for me. Given my situation with my mom and given the fact that I didn't have a real father figure in my life until I turned eighteen, I found myself growing up quickly.

Part of me wonders if that's what attracts me to Cooper. Is going for an older man part of the fallout of growing up fatherless?

It's a strange question to ponder, but there it is, taking up space in my brain.

It can't be true. The way I feel about Cooper is powerful—more powerful than anything I've felt before in my twenty-one years.

But marriage? Am I ready for that step?

I haven't even graduated college.

And kids? I *know* having a family is important to Cooper, and I figured it would happen down the line someday in the future. I haven't given it much thought at this stage of my life. Could I be ready for that?

Kaylee looked miserable, but she said over and over how this life she lives is everything she ever dreamed of. Would I feel the same?

Would I even make a good mother?

I don't exactly have a shining example to look up to. My mom got pregnant with me when she was eighteen, and maybe she did the best she could, though I'd argue including the father in my childhood might've made more sense. But my parents were young when they had me, younger than I am now.

If I got pregnant today, nine months from now would put us in mid-June. I'd be out of school, potentially working a new job. Or maybe I'd want to stay home with the baby and not work at all, but I'd be largely alone while Cooper would be in season.

I ponder that for a beat.

And on the other side of the coin, Cooper does have that good maternal example—or so he says. And it's with that thought I realize I'm going to meet her today.

I could be meeting my future mother-in-law today.

Oh, God. The thought sends a whole new host of nervous energy racing through me.

I didn't think this through. I shouldn't be here.

And yet, as the wheels touch down and the plane careens down the runway as the pilot slams on the brakes…I am. I *am* here. I'm about to see Cooper after the way our conversation ended last night.

Somehow the thought fills me with hope.

It's too soon, and I didn't think about actually marrying him until I saw that ring.

But after three and a half hours to contemplate my future, I arrive at a conclusion as the *fasten seatbelt* sign turns off and everyone on the plane immediately jumps up even though we still have a good ten minute wait until we can actually get off.

I don't want a future without Cooper in it.

Maybe it's too soon, but maybe I don't care.

I know what I want, and it's him. It's *us*. And maybe I don't have a stellar maternal example to look up to, but maybe I don't need one because I'll have Cooper by my side, and with him, anything is possible. Anything.

He's made me see at twenty-one that I want the fairy tale. I want the sexy baseball player to put a baby in me. I want a future where we work together and play together and laugh and love. I want the banter we had the weekend we met.

I want to hold his hand as he unleashes his emotions on me. I want to be his first phone call with good news or bad.

I want to cry with him and celebrate with him and eat Slim Jims with him and love him for the rest of my life. I want a future where we create new life to carry on a legacy of love that began at a blackjack table.

Maybe not today or tomorrow, or next week or next month, maybe not even next year. But once I graduate and get a job, once he plays a season—or three—with the Heat, once we're both settled into our lives in Vegas together…then maybe that will be our time.

It's not so far off, and now that the truth has come rushing at me, I'm ready for it to begin.

I order a car to the address my dad sent me, which is Cooper's sister's house in Oak Brook, and I arrive on the doorstep of a beautiful white and gray stone mansion a little after nine in the morning. My hands tremble and my heart thunders nervously as I press the doorbell.

I hear it chime inside, and a moment later, an older woman who has Cooper's bright blue eyes stares back at me with a little confusion and a little curiosity as she glances down at my suitcase. "Can I help you?"

"Mrs. Noah?" I ask.

She nods, and she narrows her eyes and tilts her head like she's trying to place me.

"My name is Gabby. Gabby Grant." My voice trembles. "I'm, uh…I'm here to see Cooper."

"Gabby?" she repeats. "As in *Gabby*-Gabby?"

"Well, not Gabby-Gabby like in *Toy Story Four*, but Gabby-Gabby as in hopefully the Gabby who Cooper has mentioned at least once," I say.

"Oh my goodness!" she squeals, and she grabs me into a hug. "Yes, yes, Cooper has mentioned Gabby-Gabby *more* than once." She's still squeezing me and it's the kind of hug that feels maternal even to *me* and I feel tears pinching behind my eyes. "Oh, he's just going to be so tickled that you're here!"

"Mom?" I hear his voice calling from another room. "Who was at the door?"

I hear footsteps on the hardwood floors, and then he appears and it's like something out of a movie when he steps into a ray of light the sun is casting into the room and he's illuminated like a freaking angel.

Like the sunshine.

Like the center of my damn universe.

"Gabby?" he says, shock evident in his tone. His mom lets me go, and Cooper and I stare at each other across the room for a beat—a beat filled with nerves and fears and anxiety that he doesn't want me here. But then he rushes across the room and grabs me up into his arms, and everything tilts back to the way it was always supposed to be.

Because I'm here in his arms.

I'm where I belong. I don't know what that means for our future, but I'm ready to figure it out.

Chapter 22
Cooper

"What are you doing here?" I say into her neck, my words muffled and emotional.

"I'll give you two a minute," my mom says, and I assume she leaves the room but I'm so consumed with the fact that *Gabby is here* that I'm not really sure.

"I came to see you," she says, and her voice trembles.

I pull back, and I stare down at her a beat. It's in that moment I wonder how the fuck I could have ever questioned it.

God, I love her.

She's here.

She came for me.

She will *always* come for me—and I don't just mean that in the sexual way, though I'm not currently opposed to that particular notion.

My mouth crashes down to hers as I hold her in my arms. A feeling like I'm home even though I don't currently have a home washes over me. Whatever it takes, whatever I have to give up, whatever notions I had about the future once upon a time…they all melt away as I hold her in my arms, as my lips move over hers, as the love I feel for her seems to come at me from every angle imaginable.

We have to find a way to make this work.

End of story.

We'll compromise, and we'll fight and argue, but I can't retreat from her when things get tough. Just holding her in this moment is enough to make me very well aware of that.

This is it. *She* is it for me, whatever that means.

"God, I love you," I say against her lips, and she pulls back but only to bury her face against my chest and squeeze her arms more tightly around me.

"I love you, too. I'm so sorry I couldn't get here sooner."

"You're here now," I say, dropping a kiss to the top of her head. "And somehow it's everything I didn't know I needed."

We cling to one another for a few more beats, and I hear my mom talking to someone in the other room. I assume it's either her phone or the television since we're home alone, and I grab Gabby's hand and drag her with me toward the kitchen, dropping the suitcase by the stairs to take up the next time I go.

"We'll be right there," my mom says as she ends the call. She glances over at us and blows out a breath. "I guess he got an infection from the catheter and he's on an IV with meds now. Marissa isn't handling it well but he's doing okay."

I nod. "Let's go. I'll drive."

"I'm so sorry this is how we're meeting," my mom says to Gabby. "I'm Cheryl. You can call me Cheryl or Mom, whatever makes you feel more comfortable."

"Thank you. It's lovely to meet you in person, but I wish it was under better circumstances," Gabby says.

"So do I, honey. But the fact that you showed up for my baby boy is everything I need." She gives Gabby another squeeze. "Gosh, you're pretty. I mean, Cooper talks all the time about how gorgeous you are, so I should have believed him. And he also talks about how smart you are, how funny…"

"Mom, we need to go," I say, my face heating with embarrassment as my mom gives away all my secrets. "And remember, her dad can't find out about us, so this is all sort of top secret." With those words, I turn to Gabby. "How are you going to explain to him that you're here?"

She winks at me. "I'll tell you in the car on the way to the hospital."

I drag her suitcase upstairs and grab my shoes, and then I quietly head back down. I pause in the stairwell as I listen to my mom and Gabby talk.

"He's a different man since you came into his life, honey. Thank you for being so good to him."

"Thank you for raising such a good man. He tells me all the time how important you are in his life, and I love that you two have such a close relationship."

My chest warms listening to the two of them.

I *think* I've got my mother's stamp of approval.

I blow out a soft breath then continue my trek toward them. "Ready?" I ask.

As we make our way toward the hospital, Gabby says, "My dad called me last night, probably right after he got off the phone with you. He said he thought you needed a friend, and since he was tied up in meetings, he asked if I could fly out to see you since I'm your shadow anyway."

"He did?" I ask, surprise clear in my tone.

Maybe Troy *wouldn't* be so opposed to the idea of the two of us—not if he's pushing her on me when he thinks this is my time of need.

"Yeah. He said he's seen how close we've been getting, and he can tell I'm like a little sister to you."

I wrinkle my nose as I look at her in the rearview. She's in the backseat, and my mom is up front in the passenger seat. "He said that?"

She giggles. "Yeah, and then he said something about how he's like an older brother to you if it was a really messed up family."

I laugh, and my mom does, too.

"Gosh, he really has no idea about the two of you, does he?" my mom asks.

I shake my head. "He's caught up in a lot of his own stuff right now, so we've been flying under the radar I guess. And I move into my new place soon, so even less chance of him finding out."

"But you can't hide this forever. Can you?" she asks.

"Neither of us wants to hide it *forever*, but it's still in the early stages. There's no harm in keeping it between us as it develops and grows," I say. I glance back at her, and her eyes meet mine in the mirror. I spot a little relief in hers at my words, as if she understands my meaning that we're still on track to develop and grow even though we haven't had a chance to talk about it yet.

We will.

She's here now.

We've got all the time in the world.

We arrive at the hospital, and we head to Connor's new room on the telemetry floor. An IV is shoved into his arm, and he rolls his eyes as he looks over at us when we walk in, my mother first, then me, and Gabby at the back of the pack.

"Well who do we have here?" he asks as his eyes fall down onto our connected hands.

She waves. "I'm Gabby."

"She's my…" I turn to look at her, and she glances a little nervously at me as she waits for me to finish that sentence. "She's my girl." I lean down and press a kiss to her lips, and Marissa cheers as Connor makes some whooping noise. "But we're keeping it quiet. We can't let her dad find out."

"Why not?" Marissa asks.

"My dad is Troy Bodine," Gabby announces, and Marissa gasps while Connor's jaw drops.

"Whoa," Marissa says.

"Yeah. It's complicated," I say. I lean down and rest my forehead to hers for a beat. "But when it's this right, we'll sort the complications later."

"Oh my God," Marissa says, clapping her hands together. She rushes over to wrap me in a hug. "I'm so frickin' happy for you."

"Me too, man. Well, as happy as a guy can be with a catheter shoved up his dick," Connor says.

"Not the first time you've had a dick infection, is it?" I ask Connor, who balks at my joke while my mother tsks me.

Marissa hugs Gabby next. "Thanks for being here for my brother-in-law. I've known the kid a long time, and he seems much calmer with you here already," Marissa says. She turns toward me. "Back to your old jokester self."

"I'm not a jokester. I just call it like I see it," I say, and Connor laughs while my mom continues to pretend like she isn't listening to any of this.

"You're one to talk. You've been with like thirty-five times as many girls as me," Connor says.

Gabby wrinkles her nose. "Too much information," she says, holding her hands over her ears.

"Connor's been with one," Marissa says, leaning in and touching her chest to indicate herself. "And I bet Coop's been with more than thirty-five."

I glare at Marissa, and I slide my arm around Gabby's shoulders as I pull her closer to me. "Numbers don't matter. All that matters is you top my list."

She eyes me skeptically, obviously able to tell I'm simply trying to divert the attention from the underlying accusation in my sister-in-law's words. She gives me a look that tells me we're probably going to have an uncomfortable conversation later.

Which is fine.

I'll have any uncomfortable conversation in the world with her. I'm just happy she's here.

Even if I don't really want to get into the specifics of my number.

Age is just a number, right? So maybe the exact number of sexual partners I've had is just a number, too.

I went through a phase or two. I'm over it now.

I know what I want, and I squeeze her to my side again. She's right here with me, and I'm not letting that change any time soon.

Chapter 23
Gabby

W e stayed at the hospital as long as they let us. Marissa headed home to pick up the boys, and she brought them by to visit their dad. He's doing much better, but with the infection, he needs to stay a couple more days, which means Cooper is staying a couple more days, too.

Which I suppose means *I* am staying a couple more days as well.

I texted my dad to let him know I arrived, and later in the day Cooper texted my dad to thank him for sending a friend.

My dad is practically pushing us together at this point, though I'm certain that's not his intent.

The entire time we sat in Connor's room, Cooper found ways to touch me. We were either holding hands, or his arm was around my shoulder, or we were sitting close enough that our legs were touching. At one point, he even pulled me down onto his lap while we sat on a bench near the window. We ate dinner at the hospital cafeteria, and Cooper laughed and joked with his brother, and everyone in the room—including Cooper's mom—made me feel like an immediate part of the family.

It's as if everything is fine between Cooper and me, yet part of me fears it's not. He nearly bolted because of the age thing, and I'm not totally sure he's okay with where we stand right now. So for as much as I've forced myself to live in the moment all day, a little tremor of fear took root in my stomach this morning and it seems to have grown and grown as we make our way toward the conversation I know we're going to have once we're alone.

Part of me wonders whether he's stayed as long as he has at the hospital today as a way to *avoid* the talk, but the other part of me logically knows he's here to spend time with his brother—to soak it all in while he can.

It's not until we've said goodnight to Cheryl, who went back home, and Marissa, who's exhausted after a long day, that we head up to Cooper's room to finally have that talk.

He sits and leans against the headboard and pats the bed beside him. I climb in and mirror his position.

"I guess we need to talk," he says.

I nod and stare straight ahead, that fear that took root this morning exploding out into a tree of nerves.

"When all this happened with Connor, I felt myself retreating," he begins. "It's an old habit. I did it when my dad passed, though I was too young to recognize it then. I did it when I hurt my elbow, and again when Stacy and I ended things. And I started doing it with you, too. My first thought was how short life is, how I need to get a jump on the future I always wanted." He reaches over and clasps my hand in his. "But when you showed up today out of nowhere, the truth slammed into me like a ton of bricks. Maybe the future I dreamed of is just that—a dream. But an even better dream is what I see in the future with you." He turns toward me, and I slide my head toward him, too. "But the thought of a future without you feels like my worst nightmare come to life. So if you're not ready, then I'm not ready. If you are, then I am, too. Whatever it takes to make this work, I want to do it. I don't want to waste time, but if it means I get to be with you, then it's not time wasted."

I press my lips together in part to keep from crying and in part to keep from responding for a beat. "I don't want you to settle for less than everything you want. I think somewhere in there we can meet in the middle."

His brows rise in surprise.

I found the ring.

I almost say it, but I stop myself. Instead, I say, "I had a lot of time to think on the plane, and I felt it, Cooper. I felt you pulling away the second you found out your brother had a heart attack, and I need to make one thing crystal clear. You never, ever pull away from me. We're in this together, and we face these things together. You talk to me, and you cry with me and yell at me and let it all out, but you don't ever turn the other way. Do you understand me?"

"Yes ma'am." His eyes look a little heated at my aggressive speech.

I sit up and turn toward him, pulling his hand in mine and staring down at it as I talk. "I don't want a future without you in it, and I want you to have everything you've ever dreamed of having.

I want to give you those things. Maybe not today or tomorrow, maybe not next week, but when we're ready." My eyes flick up to his. "And I don't think it's that far off. My goal was always to start and establish my career before I settled down, and that could be next year or five years down the road. But we compromise. We talk. We fight. We do it together."

He leans in and kisses me. "I missed you that night I was in Boston and last night, and that time we were apart when I thought you were with Justin. I miss our banter, and our dirty jokes, and your body. But most of all, I missed the way we can both be so open with each other about everything. I've spent most of my life just keeping it in, but you make me want to let it out."

"Right, and on that note…you've slept with thirty-five times more women than your brother?" I ask, raising a brow.

He wrinkles his nose. "Are you sure you want to have this conversation?"

"My number is four," I say without missing a beat and without answering his question. I purse my lips.

"Four?" he practically thunders. "Who are these other three men I need to murder?"

I laugh. "You only have three to take out. I have thirty-five?"

He holds up both hands in surrender. "Connor was just teasing me. I haven't slept with that many women. Besides, it doesn't matter. You won't be my first, but you'll be my last."

"How am I supposed to measure up to all that?" My insecurities are showing, but it doesn't feel scary since we just finished a conversation about how we're supposed to be honest and we're in this together.

"To be honest, I haven't kept count. It's somewhere between ten and twenty, probably. I was with Stacy for five years, had a few one-night stands before and after her. And nobody, I mean not a single one of them, gives head the way you do." He raises both brows as if he's raising a challenge.

I roll my eyes. "You're just saying that so I'll suck your dick."

He holds a hand up to his chest in mock disbelief. "How could you accuse me of such a thing?"

"Because it's true."

"Fine. But you thought about proving it for a minute, am I right?"

I shake my head. "No."

He laughs. "That reminds me, want to hear a joke about my dick?"

I raise my brows.

"Never mind. It's way too long."

I giggle and shake my head. "I swear, your dirty jokes are the cheesiest."

"You love them," he says, and he shifts so he's suddenly hovering over me, forcing me back into position beneath him...exactly where I want to be.

Exactly where I love to be.

I sigh with contentment as I stare up at him, a little of his weight warming me and holding me in place. His blue eyes are clear and sure as they focus down on mine. He drops his lips to mine and thrusts his hips at the same time, and he's already activating multiple pleasure points all in one smooth move.

I let out a soft moan, and he chuckles before his lips move to my neck.

"You think you can do this quietly?" he murmurs.

"Not the way you fuck," I whisper back.

"God, I love it when you talk like that." He pushes his hips against mine again.

"I love it when you do that." I tighten my grasp around his neck, and he drives toward me again, humping me on the bed in the guest room.

His lips find my ear and he sucks on my lobe for a beat. "I want to do it naked."

"Then do it."

He pulls back, his eyes hooded and heated when they land on mine. "I don't have any condoms."

My thought process on the plane returns to me. What would life be like to be a young mother, fresh out of college, having Cooper Noah's baby?

The thought even in the heat of the moment makes me feel a shocking craving I'm not sure I've ever felt before. It's a craving for this man, for a future with him, for things I wasn't sure I really wanted until he stepped into my life.

I want them now. I want them with him. But I also know that's part of a bigger conversation we haven't had yet.

"I brought some," I murmur. "They're in my suitcase."

His eyes light up like a kid on Christmas morning. "You are seriously the best."

I lift a shoulder and shoot him a cocky smile. "I know. And it probably merits mentioning before you get overly complimentary that I stole them from your underwear drawer."

He laughs and shakes his head a little, and then he leans down and presses a kiss to my neck. He drags his lips down toward my cleavage, and then he sits back on his knees and pulls my shirt over my head. He buries his face between my breasts, still covered in my bra, and he breathes deeply. "What's mine is yours, Sunshine." He moves off me and heads to my suitcase and locates the strip of condoms I grabbed just in case.

"Four?" he says, holding up the strip and letting them fall down in a row.

My cheeks heat. "I mean, I didn't *count* them. I just grabbed some."

He tears one off the strip. "Liar. You think we're going to fuck four times while we're here." He unbuttons his jeans and pulls his cock out. He strokes it a few times before he tears open the condom, and I can't help but watch as the ache between my legs intensifies and my body moves from wet to drenched with arousal for him.

"A girl can dream, can't she?" I watch as he rolls it on, and then he jumps back onto the bed and hovers over me.

"We'll run to the store tomorrow and get more." His lips drop down to mine, and we kiss as if our lives depend on it as we seal all the promises we just made.

He backs away and helps me out of my pants and panties, and then he gets rid of his own jeans while I shimmy into a comfortable position. And then he's back, his heat perched over me, that beautiful sensation where he bears down some of his weight and I breathe him in, his fresh, woodsy scent combined with the element that just makes him *him*, and I tilt my hips up to try to gain some friction from the erection hanging between us. He grips onto it and slides it through me, pumping it against my clit a few beats, and my eyes roll back at the feel as I let out a soft grunt.

"We have to be quiet." He whispers the reminder close to my ear, and I nod, my eyes shining with lust as they connect with his. And then he pushes himself into me. His hand glides along my torso and lands on my breast, which he massages as he drives his hips against mine. His grunts are soft as he buries his face in my neck, and he lets go of my breast so he can lace one arm around me, pulling my body close against his as he makes love to me. His lips move along my collarbone as he whispers softly to me.

"Fuck, you're so tight and wet for me, so fucking hot and gorgeous."

My moaning gets a little louder at his dirty talk.

"Be my good girl and be quiet," he says. "Take my cock, baby. Keep taking it so deep." As he says those words, he pushes in as far as he can go and doesn't move, but he lifts his face from my neck. My eyes are shut tight as I drink in the pleasure, and I only know he's moved since I feel the cool absence of his mouth there. "Look at me," he says. "I want to see your beautiful face twisted in pleasure when I make you come."

My eyes open and meet his. His words and his face in my view and the feel of his cock as it twitches so deeply inside of me combined with the fierce love and adoration I see in his eyes is everything I want to live in forever, and it's everything I need to catapult me into a vicious climax.

I can't help it. I close my eyes, and I sink my teeth into his shoulder as I dig my nails into his back. He grunts loudly as he starts to come, too, the two of us thrashing our way through the ecstasy as one.

When it's all over and our bodies start to relax, worn out and sated for now, he collapses over the top of me for a beat, his cock still inside me as neither of us moves to break the connection. It's not a connection I want to break. It's the way our bodies seem to speak best in the language that's theirs and theirs alone. It's the way I can feel physically closest to him as our emotional and spiritual bond strengthens and ties us together in a way that feels very much like forever.

It's pure and utter perfection, and as he slips out and I start to fall asleep after a long, exhausting day, I can't help the last thought that rushes through my mind before sleep overtakes me.

It's a picture of the future, of him getting down on his knee and presenting that Cartier box to me, and me nodding my head as I accept his proposal.

I don't want it to be the future, though.

I want him forever, and I want our forever to begin right now.

Chapter 24
Gabby

"How come Barbie isn't pregnant?" Cooper asks.

My brows dip as he glances at me in the rearview mirror. His mother is in the passenger seat beside him.

"Why?" I ask.

"Because Ken came in another box." He cracks up at his own joke, and my cheeks flush that he just told a dirty joke in front of his mother.

"Cooper Michael!" she says, smacking him in the arm, and he holds the spot of the offense for a moment in the sort of dramatic acting I always thought athletes were taught in athlete school to make any injury appear far worse than it actually is.

"What? It's funny!" he says, still laughing.

"It's disgusting. I didn't raise you that way," she scolds, pursing her lips even though they're tipping a bit into a smile, as if she's thriving having both her boys in town at the same time.

"Connor told it to me," he says defensively, and I giggle at that.

"I love how you're both adult men in your thirties and you still blame each other," I pipe up from the backseat.

Cheryl turns around to look at me. "Girl, I have about a million stories of these two stinkers getting into trouble. Being a boy mom is never a walk in the park, let me tell you. More like a leap through the park and climbing a rock wall before jumping into a den of lions."

Cooper rolls his eyes. "That's a little dramatic."

"Dramatically accurate," she counters.

I giggle at the two of them, and my heart twists for a beat that I don't have that same kind of bond with my own mother...that I don't have siblings to get into trouble with.

At least I have my dad, and he's been so incredible to me.

My heart twists the other way for a beat as I think about how he'll really feel when he finds out about Cooper and me.

What if it hurts my relationship with him? It's still so new, and the thought of doing anything at all to compromise it has me feeling a certain way.

We arrive at the hospital, and Cooper grabs my hand once we're inside. He's careful outside when he could potentially be spotted by the media, but once we're inside, it seems like he's more comfortable with the idea of being close to me. Or maybe he just *needs* to be closer to me to help carry him through whatever internal feelings he's experiencing as he watches his brother get stronger each day.

When we arrive at Connor's room, we find there are already some guests in there. Cooper grins at a woman holding a baby plus a man standing beside her, and he pretty much ignores his brother in favor of greeting the couple while Cheryl moves over to talk to Connor and get a read on how he's feeling today.

Cooper glances back at me while I stand awkwardly by the doorway. "This is Gabby," he says to the couple. "She's, uh…she's a good friend here visiting." He leaves it at that, and I get the very clear sense that he's not ready to share our status with these people. "Gabby, this is Marissa's best friend Isabel, her husband Bryce, and their daughter Olivia."

"Nice to meet you," I say with a wave.

"May I?" Cooper asks, and he nods toward the baby.

"Of course," Isabel says, and I stare as she hands the baby over to Cooper, who takes her like a natural into his arms.

I watch as he bounces a little while he stares down at the baby girl wrapped in a pink blanket, and then he smiles at her.

And holy shit…my fucking ovaries explode.

It's like all the estrogen in my body rushes to the same place at the same time and causes an explosion of epic proportions.

I watch as if I'm watching my future, as if I'm seeing Cooper hold our baby girl wrapped in a pink blanket as he bounces and smiles down at her and whispers sweet gibberish to her.

I want it.

I want the picture I see. I want to create life out of this bond we share that will leave behind a legacy of our love. And I want to do it over and over.

I know very little about babies and what it takes to care for them. I know there are sleepless nights and a whole host of new anxieties and worries that accompany them, but as Cooper glances up, that smile still playing at his lips, and meets my eyes across the room, I know for sure that he's the man I'm meant to do this with.

My God, he's gorgeous as he stands there holding her, and it taps into some different sort of need I didn't know existed.

The need to give him children. The need to protect them and care for them because they are part him and part me. The need to see him as a daddy, to give him the family he's always wanted. To give him *everything* he's always wanted.

Maybe that's the thing about finding your soul mate—you start to want the same things at the same time because you're connected by the thread holding your souls together.

I don't care that I'm young. Hell, my parents were young, too, and as it turns out, they didn't plan for me. Imagine what a life would be like for babies who are wanted, who are planned for, who are loved beyond all measure by both their parents?

I want to do that with him, and I hardly can even stand waiting another moment for it all to begin.

I mean…I know I need to wait. Obviously. We're in a hospital right now, so I can't exactly just have him knock me up right this second.

I scroll in my memory down the hallway we just walked. There was a closet, some offices, other rooms holding other patients…my mental rewind pauses on the offices.

No. Not in a hospital.

But in the guest room at Marissa and Connors house? That's a maybe.

Or the closet down the hall.

The bathroom?

No.

The elevator? Maybe…

"You want to hold her?" Cooper asks, breaking into my totally inappropriate thoughts.

I nod. "Do you mind?" I ask Isabel.

She smiles and nods as if to say *go for it*, and Cooper carefully hands her over.

I'll be honest.

I've never held a baby this small before.

I've held very few babies in my lifetime, in fact.

I've never changed a diaper.

I've never understood that new baby smell people talk about.

I've never wanted much to do with babies at all, really.

But having Cooper hand over this little bundle feels like it changes everything.

"How old is she?" I ask, smiling down at her as she looks up at me.

"Two months," her mother says.

Two months.

God, two months ago I didn't even know Cooper. It's sort of amazing how much has changed in my life in such a short time. I went from a single girl about to start her senior year of college to thinking about how I want babies and marriage and a future with a man twelve years older than me.

Life moves at an alarmingly fast rate, and I want to cling on and enjoy the ride with Cooper.

I glance over at him as I hold the baby, and I see it there in his eyes.

The same things I'm feeling.

Is this real life? I'm not quite sure, but I've never experienced a pull like this before. He *is* experienced, and he's never felt it, either.

Whatever the case, one thing is for sure.

It's time to start rethinking the priorities and expectations I've outlined for myself. I don't want to jump into anything without thinking it through first, but I've had the last six weeks to think it through.

And I've never been more sure about anything in my life than I am about a future with Cooper.

I reluctantly hand back Olivia, and Cooper asks if he can talk to me for a minute out in the hallway. We head out there together, and then he presses his hand to the small of my back and guides me toward the elevators. We get in, my brow furrowed as I wonder where the hell he's taking me, and I'm about to ask when someone else steps on, too.

Damn. I was hoping we could make out a little.

We get off on the level where we parked, and he guides me toward his mom's car. He gets into the backseat instead of the front, and he pulls me in next to him.

"What the hell was that back there?" he demands.

My brows knit together. I have no idea what he's talking about, and I can't tell if he's angry or joking or…something else. "What was what back where?"

"You being all sexy holding that baby like you wanted me to put one in you. Don't you look at me like that if you're not ready, because I will fuck you right here, right now, and get the ball rolling."

I gasp a little, and I shift as his words press an unbearable ache between my thighs. "I, uh…" I pause as I try to collect my thoughts, but the fact is I was thinking of a place we could screw and suddenly we're out here in the privacy of his mom's car. The backseat has tinted windows, and he parked sort of at the end of a row, and it wouldn't be that hard for me to get on top of him. I shake the thought out. "I don't know what I want, but I do know I want you."

He leans over toward me, and then he shifts us so he's hovering over me. His lips drag along my neck. "I want you, too. I want a future with you, Gabby. I want everything, and I feel like it's all within our reach." His mouth moves over to mine, and he kisses me like he's starved and my mouth is what's going to give him sustenance.

He doesn't have much room, but somehow he manages to drive his hips to mine. "I don't have a condom, but I need to feel you."

"I don't either, and the pull out thing worked last time." My words are breathless against his lips.

"It's risky," he warns.

"I know."

He won't come inside me.

We're fine.

I gaze up into his eyes, and the thought of little feet pitter-pattering down the hardwood floors in his new house, of an angelic face with Cooper's bright blue eyes looking up at me with love and adoration, of creating something out of this incredible thing we share…it doesn't sound so bad.

Either way, I know how it works. Mia had a scare our freshman year of college, and we learned all the things. I'm not in the ovulation zone right now. It would be safe for him to pull out.

He shoves his hips against me again, and he's so hard and ready. He wants me. I want him. I *need* him. I need to feel him, especially after the realizations I've had today.

He stares at me for a few hot beats as if trying to get a read on what I'm thinking, and then he nods. "You're sure?" he asks one more time.

"I'm sure," I say, and I pull his neck down so his lips are on mine again. I pause and pull back. "But just for the record, I did start the pill."

His jaw drops open. "And you didn't tell me?"

I shrug. "Just wanted to see where you were at. And it's noted."

He raises a brow then starts to grapple with my jeans, which I pull down and kick off, and he unzips his own pants and pulls out his cock, already leaking at the tip with desire for me.

God, I get hot when I think about what I do to him.

He strokes himself a few times before he slides his cock through my slit, up and down, hitting my clit a few times before he slides in.

"Oh my God," I shriek as he drives all the way in.

"Fuck, baby, you're so goddamn perfect," he says, and his lips move to mine.

There's just something gloriously magical about his hard, thick cock pumping inside me with nothing between the two of us. He holds onto me as he drives his hips to mine, and I feel the pleasure mounting as he fucks me in the back of his mom's car like we're two horny teenagers who can't wait another second to be together.

"I fucking love your hot cunt," he murmurs close to my ear. "It's all I think about when I'm not with you."

"Oh God," I moan again. "Fuck me harder, Cooper. Harder!"

He slams into me, and something about this entire experience is explosive and sexy and hot all at once, and the feel of him and his cock and his mouth and his dirty words drive me right to a climax.

I'm mid-orgasm, my body clenching and contracting over his, when he starts to pump harder and harder. He spills into me, the first time he's come inside me without anything between us, with a mighty and fierce growl.

He gently pulls out when it's all over, his pleasure leaking from me. He stares down at the mess we made together, and then he reaches in the front seat where his mom keeps a little pack of tissues. He cleans me off first and then himself, and we both get dressed and straighten ourselves up for a minute, drawing in deep breaths as we hold hands in the backseat.

And a tiny little part in the back of my brain that absolutely defies my normal logic can't help but wish I wasn't on the pill at all since we just wasted a chance at creating a new life together.

Chapter 25
Gabby

When we return to Connor's room, he narrows his eyes at us. I have a feeling he's about to call out what we just did when a doctor walks in, shooing all the visitors from the room for a bit.

Saved by the doctor, I guess.

A text from Kaylee comes in as we're hanging out in the waiting room, and that's when I realize I never told her I was leaving town.

Kaylee: *Tell me the twins didn't scare you off from being my friend.*

I laugh as I show the screen to Cooper, and he chuckles as he turns his phone toward me to show me the text Kaylee just sent him.

Kaylee: *I think I scared Gabby off. I haven't heard from her since she made a run for it the other night.*

"Let's call her together," Cooper suggests, and I nod. We head out of the waiting room to respect others who are sitting in there, down the elevator, and out toward the parking garage, where he dials her number and puts the phone on speaker so I can hear, too.

"What's up Coopey-Coo?" she answers.

"That's not a thing," he says. "And Gabby-Gab is here with me, too."

She laughs. "Hi Gabby-Gab."

"I promise you didn't scare me off. I'm in Chicago with Cooper," I explain.

"What are you two doing in Chicago? Spending lots of time at the Bean?" she asks, referring to a mirror sculpture that resembles its nickname—though her suggestive tone makes me think she's referring to something else entirely.

"You let me worry about the bean," Cooper says, wiggling his eyebrows at me, and I laugh. "My brother had a heart attack while I was in Boston, so I flew here."

"Oh shit, I'm so sorry. Is he okay?" she asks.

"He's fine. Probably getting out of the hospital today or tomorrow," Cooper says. "Troy couldn't come with me so he asked his lovely daughter to be a good friend and make sure I was doing okay."

Kaylee lets out a low whistle. "Damn, that man has no idea, does he?"

"Nope," we say at the same time.

"Wow. Well, I won't bug you with SFK stuff now then," she says.

"Please, bug away. We're just sitting up in a hospital waiting room, well…waiting," Cooper says.

She launches into some details about how she feels like they've stalled on new memberships, which is affecting the way SFK runs in the fitness clubs. I listen intently as I pull on my marketing hat.

"I have a few ideas," I say once she finishes. There's a pause, so I jump in with more. "From what it sounds like, you've relied solely on Ben's popularity to grow the clubs, and that's great. It obviously worked well, and his fans are members. But now you need to attract a different sort of clientele. Have you run any ad campaigns that don't star Ben?"

"No," she admits. "Everything we've done has his face plastered all over it. Or his abs. Mm, those abs." She takes a moment of peace for her husband's abs, and then she says, "Do you know anybody who could pitch some ideas?"

"Uh, hi. I'm a marketing major and your new best friend, remember?" I tease.

She laughs. "I fucking love you, Gabby. Send me some ideas when you get a chance and we'll go from there. And honestly, if you're too busy, we can look into hiring out."

"Look no further," I say. "I'll sketch out some ideas to see what you think, but last I heard I was all set up to work for you anyway, so let's get the ball rolling there. I can totally handle maybe ten to fifteen hours a week between the internship and my classes."

"That'll be a huge help," she says, and Cooper just stands by listening as we hash out the details. "I'll get a contract to your inbox in a bit, and you can just fill it out when you get a sec and shoot it back over to me. I'm going to hire you on as my assistant for now, but we can change the verbiage as needed."

"Deal." I nod even though she can't see me, and Cooper grins.

"And I can share some ideas for ad campaigns, too," he offers.

Kaylee laughs. "I think we're good. We don't need ads with beef sticks and baseballs in them."

I picture her rolling her eyes at Cooper as she giggles, but I already know I'll be running everything by him before I send it over to Kaylee. SFK is, after all, important to him, too.

We hang up with her, and when I pull out my phone, I spot a text from my dad.

Dad: *Everything okay in Chicago?*

Cooper peers over at my phone. "He texted me, too," he says, and he flashes me his screen.

Troy: *You taking care of my girl in the windy city?*

"Oh, I'm taking care of her, all right," Cooper says suggestively. I laugh as I text my dad back.

Me: *Everything is going well. Looks like Cooper's brother will be released soon, and you were right. He needed a friend. [smile emoji]*

I watch as Cooper types out a text, too.

"What does yours say?" I ask once he hits the send button.

"Wouldn't you like to know?"

"Uh, yeah, that's why I asked." I say it like the answer is obvious, and he chuckles.

"I told him I took care of you in my mom's backseat. Should I not have said that?"

I smack him in the shoulder.

He grins at me. "I told him you're fine and it was nice of him to send moral support from the Heat."

I narrow my eyes into a glare. "Is that all I am to you? Moral support from the Heat?"

He plants his hands on my hips and pulls me into him, and then he backs me into the brick wall beside us and lowers his mouth until it's centimeters from mine. "I think you know you're more than that to me."

His mouth doesn't touch mine, and the fact that he's so close yet so far grates on me as butterflies coast through me. I tip my chin to try to catch his lips, and he backs his mouth away. When his eyes fall to mine, they're heated and genuine. "You're everything to me, Gabriella Grant. *Everything.*" His voice is rich and raspy, and I melt into a puddle of lust as he presses a soft kiss to my lips.

"Right back at you, Captain," I say when he lets go of me, and he winks before we head back inside.

Once we're back up in the waiting room, a text from Justin comes through.

Justin: *You're in freaking CHICAGO with CN? What's that like after all the D-R-A-M-A? I need all the details stat.*

As I'm reading the one from Justin, one from Chloe comes through, too.

Chloe: *Joanie just told us your dad sent you to Chicago and that's why you haven't been in. Is everything okay?*

I write back Justin first, but I'm vague just in case he's with the other interns.

Me: *Drama averted, back together. [wink emoji]*

I write back Chloe next.

Me: *Cooper Noah's brother had a heart attack and my dad asked if I could be moral support from the Heat since he couldn't be there. Everything is okay. His brother should be released in the next day or two and I'm guessing I'll be back by Monday. How's everything there?*

Justin's reply comes first.

Justin: *OMG WHAT? WHEN? You didn't think to call your best friend to tell him?*

I giggle.

Me: *I'm so sorry. It's been a whirlwind. I'll call you later tonight, k?*

Chloe's next text comes in, and I flip to her message.

Chloe: *Oh man, glad he's okay. M is being a total bitch and I can't stand it here without you. Hurry back!*

I take M to mean Mackenzie, and I thought she was just a bitch to me. I guess I was wrong.

Me: *I always thought she hated me because I'm Troy's daughter. Guess she's like that with everyone?*

Chloe: *Girrrrl, you have no idea. Call me later, I'll fill you in.*

As much as I'm enjoying this retreat with Cooper and his family, I'm also finding myself excited to get back home to my internship. What if all three of us are hired on in the social media department? I realize it's unlikely given the fact that Justin doesn't want to work in baseball, but maybe I can convince him to change his mind. It would certainly be a fun work environment—especially if we delete Mackenzie from the equation.

Which reminds me—I text Justin again.

Me: *What's the latest with B?*

His response comes quick, and it's simply a fire emoji.

I laugh.

"What are you laughing at?" Cooper asks, leaning over to get a peek at my phone.

I hold it a little closer. "Noneya."

His brows dip. "Noneya?"

"None-ya business."

He barks out a laugh, and it's the hearty, deep laugh that I fell in love with in the matter of one weekend.

I giggle at the laugh. "It's Justin. He's been hooking up with someone and he sent me the latest." I flash him our text chain and he spies the fire emoji.

"Good for him. I always liked that kid."

I think back over the short time Justin has been a part of my life, and it's definitely my turn to bark out a laugh at that statement.

Chapter 26
Cooper

We've spent the last three days with my family, and it's literally better than I could have imagined...you know, minus the whole *my brother almost died* thing. They spring him from the hospital Friday morning, and Friday evening, the adults are sitting around Connor and Marissa's table eating dessert after a huge but heart healthy meal. The boys are up in their rooms on their tablets, and Marissa just ran upstairs to grab some of the journals she's been selling on TikTok.

Gabby excuses herself to the restroom after she finishes her cake, and my mom leans in close to me as she sits between my brother and me.

"You better marry that girl."

I choke on my bite of ice cream, my eyes bugging out as I glance at my brother for interference.

He nods. "She's right, you know. And knock her up good and quick before some guy better than you swoops in and steals her out."

God, he's so fucking useless.

My mom mock smacks him in the arm. "Stop it." Then she turns to me and claps her hands a little. "But do it! I need more grandbabies. Maybe a girl at some point."

"Jesus Christ, you two," I say, a warning edge to my tone.

"When are you going to do it?" my mom presses.

I roll my eyes. "When we're both ready."

"So you're gonna do it?" Connor asks.

"Do what?" Gabby asks, walking back into the room.

I shake my head. "You leave the room for two seconds and these two are all, *you need to marry her.*" I raise my voice a few octaves to imitate my family.

My mom has the grace to look embarrassed that I outed her, but Connor sure as shit doesn't, the fucker.

"We told him to put babies in you, too," my brother says.

You'd think I'd be embarrassed by him, but I'm just used to him.

I roll my eyes and jut my thumb in their direction as I wait for Gabby's reaction. "See what I have to deal with?"

"I think it's sweet." She reaches over and squeezes my bicep. "They just want you to be happy."

"And it's clear she makes you happy," my mom adds. "She makes all of us happy. She brightens the room when she walks in it."

I toss an arm around Gabby's shoulders. "She does. And I'm confident all that is in our future when we're both ready. Gabby wants to graduate college and establish a career before she has to deal with a husband and taking time off for a newborn." I glance at her and nod, confident I've said enough to shut off the peanut gallery beside me, and I take a bite of my cake.

"I'm flexible on that," she says, and goddammit, I choke on my cake again.

"You're flexible? I mean, I know you're flexible, but you're *flexible?*" I say after I chug down some water to clear the pipes, and my mom lets out a little giggle at my double meaning even though this certainly isn't the kind of conversation I want to be having in front of her.

"I'm flexible." She offers a small smile and a raised brow, and I have no idea what she means but my jaw hangs open as I try to figure it out.

"You got any wedding planners in there?" Connor asks as Marissa chooses that moment to return to the kitchen with her journals. "Sounds like we've got a wedding to plan."

"A wedding?" Marissa asks, looking around.

Connor nods toward Gabby and me, and her cheeks flush as I'm certain mine do, too.

I haven't proposed...yet.

But the last three days have pushed us even closer than we were before, and seeing how she fits into my family in a way none of my exes ever did is just the icing on the cake. When I saw her holding baby Olivia, it was like divine intervention stepped in and I just knew.

This is it.

This is the right fit for all of us—for me, for Gabby, and for my family. I already know I fit in with her father, but exactly how we're going to tell him still eludes me.

I guess we've gone from semi-serious to really serious over the last few days. We've talked about how short life is, and not just from my own perspective given my father's early death and my brother's health scare, but also from hers. She lost a grandmother she misses every day, and she lost eighteen years with her father.

Her main concern in getting serious with me at this point is how to ensure she won't lose more time with him. I told her it's not like she has to choose between him and me, that we can figure out how to coexist, that we need to tell him...but she's not ready.

She *is* ready for other things, though. Things she didn't think she was ready for. Things she's spent the last few days around, like Olivia and my nephews and my family and a life we'll build with each other.

Still, to get to that destination...we have to tell her dad. There's no way around it.

It isn't until we're on the flight home that I bring it up. "When do you think we should tell your dad?"

We're at ten thousand feet when the question falls from my lips.

She sighs as she turns to look at me. "I feel like we've had a lot of heavy conversations over the last few days, and this still feels like one I'm not ready for."

I reach over and grab her hand in mine, lacing my fingers through hers. I clasp it tightly, and I nod. "Okay."

Maybe I should object, but she's right. We *have* had a lot of heaviness, and we've come to some new revelations about our relationship and where we want it to go from here. Still, it bothers me that she's not ready to tell her dad.

She's ready to talk about marriage and babies in front of my family, but she won't even tell her father that we're in love.

How can we move forward to those other things without that part of the equation?

Maybe I'll change my mind once I'm back in the same state as him. We've sort of lived in bliss the last few days, and even though Gabby seems to be on the same page as me, that doesn't mean we have to rush into anything.

This entire thing has been rushed. I suppose her not being ready to tell her dad might be the one thing that slows us down to a normal speed for a minute.

That's not necessarily a bad thing.

"I'm sorry," she murmurs, her head sliding over to face me as she leans back on the seat.

"It's okay." I mirror her position, our eyes meeting in the middle.

"I feel like you're upset. I just feel like we need to come up with a good plan for when and where and how to tell him."

"You're right." I know she is, even if it's hard to admit—especially as I stare into her pretty eyes. "And it might be better to wait until we're in season. Right now we have a lot going on with the expansion draft coming up in a month and a half, and I don't want to pull his focus from that. We have too much to hash out before then for things to get awkward between us."

She nods. "I'm kind of sad we're going home."

I raise a brow. "Why?"

"I really love your family."

My lips quirk up. "They loved you, too."

"Really?"

I nod, and I lean over and drop a soft kiss to her lips. "Really. You fit in like the missing piece." I pull back.

She studies me for a beat before she asks, "Wanna go join the mile high club?"

I laugh, not sure how to tell her I'm already a member, but she narrows her eyes at me.

"You're already a member, aren't you?"

I twist my lips. "Guilty. But I'd love to upgrade my membership if it means I get to bang you on a plane."

She laughs, and it's just one more thing to love about Gabby Grant. Everything feels so blissfully easy right now.

I just wish I could shake the feeling that it won't last long.

Chapter 27
Gabby

My dad lifts his glass in a toast on Sunday evening at dinner. "To the future," he says, and Joanie and I clink our glasses to his.

We're back at Desmonds, Dad's favorite steakhouse in Vegas, and I think he chose this place because he feels comfortable here.

It's the first *official* dinner with my dad and his girlfriend, and I don't waste the opportunity to point that out after I set my wine glass down. "So did you invite me to this dinner tonight so we could talk about the future?"

He glances at Joanie and offers a sheepish smile. "Maybe."

I giggle. "Well, don't beat around the bush. Hit me with it."

He clears his throat, and I smile as I note how Joanie seems to enjoy watching him squirm. "Joanie and I have been together a long time now," he begins, and she leans into his side a little, which seems to settle him.

It's in that moment I know these two are going to make it the long haul. It's hard to look objectively at a relationship one of your parents has, but in this case, I can see the love between them. I don't know what their dynamic is like as a couple, but she seems to be exactly what he needs.

And it's as I study her with him that I realize she might be an entire decade younger than he is. I don't know her exact age, but I'd put her in her early to mid-thirties.

He's forty-one.

Why would it be okay for *him* to date someone younger than him, but not okay for Cooper?

"I've been wanting to have this dinner for months, but you know how it goes," he continues. "At first, I thought we were just playing around. Then as things started turning more serious, I wasn't sure how to introduce her into what still feels very much like a new equation between the two of us." He nods toward me. "But then you got the internship, and when I see you two working together, I just know the dynamic is going to work."

He pauses as if he's waiting for one of us to fill the gap, so I speak up despite the whole *playing around* comment that is a clear reminder this man owns some sort of sex club. I shake off the thought.

"It *will* work, Dad. I'm so happy you've found someone that makes you happy. That's all anyone deserves."

He presses his lips together and nods. "It is. And someday when you're a little older, you'll find the right man, too." He shakes his head a little wryly. "As long as it's not a baseball player." He holds his hands up in silent prayer, and I think he expects to hear my laugh along with Joanie's, but instead my heart sinks.

Too late, I realize my expression might give away my thoughts. And it's too late because I suspect Joanie caught it by the way she narrows her eyes at me.

A server comes by to take our order, causing a shift in subject after he leaves.

"How was Chicago?" Joanie asks.

I clear my throat. "It was fine. Cooper's brother is doing much better, and his family was lovely and so welcoming."

The way she eyes me tells me she definitely has her suspicions, but if she does, she doesn't say anything.

"And Coop?" my dad asks.

We got back last night, but my dad hasn't been home since. He texted me earlier asking if I wanted to meet for dinner, and here we are.

"He's doing well," I say. "I think he was just scared his brother was going to take the same path his dad did."

"The same path my own father did," my dad admits, and his eyes look a little pained for a beat. "That's why I wanted you to go. I know what it was like when I lost my own dad to a heart attack, and I didn't have a friend with me to lean on. It was tough, and I hated for Cooper to go through this thing with his brother alone. He's really started to see you as a little sister, and I appreciate that sort of friendship."

Joanie must see my face give me away again at the *little sister* comment, because she jumps in. "I don't know about a little sister, but they do seem like they've gotten closer."

"As friends," my dad amends. "Sure. Even though I'm sure it's hard to find much in common with a man twelve years older than you."

"You're seven years older than me and we have plenty to talk about," Joanie points out, and I almost shoot her a grateful look before I realize I haven't confirmed a thing to her—yet—and a grateful look will only be an admission of guilt.

Not that there's anything to be guilty about.

You know, other than lying.

"Right. Seven years. There's an entire *decade* plus two between her and Coop. It's just different worlds. Different generations, you know?" he says.

I guess that answers my whole age gap question from earlier.

"How are you enjoying the internship?" he asks, shifting the subject again as I try not to feel the whiplash even though I'm glad for the subject change.

"I'm loving it," I say. "Most of the other interns are great and some have already started becoming good friends."

"At tomorrow's meeting, we're going to talk about your project for the week," Joanie says, excitement in her tone. She glances at my dad. "It's the one you helped me come up with."

His eyes light up a little. "Ah, yes. It's a good one," he promises.

I laugh. "I can't wait to learn all about it."

"I'd tell you now, but I wouldn't want to give you any advantages the other interns don't have," Joanie says, and she winks.

I'm not sure what the wink means. Does she think I have an advantage because of my dad—like Mackenzie seems to think? I blurt it out before I can stop myself. "Some of the other interns already think I have advantages they don't have."

"They do?" my dad asks at the same time Joanie asks, "Who does?"

"I don't want to say," I begin, but I guess blurting it out might have not really given me much of a choice.

"Honey, if someone isn't playing fair…" my dad begins, but I cut him off when I hold up a hand.

"I can handle it. I don't want to change the dynamic or make you think less of any of the interns. I want us all to have a fair shot. It's just that some think I have an advantage at the Social Media Manager position because of who you are." I nod toward my dad.

"Pfft. That's ridiculous," my dad says, and he holds up his whiskey glass to the waitress across the room to indicate a refill.

"Is it?" I ask.

"We will select the best person for the position," he says, and I hold my tongue even though I wonder who the *we* he's referring to might mean. Is it him and Joanie? Or does he mean *we, the Heat* as an organization?

Why would he be involved in these sorts of decisions when he's in charge of player management and there are others in place for front office management?

I get that he's an important man and somehow all these pieces fit together, but it just feels like he runs a lot more than his position entails.

I'm just not sure what that means if I *do* end up with the position, and I'm not sure I'll ever feel like I got it on my own merit or because of who my father is.

Chapter 28
Cooper

"**P**ocket rockets," Rush says, tossing down a pair of aces.

"A bachelor's dream," Danny says, laying down four queens.

I laugh as I toss my cards face down on the table. I can't beat four queens, that's for sure. "I have jack and shit."

"Same," Nick says, tossing his cards on top of mine. Danny rakes in the chips in the middle of the table, and the deck passes to the left so it's my turn to deal. Everyone antes up another chip while I shuffle.

"Jacks or better, trips to win," I say, naming my game as I start dealing five cards to each of the four of us. We're at Danny's place, an apartment he's renting not terribly far from the Strip until he figures out if he wants to settle here or not. We've eaten pizza and drank a lot of beer, and even though Nick continues to tell us we shouldn't put that shit in our bodies, he's not exactly leading by example.

We're all a little buzzed, and the night has been full of laughter, teasing, and dirty poker terms. It's been the kind of evening with buddies I sorely needed after the heaviness that met me in Chicago, but that doesn't mean I'm not ready to bolt the fuck home and get back to my girl.

I miss her.

I realize we spent the last four days together, but it doesn't matter. I fucking miss her. I want her here with me. I want her sitting on my lap, laughing along with me and the guys, being part of this group even though it's boys' night out.

This is good for us. It's good for *me*.

"By me," Nick says first to my left.

"Me too," Rush says.

"I can open," Danny says, and he tosses a few chips onto the pile. As always, he tries to distract the rest of us. "Just for the record, I shouldn't even be here tonight, but I got clam jammed."

"Clam jammed?" Nick repeats, clearly asking the question the rest of us are wondering.

"You know, clam jammed. The female equivalent of cock blocked. I was talking to this girl, her friend came over crying about how her dude is a d-bag, and the rest is history. She had to go be with her friend, of course, and here I am with you douchebags instead of sporking her right now."

"Sporking?" Rush asks this time.

"You know, like spooning, but when you're sporting wood and hoping it leads away from the spoon and over to the fork." He wiggles his eyebrows, and I offer a chuckle.

"It's a real wonder why you're still single," I say dryly.

He raises his brows pointedly. "You're one to talk, asshole."

Oh, right. He still thinks I'm single...and he's the only one in this room who knows I was with Gabby. I think that also means his words were actually meant to hurt, not just to insult, and I should probably not say my next words since we've all been drinking and I know he's going to blab about me and Gabby, but I do anyway. "I'm off the market."

Everyone's heads swing toward me this time, but I just quietly check my cards. I have a pair of kings...not bad to start, but since I called trips, or three of the same card, to win, that means I need three kings to win the pot.

I up the ante anyway, bluffing my way through. I'm losing a lot of money right now, and Danny has way more chips than he knows what to do with. It's time to get some of those back.

When I go to draw my next cards, I up the bluff by only drawing two even though I have a better chance of pulling a king with three cards than with two. But this way, Danny thinks I've already got it in the bag.

He pulls three, so I know he doesn't have trips. His face is stone as he looks at his cards, and suddenly a friendly game of poker between friends has gotten a bit more serious.

"What's this off-market bullshit?" Danny asks.

"I'm not at liberty to discuss it." I give him a pointed glance that he totally misreads.

"Are you back together with Gabby?"

Fuck.

I should've trusted my gut.

The more people who know about this, the more likely it's going to get back to Troy before we're ready to tell him.

I blow out a breath as I stare down at the cards I drew: a three to match the three I held onto along with a third king.

A fucking full house…a sure winner in a five-card game with no wild cards.

I push a large stack of chips to the middle of the pile to sweeten the pot. "What if I am?"

"Gabby the intern?" Rush asks at the same time Nick says, "Troy's *daughter* Gabby?"

I lift a shoulder, pleading the fifth, and both Rush and Nick fold out of the hand by tossing their cards onto the table. It's Danny's turn, and he matches my pile of chips. "Call."

I set my cards down on the table to show my full house to Danny's muttered curse. He tosses his cards a little angrily onto the table facedown to indicate that he lost, and I rake the chips toward my side of the table.

I pass the deck onto Rush, who starts to shuffle while I organize my chips. I'm winning now, and Danny's losing, and I chug down another beer. When I set the bottle down, Rush sets the cards down and studies me.

"What?" I ask, glancing over at him.

"Are you banging Troy's daughter?" he asks.

"It's not just banging," I say, a little defensiveness in my tone.

"Oh, it's sporking and forking and licking and sticking, if you catch my drift." Danny makes a rude gesture as he slams the sides of his hands against his thighs as he sticks his tongue out.

"Subtle," I mutter. I sigh. I guess I may as well be honest here. "Look, I met her before I knew she was Troy's daughter. She left that fact out of the conversation just as I left out the fact that I used to play ball. She didn't seem to know who I was and I kind of liked just being a guy who worked for a kids' organization to her. She got to know the real me rather than the me that women tend to think I am, and then I found out she was Troy's daughter when she was standing in his kitchen the morning after I moved here. I told her I couldn't be with her, and we were apart a while, but it was all wrong."

Rush lets out a low whistle.

"Does Troy know?" Nick asks.

I shake my head. "And I need you fuckers to keep this quiet while we figure out how we're going to tell him."

"Oh Jesus, please please *please* let me be there when you tell him," Danny begs as he slams his palms together in prayer.

"That's a hard no," I say. "We're going to do it after the draft sometime. Or maybe after the season starts. There's too much on the line right now to complicate things with him, and this is all so new anyway. We're just taking it slow and giving it time."

"Damn, though. Isn't she like barely legal?" Rush asks.

My brows dip as I shoot him a little glare. "She's twenty-fucking-one."

"Your number," Danny says. "But more suitable for someone, say, six years younger than you."

I blow out a breath as my hackles rise, and my glare turns on Danny. "Stay the fuck away from her," I hiss.

He holds up both hands. "Okay, okay, man. I'm not going after your girl. I see the way she looks at you, anyway. She'd never give me the time of day. But if someone as clueless as *me* can see the way she looks at you, you best tell her to cool it in front of her daddy."

"Good point," I concede.

He's probably right.

And that brings up another point. If *he* sees it…who else has?

Chapter 29
Gabby

"Your challenge this week is to create an advertising campaign pitch that will fill seats in this stadium. That's all the direction I can give you. Take your time, be creative, and have your storyboards ready to go by Friday at noon." Joanie looks around the circular table as she gives her instructions, her eyes landing on me last.

I'm not sure why that makes me just the tiniest bit uncomfortable. It's the scrutiny, maybe, or the feel of a motherly-type even though she's a mere thirteen years older than me according to my calculations. But she's my dad's girlfriend, so I guess in a way if she marries him, she'll be like my stepmom.

This is weird. I went from not having a father at all three years ago to suddenly having an entire family. I went from having a narcissistic mother who taught me that the silent treatment is an effective way to deal with an argument and that being anything less than perfect just isn't good enough to having people who seem to love and accept me with open arms.

But my mother also taught me that love is equivalent to manipulation, and it's as that thought occurs to me that I suddenly understand why Mackenzie is such a bitch.

Is Joanie favoring me because I'm Troy's daughter?

Is Joanie going to give me the job regardless of who wins the most challenges because of my bloodline? Is it her way of manipulating my father—by buying into his good side through me?

I hate that the thought even comes to mind, but my mother left me with plenty of scars I'm still trying to live with.

"Are there any questions?" she asks, her gaze lifting from me and in turn taking with it the extra weight of it.

"Group or individual?" Justin asks.

"Individual this time, though you're welcome to brainstorm with your peers," Joanie says.

Justin wiggles his eyebrows at me, and I stifle a laugh.

"You're free to get to work. I have additional tasks for each of you within various departments this week, so don't forget to tackle those tasks first before you work on your challenge." She passes out sheets of paper with everyone's tasks for the week, and I'm lucky enough to have been assigned to the Marketing and Broadcasting department this week. Just browsing through what goes on in the department might get me some insight into where to go with this project.

Justin and Mackenzie are in Finance and Accounting, and no sooner do we all spot her name on the list than I hear her heavy, frustrated sigh.

"Is something the matter, Mackenzie?" Joanie asks.

She glances up from her paper at Joanie, pressing her lips together as if she's forcing herself not to say what she wants to say. "No ma'am."

Joanie studies her for a beat, and then she nods. "All right. Head on out, kids. Have fun!" She wiggles her fingers, and we all head out into the hallway. I'm trailing the group, and I hear Mackenzie complaining to Chloe as I walk out of Joanie's office.

"Freaking *finance*? While the golden child over there gets *marketing* all by her lonesome this week? I call BS."

"It's just the way the chips fell. Nothing to get upset about," Chloe says to her. I turn toward Justin and roll my eyes as he stifles a laugh.

"Want to brainstorm together?" he asks.

"Like I'm going to give up the goods on the ideas I already have?" I thin my lips and shake my head as I offer a mock glare in his direction. "Not a chance."

"Me-ow," he says, holding up a claw to indicate I'm being catty.

I nod over toward Mackenzie's direction, and he nods with a laugh.

"This is why we're besties. You just *get* me," he says, and he links his arm through mine.

"I need to get back in there and see what Joanie has on tap for me this week, but good luck in freaking finance with Mackity-Mack." I lower my voice so just he can hear, and he doesn't bother stifling his laughter this time.

I head back into Joanie's office. "What do you have for me, Ms. Sapphire?" I ask.

"I have some marketing analysis on the competition I'd like for you to study this week," she says. She clicks a few buttons on her computer. "I just sent you over a few different links so you can take a look at what different teams in the MLB are doing in their ad campaigns. I'd like you to study them and analyze the similarities and differences of each. Tell me what you think is working and what you think is a miss."

"Won't this give me an unfair advantage in this week's challenge?" I ask.

Joanie's brows crinkle as if she hadn't thought of that. She shakes her head. "Everyone on the intern team has the same access to the internet that you have, right?"

I nod.

She shakes her head. "Then no, I don't believe you're getting any sort of advantages over anybody else."

I twist my lips and nod, and then I get to work even though I know if Mackenzie saw what I had to do this week, she'd flip her fucking lid.

I study each of the ads Joanie sent along and make notes summarizing them. Then I draw my comparisons. Some common themes I find among the advertisements are teamwork, fan focus, and family. I start to brainstorm those ideas.

I could start the campaign with a family heading into the ballpark. Maybe a mother is carrying an infant while a dad holds a toddler's hand and their elderly parents walk in with them, too. Maybe we see the crowded lobby where friends meet and gather before entering the stadium to find their seats. And maybe we follow this family through the crowd, to the concession stand, up through the SFK area, and back down to their seats. Then we can watch as the players warm up on the field, the pillars of teamwork as they throw balls all over the place in an organized, rhythmic pattern. And then Cooper can take off his shirt and...

Oh wait. That's a different advertisement.

Focus, Gabby.

Cooper slices the bat and sends the ball flying into the outfield. He runs the bases as the three men in front of him score, and he slides into the plate with a grand slam.

He's the star of my video, obviously, just as he's the star of my dreams.

And then we pan back to the family sitting in the crowd, popcorn flying everywhere as they all stand up and high-five since their favorite player on their favorite team scored a grand slam. And a possible tagline at the end? *Bringing the Heat to Vegas.*

I like it as a first idea. It hits on all the major tenets that the successful ads Joanie sent me have. It feels a little predictable, but part of marketing is using what has traditionally worked in an innovative way. So I have a good idea, but I need to figure out how to inject something fresh and new into it.

And that's what the rest of the week is for. Well that *and* shenanigans with Cooper. Cooper also closes on his house with a final move-in date scheduled for Saturday with all his furniture scheduled to be delivered before then. I'm thankful he isn't moving this week because all my free time has been dedicated either to homework or to my ad campaign.

By Friday, I've figured it out.

It was a busy week since Kaylee asked if I could meet her on Tuesday and Thursday mornings at Tight Fit to get to know the fitness club a little better as we continue to work on marketing ideas, but the kickboxing class and the circuit training we did together were excellent stress relievers as I worked hard on my storyboards. Not only did I grow closer to Kaylee as we talked about the gym, SFK, my internship, and our boys, but I'm also damn proud of my idea.

It's an innovative approach on a traditional marketing plan, and it's almost time for my presentation.

Justin goes first, and his campaign is good. He uses dogs running around the bases in his video since we all know that animals sell products.

Mackenzie focuses on the players as she clearly thinks their level of sexiness will win her the challenge.

Chase, Dylan, and Brian's campaigns are ordinary, too, and Chloe is my biggest competition with a campaign that shows friends at home watching the game versus friends at the stadium watching the game. Her tagline says, *Heating up Vegas in person or at home.*

And then there's mine.

It starts with a video of a mom taking a video of her little boy playing a little league game, and then we pan to the little boy as he grows up into a professional ballplayer. It's a dual timeline as the family with the little boy goes to the game and runs around the SFK area before he watches eagerly from the stands. He morphs into the player on the field, hitting a grand slam for his team's win.

The tagline at the end says, *The Vegas Heat Makes your Family's Dreams Come True.*

Joanie wipes a tear from her eye when I'm finished presenting, and I can't help but wonder whether she wants kids…maybe even with my father. Isn't he a little old to be having kids at this point when he has a twenty-one-year-old daughter? What if Joanie and I got pregnant at the same time?

That would be weird.

I push the thought away as everyone in the room claps for my campaign.

"The judges will now vote for their favorite campaign," she says, and she nods toward the ten judges which include Cooper, Danny, Rush, Nick, Caitlin, Zelda, and four others from Baseball Operations. She doesn't vote this time, and she has all the judges put their votes into a bowl. She pulls them out one by one and reads the name on the paper.

The votes begin with two votes for Chloe, and then Joanie reads the rest. It's a clean sweep for Gabby.

Holy shit. That's me.

It's my second winning competition, and neither my father nor Joanie were able to swing the votes this time.

I won fair and square.

But Mackenzie doesn't seem to think so.

Once the congratulations die down and our guest judges head out, Mackenzie confronts Joanie. "Can we puh-*leez* have a blind comp next week so the golden child over there doesn't constantly have an unfair advantage because of her last name?"

"My last name is Grant," I point out, doing my very best to sound sincere and leave all the smugness out of my tone. I'm sure I fail.

"Whatever," she practically hisses at me.

"I'm sorry you feel the competitions haven't been fair," Joanie says to her. She lifts a shoulder. "But maybe you just need to step up your game." She says it sweetly even though the words are anything but sweet.

Mackenzie fumes at the words but knows better than to reply. Still, I fear she'll find some way to cause trouble for me.

"You're all released to your assignments for the afternoon. Gabby, I won't be needing anything if you'd like to find Cooper and continue shadowing him."

I nod. "Thank you."

The interns all disperse toward their assigned departments, and I head down toward the weight room. I find Nick in there with Rush, but Cooper is missing, and so is Danny.

"Have either of you seen Cooper?" I ask Rush and Nick.

They glance at each other, and my brows dip.

"What?" I ask.

"Is this, uh…is this *business* or *pleasure*?" Rush's tone reeks of inappropriate suggestion, and I'm sure my cheeks turn bright red.

Does he know about us?

Cooper wouldn't have told him…would he?

The more people who know, the better the chance there is of my dad finding out before we're ready to tell him.

"Business!" I practically shout, but it only makes me sound guilty. I draw in a breath and clear my throat. "Joanie told me I'm supposed to be shadowing him to learn more about baseball. Have you seen him?"

"Yeah," Rush says. "He's in the cages with Brewer." He nods toward the door that leads to the batting cages, and I head in that direction. "Have fun, but don't play with him, okay?"

"Excuse me?" I ask, turning around to face him again.

"He's a good guy and he's been burned plenty of times. Just take care of him because he really seems to have a thing for you."

Whoa. I was wholly unprepared for that conversation, and I have no idea what to say.

"Okay," I answer a little weakly, and then I head out of the room to find Cooper so I can figure out why the hell he thought telling his friends about us was a good idea.

Chapter 30
Gabby

I feel like I might actually be seething as I yank open the door to the batting cages. I glance around and find Danny's not in here. It's just Cooper.

And he isn't wearing a shirt.

He. Isn't. Wearing. A. Shirt.

I'm not sure why he'd be practicing hitting the ball without a shirt on, but all coherent thought leaves my mind as I watch him wait for the pitch then swing the bat. He slices the wood through the air and makes contact with the ball before lining up again. He wears a batting helmet, batting gloves, and athletic shorts, and the muscles in his chest and abdomen ripple with movement as he makes contact with another ball.

I've never watched him bat before. I don't even know if he's actually been in here practicing before. But I stand mesmerized, transfixed, riveted to the spot as I watch the shimmer of his body while he does what it was clearly made to do.

And he's mine.

It's a fact I haven't quite grasped yet. He wants me. He loves me.

Somehow watching him do something he's so completely passionate about causes a deep ache to pulse inside me as I feel myself falling, falling, falling even further into him.

Is there anything in the world I'm *that* passionate about?

Maybe him.

There are many things I enjoy, but nothing I can think of that I'd want to spend the rest of my life doing…other than him.

The pitching machine must run out of balls because he sets his bat down and starts to pull his gloves off. That's when he spots me standing there with my jaw practically dragging on the ground.

He lets out a soft chuckle. "Hey. I didn't know I had an audience."

"Sorry. I, uh…" *Forgot what I came in here for, I guess.*

"It's okay. If it was anyone else but you—"

"You want to be alone?"

He walks over toward the chain link fence separating us, and he rests his fingers through some of the links. He shakes his head. "I asked Danny to give me a few minutes to myself in here. It's just…it's the first time I picked up a bat since…" He trails off, leaving me to imagine when that was.

"Since your injury?" I guess, filling in the blank, and he nods as he glances away from me. "Well? How did it feel?"

He blows out a breath then pulls off his helmet and runs a hand through his hair. He doesn't meet my eyes for a few beats, and then he turns toward me. "You know how in life you sometimes put off doing something because you think you're only going to hurt yourself by doing it?"

My brows knit together as I wait for him to finish.

He sets his helmet down and tosses his gloves on top of it. He moves toward the gate and lets himself out, and when he's standing in front of me, he shakes his head a little. "It wasn't like that at all. It was pure fucking magic. I feel like *I'm back.* I feel like I'm *myself* again. And I'm not sure I could've opened those doors without you by my side."

My hand flies to my heart. "Without *me?*"

His eyes soften as he gazes at me. "I wasn't happy my last year playing. There were a lot of factors that led to that, and they seem to keep uncovering themselves at every turn lately. But one thing is for sure." He takes a few steps toward me as he talks. "When I'm out there on that field this year, I'm going to be happy, and it's not just because I get to play the game I love. It's not just because I'm leading a brand new expansion team. It's not just because I'm back on third where I was born to be." He takes another step toward me, closing the small gap between us, and he lifts his fingertips to my jaw before they curl around my neck. "But it's because I know you're cheering for me somewhere out there, and that's more than enough for me to give it my all."

"Wow," I breathe, and he chuckles as his lips drop to mine.

I fold myself into him, wrapping my arms around him as he leads the kiss from slow and tender toward urgent and passionate, needy and fiery.

It's full of everything I want, everything I *need*, and if three of his friends weren't milling around here somewhere, if other players and staff members and grounds crew and interns weren't just on the other side of those doors, I'd let him take me right here. I'd give in to every carnal desire I feel.

But we can't. It's not just unprofessional, but it's risky. We're trying to hold onto this secret that seems to keep getting bigger and bigger, and while neither of us feels ready to tell my dad, I know the time is inching in on us when we're going to *have* to.

And nothing drives that point home more than when I finally pull myself away from him, knowing our time here is limited in this space.

A throat clears behind us, and Cooper's eyes move over my shoulder as I spin around, my heart leaping up into my throat.

"So you're not just Daddy's little girl. Apparently you're also Cooper's little girl," Mackenzie says with a snarl. "One more advantage for you, one more strike against the rest of us." She folds her arms over her chest.

"Mackenzie, I can explain," I begin, but I can't. I can't explain that she's probably right. Cooper has been on the judging panel of most of our challenges, and I've come out victorious. It doesn't look fair even though he has assured me it absolutely is, that he's simply voting for the best presentation.

"How many others on the judges' panel are you kissing in not-so-private hallways?" she demands.

I purse my lips. "It's not like that," I begin, my tone one of begging and apology at the same time.

"Oh, it's exactly like that," she says. "You won't get away with this."

She spins on her heels and bolts out the door, and I'm left to wonder what the hell I'm supposed to do now…and what the hell she's off to do now.

I don't have much time to think about it because a text comes through from my dad.

Dad: *Do you have dinner plans tonight?*

It's a Friday night, and my only plan was to curl up in bed with Cooper.

Me: *Not yet.*

Dad: *Desmonds at eight?*

Me: *I'll be there.*

Cooper pulls his phone from his pocket and flashes the screen at me. He got the same text from my dad.

My eyes widen as guilt slices through me. "Do you think he knows?" I whisper.

"There's no way Mackenzie works that fast," Cooper points out. "I don't even think your dad is here right now."

I nod, my mouth going dry as nerves kick in. "We really need to tell him. I can't risk him finding out from someone else. It wouldn't be right."

Cooper nods, and he slings an arm around me. "You're right. We'll tell him at dinner tonight."

"Okay." I nod, and thus begins the nerve-racking countdown to eight o'clock tonight.

Chapter 31
Gabby

The day drags. I left the stadium around five, went home, and changed, and it's only six. I have two more hours to be nervous. Two more hours to let the tension build. Two more hours to wonder why my father would possibly want both Cooper *and* me at dinner.

There's only one possibility.

He found out. He's going to confront us.

I'm not sure why he'd pick his favorite restaurant to do that, but maybe it's because he wants a good meal after he blows up at the two of us.

Our relationship is still relatively new. My father hasn't had to discipline me. He hasn't had to show disappointment in me. In the few years we've gotten to know one another, I've been an adult acing my college classes. The worst he's had to deal with was a few drunken nights, and even then, I wasn't exactly out of control.

But this…this is something different. This is something he surely disapproves of. This is something I've done that might disappoint him, and I'm not sure how to handle that.

I take a shot of vodka to calm my nerves, but it doesn't help. And wouldn't you know it? Cooper walks into the kitchen as I slam my shot glass down.

He chuckles as he watches me. "Nervous?"

"Is it that obvious?"

"Both the shot and the shaky hands give you away. Need me to do something to calm you down?" He eyes me salaciously, and I set my hand on my hip as I purse my lips and cock my head at him. He chuckles. "Not *that*, although now that you mention it…"

I smack him in the arm.

"I meant some deep breathing exercises. Or you could just, you know, get drunk. I'm sure that'll help."

"Cute, smart guy." I roll my eyes. "Why do you think he wants both of us to be there?"

He shrugs. "We'll find out in a couple hours."

"Aren't you nervous?" I demand.

He shakes his head. "Not really."

"Dude, you're the one who *ended* things with me because you didn't want him to know. And now I think he might know and you're not freaking out?"

He chuckles. "I'm not freaking out. What good would that do? We already agreed we're going to tell him tonight anyway, right? So maybe he found out first. Either way, we should get ready to celebrate. We won't have to hide this anymore."

Maybe he's right. I blow out a breath, slam another shot of vodka, and stare at the clock until eight inches closer.

We decide to go together since we'll certainly be leaving together, and I spot my dad's Bentley in the parking lot. Cooper pulls in beside it, and I draw in a deep breath as I wring my fingers together.

"Hey," he says quietly. He reaches over and squeezes my hands. "It'll be fine. Whatever happens, it'll be fine."

I blink a few times and nod, and then we get out of the car, my heart pounding in my chest.

The hostess takes us to the table where my dad and Joanie are already sitting. It's a booth, and the two of them sit on one side while Cooper slides onto the other side and I'm forced to sit next to him.

A table with four chairs might've served us better. Now we'll be stuck beside one another once we break the news, and he'll surely stare us down as he contemplates his next move.

Why am I so scared of him?

Oh, right. Because he's a big, powerful man, and he's my dad, and I'm terrified of disappointing him the way I've disappointed my mother my entire life.

He's not like her, a tiny voice in my head reminds me.

The hostess takes our drink orders, and as she walks away, I see my dad is grinning at the two of us.

"I'm so glad you're both here," he begins warmly. He glances over at Joanie, who's also smiling. Does she know, too? I mean, I had my suspicions that she knew, but this would confirm it.

I clear my throat, and I open my mouth to just get on with it, to get the words out, to confess so we can move forward, but my dad continues before I fully get the words out. At the same time I begin, "Cooper and I—" my dad announces, "I asked Joanie to marry me, and she accepted."

I gasp, my hand flying to my chest. "You…you *what*?"

Joanie holds up her hand to show off a huge, sparkling, *pear-shaped diamond set in a platinum band.*

I gasp again, my heart racing as recognition dawns.

I've seen that ring before. It was in the back of Cooper's underwear and sock drawer. I shouldn't have been looking.

It wasn't Cooper's ring.

It's my dad's ring.

For Joanie.

Cooper was holding onto it for him.

Holy. Shit.

Seeing that ring in Cooper's drawer was the cornerstone of my decision to move things along with him. I decided I was ready for marriage, ready for kids, ready for all of it if it means I get to have it with him even though I fully realize I'm young to be making these sorts of decisions.

But the ring wasn't even for me. It was for Joanie.

The ring wasn't even Cooper's. It was my dad's.

My jaw hangs open as these facts plow into me.

How close are my dad and Cooper, exactly?

"I wanted my baby girl and my best friend to be the first to know," my dad says.

Oh. So pretty damn close, then.

"Gabby, I'd love for you to be my maid of honor," Joanie says.

"Oh, of course!" I manage, still reeling from the shock of it all. I slide out of the booth to give them both hugs.

"And Cooper, I'd love for you to be my best man," my dad requests. Cooper slides out of the booth, too, and then it's hugs and congratulations and handshakes and I'm definitely starting to feel the whiplash of the last few hours as the truth dawns on me.

He still doesn't know.

That's not why we're here tonight.

I exhale a long, calming breath as Cooper and I hug, too.

"Not tonight," he murmurs softly in my ear, and I nod discreetly in agreement.

Not tonight.

But if not tonight…then when?

Chapter 32
Cooper

I draw in a deep breath as I wake up on Saturday morning for the last time at someone else's house.

I'm ready to move into my new place. It's been a whirlwind of a month, and having to hide what I share with Gabby even while we're at home has been some level beyond frustrating.

My new bed was delivered yesterday along with furniture for the rest of the place, things picked out by some designer at Kaylee's sister-in-law's firm. When I first got to town, she sent me some choices of furniture to order. I barely glanced at it, balked at the bottom line, and signed off on all of it anyway. It's one less thing to have to worry about, and now my new place will be all set up when I walk in this morning with Gabby on my arm.

She didn't sleep in my arms last night, and I hope it's the last night for a long time that's the case. We weren't sure if her father was staying the night with Joanie or if he was coming home, and we figured we should play it safe on our last night in his house.

But once we're in my house? All bets are off.

And speaking of my house, I need to get over there. The pod where all my shit has been stored for the last month is arriving before noon, and I'd like to be there to unpack everything as soon as it arrives. I suppose then it'll really feel like home.

My phone rings just as I'm contemplating getting out of bed, and I see it's my mother.

"Good morning," I answer, my voice a little groggy on the first words I've spoken today.

"Oh, honey, I'm so sorry. Did I wake you?"

"No ma'am, I was up. What's going on?"

"Just checking in on you. It's been a few days since I've heard your voice and usually you're a *call Mom everyday* kind of kid," she says.

"I'm sorry. Things are heating up out here with the expansion draft just a month away now," I say. "Troy's been keeping me busy researching every player on every team so we can assemble the best team possible. And all that on top of workouts, closing on the house, Gabby…"

"How's Gabby doing?" she asks, and I sense something in her tone that tells me she really cares. I never sensed that with Stacy, that's for sure.

"Great. She's excelling in her internship, and she's managing to do it on top of all her schoolwork. She's just incredible."

"Well I already knew that part. What about you? You holding up okay or do I need to have a chat with Troy?" she asks.

I laugh. "I'm holding up just fine. Guess what I did earlier this week?"

"What?"

"I stepped into the batting cages." My voice is just above a whisper as I say the words, and it's sort of unbelievable to me how emotional picking up a bat again made me feel.

"Oh, wow. How'd it go?"

I blow out a breath. "It was…God, Mom. It was everything I was hoping for. It was like getting back on the bike after far too long away and I already feel myself becoming addicted to that feeling again."

She doesn't respond right away, and then I hear a sniffle.

"Mom?"

When she finally answers, her voice trembles with emotion. "I'm just so happy for you, honey. It's good to have you back."

"I never went anywhere," I say.

"Yes, you did. You had a hard couple years, and you're proof that you can get through those hard times and come out the other side. What an inspiration you are, my sweet boy."

"I don't know about that." My words are modest, but I will thrive on the compliment she just gave me for a good, long time.

"Well I do, and I'm proud of you."

"Thanks, Mom."

"Okay. Enough with the sappy stuff," she says, her voice returning to all business, and I chuckle. "Good luck with move-in day. Send pictures and let me know when I can come out to visit."

"The door is always open for you."

"Are you busy Thanksgiving?" she asks. "I was thinking of coming out and bringing Connor and his family with me if it's okay with you."

"I'd love that. Send my love to Connor and everyone."

"I will. Love you, Cooper," she says.

"Love you back, Mom."

We hang up, and I'm just about to get out of bed when I hear a soft knock at my door. "Come in!" I yell, and the door opens slowly. Standing in the doorway is the woman I've fallen so deeply in love with that I'm no longer certain where I end and she begins. It doesn't make any sense, but she's somehow become a part of me that feels like it was always there just waiting for her arrival.

And yet…there are things that still weigh heavy on my mind.

She said she was ready for marriage and a family, but I need to know whether those were just words or if she meant them.

I saw her face last night when her father said he'd proposed to Joanie. I saw the way her eyes bugged out when she saw the ring, and for a fleeting moment, I wondered whether she saw the ring in my drawer before she came to Chicago with clothes for me.

She would have to have seen it if she was in that drawer. It wasn't well-hidden, but I didn't expect Joanie to go rifling through my unmentionables. And if she did see it, she had to have thought it was meant for her, but she never mentioned it if she did.

Still…she seemed more *ready* for that sort of future when it came up in Chicago, and I can't help but wonder if it was because of that ring.

"Good morning, Sunshine," I say as she walks into the room. She slides into bed beside me, and I wrap my arms around her.

"Good morning, Captain." She giggles when I thrust my hips against her backside.

I've gone back and forth since last night about whether to bring up the ring, and for some reason, the words just drop out of my mouth first thing this morning.

"Can I ask you a question?"

"Of course." She wiggles her ass a little against my cock, and the question nearly darts right out of my mind.

"Your eyes got real wide last night when you saw the ring your dad gave Joanie. Did you, uh…" I trail off as I never really ask the question.

She clears her throat, and then she turns around to face me. "Oh, God. I'm so embarrassed." She sets her hand on her forehead. "I swear I didn't mean to snoop, but I saw it in your drawer, and of course I never wanted to bring it up especially because I thought it was yours and if you were going to surprise me, but now I know it wasn't intended for me, and I can't believe you just brought it up because—"

"Hey," I say softly, interrupting her babbling. "It's fine. I guess I just wanted to know what level of snooping I'm dealing with here, you know, in case I ever need to hide one of those myself..." I try to play it off as a joke, but instead, she takes it absolutely seriously.

Her eyes widen. "I swear I'm not a snooper! I just saw it when I was trying to do something nice for you, and I knew my curiosity would *kill me* if I didn't take a look, so I peeked real quick, and then it became this, like, *huge thing* to me because it made me think about what I'd even say if you gave it to me. And that was what made me realize that's *exactly* what I want. I want you, and I want a future, and I want a marriage. I want a house full of laughter and pitter-patters and maybe a kitty and T-ball and babies that have your blue eyes. I want a job with the Heat so we can be together even when we're apart, and I want to build my life not just *with* you but *around* you. And then I saw my dad give that ring to Joanie and I realized I'm way off base here because you're clearly not where I am."

My brows dip at the end of her babbling. "Hold on a second there, Sunshine. I'm clearly not where you are?"

She lifts a shoulder. "Well...no. I was ready to put that ring on my finger, and it wasn't even for me."

"Whoa whoa whoa. Just because that particular ring wasn't meant for you doesn't mean I'm not ready to give you the exact kind of life you just described." I lean my forehead to hers for a beat and close my eyes. "It's all I think about, Gabby." I pull back and my eyes meet hers. "I want to build my life around you, too. But I also need you to know what you're getting into with me. I signed a contract that says I promise to be married to my job for the next three years, and even if you're working with the Heat, that doesn't mean we'll get to be together all the time. If I were to knock you up, and believe me, I want to knock you up good and hard, you'd have to do most of the heavy lifting when it comes to our kids without me until my contract is up and we decide what we want to do next."

Her eyes glaze over a little at my words.

"What?" I ask.

"You just said *our kids* and it hit me that we're really having the sort of conversation that I thought was many years off into my future."

"How does that make you feel?" I ask.

"It makes me feel..." She pauses as she trails off to search for the right word. "It makes me feel *ready*." She presses her lips to mine, and then there's no more talking as we revel in each other's body as the words we just shared play on repeat in my mind.

God, I love her, and I can't wait to start our future together.

I just hope we actually get the chance to start it.

Chapter 33
Gabby

I open another box labeled *Kitchen*. "Where do you want these?" I ask, pulling out a wooden spoon.

He shrugs. "Wherever you want them is fine with me."

Heat fills my cheeks as I think about those words. He wants me to put his kitchen utensils wherever I want them since we'll both be using them. He's making me feel a part of this move-in day even though I'm not moving in here…yet. We both know that I'll be spending plenty of time here, but since we're not telling my dad yet, I guess we can't really make the move official.

Someday, we will. We'll get there. But on the heels of my father's engagement to Joanie is definitely not the right time.

Cooper is unpacking some boxes upstairs, and there are several service workers here setting up his internet and connecting his televisions in all the different rooms. We didn't have much time this morning to inspect the place since the pod was already here when we arrived, so I'm glad we had that morning quickie before we took showers and headed over.

And man, was that a good morning quickie.

The way he kissed me after our words to each other about building our future together made me confident that he's the last man I'll ever kiss. He's it for me, and he's made it clear I'm it for him.

We have some obstacles to overcome, but what couple doesn't? We'll take them as they come, and we'll emerge stronger for battling through them together.

My dad's words about not wanting me with a baseball player ring through my mind.

But if he knew it was Cooper, certainly he'd approve…right?

It's his best friend. It's a man he trusts with his daughter since he's been pushing us together.

Maybe that's the point—maybe it's exactly why he would be even more against what's really happening between us. He'd never even see it coming since it's his best friend and his *daughter.*

"Can I ask you a question?" I ask once Cooper reappears in the kitchen and the workers are out of earshot.

"Always." He grabs some plates out of another box and chooses a cabinet at random to stack them in. He glances at me before he places them on the shelf, and I shake my head a little, nodding at the cabinet where I already started putting plates and bowls. He chuckles and moves to that one, and I love how we can already have silent conversations with one another.

"Why'd you tell your friends about us?"

He sets the plates into the cabinet with a rather loud bang, and then he turns toward me. "Uh…"

"You just seem to want to keep it a secret from certain people, yet the more people who know, especially people who are close to my dad, the more likely he is to find out before we figure out how to tell him," I point out.

He draws in a deep breath. "Danny asked if I'd gotten back together with you at poker the other night. He was there when I, uh…helped you home when you were drunk at the bar, and I'd confessed what was going on between us to him. Rush and Nick heard the question and I couldn't exactly back out of it, so I went the honest route. They'll be discreet about it."

"Yeah, Rush was real discreet when he asked if it was *business or pleasure* when I was looking for you in the weight room the other day." I set my hand on my hip, and he takes a few steps toward me to close the gap between us. "They know, Mackenzie knows, Justin knows, and I swear I think Joanie knows. How long until he finds out before we're the ones to tell him?"

"Hey," he says softly, and he loops one of his arms through mine where I'm still holding onto my hip. He pulls me into him. "Chill, babe. We're fine."

I'm sure he's right. I'm overreacting. I'm trying to be careful since the last thing I want is for my dad to find out about us from someone other than, well, *us.* But it just seems like every time we're ready to tell him, something stands in our way.

Is that a sign?

"Maybe we should just tell him," I say.

"Or maybe we should break in my new place since the internet guys just left and we're all alone."

"You want it again?" I ask.

"I *always* want it with you."

I can't help a little giggle at that.

"Before we do all that, though, I have something for you." He opens the drawer closest to the fridge and pulls out a key. Looped onto it is a keyring that says *Captain's House.*

I giggle as he presses the key into my palm, but his eyes are serious.

"This doesn't have to be a big deal, but it sort of feels like one to me. I want you to feel free to come over any time you want. I want this to feel like home for you, too."

My eyes fill with tears as I close my fingers around the key, and then he leans forward and nibbles on my neck a little. It has the effect of completely clearing my mind of pretty much anything and everything except more of Cooper on top of me, and he grabs me suddenly and perches me on the edge of his countertop. He pushes his way in between my legs so they're spread open for him. "Mm," he murmurs, his face level with my breasts. He looks up at me, and I set the key on the counter beside me. I loop my arms around his neck, our eyes sharing some mutual understanding before I drop my lips to his.

He wraps his arms around me, and I wrap my legs around him as his mouth opens to mine. I'm not sure how every kiss with him turns from sweet to fiery nearly in an instant, but the urgency and the passion between us is hot and heavy.

We kiss like that a few beats, but he's a man on a mission, and it's mere moments later that he's pulling my jeans and my panties down my legs and tossing them on the kitchen floor before he makes a meal out of me right there on his kitchen counter.

He sucks on my clit before sliding his tongue down, dipping it into me, and then adding his fingers as his tongue laps at my clit some more. I lean back, my palms flat on the counter behind me, and I find myself completely lost in the sensations of his tongue and his lips and his fingers as he drives me closer and closer to my climax. "Oh my God," I yell out, and then "Oh yes, Cooper, yes, yes, yes!" I scream as he carries me over the edge of bliss, my thighs clamping around his ears as my body thrashes against him. It's brutal and violent and beautiful all at once, and he hums softly against my body as he drives me all the way to the finish line.

I collapse back onto the counter, panting as my body comes down from the high, and he rises to a stand. He leans over me and presses gentle kisses to my neck, and it's a pure moment of sweet delight as I think about how many times over we'll do this right here as we fall deeper and deeper into each other.

And then, someday down the road once all secrets are revealed, we'll live here together and we'll create the kind of future we've already promised each other, the future we've dreamed about together.

We'll do that as many times as we want right here in this kitchen. We'll be as loud as we want, and we won't have to hide from anybody.

I live in that bliss for all of a few moments before we hear the doorbell ring.

"Dammit," Cooper mutters under his breath. He straightens, pulling his weight off me, and he helps me sit up again. He reaches down and picks up my clothes, and he helps me down from the counter before handing them over.

"My legs are still a little shaky after that one," I admit, and he chuckles.

"I'll go get rid of whoever's at the door," he promises.

I quickly pull on my clothes as he disappears, and I hear the door open a few seconds later. I'm pulling up the zipper on my jeans when I hear it.

"How's the new place, man?"

My dad's voice.

Oh, shit.

He had to have seen my car outside.

How the hell do I play this one off?

Cooper just gave me an orgasm on his kitchen counter and I was about to return the favor when my freaking *dad* showed up.

I sigh.

The bliss wasn't meant to last forever, I guess.

I smooth my hair down and dive back into the box I was unpacking before Cooper came in with that little...*interruption.*

"I called in for some help from my shadow," Cooper says, his voice carrying down the hall and into the kitchen, where I stand as they walk into the doorway.

"There she is," my dad says, and he walks over and grabs me into a hug.

Jeez. My legs are still shaking from the vicious orgasm his best friend just gave me, and now I have to act like everything's normal.

399

"Hey, Dad," I say, my voice shaky and high-pitched. "Just, uh, taking out Cooper's equipment." My eyes widen at the potential euphemism. "Utensils! I'm unpacking his utensils." I'm not sure if that's any better, and my dad gives me a strange look while Cooper laughs.

Oh my God. Can he smell me on Cooper's breath? I'm not sure why the thought darts through my head, but now I can't make it go away.

"She's been a huge help." He opens a few cabinets to show my dad how much we've accomplished, my climax on the counter thirty seconds ago notwithstanding.

"Glad to hear it," he says. "My little girl is a great helper, isn't she?"

He musses my hair a little, and I get the sense he will *always* see me as his little girl. Maybe it's because we missed so much time together, but every time I'm around him and Cooper together, I just get this weird premonition that he would *never* be okay with what's happening between us. It would come as way too much of a shock when he truly thinks I'm nothing more than a much younger little sister to Cooper.

And I'm scared it has the potential to spell the end for us before we even really get the chance to get started.

Chapter 34
Cooper

Kaylee peeks behind me, and I turn around to see what she's looking at.

There's nobody there.

"What?" I ask, holding up both hands in confusion.

"Where's Gabby?"

My brows knit together. "I didn't invite her."

Kaylee huffs out an agitated sigh. "You were *supposed* to. I was excited to see her again and, you know, scare her off from ever having kids."

I laugh. "Why do you think I didn't bring her?"

Kaylee punches me in the arm, and I grab the spot of the offense.

"It has nothing to do with you, Kay. I swear. We're still hiding it from her father, and she needed to spend time at home before he starts asking questions about where she's been."

She narrows her eyes at me. "You're still hiding it?"

I lift a shoulder. "It's complicated. Can I come in or are you planning to have me eat out here on your front porch?"

She laughs and opens the door a little wider, and I spot Kaylee's entire extended family gathered in the kitchen along with Aces wide receiver Tristan Higgins and a woman who's presumably his wife. They all turn toward me as I walk in, and then a chorus of *Cooper* and *Noah* follow as everyone greets me. Kaylee's mom and Ben's dad are in the family room with the twins, and they both wave before turning their attention back to the kids.

Ben tosses me a can of beer, which I promptly open, and then together we chug until our cans are empty.

"Victory Monday, baby!" Ben says, and he tosses me a second one. Victory Monday is a football term—something we don't have in my sport where the team gets the day off practice if they win on Sundays.

"Good God, you're a freaking caveman." Kaylee bumps into his hip with her ass, and he laughs as he grabs her ass and makes a lewd gesture.

"Dude, that's my fucking sister." Jack, the quarterback of the Vegas Aces, makes a face of disgust at his teammate-slash-brother-in-law.

"Oh, stop it. It's cute," Kate says, swatting playfully at her husband.

I walk over and give Kate a hug. "Thanks for everything you did to get me into my dream home. I moved in two days ago and it's even better than I'd hoped."

"I'm so happy to hear that," she says, giving me a squeeze.

"And that couch you picked out for me? Fucking heaven," I tell her.

"Sounds like Coop's volunteering for a Dalton Family Fun Night at his new place next Monday," Kaylee jokes. At least I hope it's a joke.

I shake my head with a modest laugh. "I don't think I have the stamina to handle this entire crew."

"Seriously, though. Bring the girl next time," she scolds.

"Ooh, there's a girl?" Ellie asks next, sidling up beside her sisters-in-law. "Tell us more."

I laugh, and then I'm saved by the bell…literally. The oven timer beeps to let us know dinner is ready, Ben tells everyone to take a seat in the dining room, and chatter and laughter follow us in.

Kaylee and Ben serve the steaks and potatoes, and I listen as the family chats around me. I'm sandwiched between Kaylee and Tessa, the girl here with Tristan. It's split pretty evenly between football talk and baby talk with this crowd since there are seven little ones sitting around the table, but regardless of the topic, they make me feel like I belong here.

I know they'd make Gabby feel the same way, but something stopped me from bringing her tonight.

Kaylee already knows her, but it's a big group to walk into, and while I've gotten to know them pretty well, they can be intimidating. Plus there's all the babies here, and it's just another reminder that she might not be ready for those things while I am. It's smacking me right in the face as Jack's kid JJ tosses mashed potatoes at his dad and Luke's daughter cries because she wanted apple juice instead of milk.

This is family. This loud, raucous group gathers every Monday just to be together, and this is something I always wanted for myself, too. Baseball took me away from my family, so we've never been able to have these sorts of gatherings other than during the holidays.

I'm not sure if I was protecting her or protecting myself by not inviting her. The people in this room are all good friends of mine, but that doesn't mean I'm ready to listen to their judgment about the difference in our ages. Ben and Kaylee get it, but it's because they also have an age gap between them…though not as wide as ours.

Maybe a small part of me actually *likes* keeping what we have on the down low. She's my secret, and I'm hers. There's something romantic about that, right?

Plates are emptied but the laughter remains, and when we're finished and the plates have been cleared, Ben asks, "Anybody in for some poker?"

Jack, Luke, and Tristan raise their hands, and I follow suit even though a part of me is ready to head home so I can call Gabby.

Mrs. Dalton and Mr. Olson manage the kids, the ladies all head into the kitchen to talk about Ellie's latest adventures with her public relations firm—a firm which every woman in the room has worked with for at least for a short period of time, and Ben takes us to the game room, where a poker table is already set up. We each throw a hundred dollar bill into the middle, and he distributes the chips.

Luck is not my friend tonight.

I'm out of money after the first half hour, and so is Luke. It's down to Ben, Tristan, and Jack, all who are on the starting roster for the Aces.

I lose interest in watching since I'm out of money and can't play. I head over to the small fridge in here to grab another beer, debating whether I should just call it a night, when Luke asks, "You liking it here in Vegas so far?"

I nod as I crack open another can, and I hand him one, too. "I've only been here about a month, but so far I can't complain."

"Kaylee mentioned a girl?"

I huff out a laugh. "Your sister is not subtle."

"Subtlety has never been her strong suit."

"There's a girl, and she's the boss's daughter, and we're keeping it on the down low." I chug some more beer as he processes my words.

"I knew all that, but you know we'd keep your secret over here." He wiggles his eyebrows, and I chuckle.

"I don't doubt it, but when there's a group this big, it's easier just to blend into the backdrop."

"Cooper Noah blending into the backdrop?" he asks as he shakes his head. "I don't think that's a thing."

I shake my head, too. "I think you might be right about that."

The question remains, then: how do I protect what Gabby and I have?

Chapter 35
Gabby

"You didn't get enough last night?" I murmur against his neck.

"I will *never* get enough of you," he murmurs right back. His lips drop down to mine, and he kisses me as he wraps his arms around my naked torso.

We're back in the training room, and he tore my shirt over my head and I think we're supposed to be up by the SFK kid's area checking on things, but instead we found an empty weight room so we decided to take advantage.

I know we're tempting fate here, but I can't get enough of him, either.

We spent all night naked. We woke up and did it again. And now, a mere two hours into the workday, we're in the training room about to have sex *again*.

I've never been with a man who had this much sexual vitality, but I've also never been with a man who made me feel this needy *all the time*, either. When I'm not around him, I ache for him. When I am around him, I become, well…

"I love how greedy your cunt is for me, baby. Let me fill it one more time before lunch."

He's not wrong. It is greedy and I do want him to fill it, and if I didn't feel the soft slide of his teeth against my nipple a moment later, I'd wonder whether this was real or a dream.

It's real.

I cry out with pleasure lined with the gentlest bite of pain.

"Shh," he warns, biting down a little harder.

I gasp as my hips thrust against his of their own volition. "Oh my God, Cooper," I moan.

"That's right, baby," he whispers. He pulls his cock out, and a second later he's driving into me. He adjusts us so he's holding on under my thighs, and he bounces me up and down as he thrusts into me. Holy fuck, it takes an athletic man to do what he's doing, but he's doing it incredibly.

I can't take it.

Between the feel of him, the sweet sensation of him rocking into me, the emotions coursing between us, and God, even the smell of him, I lose all control. My body spasms under his touch, like it was made to be handled by him and him alone.

I come with force as I jerk and twist over him, but he holds tight onto me before he explodes into his own orgasm with a mighty roar.

"Shh," I remind him lazily as I come down from my high, my mouth close to his ear since I've gone limp in his arms. I feel like a noodle, or jelly, or some sort of jelly noodle.

How the hell am I supposed to just get dressed and head back to work like he didn't just give me the most blissful few minutes of my entire life?

He chuckles as he gently sets me on the exam table, and I feel like I could curl up in a ball and take a nap. Instead, I sort of slump against the wall wishing I could just get a few minutes of sleep.

But I can't. Because I'm here working.

He cleans himself up and tucks the pleasure stick back into his shorts. "Does that get better every time?" he asks as his brows knit together. He reaches over and hands me my bra.

I sit up and nod as I start to pull it on. "Seems impossible, but yes, I really think it does."

He hands me my shirt next, and he covers up his glorious body with his own shirt to my dismay.

I force myself off the table to grab the rest of my clothes.

As has become our routine, Cooper opens the door first to make sure the coast is clear once we're dressed.

"Joanie," he says loudly as soon as he walks out of the room.

Shit.

I slink back into the room, moving into the shadows as much as I can.

"Where's Gabby?" she asks.

"How should I know?"

"Because I sent her off with you to check on the StrongFitKids progress over a half hour ago and nobody up there saw you. What were you doing in the training room?" she demands. She's onto us, I just know it. I can hear the suspicion in her voice.

"I was, uh…taping my finger."

"There's no tape on your finger, Cooper," she says sternly.

"No, Joanie! Don't go in—" his voice trails off as the door opens and Joanie stands there staring back at me. "—there."

I wave a little sheepishly. "Hi."

"What are you doing?" she asks. She takes a step toward me, and she smooths my hair down on one side.

I clear my throat, but I can't seem to find the words.

"She was getting tape for my finger," Cooper says, inflecting it at the end like a question.

God, he's a bad liar.

"Are you two…" Joanie asks, looking between the two of us.

I blow out a breath, and when I look at Cooper, I can't help but think it's all going to be okay. He gives me a warning look, but I can't keep lying to her—not when I've started to feel a closer connection to her. Maybe she'll have some insight on how to break this to my dad, anyway. She seems to know him pretty well given the fact that she's wearing his pear-shaped engagement ring on her finger.

"Yes," I finally say softly. "We are."

She purses her lips as if she's torn between scolding me, expressing her disapproval, or showing support.

"We first met before I knew he was playing for my father…before he knew I was Troy's daughter. We tried to fight it, but we couldn't," I admit.

Cooper just stands there silently, clearly letting me take the lead on this one.

She nods. "I had a feeling." She draws in a long breath before she lets it out. "Your father can't find out. And for fuck's sake, you can't be doing this here at the stadium. Look at the two of you, those relaxed looks on your faces." She shakes her head with disapproval. "If this was anyone else, you'd be fired. You realize that, right?"

"I know, ma'am," I say quietly. "I'm so sorry." I have no defense. My boss-slash-future stepmother just caught me banging her future husband's best friend while we're both supposed to be on the clock.

"You said Troy can't find out," Cooper begins, finally joining the conversation. "Why, exactly?"

"Lots of reasons, Cooper. For one, you're, what—at least a decade, maybe more, older than her. You're in two totally different generations. You're probably three years away from retirement, and she's not even out of college yet. And aside from that, the last thing he wants is for his daughter to get caught up with a ballplayer. He knows what sort of commitment it takes from you. It's something he and I have talked a lot about over the last year as he moved into this management position. His first commitment will be the game, and I understand that. I support that. But he doesn't want that for you, Gabby. He wants better for you. You're his little girl, and—"

"And I'm afraid that's all I'll ever be to him," I say, cutting her off. "I'm an adult, but he'll never see me as one."

"You're absolutely right, honey. He missed out on all that time with you, and we both know how protective he is." She shakes her head a little as she wrestles with that last thought, and I wonder exactly how protective he is and why she seems to react the way she does to those words. "What is this thing between you two anyway?" The subject change is both abrupt and jarring.

Cooper and I exchange a glance.

"It's..." he begins.

"Everything," I finish, going for total honesty and transparency. She already knows, so what good would diminishing what has blossomed between the two of us do?

He nods. "Everything," he repeats, and our eyes lock across the small space separating us.

Joanie blows out a breath. "Oh hell. Then I guess I'll do what I can to hide it, but your father can never know I know. This is going to make the wedding plenty awkward." She mutters the last part under her breath, and I can't help a small giggle.

Cooper chuckles, too, and then Joanie looks between the two of us a little wryly at first before she bursts out into laughter, too.

Maybe it doesn't make sense, but somehow now that she knows, I feel just a little closer to her.

"Now get your ass back up to my office, and no more stadium shenanigans, do you two hear me?" She shakes her head as she spins to walk out of the room, muttering the whole way out. "If he only knew what putting you on Cooper as a shadow really meant..."

Cooper and I both laugh as she walks out, but he turns serious for a beat. "Are you okay?"

I nod. "I'm fine. It's sort of a relief, really. One less person to hide it from, though I'm sure it's not going to be easy for her to keep something like this from my father."

"She's right, though. I know I can't keep my hands off you, but it's probably in our best interest to resist this when we're together at the stadium," he admits.

"No more stadium shenanigans," I say sadly, even though I hate the idea of resisting him anywhere, anytime. "You're right. Too many people already know. It's only a matter of time before it gets back to my dad."

"Then let's cut it off. Do we need to stage some big break up and really keep this thing secret?"

"Maybe just in front of Mackenzie. I don't trust her," I say. "But I'm okay with your friends knowing as long as you trust them."

He nods. "I do. But next time she's around, we'll fake a fight and end it."

"And it would be even better if you hit on her," I add.

He wrinkles his nose. "Do I have to?"

"As long as you come home to me, pal."

He laughs, and he taps the tip of my nose. "Always."

I wish we hadn't just vowed no more stadium shenanigans, because I'd love to seal that promise with some more time in the training room.

Chapter 36
Gabby

The closer we move toward the expansion draft, the busier Cooper gets.

And that also means he's been spending a *lot* more time with my father.

They're analyzing players, watching games, and strategizing, and my dad has been spending more and more time at either our house or Cooper's, which means I've been spending less and less time with both of them. My own schedule has started filling, too, as the internship has suddenly become like a full time position, I've been working more and more with Kaylee, and my school schedule only gets in the way.

We're a week out from the expansion draft and I'm editing a video to give Zelda to post to the Heat's TikTok account when Mia calls me in tears.

I haven't spoken to her outside of class in weeks, and Dylan has been avoiding me at the stadium. We haven't been put on any projects together, so I haven't even had a chance to ask him how Mia's doing.

"I'll be right over," I say before she can even get a word out.

When I show up at her apartment, she's positively distraught.

"What's going on?" I ask, squeezing her in a tight hug.

She gulps for breath for a few beats, and I grab the box of tissues and direct her over to the couch, where she promptly bursts into tears all over again.

"Sorry," she sniffles as she tries to pull it together. "There's just so many memories here on this couch."

I wrinkle my nose as I eye it suspiciously, but I let it go. "What happened?"

"I think Dylan might be cheating on me," she manages.

"Oh no," I say, racking my brain for anything I might've seen at the stadium. "What makes you think that?"

"He's going home for Thanksgiving and I saw a text in his phone about how this girl wants to hook up with him while he's there, and I asked him about it and he got real defensive about how she's just a friend, like *too* defensive and it feels like he's lying. So we got into a huge fight and I told him maybe we should just start seeing other people."

"When was all this?" I ask.

"A couple hours ago. We haven't spoken since he slammed the door on his way out."

"Do you have any proof he's lying?" I ask, trying to remain calm even though I have about ten thousand things I know I need to do at home and this sounds like either a simple miscommunication or a silly fight that they could work out. Still, I know my friend needs me, and she deserves my attention even though we've barely spoken recently since we've both been busy doing our own thing.

She shakes her head forlornly, but at least the tears have stopped. "No proof. Just a strong gut feeling."

"I always say trust your gut, but I think you and Dylan are really solid."

"I thought we were, too, and that's why this is all so upsetting." She sniffles, and I hand her a tissue.

"What are *your* Thanksgiving plans?" I ask.

She shrugs. "My mom and dad are going to my brother's house in Florida and it just feels like a long trip to make for a few days."

"Stay here and celebrate with us," I suggest.

"That's really sweet of you. I might take you up on it. I just don't want to impose or get in the middle of things with you and your dad or anything." She leans back on the couch and draws in a shuddering breath.

"It's not imposing when I invited you." I nudge her elbow.

"How are things going with Cooper? I've been such a bad friend. I'm sorry. I've just put all my eggs in Dylan's basket because I really thought we had a future, you know? I thought he was the one. I thought I'd graduate in the spring with an MRS degree, you know?"

"Maybe you will," I say, ignoring the fact that she started her rant with a question about me and ended it by turning it back to herself. She's going through something, and she doesn't want to hear about how great things are in my own relationship.

Although they *are* pretty great. Even though time has been limited for us over the last few weeks, we've made the most of our time when we get to have it.

There's a knock at the door, and I get up to answer it.

My eyes widen when I find Dylan standing there. He looks as sad as she does. I open the door a little wider without saying anything, and he steps in with a friendly nod.

He beelines for the couch when he sees her sitting there, and he kneels beside her. "I don't want to see anyone else."

She bursts into fresh tears again as he takes her cheeks between his palms.

"I love you, Mia Delgado. Come home with me for the holiday. Meet my family. Meet my friend who I swear is nothing more than a friend." He's begging, and Mia starts to calm down.

I take that as my cue to slip out the door.

I try calling Cooper on my way back to my dad's place, but he doesn't answer. He's busy, though, and he's probably *with* my dad, and he can't exactly answer when they're together. I call Joanie next.

"Hi honey," she answers, and in the last few weeks, we've grown closer and closer as we've been spending more and more time together. She's sort of become like the mother that my own mother never was. In fact, I haven't even spoken to my actual mother in months. She called the day before my birthday to wish me a happy birthday and to remind me how she was in labor with me for a full sixteen hours before I came out, as if she still blames *me* for the hard labor that happened twenty-one years ago.

On the other hand, Joanie is supportive and kind, and she's a good boss, too. She praises me for a job well done, and she's never critical when she shows me where I can improve.

I feel like I'm a lock for the social media manager position, and not just because Troy is my father and Joanie is my future stepmother. It's because I'm putting in longer hours than the other interns. I'm studying the craft of marketing, learning new things every single day, and I'm not afraid to try them out.

Chloe is right beside me for all of it, and in some ways, I've gotten closer with her than even Mia. But she still doesn't know about Cooper and me. Only Justin does, and he's been discreet—and busy himself as he and Brian embark on a down low relationship, too.

"Do you have any dinner plans tonight?" I ask Joanie.

"I'm all tied up tonight," she admits. "I'm so sorry."

"No worries. Maybe another time."

"Of course. Everything okay?"

"Yeah," I say. "My friend Mia just called me in hysterics because she thought her boyfriend was cheating on her, and he showed up apologizing. I guess it just drove home the fact that the season hasn't even started yet and I already feel like they're gone." Joanie and I don't talk much about my relationship with Cooper, mostly so it doesn't get awkward for her where my dad is concerned. But on the rare occasion I bring him up, she's always there with good advice. And she's an especially good person to talk to on this topic considering she's in the same boat with my father where time is concerned.

"It's going to get worse before it gets better. I suspect you already know that, though, and only you can decide if that's a sacrifice you're willing to make."

I think about how good things are between Cooper and me. "Of course it's worth the sacrifice. But it doesn't make it any easier going through it."

"Then it's a good thing you have me since I'm going through the exact same thing."

"Thanks, Joanie. You really are the best," I say.

"Right back at you, sweetheart. Oh, and if you see your dad when you get home, can you tell him I'm done with the task he gave me?"

"Sure thing. Talk to you soon." I wonder for a beat what that task is all about, but I'm sure it has something to do with the marketing department.

But then the thoughts filter in about the club my father supposedly owns, and I can't help but wonder what his relationship with Joanie is really like.

I don't think I want to know.

Chapter 37
Cooper

Troy asked me to stop by to review some more film with him, and I decide to run over since it's only a mile away. By the time I get to his house, I'm sweating and panting as I spot a little red Toyota in the circular drive and a woman standing by the front door.

I run up toward the door. Troy probably gets random fans stopping by all the time, but the gate at the front of the community seems to help with the majority of onlookers.

Somehow this one got through, I guess. "Can I help you?"

"Hello, yes," the woman says, turning around to look at me. "I'm looking for Gabby Grant."

"May I ask who you are?"

She raises an eyebrow. "Who are *you?*"

"I'm Cooper," I say, leaving it at that. She doesn't need to know more, but the fact that she doesn't know me tells me a lot about who she is. She must be a Troy fan, not a baseball fan. "Your turn to tell me who you are now."

She clears her throat and lifts her chin, and it's in that moment I know exactly who she is. The dark hair, the dark eyes, the mannerism she just exhibited…it's all so clear before she even speaks the words.

"I'm Gabriella's mother."

My hackles rise as I want to do everything I can to protect Gabby from this woman.

"What are you doing here?"

"I came to see my daughter." She folds her arms across her chest, and I get the impression she's not budging.

I glance out at the driveway and find her car isn't here. "She's not home, and she doesn't want to see you. You can go now."

Her brows shoot up in surprise at the venom in my voice. "Who the hell do you think you are?"

The man who's going to marry her someday.

I don't say that. I can't. I wish I could, but we're still fucking hiding it and I hate it more and more.

Telling her mom and not her dad would be absolutely toxic, though.

"I'm a good friend of hers."

She rolls her eyes. "Right. And you're at least a decade older than her, so her being here with her father is even worse than I imagined."

"Oh, she's told me all about you, Christine. And so has Troy." I raise my brows pointedly, and she practically snarls at me.

"I'm here to save that girl from her father. He's a terrible, terrible man."

I can't help my laugh. "You don't even know him, and you better watch what you say about my best friend."

A silver truck comes pulling up, and my one regret is that I didn't get rid of this woman before Gabby arrived home.

She steps down from her truck and approaches the front door, where she sees me talking to her mom.

"Mom?" she asks tentatively.

Christine rushes toward her daughter. "Oh Gabby, I can't believe you left me! I've missed you so much!" She wraps her arms around her.

"I didn't leave you, Mother. I went off to college and I chose UNLV, remember?"

"You left to meet your father, something I never agreed with." She pulls back and looks at her daughter, and I can't help but study every single move she makes. "You're too skinny. Are you eating enough?"

Jesus. This woman is the classic definition of a narcissist, and her poor daughter still emerged as a ray of sunshine despite her.

"I'm eating plenty. What are you doing here?" Gabby asks, rolling her eyes at me over her mother's shoulder.

I stifle a laugh.

"Well first I was just fending off this beast who claims he's your friend," she says, looking at me as if *I* am the problem.

"He's not a beast," Gabby says, and then she raises her brow at me as if to say *well, except in the bedroom.* "He's a great man with a wonderful heart and he's become very important to me in the last few months, so please stop insulting him right now."

"Oh, don't be so dramatic." She pulls at Gabby's arm, and Gabby looks incredibly uncomfortable. "I came to finally tell you all about your father."

Gabby's brows dip. "I've been living here for three years. Why are you doing this now?"

It clicks in my head before Christine says a word. She's here because the expansion draft is one week away. She's here to fuck with Troy because she thinks he stole her daughter away when the reality is that Gabby left because her mother was so goddamn awful to her.

"I felt it was time for you to know," she says.

I let out a snort I meant to keep quiet, and her mom raises a brow at me as if to ask what that's all about.

I decide to go for honesty. I'm not a fan of this woman after everything Gabby has told me. "You're here to fuck with Troy. You don't give a shit about your daughter."

Her hand flies to her chest in total defensiveness. "Excuse me, sir, but I'll have you know Troy is a very bad man. He tried to do dirty things to me on more than one occasion!"

I blow out a breath as I scramble to come up with how to protect Gabby from all this. She's already semi-aware of the club her father owns, and while I've never witnessed anything firsthand, I had my suspicions he and Joanie might be into the BDSM lifestyle.

I don't know Troy's exact sexual proclivities, but I do know he'd never beat a woman. But if this was over twenty years ago and he was exploring the idea of a dominant-submissive relationship, he very well may have been experimenting. Still, he's not the kind of guy who would have done any of that without total consent.

"Maybe we ought to let Troy give his side of the story," I suggest dryly.

Gabby's eyes are hooded out here on the dark porch as she studies her mother. "Go ahead, Mom. Tell us your side of the story."

"It's…it's so embarrassing," she says, shielding her eyes a little. "He was young, playing in the minors and thought he was hot stuff. We met at a bar, and we had one night together. And then another and another. Eventually we sort of became an item, or at least I *thought* we were an item, and one night he asked if he could…*spank* me. It felt wrong but I agreed to do it since he was who he was. The next night he wanted to use a whip." She closes her eyes as if the memory is too painful to bring up. "I found out I was pregnant, and the night I was going to tell him, I learned he was cheating on me. I knew I couldn't allow someone like him—a lying, cheating, violent man—around a baby. I ran off, wouldn't talk to him, wouldn't see him. He saw a photograph of me when I was around six months pregnant, and I lied and said it wasn't his."

She *agreed* to it. That's consent. Just because she didn't like it doesn't mean Troy is violent. It means he likes certain things in the bedroom, and that's his business. And beyond that, if what she's implying is true…why would she show up at his house over twenty years later?

A narcissist will twist and turn things to make anyone believe her narrative. I can't let her turn Gabby against her father, not when I know how close they've become.

Gabby looks like she's going to be sick. She doesn't say anything, so I jump in.

"I gotta tell you, it sounds consensual to me." I lift a shoulder. "And he doesn't strike me as a cheater."

Christine turns a glare on me. "You obviously misheard what I said."

"In what way? You said you agreed to the spanking." I shrug. "That's consent."

"But it felt wrong to me," she insists. "I agreed to it because I thought I was in love."

"Should we let him tell his side of the story?" I ask, setting a hand on the door handle to let myself in.

"No—uh, just wait a second," Christine says.

I turn around to face her. "For what?"

"Can I just have a moment with my daughter?" she asks.

I glance at Gabby first, and she's got a look of determination on her face. It's in that moment I know she isn't going to let Christine get to her. I sigh. "Go for it. I'm heading in."

I'm curious what she wants to say to her daughter, but it's between them. "Troy?" I yell, and he walks into the kitchen a beat later.

"Hey, man. I've got some film loaded up on the big screen in the game room if you want to join me in there." He turns to head back that way.

"Hang on a second," I say, and he freezes as he turns back around. "You have an unexpected visitor."

"I do?"

I nod toward the front door. "Gabby's mother was out there when I ran up."

His face blanches a little. "Gabby's…mother?"

"Christine," I confirm.

"Fuck," he mutters. "What does she want?"

"She claims she wants to see her daughter, and she just unloaded the entire story of why she never told you she was pregnant on both Gabby and myself."

"I'm certain it was her version of events," he says dryly.

"She basically claims you're a violent man who tried to beat her into submission." I lay out the facts of what she just said so he knows what he's dealing with before she even steps foot into his house.

"That same fucking story?" he practically roars, and he storms over toward the front door.

"Uh, Troy?" I say quietly, and he freezes. "Might want to tone down the anger given her accusations even if they are twenty years old."

"Shit," he mutters, and he draws in a deep breath because he knows I'm right. He moves toward the door and opens it, and both women whirl around to see him standing there. "Christine, hello," he says with the fakest hospitality I've ever heard. "Heard you're still spouting the same old lies but this time to our daughter. Come on in."

Well, this should be…interesting.

Chapter 38
Gabby

My instincts are usually spot on, and right now, my gut is telling me that my mother is lying.

I could be wrong, but I've lived with Troy Bodine for the last three years, and not once has he ever shown even an ounce of violence. I've worked with him at the stadium for the last month, too, and even there he's calm and rational.

I have to believe in my own experiences with these people, and my mother has proven to me more than once that she's a liar while Troy has proven to me over and over that he's a good man and a good father.

It's a little gross as his daughter to hear that he's a…*dominant* in the bedroom, but that's between him and his partner.

Oh, God. Joanie just told me to tell him she finished his task. Was it something sexual? She specifically said she was *all tied up* and that was the reason she couldn't do dinner with me tonight.

I feel a little sick at the thought.

"I didn't say anything that wasn't true," my mother hisses at my father.

"There's another lie." He shakes his head. "Do you even know *how* to tell the truth?"

"What a lovely family reunion," I mutter dryly.

"Come on, Christine. You told me the baby was someone else's, and eighteen years later, that baby shows up looking for me…looking for the truth." He slings an arm around my shoulders and draws me in close. "The truth that was kept from her for her entire life."

"I was protecting her from the monster you are," she says.

"You were protecting yourself from your own embarrassment. If you truly thought you were protecting her from me, you would've sent the checks I sent to help you with your child back rather than cashing them the moment they arrived."

Cooper watches them like he's watching a tennis match, his head bobbing back and forth between them, and I feel awkwardly sandwiched in the middle.

"Why are you here?" Troy asks. He drops his arm from around me.

"To make sure she knows the truth."

"But why *now*?" he presses, a question I'd love to hear the answer to as well. "Is it, oh, because I have an expansion draft next week and you want to try to ruin my life again? Or is it because you somehow found out I recently got engaged and I'm actually happy for once in my adult life?"

My mother sniffs as she juts her chin up high into the air. "It's none of those things. Coincidences, if that. I want her to know the real man you are, and I want her to decide whether she wants to stay here or come home with me."

It might be that moment when I realize just exactly how delusional my mother actually is.

Does she really think I'm going to give up everything I have going here in Vegas and head back to Colorado to be with her one semester shy of graduating from UNLV?

My dad turns to me. "I just want you to be happy, Gabriella."

And that's the crux of it, isn't it? My mom wants to play games and put me in the middle, and my dad wants me to live my life and be happy.

I just want you to be happy.

How would he feel if I told him it's his best friend that makes me happy?

I glance at Cooper, and his eyes are on me, but I can't quite read what's in them. Is he having the same thoughts I am about my dad's words?

Regardless, I draw strength from his gaze before I turn to my mother. "What's there to decide?" I ask softly. "My life is here now. Dad and I have grown close. I've made friends." I nod toward Cooper. "I'm working an internship that might open big doors on my career. I'm happy here, Mom." *And I was never happy with you, but I'm thriving despite that.*

I leave that last part out.

Silence falls over the room as we all await whatever she has to say to that.

When her words come, they're the epitome of why I left Denver in the first place. "Of course you're happy here. You have no responsibilities, and your father hands everything to you on a silver platter. You know, when I was your age, I had a two-year-old I had to care for as a single parent. I gave up everything to give you a good life, and you don't even care."

I set my hand on my hip, ready to defend myself, ready to tell her that I do, in fact, work hard and I do, in fact, have plenty of responsibilities, when I realize…I don't have to.

It doesn't matter what she thinks. I know the truth, and I'm happy with it. I drop my hand so I'm in a less defensive stance, and I keep it simple. "I'm sorry I ruined your life."

She juts her chin up again. "I never said that."

"You sure as hell implied it," Cooper says, and I hear the venom in his tone. I glance over at him, and our eyes lock again. He seems to calm when he sees that I'm not upset.

I would have to respect her in order to be upset, and after all this time…I just don't.

"Stay out of this," she hisses at him.

"He's been a great friend to me since he moved here, Mother. Don't talk to him like that," I say, and this time I can't keep the defensiveness out of my tone. It's not her place to come here into my father's house and disrespect his friend.

"What are your plans while you're in town, Christine?" my dad asks her, clearly trying to save this whole fiasco.

"I figured I'd just stay with Gabby," she says.

I blink at her a few times, completely dumbfounded. "You know I live with him," I say, jutting my thumb toward my father. "I don't think you're exactly welcome to stay here."

"She can stay here," Troy says. "I've got work to do, and then I'll be heading over to my fiancée's house."

"Hm," my mother hums. "Abandoning your child to run off to another woman. Shocker."

My dad just stares at her a long beat before he says, "I have work to do. If you'll excuse me," and he walks out of the room. Cooper shrugs and follows him, and I stand staring at my mother.

"Care to tell me what really went down between you two all those years ago?" I ask. "But, like, the truth this time?"

She lets out a long sigh. "You've heard the story before."

"Tell me one more time." I walk over to the couch and flop down, and I can't believe she really thinks she'll be staying here with us.

I don't want her here.

I don't even want her in Nevada.

"I'd just found out I was pregnant, and I'd planned to tell Troy after the game. He'd gotten me a seat just above the dugout, and there was another woman in my row who kept trying to get his attention. She told her friend how she'd been intimate with him, and after the game, she ran down to the dugout and hugged him. He was talking to his manager, and then he left without so much as a goodbye. He ghosted me, sweetheart. Is that what they call it? He didn't call me, didn't get in touch. As far as I knew, he ran off with that other woman, and I was embarrassed and alone and filled with shame for what I allowed him to do to me."

I know she's leaving out parts of the story, and I assume they are parts my father will fill in later for me.

But one question remains: why is she here *now*?

I suspect my father may be right. She wants to mess things up for him ahead of the draft, ahead of his wedding…and I pray that's the answer, because if she's not here to mess up *his* life, she might be here to mess up mine.

And her next question confirms that hunch.

"So what's really going on between you and that Cooper jerk?"

I blow out a breath.

Is it wrong to kick your mother out of your father's house?

Chapter 39
Cooper

I pop the last bite of the salty, savory stick into my mouth and munch on it as I stand on Troy's porch. Troy took off to meet up with Joanie, and I think we're both on the same unspoken page right now that we want to soak up as much time with our women as we can before the chaos next week begins.

Obviously unspoken considering he doesn't know I even have a woman, much less that it's his daughter.

The expansion draft will really be the start of a new era for the two of us. It'll mean later nights and longer days. It'll mean the real work can begin...but it's also the fun work.

I'd planned to just run back home once Christine showed up, but Gabby and I texted a bit before, and she said she'd give me a ride.

I think she wants to get away from her mom, and I don't blame her.

Her mom is sleeping in my old room, but if it were up to her, she'd be shacking up with my girl.

The door opens, and Gabby steps out, a beautiful vision as always. My instinct is to close the gap between us.

"Hey," I say. I'm about to lean in for a kiss when her eyes widen and she inclines her head toward the house.

"Your dad just left," I assure her.

She shakes her head. "My mom didn't." Her voice is a low whisper.

I nod in understanding. We can make out in my driveway. Or on my couch. Or in my bed.

"And you smell like pepperoni," she adds.

I can't help laughing at that as we hop into her truck.

"Did my dad say anything?" she asks.

"He said a lot of things," I admit.

"What was his side of the story?"

"He told me he'd just finished a game when he got called up from the minors. He'd planned to take your mom out after the game, but he was swept away in the frenzy and had to head straight on the road. He tried to get in touch with her to let her know he wanted to celebrate with her when he got back to town, but she wouldn't answer his calls. Your mother ran to the media with an exclusive story about how Troy Bodine was a sick, twisted, abusive cheater while he was on the road. His brand-new contract was nearly pulled because of her lies, and he had to work hard to fix his image."

"Why would she do that?" she asks.

I shrug. "I guess she thought he was cheating on her and she was humiliated, so she wanted to humiliate him back."

She shakes her head. "Wow. So her ego came between them."

I nod. "That's what it sounds like. Troy had a friends with benefits thing going with some woman before he met your mom, and your mom thought it was a current thing. She assumed she was in the right and he was in the wrong. She didn't take a step back before jumping to a conclusion and acted on it rather than waiting to talk it out with Troy. He should've been celebrating his new contract, and instead he was battling your mother to clear his name. And then he found out she was pregnant, and she lied and said it wasn't his. He's never forgiven her."

"Nor should he," she says, pulling into my driveway. She puts the truck in park. "It's so messed up."

"It is, and I'm sorry you have to deal with it all these years later. What story did she tell?"

"The same thing she told us outside. She said he was a cheater and a liar and blah blah blah." She leans her head back on the headrest and closes her eyes. "She also said she doesn't trust you, and I don't trust her. I'm afraid she's going to make trouble for you."

"I won't let her." I reach over and grab her hand. "If anything, her being here is only going to drive us closer together."

She opens her eyes and slides her head over to look at me. "I hope you're right."

I squeeze her hand. "Do you want to come in?"

"It's all I want, but knowing my mother, she's counting the minutes on the clock until I walk back in the door." She sighs.

"How long is she staying?"

She lifts a shoulder. "No idea. Until I agree to go back with her?"

My brows draw together.

"Don't worry," she says. "That will never happen. My life is here. It's with you, even though we're hiding it. I don't want to hide it anymore."

"I don't, either. Let's just tell your dad."

She sighs heavily. "The expansion draft is a week away, and I know he's stressing about that. Let's tell him after the draft."

I nod, and then I lean across the armrest and press a soft kiss to her lips to seal the promise. She grabs the back of my head and holds on for a beat. We don't deepen the kiss, don't intensify it. It's not urgent and needy like they usually become, but it's a sweet expression of the love that's grown between the two of us.

"Are you sure you can't come in for a little while?" I ask softly, leaning my forehead against hers. I want to deepen it. I want to intensify it. I want to give her everything I'm feeling as we let our bodies speak in the language they've perfected over the last two months.

"I wish I could." She pulls back and brushes a tear away, and my heart breaks for her.

"You can, Gabby. You're an adult, and she can no longer control what you do."

She lets out a little snort. "I wish that were true. But if we're keeping this thing under wraps from my dad, then we need to play her game until she leaves."

I nod, forcing myself to hold my thoughts about that in. I will support her in whatever way she needs me to. "I love you."

"I love you." She leans over for one more kiss, and then I jump out of her truck. She speeds away, and I can't help but wonder what sort of hell she's heading back into.

Chapter 40
Gabby

When I get back home, my mother is waiting in my room. On my bed. Like we're going to have some sort of sleepover or something.

I sigh as I walk into the room that should be a sanctuary and instead has turned into some strange nightmare.

When I left Denver, I didn't look back.

It's not like my childhood was *all* bad, but once I learned the truth about my mother, I knew that not only had my entire life been a lie, but my relationship with my mother had been incredibly toxic.

I knew she did the best she could, but I also can't say I've missed my life with her since I moved to Vegas.

It was hard at first as my dad and I got to know one another and I was starting school away from pretty much everything I'd ever known, but I found a good group of friends pretty quickly. My relationship with my father grew while I found myself busier and busier—oftentimes too busy to make the call back home to my mother. We grew apart while the people here became my family, and I'm happier than I've ever been—in particular since I first met Cooper.

But seeing my mother lounging on my bed like she belongs here seems to negate everything I've worked so hard for.

She'll tell me I'm wrong for wanting to be here. She'll make me feel like I've made all the worst possible decisions. She'll spout more lies about my father.

And I don't want to hear any of it. I don't want to deal with any of it. Whatever issues she has with my father are between the two of them.

"So tell me about this woman your father proposed to," she says flippantly as I walk in.

I blow out a breath, and I collapse onto my desk chair since I don't want to share the bed with her. "I don't really think it's any of your business."

"Of course it is!" She sits up and stares at me in horror. "You're my daughter! She's going to be your stepmother! I deserve to know these things."

She doesn't deserve anything, but I tell her anyway. "She's a lovely woman who I've grown very close to over the last couple months. She's the head of marketing for the Vegas Heat, and she—"

"She's the head of *marketing*?" she practically screeches. She shakes her head, and she mutters something under her breath that sounds like, "That should've been me."

"From what I know, she achieved the job on her own without Troy's assistance."

She purses her lips and rolls her eyes. "Right. Just like how you got the internship on your own merit. You know, when I was your age, I was taking classes toward a marketing degree myself. I had to give it all up when I got pregnant."

I clench my jaw as tightly as I can before an inappropriate retort comes flying out of my mouth, and then my mouth opens anyway. "I'm so sorry I ruined your life." I spit the words out as I stand. "Why are you here? Did you just come to make everyone miserable? Go back to Denver. Go home, and leave us the hell alone." I grab my purse and storm out of the room.

I seethe with anger as I get into the truck, and less than two minutes later, I'm pulling into Cooper's driveway.

Because of course I run to Cooper when I'm upset. I run to him when I'm happy, or when I'm sad, or when I'm angry. I run to him first because he's become the most important person in my life.

He's wearing nothing but basketball shorts when he opens the door, confusion on his handsome face. "What are you doing—"

He doesn't get the chance to finish his sentence because I burst into tears as I plow into him. He wraps his arms around me for a beat, and then he sweeps my feet out from under me as he lifts me up. He kicks the front door shut as he carries me through the house and into the family room, where he sits on the couch with me still wrapped in his arms.

"Shh," he soothes, and he presses a kiss to my temple. "It's okay. You're okay. You're here now, and I've got you."

"I know you do," I sob, and his arms tighten around me.

"Do you want to talk about what happened?"

I shake my head. No, I don't want to revisit the conversation where my mother told me yet again how she had to give up her entire life when she got knocked up, how I ruined her life, and what a disappointment I am.

It's as Cooper holds me in his arms comforting me that I realize this is why I've never been totally sure whether I want kids of my own.

I don't want to make another human feel like they're nothing but a burden to me. I realize I'm not my mother, and likewise I realize I would not be the same type of mother she is. But I was raised thinking my father didn't want me only to learn later in life that it was really my mother who never did.

Is it any wonder I've spent so much of this relationship questioning whether I'm good enough for Cooper?

"Why are you with me?" I ask, my voice demanding and completely out of left field.

He looks surprised for a beat at my question, but he recovers quickly...and his answer tells me he's already thought an awful lot about it. "The night at the blackjack table, I'd made a vow to get back into the dating game literally five minutes before we met. You intrigued me the moment you sat down. I didn't care about how old you were or whose daughter you were. I was wrestling with whether to take the job offer from Troy, and you simplified it down to what would bring me joy."

He draws in a fortifying breath before resuming. "I realized the more I talked with you that it was *you* who would bring me joy. Wherever you were, even though I hardly knew you. And then the next morning in my hotel room, you were standing in this stream of light that surrounded you like a halo, and I knew you were an angel sent to this earth to save me. My Sunshine. The center of this new world I found myself in. That was the moment I fell in love with you."

He presses his lips to my forehead for a beat, and I brush away a tear.

"Every second I've had the privilege of spending with you since, I've fallen deeper and deeper into you," he continues. "You're smart, and you're funny, and you're not afraid to tell me my breath smells like pepperoni even though you secretly love it. You're brave, and you're fierce, and you're creative. You're passionate, and you're gorgeous, and you challenge me. Plus you really know your way around my cock."

I giggle at the last part.

"Why am I with you?" he asks, and the way he says the question makes me wonder why I even had the audacity to ask it. "For all those reasons, Gabriella Rose Grant, but most especially because you make me a better man. You make me want to sacrifice everything to be with you. You make me see what's important in life in a way I've never seen it before. I've never been with someone who made me feel like I can conquer the world the way you do. But I don't want to conquer the world. I just want to conquer this life with your hand in mine."

By the time he finishes talking, I'm a sobbing mess again, but this time it's for completely different reasons.

He holds me in his arms, and then he takes me upstairs and holds me while I fall asleep in his bed.

It's not a night of raunchy sex or hot naked time. Instead, it's the kind of intimacy that strengthens the bond we've started to grow.

I think he might be right. My mother may try her hardest to break me, to break *us*…but her being here is only going to drive us even closer together.

Chapter 47
Gabby

I detour toward Mia's on my way back home, in part
because I don't really want to face my mother right now
and in part because I haven't spoken to her in weeks.

Dylan's there, too, but when he heads toward the bathroom, I
strike up a conversation with my best friend as I unload how I'm
feeling about continuing to keep Cooper a secret from my dad.

"It's eating away at you, girl. Just tell him already." Mia glances
over at Dylan as he walks back into the room, his time away
woefully too short, and I get the distinct feeling that if I wasn't
here, they'd be naked on the couch where I'm sitting.

I suddenly feel like a third wheel. I came by to visit my best
friend, but Dylan was already here, so it's not like we've had the
chance to have our girls-only chat.

"Where's Chelsea?" I ask, changing the subject since Mia just
doesn't seem to get it. I want to tell him, but I've already felt plenty
rejected by him once in my life. What if he pushes me away again?

I think about mentioning that to Mia to get her take on it, but
with Dylan here...I guess I'm just not comfortable bringing it up.

"Didn't you hear? She's dating Greg!" Mia says.

My brows knit together. "Greg *Hansen*?"

Mia and Dylan both nod at the same time.

"He found his girl-gamer?" I ask.

They both laugh. "Turns out Chelsea has a secret Minecraft
thing. They're all into freaky shit with their games. They do naked
competitions, and he even got her a gaming chair that fits right next
to his in his room," Mia says.

I whistle. "Just goes to show you there's a match for everybody
out there, right? Some people get lucky and find them at the right
time."

"So is Cooper your match?" Mia presses, snuggling closer into Dylan as if to tell me not in so many words that Dylan is hers.

I nod. "I know the season will change the dynamic, but yeah. He's definitely my other half."

"But he's so…" Mia trails off.

"Hot?" I fill in.

She nods, conceding, but she adds, "Old."

"He's not *old*. He's thirty-three." My tone is far more defensive that I mean for it to be, but thirty-three isn't old.

"Exactly. He's three years away from retirement, and you haven't even graduated college. Don't you think that difference will cause problems?" Mia asks.

I know she's just trying to be a good friend, but this is all the same shit we've been over a million times, and frankly, I'm tired of defending it. "No, I don't."

She presses her lips together and nods. "Okay. I hope you really, really believe that and you're ready to defend it to the media since you know that's what's coming."

Maybe she's right, but I can't take it anymore. I'm sure it'll be far worse when it's not my best friend asking once the media gets wind of it, but she's supposed to be my *best friend*.

She's so busy being wrapped up in Dylan that she hasn't been much of a friend *at all* to me lately.

"I don't need to defend it to anyone," I snarl, standing up. "You're supposed to be my friend, and instead all you've done lately is pick at my relationship. You're looking for holes rather than standing by me. And frankly, I'm sick of it."

With those words, I whirl around and storm out of her apartment. I practically run to my car, and I slide into the driver's seat upset and angry as I head toward home.

It's not any better once I arrive.

"Where were you all night?" my mother demands the moment I walk in through the front door, as if she sat up waiting for me to come home.

"Out," I answer flippantly, a large part of me regretting leaving Cooper's house as early as I did. He and my dad are meeting for brunch in a bit, though, so I had to leave.

She stands from her spot on the couch and folds her arms across her chest. I walk past her and into the kitchen.

"You kept me up all night with worry!"

I blow out a breath as I reach into the pantry for a box of Honey Nut Cheerios. "I'm twenty-one years old, Mother, and I live in a different state than you. I no longer have to answer to you."

"I'm your mother and you will *always* have to answer to me, darling." Her words are riddled with impatience, as if I'm the problem here.

"I guess we'll have to agree to disagree on that front." I hold up the box as if to offer to make her a bowl, too, and she shakes her head.

"That stuff is full of sugar," she scolds, and I remember how we *never* had any good cereal in the house growing up. My options were usually either dry wheat cereal or plain yogurt, neither of which appealed to me.

I want to ask how long she'll be hanging around, but I hold myself back. Barely. "Is Dad home?" I ask instead.

She shakes her head. "You two left me all alone in this big old house all night," she whines.

"I hadn't realized you came here so we could entertain you," I say dryly as I reach into the fridge for the milk. "I hate to be the one to break this to you, but we both have lives here in Vegas that don't revolve around you." I mentally pat myself on the back for standing up to her, but she isn't having it today.

"How dare you?" she asks. "I came to visit you and you can't be bothered to spend any time with me at all!" She's immediately on the defensive again, never a good place for her to be. That's when she strikes out.

That's when things turn nasty.

I slide into my usual chair at the table and shovel a huge spoonful of cereal into my mouth.

She narrows her eyes at me. "Were you at Cooper's house?"

The question takes me so off guard that I choke on a Cheerio. I grab a bottle of water from the fridge to clear it out, and by the time I've chugged half of it down, she's pursing her lips and shaking her head.

"I knew it. I *knew* there was something going on between the two of you. And your father doesn't know, does he?" She looks up at the ceiling with a menacing laugh. "God, men are so stupid. Even that Cooper guy, to act around you the way he does, all protective, and your father is so blind to all of it. You're hiding it from him, but why?" She taps her chin, and the horror that planted in my stomach last night at the thought that she might try to come between Cooper and me seems to blossom in my chest.

Her being here is only going to drive us closer together.

I repeat the mantra in my head.

But what if she spills it to my dad?

"Let's see, why wouldn't you want Troy to find out about you two?" She stands and paces around the kitchen a little as that horror in my chest continues to bloom. "Could it be because you're so much younger than him?" She shrugs as she contemplates that thought. "Or is it because Troy is close with Cooper? Hmm..." She trails off as she thinks that one over, too. "Or maybe it's because daddy's little girl doesn't want to disappoint him with her terrible taste in men." She cackles with delight at her suggestion.

"Before you take your little fictional story any further, I should jump in to tell you I was at Mia's place," I lie, pouring weedkiller all over that blooming horror to cut it off at the source.

I mean...technically, I did stop by there. It's not a lie.

The only problem is that I know my mother, and once she thinks she's onto something, she will continue to pick and gnaw at it until she proves it to be true. More than once I could have sworn she manifested something out of thin air just because she believed so heartily in it.

"Oh, Mia. How's she doing? I always thought she'd be so pretty if she just cut and colored her hair." She tsks as if that's a bad thing, as if one's entire worth depends on how attractive my mother finds their hair.

"She and her hair are doing great, and she's gorgeous and perfect just the way she is."

She misses my tone, but that's pretty standard. She's too lost in her own little world to get it.

"That's nice," she says, offering a fake smile. "So tell me more about this internship."

My first thought is that it'll be nice to talk about something other than where she thinks I was last night, regardless of whether she's right or not. But then I realize she's asking for one of two reasons. Either she wants to get some intel on my father and his fiancée, or she's trying to find some nugget of information to prove Cooper and I are an item.

I steer clear of those topics. "It's a general internship with the stadium, so I along with six other interns have had opportunities to work in several different departments. Because of my major, mainly I've been working with business and marketing. We're currently competing in a marketing challenge, and the top two winners have a shot at interviewing for an open full-time position."

I keep it generic, and I leave out the parts about me shadowing Cooper.

And the stadium shenanigans. Those I *definitely* leave out.

"And how much time do you spend with Cooper there?" she demands.

I shrug. "Not that much. He's sponsoring a kids' play structure, and part of my internship has been working on that with him. That's about it."

She narrows her eyes at me as if she doesn't believe me. "And this woman your father has decided to marry? What do we know about her?"

"Mom, if you want details on her, you should ask him. I'm not playing this game." I shove my cereal into my mouth, trying to finish as quickly as possible to get myself out of this situation.

She gives me a look that clearly tells me she's hurt by what I'm implying, but I'm beyond the point of caring. I stand and head toward the sink to rinse my dish, and she sighs rather dramatically.

"What are we going to do today?" she asks.

I lift a shoulder. "*We* aren't doing anything. I have a paper due tomorrow that I haven't started, so I am going to head to campus to work at the library."

She purses her lips again. "You haven't started yet? Same old Gabby."

I spin around to face her. "*Same old Gabby*?" I practically screech. "Mother, I was salutatorian and you made me feel like I wasn't good enough because I wasn't number one. My entire life you've made me feel like a failure, and I will not let you come into this house, into a place that has very much become a sanctuary for me, and ruin this for me. I'm an adult. I'm earning straight As while I'm working hard to line up a job I deserve after graduation. And instead of being proud of me, you're accusing me of things that aren't true. You're making me feel like I'm not good enough just like you've always done."

She looks shocked by my words, as if this comes as some huge surprise to her that I feel this way.

And maybe it does. Maybe I've never voiced those things because I was raised to respect my elders. And I *do* treat my elders with respect, but I draw the line at being insulted by my own mother. I've grown a backbone since I've been here in Vegas.

She sniffs and juts her chin up. "Well, I'm sorry I've been such a terrible mother to you."

I grit my teeth and sigh at her sarcasm. She just doesn't get it, but that's the problem with selfish people, isn't it? They never see beyond their own egos. I guess I forgot what it was like since I moved away. I've seen her less than a handful of times in three years, and it's been months since we've spoken.

There was a reason for all that, but she'll never see that it was because of the way she treats me.

And yet...here I am, successful and independent, feeling like a failure after my mother's been in town all of half a day. The old familiar feelings of rejection and abandonment are creeping back in on me as the quiet little voices start to speak up again. I don't deserve Cooper. My father never wanted me and he just puts up with me now because he has to. I need to be perfect, to do better, because one mistake will prove to everybody that I'm not good enough.

And it's with those voices in mind that I walk out the front door and head to the university library, where I work my tail off to write the best goddamn paper I've ever written.

It's where I spend extra time researching some of the marketing tactics Joanie shared with me.

It's where I stay far too late because maybe she's right—the *same old Gabby* just isn't working hard enough.

And it's where I am when the text from Cooper comes through.

Captain: *Hope you're having a good day. I miss you.*

And then, because I've been lost in work and haven't been watching the clock, hunger plows into me. I stand to stretch, and all the blood rushes to my head.

I don't even realize I've passed out until someone starts shaking me awake.

Chapter 42
Cooper

"I can't fucking believe her." Troy tosses his phone angrily on the table. The rest of the crew are in the kitchen grabbing another drink, so it's just the two of us.

I've spent the whole day with the scouting director, the team manager, the general manager, and the three team owners, and there's still more work to be done as the draft is only a few days away now. We started with brunch at Mike's place, and then we ordered in a late lunch. We just finished the dinner Joanie sent over.

I haven't spoken with Gabby since she left my place this morning, and my day feels incomplete without her. A strange sensation passed over me as I texted her, and I have a weird feeling in my chest.

She was really distraught last night, and I hate that her mother has this sort of power over her. From what I understand, she has the ability to make Gabby question everything—like why I'm with her.

My chest ripped wide open when she asked me that last night.

She doesn't feel deserving of my love, and that only makes me want to try harder to prove how much she *does* deserve it. Maybe just experiencing unconditional love and support from someone like me—and even her father—will help heal the wounds her mother inflicted.

"What's going on?" I ask.

"I'm checking in on the video monitor on my back porch at home and Christine is helping herself to my Port. My fucking Port! Do you know how expensive that shit is?"

I can't help a chuckle at his reaction. He's got plenty of money, so I know that's not the real root of the issue. "What can you do to get rid of her?"

He shakes his head with disgust. "She's a fucking leech, man, but she's Gabby's mother. I can't just kick her out."

"How does Gabby feel about it? Does she want her here?" I press, knowing full well that she most certainly does not.

"It's her mother," he says. "Of course she does."

"Have you asked her?"

He shakes his head. "I'm trying very hard to be the adult here."

"Maybe start by finding out what your daughter really wants," I say.

He nods. "She's been so busy lately, and so have I. It's going to get harder before it gets easier, and I'm not ready for the wedge the season will inevitably drive between us." He's quiet as he speaks, and I can't help but feel the exact same way.

He's right. It's inevitable. A wedge will form because it's time away from each other. Time focused on things other than our relationship. And time is the one thing we can't get back once we spend it.

We turn quietly back to the film we were just watching, but I'm no longer concentrating on the plays as I think about Gabby.

As far as the team is concerned, I'm not too worried. We're in good shape. We've already built one hell of a team, and the draft will only help fill in the gaps. Pete has worked hard to earn his position as our scouting director, and he knows virtually everybody in baseball. The Heat will be a force to be reckoned with, especially once the team is complete after the draft.

Then the real fun begins…but then the late nights begin, too, and I'm not entirely sure I'm ready for all that entails, especially if I can't be with Gabby, and especially if we're still hiding this from her father. He's already concerned about the wedge the season will drive between them. I can't imagine how he'd feel about the wedge of lies on this side of the bridge.

As much as I want to tell him, the universe seems to keep delivering signs to the contrary. Besides, I don't want the media attacking us for our age gap. Maybe this is best kept hidden a while. We can allow the attention to be on baseball, on the new team, on the season…rather than on my personal life. I'll deflect questions, and when the time is right, when we're both ready to take the next step, then we can tell Troy before we go public. After the draft— just like we promised each other.

Mike, Pete, Dave, and Victor walk back into the room just as Troy's phone starts to ring. His brows dip as he glances up. "I need to take this."

He ducks out of the room for a beat, and when he returns, he says, "I need to go. My daughter was just rushed to the hospital."

All the breath is squeezed out of my chest as fear sets in. "Is everything okay?" I ask.

He blinks a few times as he focuses in on me. "I—I think so, but…I don't know."

"I'll drive. Let's go," I say, and I realize it might not be my place to do that, but it fucking *is* my place and fuck this nonsense about keeping it from her father.

I need to know whether she's okay.

He nods, as if I'm just being a good friend to him by offering him a ride when the truth is that there is absolutely no place more important than beside her right now.

I rush to the hospital, and I walk a few paces behind Troy to allow him to take the lead.

Jesus, this is all so fucked. I should be rushing to the desk instead of pretending like I don't have a stake in this. I want to be by her side. I want to be holding her hand. I want to be the one who's informed of her condition when I walk up beside her father.

I want to be her emergency contact.

It's a strange realization as I stand in an emergency room waiting area, but it's the truth. I want to be her *everything*.

"Patients are only allowed one visitor," the woman at the front desk of the emergency room says. "It looks like someone is already back there with her."

"Well tell whoever the fuck it is to get out of there because I need to see my daughter," Troy demands. "And get her in a private room!" He throws a couple hundreds on the counter as if money will solve the problem.

I grab his shoulder, feeling as angry as him at the stupid policy but knowing it's not this poor woman's fault. "Hey," I murmur. "It's their policy." I turn toward the woman and offer up the charm even though I'm scared out of my mind right now. "Can he get in to see her, or can he at least get an update on how she's doing?"

She purses her lips. "I'll see what I can do."

Joanie comes rushing through the doors as the woman leaves her post to go check on the visitor situation, and she flies right into Troy's arms. "How's she doing?"

"They won't fucking let me back to see her, so I don't know!" he roars, and some woman sitting beside a small child picks up the child and moves to the other side of the room.

Joanie looks worried, too, and she looks up at Troy, grabbing his cheeks between her palms. "I know you're worried, but you have to take a deep breath. Okay, boss?"

He draws in a deep breath, and he seems to calm a little at her touch. "Yes, kitten."

Boss and *kitten*. Wow. If I wasn't in a hospital worried about the woman I love, I might be able to come up with some sort of snarky comment or two on those nicknames.

The woman at the desk reappears. "A third now?" she asks, folding her arms across her chest. Joanie offers a small wave. "I can take two of you back as soon as the woman in there exits. For the record, your daughter is awake and doing fine. We're just completing some paperwork now."

The woman in there. The last person Gabby needs to see when she's in distress is her mother.

Still, a pulse of relief darts through me.

"You two go," Joanie offers, giving me a meaningful glance Troy doesn't catch. "I know how close you both are with her."

Thank you, I mouth to her, and she offers a slight nod.

Christine walks out a moment later. Her eyes are red as if she's been crying, and I can't help but wonder if she's crying because she had to leave her daughter's side or if it's because something's wrong with Gabby.

Troy doesn't say a word to her as he walks through the door Christine just walked out of, and I follow close behind him as the front desk woman walks us back to Gabby's stall.

"This is unacceptable," Troy mutters to the poor woman. "Get my daughter into a private room."

"Sir, she's being discharged as we speak. You're lucky I was able to pull enough strings to get you back here."

I just keep my mouth shut and my eyes focused down on the floor so I don't accidentally see anything I'm not supposed to see.

"Daddy," Gabby says when he peeks his head around the curtain. "Don't worry, I'm totally fine."

I walk in behind Troy, and Gabby's eyes seem to soften a little as they land on me. She gazes at me for a long beat, and I can see plainly for myself that her words are true. She really is totally fine. It's like we have some silent conversation in that split second—one where she tells me everyone is making way too big a deal out of this, but she's still grateful we all showed up for her.

I love you. I say the words in my mind, and I hope she can read them the way I can read what she's saying to me.

One side of her mouth tips up in a smile for a moment before her father points to her arm and booms out his next words.

"You've got a needle in your arm! You're not fine."

"I stood up too fast and hadn't eaten all day, and the librarian found me passed out on the floor of a little private room. She freaked out and called an ambulance, but I swear, I'm fine. I don't even need to be here. I just want a cheeseburger and a big cup of water," she says.

"Why didn't you eat all day?" Troy demands, and I just hang back quietly as I look at her on the bed. She looks a little pale, a little tired, and as beautiful as ever—no worse for the wear considering where she is. Still, Troy's right. She's got an IV in the back of her hand, and seeing her here like this does something to me.

Something strong and powerful. Something fierce and emotional.

It's love, plain and simple. It's the type of love I've never felt before, and I already knew that about the two of us, I already knew that these feelings were different and intense and forever. But this seals it. Whatever's happening in my chest right now, between the relief I feel at seeing for myself she's okay and the way her eyes found mine the second I walked in, I'm filled with love in a way I never even knew existed. It's like a wave that washes over me, like a bubble that surrounds me, like a new fire that swims in my veins.

The question now remains.

What the fuck am I going to do about it?

Chapter 43
Gabby

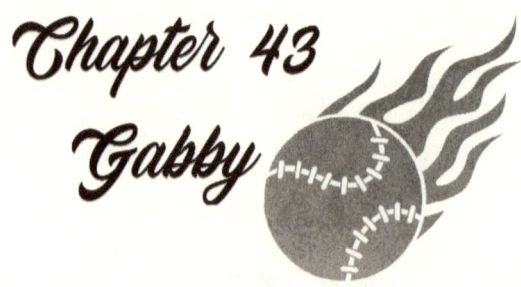

I'm embarrassed more than anything. I'm smart enough to know I need to eat, but I got so caught up in my work and staying away from my mother that I spent too many hours in one place.

And wouldn't you know it? My emergency contact is my mother.

She called my dad, and I'm not sure how Cooper showed up here, but something shifted inside me the moment he showed up.

He showed up, for one thing.

I'm not sure I've ever had someone's unconditional support the way he showed up. He didn't have to. He's busy with the draft. But he got here quick. He made sacrifices to be here.

My mother didn't always show up for me. She couldn't. She blamed having to work hard to afford things for me, for *us*, and the timing didn't work out for her to be there for things like my National Honors Society induction or my volleyball games. On top of that, I grew up believing I wasn't good enough to have my father's unconditional support. I've only slowly grown accustomed to it over the last three years.

But as Cooper gazed at me when he walked in and I felt all the love he has for me even with my dad standing in front of him, that thing that shifted for me was the strange feeling of knowing my relationships will always fail if I don't resolve that fear inside me like I *won't* always have that unconditional support.

In some strange way, Cooper showing up today seems to have started healing that wound. I want to talk to him. I want to be alone with him.

But I'm not sure how to get my dad out of the room. I don't want to hide it, but lying in a hospital bed hardly feels like the right time to break the news to my father that I've fallen for his best friend.

A man who doesn't look much older than me wheels in a cart with a computer screen on it. "How would you like to pay for today's services?" he asks.

"Are you kidding me?" my father yells at the poor tech who probably doesn't get paid nearly enough to deal with this. "Out in the hall. Now. She doesn't need to be worrying about *payment* at a time like this!"

My dad follows the young man out to the hall, and he pulls the curtain around my stall closed as he exits. I can still hear him in the hallway. The curtain isn't soundproof, and Cooper offers a small chuckle as he steps toward me.

He quickly presses his lips to my forehead. "I love you." He whispers the words, and I gaze up at him with total adoration as love seems to explode within me.

"I love you, too."

"I was so worried, Gabby."

I shake my head. "I'm sorry. Nothing to be worried about."

He nods and presses his lips together as he straightens. He takes my hand gently in his—the one with the IV still plugged into the vein on the back. He presses a gentle kiss near the needle. "It's already bruising."

"It'll be okay. Now about that cheeseburger…"

He chuckles and pulls his phone out. "Where do you want to go? There's an In-N-Out not far from here. Want to grab something on the way home?"

"How much longer do you think I'll be stuck here?"

He shrugs. "With your dad out there yelling at everybody, I'd imagine they'll get you out of here quick."

I nod. "Can you just go get me something from the cafeteria maybe?"

"Of course. Cheeseburger, anything on it?"

"Everything. And fries."

"You got it." He leans down and kisses my lips this time, softly and quickly, but he doesn't straighten as he talks to me. He's hovering over me, and we both still hear my dad in the hallway, but I'm not sure he'd move even if my dad walked back in. "Thank God you're okay. I can't explain to you what happened to me when your dad said you were in the hospital. It was…" he trails off and shakes his head. "It told me a lot."

I grab the back of his head and kiss him again, not sure I'd want him to move if my dad walked in. "Thank you for being here."

"There is literally nowhere else in the world I would be right now," he says softly. He straightens, and then he chuckles. "Except the cafeteria to get that cheeseburger as requested. Be right back."

I grin as he heads out, and I hear him tell my dad where he's going in the hall.

"You're the best, Noah," my dad says to him, and my chest swells.

He really is the best.

My dad returns a minute later, and he sits with me. A nurse comes in to remove the IV from my hand, and I wince at the pinch. She gives me my discharge instructions, reminds me to eat regular meals, and tells me I'm free to leave. My dad helps me up, and while I feel a little weak, overall I feel fine.

I just want to see Cooper again.

He walks into the waiting room with a bag of food just as I walk into it from another door, and I grab the bag from his hands. I can't even wait to get to the car to open it. I plop down in the closest chair and scarf down the entire burger in about ten seconds flat. I glance up at Cooper, who shifts on his feet like watching me eat that burger was an actual turn on.

"Whoa. Slow down," Troy says, and I can't help a small giggle as Joanie sidles in beside him.

Did she introduce herself to my mother? Or is this Mom's first clue that the woman in the waiting room is, in fact, her baby daddy's fiancé?

"Fries in the car," I announce before this family reunion gets any more awkward. "Get me out of here."

"Come on, honey, let's go," my mother says at the same time Cooper says, "My truck's just out front."

I look back and forth between everyone.

I hate this shit.

I want to go with Cooper, of course. But I'll feel like I'm letting my mom down if I don't go with her.

Given the fact that I was just discharged from the hospital, I decide to go with what I want. I force away those voices in my head telling me I'll only disappoint her.

I'll disappoint her either way, so I may as well do what I want.

"I'll head home with Cooper," I say.

She looks hurt, but for once in her life she keeps her mouth shut.

"Why don't I take you back," Joanie says to my dad, and I silently thank her for the suggestion. "That way Gabby can spread out in the front seat."

"Great idea," my dad says, and that's that.

I climb into Cooper's truck, and I immediately open the bag of fries. "Want one?"

He shakes his head. "All yours. I ate an hour or so ago. By the way, you attacked that cheeseburger with the same enthusiasm I've seen from you when my cock is in your mouth, so that was hot."

I gasp at his words as a rocket of need plows into me. I'm feeling more like myself after that cheeseburger combined with the heavy emotions surrounding us. "Speaking of your cock..." I say, and I pop another French fry into my mouth.

"Yes?" he says, and his voice is all gravelly and deep.

"I'll be needing some dessert, you know."

He laughs. "Shall we stop for some ice cream?"

I purse my lips.

"Babe, you just got out of the hospital. I know it wasn't serious, but you still need to rest at least for tonight before I plow you with the captain."

I sigh. "Yeah, yeah. I just wish I could go home with you to your house instead of back to my dad's."

"Then come home with me. I'll tell them I wanted to keep an eye on you."

"They'll want to keep an eye on me, too," I say softly. I reach over and grab his hand. "We should tell them. My mom guessed it earlier anyway. I managed to throw her off, but me going home with you over her isn't going to send the message that she was wrong, you know?"

He threads his fingers through mine and squeezes my hand. "I don't care what she thinks. But your father's got a lot of stress right now between the draft and your mother being here. Let's just wait until after the draft, okay?"

I press my lips together and nod.

"Can I tell you something?" he asks.

I turn and look at him. "Anything."

"This whole thing...it's told me a lot about my feelings for you."

My heart races at his words, and my first thought is that it made him realize he doesn't love me as much as he thought he did.

It's my damn issues talking to me again, and I force a deep breath to calm those thoughts down.

"What did it tell you?" I ask quietly. I stare out the windshield as I brace myself for his answer, the deep breath doing nothing to calm my racing fears.

"I want to be your emergency call," he says simply. He raises our joined hands to his lips. "I want to be your *everything*."

Tears fill my eyes as relief fills my chest.

"You are."

He shakes his head a little. "I can't be until we tell your father."

"The draft is Saturday, right?"

He nods.

"Then we plan a celebratory brunch for Sunday and tell him then," I suggest. "And it gives you the rest of the off-season to help him come to terms with it since we already know he's not going to react well."

He nods resolutely. "Okay. We have one week to brace ourselves."

"One week," I echo. One week to brace ourselves…and one week to worry and fret over what his reaction is actually going to be.

Chapter 44
Cooper

It seems like so much is hanging in the balance. Christine thinks she knows something about Gabby and me. Mackenzie and Joanie do know along with Nick, Rush, and Danny. It's secrets piled on top of secrets, and it's starting to feel like lies piled on top of lies. I'm ready to just get it out in the open so we can stop the madness and get a start on living our lives.

Between meetings with the Heat brass and player research, the next week both flies and drags. It flies because I'm so busy, but it drags since I don't get to spend much time with my girl.

In fact, I haven't spent the night with her since the day her mother arrived in town, and I haven't had the chance to enjoy her naked body for even longer.

I'm getting antsy.

It's not just the draft, and it's not just the fact that we agreed to tell her father about us the morning after the draft.

It's that I haven't gotten my Gabby hit, and I'm struggling without it. Without *her*. It feels like it's affecting everything.

So when draft day rolls around, it's no surprise Troy calls me on it.

"What's going on with you, man?" he asks as I pace Mike's kitchen. We just finished a catered breakfast—Mike and his wife spare no expense to keep us happy, and we've spent the majority of our time at the GM's house over the last week.

If we were at Troy's, at least I'd have the chance of running into her. Here, though? Not so much.

Tomorrow. Tomorrow we tell him. Tomorrow the secrets and lies will end.

I can't fucking wait.

The draft tonight is being held on a newly constructed stage outside a popular hotel on the Vegas Strip. I'll be there along with Mike, Troy, a couple assistant coaches, and Pete, though Pete will be the one making the official calls. It's being broadcast on ESPN, of course, because why the hell wouldn't it be since the World Series just wrapped a couple weeks ago and there's no new baseball news to cover at the moment.

I blow out a breath. "Just ready for the draft. Ready to kick off this whole thing," I lie. "Ready to get our team in line and start running drills and winning games, man."

He draws in a deep breath and nods. "I know what you mean. I've had this strange feeling since late last night."

"What kind of strange feeling?" I ask, happy to deflect the attention from myself.

"Just nervous I think. Exhausted from all the planning. I'm not the young buck I once was." He wipes his forehead with his napkin and tosses it in the trash. "And my back is stiff today. I think I just slept all wrong."

"Deep breaths, Coach," I say. "And lots of H-two-O."

"I know, I know. Nothing to worry about here, but I have a gut feeling about our last three picks. I need to touch base with Pete."

"I haven't seen him yet, but you know he's been skipping breakfast to sleep in." I put air quotes around *sleep in* since he just got married a few weeks ago. We all know what he's really doing with his mornings.

The same thing I'd like to be doing with mine, if I'm being honest here.

I think for a beat about what it would mean if we told Troy. Would he always assume that's what we were doing if we didn't show up to breakfast? Or if Gabby spent the night away from home?

Troy and I aren't exactly shy around each other. Back in the day, we'd share stories about our conquests. But we're both different men now. I've settled down...and he's a father now. I guess he was then, too, he just didn't know it.

And then there's the whole sex club that isn't *really* a sex club angle, where he does the things he does that are typically reserved for private, intimate moments in front of anyone who wants to watch.

So how would he really feel about his best friend sleeping with his daughter?

Would it make it any better to know that we've actually fallen in love? That there are real feelings here that go far beyond just sex?

I guess we'll find out tomorrow.

Pete shows up and steals Troy away, and we hammer out the final details before we each head home. I take a quick shower since I need to get down to the Strip, and I'm shocked when I step out of the bathroom and into the bedroom wearing nothing but a towel only to find Gabriella Rose Grant lying on my bed.

And she's wearing nothing but a smile.

"Hey there, Captain," she says, and she's holding the keyring I gave her on her fingertip. She drops it on the nightstand beside her.

I chuckle. "Well this is certainly a nice surprise."

I drop my towel and pounce on my girl. She dissolves into giggles as I dive right for her tits, and she wraps her arms around my neck.

"I missed you, so I thought I'd rectify that," she murmurs into my hair.

"I've missed you, too." I suck one of her nipples into my mouth, and her body arches off the bed as she searches for friction to relieve the ache pulsing between us.

I don't waste any time. I slide into her, and we immediately find the beautiful rhythm our bodies have become so accustomed to.

She cries out my name, and I murmur hers into her ear as my lips connect with the sweet skin of her neck as I drive into her addictive, tight body. I could do this all day. I could do this forever.

I *want* to do this forever with her and only her.

That wave of love that's starting to become familiar to me when I'm around her flows through me, and it's enough to cause my body to plow into the wall of pleasure.

I grunt out some curse words and her name as I come, and her body tightens around me as she flies over the edge right along with me. When our bodies start to slow, my lips find hers, and I kiss her with all the adoration and love I feel inside me. We kiss slowly, sensually, erotically with our bodies still connected, and eventually I know I need to stop. I need to get dressed. I need to get down to the Strip.

But I never want to leave this bed.

"You need to go," she says softly as she collapses back, and I climb off her and slide in beside her. "I think I'll just wait here for you."

I laugh as I lean up on my elbow and peer down at her gorgeous face. "Aren't you going?"

"Oh, yeah. I guess I have to." She rolls her eyes with a laugh.

"I wish I could take you," I murmur, leaning down to press a soft kiss to her cheek. "I wish you could walk in on my arm and we could go public with this."

"Aren't you nervous about that?" she asks, her earnest eyes on mine.

I lift a shoulder. "Any time someone like me goes public with a relationship, it's a gamble. Most people out there will want to tear us apart, which is why growing this in private has meant so much to me. It's why I loved how we first connected, when you had no idea who I was. It made me feel like I could immediately trust you, like you weren't just saying shit because you thought it was what I wanted to hear."

She reaches up and runs a fingertip along my jawline. "Even if I had known, I wouldn't have done that."

I chuckle. "I know. And that's why I fell so goddamn hard so goddamn fast."

"I love you."

"I love you, too. Now get the fuck out of my bed before I take you long and slow."

She narrows her eyes at me. "Is that supposed to make me want to get out?"

I shake my head and grin. "Nope. It's a promise for later."

She winks at me. "I for one can't wait."

She heads home to get ready for tonight, and I fish a suit out of my closet, throw it on, and I'm ready to go in a few minutes. I head over to Mike's since I'm supposed to arrive with the rest of the group I've been working so closely with over the last few weeks, and I find everyone else is already here.

"Why do you look so relaxed?" Troy demands when I walk in last. "You get laid or something?"

Oh Jesus. What the fuck am I supposed to say to that?

Yeah, by your daughter seems inappropriate even though it's the truth.

"Fuck off," I say instead. "Are we ready?"

Troy shakes his head and wipes his brow. Wasn't he sweating earlier today in this same place? I wonder if he's stopped sweating all day.

It's a big deal, but I'm more excited than nervous. We're guaranteed most of the players we want since we're the only team taking part in this draft—except for the first two picks that Troy traded. It's an historic occasion as the last time the league expanded, two teams were added. This time, it's just us, which means we have our choice of all the men the teams in the league put up.

We've already talked to most of them. Most of them even know what position they'll be drafted in. With the men we've already put on the team, we're adding eighteen more to get to the forty-man roster—some of which will end up in the minors since the active team only has twenty-six men on it.

The resort sends a car that will deliver us right to the stage, and as it pulls up, the first face I see in the crowd gathered is AJ Winters, who agreed to play with us.

Excitement fills my veins.

I spot Gabby standing next to Joanie. They're both clapping as they clamor to get a look at the car, knowing the men they love are waiting inside, excitement and anticipation on their faces.

Gabby's mother stands on her other side. She's still here, but it doesn't matter. All that matters is what tonight represents, and after that, tomorrow morning we'll tell Troy the truth and then our relationship will be out in the open. I'll be able to hold her hand in public. I'll be able to kiss her in front of her parents. It's more to be excited about even though it comes with a healthy dose of nerves.

There's so much excitement, in fact, that I don't even notice what's happening in the car right beside me. The man who has spent the majority of the day sweating is now panting.

"Hey, man, you okay?" I ask Troy, my brows pinching together as I study him.

He nods. "Fine. Just nerves."

It's the same thing he's said to me all day.

The car pulls to a stop, and Mike gets out first. We all file out behind him, and as we walk up the red carpet to the stage, Troy stumbles a little.

And then he grabs his chest right before he collapses.

To be continued in Book 4, GROUNDBALL

Groundball

Chapter 1
Cooper

"**S**omebody call nine-one-one!" a voice nearby yells.

No.

Not *somebody*.

Every CPR training course I've ever taken tells us we need to pick a person to make the call. Yelling *somebody* means *nobody* will call.

"AJ, call nine-one-one," I say when I spot the first person I recognize nearby. He nods and grabs his phone out of his pocket.

"Stand back! Give him some room!" a security guard yells, and a circle seems to form around the man lying on the ground, mostly of those of us who shared the car on the way here. We're trying to shield him from onlookers, shield him from those taking videos to make a buck off whatever's happening, shield him from the chaos of the crowd.

He's still clutching his chest, and he's wincing in pain, but he's conscious. That has to be a good thing.

Gabby and Joanie break through the crowd, and Gabby kneels by his side, taking his hand in hers. She's murmuring something to him, and Joanie kneels on his other side.

Fuck it. I rush over and drape an arm around Gabby, squeezing her into my side to let her know I'm here.

"Daddy, it's okay, help is on the way," she murmurs softly to him.

His eyes flick to mine, and I can tell he's scared about what's happening to him. "Get up there and stand in for me, Coop," he says, and I nod. "The draft must go on. Make the right picks. I'll be back at it soon." We've got a mutual understanding about what this team needs, and I'm more than capable of doing what needs to be done.

"Of course. Get yourself well and then we'll kick some ass on the ballfield," I say with a wide grin that I don't really feel. Keep him calm, though. If it's his heart, he needs to remain calm and relaxed.

Managing a professional baseball team isn't exactly conducive to calm and relaxed—which might be what landed him in this situation to begin with. It's traveling and stress and not having a regular sleep schedule and eating whatever is available on the road. That combined with genetics could cause health problems for anybody.

I'm not just worried about my best friend. I'm worried about my girl's father. The way he grabbed his chest combined with the other symptoms he's had all day tell me this isn't just nerves. I've seen it before.

He's having a heart attack, and there's been too goddamn many of those in my life. I nearly lost my brother to one not so long ago. I'm not losing Troy to one.

Gabby's not losing her father to one.

It runs in the family. Troy lost his father too young just as I did to the same disease.

But he will get the care he needs, and he will come back to manage the fuck out of this team.

I refuse to allow my brain to have any other thoughts on the matter. I'm manifesting only positivity right now.

Gabby keeps her eyes on her father, and I squeeze her once more in solidarity before I straighten and walk over to address the crowd staring in this direction. I hold up both hands. "Everything's fine. The draft must go on." I repeat the words Troy just said to me, and it seems to calm the crowd down a little.

Sirens scream moments later, and Troy is taken out on a stretcher. Gabby glances at me before she climbs into the ambulance to be with her father, and I nod at her when our eyes meet before I'm forced to head up to the stage.

I stand beside Pete and Mike as we wait for the two announcers from ESPN—Carl and Doug, the hosts for tonight's draft—to announce our arrival.

"We'll keep you updated with the latest on Troy Bodine's condition throughout the evening as updates come in," Carl says. "And now, it's the moment we've all been waiting for! Please welcome to the stage Vegas Heat scouting director Pete Holt, general manager Mike Perry, assistant coaches Chris Jarrett and Joe Buchanan, and third baseman Cooper Noah!"

The crowd goes wild for our arrival, and we take our seats on the long stage, bright lights blaring into our eyes as we pretend we didn't just watch one of the men we all respect most in the world go down clutching his chest.

Fuck.

We're supposed to concentrate on the draft. We're supposed to hold it together.

We're supposed to act like everything's fine while we're here on this live broadcast.

But it's not fine.

My best friend was clearly in the middle of some cardiac episode, his daughter is worried sick about him, and I'm sitting up on this stage as his stand-in since that's what he told me to do.

The hosts ask us each a few questions, and I don't even know what the fuck I'm saying as I hide the fear behind the charming smile people have come to expect from me.

We cut to commercial, and I blow out a breath as I slide my phone out of my pocket and send Gabby a covert text.

Me: *My heart is with you. Keep me updated.*

I slip my phone back into my pocket, and when I glance up, I see the man sitting beside me—the team's general manager—as his eyes meet mine.

He absolutely just saw what I typed.

The contact in my phone is *Sunshine*, but it doesn't take a genius to figure it out.

Mike raises both brows. "Joanie?"

Oh fuck.

I weigh my options here.

Is it worse to admit the truth or to let him believe the lie? It's a tossup between fucking my best friend's daughter or fucking his fiancée.

The broadcast returns, so I don't get the chance to make that choice.

We talk for another few minutes, and I feel my phone buzz in my pocket with a potential reply from Gabby. I can't take it out to check since we're on live television.

As soon as they run the pre-recorded package on a few of the potential first picks, Mike turns to me again with raised brows.

"Gabby," I admit softly.

"Fuck."

I slide my phone out of my pocket and read the text from her.

Sunshine: *Just arrived and he's getting checked in. The paramedics said likely two blocked arteries. They were talking emergency double bypass. I'm scared.*

I flash the phone to Mike for him to read it, and he presses his lips together. He glances around us, and Chris and Joe are deep in conversation beside me while Pete is chatting with Doug and Carl.

"Thanks," he says.

I reply as fast as I can while the broadcast cuts to another commercial.

Me: *It's a very common surgery. He's in good hands now.*

Mike looks at me again as I slide my phone back into my pocket. "Is it serious or are you just playing around?" His voice is low and just for me even though we're surrounded by people.

I blow out a breath. "Serious."

"You know you can't tell him. Especially not now."

"I know not now. But not ever?"

He raises both brows. "I'd keep it to myself until you're about to walk down the aisle. If it's not as serious as that, he doesn't ever need to know."

I get the feeling he's not wrong about that.

"We'll talk more later, but let me leave you with this. It's not just the fact that she's his daughter. It's not just the fact that you're his good friend. You're a player on his team now, and if ever there were bad feelings between you and her, that will be reflected in every aspect of your game play, of his management, of simply *everything*. If he has to choose sides between you and her, guess who it'll be?"

The cameraman signals that the broadcast is about to return. But even though I don't get the chance to respond, the answer is clear.

If it ever came down to it and Troy had to choose between his daughter and me, there would be no contest, and there shouldn't be.

But what would that mean for me?

Chapter 2
Gabby

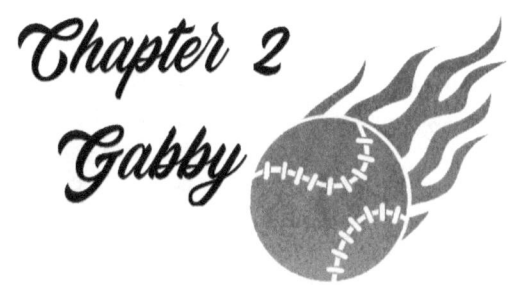

I t feels like I've been sitting here forever when Cooper walks
through the doors, but in reality it's only been about four
hours.

He's still in a suit from the broadcast, though he's removed his
jacket, and if I were anywhere other than a hospital fretting about
my father as he undergoes emergency surgery, I might take the time
to appreciate the feast laid out before my eyes.

"How is he?" Cooper asks.

I shake my head as I rush into his open arms, and the moment
he folds me into him, I feel a sense of peace wash over me. "Still
no update." My words are lost in his chest, and I feel him lean
down to press a kiss to the top of my head.

"The doctor should be out soon," Joanie says.

I'm not sure anything could draw two people closer than
holding hands and praying in a hospital for a successful surgery.
We've cried together, we've shared stories about him, and we've
discussed ways to help reduce his stress going forward, a seemingly
impossible feat.

He lets me go to give Joanie a hug, too.

"Can I get either of you anything?" he asks, and just as I open
my mouth to tell him I could use some water, a doctor walks into
the waiting room.

"The Bodine family?" he says, and we all turn to face him. He
walks us back into a private room. My heart pounds and my mouth
goes dry as we wait for the news. I just found him a few years ago.
I can't lose him already. He's too young at only forty-one. He's fit
and athletic and handsome. He eats a fairly healthy diet with maybe
too much sodium but I guess I just don't understand how this
could even happen to him.

Why is the doctor taking us to a private room? Why can't he tell us out here?

I get it. My dad's a celebrity. This is for his protection.

Still, it feels ominous, and I don't like it.

The doctor finally speaks. "We were able to remove the blockages successfully." Joanie and I both let out loud breaths of relief. "He's stable and resting now. He'll need to stay here a few days, and then it's a four-to-six-week recovery at home."

"Thank you, doctor. What can we expect at home?" Joanie asks.

"He will need someone with him the first week to ten days after he's released. He'll have some pain around the incision as well as his legs from the vein graft. He'll be tired and weak, but he'll be okay to take walks and slowly build his strength, and he may have episodes where he feels depressed, so keep an eye on his mental state. He shouldn't drive or travel for about a month, and he will likely push back on that. If you need any assistance at home, we can recommend some great in-home care."

"Thank you," Joanie says.

The doctor pats her shoulder lightly. "He's going to be fine. He's young, and he's otherwise in good health. Keep him on a heart-healthy diet and help him reduce his stress."

Joanie shakes her head a little. "I'll do what I can from home, but his career isn't exactly conducive to a low-stress environment."

The doctor chuckles. "No, it isn't. But if he can manage his stress at home from now until he needs to be at the stadium more regularly, he'll be in better shape when the season comes. The drive for success is hard on the heart." The doctor pats his chest. "Coaches tend to have irregular sleep and eating habits, and they can't work it into their schedules to see a doctor. They often wait until it's past the point of good sense, which is what happened with Troy. I suspect he's been ignoring symptoms for weeks, even months, and there were enough events colliding into each other at once to trigger tonight's attack. So do whatever you can to reduce stress. Get him a dog. Make him take walks to build strength back. Have him give something up, or it might cost him more than a night in surgery and a few weeks off work." He presses his lips together and nods meaningfully, and Joanie nods back.

"Will do," she says dutifully, and I have no doubt she will try her hardest...but my father can be awfully stubborn when he wants to be.

"I can take one of you back to recovery to see him," the doctor says.

Joanie looks at me, and I nod.

"You go ahead," I say.

"Thank you," she whispers, and she follows the surgeon out of the room.

I practically collapse onto Cooper, and he just barely catches me.

"Whoa," he grunts quietly. "You okay?"

"I've been trying to stay strong for Joanie," I admit. "But the second she left the room and you were here, I knew you'd catch me."

"I will *always* catch you, my Sunshine," he murmurs against my temple. He sweeps me up into his arms, and I start to cry. I've been brave all night for Joanie, but here in Cooper's arms where it's just the two of us feels like the comfort of home where I don't have to put on a façade anymore.

It's just one more sign pointing in the direction of *right* for the two of us.

Everything about this feels *right*.

The only thing that would make it feel wrong is if my dad were to catch us here.

He walks over to some chairs and sits down with me draped across his lap and clinging to his neck, and he quietly holds me as I let it all out.

Eventually the feeling of overwhelm starts to subside. "How'd the draft go?" I ask with a sniffle, and he reaches over to a box on the table beside us and grabs a tissue for me. I wipe my face and blow my nose.

"As expected," he says, and his tone is clipped.

My brows dip. "Is that a good thing?"

He nods. "It went well. But Mike caught me texting you."

I blow out a breath. "So now he knows too?"

"I have you in my phone as *Sunshine* but he thought I was texting Joanie. I either had to let him believe I was committing adultery with my best friend's fiancée or fess up to the truth."

"Quite the dilemma," I say dryly.

"He was another vote in the *don't tell him* column, just for the record. And after what the doctor said, I don't think brunch tomorrow is a great idea." He presses his lips to my cheek.

"More secrets. More lies. More people involved."

He nods. "I'm so sorry. Believe me, Gabby, all I want to do is shout from the rooftops about the two of us."

"I know. And someday, we will."

We have to…because I don't even want to consider what the alternative would be.

It feels like I've been sitting here forever when Cooper walks through the doors, but in reality it's only been about four hours.

He's still in a suit from the broadcast, though he's removed his jacket, and if I were anywhere other than a hospital fretting about my father as he undergoes emergency surgery, I might take the time to appreciate the feast laid out before my eyes.

"How is he?" Cooper asks.

I shake my head as I rush into his open arms, and the moment he folds me into him, I feel a sense of peace wash over me. "Still no update." My words are lost in his chest, and I feel him lean down to press a kiss to the top of my head.

"The doctor should be out soon," Joanie says.

I'm not sure anything could draw two people closer than holding hands and praying in a hospital for a successful surgery. We've cried together, we've shared stories about him, and we've discussed ways to help reduce his stress going forward, a seemingly impossible feat.

He lets me go to give Joanie a hug, too.

"Can I get either of you anything?" he asks, and just as I open my mouth to tell him I could use some water, a doctor walks into the waiting room.

"The Bodine family?" he says, and we all turn to face him. He walks us back into a private room. My heart pounds and my mouth goes dry as we wait for the news. I just found him a few years ago. I can't lose him already. He's too young at only forty-one. He's fit and athletic and handsome. He eats a fairly healthy diet with maybe too much sodium but I guess I just don't understand how this could even happen to him.

Why is the doctor taking us to a private room? Why can't he tell us out here?

I get it. My dad's a celebrity. This is for his protection.

Still, it feels ominous, and I don't like it.

The doctor finally speaks. "We were able to remove the blockages successfully." Joanie and I both let out loud breaths of relief. "He's stable and resting now. He'll need to stay here a few days, and then it's a four-to-six-week recovery at home."

"Thank you, doctor. What can we expect at home?" Joanie asks.

"He will need someone with him the first week to ten days after he's released. He'll have some pain around the incision as well as his legs from the vein graft. He'll be tired and weak, but he'll be okay to take walks and slowly build his strength, and he may have episodes where he feels depressed, so keep an eye on his mental state. He shouldn't drive or travel for about a month, and he will likely push back on that. If you need any assistance at home, we can recommend some great in-home care."

"Thank you," Joanie says.

The doctor pats her shoulder lightly. "He's going to be fine. He's young, and he's otherwise in good health. Keep him on a heart-healthy diet and help him reduce his stress."

Joanie shakes her head a little. "I'll do what I can from home, but his career isn't exactly conducive to a low-stress environment."

The doctor chuckles. "No, it isn't. But if he can manage his stress at home from now until he needs to be at the stadium more regularly, he'll be in better shape when the season comes. The drive for success is hard on the heart." The doctor pats his chest. "Coaches tend to have irregular sleep and eating habits, and they can't work it into their schedules to see a doctor. They often wait until it's past the point of good sense, which is what happened with Troy. I suspect he's been ignoring symptoms for weeks, even months, and there were enough events colliding into each other at once to trigger tonight's attack. So do whatever you can to reduce stress. Get him a dog. Make him take walks to build strength back. Have him give something up, or it might cost him more than a night in surgery and a few weeks off work." He presses his lips together and nods meaningfully, and Joanie nods back.

"Will do," she says dutifully, and I have no doubt she will try her hardest...but my father can be awfully stubborn when he wants to be.

"I can take one of you back to recovery to see him," the doctor says.

Joanie looks at me, and I nod.

"You go ahead," I say.

"Thank you," she whispers, and she follows the surgeon out of the room.

I practically collapse onto Cooper, and he just barely catches me.

"Whoa," he grunts quietly. "You okay?"

"I've been trying to stay strong for Joanie," I admit. "But the second she left the room and you were here, I knew you'd catch me."

"I will *always* catch you, my Sunshine," he murmurs against my temple. He sweeps me up into his arms, and I start to cry. I've been brave all night for Joanie, but here in Cooper's arms where it's just the two of us feels like the comfort of home where I don't have to put on a façade anymore.

It's just one more sign pointing in the direction of *right* for the two of us.

Everything about this feels *right*.

The only thing that would make it feel wrong is if my dad were to catch us here.

He walks over to some chairs and sits down with me draped across his lap and clinging to his neck, and he quietly holds me as I let it all out.

Eventually the feeling of overwhelm starts to subside. "How'd the draft go?" I ask with a sniffle, and he reaches over to a box on the table beside us and grabs a tissue for me. I wipe my face and blow my nose.

"As expected," he says, and his tone is clipped.

My brows dip. "Is that a good thing?"

He nods. "It went well. But Mike caught me texting you."

I blow out a breath. "So now he knows too?"

"I have you in my phone as *Sunshine* but he thought I was texting Joanie. I either had to let him believe I was committing adultery with my best friend's fiancée or fess up to the truth."

"Quite the dilemma," I say dryly.

"He was another vote in the *don't tell him* column, just for the record. And after what the doctor said, I don't think brunch tomorrow is a great idea." He presses his lips to my cheek.

"More secrets. More lies. More people involved."

He nods. "I'm so sorry. Believe me, Gabby, all I want to do is shout from the rooftops about the two of us."

"I know. And someday, we will."

We have to…because I don't even want to consider what the alternative would be.

Chapter 3
Gabby

I went in to see him.

He was sleeping.

He looked weak in that hospital bed, but he still looked like my father.

When I first met him, I thought he was way too good looking to be my dad. He didn't seem old enough to have an adult daughter, and furthermore he seemed way too sophisticated to have any relation to me.

But the more I studied him, the more I saw of myself in him. My green eyes and straight nose are all similar to his, while my jawline and cheekbones come from my mother. A true combination of both parents, though I feel like I tend to act more like my father than my mother when it comes to our personalities.

At least I hope that's true.

He's passionate and fiery when something is important to him, and he's determined and will always take what he thinks is the right path. He's Type A, a true perfectionist like me, and he's worked incredibly hard to get where he is. He enjoys the finer things in life, and he loves with his whole heart and will protect those in his inner circle no matter the cost.

On the other hand, my mother will always put herself first. She believes she's right no matter what, and she can often be too hardheaded to see past her own desires.

Determined and hardheaded are just synonyms for stubborn, but somehow my dad's stubbornness comes off like a positive thing while my mother's feels very negative.

Maybe I fall somewhere in the middle of those.

I know I should go home since that's where my mother is, but as I leave the hospital with Cooper, I find that I don't *want* to go home. I just want to feel the calming tranquility that I feel when I'm with the man I love. It feels like everything's going to be okay, versus the complete opposite feeling when I'm in the same room as my mother.

And so I don't go home.

Joanie forced me to leave after I went in to see him, citing my need for sleep as the reason. She said she'd stay with my father, and I could come back tomorrow once they got him out of recovery and into his own room.

Cooper agreed with her, and I knew they were both right.

Once I'm buckled in the passenger seat of Cooper's truck, I text my mom to let her know the doctor said Troy is stable, and I leave it at that. I don't tell her I'm leaving the hospital as I let Cooper take me to his home, where he plants me in a bathtub and slowly washes me by candlelight. It's not for romance, but it's exactly what I need to relax after the terrifying moments of tonight.

I haven't been able to stop replaying the part in my mind when my dad just crumpled to the ground.

He's such a strong man. Young and full of life, energetic and important. He's not supposed to fall to the ground in pain. He's supposed to stand tall like he always does, a pillar both in the Vegas community and the baseball community. He's a legend.

And now, people will remember the moment when he grabbed his chest and collapsed. I'm certain that's not how he'd want people to think of him, but it's the image that keeps coming to my mind—at least for tonight, anyway.

He's okay. He's stable. The bypass was a success, and while there's certainly a healing period, he's on the road to recovery. He'll know how to care for himself better now—we *all* will, but I also know that the stress of his career will continue to stress his heart to the point at which we may end up losing him far too early.

And that's a terrifying thought to have.

"What are you thinking about?" Cooper asks me once we're settled into his bed. He's the big spoon as his front aligns with my back, his arms around me and his face near my neck. I'm wearing one of his old Dodger t-shirts, and it's big enough that it feels like a nightgown. I don't know if I've ever been so comfortable in my entire life as I am right in this moment.

I only wish that comfortable feeling extended to my mental state.

"About how my dad's career is going to take him from me far too early," I admit.

He presses a soft kiss to my neck. "I won't let it."

"You shouldn't make promises you can't keep."

"Who says I can't keep it?" he asks. "I heard what the doctor said. We all need to work together to reduce his stress, and I can help out on the field. You can help at home. You're not losing your father, and I'm not losing my best friend." His voice is fierce and determined.

"I don't want you taking on the brunt of it and burning yourself out, either."

"I won't. I've got a gorgeous woman keeping me young, virile, and virtually stress-free since August. You know, barring a few instances." He thrusts his hips against my ass.

"You think sex is going to keep the stress off?"

"It can't hurt," he points out.

I giggle, but it fades to serious pretty quickly as a sobering thought plays in my mind. "What about the club my father supposedly owns, then?"

"He's stressed by the business side of it, not by the activity that may or may not happen inside it. But he already admitted to me a few weeks ago that he's stepping back from the club a bit once the season gets underway. He's going to be the silent partner for a while. Besides, he and Joanie need to lay low since the news of their engagement will likely hit the media any time now."

I wrinkle my nose at the idea of him and Joanie *not* laying low. What exactly were they doing at his club?

Never mind. I don't want to know.

When morning rolls around, Cooper offers to drive me home. After he makes me breakfast, I change back into the gown I wore to last night's event even though I want to wear his shirt forever. He takes me home.

"Do you want to come in?" I ask once we pull into the circular drive.

"That's a loaded question. I mean, I want to spend time with you, but your mom's already suspicious of us. And I should get over to Mike's place to see if there's anything they need me working on before I head to the hospital to visit your dad."

"I'll see you there," I say, and it's an automatic response to lean in and press a soft kiss to his lips.

He leans his forehead to mine. "Love you, Sunshine."

"Love you more, Captain."

He grins as I get out of the car, and I head inside.

"I knew it!" my mom exclaims without preamble the second I walk in the door. She flashes her phone screen at me. "And the evidence."

I stare at the photo on her phone. It's a little grainy and hard to see since it's a picture taken from a window and through a windshield, but I see the back of my head as I lean toward Cooper in his front seat. I know what I'm looking at since it just happened, but if I didn't know, it would probably take me some time to piece together what it was.

"Good morning to you, too," I say with fake brightness. "Why, exactly, are you looking for evidence on your daughter?"

"Because I knew I wasn't crazy!" She waves her phone around in the air. "You've been lying this entire time and I just watched while you smooched your boyfriend in your father's driveway with him none the wiser while he recovers from open heart surgery miles away in the hospital."

"Way to lay it on thick," I mutter dryly, and then since I'm not really sure how to handle it, I divert the subject completely. "I need you to go back home to Colorado."

Her jaw drops open. "What?"

"You need to go home," I repeat, enunciating my words as clearly as possible this time around.

"What are you talking about? You need me here now more than ever!"

My brows knit together. I know who I'm talking to here, and I know I need to be careful, but I can't help the words as they come tumbling out of my mouth. "In what sort of delusional universe might that be true?"

She looks supremely offended by my words.

"I know you're trying to help," I say, going for a different tact, "but the doctor said we need to do everything we can to reduce Dad's stress at home. And I'm sorry, Mom, but I don't think having you here is conducive to a relaxing environment for him." *Or for me.*

She presses her lips together as she swipes away a tear, and the act is frankly getting a little tiresome. "Fine. You don't want me here? I'm some nuisance that triggers stress? Right. I'll just go then."

I blow out a breath, and I'm about to say something along the lines of *this isn't about you, Mother*, when I remember who I'm dealing with.

She's the narcissist to end all narcissists, and telling someone as self-centered as her that any given situation isn't actually about her isn't the way to diffuse the situation nor is it the way to draw the line in the sand to tell her what's okay and not okay to put on me. It's time for me to set those boundaries.

To that end, I say, "I'm so sorry you feel that way. I apologize for making you feel sad, but your anger and your sadness are not my responsibility."

She huffs out a breath before she spins on her heel and stomps up the stairs like a pouty teenager, and while I don't want my mom to be mad at me, I'm at a point in my life where I can decide what's best for me…and she isn't it.

I've done my service. I was a good and respectful daughter to her my entire life, often giving up things I wanted in order to accommodate her. But when I learned who my dad was and found out about her lies—both about *who* he is and the fact that she told me he never wanted me—she gave up the right to my respect. And in the three years that have passed, she's done literally nothing to try to earn it back.

And so, like I just told her, I can no longer take on her emotions as my responsibility. Maybe it's all part of growing up—of becoming an adult and realizing that your parents are people, too, and that you have choices on the table you never really considered before.

I stay out of her way while she packs up. It's an eleven-hour drive back to Colorado, so she can be back home as early as late tonight.

She comes down the stairs a full hour later, and I'm positive she was taking her time to see if I'd come up and apologize. But I won't. I'm not going to back down on this one. It's time I stand up for myself when it comes to her.

"I guess I'll be leaving, then," she says.

I nod, and I walk over to give her a hug that isn't returned. "Have a safe trip back."

She narrows her eyes at me. "Let's not forget I have some evidence on you, young lady." She holds up her phone, and I really thought maybe we could do this civilly. Clearly not.

"Seriously, Mother?" I roll my eyes. "I'm your daughter. It would be great if you could, you know, just hope for the best for me instead of always trying to prove you have the upper hand."

"Or you could just admit what I've suspected all along rather than lying about it," she says.

Oh, right—I forgot. She's *always* right and will do *anything* to prove it.

"Fine. Yes. I'm in love with Cooper Noah, okay? I love my father's best friend with my entire heart and soul, and no, Dad has no idea, and yes, we're doing this in total secret because every time we try to tell him, something comes up. Are you happy now?"

She purses her lips, clearly *not* happy despite being proven correct. "You could've just told me from the beginning."

Oh my God. Nothing is *ever* good enough for her.

"Yeah, I could've. And maybe if I trusted you, I would have. Now if you'll excuse me, I have a lot I need to get done today. Have a safe trip back home." *Don't let the door hit you on the way out.*

I omit that last part as I spin on my heel and head up the stairs to take a shower before I head to the hospital to check on Dad.

But something tells me my mother isn't done with the secret she's suddenly privy to.

Chapter 4
Cooper

We have a huge welcome party for our new teammates on Tuesday. We've already planned a big fanfare, a parade, the whole nine yards. Rules state the new players have seventy-two hours to get here, but I think most will arrive today. Coop, can you help lead the stadium tour? Joanie had planned to do it but it's looking like she'll be out this week," Mike asks.

"Absolutely. I'll touch base with Joanie and see what she had planned."

He nods. "We'll welcome everyone into the front offices at nine and I'll make the introductions there, and I'll talk a while in one of our classrooms. Then the tour, a luncheon, and the parade at noon. Players will spend the rest of the day at the stadium completing their paperwork and getting added to all the appropriate systems, and we'll do player photos as well. Dinner is being catered in. It'll be a full day event."

"Any word on Bodine?" Chris asks.

"He was stable when I left last night. I'm heading there next. I'll touch base with Joanie and see if I can put her interns to work on Tuesday's events," I say.

"Fine," Mike says in the tone of voice that really means *great idea, man.*

I go to the hospital once our meeting is over. Joanie texted to let me know Troy was moved to a private room last night, so I head right up to his new room.

He's sitting up and drinking some water when I walk in, and he looks pretty good all things considered. A little weak, a little tired, but not lying on the ground. That's an improvement.

"Hey, he's awake," I say when I walk into the room.

"Tell me about the draft," he begs without greeting. He winces a little as he readjusts in the bed, but whatever painkillers are being pumped into his veins via the IV seem to be helping him to manage it.

"No work chatter in here," Joanie warns.

"It all went fine," I assure Troy, doing my best to assuage his concerns and appease Joanie as I flip the subject. "Now listen, how many days are you stuck up in this joint? Because you can borrow my passwords to my porn sites if you need them."

Troy chuckles. "Don't worry, I've got plenty of apps for that. I'm in here a few more days at a minimum and can you believe this bullshit? They said I can't travel for *four weeks*. Four weeks!" He shakes his head in disgust.

"Dude, four weeks puts us just before Christmas." I shrug. "Enjoy the holidays with your family, get healthy, and then we hit it hard January one."

"Yeah, yeah," he mutters. "What's going on with the stadium welcome on Tuesday?"

"Joanie said no shop talk," I remind him, but he just rolls his eyes. "Mike tapped me to lead the tour, so I'll need to borrow Joanie later for the details."

"Use the interns," Joanie pipes in. "Oh! And can you get signed items from our new players that we can donate to the sponsors who are participating in the parade?"

"Great idea," I say with a grin. "That must be why you're the head of marketing."

She laughs and holds a modest hand to her chest. "Oh, I don't know about all that."

The door opens, and Gabby walks in holding a bouquet of flowers. "How's Daddy feeling?" she asks around the bouquet, but it's so big it's blocking her view of me.

Every time I hear her say the word *daddy*, I can't help where my dirty mind wanders.

"Better than yesterday," Troy says.

She sets the bouquet down and turns around, and that's when she sees me. "Oh, hey," she says nonchalantly, like she didn't wake up in my arms a few hours ago.

"Hey," I say. I force my gaze off her before Troy starts to suspect anything, but an immediate calmness flows through my chest the second our eyes connect. "Can you and the interns help me with the stadium tour for the new draft picks this Tuesday?"

She nods. "Of course."

"I'm going to take this week off to be with your father," Joanie says to Gabby.

"Nonsense," Troy says. "I'm fine."

She turns toward him. "In sickness and health, right?"

He sighs with a bit of frustration.

Joanie turns back to Gabby. "Can you step in for me this week? I'll have my phone on me and I'll be available to answer questions or video chat or whatever you need, but once your father is discharged, he'll need someone with him. I know you have classes in the mornings, but I also know you have a better handle on my job than anyone else, and I wouldn't trust anyone aside from you with the keys to the kingdom."

Gabby walks over and pulls Joanie into a hug. "I'd be glad to do whatever I can to help. I'm sure my professors will understand."

"You will *not* miss class over this," Troy booms, and Gabby turns toward him. "You already missed when you were in Chicago with Cooper. No more."

"Okay, fine. I won't." She turns around and gives me a look that says *oh hell to the yes I will*, but obviously we're not going to allow Troy in on that nugget since we don't want him blowing a gasket twelve hours post-op.

That's Gabby. She's stubborn, and she tends to do whatever she wants, preferring to deal with the consequences as they come.

It's one of the things I love most about her, but it's also potentially one of the things that's going to get us into trouble.

"You two go get to work," I say to Joanie and Gabby. "I can stay with Troy a few hours while you fill Gabby in on what you need from the interns this week, and I can switch out with you whenever you're ready."

"You have workouts to get to, Noah," Troy grunts.

"And you need your rest. I expect you to take a good, long nap while I watch *Top Gun.* Have you seen it?" I fold my arms over my chest in a power play that Troy can't do much about given the fact that he's laid up in a hospital bed tied to a bunch of monitors, and so he blows out a frustrated sigh while his daughter walks over to grab his hand.

"Get some rest while we work out the details, and I'll have Joanie back in a flash," she says. He kisses her hand, and it feels like it should be my place to kiss her goodbye next.

"Thanks, baby girl," he says.

Joanie kisses Troy next. "I'll be back in a few hours. If you need anything, you call me. Okay?"

He nods and narrows his eyes at her as he says, "Yes ma'am."

They both chuckle softly as she leans in for another kiss, and I gaze across the room as I wonder when it'll ever be okay for me to kiss Gabby goodbye or share a soft chuckle with her in front of her father.

Chapter 5
Gabby

I drive Joanie and myself to the stadium, and she scribbles notes while we make our plan of attack in the car, not wasting a single moment.

"I wish Dad could be there on Tuesday," I muse.

"It'll be hard on him missing it, but it would be harder if he wasn't here at all," she says as I pull into the parking lot. Security waves me through, and we head up to her office.

She makes me a list of her passwords and tells me everything I need to know in order to effectively do her job while she's out this week, and she also gives me a list of tasks for the interns.

"Mackenzie is going to *love* having me call the shots," I murmur, and Joanie laughs.

"You've got nothing to worry about, Gabby. All personal feelings aside, your ideas and creative content are in a completely different league than hers."

"She knows about Cooper and me," I admit.

She twists her lips. "Is she using it against you?"

"She hasn't yet, but I don't doubt this will tip her over the edge."

She picks up her phone and taps on it a few beats without responding. "There." She sets her phone down and wipes her hands as if she's taken care of the situation, and my phone buzzes with a new text.

I lift it to read what Joanie just sent.

Joanie: *Hi Interns – I will be taking the week off for personal reasons. I've selected Gabby to fill my place for the week, and she will hand out your tasks. If any of you are available to come in right now, we're working on the new player welcome day on Tuesday and we could use all extra hands on deck. Thanks!*

She lifts a shoulder as she raises her brows. "Let's see who rushes over, shall we?"

I laugh and shake my head. She's got a point, though—if the others aren't willing to drop whatever they're doing to come in on short notice, then do they really deserve a full-time position here after all?

Likely not. This sort of career isn't just a *job*. It's a lifestyle, and I'm already living it.

The others…they're just not. They're living as college students working an internship, but I've got different stakes in the game than they do.

It's not that my father is the manager or that his future bride is the marketing director. It's not even that I'm hot and heavy with the third baseman, though some combination of those things are what landed me here.

I want the job, and I think I want it more than the others do.

It's that I *want* this to be my lifestyle. I want it *more* than the other interns do *because* of how I landed here. I want to learn everything about the game. I want to watch film and get to know the strengths of every player. I want to film behind the scenes footage and brag about how the Heat are the best team in the league. I want to travel with the team and show the world what it's like. I want to be a part of this organization.

Do I have advantages? Certainly. And I'd be stupid not to use them.

"Do *we* have a float?" I ask.

Joanie's brows draw together. "We have three double decker buses for the players."

"No, not the players," I say, shaking my head. "Not the coaching staff, either. I mean *us*." I wave my hand between Joanie and me. "The marketing department. The front office staff. The interns."

She sighs as she looks down at her desk. "I mean…no. It's a great idea, but it's not a necessity and I should really get back to your dad."

We both turn toward the door when we hear a knock on it. "Then it's a good thing you ran into me."

I smile broadly at Justin. "You have experience with floats?"

"Oh, not only do I have *experience* with floats, I was president of my high school's student council, and I oversaw the most *epic* float to ever grace the football field at Sunrise Academy's Homecoming

Game." He raises both brows arrogantly, and he steps into the office as both Joanie and I laugh.

"Joanie, can we get into the swag closet?" he asks.

She narrows her eyes at him. "How do you know about the swag closet?"

He laughs. "I may play dumb, but I'm a good listener." He winks, and she grabs a key. "You know where it is?"

He nods. "Am I free to take what I want from it?"

She nods. "Sure, but first you need to organize and inventory the stuff I haven't gotten to yet. I had it on the list for next week, but it looks like it's not happening."

"Oh, it's happening. I'll get it done *today*," Justin promises.

"What's the swag closet?" I ask, looking between the two of them.

"It's a storage room downstairs near the clubhouse where we house giveaway items and decorations for events. Some stuff is still on order, and I've gotten some new deliveries down there but haven't had time to go through them," she says.

"Then it's a good thing you have a team of interns. You got this up here?" I ask, and she nods. "I'll be back." I head down to the swag room with Justin, and we discover a room filled with shelving units and boxes stacked on top of each other.

It's a little chaotic, a little disorganized, and filled with stuff we can use to make our float.

"My dad has a large trailer we can decorate." He walks to a far wall where a bunch of boards are stacked, and he reaches between them. "I saw these the other day." He unrolls long clings with the Heat logo on them and holds them up to show me.

"Oh my God, Justin. This is perfect!"

He grins. "I know! And we can toss these at the people in the crowd." He pulls a box down and shows me a whole bunch of mini stress balls in the shape of baseballs with the team logo on them.

"You mean toss them *to* the people in the crowd, right?"

He shrugs. "Potato, po-tah-to." He winks at me, and I get the mental image of him whipping balls at unsuspecting fans. "I'll be good. Promise."

"I mean, feel free to fire a few off at Mackenzie," I mutter, and he laughs.

"That's what the t-shirt gun is for. So how are you going to handle her over the next week?" he asks.

"I'm not sure," I admit, but with Justin by my side, I have a feeling I'll be okay.

Chapter 6
Cooper

*T*op *Gun* was pretty good, but Troy slept through most of it, and I just started some James Bond movie when Joanie appears in the doorway. She's quiet so as not to wake the sleeping Troy, and she smiles at me as she sits nearby.

"Thanks for staying with him," she whispers. "Did I miss anything?"

I shake my head. "Not a thing. And I haven't had a break in the last few weeks, either. It wasn't hard to sit back and enjoy a movie."

"If you two would stop jibber-jabbering, maybe a guy could get some rest," Troy mutters from the bed.

"Good morning, Sunshine," I say, the word out of my mouth before I realize that's his daughter's nickname.

He glares at me.

"Is he always this grumpy when he wakes up?"

She nods. "Unfortunately, yes. But I usually have my ways of dealing with it."

"Can't get the old ticker moving too fast yet, Joanie," I warn, and she giggles while Troy continues to glare.

"Well, I'll be on my way," I say as I stand and stretch. "I hear the interns may need some help."

"They do. They're in the swag closet now planning a Heat float," Joanie says.

"Thanks for sticking around," Troy says gruffly.

I nod as I offer him a fist bump. "Hey, you just keep getting better. I'll always stick around, man."

He nods his thanks, and I head out. I decide to surprise Gabby at the stadium, and I find her, Justin, and Chloe working hard in the swag closet. They appear to be organizing and taking inventory of supplies, and they have a whole system down where Justin opens the boxes, Chloe unpacks them, Gabby inventories them, and Justin finds shelf space for them.

I jump in by helping break down the empty boxes, and the process moves pretty quickly. They grab the items they want to give away during the parade, and Gabby sends a text out to the interns to let them know they're moving over to Justin's place to work on the float.

"Can I do anything?" I ask.

Gabby nods. "Get started on signed stuff from the players. We want to gift at least one item to every business who volunteers a float."

I nod. "You got it." I glance around the swag room and find a variety of things I can have players sign, and then I head to the clubhouse while Gabby and the interns gather up what they need for the Heat float.

I find Danny and Rush in the weight room with Nick, AJ, and a few guys who must've rushed right over after the draft. Overall the tone in here is one of enthusiasm and excitement, like we're a group of men ready to spend all our time together over the next several months working toward a common goal.

I talk to the handful of new guys about the housing options. I know very little about the accommodations the team provides since I opted to buy my own place, but not everyone has that option, and not everyone on the team has the same paycheck I have.

I realize how lucky I am not for the first time.

I hand out a few items and some sharpies I found in the swag closet, and the guys start signing. I force in a quick workout, drop the signed items in Joanie's office, and head to dinner with Danny.

Dinner goes late as we talk about the draft picks much longer than I was expecting, and it's nearly eleven by the time I'm getting in my truck to head home. I call Gabby while I'm on my way.

"Hey," she answers, her voice warm like honey.

"Hey yourself. Are you still working on the float?"

"I'm just heading home, actually. It all came together beautifully and Justin's taking over in the morning so I won't have to miss class."

"I know it's late, but I'm on my way home if you'd like to stop by," I offer.

"Mr. Noah…is this a *booty call?*" Her voice is filled with shock, but I know she's just teasing me.

"Hey, a guy's gotta fit it in when a guy can fit it in, you know what I'm saying?"

She laughs, but the sound sobers quickly. "That's how it's going to be, isn't it?" she asks.

I clear my throat. "I mean...I can't sugarcoat it. Yes, it's going to be squeezing in time when we can. Having to do it on the sly will complicate things, but it's you and me. We'll manage. Thanksgiving, Christmas...then it all starts. Spring training is voluntary but since it's a brand-new team, we'll all be there. We'll want to start running drills long before that, too, so even like I told your dad earlier, we get through the holidays and it all begins January one."

"Get through the holidays," she murmurs. "How am I supposed to get through the holidays when I have to pretend?"

I sigh. "I wish I had the answer to that."

We haven't talked about Thanksgiving even though it isn't far off. I sent plane tickets to my family, and they're coming for the long weekend. I haven't thought as far ahead as Christmas yet.

But she's right. I don't want to pretend anymore, either. We both braced ourselves for today to be the brunt of it, and then her father had to go and have a fucking heart attack.

I don't want to pretend, and I also don't want to spend these important moments without her. But we're back to square one where we don't have a choice.

We pull into my driveway at the same time, and it's a relief to be home with her here. It's the one place where we *don't* have to pretend, where we can be ourselves, where we can do whatever we want however many times we want as loudly as we want.

She follows me through the garage and into the laundry room, and the moment the door closes behind us and seals us into privacy, I pull her into my arms.

She wraps her arms around me, too, and she clings to me. We simply stand there in the laundry room holding tightly to one another—something she needed after the long twenty-four hours of worrying about her father, and something I needed after the long twenty-four hours of worrying about both her and my best friend.

And in this moment, whatever secrets or lies or fears lie ahead of us, I truly feel that as long as we find our way back into each other's arms, it'll all turn out okay.

It's not until much later I discover how very, very wrong I was.

Chapter 7
Gabby

I don't want to let go. I know if I let go, all the other stuff that keeps getting in our way has the potential to sneak back in. If I stay right here, it's just the two of us. We don't have to worry about the secrets we're keeping. We can just *be*, and there's something so magical and comforting about that— something I'm not ready to let go of just yet, and so I continue to cling onto him.

My brain knows the truth. Eventually we'll have to let go. I have classes in the morning, and he has responsibilities to get to as well. We'll need to see my dad. I'll need to lead the interns this week while I fight for the social media position. There's a million things on each of our plates, but somehow they all fade into the ether when I'm with him and all that matters is *this*.

He pulls me up by placing his hands under my thighs, and I lay my head on his shoulder as he carries me through the house to the couch. He sets me down onto the sofa lounger seat, the longer cushion that can accommodate both our bodies, and he climbs up to hover over me, his lips inches from mine as he peers down at my face.

I stare up at him, totally content and comfortable here in this place.

"Every time I look at you, it's like this wave of something just washes over me," he says softly as he continues to gaze down at me. "At first I thought it was love, but I think it's something so much bigger than that. It's just fucking *home*, Gabby. I've bounced around the last few years, and honestly nothing has felt like home since my dad died. But you...you're *home*. You're the place the compass points to when I get lost, and I don't want you to ever forget that."

His words touch a place in my chest that goes far deeper than just my heart. They brand onto my very soul, and there is where they will reside until the day I die.

"I love you, Cooper Noah," I whisper, tears trickling from my eyes.

"I love you too, Gabriella Rose Sunshine Grant." His lips drop to mine, and he kisses me so tenderly and with the kind of authenticity that only serves to validate the words he just spoke.

He breaks from me long enough to pulls his shirt over his head, and I run my fingertips along the cut ridges of his abdomen before he pulls my shirt over my head, too. He unhooks my bra and helps me out of my jeans before taking care of his own.

And then he's making love to me right there on his couch, our bodies racing toward the brink of pleasure as I dig my nails into his skin and he growls my name into my ear, our quiet whispers and moans speaking our language for us as he rocks into my body. His lips find my nipple as my body bends and bows under his touch, and he continues to drive into me as he manages to thrill every single erogenous zone seemingly simultaneously. The words we spoke hover around us like a warm blanket, and as I tip over the edge into the abyss of pleasure, I know this is it for me.

There will never be another man like him. Not for me. I will never love like this again. No one will ever make me feel the way he does—not just in moments like these where he physically knows my body so well, but in every moment where we connect beyond the level of physicality. He just gets me, emotionally, mentally, and spiritually, and we have to find a way to go public with what we have because I can't keep living with the best thing that ever happened to me as my best-kept secret.

My alarm wakes me too early the next morning as I scramble to shut it off, forcing me out of the warm cocoon of Cooper's arms.

I spot a text from Justin that must've come in late last night.

Justin: *FYI Mackenzie was on a rampage last night. I'm faking a friendship with her to get her to keep her mouth shut for you, but she told me you're fucking CN. How does she know? Delete this text.*

"Shit," I grumble.

Cooper reaches over for me and bats my phone out of my hands as he pulls me closer into his body, and I giggle.

"I need to get up and get ready for class," I remind him.

"What are you cursing about at this ungodly hour?" he asks.

"It's not like it's five in the morning," I point out. "It's six-thirty."

"It's still dark. I don't do dark mornings."

"If I got naked, climbed on top of you, and called myself Dark Morning, would you change your mind?"

That draws a sleepy chuckle from him. "Yes, then I would definitely do dark morning." He thrusts his hips against me.

"Are you ever *not* hard?" I ask.

"Yes. I am not hard in the three minutes after you've made me come. But otherwise, when you're around…all the blood seems to run straight down to the big man as he begs for a chance to score with the hottest girl he's ever seen."

"That's quite a speech coming from someone who still has his eyes closed."

"Five more minutes," he demands, and he pulls me back down, peppering my neck with kisses.

"Sorry, pal. I set the alarm for as late as I possibly could. I need to get up, and I need to deal with something."

"Fine," he mutters, and he finally lets me go. "What do you need to deal with?" He sits up.

I wave at his abs, and he gives me a funny look.

"What are you doing?"

"Waving to the abbies," I say. I walk over and point out one of the muscles near the bottom. "This one's my favorite, but don't tell the others."

"He wants a kiss," Cooper says, and I lean down to kiss my favorite ab. He takes the opportunity to grab the back of my head and tease me like he's pushing me down, down, down.

"Too early to get up, but not too early for a blow job?" I ask with a raised brow when he lets go.

He grins and shrugs innocently. "It was worth a shot."

"If you behave, maybe later, but I really do need to get to class."

"And you have to deal with something that caused you to curse. What was it?" he asks.

"Justin said he's faking a friendship with Mackenzie to help me out. She told him we're sleeping together."

He sighs. "We need to stage that breakup pronto, then."

I nod as I put on my clothes from last night. "Do it today. I'll be in after class, and I'll ask her if I can talk to her, and then you just walk up and do it."

He twists his lips. "Why do I have to be the one to end it?"

"Because she'll never believe that I'm the one ending it with you. It just wouldn't make any sense."

"Why not?" he asks.

"Because we're not playing in the same league, Cooper. You're the older, worldly, all-star athlete, who could have his pick from any woman in the world, and I'm…me. I'm the younger, inexperienced college student who's more well-known for her famous father than on her own merit."

"I hate it when you talk about yourself like that. I wish you loved yourself the way I love you."

"My vagina couldn't take that sort of workout, my friend," I say dryly.

He laughs, and I press a kiss to his lips before I take off for home, praying that our plan works.

Chapter 8
Gabby

I arrive at the stadium after my morning classes to find Joanie's office filled with banners and signs welcoming the new players. Justin put the interns to work, capitalizing on each of their strengths. Mackenzie has perfect handwriting to create the words, Brian and Chase are busy painting in the letters after she finishes, and Chloe is adding the artistic flair while Justin directs and manages the supply chain. Dylan was in class with me this morning, and he should arrive any minute.

"You guys! This looks amazing!" I glance around at all the signs.

"We've been hard at work all morning," Justin brags. "Those are dry," he says, pointing to one pile. "The ones leaning up on the walls are wet. I've got the stack we worked on last night in the office next door, one with each player's name on it for the clubhouse. We can start hanging them up whenever you're ready."

"Let's do it," I say, and together we head to the office next door to grab the stacks of already dry posters. We take them down to the clubhouse and start hanging them up all around. It looks festive and exciting when we leave, and I spot Cooper walking in just as we're walking out.

"Is now a good time for the fake-up-break-up?" he murmurs as he passes by me.

I nod. "Be gentle, though."

He chuckles, and Justin and I head back up toward Joanie's office.

"What was that about?" he asks.

I roll my eyes. "We decided to stage a break-up in front of Mackenzie so she keeps her damn mouth shut."

"Smart. She was yammering on about telling Joanie."

"Joanie knows," I mutter.

Justin's eyes widen. "And she hasn't told Troy?"

I shake my head slowly, and he lets out a low whistle.

"Oh, that ain't gonna be pretty when he finds out she knew."

I twist my lips. "I know. But maybe he never has to know she knew."

We arrive at her office and step in, and the production line just keeps churning out more and more posters. I help make a few, and since I know Cooper's on his way up, I ask Dylan, Brian, Chase, and Chloe to go hang some posters around the hallways and weight room so it's just Justin, Mackenzie, and me up here.

"Gabby, can I talk to you?" Cooper asks.

I purse my lips. "What is it? I'm kind of in the middle of something here."

"I, uh...can you come out here?"

"Just say whatever it is." I go for the bitchiest, most exasperated tone I can muster.

"Really? You *really* want me to do this here in front of everybody?"

I blow out a breath. "Go for it."

"Fine," he mutters. "I can't do this anymore."

I freeze as I glance up at him, and his eyes are cold and hard. It's quite the act he's putting on. He's even got me convinced.

Mackenzie freezes, too.

"It's been a fun few weeks, but it's over," he says.

My brows dip as I finally force myself into motion. I take a few steps toward him, abandoning the paint brush I was just using. "What do you mean?" I ask, forcing a little bit of begging into my tone.

"I mean this shit between us is not worth it," he says, and even though I know we're staging this, his words still cut into my heart. "You're too young for me, too clingy, and I'm just...done. I'm here in Vegas, baby. I just want to have a good time in a brand-new city with my brand-new team. I'm out."

Too young.

Too clingy.

Does he mean those things?

It's like he's choosing my deepest fears and laying them out on the table in front of Mackenzie, and that hurts my heart more than I thought it would.

Tears fill my eyes, only they're not fake. "Oh."

He shrugs. "It was fun while it lasted." He shoots Mackenzie a grin and raises his brows as if he's issuing an invitation, and then he disappears from the door.

Justin walks over and puts his arm around me. "I'm so sorry, baby girl. Are you okay?"

I shake my head. "No. What a dick," I mutter, and then I actually do allow myself to cry for a beat.

What if that was real?

What if he meant those things?

He didn't, and I know he was doing this on the fly. The words he said to me last night are far more meaningful than these fake ones. But that doesn't lessen their impact.

Just the mere thought of him ending things with me has me feeling this way. I can't imagine how it might feel if we *actually* ended things.

"I'm so sorry, Gabby," Mackenzie finally pipes in. I sense just the tiniest bit of smugness in her words.

I suck in a breath as I remember *why* I talked him into doing that. "Thanks," I mutter, and she walks out of the room.

I have zero doubts in my mind that the reason she walks out of the room is in order to track him down and shoot her shot, and I've never hated someone more than I do in this moment.

"You okay?" Justin whispers while I blow my nose.

I nod. "I'm fine. It just cut a little deeper than I expected it to."

"You're really in deep." He raises his brows pointedly.

"Deeper than I've ever been into anything before," I admit.

We get back to work, and by the time we leave, the stadium is decorated beautifully with tons of welcoming messages, and we have a pile of posters drying that we can pass out to people watching the parade.

It's not until I'm on my way home that I finally get the chance to call Cooper.

"Hey babe," he answers, his voice filling my car speakers.

"Hey," I say quietly.

"What's wrong?" he asks immediately.

"Your little speech hurt more than I was expecting."

"Oh, God. I'm so sorry. I didn't mean any of it, and I felt like shit as the words came out of my mouth. Come over so I can prove how much I didn't mean it."

"I'm the one who told you to say it. I guess I just didn't realize how invested I am until I thought about a real end."

"It's not something you have to worry about, Gabby. I promise. I'm not going anywhere."

"But you called me too young and clingy." I sniffle at the memory.

"If anyone here is clingy, it's me. I'm sticking to you like plastic wrap, baby, and you are not getting rid of me easily."

I giggle at his comparison, and I decide to let it go as I head toward his house to let him prove to me how he really feels.

Chapter 9
Cooper

We both oversleep the next morning, unsurprising considering we were up late "making up" after our fake fight.

At least we're both waking with smiles on our faces, but hers doesn't last long when she spies the clock.

"Shit!" she yells, jumping out of bed and grabbing her clothes. "I'm late for class!"

"Take the day off," I suggest sleepily. "You're already missing your later class anyway for the parade. Besides, I'm going to need help corralling all the new players."

She sets her hand on her hip. "And you think *I* can help with that?"

I laugh. "No, but I do think seeing your sunshine face there will help make it easier on me."

"You think it's going to be rough?"

"Gabby, these are players coming to *Vegas*. Imagine playing in, I don't know, Minnesota or Cleveland or Milwaukee and getting called into a town like Vegas. You're leaving cold, harsh winters for fucking Sin City. Some want to be here, and others won't, but either way, they're stepping immediately into a party. Somehow I've been tapped as the guy who's supposed to keep them from getting arrested." I shake my head. "It's going to be an uphill climb."

She blows out a breath and perches on the edge of the bed in serious contemplation, and I can tell she's the type of student who *never* misses class unless it's an absolute necessity. I reach over for her and pull her into my arms, toppling her over so she comes back down on top of me.

She giggles. "You really do have your way of convincing me to see things your way, don't you?"

I press a kiss to the back of her hand and thrust my hips toward hers. "Did it work?"

She sighs. "Yeah, it worked."

"Good. Now get that cute ass of yours naked again so I can work you over in the shower before we have to get to the stadium."

"Yes sir," she says, stripping out of her clothes again, and then I make good on my promise.

After pumpkin pancakes that she makes and I pretend to like, we head toward the stadium together in our separate cars. She goes up to the marketing department to make sure everything is lined up the way Joanie wants it while I move toward the clubhouse, and I'm met with Danny Brewer shotgunning a beer.

"Dude, it's eight-fucking-thirty in the morning!" I say, and Rush stands beside him laughing.

"It's parade day," he says with a shrug, and as I glance around, I find a clubhouse full of guys who are starting their avenues toward being either drunk or high. Danny appears to be some sort of ringleader, which isn't shocking, but I thought since the two of us had become so close in the last few weeks, maybe he'd err on the side of responsibility.

Turns out I was dead wrong.

I spot cans already filling the garbage can beside him, and the glassy look in his eyes tells me a bunch of them belong to him.

Add to that the fact that the league removed marijuana from its list of banned substances a couple years ago, and now it's treated the same way as alcohol...that means it's fairly commonplace among players.

And weed is legal here in Vegas.

The combination of that means players in the off-season are already taking advantage of all Vegas has to offer with little to no concern as to what sort of impression they're making with their new ball club, going so far as to actually drink beer *inside of* their new clubhouse.

"If Troy was here, he'd kick all your asses," I say.

"Well he's not," Danny counters.

"No, but I am." I grab the case of beer behind him and carry it with me out of the clubhouse despite the protests following in my wake.

Troy brought me in to be a leader. This is where it starts.

I hide the beer in the backseat of my truck, seething the entire way that this is somehow where I ended up. A few months ago, I was working happily with kids and living a fairly quiet, private existence.

And now I'm tapped to lead this team, in charge of babysitting a bunch of drunken idiots.

I swing by the marketing department to see Gabby. She's the light at the end of this tunnel, and she's all alone in Joanie's office. She tilts her head when she sees me.

"What's wrong?"

"Danny was shotgunning a can of beer when I walked in, and half the players down there are on something or other."

She closes her eyes and draws in a deep breath. "What can I do?"

"I think I've got it handled. I need to fend them off at least until after Mike talks to them, and what they do during the parade is their business." I think back to all the parades celebrating victories that I've seen or participated in over the years, and sobriety was never in sight for the majority of people on the bus.

But never once did I partake in one in Sin City, either. I have the sudden feeling that today's parade is going to be like literally no other.

When I return, Danny is sulking. "Do you really want the front office seeing you like that?" I ask him.

He glares at me a little, but eventually he purses his lips and looks away, which tells me that even though he might be a little on the wrong side of sober, he's not stupid and he sort of gets my point.

"Let's head to classroom A for Mike Perry's opening statements," I call out to the men gathered, and they actually listen as they all start to make their way for the exit with Rush leading the pack since he knows his way around.

Mike drones on and on, which isn't a bad thing since it kills the buzzes that started down in the clubhouse. Eventually he releases everyone for the tour, and I take the pack around the stadium, showing them all the key places they need to know. Gabby and her team did an amazing job with the welcome banners, and every time I see one, a little tingle runs along my spine as it makes me think of her and all the work she's putting in here.

I lead the players through the front offices and introduce them to everyone on staff, including the interns.

I catch Cade Barrett, one of the minor leaguers with lots of potential to get called up, giving Gabby the eye, and I'm sure he's not alone. I force my hackles down even though the thought of any one of these guys hitting on her seems to flip a violent sort of switch in me.

None of them are good enough for her.

Her father's right. She deserves better than a baseball player. She deserves better than *me*.

But I'm what she's got, and I hope it'll be enough.

We end the tour down in the clubhouse, where I give the speech I've gone over in my mind a few times.

"Welcome to the Heat!" I begin, my goal to make eye contact with every guy in the room during my short speech. My opener is met with cheers from the guys gathered here, some sitting by their lockers, some standing. "We all came from somewhere else, and today we're a team. Think about what that means to you. To me it means we're working together toward a common goal, and that goal is going for Ws. But today is where we start to build the brotherhood that lies behind what we do on the field. It's where we start to build trust in each other, where we get to know each other and create bonds that extend far beyond our time here with the Heat. I can't wait to build this thing with each and every one of you, and I know if Troy were here, he'd speak to the brotherhood we're building, too. We're a team, and we have four months to get ready to fucking win! It all starts today, so get out there, have fun, and please don't get arrested."

The end of my speech is met with laughs even though it's a fair warning, and then I get a standing ovation.

I hold up a modest hand until they quiet down, and then I say, "Lunch is served up on the Diamond level, so get some food and then let's rock this parade."

The guys filter out of the clubhouse and head up to the Diamond level, and Danny hangs back.

"Sorry about this morning," he says. "I feel like an asshole, but I do want you to know I respect you."

"I know you do, man," I say, and I slap his back. "Do what you want, but I didn't want you wasted when Perry was talking to everybody. And remember the parade is public, so people will be watching—and filming."

"I'll be on my best behavior." He holds up a solemn hand, but the second I walk up to the Diamond level, I realize how fucked we are.

Whoever thought it was a good idea to serve beer at the player luncheon right before the parade should be fired.

Chapter 10
Cooper

I t was supposed to be a family affair.

Somehow it got off track.

I'm on the top of the double decker bus carrying the players, and Danny is currently tossing those little shot bottles of Fireball out into the crowd. I don't even know how he got his hands on them, but he's tossing them to the most attractive women in the crowd.

"Show me your tits!" he yells to a woman in a sequined bikini top with a matching skirt.

Jesus Christ. It's sixty-seven degrees out here, but that doesn't stop the woman from lifting her top, and Danny tosses her a bottle of Fireball.

Rush stands on his other side goading more women out of their shirts, and these two are Vegas's newest dynamic duo. Or dangerous duo. I'm not really sure yet.

AJ was up here a minute ago, but now I don't see him, and I watch as Cade climbs down the stairs with Colton Everett and Vince Finley, two more younger men on our forty-man roster who are playing in the minors. These are guys with a lot to lose, but when in Vegas…I guess the goal is to get fucking wasted.

I follow them down the stairs since I've lost all control up here, and I close my eyes for a beat at the scene on the first floor of the bus.

AJ is making out with some woman who he must've pulled out of the crowd. She's topless, and his hand is firmly planted on one of her breasts.

A bunch of other women have somehow made their way onto our bus, and I spot some players with women gyrating on top of them while others aren't quite as raunchy, but by the looks of things, they'll be getting there soon.

I go back up to the top. It was safer up there.

And that's when I spot Danny crouching down as he lights up a joint in the middle of the bus. At least he isn't doing it where the crowd can see him…but that's about the only positive I can find in this particular situation.

"Put that shit out!" I warn him.

"Why? The big bosses aren't on our bus."

"You're a fucking idiot," I say, shaking my head and grabbing the joint out of his hand.

"Hey!" he protests as I toss it on the ground and snuff the flame with my shoe.

"Go back to throwing alcohol at the topless women."

When I woke up this morning, I never thought those words would be leaving my mouth today…or that throwing alcohol at topless women from the top of a double decker bus would be the lesser of two evils.

I move to the opposite side of the bus and wave to the crowd. I'm pretty sure I'm the only player on either bus who's totally sober, and maybe that's where I went wrong.

I could've had a beer or two. It might've taken the edge off since now I'm chasing these dickheads around. Maybe I wouldn't care as much if I was a little drunk myself, but instead I'm thinking about Gabby and how much work she put in to pull this thing off today. I'm thinking about how upset she might be if these idiot players ruin the parade being thrown in their honor.

And I'm thinking about all the headlines that could potentially come out of this. I'm thinking it's not going to be pretty.

My brain is already scrambling with ways to fix it, and we haven't even seen the extent of the damage yet.

A community service day? That might be one solution. Something to bond us together in a wholesome environment instead of each new scandal that seems to be popping up by the minute.

I can't help but wonder what's going down on Gabby's float. It has to be calmer than this shit show.

I watch as some dude from the crowd crosses over the police barricade for our bus and storms onto it.

Fucking hell, what now?

I make my way back downstairs as I watch the rather large man push AJ off the woman he's making out with, and then I watch as AJ winds up and throws a punch at the guy.

God dammit.

Cade bounces into action first, and he goes to pull AJ away from the large man, and I move into action as well, racing toward them to help fend off the big guy along with Colton and Vince.

The parade literally lasts a half hour, and it feels like a lifetime. By the time we get off the bus, police are waiting to arrest the man who stormed the bus as well as AJ since it was fairly easy to see that he threw the first punch.

I shake my head and blow out a breath as I watch the police shove AJ into the back of the car in the player parking lot where the bus parks once the parade is over. At least it's in the player lot with no public access versus one of the public lots. That's the only saving grace here.

I yell to AJ that I'll be down soon to bail him out as I scramble to figure out who the hell to put in charge while I'm gone.

I really wish Troy was here. He never would've let this happen.

I turn to the players gathered in the parking lot. "I'm disappointed in how that went," I say, not that anybody gives a fuck. "Head back to the clubhouse. You're free to check out the stadium or fucking sober up until dinner, which will be served at five. Don't do anything stupid while I'm gone." I glance around, and I spot Rush and Danny.

Nope.

That's when Holden Thatcher, one of our pitchers signed during free agency, steps forward. "I've got this, man. I'll keep an eye on things here while you're gone."

I look to him gratefully, and I realize he may be the only guy here aside from me who didn't make a fool out of himself during that parade. "Thank you."

I hop in my truck and take off for the jail where AJ is being processed wishing this day would just fucking come to an end already.

Chapter 11
Gabby

"Hey," I answer after I see Cooper calling me. "Where are you?"

"On my way to bail out AJ Winters." His tone is filled with disgust.

"What?" I screech. "Why?" From my float, everything seemed to go off great. We were five or six floats in front of the team bus, and I couldn't see them from where I was. "What happened?"

"It was a disaster, Gabby," he says. "I'm so sorry these assholes ruined your parade."

"They ruined it?" I ask.

"Fucking Brewer and Ross were tossing alcohol out to the crowd and getting women to flash them. Somehow guys on the first floor of our bus were pulling women out of the crowd, and I guess AJ pulled the wrong woman because he was making out with her and some beast of a guy didn't like it and stormed the bus to give him a piece of his mind. AJ threw the first punch and the cops hauled them both off when we got back to the parking lot."

"Oh my God, Cooper! I didn't know any of that!" I realize there's loud panic in my voice, but this was not what I was expecting.

I thought everything went fine.

Instead…I'm going to have to figure out how to explain this to my father, who most certainly will see any news there is to see from his hospital bed where he's supposed to be recovering.

I'm on Joanie's computer, and I pull open a browser and type in a search. "Shit," I mutter when I see results already populating. I force my brain to focus. How the hell can we fix this? "I think I have an idea to mitigate the damage. When will you be back?"

"However long this takes. Hopefully before the dinner," he says. "Holden said he'd keep an eye on the boys."

"I'll take care of things here. Don't worry, okay?"

"Thanks, Gabby," he says, and his voice is filled with relief.

"I love you," I say, and he says it back before he cuts the call.

I grab Justin and race down to the clubhouse without thinking twice—without allowing myself to get nervous for what I'm about to do. I find a whole bunch of hot baseball players laughing or talking or playing poker or video games. Others are just sitting around scrolling their phones, but in general it's low-key in here. Not everyone is here since some are getting their player photos taken and others are filling out paperwork, but there are enough in here for me to get the message across.

I put my fingers between my lips and blow a loud-ass whistle the way my dad taught me when I first moved to Vegas.

The room fades into quiet slowly as the attention turns to me, and with a shaky voice, I begin a speech I haven't planned. "Hi everyone. We met upstairs, but in case you forgot, I'm Gabby…uh, I'm Troy Bodine's daughter. I have to tell you, he'd be pretty disappointed with your behavior at today's parade if he was here, and I'm going to need you to figure out how to fix what you've done."

The room remains silent.

"I think a good first step might be allowing me to film you explaining why you're excited to be here playing for the Heat. A good second step would be selecting a leader who can put something together for my father to let him know you're here thinking about him and wishing he was here as part of the welcome committee. And finally, I'll be putting together a list of community outreach events. You can swing by the marketing department to sign-up, or once you've all been set up on the Heat email system, you can sign up from there. Any questions?"

The room remains silent.

"I'm going into the weight room. There's a backdrop there where you can tell me why you're happy to be here with the Vegas Heat. I'll set up shop in there for the next hour, and then I'll be working to splice together a video to try to mitigate some of the damage you've done." I shake my head and purse my lips as I walk out of the room, and it's silent as I leave.

Still, just before the door closes behind me, I swear I hear, "Damn, that girl got some sass for such a fine little package."

I can't help a huge grin at Justin, who high-fives me.

"They aren't wrong," he says with a laugh. "You are pretty damn sassy."

"Don't forget damn fine in this little package." I toss my hair haughtily over my shoulder and head over to the weight room to set up my phone to grab some footage.

They give me exactly what I need.

I go live in the weight room for a little while, and Justin warns players as he ushers them in. Some of their kind words are caught during the live, and others will appear on the video I'll edit together and post later.

I'm excited to build a brotherhood from the ground up.

I'm excited to play for Troy Bodine.

I'm excited to be here to collect as many W's as we can.

I'm excited to live in a place with palm trees.

I'm excited to play with Cooper Noah.

I'm excited to bring the Heat to Vegas.

I'm excited to be here to launch a new legacy.

They're all wholesome after a wholly unwholesome parade, and it's the type of content I was expecting rather than the boob and beer fest we ended up with.

I record additional footage as I ask players questions about my dad, and I work on that video first when I head back to Joanie's office.

I also pull together some charity events and community service opportunities for the players on the team. I text Kaylee to see if she has any leads, and she puts me in touch with her sister-in-law, Ellie, who knows everything there is to know about local events.

Cooper makes good on his word, returning with AJ a little before dinner time, and I take that as my cue to head out. He's got it from here, and I'm freaking exhausted after a long, long day.

Besides, it's time to head to the hospital to visit my dad and face whatever wrath awaits there.

Chapter 12
Gabby

My dad was sleeping when I arrived, but Joanie was not. She kept him from seeing any of the coverage of the parade today, in part because a doctor came in to examine him right at noon, but *she* saw it.

And she was *not* impressed.

I told her I took care of it, and when I told her what I did, this time she *was* impressed.

"The players also signed a card for Dad," I say, handing over three Get Well Soon cards in an envelope along with some additional handwritten notes to my father.

I didn't read them.

I couldn't—not because they were sealed, but because it felt too personal to him and I knew that reading them would only slay me. I know how important this was to him to be there, but sometimes things happen out of our control. His body needed to slow down, and this was its way of warning my father that if he doesn't take these issues seriously, he won't be here at all.

She tears up and pulls me in for a hug.

"They were really sorry," I say. "I have a video to show him."

She nods. "I wish I could've been there today, too."

"You were there in spirit."

She offers a smile and waves me toward his room.

"One more thing before we go in," I say, and she turns back to me with eyes narrowed in my direction. "The doctor said getting a pet can be good for helping lower stress, and I think we should get Dad a dog. I can take care of it when he's not home."

She smiles broadly. "I think it's a lovely idea. I have a niece who's a veterinarian. I'm sure she can recommend the best place to get a dog, along with top trainers and caretakers when we can't be around. I wouldn't want to put the entire burden on you since, you know, you'll be traveling with the team, too." She winks at me, and my hand flies to my chest as my brows knit together.

"I'll be traveling with the team?"

She nods. "We still have to conduct interviews and blah blah blah, but you're a lock for the social media position, Gabby."

She doesn't say it, but I get the feeling I'm a lock because they think it will be good for my father if I travel with the team. Maybe it's just my own insecurities showing again, but part of me hates the idea that I'm potentially getting a job like this just because of my genetics.

"And lest you think your father has anything at all to do with this, I want you to think about what an asset you've become to the marketing department. Not just to me, but to the entire team. Your talent and your attitude are what got you here."

I'm using the team's social media accounts to mitigate the damage the new players might've caused today. I'm using social media to showcase the good in this team, to show the excitement and the optimism.

None of the other interns today were taking footage all day. None of the others were posting TikToks from the float. They were waving and throwing out candy and laughing and having fun while I was working.

I feel like I'm always working lately, and that's the kind of dedication the Heat is looking for in their next social media manager.

Maybe I *am* deserving of the position, and maybe it's time I start believing in myself.

I hope that sentiment continues to grow stronger as time marches forward.

My dad is released from the hospital a week after he entered it, and he's been resting at home, which has made it harder to have secret rendezvous with Cooper.

The Monday before Thanksgiving, my dad calls me into the family room, where he's resting on the couch with Joanie sitting on the cushion beside him.

"Can we talk?" he asks.

I nod, and I perch on the edge of the recliner nearby.

"Joanie and I were talking about what comes next for us, and with the wedding in our future and the fact that she's practically been living here anyway…well, we think it's time for her to sell her place and move in here, but we wanted to run it by you first," he says.

"By me?" I ask, my hand moving to my chest in surprise.

"Of course. You live here, too, and you deserve to have a say in it," Joanie says.

"I'd love it if you moved in here," I say with a wide grin. I'm just happy my dad has found happiness with someone who is so dedicated to caring for him. I can see how much she loves him, and it's the kind of love we all deserve.

I finally dial up Joanie's niece, Nicole the veterinarian, later that day.

"I have a client who has a litter of eight-week-old Golden Retriever puppies if you're interested. She's here at my clinic right now if you want to swing by and take a look," she offers. "They're all vaccinated and microchipped, and we've also been working on potty training and leash training. I have everything you'd need to care for the pup right here in the office."

It feels serendipitous—like I finally called her, and she has a puppy ready for me. I hop in the car and head over to the address she gave me, and I spot a little puppy play area fenced off in the middle of the clinic's lobby.

Two puppies are racing around playing with each other. Another is chasing its own tail. And a fourth is lying off to the side, apparently resting after a busy morning with the other three.

A woman walks up beside me. "Can I help you?"

"I'm Gabby," I say. "I called and spoke with Nicole a little while ago."

She gives me a broad smile. "Nice to meet you. I'm Nicole."

I shake her hand and echo how it's nice to meet her, too, and we turn our attention back to the dogs.

"The three playing are male, and the cutie resting over there is the lone female. There were eight total in the litter, and these four are all Darlene has left."

I head over toward the female. "May I?" I ask, indicating that I want to pick her up.

Nicole nods. "Go right ahead while you can. That little cutie could get all the way up to seventy pounds when she's fully grown."

I can picture Cooper and myself hiking up a mountain with a sweet seventy-pound Golden Retriever...and then I remember that this dog isn't for me.

She's a gift for my dad.

Still…I live with my dad, so I'll get the chance to fall in love with her, too. And she'll still need walks when my dad isn't home.

Okay, fine. Maybe I'm *sort of* getting the dog for me, too.

Her big brown eyes lock on mine, and she licks my chin.

"I'll take her," I say, and Nicole sets me up with Darlene so we can get the paperwork rolling.

She sets me up with all the supplies I need, from toys and food to a bed and a crate to keep her safe in the car, and the house is empty when I get back home.

I set up her bed in a corner of the family room, and I find a spot for a food bowl and water dish in the kitchen. I take her out to the yard to do her business, and I reward her with a treat when she does her thing. She snuggles onto my lap, and when the door opens a short while later, she jumps down and starts barking.

"Is that…is that a dog I'm hearing?" my dad asks when he walks in.

I giggle as the puppy runs over to him and starts running circles around his legs. He reaches down to pick her up, and she licks his chin.

"Oh my God, Gabby, she is the most adorable pup I have ever seen!" Joanie squeals.

"She's yours, Dad," I say.

He looks from the puppy back to me. "She's mine?"

"The doctor said having a pet is a great way to reduce stress, so Joanie and I thought it would be a good idea to get you a puppy," I explain.

"I love her already," he says.

"What are you going to name her?" I ask.

He glances at Joanie, and then he says, "Ruby Sue."

She bursts out laughing. It must be some inside joke between the two of them.

"Does that have some significance?" I ask.

"It's after the girl in *National Lampoon's Christmas Vacation*," Joanie says. "It was on TV last night."

I giggle. "Ruby Sue it is, then." I watch my dad with her and Joanie, and I can't help but think what an adorable little family they're creating together—a family I'm a part of.

Now if I could just get the nerve up and find the right moment to tell my dad about the next generation of this family that I'd like to create someday with Cooper, we'll be all set.

Chapter 13
Gabby

J oanie calls her realtor friend to get her house up on the
market then heads home to pack a few boxes of essentials.

Cooper helps since my dad isn't supposed to be lifting
heavy things, and we order in dinner from Desmonds. It's as we're
sitting around the dinner table that Cooper says, "My family is
coming into town for the holiday. I'd love if you all joined us for
Thanksgiving on Thursday."

My heart pounds in my chest. I love the idea of spending the
holiday with Cooper, but what I don't love as much is the idea of
doing it with my dad there. That would mean Cooper's entire
family would have to keep up the lie about our relationship in front
of my father, and that's just not fair to anyone.

Joanie glances at me first and then my dad. "I think it might be
a little much for Troy, but you should go, Gabby."

Relief rushes through me.

My dad nods. "I agree. It hasn't even been two weeks since the
draft, so I should probably stay home a bit longer. But bring me
some turkey."

"I bought a turkey," Joanie protests. "I'm cooking for you!"

My dad winks at me. "Bring me some turkey," he whispers.

We all get a laugh out of that, and I turn toward Cooper. "Count
me in. I'd love to see your family again."

He nods. "They adored you when your dad sent you to hang
with us in Chicago." He says the words carefully—as if he
purposefully chose to remind us all that my father was the one who
pushed me to go to Chicago.

"I adored them as well. I can't wait to catch up with Marissa."
I was only there a few days, and most of it was spent at the hospital,
but I felt a bond form between Marissa and me in that short time,

like if we had the chance to get to know one another in a different environment, she could become like a sister to me.

And maybe someday she *will* become like a sister to me—a sister-in-law. It's a strange thought to have as I shove another forkful of lemon chicken in my mouth beside my father who is still oblivious to everything.

"How's your brother doing, Cooper?" my dad asks.

"It's been two months since his heart attack and from what he said, he's doing great. Seems like it was a wake-up call and he's been avoiding salt ever since. Marissa tells me he hasn't backed off work much, though. Still vying for partner." He shrugs as he says it.

Joanie purses her lips and inclines her head toward my father. "Sounds like this one. You can avoid salt all you want, but the stress of the job isn't going to go away."

My dad barely refrains from rolling his eyes as he blows out a breath. "I know, I know. And I'm taking it easy as promised."

"Yeah, but for how long?" I ask pointedly.

"I'm not giving up my career because of this," he says. "It's one setback. I'm fixed now. I've got a lot of years ahead of me."

"You better," I say, reaching over and squeezing his forearm. "I just found you. I'm not losing you anytime soon."

He grabs my hand and squeezes it, and Ruby Sue breaks the tension in the room by setting a paw on top of our joined hands.

Cooper leaves after dinner, citing house preparations as his reason since his family is arriving tomorrow. He has spare bedrooms to check and grocery lists to make.

"Need any help?" I ask, and he nods.

"If you don't mind, I could definitely use some help with the meal planning for Thursday."

"It's Monday, Coop. You haven't planned your Thanksgiving dinner yet?" my dad asks.

He shrugs. "Been busy picking up all the slack at the stadium. I could use some help with putting the guest rooms together, too. I have clean sheets but none of the beds are made."

My dad narrows his eyes at Cooper, and I giggle.

"Good thing you ran into me, then. Let's head over to your place," I suggest.

We leave shortly after that, my dad none the wiser to our real intentions this evening.

Or at least *my* intentions.

He really does need help with the meal planning. "So…I have no idea how to make a turkey," he begins as we drive together over to his place. "I was thinking about those meals grocery stores and restaurants offer where you just pay per person and get everything you could ever want."

I wrinkle my nose. "Yeah, but that's no fun."

"You know how to make a turkey?" he asks.

I laugh. "Uh...no. But I have this funny little rectangle thing that I can fit in the palm of my hand that will tell me how."

He thins his lips as he gives me a look, and I laugh again.

"YouTube, baby. It has all the answers." I shrug.

"You want to *YouTube* a Thanksgiving dinner when neither of us have any idea how to cook a turkey?" he asks, total disbelief evident in his voice.

"I think it could be fun," I admit.

"Okay, so we make a turkey together. What else?"

"What are the other traditional sides?" I start numbering them off on my fingers. "Stuffing, mashed potatoes, gravy, biscuits, cranberry sauce..."

"Sweet potato casserole, green bean casserole, macaroni and cheese casserole," he adds.

I glance over at him. "You're really into casseroles."

He lifts a shoulder. "My mom's a good cook, which is why I feel like I should order in. I never learned how, and I want to impress her."

"Don't you think she'd be more impressed that her son and his girlfriend cooked for her?" I press.

"Oh!" He snaps his fingers. "And pumpkin pie."

"Right. We can totally do this. It's only like ten dishes plus the turkey." I lost count, but I'm trying to minimize how much work this is actually going to be.

"Do you know how to cook?" he asks.

I shake my head. "Nope. But you're never too old to learn." I glance over at him and study him for a beat. "Well, maybe you are."

"Hey!" he protests, and he reaches over and grabs my knee in the exact right spot that sends me into cackles.

Yeah...this is going to be fun.

Chapter 14
Cooper

She is incredible.
Truly.
In every way.

My refrigerator is filled with all the items we need to make our Thanksgiving dinner a total success, the guest bedrooms are ready for occupancy, and I'm lying back in total relaxation after she just swallowed my come, my own breath hot with the tang of her pussy.

And it's not just that we finished a round of top-notch sex a minute ago, but it's the fact that all the small tasks that I needed to accomplish before my family came to visit got done…and we had *fun* doing them.

That's part of what I've found with Gabby: fun.

My last relationship was never fun. It was a chore. It was avoidance and dread, and the more I'm able to look at it with the ability of hindsight, the more I see how wrong Stacy and I always were for each other.

With Gabby, it's light and easy. We've had our hard times, and certainly there will be even harder times ahead, but I feel so *free* when we're together—ironic since I'm not free at all but instead I'm wrapped around her finger.

She just has this way about her that's fucking addictive.

"When does their flight get in again?" she asks on a yawn. She's settled into my side, her head on the nook of my shoulder and my arm around her.

My fingers flex on her arm, and I lean up to glance at the clock. "About an hour. We have maybe twenty minutes before we need to get dressed and head out the door."

"K. I'm just gonna take a quick nap."

She's asleep maybe twelve seconds later, and I thought she was just kidding.

Moving as little as possible so as not to disturb her, I lean back so I can look at her. My view is from an odd angle—the slide of her nose, the tops of her lashes—and somehow even from here there's a simple beauty about her. It's in the way she can just be. Whatever we're doing doesn't have to be loud and flashy. Instead, she knows how to be quiet and understated, a quality the women in my previous relationships just didn't have. A quality I've fallen for in a way that terrifies me.

I let her sleep until we have to get dressed, and I spend the time studying her as the overwhelming feelings rush through my chest. I didn't know something like this could exist, and it would be absolutely perfect if we just didn't have to keep hiding.

But we do.

And the tragedy in that slices through me.

I order a car big enough to carry my entire family back to my place, and she comes with me.

On the way to the airport, she reaches over and grabs my hand in the backseat. "You're quiet."

I look over at her, one side of my mouth tipping up in a smile. "Just thinking about how much I love you."

Her eyes soften and even get a little misty, and she squeezes my hand where she holds it. "I love you, too."

It's only been two and a half months, yet it's been enough time for me to know I want forever. I want to tell her that, but how can I when we haven't even told her father?

I think about Mike's words about not telling Troy until we're about to walk down the aisle. It's not like we're going to get married before the season starts, and with Troy's recovery, actually telling him seems to keep getting pushed further and further down the road.

I squeeze her hand back. It's okay. As long as her hand is in mine, I guess we'll figure out the rest when we need to.

The flight is on time, and I spot Connor first. He's six-five, so he tends to stand out in the crowd, and his boisterous laughter announces his arrival as my family makes their way down the escalator toward baggage claim, where the two of us are standing.

Marissa holds Jacob's hand like he's still five and not nine, Ethan is talking to his dad, and my mom looks all around before her eyes land on me with Gabby by my side.

I'm semi-incognito with my baseball hat on, doing my best to blend into the crowd, but the moment my mother spots me, her face breaks out into a wide smile.

This is going to be a fun weekend.

And I'm not wrong. My mom practically runs across the airport to grab me up in a hug. Gabby's next, and everyone seems excited to be here.

"When can we hit the tables?" Connor asks as he pounds my back, and I chuckle.

"You're the one toting around two underage boys, so you tell me."

He shoots his wife a pleading look, and I can't help but laugh when she glares at him.

"We just landed, Connor!" Marissa says, total exasperation in her voice. "Give it a break. Besides, don't you think the tables will cause your blood pressure to spike?"

Connor rolls his eyes. "I'm fine. We're in Vegas, baby! You gotta let me have *some* fun while we're here!"

My mom squishes his cheeks between her fingers. "We'll have *lots* of fun. Family fun."

He huffs out a sigh that's mostly for show.

I lean into his side and tell him not very quietly, "Don't worry. We'll find some time for brotherly bonding."

He fist bumps me, and then we head toward baggage claim to grab their luggage before we hop back into the car waiting for us and travel toward home.

The car is filled with warmth and laughter. My hand clutches Gabby's, and I take a minute to sort of mentally step back and just enjoy the moment. It feels perfect—Gabby laughing and joking with my mom, the boys in awe of the huge backseat we're sharing, my brother with his arm tossed around his wife, whispering something to her as she giggles.

This weekend will be filled with these warm feelings, and it all starts now. I just can't wait to keep them going for, say...the rest of our lives.

Chapter 15
Gabby

"I'd love to see the hotels," Cheryl says as she hands me the bowl of mashed potatoes. "It's been *years* since I've been to Vegas."

I scoop a dollop onto my plate, and the gravy comes next, which I pour all over the potatoes.

I'm excited to taste everything—and not nervous like I thought I'd be.

Since Cooper's family came in last night, his mom was here to oversee the cooking. She scolded Cooper when he shooed her out of the kitchen, telling him that it was her favorite place to be. She insisted on helping, and in the process, she taught us both a thing or two—things we couldn't have learned from our YouTube tutorials, like how to cook with *love*.

Cheryl really is the best.

She's across the table from me, and Cooper's going to sit at the head of the table between us, but he's currently walking around the table pouring wine for the adults and *kid wine*—or sparking grape juice—for the kids.

"I want to go on the High Roller," Marissa says. "That big Ferris wheel thing. I think the boys would like that."

"I think they'd like the Stratosphere," Connor adds.

Marissa gives him a look of horror. "Those rides are way too much for them, dear."

"Some have age requirements, too," Cooper says. "And the High Roller and the Stratosphere aren't exactly close. It's like a four-mile walk."

"Good thing we're here through Sunday, then, right?" Connor follows his words with his boisterous laugh.

"We've got a full schedule, Connor," Marissa reminds her husband. "Turkey today, stadium tomorrow, tickets to that magic show on Saturday…"

"Right. One thing for each day? Let's pack this trip up with events," he says.

She rolls her eyes and glances at Cheryl. "He's always like this. Go go go, never take a five-minute break."

"That's how he's been since he was a little boy," Cheryl admits. "What if we went for a walk on the Strip tonight after dinner to check out some of the hotels and maybe ride the High Roller? Then tomorrow Connor can choose something else to do after the stadium tour."

"Good compromise, Ma," Connor yells from his side of the table with a giant thumbs up. He leans in toward his brother. "Gentlemen's clubs, blow, and poker, am I right?" He doesn't exactly mask his words, but I'm pretty sure his nine- and eleven-year-old sons have no idea what he's talking about.

Cooper smacks him in the back of the head, much to the delight of his nephews. "No, you're not right."

"Okay, fine. You're heading toward a new season, so no blow. See? I can compromise, too." Connor brushes off his shoulders with zero modesty.

Cooper smacks him in the back of the head again, and Jacob and Ethan both crack up. "I'll hit some tables with you, but you're on your own for the rest."

Connor rolls his eyes, but it's all good-naturedly and in good fun as Cooper slides into his chair. He reaches under the table to squeeze my knee, and I smile at him.

A warm and fuzzy feeling fills my chest as a ripple of love travels up my spine. I'm so happy to be here, so happy with Cooper, so happy with how I fit in with his family. It all just feels natural, like everything is exactly how it's supposed to be. I wish my dad and Joanie were here, too, but then the warmth I'm feeling wouldn't be there since Cooper and I would be acting once again.

I take a bite of potatoes. They're light, and they're buttery, and they're whipped to perfection.

Damn, Cheryl's a good cook, and damn, Cooper and I are fantastic sous chefs.

"Ethan, tell Uncle Coop about your baseball team," Connor tells his son as I force myself not to have an orgasm over mashed potatoes.

"You tell him," Ethan says, shoving a rather large forkful of green bean casserole into his mouth.

"His team went eleven and one," Connor says proudly. "He was a *star* on third, just like his uncle. And he hit three homers this season."

"Four," Ethan corrects him around his mouthful of food.

"Oh, right. Four." Connor holds up four fingers.

"And look at him eat!" Marissa adds with glee. "Remember when he'd take one tiny bite of everything and ask to go play his Nintendo? Now he's eating like a horse!"

"A growing horse," Cheryl says with a smile.

All the attention is on Ethan, and I can't help but glance over at Jacob. Having never grown up with a sibling, I have no idea what it's like to feel left out, but I see it there on his little face.

"Weren't you on the swim team?" I ask him. He's the younger brother, and since this family is most definitely a baseball family, I get the feeling he often feels left out.

His eyes light up at the attention. He nods as he sits up a little straighter. "I set a personal best on the freestyle at our last competition." The pride in his tone is nothing short of adorable.

"Four homers was a personal best in one season for me, too," Ethan interrupts.

"You're both doing a great job," Marissa says, nodding proudly at her boys.

The meal is a total success, and we're all so stuffed that a walk down the Strip sounds next to impossible. And that's when Cheryl says, "Okay, everyone. Shoes on. Let's head to the Strip to burn off some calories and take in the flashy Vegas sights."

She's met with a chorus of moans and groans, but eventually everyone gets up to make her happy. Forty-five minutes later, we're walking along Las Vegas Boulevard. Cooper and I each drove a carful of people and we parked in the Harrah's garage since it's close to the High Roller. As much as I want to hold Cooper's hand while we walk down the Strip, we both know we can't just in case somebody recognizes him.

So I walk and chat with Marissa and Cheryl, and Cooper walks and chats with his brother while the boys are sandwiched somewhere in between us.

Marissa and Cheryl head up to the booth to purchase tickets for the High Roller, and I hang back with Cooper. I spot Ethan as he's talking to Connor near the front of a store, but I don't see Jacob anywhere.

"Is Jacob with your mom and Marissa?" I ask Cooper.

He cranes his neck to try to get a look, and then he looks at me and shakes his head. "I don't see him." He glances over toward Connor, and then he makes his way over with me right behind him. "Where's Jacob?"

Connor looks around and checks the line where Marissa and Cheryl stand. His brows dip, and he strides over to them.

I turn around in a circle, panic starting to climb up my spine as I don't see him in the near vicinity.

There's a lot of people walking around. It would be easy for a child to get lost...or worse.

I don't let that thought form, but fear takes an icy grip onto my heart.

"Jacob?" Marissa yells, jumping out of line and looking around like I am—but in a different way. With motherly panic that her son is missing. "Jacob?"

"Let's look around and meet back here," Cooper suggests, somehow staying calm even though I feel on the verge of tears and this isn't even my kid.

"I'll retrace our steps back," I volunteer. "I'll text you if I see him."

He nods, and I take off from the way we just came while he formulates a plan with the rest of his family. I draw in deep breaths while my eyes dart everywhere looking for him.

I try to think back to the last time I saw him. I just noticed he was missing when we got into the line at the big Ferris wheel, so he can't have wandered too far off.

I duck into the souvenir shop we just came out of. He was with us when we walked in there. Maybe he stayed behind to check things out, but the store is filled with loads of junk he wouldn't really want, and I don't see him anyway.

Come on, Gabby. Think.

And that's when it hits me. I remember he was tugging his mom's arm when we passed by a candy store a block or so ago, but she was talking to Cheryl as she ignored his request to go in.

I race back to the candy store, darting in and out of people as they walk in the opposite direction as me. They're cursing at me and glaring at me and I couldn't care less as I work my mission to find the missing boy.

I throw the door open and glance wildly around, and I see the top of a little head over a bin of candy.

I walk in that direction, and sure enough, he's sitting on the floor munching on some chocolate covered raisins. I send Cooper a quick text.

Me: *Found him. Sugar Shack. He's okay.*

I slide down the bin and take a seat next to him. "Can I have one?"

He hands one over, and I chew it. "Your family is worried about you."

"I don't care."

"You don't?" I ask.

He doesn't answer right away as he chews thoughtfully on his raisin, and then he glances over at me as if his nine-year-old mind is judging whether he can talk to me about this or not.

And then he does. "Nobody ever listens to me. Nobody ever wants to do what I want to do. It's always Ethan Ethan Ethan, baseball baseball baseball. I'm sick of it, and I wanted to see what was in this store."

"I get that," I say softly. I hold out my hand for another raisin, and he hands one over.

"Aren't you going to yell at me?"

I shake my head. "It's not my job to punish you, buddy. You shouldn't have run off, and you shouldn't be eating candy you haven't paid for—"

"You're eating it," he points out.

I laugh. "I'm going to pay for it. Fill the bag, and you can pick out one other thing, okay?"

"Aren't you mad?"

I shake my head. "I'm glad you're okay. That's all that matters right now, and I'm sorry you felt like nobody was listening to you."

"Nobody *ever* listens to me."

"I'll listen," I offer. "And you know what? I didn't have a brother growing up—or a sister—so I don't know what it's like to feel what you're feeling right now. But it wasn't exactly fun having all the attention all the time, either." I wrinkle my nose.

"It wasn't?"

I shake my head. "Nobody to blame. Nobody to throw the attention to. Nowhere to hide. But you've got a lifelong friend in your brother. Only you two know what it's like to grow up with your mom and dad. You two share a bond nobody else in the world has, and that's pretty darn special, don't you think?"

He twists his lips. "I guess."

"Pick out your candy, and we'll take it up to pay," I suggest. "Then we get to go on the big Ferris wheel."

"Do we have to?" he asks.

My brows crinkle. "You don't want to?"

He shakes his head as he blanches a little. "I'm scared," he whispers.

"Then I won't go either. We'll hang out here in the candy shop." I lean in and lower my voice to a whisper. "Or even better, I saw an ice cream shop by the wheel."

His eyes grow round as he draws in a loud, excited breath. "You did?"

I smile and nod as he picks out chocolate pretzels next, and we head up toward the register just as Marissa comes bursting through the doors.

"Oh my God! Jacob Joseph Noah, you are in big trouble!" she cry-yells at him, grabbing him up into her arms like she's never going to let him go.

I bring the candy up to the register. "Add a little weight to the raisins, please. We sampled a few," I say to the cashier as I set the bags down on the counter.

He nods and rings me up while Marissa smothers her boy, and then we head back toward the wheel where the rest of our group waits for us.

"You're a hero," Cooper whispers into my ear, his voice warm and proud.

I grin, and then the rest of them head toward the wheel while Jacob and I hang back to get our ice cream sundaes, Cooper's words wrapping around me like honey the whole time.

Chapter 16
Gabby

The weekend goes far too quickly, and suddenly it's Monday and I'm back at the stadium—earlier than usual since it's the week of final exams and I don't have class this morning.

"I'm back!" Joanie says with a little too much glee as the interns gather around the table in her office. "And I'm here with your final competition for those of you still interested in the full-time social media position. Once we tally the points after this comp, we'll select our top three candidates to interview." She does a great job avoiding eye contact with me, something I appreciate considering she just told me the other day that I'm a lock for the position. It seems like the rest of this is just a formality.

"We've done a variety of challenges over the course of this competition, from profiles on our players to scavenger hunts for free tickets, and I'm so excited to see what you come up with for this final challenge. The winner will be awarded ten points since it's the final one, and just to remind you, we have a tight race for the top three," she says.

I glance over at Dylan ready to smile, and I spot him glance away from me just as our eyes meet.

My brows dip a little.

Is something wrong? Is Mia mad at me?

I haven't spoken to her in a while, and I get the sudden feeling that something is off.

But it's something I'll have to deal with later since Joanie continues on.

"For the final challenge, your goal is to come up with a pitch for a single day promotion by Wednesday. This can be a game day promo or something you put together in the off-season, but the goal is building a community and your theme is *Heat Wave*." She glances around the interns with a touch of glee. "Any questions?"

Chase looks monumentally confused. "Heat Wave?" he repeats, his brows drawn together.

Joanie nods. "Take it and run with it. Whatever that means to you."

He makes a funny face. "Okay," he says, drawing out the word, and the rest of us laugh. I can't wait to see what it means to him.

I basically lock myself in the library to work diligently on my plan for the next forty-eight hours—barring the two final exams I have to go take. Cooper texts me with encouragement, and I pop by his place for a quick kiss before heading home to call it a night. I don't want to tell him or my father what I'm working on because I want to win this on my own ideas.

And when Wednesday morning arrives, I find out where Chase's mind went when she said *Heat Wave*.

"We'll call in the *Guinness Book of World Records* during one of the hot summer months to do the biggest fan wave in a stadium ever recorded." He looks so proud of his idea, and while it's cute, and I suppose it does build community, it's not exactly a winner.

Mackenzie's pitch is about a contest where fans create artwork and posters to hang around the stadium, and Justin pitches multiple giveaways at the gate from a variety of sponsors. Chloe suggests a family fun day, and Ben's idea is to have a *bring your pet to the stadium* day. Dylan pitches a player and fam community service day, which is actually a pretty awesome idea.

I pitch last, and I'm nervous as I stand to present my idea. I feel like it's good. I feel like the hard work I put into it will shine through.

But I also feel like Mackenzie will assume I got input from my father when that couldn't be further from the truth.

"Close your eyes with me for a moment and picture this."

I glance at the other interns, and only Justin and Chloe have actually closed their eyes. Joanie's eyes are closed, too, and Zelda's and Mike's—our three judges for this competition.

"It's a Saturday," I continue, "and we're in town but don't have a game. The stadium is full of fans who bought a ticket to access a stadium tour, a pitching clinic with a Heat player, live press conferences, the chance to interact with players and coaches, bounce houses on the field, arts and crafts stations, and more. Our vendors are here selling their products and we invite others in the community to set up booths. Think spin the wheel to win, contests and games, whatever anybody wants to do to get people to their booths. We mark all the open seats still available for season tickets with their price structure and sell those out mid-season. We have a garage sale to clean out the swag closet of the previous year's items. We discount merch, or we offer special merch only available for that one day. We call it Fan Fest, and it's the Heat's way of waving to other businesses in our community as well as opening our home to our fans while promoting everything we can about our brand."

The room is silent when I finish speaking, and I wait nervously for someone to tell me it's a silly idea that will never work.

Instead, Mike starts clapping.

The general-freaking-manager of the Vegas Heat *claps* for my idea.

I draw in a deep breath, and Joanie and Zelda join him. Justin does, too, and he stands, and Chloe is next, standing beside him. Brian and Chase join in as well. Dylan seems reluctant, but eventually he joins, and Mackenzie stands but never claps.

It feels like a victory.

It feels like a win.

I keep waiting for someone to tell me what's wrong with my idea.

I keep waiting for someone to explain why it's really second best…because it seems like I've always been second best—or at least my mother has made me believe that.

Instead, Mike stands and reaches out a hand to shake mine. "I don't think we need to vote, Gabriella. This idea is outstanding, and regardless of who wins the chance to interview for the social media position, we will be implementing this fan fest idea in our inaugural season. I see it becoming an annual event, and I could not be prouder of what you've come up with here today."

Tears spring to my eyes as one of the most important people heading up this organization compliments my idea. Other teams do fan fests, too. This isn't a new idea, but it's new to the Vegas Heat, and as we establish our team and our place in this community, it'll hopefully become an exciting annual event both for locals and for tourists.

And the longer I intern here, the more I hope it's me who gets to document it all as the social media manager.

Chapter 17
Gabby

Final exams come and go, and I ace all my classes.

Our internship comes to a close with a big party at our favorite bar. Chase and Brian aren't able to return after winter break since they both have fully loaded spring semester schedules, but Chloe, Mackenzie, Dylan, Justin, and I will all be back. The StrongFitKids section at the stadium finishes construction, and it's beyond amazing.

I'm spending more and more time with my dad and Joanie and less and less time with Cooper, but text messages throughout the day let me know he's thinking about me as much as I'm thinking about him. He comes over for lunch or dinner a few times a week to fill my dad in on the latest from the Heat, but overall, my dad has been well-behaved when it comes to his recovery.

Classes are over and I'm in the thick of Christmas shopping as I try to figure out what to get for the men in my life—two men who have virtually everything.

Two men who are both intent on living life to the fullest given that they've received different but still very real warnings about how preciously short life can be.

And that's when it hits: the winter bug that seems to come for me every December. Classes are over, and my body finally has a second to relax as the front office of the Heat goes on hiatus for a couple weeks as well.

It infiltrates me and knocks me down to the point that I don't even want to get out of bed.

Mia calls me, but I don't answer.

I stay in my room since the last thing I want to do is get Joanie or my dad sick. Joanie's family comes into town to visit prior to the holidays, and my dad and Joanie stay with them in their rental place to keep away from my germs. Cooper comes over as soon as the coast is clear to take care of me.

He makes me soup and tea, and he brings me a box of Kleenex along with an assortment of cold remedies. Just seeing him makes me feel a whole lot better.

Still, the bug knocks me down for nearly an entire week. For an entire week, Cooper comes over to check on me, to feed me, and to take care of me. He takes me to the doctor, who prescribes an antibiotic, and he makes sure I take it every day. He heads home at night just in case my dad comes back, and by the time I wake up on Sunday morning—a week before Christmas—I'm feeling back to my old self again.

So much myself, in fact, that before Cooper arrives, I change my sheets and spray Lysol everywhere to clean the place up. I vow to be ready when he gets here.

While I was lying in bed sick, I did some online shopping. I pull out the racy red lingerie I grabbed for myself, and I set up the pre-lit Christmas tree I ordered in one corner of my bedroom on top of a fuzzy red rug that came in the same delivery.

I force my way into the strappy contraption held together by a bunch of ribbons tied into bows—complete with a row of festive white fur above my boobs, by the way—and position myself beneath the tree.

When Cooper walks in, he finds me under the tree, wrapped in red silk and white fur.

His jaw slackens. "Feeling better?"

I nod slowly as I run my tongue along my lower lip. "Would you like to unwrap your gift?"

He just stares at me for a few beats, and then he strides across the room and sinks down to his knees in front of me. "Fuck yes I would." He pulls at one of the ribbons near my hip holding the scrap of fabric together, and then he unties the other side as well.

His movements are slow and meticulous, and he unties the ribbons holding my top together next. Soon I'm naked under the tree, and he runs his hands along my skin, starting up on the sides of my breasts and down along my torso to my thighs. He rubs them along my inner thighs and up across my hips to my stomach, and then up between my breasts, gently trailing a pattern along my skin, carefully avoiding the places that I most need him to touch.

He does it again, this time running his hands all the way down my calves to my feet, and he takes a moment to massage my feet before working his hands back up my legs. He massages my calves, and then my thighs. It's both relaxing and infuriating as I wait for him to make his way toward the places that have been aching with need for him for the last week.

My lips want his on mine.

My breasts feel heavy as they wait for his touch, and my pussy throbs with need as he builds the tension between us.

It's been too long. Between the holiday and his traveling combined with how busy he's gotten introducing new players to town as he works to build the bond between teammates—and then me taking care of my dad and suffering through my own bout with a winter cold, we've only snuck in two quickies since right before the parade.

"I've missed you," he murmurs softly, and then he leans over me, pressing a soft kiss to my lips before trailing his mouth to my neck, and then down to my chest, between my breasts and down to my navel, along my hips and down to my thighs.

My hips buck toward him, silently begging him for any sort of friction, any sort of relief as I become desperate for his touch, and he trails the softest kisses along the inside of my thigh as butterflies seem to batter around my stomach. He moves so slowly, so deliberately, and I shiver from the anticipation. He's fully clothed and he's only just barely kissed my lips and yet somehow this is the single most erotic moment of my life.

I allow my legs to fall open to give him the access he needs as he continues kissing his way along my thigh, and then I can't help it. I grab onto the back of his head and direct him between my legs.

He dives right in, his tongue darting out to flick along my clit before he moves it down, dipping it into my pussy for a beat before moving it out and back up. He sucks on my clit, and then he reaches up to push a finger into me while he does magical things to my clit, his tongue working in time with the pressure of his finger as he thrusts it into me.

God, this feels good. *He* feels good.

I grab a fistful of the fuzzy rug beneath me, clenching it between my fingers as I feel my body start to tense up at his touch, and that's the moment he pulls back. I'm right there, right at the edge, ready to explode into the type of orgasm my body has needed for weeks, and he stops what he's doing.

I'm too needy, too desperate, too insane with hunger to even form words to ask what the fuck he's doing and why the fuck he's stopping, but just because he stops what he's doing to my vagina doesn't mean he stops entirely.

He goes back to kissing my thighs softly, and then he moves up my body toward my breasts, trailing kisses the entire way, like he's worshipping my body. My body is eager for any tiny sort of friction against his jeans, and I wrap my legs around him, my pussy wide open as I desperately try to find some relief. His mouth latches onto my breast, his magical tongue swirling around my nipple. The feeling only intensifies the ache and the desperation.

He sits up and reaches down to unbutton his jeans, and he pulls himself out, hard and heavy. I want to taste him, to feel him in my mouth, the salty sweet tang on my tongue, but I'm too desperate to suggest it. Instead, I watch as he stokes the head of his dick a few times before he lines it up with my pussy. He swipes it through a few times, and then he jerks himself off against my clit, driving me closer to the edge again, before he dips inside. He lets out a loud grunt as he holds himself steady for a beat, and then he pushes in, dropping some of his weight down on top of me as he balances on one arm and grabs my breast with the other hand.

He doesn't speed up, though, instead opting to take his time as he pulls out and pushes back in. It's slow and luxurious, and part of me forgot just how incredible it actually feels to have nothing separating our bodies as we do this. This is something sweeter than fucking yet something far beyond making love. It's some sort of communication that I've never experienced with anybody else, an intimate way for us to connect that transcends words. It fills a need and a void I didn't know resided within me, and it somehow colors the gray as he drives me closer and closer to the edge again.

This time he lets me tip over it, picking up speed as I ride him through my body's wild contractions over him. I moan through my release, my body clenching up like a tight coil as it releases with pulses and pulses of pleasure.

"Fuck, Gabby," he grunts. "Yes, baby. Come for me. Come all over my cock," he murmurs as I come. "Fuck, you feel so good. I could stay in here forever." He thrusts a little harder as my body starts to calm, and then he slows as his grunts turn to growls that tell me he's coming, too.

He finishes with a mighty roar, a sound that has quickly become my favorite thing to hear, and then his mouth finds mine.

He kisses me like I'm holding onto his last breath, and it's beautiful and slow and tender as we lose ourselves in each other.

"You didn't even take off any clothes," I say after he pulls out and starts to move off me.

He chuckles and pulls his shirt over his head.

"Hi abs," I sing, and I run my fingertips along them as he moves to settle in beside me.

"I'm glad you're feeling better," he says. "Come spend the night at my place. We can do that at least a few more times, and I'll even whip something up for lunch."

"Don't you have somewhere to be today?" I ask.

"Yeah, I do," he says with a resolute nod. "And it's wherever you are."

It's cheesy, but it does the trick. It hits me square in the heart.

"I know I've been busy, and we both know it's going to get worse once the season starts, but I want you to know that wherever I am, whatever I'm doing, I'm carrying you in my heart and my thoughts. Always."

"Right back at you," I whisper as a sudden intense emotion rolls over me. "I wish we could spend Christmas together."

"We are," he says, turning toward me brightly. "I told Troy I was bringing over Christmas dinner."

"Oh, that's so nice of you. But that's not really what I meant."

"I know what you meant," he murmurs. "And maybe next Christmas will be different. But I figure it's better than nothing, and your dad is getting stronger every day."

I nod. "He is, but I still don't think he's ready to hear about us."

"I agree with you. Maybe it'll be different as we get closer to the season starting. He'll watch us as we keep growing closer and it'll be like some natural progression. If he's there to witness it, maybe the blow won't be so hard. And someday down the road, like a long, *long* way down the road, we can admit the rest of it to him about how we really met."

"You think so?" I ask a little doubtfully.

He shrugs. "We can hope so."

If only it all went down quite that easily.

Chapter 18
Cooper

I finally came up with what I think is the perfect gift for her, and we've agreed to exchange gifts on Christmas Eve since Troy has been medically cleared to attend the huge party Victor is throwing at their club, so he and Joanie will be out for the night.

She walks in my front door a little after six, and I'm ready for her. A fire crackles in the fireplace, lights glitter on my Christmas tree, and soft instrumental Christmas tunes play in the background.

It smells delicious in here, too. I ordered in a romantic dinner for the two of us, and it's currently heating in my oven.

I can't help but think of how different this Christmas is compared to the ones I celebrated with women in the past. There were expectations and pressure. This feels...fun. It feels calm and peaceful, and rather than be nervous about my girl liking what's wrapped under the tree for her, I know with us that the real gift is just having this time alone together.

It feels like the start of a new tradition. I can see future Christmas Eves with just her and me, and maybe in the years that follow us down the road, our children as their eyes light with excitement knowing Santa is on his way, and the two of us exchanging presents after they go to bed, the only quiet moment we might get to share in the chaos of the day.

She carries a huge box in her arms, and I narrow my eyes at her when she walks in.

"Need some help with that?" I offer, and she just shakes her head and sets it under the tree. I stand and walk over to her, and I pull her in my arms. "What did you do?"

She just offers a sassy little shrug and a smile, and I laugh.

"It smells fantastic in here. What did *you* do?" she asks. She tips her chin up for a kiss.

"I turned on my oven and popped it in," I admit. "We're having crab cakes and filet with a side of mac and cheese."

"Fancy," she says, and I twirl her once before pulling her back in.

"How was your day?"

"Fine. I took Ruby Sue for a hike, and I spent some time with my dad. He told me more about his club," she admits, and I raise a brow.

"Did he tell you...everything?"

She laughs. "Not in so many words, but after the accusations my mother hurled when she was here last month, he couldn't exactly deny that he enjoys a particular lifestyle. I told him that was his business, and he told me I was welcome to visit Coax any time as long as I promised to stay on the first floor."

I wrinkle my nose at the thought. "Do you want to go?"

"It might be interesting to see it, say, during the *daytime*, but no, not really. How was your day?" She changes the subject rather abruptly, and I don't think she's totally okay with knowing these intimate details about her father's life, but it's one of those things I think she'll figure out how to compartmentalize over time.

"It was good. I went for a run, wrapped some gifts, talked to my mom..."

"How is she?"

"Great. She convinced me to come to Chicago for a couple nights next week. I wish you could come."

She pouts for a beat. "So do I, but I'm glad you get to go."

A buzzer dings in the kitchen, and I head over to pull the food out. We eat and talk, and this warm feeling of comfort and home washes over me.

I want her here with me all the time. I want her in my bed when we wake together in the morning, and I want her in my kitchen when I serve her dinner, and I want her lying across my couch as we both stare into the crackling flames of the fireplace. I want to make a life with her.

Everything is going so well. My life is damn near perfect right now except for having to hide the love of my life, and it should be the signal that a storm is brewing.

I force the thought away, instead choosing to focus on what's going well.

We laugh and bake cookies together after dinner while we toast with eggnog mixed with Fireball, which she claims tastes much better than eggnog with the more traditional brandy, and after two or three where the ratio of Fireball to eggnog seems to be getting higher, I'm buzzed enough not to care too much that the drink tastes pretty damn gross no matter what we add to it.

In fact, I want to pour Fireball eggnog on Gabby's tits and lick it off.

Now *there's* a Christmas idea for later. Way to make the holidays merry and…hot.

"More Firenog?" she slurs, and I laugh.

"Are you drunk?"

She shakes her head. "Just enjoying the Christmas spirit."

"Firenog…not Eggball?"

She makes a face. "Definitely not Eggball."

Once the cookies are in the oven, Gabby claps with excitement. "Let's open presents!"

I grin. "Let's do it. Is this the same gift you gave me last week?" I reach for her to run my fingertips up her torso, but she giggles as she bats my hand away.

"If you're a good boy, maybe we'll find time for that later."

"You can come sit on Santa's lap," I say with an exaggerated wink. "Ho ho ho."

She rolls her eyes as she makes her way over toward the tree, and I can't help that feeling as it washes over me once again.

God, I love her. It's so strong, so pure. So unlike anything I've ever felt before.

She sits on her knees by the tree and reaches for the big box, and I shake my head.

"You first," I say, and I sit close to her and hand her a small box.

She narrows her eyes at me, and then she rips the paper off the box with all the glee of a small child. She pulls out a jewelry box and opens it, and she looks up at me when she sees what's inside.

I decide not to mansplain the gift and opt instead to carefully watch her reaction as she pulls out the necklace with two simple charms on it—a silver outline of an ace and a jack of hearts, both glittering with diamonds.

"This is so sweet," she says softly. "So meaningful since we met at a blackjack table on my twenty-first birthday, and these two cards add up to twenty-one—the number you wear on the field."

"I wanted to give you something with my number on it, but I didn't want that to be what tipped off the people we're trying to keep this from," I say.

She pulls it out of the box and holds it out to me. She turns around, and I clasp it on her. She turns back toward me and sets her hand over it. "I'll wear it always." She leans forward for a quick kiss, and I grab her head and hold it there for a beat, never wanting to let her go. "Now you open one."

"The big one?"

"Sure," she says, and she seems nearly giddy.

I tear the paper off the box in a similar way to how she did it, and then I rip open the box.

Inside I find a huge gift basket filled to the brim with Slim Jims. I laugh as I lift it out of the box, and she giggles along with me.

"This is absolutely perfect," I say. There must be a hundred meat sticks in there, and it should satisfy my anxiety over running low on my favorite snack for at least a month or two. "I love it, and I love you." I kiss her again, and I'm about to push her onto her back and give her a real gift when she pulls back, panting a little.

"I have another one for you."

"I have another one for you, too," I say. I'm panting a little myself as I hand her the next box, and then I gulp down some more Firenog.

She tears this one open, too, and she stares at the random numbers printed in fancy font in the framed black and white photograph. "Thirty-six point eleven sixty-two degrees north, one-fifteen point seventeen forty-five west?" she asks.

"The coordinates for the place where I first fell in love with you."

She brushes away a tear. "This is incredible, Cooper. The most thoughtful gift anyone has ever given me."

"Get ready for a lifetime of them."

She pounces on top of me, and I laugh as I fall back to the ground with her body on top of mine...just where I wanted it. She presses her lips to mine, and the kiss turns pretty intense before she pushes herself up, balancing with her palms flat on my chest.

"You have one more gift to open, and I know we're sitting right next to a fire and we're creating some of our own, but do you smell smoke?"

I grab onto her back and sit up, sniffing the air, and she laughs at me.

And that's when I turn toward the kitchen. "Oh shit! The cookies!"

She leaps off me and we both run toward the oven. We catch them in time before they set off the smoke alarm, but they're definitely a little…crispier than I prefer my chocolate chippers to be.

She giggles as we inspect the cookies to determine whether there's anything edible, and then we throw more dough onto another pan and this time, I set a timer rather than relying on thinking we'll actually watch the clock.

We head back to the tree, and she hands me my final gift, which happens to be in an envelope. I bend it a little to try to guess what's inside. "Did you get me a…gift card?"

She giggles. "Yes. I bought the man with a ginormous bank account a gift card because I couldn't think of anything else." She rolls her eyes with mock exasperation, and I laugh. "Just open it! No guessing!"

I gently slide my finger along the sealed paper and slide out the card inside, and attached to it is a sort of metal photo card.

It's the first picture we ever took together, a selfie from the room at Caesar's Palace. We didn't know the true identity of each other back then. She had no idea I played baseball or that I was moving to Vegas to play for her father. I had no idea that she was the daughter of one of my closest friends.

It was easy back then even though at the time, it felt impossible. We'd just met, and we'd both somehow fallen in love in one weekend. It didn't matter that we were from different worlds—nearly even from different generations. What mattered was how we felt, and that remains true to this day.

"It's small enough to slide into your wallet so you can carry us with you wherever you are, and I figure if it's tucked in there real good, nobody will ever see it," she says a little nervously.

"I love it," I whisper, and then I flip it over where I find a personalized note engraved onto the back in Gabby's handwriting.

To my Captain. I love you always. Forever Your Sunshine

I chuckle at her words. "So we're settled on Captain Orgasm, then, as my nickname?"

She dissolves into giggles, which then turns into more kissing, which is only interrupted once again by the damn cookies.

But at least this time, we salvage them in time to be able to eat them with another round of Firenog.

Chapter 19
Gabby

I told my dad I was hanging with Mia to ring in the new year, but instead I rang it in wrapped in Cooper's warm embrace in front of his fireplace.

I've spent more and more time at his place lately as we soak in every moment we can together, but with the start of the new semester for me also comes additional responsibilities for Cooper at the stadium. In his words, it all starts January one.

He's not an assistant coach, but as the team leader, he's there mentoring players as much as he can be. He's on the field practicing, working out, or talking players through different issues both related to the game and not. My dad's time there has been limited as he slowly starts building his strength back, and Joanie and I—along with Ruby Sue—have spent a lot of time making sure his environment is as stress-free as possible.

And I've gotten busier, too. As we ramp up toward the season, I've been tasked with social media posting. Zelda is officially on maternity leave, and I've been tapped as her temporary replacement. Joanie put everyone in different departments this semester—Justin has been working more with the business department, Mackenzie has been working in operations (thankfully since it's on the opposite side of the office from my department), Dylan has been in finance, and Chloe has been focusing on human resources, so I rarely see the other interns as I go about my day gathering any sort of news worthy of a social media post.

And I freaking *love* my job.

I have access to every square inch of the stadium, and I take pictures and videos all day of the players and the staff to give fans an inside look at what we're doing to prepare for our inaugural season.

Our social presence is growing, and Joanie credits me with that growth.

I couldn't be prouder of the work I've done, and from everything I've heard, spring training tickets are completely sold out, and so are the home games for the entire months of April and May.

The feeling of excitement only gets stronger every morning when I rip the page off my daily calendar.

But a feeling of fear sneaks in, too.

At the end of February, the entire team will take off for Phoenix, where they'll stay for an entire month for spring training games.

I'm not going.

It's not that I don't *want* to go, but I still have that one class I need to attend each week, and since my dad is still technically recovering, Joanie has decided to go. Any guesses who she decided to leave in charge of the marketing department while she's gone?

By now it's public knowledge that she and my dad are engaged, especially after she stayed by his side the entire time he was in the hospital. And while there are probably people more qualified to run the marketing department than me, I'm the one she most trusts with her office.

I couldn't say no. Not when I want to be hired on for the social media position.

So I'll be stuck here in Vegas while Cooper is in Phoenix for a whole month.

It's a few days before Valentine's Day when Cooper tells me he wants to take me somewhere special. We drive until we hit Red Rock Canyon, and then he takes us through the park to nearly the exact same spot we parked when I took him here to show him a side of Vegas he'd never seen before.

He rolls out a mattress pad in the bed of his truck and produces a basket filled with goodies from his backseat—including a few blankets, which are quite needed in the chilly desert air.

"What's all this for?" I ask once we're settled in, our fingers linked together beneath a blanket as we gaze up at the stars.

"Do you know what today is?" he asks.

My brows knit together. "February eleventh?"

He nods and chuckles, and then he turns toward me. "We first met six months ago today. It's our anniversary. I've spent half a year loving you, and I can't wait to spend the rest of my life doing it."

It's hard to believe the last time we were here was six months ago.

Six months of Gabby and Cooper. The best six months of my life.

But also six months of hiding. Six months of fear that someone will find out, or that someone who already knows will spill the beans. Six months of worrying how my dad will take the news when we'll inevitably have to tell him. We're not screwing around anymore. Six months marks a fairly decent amount of time, and there's no end in sight for either one of us.

"Aww Cooper," I sing, tears rushing to fill my eyes. I didn't expect *him* to be the sentimental one in this relationship. "That's so beautiful."

"I mean it, Sunshine. You have become the literal center of my universe. There's no one else in the world I'd spend six months under the radar with. There's no one else I want to wake up next to and fall asleep holding. There's no one else I think about all day every day."

I lean my head toward his, and he rests his forehead against mine for a beat as he draws in a deep breath.

"I think it's time we tell your dad. He's better, and he's stronger, and I'm so goddamn tired of hiding the best thing that's ever happened to me."

A shudder races through me at the thought of actually telling him. We've gotten so good at keeping this just between the two of us that I'm almost scared what it'll mean to go public.

It's not just telling my father.

We'll be opening ourselves up to public scrutiny, to comments about the difference in our ages, to judgment from people who know nothing about us. And that's sort of terrifying.

But knowing I'll be doing it with his hand in mine means we'll get through it. We've built a strong foundation over the last six months.

"I think you're right," I finally agree. "It's time."

He kisses me softly, and it quickly turns urgent and passionate as our kisses always seem to. It hasn't worn off over the last six months. If anything, the flame has only grown brighter.

I just hope that the flame continues to burn once we allow others who have the potential to smother it in.

Chapter 20
Cooper

We both agreed we should tell him, but we didn't agree on *when*.

It's still hanging in the air around us as we celebrate our first Valentine's Day together—mostly naked and a little drunk on wine and each other.

Part of the problem is that we've all gotten busy. Gabby and I sneak in moments when we can, and it's often when Troy is busy with player management, when he's working with Mike, or when he's at Joanie's place or his club.

When we're not sneaking in moments, I'm usually working, and often with Troy—but it's also when Gabby is either working or at class. Over the last few weeks, it's become pretty rare for the three of us to be in the room at the same time with nothing else going on where we could have this sort of huge conversation.

And so Gabby and I stay comfortably in the zone where we've resided for six months.

I want to tell him before we head to Phoenix. I want to get it off my chest before the real game play begins. I want to go into the season with a clear conscience, with nothing standing between my manager-slash-close friend and me, and I want to be able to call my girlfriend without worrying her father is going to catch us.

It's been six months. We've managed to keep it from him this long, but once the season begins and she's traveling with the team, I just don't know how we'll continue to keep it up. And even if we could, I'm not sure it would matter. I don't *want* to keep it up anymore.

And now even my friends who know are starting to harp on me.

"When are you planning to tell Troy?" Danny asks when it's just the two of us at the bar on a Wednesday night. We're a few days out from leaving for Phoenix, and Gabby's working late again while I'm working on...*player relations*—also known as drinking beer at a bar with some teammates before we wind up at someone's place for a few hands of poker.

I sigh, and then I chug down half my beer.

"That soon?" he teases, and I shake my head.

"I don't know, man. We talked and we agreed we should tell him soon, but things are just...out of control right now. I'm here with you, she's working late. Tomorrow I'm at the stadium all day and then I'm interviewing on a couple different podcasts, and she's got a paper due that she has to work on tomorrow night. Troy will be at a charity event the next night. We just can't seem to find a good time to do it."

"Or you're not actively searching for one. Isn't it easier not knowing his reaction versus getting a bad one?" he asks.

It's sage advice from the idiot who was shotgunning beers the morning of the parade, but he's got a point.

I don't admit to that, though, and I really don't have to since he opens his mouth again.

"Or, you know, cut it off and find a different pair of legs to slide between every night." He wiggles his eyebrows, and I roll my eyes.

He's younger than me, and he doesn't get it yet. He hasn't had that pull to want a wife and kids and love. I've been where he is, and there's nothing satisfying or fulfilling in sleeping with a different woman every night. It's fun for a while, but it ends up leaving a giant void of loneliness. I'm sure it's just down the road for him. It'll hit him when he's least expecting it.

Rush slides back into the booth and Nick follows a moment later, cutting our conversation short. The rest of the night, though, my brain focuses on what Danny said.

While I deal out the cards once we're at Rush's mansion, I can't help but wonder what if we *do* get a bad reaction? What's the worst thing Troy's going to do?

I keep circling back to that as I push chips out onto the table and lose my ass since I'm totally unfocused.

I'm usually a fairly optimistic guy, but I force myself to go down the road of the worst possible scenario.

Let's say he gets mad about it. Maybe I lose a friend. Am I prepared for that?

This is the guy who lured me to Vegas with a ninety-million-dollar payday, and I've been betraying him for six months. How the hell do I *think* he's going to react to that?

How would *I* react to that?

Not well, but I'd like to think we're all adults here. He'll come around eventually…right?

It's not like he's going to make trouble for me on the field after convincing me to come play for him. He's a professional first, and he wants the Heat to win. Whatever happens, it won't affect our professional relationship.

It's another lie I tell myself as I go all in against Nick when I'm holding shit in my hands.

I lose a hefty sum of money at the table since we're gambling high stakes tonight all because my mind is wandering to these scenarios where I tell myself everything is going to be fine.

I even lie to myself when I text with Ben Olson the next day. His season is over, and he and Kaylee are in Montana with their girls for the next month.

Ben: *You doing okay in Vegas without us there?*

Me: *Did your wife put you up to texting me?*

Ben: *Yes.*

I laugh at his honesty.

Ben: *I mean no. I'm genuinely checking up on you.*

Me: *Did she tell you to say that, too?*

Ben: *Yes.*

Me: *I'm fine. Trying to figure out the best time to tell her dad.*

Ben: *I don't know if there's ever a GOOD time for that convo. Rip off the bandage, man.*

He makes a good point. There won't ever be a good time for it, and the sooner we get it over with now that we've decided to tell him, the better.

Too bad I don't realize I should have stuck with the lies until it's far, far too late.

Chapter 21
Gabby

I decide to swing by Mia's apartment after work, and when she answers, she looks less than delighted to see me. She barely grunts out a hello, but she opens the door a little wider anyway. Dylan isn't sprawled on the couch, so this feels like a good time to talk.

"Is everything okay?" I ask.

She folds her arms over her chest. "Not really."

"What's wrong? Are you mad at me?"

"You mean aside from ignoring my calls and texts for weeks in favor of your boyfriend?" she demands.

I'm still standing in the doorway as she hurls that particular accusation at me. "Are you serious right now?"

She raises both brows pointedly.

I blow out a breath. "Mia, you've been so wrapped up in Dylan that you haven't had time for me, either."

"Don't you dare bring up Dylan," she hisses.

"Why can't I talk about Dylan?"

She purses her lips for a beat before she plows forward with it. "What you're doing to him, to *all* the interns…it's so, so unfair."

I feel sucker punched, and I actually take a step back at her words. "What I'm doing to him?" I repeat. "What, exactly, has he said I'm doing?"

"You've got connections the others don't have, and you're going to get that position because of who you're related to when you don't even care about baseball. You don't deserve it."

"Excuse me?" I say, my hand moving to my chest defensively. "I have worked my ass off to try for the position. And I do care about baseball. A lot."

"More than our friendship," she mutters.

My brows pinch together. "Are you kidding me? We've all been busy! You've got your own internship, too, and you're always with Dylan—"

She cuts me off. "I already told you to keep his name out of your mouth. You should take your name out of contention for that position. Give someone else a chance instead of getting it because you're related to the manager and you're fucking a player."

Tears pinch behind my eyes. I can't believe she just said that to me, and I have no idea what Dylan has been coming home to tell her, but there's no way it's the truth.

I've worked really fucking hard to get to where I am. Do I have connections? Absolutely. Have I used them?

Not really.

Yet her words press on every insecurity I have. She confirms that I'm not good enough—not deserving enough—and it causes my chest to feel a little hollow.

It also makes me feel like my friendship with her has run its course. We've been friends a long time, and we've gotten into fights before, but we always find our way back.

This, though? I'm not sure we can come back from this one.

"Wow," I murmur. "Great knowing what you really think."

I spin on my heel and head back out the front door that we never closed behind us, and I rush down to my car. A text comes through just as I draw in a shaky breath in my driver's seat.

Captain: *Where are you?*

I'm looking blindly through tears as I read it.

Me: *Just leaving Mia's. You?*

Captain: *Just got home. Do you have time to come over?*

Me: *On my way.*

I decide to call Justin on my way to Cooper's as a distraction from what just went down.

"Hey girl hey," he answers.

"Hey boy hey. What's going on?" I ask.

"Nothing. Just waiting for Brian to finish dinner with his parents before he comes over."

"Do his parents know about you two?"

"His do. Mine still don't," he admits.

"Are you ever going to tell them?"

He clears his throat rather pointedly. "Are you ever going to tell your dad about you and Cooper?"

I blow out a breath. "Touché. But the answer is yes. We agreed to tell him."

"You did? When?"

"We don't have a *when*. I guess I'm just…"

"Scared?" he guesses.

"Well, yeah."

"Of what?"

I'm quiet a beat while I try to put it into words. "I spent the majority of my life thinking he didn't want me thanks to what my mother told me. What if he doesn't want me after he finds out I've been sneaking around with Cooper for the last six months?"

"Oh, honey," he says softly. "He's your father. He will *always* want you."

"And so will your parents."

"You don't know Dean and Laura Larson the way I do," he says. "They're very conservative, and I hear the things they say when they think I'm not listening. I know they love me, but they will *never* understand me."

"That's only true if you don't give them the chance to understand," I point out.

"We're a couple of hot messes, aren't we?" He chuckles, but the truth is that none of this is very funny at all.

"I think we're both well within our rights to be scared about telling the truth, however different those truths may be." I brake for a red light, and my heart breaks a little for my friend as I try to push what just happened with Mia out of my mind.

"They're not that different. Neither of us thinks our parents will approve of the man we've fallen in love with. The root of that might be different, and the results, and the reasons and reactions…but the fact remains that we can't choose who we've fallen for."

"Love?" I shriek. "You love Brian?"

"Dude, have you been paying any attention at all? We've been together almost as long as you and Cooper have!"

I can't help but feel a little shocked at that, but I guess it's true. "I haven't been a very good friend lately," I say. "I'm sorry. I've been so caught up in my own problems and work and school that I haven't really looked around me much lately." Is that true of my relationship with Mia, too? I don't think so. I think I am genuinely upset with the way she chose Dylan over me just now. On the other side of the coin, Justin has been nothing but supportive.

"You're happy, babe. That's all I care about. And I'm happy, too. And if I have to keep that happiness a secret anywhere from a little while until forever…then so be it." His voice carries some dejection to it.

"It won't be forever…for either of us. You'll tell them when your timing is right, and so will I. I can't sit here and tell you everything will be okay for you and not believe it for myself, too." And it's the first time I really try to believe in those words.

I've spent my entire life trying to be perfect, and it still wasn't good enough for my mother.

But my father isn't the man she painted him to be my entire life.

So now I just need to get past those fears—not of just admitting to him that Cooper and I are in love but admitting that we've been lying to him for six months now.

It'll be okay.

It has to be.

Because I'm not ready to face losing either of the two most important men in my life, and I'm also not willing to make a choice between them.

I just hope I'm not forced to.

Chapter 22
Cooper

She's on her way over when my phone rings, and I see that it's Troy calling.

Maybe I can tell him to come here, too, and we can just get this over with already.

"Hey man, what's going on?" I answer.

"I have some news. Are you sitting down?" he asks.

Oh, shit. What the hell is going on now? "I am, in fact, sitting."

"Are you free tonight and tomorrow evening for best man duties?" he asks.

"Best man duties?" I repeat.

"Joanie and I booked a chapel at the Bellagio tomorrow night. It's going to be small and intimate. Just a few close friends and family, those who can keep quiet since we'd like to do this under the radar and before we leave on Sunday. And if you're available tonight, I'm throwing my own bachelor party."

"Whoa," I murmur. "Yeah, man. I mean—of course. I'll be there. Wherever you need me, whatever you need me to do." Shit. I was hoping to soak in a few Gabby hours, but it looks like that might be out.

"Great. I'll text you everything you need to know. The party tonight will be at Coax starting at ten, sort of a bachelor party slash going away party since it'll be a while before I'm able to get back there. I'll send a car so you don't have to worry about driving."

Coax.

His club.

The club where sex happens on the third floor, strippers strip on the second, and business takes place on the first.

It's all secretive and exclusive, so it's not like the paparazzi is going to see me walking in and it'll be splashed all over the tabloids tomorrow. Still, I feel uncomfortable going there as I assume the things that happen on the third level with my girlfriend's father and his fiancée…and whoever else they invite into their circle.

I glance at the clock. The timing gives me a couple hours to spend with Gabby, but if he's calling me to be at his bachelor party, I have a fairly good inclination that she'll be needed at the bachelorette party as well.

Unless Joanie chooses Coax for her party, too. I doubt Gabby will be invited in that case.

When she shows up a few minutes later at my door, there's a look of determination on her face.

"Let's call him right now. Let's just get this over with," she says, her jaw clenched.

"Whoa," I say for the second time in the last ten minutes. "What's got you all fired up?"

"I just got into a huge fight with Mia followed by a great conversation with Justin, and I realized as I'm sitting there telling him to admit to his parents that he's dating Brian that I'm a total hypocrite! I can't try to convince him to do something I'm not doing myself. We said we were going to do it, so let's just freaking do it." She pulls her phone out of her pocket as if she's about to pull up her father's number, and I grab her wrist.

"Hold on. Have you spoken with your father tonight?" I ask.

Her brows knit together. "No. Why?"

"Well, tonight might not be the best time for our confession."

"Why not?" The crease between her brows deepens.

I blow out a breath. "He and Joanie are getting married tomorrow. They want to do it before we leave for spring training."

Her jaw slackens. "Are you fucking kidding me?"

I grab her into my arms, and I shake my head. "Tonight's the bachelor party, and I assume Joanie will be calling you shortly to attend the bachelorette party."

She touches her forehead. "Jeez, this is a nightmare. So when are we going to tell him? We pushed it and pushed it, and now it's too late and there's no time to talk before you all leave for the next month, and then you'll get back and it'll be games games games and you'll be on the road and I'll never see you except when I'm able to travel with the team and—"

I cut her off by pressing my lips to hers.

"—and this is not how I pictured this all going down," she finishes.

"I know," I say softly, going for a soothing tone. "I know. We will figure it out, but I don't think the night before his wedding or his wedding day are a good idea. Maybe Sunday morning before we go?"

She lifts a shoulder. "Maybe." She looks a little hopeless. "Or maybe we just never tell him and keep this a secret forever."

"It won't be forever." My tone is resolute, and she just looks like she doesn't believe me. I lean and rest my forehead against hers. "It can't be forever. Someone's going to have to walk you down the aisle toward me someday, and it better be him."

She closes her eyes and draws in a deep breath, and then she pulls back. "You really mean that?"

"Of course I do, Gabby. What we're building here is meant to last."

Her phone starts ringing, and she sighs. "That's Joanie's ring tone."

"You better pick that up then." I drop my arms from around her.

She slides her phone out of her pocket. "Hey Joanie." I watch her as she paces around a little. "Oh, hey, Dad."

I take it they're together as they share the news with Gabby.

"Yeah, I can be there in a few minutes. Is anything wrong?"

I watch as she puts on her actress shoes, going for what sounds like a natural question in this situation. "Okay, I'll be right over." She hangs up and looks up at me. "They want to talk to me in person. And I have to pretend I don't know they're getting married and throwing parties for themselves tonight."

I grab her hand and squeeze it. I wish I had the right words for this situation, but there aren't any. Sorry you have to go lie to your father some more just doesn't seem right. Instead, I simply grab onto her and hold her for a few beats.

"I better go," she says against my chest.

"I know," I murmur down into her hair. I breathe her in, and then I let her go.

She tips her chin up for a kiss. "Good luck tonight," she says.

"Same to you."

And then she turns out the door she just came through a few minutes ago as I force thoughts of what I wanted to happen tonight with her from my mind and instead focus on getting ready for a night out ahead of my best friend's wedding tomorrow.

Chapter 23
Gabby

"We decided to get married before we leave for spring training. The wedding is tomorrow," my dad announces as if I don't already know.

I force my jaw to drop open. "What?" I gasp dramatically.

"Life's too short to wait," my dad says, looking lovingly at his future bride.

Life's too short to wait. You'd think maybe by this point *I* might've picked up on that lesson myself considering everyone around me is getting pounded with it, but here we are.

Another opportunity to tell him *poof!* Gone.

"Congratulations!" I say, hugging both of them. "This is so exciting! What do you need me to do?"

"Do you have a black dress?" Joanie asks.

I nod. "It's a staple in any woman's wardrobe, am I right?"

She laughs. "You're absolutely right. Wear it with black heels tomorrow. That's all I need you to do."

"But I'm your maid of honor! Surely you have other duties for me!"

"I do. I've decided to have a low-key bachelorette evening with a few of my closest friends, so we're just going to do dinner at Desmonds. I'd love for you to be there," she says.

"I would love to," I lie. In truth, I'd rather be curled up under a blanket watching Netflix with Cooper in front of his fireplace with my cozy socks on, or, you know, walking through hot lava rather than listening to Joanie and her girlfriends discuss whatever it is people discuss the night before they get married, but I guess that's not in the cards tonight.

"I have my own party to attend," my dad says, standing and planting a kiss on Joanie's lips. "You ladies have a lovely time at dinner."

"I'll see you after," Joanie says.

My dad nods once, and he raises a brow. "Room three-oh-eight, say…eleven?"

She offers a sly smile. "Three-oh-nine at eleven."

Oh God. I don't even want to know what they're talking about, but my stomach turns over at the thought of the *three* being the *third* floor at my dad's club. And the eight or nine…is that, like, in front of other people versus behind closed doors?

My stomach twists back at that new thought, and I push it away.

"Well, I'm going to go freshen up before we head out to dinner," I announce, my voice a little louder than I intend for it to be, but something's got to break up the weird sexual energy in here. I bolt out of the room, change my clothes, fix my face, and chug some water because whatever twists they just made my stomach do have *not* straightened out yet.

I drive separately from Joanie since she's heading to dear ol' Dad's club afterward, and we pull into the parking lot at the same time.

Is this weird?

Absolutely.

But I'm doing it for my dad. I'm happy he's happy, and I've grown close to Joanie over the last couple months.

A small group of women waits in a private room for us, and I'd peg them all to be in their early-to-mid-thirties like Joanie. And like Joanie, they're all gorgeous, blonde, and probably members of the same club she belongs to. She introduces them as Jade, Raven, and Amber, and I can't help but wonder if she met them at the club or if she knew them before.

"This is Gabby…Troy's daughter," Joanie says pointedly as she sets a hand on my shoulder, introducing me in a way that tells them not to talk about the club in my presence.

Maybe it's just my imagination.

We sit, we look at the menu, and the ladies all order wine…except for me. My stomach is still in knots, and I'm not really in the mood to drink. Besides, I drove here and need to drive home afterward, so I decide to pass on the booze.

We chat a bit after we order, and I learn Jade and Raven are both dancers in shows on the Strip while Amber is a back-up singer for a well-known band who has a residency here in Vegas.

So all three of them might be considered local celebrities, which makes me lean even harder into the idea that she knows them from the club.

"Did you hear about Brandi?" Jade says as she leans in toward Joanie. I'm half-listening to Amber and Raven as they talk about how the crowds have dwindled since Christmas at their shows, but Vegas is pretty much always packed and full of action. I pretend like I'm still listening as Amber talks about the lead singer's antics in the band she sings with, but my attention is really on Jade and the way she's angling her body so her conversation with Joanie is more private.

Who's Brandi?

"No," Joanie says, lowering her voice but not so low that I can't hear her. I feel her eyes on me, but she must be satisfied that I'm paying attention to Amber because she turns back to Jade. "Ever since Victor booted her, we lost touch. What's going on?"

"She's *pissed* that she got kicked out, and she's threatening to expose everything."

I glance up to see Joanie's eyes grow wide. "Like…*everything* everything?"

Jade nods. "Ev-er-y-thing."

"Whoa. We need to stop her." Joanie sounds nervous, but I don't look over at her to see if she actually is.

"Victor's on it. He didn't want to burden Troy with it, but I also thought maybe you could reach out and talk some sense into her."

"I mean, legally if she breaks the NDA, Victor will definitely press charges," Joanie points out.

"Yeah, but what's really the consequence for a broken NDA? A lawsuit for breach of contract? The courts have plenty of other cases they're dealing with. They won't give a fuck about a silly girl outing an exclusive club," Jade says.

"But Troy will. Victor and James will. *I* will," Joanie says.

"We *all* will have to deal with it if she says something to the media. That's why I thought maybe you could stop her," Jade says.

"I haven't spoken to her in months." Joanie picks up her glass of wine. "God, it's probably been close to a year since she was kicked out."

I wonder what this Brandi girl did to get kicked out, but not enough to admit I've been eavesdropping.

I glance up at Amber and see that she and Raven are both looking at me as if they're waiting for me to say something. "I'm sorry," I say, shaking my head. "What?"

"I asked if you've been to the show," Amber says.

"Oh, no, I haven't. Not yet." I offer a smile. The band she sings with isn't really my jam, but I'm not going to admit that to her.

And that's that. They ask me more questions about the shows I *have* seen, and I admit I haven't seen any, and they spend the rest of the meal trying to convince me to come to their shows when I actually didn't move to Vegas for the world class entertainment.

Our meals come, and we all enjoy them, but I feel a little out of place here. I realize I'm Joanie's maid of honor, but surely she wants to talk about things with these other women that she can't talk about in the presence of her future stepdaughter, so I excuse myself after the meal to head home.

Joanie gives me a big hug and thanks me for coming, and I tell everyone I'll see them tomorrow night.

I head home, my stomach still a little twisted up as I try to get some rest ahead of tomorrow.

Still, I can't help feeling an ominous sense of gloom as I toss and turn. This Brandi woman sounds like she could cause a lot of trouble for my father, and we're still trying to keep things relatively stress-free for him as he continues to recover and heads into a very stressful season at his job.

It's a huge part of the reason why we haven't confessed our love story to him just yet...and I just wish I could protect him forever. But as it turns out, I can't.

Chapter 24
Cooper

This really isn't my scene, but I've drank enough that I'm starting not to care.

I've spent the night on the first floor, though I did venture up to floor two for a bit, which is the floor the gentleman's club is located since it's my best friend's bachelor party and the strippers really put on a show for him.

I declined the lap dances, and Troy wanted to know why.

I told him I was seeing somebody, and then I headed back to the first floor, grabbed some more whiskey, and decided to go out front to call the car to come take me home.

And that's where I am now, waiting to leave just as Joanie pulls up in a car carrying a few other women. Gabby is noticeably absent.

As she walks by me, she leans in while the other women step inside the front door. "Gabby went home. She seemed quiet. You might want to check on her."

"Thanks," I murmur, and just as Joanie turns to head into the club to find her future husband and probably take him up to the third floor where they have some very public sex for the last time as single people, another car pulls up and a woman practically jumps out of the backseat as she stalks up the sidewalk toward Joanie.

"Brandi," Joanie says, clearly surprised to see her here.

"A bachelorette party and I'm not even invited?" she demands.

I hang back as a witness to whatever's coming next, and Joanie glances at me. That little glance tells me everything I need to know. Whoever this Brandi woman is…she shouldn't be here.

"Honey, we haven't spoken in nearly a year," Joanie says quietly. "You're not allowed to be here."

"You could've invited me to dinner. Hell, you could've invited me to the wedding. Instead you keep it a secret, and after all we shared." She shakes her head in disgust.

"I'm sorry," Joanie says gently. "People grow apart as life changes. I don't know what else to say, but I'm here to see Troy and he's waiting for me."

"Remember what we used to get up to on the third floor with Troy, when we'd both be waiting for him? How the tables have turned."

Joanie blows out a breath, clearly perturbed by this woman's presence. I'm debating whether to take a step forward and get involved or just leave it be, and that's when the door bursts open and Troy comes barreling through it.

"Get the fuck out of here," he snarls, and Jesus this can't be good for his heart. "You were told in no uncertain terms that your membership was revoked and you were not welcome here. So kindly leave. Now."

"Troy, honey, it's okay," Joanie says. "Look at me." He finally turns to look at her, and she moves in toward his chest, taking his face between her palms as her body aligns to the front of his. "It's fine. She's leaving, and we're going upstairs." She presses a kiss to his lips, but he doesn't budge as he stares down the woman who does not look the least bit intimidated by him.

"If you breathe a word to a soul, I will take everything away from you so goddamn fast your head will spin." With the threat issued, he grabs onto Joanie's waist then strides back inside without waiting for her response.

I wonder how many other people he's had to threaten—and not just him, but Victor and James, the other owners of this club, too. People sign nondisclosure agreements, but every time he invites new people into this club, he's taking a risk that the word will get out.

It's meant to be private. Secret. Exclusive.

It's meant to be a place where people of means can come for a good time, whatever that means to them. It's a place to indulge in many different ways. It's out of the prying eyes of the public and the media.

But you can't keep the snakes out. Where people like us gather, crowds will eventually follow.

Word will eventually get out, whether it's Brandi or somebody else. And I don't want to be a part of the fallout. I don't want to be associated with this place even though my manager certainly will be. It'll be his issue to deal with.

I decide to have the car take me right to Gabby's since Troy is otherwise occupied, and I don't text to let her know I'm coming. Instead, I get out of the car and hope she's home since the car speeds away as I ring the doorbell.

It takes a minute before she opens it, and she stands in front of me with a freshly scrubbed face in sweatpants and a baggy Vegas Heat sweatshirt, her hair pulled back out of her face. She looks like she's ready for bed—or like maybe she just rolled out of it when she saw it was me at the door.

"What are you doing here?" she asks, opening the door wider to let me in. I step in and grab her around her waist, pressing a soft kiss to her mouth.

"Joanie said you were quiet during dinner, so I wanted to come check on you. Is everything okay?"

She nods. "I'm just tired. It's been a long week and we're capping it off with a wedding tomorrow." She shakes her head and sets her hands on my biceps. "As if we weren't already stretched to the max. And then you're leaving Sunday, and I guess I'm just not in the partying mood. Besides, it's not like I was going to go to my dad's club with Joanie."

"Aren't you the least bit curious?" I tease with a cheeky grin.

She giggles as she shakes her head. "Not even the tiniest fraction."

"Come home with me," I say, nipping a soft kiss to her neck.

"You smell like whiskey," she says.

"Is it better than the usual pepperoni smell?"

She laughs, and then she pretends to think about it while I pretend to look supremely offended.

"Pepperoni just smells like home to me now," she admits, and I press another kiss to her lips. I may be a little drunk, but those same feelings that seem to wash over me like a wave at the most random times plow into me once more. She pulls back with a soft sigh. "Let me go get my things and we can head over."

As she drives me toward home a few minutes later, she says, "You know, I was almost asleep when you rang my bell. You're messing with my beauty rest."

"I'm gonna ring your bell once we get back to my place too. And you'll be as gorgeous as always with or without sleep." I squeeze her knee, and she chuckles. "I have to be up fairly early anyway as your father has set a tee time of nine o'clock."

"You're going golfing in the morning?" she asks.

"Groom's request. I sort of have to, don't I?"

She nods, conceding, and we pull into my driveway. I take a quick shower to get the smell of strip club off me even though I didn't actually go to one, and by the time I get out, she's asleep in my bed.

As much as I'd hoped for a romp between the sheets before sleep with her, I'm just as happy to hold her in my arms tonight. We only have one of these left before I head to Arizona for an entire month, and neither of us knows what the other side of that will look like.

Of course, neither of us knew how much would change in the next twenty-four hours, either.

Chapter 25
Gabby

Something feels off when I wake up. It's almost like I'm getting hit with the flu or something, like I didn't sleep nearly long enough even though I got a solid eight hours of rest.

Cooper is still asleep beside me, and I shake him awake. "You need to be at the golf course in twenty minutes," I say.

"Fuck," he murmurs, and I laugh at his first word of the day. There's just something cute about a Cooper who doesn't want to get out of bed.

Of course *everything* about Cooper is cute. And sexy. And perfect.

I love everything about him, and I just wish today was the day we were going to come clean instead of another day where we're hiding. We should be holding hands as we skip down the aisle, the best man and the maid of honor—and instead, we're tucking away our feelings in mixed company for yet another day.

I make him some oatmeal while he gets ready, and then he leaves for the golf course after the kind of hug that makes me feel all warm inside.

I opt for eating breakfast once I get home, and it's as I'm making my way toward the stairs to grab my overnight bag that I feel like maybe I stood up too fast again.

Little black dots edge in on my vision, and the next thing I know, I'm lying on the floor at the foot of the steps.

Did I pass out…again?

If it's a blood pressure thing, and my dad just had double bypass surgery a few months ago…the thought makes my blood run cold, so I decide to head over to urgent care just to get checked out to be sure I'm okay.

I don't even need to tell anybody I went. I've been feeling a little off the last few days, so this is just preventative. Peace of mind to get checked to make sure I don't have a bug, to make sure everything's okay with my heart. I wouldn't want to spread around the flu at my father's wedding the day before the men leave for spring training. It's just a precaution.

I tell myself that over and over as I drive toward the urgent care—after I grabbed a protein bar from Cooper's stash. I repeat the mantra in my mind as I check in at the desk, as I fill out paperwork, as I ignore incoming text messages from my father and Joanie about today.

I only wait about a half hour before I'm called back. The medical technician takes my vitals, and she doesn't say anything, which only serves to drive me crazy.

"Is, uh…is everything okay?" I ask.

"Everything's looking normal," she says. "Tell me about your symptoms."

"I passed out about an hour ago, and it's the second time in the last couple months that's happened. I've also felt a little off the last few days."

"Off?" she asks.

I wrinkle my nose as I try to put words to how I've been feeling. "Kind of like something's coming on. I haven't been sick or anything, I've just felt…tired. Maybe a little nauseated, like I'm never hungry but when food is in front of me, I can't stop eating. I've been busy and stressed between work and school, and my dad is getting married tonight, and I just wanted to make sure whatever it is isn't contagious."

"Have you had to go to the bathroom a lot?" she asks.

I nod. "I've been drinking an abnormal amount of water lately, so I figured that's why."

"Any tenderness in your breasts?"

I nod. "Like *so* sore lately. Usually they get sore around the time my period comes."

"Regular periods?"

"I started birth control, so I haven't been having periods at all. I figured that's why my boobs have been sore, too."

She clears her throat. "Any chance you might be pregnant?"

"I'm on the pill." Didn't I just say that? I shake my head. "So no."

"Let's run a test just to make sure."

I shrug. "Okay. Go for it."

"The pill isn't one hundred percent effective," she says as she pulls some items out of a drawer.

"Right. My doctor told me that. But ninety-nine percent is still pretty good."

She nods. "It is, but it only reaches that rate when it's taken correctly."

My brows knit together defensively as my perfectionism takes over. "I take it correctly. Same time every day."

She hands me a cup and writes my name on it. "We'll need a sample in this cup. There's a bathroom down the hall to the right. There's a little cabinet on the wall you can leave it in."

"A sample?" I ask.

"Urine."

"Right." My cheeks fill with color, and then I hop off the table and head down the hall to grab my *sample*.

There's no way I'm pregnant.

If I was, wouldn't I know?

When I return to the room, the medical technician is gone. I sit on the table and wait.

It feels like the longest damn wait of my life before I finally hear a knock on the door.

"Come in," I yell, and a man who looks to be in his late twenties and who might pique my interest if I wasn't in love with Cooper walks in.

"Well, I'm glad you're sitting, because I'm here to tell you that you're pregnant," he says. He sits on the stool across from the table where I sit, and I'm glad I'm sitting too because what?

"What?" I voice the thought in my head.

"You're pregnant," he confirms.

"But...but...but how?" I sputter.

"How?" he asks, narrowing his eyes at me in confusion. "When a man and a woman—"

"But I'm on the pill!" I scream at him.

"The pill is not one hundred percent—"

I hold up a hand. "Effective. Right. Noted," I practically spit out at him. "How far along am I?"

He glances down at the tablet he holds. "The test you took only tells us yes or no. You'll need to schedule an ultrasound with your obstetrician to determine the answer to that."

"But how could this have happened?" I ask. "I'm on the pill. I take it at the same time every day."

"Stop taking it since you're pregnant," he says.

"Is it dangerous that I've been taking it?"

He shakes his head. "Many women still take it in the early weeks when they don't know they're pregnant. And many women also don't even know when they've taken it incorrectly. Vomiting or diarrhea could render it ineffective. Have you been ill?"

I shake my head, though I *have* felt a little nauseous lately—I attributed it to the pill, but obviously it wasn't that.

"Have you missed any at all?" he asks. "Or have you been sick recently?"

"Sick?" I repeat. "Like with a cold?"

He nods. "Some different cold medications can affect you, and many times when women are sick, they miss a pill or take it at a different time of the day."

"Cold med…" I trail off as it hits me.

It's been nearly two months since I was sick right before Christmas, and the doctor recommended an over-the-counter cold medicine to alleviate my symptoms.

Oh my God.

It doesn't really matter *how*. Maybe I missed a pill and didn't realize it back in December.

It hits me, and I nearly pass out again.

I'm pregnant—maybe as far along as two entire months…and the daddy is *my* daddy's best friend.

Chapter 26
Cooper

My phone rings as I sit in a golf cart, and I slide my phone out of my pocket to see it's Gabby calling.

I can't exactly answer it during her father's backswing, so I have to just let it ring.

I text her when I get a covert second to send it through.

Me: Can't talk. Everything okay?

She doesn't text back, and it's got me worried.

"What about you, Noah?"

I glance up at James McKinney, bassist for the band Vail and one of the co-owners of Coax. He's in the golf cart right behind me as we wait for Troy to finish teeing off, and clearly he's asking me a question but I have no idea what it was since I was texting my best friend's daughter on the sly.

"What about me?" I ask.

"You dating anyone?" he asks. "A few of my wife's friends were discussing what a snack you are the other day, so if you're looking to meet someone, I know a few single ladies who are interested."

I laugh. "A snack?"

"Their word, not mine." He shrugs.

"Is it supposed to be a compliment?" I wonder aloud.

"It means good enough to eat," Victor Bancroft, the famous actor and the third co-owner of Coax, pipes in. He wiggles his eyebrows up and down to make sure his meaning is clear—a snack is something sexually appealing, apparently.

And that's the foursome with the groom to be today. Three sex club owners plus a third baseman. It sounds like the start of some raunchy joke, but it's just my Saturday morning on a golf course.

James and Victor are Troy's closest friends outside of ball, and they're here to support him on his wedding day. He didn't ask either of them to stand up in the wedding, but he did ask them to be there tonight on the very small guest list.

Troy walks back toward the golf cart we're sharing, shaking his head at the way his ball sliced right, and I start driving to the next tee as soon as he gets in.

"Did you ever answer the question?" he asks.

"What question?"

"The one James just asked you. For as close as we are, you never talk about your personal life," he presses.

I sigh. I can't exactly do this without Gabby by my side. "It's complicated," I offer instead.

"With Stacy?"

I shake my head, my brows dipping as my head swings over in his direction for a beat before I turn back to the road as I take the curve around toward the next tee possibly a bit too fast. "What makes you say that?"

"She showed up out of nowhere a few months ago, and you went radio silent right around the same time. I figured one had to do with the other and you didn't want to admit you were fucking your nutty ex."

I turn to narrow my eyes on him. "Question."

He raises his brows as if to tell me to ask away.

"What if I was fucking my nutty ex? Do you really think I'd take kindly to you calling her nutty?"

He chuckles. "I figured I'd either get a rise out of you or you'd let it go, but either way I'd get the answer. So I take it it's a no?"

"It's a hardcore no. I want nothing to do with my ex-girlfriend and I made that very, very clear to her."

"Then who's been yanking your crank? You're in a perpetual good mood, so you must be getting it somewhere."

Jesus, this is uncomfortable. I'm trying to come up with some answer when I pull up to the next tee.

"Hey Bodine, is your daughter seeing anybody?" Victor asks when we pull up to the next tee, thankfully saving me from having to answer more of Troy's questions…but also throwing a brand-new wrench into the thick of things since I could essentially kill two birds with one stone if I answered Victor's question.

"Not that I know of," he answers, and I force myself not to freeze, to feign total disinterest…to act like I have no horse in this race even though I essentially own all the horses. "Why?"

Thank God he asked so I don't have to.

"Jade's younger brother is moving to town. He's in his early twenties, and I thought he might like a friend close to his age," Vic says.

He. He is in his early twenties.

Victor is trying to hook Gabby up with some woman from the club's younger brother, and my hackles rise all the way the fuck up to the sky.

I'm about to get involved when I realize I can't. It's supposedly not my place even though it most definitely is my place. Still, Gabby should be here for that particular conversation.

So I zip my lip and head up to tee off, tuning them out. My ball goes right into the fucking bunker because now I'm thinking about Gabby and Jade's brother and how none of this is okay.

"Look, Jade is lovely, but I just don't want Gabby involved in any way with the club," Troy says to Victor when I return to the cart and slide my club into my bag.

"She wouldn't be unless Jade invites her brother for a preview night, which I highly doubt," Victor points out.

Troy presses his lips together. "I just don't think it's a good idea. I don't know this kid. Do you?"

"You've got to let her go at some point, Troy," Victor says softly.

I'm so torn on whether or not to insert my own opinion here. Yes, he should let her go. But he should let her go to me. No one else.

"Maybe that's true. Or maybe I can spend a little more time protecting her since I missed out on the first eighteen years of her life." He shrugs, and then he grabs his driver. Before he walks up to the course, he turns back to us. "Nobody's ever going to be good enough for her, of course. But she's only twenty-one. I've got a few more years before I need to worry about any of this shit."

I fail to remind him that he was her age when she was born. It's irrelevant.

The point is...he's never going to be okay with anybody dating his daughter, but least of all a thirty-three-year-old baseball player he calls friend.

Chapter 27
Gabby

I tried calling Cooper, but to nobody's surprise, he didn't answer. He's on the golf course with my father. Of course he didn't answer. He couldn't, and I didn't expect him to.

It's not like I was going to tell him over the phone. I just wanted to let him know I passed out again but I'm okay...or something along those lines. Maybe I just wanted to hear his voice to know that everything's going to be okay.

I'm still sitting in my car staring at the steering wheel even though I got his text back that he couldn't talk nearly fifteen minutes ago.

I think I'm numb. I'm not crying, but I'm also not smiling. I'm not exactly sure what I'm feeling right now other than just a strange sense of numbness. Maybe my legs are falling asleep from sitting in the same position for so long.

I'm pregnant.

I guess it explains some of my moodiness lately. I got into that fight with Mia yesterday...was this why?

I don't even know what this means.

It means sleepless nights staring down at rosy cheeks. It means changing diapers and caring for another human. I just helped with Ruby Sue when she was a puppy, but I have a feeling that having a baby is nothing like having a puppy.

It means tough conversations when they get old enough to understand. It means deciding between sleeping in on a Saturday morning or taking the kid to soccer practice. It means learning how to live my life for someone else instead of for myself because I refuse to be anything like my mother was. It means loving somebody with your entire heart and soul, and it means sharing that love with the baby's father. It means making decisions as a unit and making sacrifices for the ultimate gift in return.

I guess it also means I need to make an appointment with my gynecologist to confirm everything and make sure all's going okay down there.

I set my hand on my stomach.

How can there be a baby in there that I didn't know a damn thing about?

I just kept taking my pills, attributing any nausea or change in mood or soreness in my boobs and even a little bit of weight gain to the pill.

I skipped the placebo weeks so I wouldn't get a period.

I had no idea there was a baby growing inside me.

I'm scared.

What sort of mother doesn't know she's pregnant? How could I not know? Am I going to be a terrible mother?

Scared doesn't really even begin to define what I'm going through. Terrified, actually…yet knowing this is part me and part Cooper sends a single pulse of relief down my spine.

And then I remember that he'll be gone for pretty much the next three years and I'll be doing this by myself, so that pulse of relief is kicked out in favor of terror once again.

The reality hasn't really hit me yet.

I don't know what all this means other than the fact that I will be tied to Cooper for the rest of my life now. We talked about this as a possibility down the road…but it's not something either of us are ready for.

But ready or not…a baby is on its way.

I keep teetering between happiness and horror at the thought.

I do the math. If it happened around Christmas, I'll be due sometime in September. I think. I have no idea how any of this works.

But I'll finish school. I'll have my degree, and hopefully I'll have my job as social media manager—a job someone else gave up because she's having a baby, I remind myself.

It's different for me, though. If I'm traveling with the team, that means I'll be with the baby's father. We can do more of it together—in theory. He'll be busy playing and doing whatever it is baseball players do between games, and I'll be busy working a job and breastfeeding—or bottle feeding? I don't even know where I stand on that. I don't know the benefits of one over the other. I don't know anything, and I think an hour must pass where I stare at my steering wheel as I try to come to grips with this bombshell.

My phone rings and pulls me out of my thoughts, and I see it's Joanie.

"Hey," I answer.

"Where are you, girl? Your hair appointment starts now, and Wendy is waiting for you at your dad's house."

"I'm so sorry," I tell her. "I, uh…wasn't feeling well, so I went to urgent care just to make sure I'm not contagious."

"Oh no! Are you okay?"

No.

Nope.

I'm definitely not okay.

"Yeah, I'm fine. Just some bad chicken, I think." I lie. I have to. I can't tell anyone about this before I get the chance to tell Cooper.

And maybe I shouldn't even mention it to him until I'm absolutely sure about this. I don't know anything—a due date, or gender, or whatever.

Maybe it was a false positive.

I need to see my doctor and confirm everything, to get all the information possible before I scare the hell out of everyone else, especially since Cooper's leaving town tomorrow for the next month. I don't want him worrying about me the whole time he's gone. In fact, that's why I haven't texted him back yet. I don't know what to say. I don't even know what made me call him other than the fact that I wanted to hear his voice in my ear.

"Okay. Are you feeling any better?" she asks.

No.

Nope.

Not even a tiny bit.

If anything, I feel a little worse.

"Yeah," I lie. "I'll be okay. I'm on my way home now."

"Be safe and I will see you soon!" She sounds so excited, and I know part of my maid of honor duties will be to share in that joy with her despite all the things weighing heavily on me right now.

So I draw in a deep breath, and I start the car. One step at a time.

I drive toward home, forcing in deep breaths at every stoplight. I guzzle down some water.

I pull into the circular drive, and I take one more deep breath before I force on a happy face. And then I head inside to celebrate my dad's wedding day as if I didn't just receive the sort of news that has already turned my entire world upside down.

Chapter 28
Gabby

Curly or straight, up or down, does it really matter?

There's a baby growing inside me, and it's anywhere from a few days to a few months along.

It's the fear of the unknown that's getting to me right now. I'm holding a secret I need to share with *somebody*, but the only person I want to tell is Cooper, who's currently getting ready to walk down the aisle as my father's best man.

I can't focus on anything except the rampant thoughts running through my brain—everything from whether the baby will have Cooper's blue eyes or my green ones to how I'm going to do this when Cooper's out of town and whether I'll travel to games with the baby or if it's better to stay home. Is it safe to bring a baby to a ballpark? What if a foul ball comes toward us? I'm terrified of those when I go to games anyway, let alone when I'm holding onto a newborn. Maybe I should just stay home. Or maybe I can watch from a box up high where I won't need to worry about foul balls. Surely the manager's family gets one of those even at away games, right?

It's early, and I get that. It'll take time to even get used to the idea, and there will be plenty of time to make those sorts of decisions.

Today's not the day to focus on it, yet it's all I can think about. When Wendy asked me if I wanted my hair curly or straight, I wondered if the baby would be born with a head full of curls or no hair at all. When Joanie asked if I wanted anything to eat, I wondered what sorts of foods the baby would like and whether what I eat now will promote different sorts of habits for this child as it grows.

Is it a boy or a girl?

What will we name him or her?

Does Cooper already have names picked out?

Some little girls dream of what they'll name their babies, but that was never me. I don't have a name in mind. In fact, when I try to think of names, I draw a total blank.

I know literally nothing about what it means to be pregnant, but when Joanie hands me a glass of champagne, I know I can't drink it. So I fake a sip when she toasts me, and I set my glass down and pretend to forget about it.

I told Wendy to decide what to do with my hair, and she's just about finished curling it. She's about to start pinning portions of it up when a text from Cooper comes through.

Captain: *Are you at home?*

Nerves race through me. Will he know by my response? How do I act *not* pregnant when I *am* pregnant?

Me: *Just finishing up hair.*

I stare at the words before I click send just to make sure there's nothing in them that he might decode as something wrong.

Captain: *Just finished golfing. Heading home to shower.*

Me: *Did you win?*

Captain: *I was doing okay until I missed your call. I was worried when you didn't text back.*

Me: *I'm sorry. Busy morning.*

Captain: *But everything's okay, right?*

What a loaded question. Is everything okay?

I'm not really sure.

I haven't come to grips with any of this yet, and somehow I think that *yes*, everything *will be* okay once I tell him and once we tell my dad and it's all out in the open.

But we're running out of time.

Why did my dad choose *today* of all days to have this wedding? There's so much to do. So much to tell him. So much to confess to. But I can't do any of that today when he's focused on getting married and we're supposed to be keeping his stress levels low as he heads into spring training literally tomorrow.

I need time alone with Cooper, and I'm still torn as to whether to tell him tonight sometime or if I should wait until I see a doctor and confirm all this is true. Can I really wait an entire month to see him? Do I *need* to tell him in person? Or can I find some way to surprise him with the news?

I *want* to tell him in person. I want to see his face when I give him the news he's wanted to hear his entire life. I want to share in that joy. I want him to take me in his arms and tell me how everything's going to be okay.

I finally write him back.

Me: *Everything's okay. I'll see you in a few hours.*

Because it's a quiet, last-minute ceremony, there's no rehearsal. Instead, we're all supposed to show up at the chapel at five for pictures. My dad and Joanie don't believe in the superstitions about not seeing each other before the ceremony, so they're doing first look photos and wedding party photos ahead of the ceremony, which starts at six. They'll have a small, private reception in a ballroom at the Bellagio where I'll have to dance with the best man and pretend like he didn't put a baby in me and I'm not head over freaking heals in love with him.

Captain: *I can't wait. You'll be gorgeous in your dress and even more gorgeous when I take it off you later. [water droplets emoji] [eggplant emoji]*

My cheeks heat at his words and his dirty emojis.

Me: *Looking forward to it, Captain. [firecracker emoji]*

Time seems to slow down, and a strange sense of nervousness sets in as the clock slowly ticks closer and closer to five.

I eat my bagel along with the cream cheese when I realize I'm being silly, and I eat some finger sandwiches Joanie catered in, and I eat a huge salad. And some cookies. And another bagel. And some yogurt. I can't seem to get full, and now I understand why.

A make-up artist comes in and works a miracle on me, and then it's finally time to go. The nerves kick into high gear, or maybe it's butterflies. I'm holding onto a brand-new secret that only two people in the entire world know about—the doctor at the urgent care and myself.

Secrets have a way of revealing themselves, though, and I wish I would've had the foresight to believe that long before the moment when it became too late.

Chapter 29
Cooper

I take a quick shower after golf and head toward the Bellagio. Troy reserved a suite, and all the tuxedos are over there for us to get dressed. But before that, he wanted to hit the blackjack tables for a bit, so I head straight for the high-limit room.

He's already sitting there with Victor, and a pile of chips sits in front of both men. I slide into the seat on Troy's left, and I wait until they both lose a hand at the same time before I set some money on the table and join in.

As I sit, I can't help but remember sitting at a blackjack table last August and my entire life changing when a beautiful woman sat down at the same table as me.

It's funny how life works in mysterious ways, and I know now that she sat there because she was meant to be in my life. If it wasn't that night at that table, then it would have been when I showed up at Troy's house. It was inevitable that we'd find each other, but the way it played out is one of the things I love most about our story—that we fell in love long before we knew so many things about each other, and that we stayed in love even after we found them out.

Troy's drinking whiskey and Victor's starting on a glass of gin, so when the waitress comes by, I order a Miller Lite. Troy gives me a look like beer is for animals, but I like what I like and I'm not about to be judged by my friend.

"Have you ever been married?" Victor asks me, and I shake my head.

"I was with someone for five years who pushed hard for it, but I knew it wasn't right." But the woman I'm with now…she's right. "You?"

He nods. "Twice, and I'm probably stupid enough to do it again."

Troy laughs. "Way to sell the concept of marriage on a man's wedding day."

Victor shrugs. "I believe in the institution. I don't regret either of my marriages, and if the right woman comes along and we agree we both want to make that commitment, then we will."

"Not Jade?" Troy presses.

Victor laughs. "No, not Jade. She's a little…"

"Young?" Troy supplies.

Victor shoots him a look. "You're one to talk. Isn't Jazz half your age?"

"She is half my age, but she's not the woman I'm marrying. She's one of the ones Sapphire and I played with to spice things up." Troy shrugs as if it's totally normal to say that—to invite other women into his bed with his future wife. "That's what you do with the young ones, right? You play, but you marry the ones who are more in line with where you are in life."

"And that's Joanie for you?" Victor asks. "She's still quite a bit younger than you, right?"

"Seven years. But we're both established in our careers. We both had our own thing before we met each other," he says.

I think about those words and what, exactly, he means by them. Would he dismiss what Gabby and I have because we're not both established? Because we didn't really have our own things before we met?

Somehow our paths have started to align. I'm not sure if she wants the social media manager position with the Heat so she can work closely with me, or with her father—or even with Joanie, or if it's because it's a marketing position that she really wants. Does she have her *own thing* as Troy just said, or are our paths aligning because *we* are aligning?

It doesn't matter to me. I love her either way. But I'm also trying to answer the questions that are sure to come up before they get asked. I want to be fully prepared when we deliver our news.

I'm still not quite sure how we've let so much time pass without telling him. Some mix of fear and bad timing, I guess. Every time we're ready to take the leap, another obstacle jumps in our path, or Gabby isn't ready because of the fear of rejection she lives with every single day.

Whatever the case, time is running short now.

"You're quiet," Troy says to me.

"Just focused on the cards," I grunt, but the truth is that I'm focused on his daughter.

The cards are up and down, and I walk away essentially even when it's time to head up to Troy's suite to get dressed. I pull on my tuxedo, and I glance in the mirror. I wear a bow tie, and I don't know if I've ever worn a bow tie. I feel like a waiter at a fancy restaurant or something.

I wait in the lounge area of the suite for Troy, and I feel nerves prattling at my chest.

I guess I'm just worried he's going to find out before we get the chance to tell him.

I've been worried about that all along, but tonight will be different. I'll be forced to escort her down the aisle. Forced to sit beside her at dinner, forced to dance the traditional wedding party dance with her. And all the while, I'll have to put on the act like she's nothing more than my best friend's daughter when the truth is that I've never known a love like this.

We head down to the chapel, and Troy stops just outside it. He grabs my arm. "I'm not supposed to go in. Can you check if they're in there and let them know I'm ready for the first look?"

I nod, and I head into the chapel.

It's gaudy in here—too many flowers, and they all mingle together to create a rather strong fragrance. The wall behind the altar is entirely glass with a door in the middle leading to an outdoor area set up for photos, but I don't notice any of that.

Instead, my eyes move to the absolute angel standing in the room all by herself. She faces the altar, and she's off to the side of the room toward the front. She turns when she hears me walk in.

I freeze for a beat, my heart racing and my chest pulsing as I stare at her. She wears a simple black dress and black heels, and her hair is pulled partially back to allow her beautiful face to be the real showstopper.

I glance back at the door as it clicks shut behind me, sealing us into privacy in the chapel.

"You're not supposed to be more beautiful than the bride on her wedding day," I say softly as I walk slowly down the aisle toward her.

Her eyes soften, and she smiles. It's demure and modest, and she shakes her head a little. "And you're not supposed to be banging the groom's daughter, but here we are."

I chuckle as I move closer and closer, and I pull her into my arms once she's within my reach. She glances nervously over my shoulder as she stiffens.

"He's waiting out there for the first look pictures, and I've needed this all day." I drop my lips to hers, and she laces her arms around my waist for a beat.

She pulls back. "We shouldn't."

"Oh, yes. We should." The overwhelming urge to feel her body against mine pulses through me, so I back her up until she bumps into the wall, and I kiss her again.

But this time, I give her everything I'm feeling as I try to pack it all into the short window of time we have left. This time tomorrow, I'll be on the road toward Arizona. We'll have said our private goodbyes, and I don't know what gets us from here to there. I don't know what awaits tonight as anticipation plows through me or whether we'll get the chance to tell her father.

None of that matters in here, not when I'm holding her in my arms.

In here, we're fine.

In here, we're *us*.

It's just us, and Troy's waiting out in the hallway until I return to give him the all-clear for his first look at his bride.

That's what I *thought* was true, anyway.

I don't see it happen since I'm still pinning Gabby to the wall with my hips, but I hear the door burst open with violence as it careens into the backstop with a loud thud.

I hear Joanie's voice before I realize what's happening. "Troy, stop!"

I jump apart from Gabby, but it's too late. Troy storms in. His nostrils are flared, his face is red, and the flint in his gaze is harsh as the truth seems to crash into him.

"What the fuck is going on here?" he demands.

"Troy, your heart," Joanie pleads, her tone full of desperation as if this one event will send him back into the ER. She grabs onto his arm to stop him, but he shakes her off.

"My heart is fine. What the hell is going on?"

I glance at Gabby, who looks like she's about to throw up, and I clear my throat to say something—*anything*—to answer his question.

I come up short, and Gabby steps in first.

"Cooper and I are together," she blurts.

Joanie gasps, slapping a hand over her mouth as the truth comes out, and Gabby and I both stand stock still as we await his reaction.

"You're *together*?" Troy asks. "What the fuck does that mean?"

"We're seeing each other," Gabby says, trying again and giving exactly zero more information.

"That's ridiculous," Troy says, shaking his head. He looks at me as if this just doesn't add up. "You're in your thirties." He turns to his daughter. "And you're still in college. What do you mean you're *seeing* each other?"

"I'm in love with him," Gabby whispers, and she reaches over to grab my hand.

We both brace ourselves for the fallout. I open my mouth to admit that I love her, too, but Troy cuts in first.

"Love?" he practically roars. "Like you know what love is. You're twenty-fucking-one!"

"You were twenty-one when you had me," she argues.

"Yes, and admittedly I was stupid," he says.

"Whoa." I hold up a hand to stop him from saying something he'll regret. Implying that his daughter is stupid because of her age is crossing the line, and I don't give a fuck *who* he is. I'm going to stand up for my girl.

But this time Joanie cuts in before I get the chance to say anything else. "You had all the time in the world to tell him, and you choose *today* to get caught? Our *wedding* day?"

"We didn't *choose* it—" Gabby begins, but her father cuts her off.

"Wait a second," he says, turning toward Joanie. "How much time did they have, exactly?"

Joanie's eyes widen as she realizes *she* is caught, too.

"You knew?" he asks her, that flint in his eyes turning even colder. "And you kept it from me?"

She sputters with something to say, but she comes up short.

"I can't marry someone who thinks it's okay to lie to me. God damn, I can't even look at the three of you right now." He shakes his head in disgust. "Fuck this," he mutters, and he walks out of the room.

Chapter 30
Gabby

All three of us stare at the door in total shock over what just went down, and the worst part is that I don't even know what comes next. Is he angry that we lied? Or is he angry that Cooper and I are together?

"Shit," I mutter. Do we chase after him? Do we give him a minute to cool off?

Is this too much stress?

Is it any more stress than the season will be?

This wasn't how he was supposed to find out.

"Joanie, I—" I begin, but she turns to me with a glare.

"Don't," she hisses. "Just...don't." Tears fill her eyes, and then *she* bolts from the room, too.

I don't know where Jade or Amber or Raven are. I don't know where Joanie's parents are—they're supposed to be here today, too.

Cooper and I exchange a glance.

"How'd he even know?" Cooper wonders aloud. "Why'd he bust in here like that?"

Oddly it's the one question I actually have the answer to. "There's a television monitor around the corner showing what's going on in the chapel to the receptionist. Some maintenance workers were over there earlier. They must've left it on."

The photographer and Corinne, the wedding planner here at the hotel, choose that moment to enter the room. "Are we ready for the first look?" Corinne asks brightly, clapping her hands together, and she glances around. "Where is everybody?"

"I think the wedding might be off," I murmur.

"Off?" Corinne screeches. "What happened?"

I blow out a breath. "Long story. I have to go find my father." I make a break for the door, and Cooper is hot on my tail.

He's not in the immediate hallway, and neither is Joanie.

We both glance around, and Cooper checks the men's room while I look in a few empty offices.

"Let's split up to search. Text me if you find him, okay? And I'll do the same," Cooper suggests.

I nod, and Cooper leans in to give me a quick kiss goodbye, but I just bolt.

It was our kisses that got us into this mess in the first place, and I guess I just need to go find my dad without wasting another second. I need to explain everything to him—how I didn't have a clue who Cooper was when I met him, how we were both shocked when we ran into each other in the kitchen that morning, how we tried to resist it but there's just something here that I can't quite explain.

I have to make him understand before he leaves for the next month. He'll be in close quarters with Cooper, and I have no idea what that means for the two of them or how it'll affect their working relationship.

I get that he's angry, and that's fine. We're all entitled to our own emotions, and he deserves to feel whatever he feels over walking in on his daughter kissing his best friend. But he just ran without letting us get a word in, and I feel like if I could just talk to him…I don't know. I don't know if I can make him understand.

But I have to try.

I don't even know where to go. Cooper runs for the elevators, so I assume he's checking the suite where they got ready. I run to the high limit area, and I check the bar.

I don't find him.

I wander around the hotel for over an hour, feeling very much like a lost little girl looking for her daddy, and eventually I wind up out by the pool, where I find Joanie sitting in a lounge chair crying.

"Have you found him yet?" I ask, sitting beside her and taking her hand.

"No," she sobs.

"I'm so, so sorry," I begin. "I don't even know what to say."

She shakes her head. "It's my fault. I never should have agreed to keep a secret like that from him."

I squeeze her hand. "We need to find him. We need to make him understand."

She shakes her head. "He *won't* understand. You don't know him the way I do, and trust me when I say that lying is the ultimate betrayal for him."

My brows crinkle. "Then why'd you do it?"

"Because I knew the truth would hurt him more than the lie. He's so protective of you, Gabby, and I didn't know what you two were up to. I didn't know if you were just, you know…doing it, or if you were more serious than that. I caught you once, and I told you not to do it at work. I assumed it was a fling, and we never talked about it again." Her voice trembles through her words.

"I've been so scared to tell him for fear that it would hurt his relationship with me or with Cooper. But you can't help who you fall for." I blow out a long breath.

She huffs out a mirthless chuckle. "No, you sure can't. Today was supposed to be the happiest day of our lives. Instead I'm afraid I've lost him for good."

"He'll come around," I say, hoping there's truth to my words.

She presses her lips together. "I don't know if he will. You're his daughter, so you've got the best chance of forgiveness. His best friend's lies?" She shakes her head. "His would-be wife's lies?" She shakes her head again. "I broke his trust, and that's not something he will let go."

"How do you know?" I ask. She just seems so…*sure*. Like she already knows he will never forgive her for keeping something from him.

"Because your mother kept you from him for eighteen years, and I know how he feels about her. He's gone on and on at length about how secrets ruin relationships. I knew what I was risking when I agreed to keep your secret for you, but I never thought he'd find out I knew." Her eyes are glassy as she stares out over the pool.

A text comes through from Cooper.

Captain: *Danny said he hasn't seen him at the stadium. Victor checked with the receptionist at his club, and she said he just walked in. I'm on my way there now.*

I read the text to Joanie, and her face crumbles into sadness again.

I don't know what that means. Maybe he's going there to work out some secret kinks without her, and maybe that's upsetting to her for whatever reason, but I can't find it in me to ask.

"Of course that's where he went. It's his home away from home. The place he can go to unwind," she says.

More words I don't want to ask about. "Do you want to go there, too?" I ask instead.

She glances at me. "I've had a few glasses of champagne and I want to go home and change first. Would you drive?"

I don't want to go. It's the last place I ever wanted to see.

But this feels an awful lot like my fault.

I need to find him, and I need to fix this.

"Let's go," I say.

Chapter 31
Cooper

I make it to Coax in record time, my tires squealing as I throw the truck in park and leap out.

God, I hope he's not on the third floor. I hope I don't catch him with his pants down—literally. I hope he's not here with some other woman as retaliation against his would-be bride's secrets. He doesn't seem like the type that would do that, but who knows what the hell goes on here?

I walk toward the front door and the security guard there recognizes me from previous visits. He waves me in. I hand my phone to Heidi, the receptionist in the front room, and she waves me into the next room. I glance around for Troy, but the place is empty and I don't see him. It's early on a Saturday evening. I'm sure this place will be hopping later tonight, but not quite yet.

I make my way into the next room—the lounge that sort of reminds me of a study with its bookcases and wingback armchairs and couches and pool tables. I glance all around. Two men sit in the wingback chairs near the window chatting with tumblers in their palms. A couple plays pool at one of the tables. Nobody stands by the bar, and the bartender appears to be looking at some paperwork. This is probably the one room I'd be most comfortable having this conversation, but no dice in here, either.

My heart pounds as I make my way up to the second floor, praying I find him watching the strippers since if I don't, that likely means he's somewhere on the third floor.

I don't. In fact, nobody is on this floor at all. The stage is dark, and I'm guessing it doesn't open until later tonight.

Before I go up to the third floor to look for him, I head back down to Heidi in reception.

"Have you seen Troy?" I ask.

"Is there a message I can deliver for you?" she asks rather than answering my question.

I shake my head. "I need to see him."

She studies me for a beat, and then she nods. "He's up in his office. I'll let him know you're here." She picks up a phone and dials in, and a moment later she says, "You have a guest in reception."

He appears a minute later. He's still wearing his tuxedo, and so am I, and I can't help but wonder how much Heidi knows. I'm not sure why that's where my mind goes, but she's always here. She has to have *some* sort of relationship with her boss, right? Does she know he was supposed to get married today? Does she know he ran out on his own wedding?

He looks…agitated. The opposite of the low-stress environment we were supposed to be providing for him. Clearly this is hitting him in some way, and I'm not sure if it's because of the secrets we've all been keeping or the brand-new knowledge that his best friend is banging his daughter.

But it's so much more than that, and I just need to make him understand.

"Can we talk?" I ask.

"I have nothing to say to you. We will communicate only on the field going forward. You are no longer welcome in my club, so you may kindly see yourself out." His tone is firm, and he turns to leave the room.

I can't let him just run away.

My eyes edge over to Heidi. Fuck it. He's not giving me a choice. "I fell in love with her before I knew she was your daughter," I say to his back.

He freezes, and I grab onto the opportunity with both hands even though Heidi is listening to us. I no longer care who knows. The one person we were trying hardest to keep it from found out, and I'm sure Heidi has signed a pretty extensive and intense NDA anyway.

"I met her the weekend you brought me to town to ask me to play for the Heat. It was an instant connection. She didn't know who I was, and there was something so pure about that. I didn't know who she was, either. I didn't even know you had a daughter."

He turns around to face me, and his eyes are hard and flinty again. His mouth is a thin line, and I can feel the anger vibrating off him from here.

"You've been with her since August?"

I plow forward. "We spent the entire weekend together, and she came to see me the next weekend in San Diego. She helped me look for a house before I moved here. You don't share the same last name, and in those three weeks, I fell for her. I didn't find out she was your daughter until the morning after you threw that party for me when I first moved to town. I broke it off with her as soon as I found out, but when the feelings are this strong, this intense..." I shake my head. "We were just drawn to one another. We couldn't fight it."

"So you're saying it's love," he says flatly.

"It's big, Troy. I've never felt like this before," I admit. "She is it for me."

"That's fucking ridiculous," he spits. "You're twelve years older than her. When she was in kindergarten, you were graduating high school. It's practically illegal. You're taking advantage of her because she doesn't know any better. It's wrong, and it's disgusting, and you better fucking believe I will choose to act in the best interest of my daughter over *anyone* else. Always. That includes you." He points at me then folds his arms over his chest. "And that includes the team. You signed a contract. You made commitments. You may have fucked up our friendship, but you will *not* fuck up our team over this. I was hired to manage game play, not players, but if you don't break it off with her before we leave for spring training, I will go to Mike and blow it up myself. What's it going to be, Noah?"

I don't know what he means by going to Mike to blow it up himself—does he mean he'll blow up my reputation? My chance to play again? Or will he ruin his own daughter's chance at the full-time job she's on track to start after she graduates?

It doesn't matter.

He's right. I signed a contract, and I can't back out of it. It's that goddamn sense of responsibility rearing its ugly head again, and I know he's right. My heart says to choose Gabby over everything, over everyone else. That's what I want to do. But my brain knows that I made a commitment to the team, and I can't back out of it...not now. Not when I have thirty-nine other guys on the forty-man roster depending on me. Not when I have an entire expansion team depending on me from the grounds crew all the way up to the front office staff. An entire fucking *city* depending on me to lead this team to victory in our inaugural season.

Maybe she can wait three years for me until I play out my contract…or maybe we're the star-crossed lovers who were always destined to have only a short time together, and maybe we're supposed to be grateful for what we were allowed to have.

It was the best six months of my life. She is the love of my life.

But I don't have a choice.

I signed a contract, and I committed to leading the team.

I have to end it with her before I leave for Arizona in the morning.

Chapter 32
Gabby

Cooper's truck is in front of a mansion when I pull up to the address Joanie gave me, and I wonder how long he's been there. I wonder if he found my dad…if he made him understand. If he explained and they're toasting and everything is going to be fine.

The nauseous feeling permeating my entire body tells me it's not likely, but a girl can dream.

"Is this it?" I ask Joanie.

She nods.

"This is the exclusive, private club? It looks like a house." I feel like I'm making conversation as a way to divert the fear zipping up and down my spine, but it isn't really helping.

"When Troy and Victor bought the place, they pretty much gutted it to build what they had envisioned," she says a little absently as we both get out of my truck.

We walk toward the front door, and I have to force one foot in front of the other. I'm dreading what we're about to find inside, and not just this whole mess with my dad and Cooper but actually stepping foot into this sex club. Will people be doing it in the foyer?

Joanie nods to a security guard standing near the front door, and he opens the door to let us in. She must be a VIP if she's the owner's fiancée. Did they meet here? Or did they know each other before this? I realize only now I have no idea how they met even though Joanie and I have gotten fairly close over the last few months.

I don't know if we'll remain close after this, though. And I don't know how my dad will feel knowing that I've been sleeping with Cooper, either.

I'm surprised when we walk in and the first room is a foyer with a tall counter in front of us. The room is painted black, but the countertop is white with lights glowing beneath them. Overhead lights are on, too, and we find Cooper and my father facing off. My dad's hand is on the door handle behind him, and Cooper stares him down with a look of complete and utter devastation on his handsome face.

It scares me.

A lot.

I'm terrified for what's coming next.

A gorgeous woman sits behind the counter, clearly pretending like she's not listening to every word exchanged between Cooper and my father, and she glances up toward Joanie and me when we walk in.

My eyes are glued to Cooper, and the tension in here is thick. He doesn't look at me—not right away.

The fear kicks up a few notches as my heart turns from pounding to thundering. It's so loud I'm certain everyone in the room can hear it.

Cooper breaks the face-off with my father first as he blows out a long breath and runs a hand along his jaw. He stares down at the ground, still not looking over at me.

"Is there somewhere private I can speak with Gabby?" he asks my father.

"There's an empty office upstairs." He grunts the words then opens the door behind him. He leads the way up the stairs, and all four of us trudge up them toward the second floor. He opens another door, and we walk down a hallway. He nods toward a dark room, and Cooper goes in first, flipping a light switch.

I follow him in, and it feels very much like I'm in trouble.

"You can leave," my father says to Joanie just before the door clicks shut behind us.

The office has furniture in it—a desk with a chair, a small leather couch, and a recliner, but otherwise it's a vacant office.

I look at the couch since my legs feel like they're about to give out, but I don't sit—mostly because I'm waiting for Cooper to make a move first. I want him to pull me into his arms. I want him to pin me against the wall with his hips and kiss me the way he did back in the chapel, but instead he blows out another breath and runs his hand along his jaw again. He's keeping his distance.

That's not a good sign. My chest starts to ache as my body prepares for what's coming.

He perches on the edge of the desk, and he won't look at me.

"What's going on? Did you talk to him?" I finally ask, breaking the silence because I can't take it for another freaking second.

"I talked to him," he says quietly, staring down at a spot on the carpet. "I told him how we met before I even knew he had a daughter. I told him how we fell in love before you knew I played ball. I told him how we tried to stay away but couldn't. I told him how you are it for me, how you are the love of my life."

His eyes finally lift to mine, and the pain in them tells me the rest of this conversation isn't going to go the way I've been hoping.

"He told me I made a commitment to the team and I need to choose between that commitment and you. I...I don't have a choice." His voice breaks, and it kills a piece of me since it tells me what decision he's already come to.

"There's always a choice," I interject softly.

He shakes his head, and I wish I knew what the hell my father said to him to cause him to act this way, but I don't press. He's made a decision.

Maybe he'd take a different route if he had all the facts, but blurting out *I'm pregnant* right now seems like it would just be a desperate attempt to hold onto something that he has already determined to be over, and I don't even have a confirmation from my doctor yet anyway. We'll cross that bridge when we get to it.

It's easy to say that to myself. It's easy to pretend the reason I'm not telling him is because it's not confirmed, or it's because I don't want to seem desperate.

It's a little harder to admit that maybe I'm more like my mother than I ever thought I could be.

To be concluded in Book 5, HARDBALL

Chapter 1
Cooper

"There's always a choice," she says. Her voice is soft velvet, and this feels like the last time I'll hear it in an intimate setting.

I shake my head. There just isn't one this time.

I could give it all up. A tiny voice sneaks into the back of my mind. I could walk away from the game, break my contract, break my commitment.

I want to do those things. I want to choose Gabby. My heart *is* choosing Gabby.

It's not how I was raised. It's not who I am. I don't break promises I've made...but I made promises to Gabby, too. I promised not to hurt her. I promised everything would be okay.

It's all happening too fast. I leave in the morning, and I have to make a decision tonight.

So I'm doing what I think is the right thing for everybody, even if it means I have to suffer right now.

Nobody wins here, but I can't just walk away from the Heat. I want it to be that simple, but it's just not.

And there's a lot more at play here than my commitment to the team.

There's Gabby's relationship with her father, and I can't help but think about my relationship with my own father.

I care about her more than I care about the team. I'd give it all up for her in a heartbeat. But my brain keeps circling back to Troy's words.

You're taking advantage of her.

It's wrong.

It's disgusting.

You signed a contract.

You made commitments.

You may have fucked up our friendship, but you will not fuck up our team.

There was nothing wrong or disgusting about the two of us together. It was right. It was perfect. It was everlasting. But he's her father. He'll never see it that way.

And others won't see it that way, either. I didn't have to worry about that so much when we were together in secret. However, it's not something I'm willing to subject Gabby to. She always deserved better than me, but it's not just *me* she deserves more than. It's the media frenzy that will attack her for being with me. It's what people will say…and while *I* don't give a fuck about what anyone else thinks, I know Gabby does. I know she'll be hurt.

I know this because I know *her*.

I've gotten to know her better than I know myself in the time we've been together. I know all her biggest fears in life, and one of them is simply falling short—of being a failure. It's why she has such a strong drive to succeed, something that's worked in her favor when it comes to the potential to secure a job after she graduates, but the media won't see it that way.

They'll see what they want to see. They'll create a story out of nothing. They'll capitalize on the twenty-one-year-old little girl sniffing around the eternal bachelor twelve years her senior. They'll see nepotism when the truth is she earned everything she has, much like some of the interns saw even though it wasn't true. She'll be hurt by those things. She'll feel like a failure. Like a joke. She'll feel taken advantage of. She'll be punished for things out of her control. These are all things she's been terrified of her entire life.

And so I have to protect her in whatever way I can.

The only problem is that in protecting her from all those things, I have to be the one who causes her the most pain by delivering on the two biggest fears she has courtesy of her mother: rejection and abandonment.

I have to end things with her. Boom: rejection.

I have to leave for Arizona in the morning without her. Boom: abandonment.

I'll be breaking her heart, and in the process, I'll be breaking my own as well.

It's broken already. Being in this room with her and not taking her into my arms, not expressing my love for her…it's too hard. The thought of plowing forward without her…it's too hard. The thought of moving on, of playing ball, of ever feeling happy again…I can't comprehend any of it.

I have nothing without her.

And yet…this is the snap decision I've made.

It feels wrong.

I know it's wrong.

But even if I had time to think it through, I'm confident I'd make the same choice. Because when you love somebody, really and deeply and truly, you do what's best for them…even if it means hurting yourself. And this is what's best for her.

She lived her entire life without her father, and I won't make her choose between him and me. I can't do that to her.

And I won't do it to Troy, either.

He may be the reason I have to do this, and our relationship may never be the same again, but what if she chooses me? I can't be the person who rips away his daughter from him after he lived eighteen years without her.

He's only had her three years.

But I only had her six months.

I guess he wins.

There are far too many factors at play for us to ever really be able to give this a fair shot. And so I have only one choice, and that's to be grateful for the time we shared. It's better to have loved and lost than to never have loved at all…right?

Wrong.

In this time of total darkness and despair, nothing has ever felt more wrong than that stupid statement. The pain I'm going to endure in the hours, the days, the weeks, the months, the *years* going forward…I'm not sure I'll be able to take it. I'm not sure how I'll come out on the other side of it.

"Not this time," I say softly. "I won't be the person who makes you choose between a guy you've known six months and the man you searched for your entire life. And trust me when I say there will come a time when you'd have to make that choice. I'm bowing out. Blood is thicker than whatever this is, and if I had the chance to spend one more day with my own father, I know I'd do pretty much anything to grab onto it."

"So that's it?" she asks flatly.

I snag my bottom lip between my teeth and bite hard, hoping to focus on the pain there instead of the pain in my heart. My eyes burn with sadness, and I keep my gaze on the carpet. I know if I look at her, I'll change my mind…and I *can't* change my mind. Not with all the cards on the table. Not with so many pieces to this puzzle.

"That's it," I whisper, unable to change the volume of my voice.

"It can't be it," she says. Her voice breaks, and I know she's crying.

I want to grab onto her, to pull her in my arms and hold her and promise her that this is all just a nightmare we'll surely wake up from any minute.

But the pain slices fresh, so I know it's real.

"I'm sorry," I murmur. And then because I'm a fucking coward, I start for the door. "I need to go."

"Sounds about right," she mutters.

I freeze and turn around, my brows knit together with a question I never voice.

"Go ahead. Leave me. Everyone else does." She folds her arms over her chest as if she's issuing a challenge.

My chest cracks wide open as my heart throbs with an aching pain. "Believe me, Gabby, this is the last thing I *want* to do. But it's what I *have* to do."

And with those words, I turn and walk out the door.

Chapter 2
Gabby

I slap a hand over my mouth as the door clicks shut behind him, and I sob into my palm.

Tears course down my cheeks as I try to catch my breath, but I can't seem to breathe. I'm not sure I'll ever be able to breathe again.

He said it's the last thing he wanted to do but that he *had* to do it.

I call bullshit.

He walked away.

I think that's the biggest shock of all. He chose the game over me. Over *us*.

And the worst part is that he didn't even admit it.

It's fine if that's what he really wants. I'm not going to chase him down, to try to stop him—to beg and plead with him.

But to blame my relationship with my dad is just the coward's way out. To bring up his own father and throw his loss in my face is such bullshit.

I'm hurt, and I'm angry, and I'm feeling my emotions in a way I've never felt them before. They're some level beyond strong. They're ferocious, and at the same time I'm somehow totally numb. None of it makes any sense, and I can't process what just happened.

He just walked out on me. He proved he's like everyone else in my life. He made me believe he loved me and cared about me, but the truth is that he was always going to choose himself over us.

My mother did it my entire life. She made me believe my father did it, too, and even though I've slowly learned over the last three years that he didn't—not *really*—those scars still run deep. It's a different type of pain, one that forces a person to construct walls tall and strong, walls that take a while to come down, walls that are firmly in place for maximum protection.

One thing's for damn sure.

I won't let those walls down again.

I was stupid to give myself over to someone who plays games for a living. It was another example of me showing my age, of my immaturity when it comes to relationships.

I don't know what to do. I don't know where to go.

I can't face my father right now. It's too fresh, too painful. Too hard. I know there's no one who should shoulder more of the blame for everything that just went down than myself, yet somehow the fact that Cooper just ended things with me feels very much like it's my father's fault.

I don't know where he stands with Joanie. I could leave this office, go downstairs, try to find her...or I could just sit tight.

Am I supposed to drive her home?

God, this is such a mess, and I feel so very alone right now. I can't call Mia. Cooper is the one I'd lean on, but he just walked out on me. My dad would come next in line, and then Joanie.

I could call Kaylee, but she'll choose Cooper's side in this. She was his friend first.

My only option feels like Justin, but as I pick up the phone, I find I can't force myself to hit the call button.

I need a minute to process what just happened.

I need a minute to cry. To mourn.

I need a minute to remember who the fuck I am.

I collapse on the couch as I set my hand over my stomach.

I got through my entire life up to this point essentially on my own. My mother was there. She provided what I needed, but nothing more. And I got away when I could. While from the outside it might look like I've grown dependent on my father, the truth is that I just like living with him as I've gotten to know him. I'll be done with college in another few months, and once I start working a job of my own, I'll move out. That was always the plan.

Except moving out now means I need to find a two-bedroom apartment instead of just one. It means quite possibly I'll be raising a baby on my own—a baby Cooper has spent years yearning for while I'm barely old enough to legally drink alcohol.

It means Cooper will be in my life one way or another, and the thought of having to see him and interact with him and be around him for the sake of the baby but not getting to be *with him* has me crying all over again.

Maybe I'm not as strong as I think I am—as I wish I was.

I'm scared to do this at all, but having to do it without Cooper seems like the sort of daunting task that I can't face.

It's not like I'll *never* tell him. I'm just waiting for the right time.

Because we all know how well the last time I waited for *the right time* went.

Sometimes there isn't a right time.

There's a knock on the office door, and then it opens. My dad walks in as I wipe away my tears.

"I don't want to talk to you right now," I say with a sniffle as my voice trembles.

"I don't really want to talk to you, either," he admits, and he sits on the chair beside me. "But you're my daughter, and whatever else went down today, whatever secrets and lies and betrayals were unveiled, that's the one relationship that won't change as a result."

I grunt, unable to form any sort of reply, and a beat of awkward silence passes between us as I start to feel like I don't really know him at all.

If he truly loved me, wouldn't he want me to be happy?

Instead, I feel like he said something to Cooper that made him feel like he didn't have any other choice but to walk away from us.

"Where's Joanie?" I ask.

He shrugs. "Not here."

"Did you talk to her?"

"Long enough to end things with her," he says quietly, his eyes down on the ground.

"What did you say to Cooper?" I ask.

He glances up at me. "That's between him and me."

I blow out a frustrated breath as an annoyed growl gurgles in the back of my throat. "Whatever you said caused him to come in here and break my heart, so I sort of feel like I'm a little bit involved."

He sighs. "I told him I would always choose you over anyone else. I told him it was wrong for him to take advantage of you, and that he made commitments to the team."

I press my lips together. "He chose the team over me, so I hope you're happy."

"I'm not. I fucking hate that you all lied to me, and I fucking hate how all this went down today."

"Like it matters," I spit. "The end result is the same. You never would've approved of us whether we lied to you or we were open from the beginning."

"I guess we'll never know if that's true." He raises his brows pointedly, and it feels very much like the end of this conversation.

"I'd like to go home now," I say.

He nods. "Of course. I will not be coming home tonight. I'll send someone to pick up my bags for Arizona in the morning."

"Right." I should tell him to have a good trip or win some games or something, but I can't seem to muster any of it up. Instead, I stand and move toward the door without another word.

"I'll miss you, Gabriella. I'm sorry for how all this went down, but trust me. It's better this way."

I freeze by the door, and then I turn around to face him. "I wish you trusted me enough to make that decision for myself."

I open the door and head for the first stairwell I find, hoping against hope I don't somehow land in a sex room on my way out of this strange place.

Chapter 3
Gabby

What have I done?
        It's the question with no answer that continues to swirl around my brain.

What have I done?

I keep trying to convince myself that I'm doing what's best for Gabby.

What have I done?

When I try to convince myself I'm acting in her best interest, I feel like I'm making myself out to be some martyr. And I'm definitely no martyr. That's for goddamn sure.

Instead, I'm driving away with my heart planted firmly in her hands. She will forever hold onto it. No other woman will ever measure up. No other woman will ever give me what she did. No other woman will ever be the other half of me the way she was.

But what choice do I have?

Her father holds the cards here. I didn't sign a three-year contract so I could sit on the bench because he's throwing a tantrum, but that's not why I had to let her go.

It's all the other pieces of the puzzle.

In the end, her father is right. She deserves better than a baseball player. And even though our age difference was never an issue for either one of us, she still deserves someone closer to her age. Facts are facts, and while not a single one of us is promised tomorrow, knowing what I know about my family history and how long the Noah men get on this earth, I can't help but think she deserves someone who has better odds at more years than I might have left.

No matter how much I throw all that around my brain, though, the fact remains: my heart is shattered. My chest hurts, and I feel nauseated. My head throbs, and my eyes burn.

I need a drink.

I need several drinks, actually. I need to drink myself into oblivion. I need to drink until I no longer feel the pain, even if it's only for tonight. It'll be worse when I wake in the morning, but the promise of just a tiny bit of relief tonight is appealing in a way I'm not sure I fully comprehend.

It feels like the opening stages of grief as I act purely on instinct, the shock of what just went down starting to wear off as the pain sets in.

The truth of the matter is that Gabby made me happy.

I haven't been happy in a long, long time.

If ever.

She made me the kind of happy that I could've lived on forever, but I walked away.

And the thought of what comes next, the thought of the days ahead without her...well, it's enough for me to pull the car over on the side of a dark, deserted highway in the middle of the desert, turn on my hazard lights, and puke my fucking guts out.

It happened when I found out my father didn't make it.

It happened when I found out I'd need surgery that would take me out of the game for a year.

And it's happening again today.

The three worst events I've ever lived through...except I haven't actually lived through the fallout of this one yet.

I try to convince myself that I made it through the first two, so I can pick myself up and do it again.

But as I wipe my mouth with the back of my hand, I can't help but think I'm not strong enough to make it through this time.

I don't want to make it through if I don't get to make it through with her.

That's the difference.

I had to be strong for my mom when I was a kid.

I had to be strong when I left the game because the media was watching.

But this time?

This time, I'm all alone. I can grieve in peace.

I sit on the side of the road and try to catch my breath. I draw my knees up, hugging them into my chest, and I tilt my head back to look up into the clear night sky.

I study the stars, but all they do is remind me of everything I've lost. All they do is make me think back to the night we sat in the bed of her truck and stared up at them as we got to know one another—as I fell head over fucking heels in love with her in what was meant to be the most important relationship of my life.

What have I done?

I ruined the best thing that ever happened to me.

I'll be okay. Eventually, I'll be okay.

In the coming days, surely I'll figure out why all this happened. Surely I'll start to understand why it's better this way. I can't see that right now, but the pain is too fresh. It'll take time to step forward from this. It'll take time to heal.

At least I have the game to fall back on. My first love. My only love now, I guess.

It's dark and depressing as I kick that dream of having a family down the road a little further…as I ponder how many—or how few—years I'll get to spend with kids if I'm ever blessed enough to have them.

If I'll ever find a woman I want to have children with the way I wanted them with Gabby.

I force another deep breath into my lungs, inhaling the cool desert evening air, but it feels like I can't quite take a deep enough breath to satisfy the need for oxygen inside me. It's like a heavy weight presses against my chest and I'm no longer able to breathe without assistance. So I suck in small breaths instead, hoping they'll be enough to allow me to carry on.

And then I force myself up.

Baby steps. I force one foot in front of the other.

I climb into my truck. I pull on my seatbelt. I fire up the truck. I put it in drive and check for oncoming cars.

The road is deserted, so I pull out onto it, the lone driver in the lone car heading toward a lonely home where I can break open a bottle of whiskey and drown my sorrows before I leave town—before I leave her—in the morning.

Chapter 4
Gabby

The house is so silent I could hear a pin drop.

I can't help but wonder where Joanie went. Are she and my father working things out?

I doubt it.

After all she did for him when he was sick, I can't believe he'd let this come between them. But it's his relationship to destroy.

Usually Ruby Sue is here to break up the peace, but she's at a puppy hotel for the night since my dad and Joanie were supposed to be walking down the aisle and none of us knew how late we'd be out.

I could really use some puppy love right about now. She'll be back tomorrow, and then it'll be back to her regular routine where Joanie's niece will stop by to take her for long walks and feed her during the day when none of us are home.

God, I need a drink. Everything hurts in a way that makes me wonder when the pain will stop. Maybe I'll numb to it eventually, or maybe this is just my new normal.

God, I want to numb it.

I walk over to the pantry and reach for the top shelf, and I grab down the first bottle I see.

It's tequila.

I spin the cap until it comes off, and that's when I remember...I can't.

I set my hand on my stomach as I realize at least I'm not *truly* alone, yet I don't know if I've ever *felt* so alone in my entire life.

I take the bottle in between my fingers and hurl it against the wall with a loud, frustrated scream.

The bottle breaks into a million pieces, shards of glass spewing all over the hardwood floors and skidding everywhere as tequila bursts out and falls to the ground.

That was dumb, but it felt good anyway.

The petty side of me hopes it was one of my father's expensive bottles.

My eyes burn with tears at the complete and utter mess the bottle made—not because I made a mess or broke a bottle, but because it's so damn representative of the mess I've made of my life.

I let myself fall for someone I never should have. It was stupid. It was a mistake.

I should have trusted my gut when it told me I wasn't good enough. Instead, I trusted my heart.

My stupid, stupid heart.

I let the tears fall with loud sobs as I stare at the mess I made, and eventually my responsibility forces me into action. I grab a towel to clean up the liquid, and I pick up the larger pieces of glass before sweeping the shards into a dustpan. I even run the vacuum to make sure I got all the pieces, and I mop the floor when I'm done for good measure.

Loud sobs escape me as I work, as I contemplate my next move.

I need to finish the semester. I'm one class shy of graduating.

I need to finish my internship no matter how painful it'll be to see Cooper at the stadium.

I need to stay here in Vegas for now no matter how hard it'll be to live in the same town as my father. I can't help but wonder if he will continue to find ways to control my life.

What's worse? An overbearingly overprotective father or a narcissistic mother?

I don't want to go back to Colorado, but maybe I should. Or maybe I should start looking for a marketing job somewhere else— away from my mother, away from my father, away from Cooper.

The tears fall harder as I contemplate that.

Just the thought of leaving makes my stomach twist violently.

Do I even want the social media position? Will Joanie continue to work at the stadium?

Only time will tell, I guess.

The floor is spotlessly clean in too short a time. I take a shower. I change my clothes. I sit on the couch, and it takes me all of five seconds to realize I don't want to be alone right now.

I want to text Kaylee, but I'm not ready to tell her what happened tonight.

Instead, I text Justin.

Me: *Are you around?*

He replies right away.

Justin: *At the bar with the other interns. Come join us!*

Me: *Not really in the drinking mood tonight.*

Justin: *What's wrong?*

I debate how to answer that. What's wrong? Only everything. I'm pregnant and the daddy just broke up with me, and my own father is probably a big part of the cause of all of it.

I can't exactly text that.

Instead, I go for the simplest answer.

Me: *My dad found out.*

Justin: *Oh shit. How'd he take it?*

Me: *About as well as you'd expect.*

Justin: *I'm coming over.*

I glance around the quiet house. I can't go out drinking, but I don't want to stay here, either. Maybe the solution lies somewhere in the middle.

Me: *No, don't leave your friends. I need to get out of the house, so I'll come there.*

Justin: *Are you sure?*

Me: *Give me an hour.*

When I get to the bar, I spot the table right away. Dylan isn't here, which means he's probably with Mia, and that's fine. That's good. I don't have to put on a happy face for him.

Everyone else is here, though, and they're all drunk already.

Which is good. It's fine. I sort of wanted to talk to Justin about what went down tonight, but he's not in the right frame of mind for that.

Tomorrow's another day.

"Let's get this girl fucked up!" Justin yells when I slide into the booth beside him.

I force away the heat building once again behind my eyes.

I can't get fucked up, but he calls the waitress over. It's loud enough in here that I lean in close to her so nobody else will hear my order. "Just a Sprite with a lime, please."

I'd love some vodka in that Sprite. I'd love to get drunk with my friends. I'm only twenty-one, right?

My dad would say I should be enjoying life, making trouble, getting drunk.

Cooper would probably agree. I'm too young to be tied down, too young to be making decisions about my future and getting married and having kids.

But I am. It's all I want. I don't want to be here with the other interns pretending that I'm just like them because I'm not.

I wonder if he's punishing himself right now. I wonder where he's at and what he's thinking.

I wonder if I'll ever be in a position where he'll share those things with me again…or if tonight really was the end.

Chapter 5
Cooper

I stare out the window silently as the team bus carries us toward Phoenix.

It's raining, a rare occurrence for both Vegas and Phoenix, but the skies seem sad today as a light drizzle follows us down the highway.

It's not doing my mood any favors, that's for sure.

I try to muster up the enthusiasm I've felt in years past as the team bus carried us toward our final destination for the month of preseason games, but I can't seem to find it anywhere within myself to feel even a tiny ounce of joy.

Instead, I keep my gaze focused out the window as I force myself to believe I'm doing the right thing no matter how wrong it feels.

But as much as I try to justify it, I'm having a hard time believing it myself.

Rush Ross asked if I wanted to stay in the same house with him and Danny, and I agreed. Now I'm wishing I would've just gotten my own place.

This will be good. It's a private residence we're splitting six ways—between myself, Danny, Rush, Duke, AJ, and Nick—while we're here, and it'll be the party house. It'll give me something to do when I'm not playing so I don't have a chance to dwell on everything I just lost.

I continue to keep my gaze out the window even when I feel someone slide into the seat beside me.

"You ever seen rain before?" Danny asks.

I don't answer. I can't turn to look at him. If I do, my gaze will catch on the back of Troy's head, and I'll just fall back down into the abyss.

"What happened, man?" he asks, his voice a little lower.

There's nobody sitting in front of me. Nobody sitting behind me. No one will overhear if I confess what went down.

But I can't form the words. I can't seem to make my mouth work. I can't seem to gather my thoughts into coherent strings of words. And I don't want to, either.

"Is it Gabby?" His voice is a whisper, and I finally turn toward him.

I press my lips together and nod. "It's over. Troy found out last night, and I don't want to talk about it."

He hisses out a breath through his teeth as if to say tough loss, man, but it's so much more than that.

It doesn't feel like a heartbreak—not the way my heart felt broken when I found out Stacy was cheating on me with a teammate.

It feels like something else entirely.

Like my entire *body* is breaking.

Like my very spirit was extracted from my body and left in the dust with hers.

I don't know how to piece myself back together to make myself work again, but the problem is that I don't have a choice. I was chosen to lead this team, and that's why I'm sitting on this bus.

And no offense to Danny Brewer—he's a great guy, but there's just not a chance this is something he would ever understand.

"I'm sorry, man," he says quietly. "I can't imagine."

And that sums it up.

He's right.

He can't imagine this sort of pain. He's the guy who will find someone different to make moan every night we're in Phoenix. He won't make any real connections, won't even give out his number, and he'll start over again when he gets back to Vegas without a single care in the world.

It's lonely, that life. But is it any worse than what I'm going through right now?

I remember those nights—and worse, the mornings. There was always the awkward moment when I had to say goodbye, or she'd hand me her number and I knew I wasn't going to use it.

There was one in particular when I woke up and couldn't remember her name. It only happened once, but it was one of those situations I still feel guilt over to this day. That's not how I was raised, and it's not how I wanted to live my life. The next woman I met after that was Stacy, and it was coincidental timing—and probably a big part of the reason why I was with Stacy as long as I was. I knew it was time to change something, and so I tried to make it work.

God, did I try.

I didn't know it at the time, but I was putting all my effort into the wrong woman.

And now, I don't even have the option to put it into the right one. I gave it up, and I'm watching it like a helium balloon I let go into the sky until it's so far that it disappears from my sight.

"Listen, the right one will come along," he says, and I know he's trying to help, but I can't help my retort.

"She did, and I was forced to give her up." My voice is short, and I think it's short enough that he'll leave me alone about it.

I'm wrong.

"Why?"

I blow out a breath, and I finally turn to look at him, wincing as I do it because I'm not kidding when I say it feels like my entire body is broken.

"Who would your hall pass be?" I ask.

His brows dip. "Huh?"

"Your ultimate fantasy. The dream girl. If you were in a relationship and could fuck any celebrity if she crossed your path and she was game, no consequences to your relationship…who would it be?"

"Anyone?"

I nod. "Anyone."

He doesn't understand why I'm asking, but his reply is immediate. "Alexis Bodega."

"The actress?"

He nods. "And singer-songwriter."

"Isn't she married?" I ask.

He shrugs. "In your scenario, you said there are no consequences."

"Right," I concede. "Why Alexis Bodega?"

"The banging body, for one thing, but also because I'm a man who can respect talent when I see it, and she's a triple threat. She can act, sing, and dance, and I would love her to do all three while she's naked underneath me."

I make a face. "That's a nice way to talk about a woman, man."

He shrugs. "What about you? Who would yours be?"

I press my lips together and blow out a breath. "Don't have one. I was with the only woman I ever wanted, and now it's over."

He makes a face of disgust. "That's stupid. Everyone deserves a hall pass."

"Everyone deserves what Gabby and I had. And I'm trying to convince myself that it was better to have had the experience than not, but right now I'm sort of feeling like I wish it never would've happened."

He shakes his head. "This." He nods toward me. "This right here is why I don't bother with that shit, man. You're fucking miserable, and it's all because of one girl."

I press my lips together. "I wish that were true, but the truth is that I'm miserable because of my own actions. I'm trying to believe I'm doing the right thing, but it feels dead wrong."

"Then fix it."

I turn my gaze back out the window.

Fix it.

If only it were that easy.

Chapter 6
Cooper

The house Rush secured is about a fifteen-minute drive from the field. Another group of guys rented a house nearby, and we rented a few cars between the twelve of us to share while we're in town. The rest of the team is staying a little closer to the stadium, but I like a little distance given the fact that most of us staying in this house together are well-known in the baseball community.

I don't know where Troy is staying. I didn't ask. I don't know if he got a place with the other coaches or what, and I'm not sure I care so long as he isn't in the same house I'm in.

This is bad.

Real bad.

I realize my best friend is going through his own version of heartbreak and maybe we should be there for each other. But how can we? How can we ever be friends again?

The entire time I was with Gabby, I was worried I'd lose either my best friend or the girl I love. I was naïve to think I wouldn't lose both of them, yet here we are.

There's supposed to be mutual respect and understanding between a team manager and a player, and I just don't have that right now. I can't even look at the guy without everything rushing back to me, but I know I can't blame him. He might have been the one who made me choose, but I'm the one who decided to keep it from him for as long as I did. He's right...we'll never know how he would've reacted to the truth. Instead he discovered the lie, and those are the repercussions we're forced to live with.

When I walk into the place that'll be home for the next month, I feel just the tiniest glimmer of respite from everything going on. It's a mansion built into a hill overlooking the valley. It's got six bedrooms, and every one of them has access to the huge back patio with a pool and a firepit.

There's a game room, too, along with a weight room and a sauna, all of which I imagine we'll spend a good amount of time when we're not on the field. Two huge side yards run along either side of the place, and one side has a batting cage while the other side is perfect for playing catch.

It's like the owners built the place with the idea in mind of baseball players hanging here for spring training season. And they're charging us enough that it'll take care of their expenses for the year, though I imagine a sweet place like this gets plenty of renters throughout the year.

Each of the six bedrooms features a king-sized bed along with a private bathroom, and we draw cards to see who will get first pick. I draw the Ace, which means obviously I take the primary suite.

I set my duffel and my suitcase down in my bedroom, and I collapse on the bed as I stare up at the ceiling.

I wonder what she's doing right now. I wonder if she's thinking of me.

I wonder when I'll stop wondering what she's doing and thinking. I wonder when any of this will get any easier.

Eventually Rush knocks on my door asking what I want for dinner. He tosses me a menu he found in the welcome binder in the kitchen, and I make my selection. He orders our food, and we meet in the kitchen to eat an hour later.

It's a good group of guys, and we're all pretty laid back. We've gotten close over the last couple months, and this next month will draw us even closer.

And that's why I shouldn't be surprised when Rush glances up at me while we're eating and asks, "What's wrong, man?"

I blow out a breath. I guess I'm not very good at hiding what's going on, but these are my best friends. They might be the only ones who can help me through it—who can help me get to the other side of it.

"I ended things with Gabby last night."

Danny already knew, and Rush and Nick knew I was seeing her, but this is news to Duke and AJ.

Danny's eyes are wide when he glances up at me, as if to say *dude, Duke and AJ didn't know.*

But it doesn't matter. Troy knows, so now I guess everyone can know.

"Oh, shit, dude. I'm sorry," Rush says.

"Gabby?" Duke asks.

"Troy's daughter," I clarify.

Duke's eyes widen, and AJ chokes on a French fry.

"Troy's daughter?" Duke repeats.

I nod. "We met before I knew she was his daughter, before she knew who I was. We've been seeing each other on the sly since August, and her dad found out last night."

"How'd he take it?" Nick asks quietly.

"Well, we broke up, so that should answer that question." I set my fork down, suddenly not very hungry anymore.

"You've been banging Gabby?" AJ asks, and I can't even muster up a sharp glance to tell him to shut his damn mouth.

"It was more than that," I say softly. "She was it for me, and now…" I trail off. Now…what?

Now I'm alone.

Now I'm not sure I'll ever find love again.

Now I'm not sure I'll ever even smile again.

I'm not sure I want to without her.

It's dark and cloudy all around me, but I made my choice.

Now I have to deal with the consequences.

"Let's get this boy fucked up!" AJ says.

I shake my head as I think about what he really means—his real motives here. He wants to go out drinking with the boys, and he wants to find someone to hook up with. Maybe he wants that for me, too, but that's definitely not something I'm game for.

"I just want to focus on ball," I say.

"Anyone else want to go get fucked up tonight?" he asks as he looks around the table, clearly not understanding my predicament.

Danny raises his hand, and AJ fist bumps him from across the table.

I'm glad they're going out and having fun, but I'm not here for that shit. I'm too old at this point.

Instead, I'm going to study the teams we'll be playing. It's what I'm here to do anyway. I'm going to look over our practice plans and tweak what needs to be tweaked before emailing my notes off to Troy because fuck if I'm going to sit in a meeting with him right now to make these decisions and have these conversations.

And then I'm going to stare out at the view this house offers and wonder how the fuck it all went so terribly wrong.

Chapter 7
Gabby

My dad calls me on Sunday, but I don't pick up. I'm not ready to talk to him yet.

I know I can't hold grudges against him. Who knows how limited our time together might be given his recent heart attack, but I need a little space and time before I'm ready to chat.

He texts me instead, and I read them all but I don't reply.

Thinking about you.

Are you okay?

Talk to me, Gabriella.

I haven't heard from Joanie. She didn't come home last night, but her stuff is all still here—including her car—so she'll be back at some point, surely, unless she ended up traveling with the team as she was planning to.

I doubt it.

Last night I pretended I was drunk along with the rest of them, and I seriously deserve an Oscar for my performance. Or maybe they were all so drunk they didn't realize I wasn't and my acting isn't really that good.

Justin went home with Brian, and I can't really fault him for that. If Cooper was here and we were still together, I would've gone home with him, too.

I didn't expect Justin to choose me over Brian, and I didn't ask him to. Still, I wish he would have.

I wish I wasn't alone.

I wish my chest didn't ache as badly as it does.

I wish I knew what was going on with Cooper, and that's when I decide to punish myself further by checking the team's Instagram page.

There's a post from an hour ago with several photos taken from the team bus as they ride in style down to Phoenix.

I flip through them until I find one of Cooper. He's talking to Danny in it, a candid shot where they seem to be deep in conversation—so deep that they don't even realize their photo has been taken.

I wonder what they're talking about. I wonder if he told Danny he's single now, and I wonder if the two of them will hit the bars in Scottsdale and take women back to their rental and have sex all night only to wake up in the morning and do it all over again.

It doesn't sound like my Cooper at all, but my Cooper also wouldn't have walked away from us the way he did yesterday.

I go through the motions to get through the day, and I can't help but wonder whether I'm supposed to go into work tomorrow. Am I still taking over the marketing department for the next month as planned?

Do I even still have an internship?

Do I even still *want* one?

I'm not really sure, but the thought of traveling with the Heat to their games, the thought of being so close to Cooper yet so far…it has me wanting to run far, far away.

I can't make any decisions right now—not until I know for sure what I'm dealing with, and on that note, I hop onto my doctor's website and make a request for an appointment as soon as possible. I get a confirmation email letting me know I'll get a call tomorrow from a scheduler, and now I wait some more.

I make myself some lunch, knowing I need to get out of the house but not sure where to go, and it's as I'm cleaning up my dishes that a text comes through from Justin.

Justin: *How are you doing today, baby girl?*

Me: *Hanging in there.*

He calls a minute later.

"Hey," I answer.

"Hey. You seemed quiet last night. Sorry we were all so wasted already when you showed up. I'm a bad friend."

"No you're not. I don't expect you to sit around waiting for me to call with my problems."

He chuckles. "Talk to me, baby girl." His voice is warm and tender, and it's a lot to pin on one person, but it feels like he's all I have left.

I can't help it.

I burst into sobs. Again.

"Oh, shit. I'm on my way over."

"No, Justin, don't. It's okay." I force in a deep breath. I don't want to interrupt his plans today no matter how much I don't want to be alone.

"No, it's not." He cuts the call, and I try to feel bad, but the only feeling I can muster up is one of total gratitude that I'm not going to be alone.

The doorbell rings ten minutes later, and I rush into Justin's arms.

"What happened?" he asks once I let go long enough to let him in. "All you said last night is that your dad found out and it went how you expected. What does any of that mean?"

I grab his hand and walk over to the couch. "It's a long story."

"I've got all day," he says, propping his feet up on the coffee table in front of us.

"My dad and Joanie were supposed to get married last night. It was all hush-hush, a secret surprise wedding before they left for Phoenix today. Cooper came into the chapel, and I was in there, and he kissed me…and my dad walked in on us. We admitted our feelings for each other, and Joanie let it slip that she knew. He called off the wedding and ran out."

"Because Joanie knew?" he asks, confused.

"I guess lying is, like, the world's worst thing to him after what my mom did to him. So he takes off, Cooper tracks him down, he says *something* to Cooper but I still don't know what, and then Cooper breaks it off with me." I rush through the rest of the story because I can't say it without breaking into sobs again if I take my time reliving every detail.

His jaw drops. "He broke it off with you? What the fuck did your dad say to him?"

"Great question." I swipe at my damp cheeks.

"Did he say why?"

I shake my head. "He spouted all this bullshit about doing what's best for me, and not wanting to come between my dad and me…" I roll my eyes. "All the things he should have been worried about the entire time we were together but we kept pretending wouldn't matter. I guess it did."

"And now he's gone for a month for spring training," he says flatly.

I nod. "And Dylan went as the intern and he's on Mackenzie's team now when it comes to me. Between being his girlfriend's estranged best friend and essentially winning the job over him, I have a feeling he's not going to be team Gabby when it comes to what he focuses on in his social media posts."

"Fuck him," Justin says, a true friend when it comes to solidarity.

"He's straight," I deadpan.

He laughs.

"Can we talk about something else?" I ask.

"I told myself I'd tell my parents when you told Troy. So I guess I need to make good on that promise."

I raise my brows. "You're sure?" I ask.

He nods. "It's time. Things with Brian are..." he trails off and shakes his head. "They're incredible, Gabs. I don't want to hide him. But I need to mentally prepare."

I nod. "Of course you do. You tell me when you're ready, and I'll be there to hold your hand through it."

"You're a good friend," he says, leaning his head on my shoulder.

"Back at you."

We spend the rest of the day watching rom coms on Netflix and snuggling Ruby Sue, which doesn't distract me as much as I was hoping it would. And bright and early on Monday morning, my doctor's office calls.

"I know it's short notice, but we had a last-minute cancellation for seven-thirty if you can make it in."

I glance at the clock. I have twenty minutes. "I'll be there."

It's time to get some answers.

Chapter 8
Gabby

The last time I had my annual appointment here was nearly ten months ago.

Ten months ago, I could never have predicted the roller coaster that would've brought me to this moment.

I sit in the parking lot for a beat as I stare at the building. It's a little surreal being here for an exam to see how far along my pregnancy is. To see whether the baby is healthy in there. To see whether I'm really pregnant.

I've had a lot of time by myself to think over the last couple days, and I've come to a few conclusions. The first, and maybe the most important, is that it doesn't matter what happened between Cooper and me. It doesn't matter that I'm alone. What matters above all else is this baby.

Ten months ago, I never would have imagined I'd be pregnant, or that I would've met the love of my life only to lose him because of the father I so desperately wanted in my life, or that I'd want this baby with the type of intensity I didn't know I could feel.

It feels like she is all that matters.

I'm calling her a *she* in my own mind for now because I have this gut instinct that Cooper and I created a little girl out of the love we shared. It's a love we'll always have for one another—or, at least, it's a love I'll always have for him. I can't speak for him or his feelings, obviously. It's a love that will never dim even though love isn't enough for the two of us to make it work.

I force the threat of tears away as I hang onto that last thought.

I wish I could find a way to get him back without using the baby he doesn't even know about. I'm terrified that I'll tell him about her, and he'll want to get back together for her sake, and it'll be all wrong. I want him to want me for *me*, not because of the idyllic family picture he always painted in his mind.

I want to fight for him, but I don't even know how. He made his choice, and he picked the game. He picked pleasing my father. He picked essentially everything else over me while he pretended like he was only acting in my best interest.

I hate it. I hate where we left things, and I hate that he knew what my biggest fears were and he did what he did anyway.

He wants kids.

I can give him that. I *will* give him that. But he also wants a family, and after the way he ended things, I just don't see how that will ever be a possibility for us.

I head inside, and I check in for my appointment. She asks me to leave a sample, and this time I know what that means.

I wait to hear my name, and then I'm taken back to a small room with a table for me to sit on, a computer, and a large screen on the wall.

"I'm Juliette, and I'll be your ultrasound tech today. Since we're not sure of the timeline, I'm going to do a transvaginal exam, which means I need you to take off your pants and underwear. I'll insert a probe that will allow us to take a look around and see what's going on. I'll give the results to your doctor, who will explain everything in detail to you. Sound okay?"

I nod, and for the first time I really wish I wasn't here alone.

But who would I have brought with me?

Even if Cooper and I were still together, he'd be in Arizona. I'm not talking to Mia. My dad is out of town, and Joanie seems like she's not an option right now. I wouldn't even consider asking my mother. I haven't spoken to my other friends in months thanks to spending my time working or naked with Cooper, and I don't think Justin and I have a *see each other naked* type of friendship.

So it really *is* just me and the baby.

Juliette shoves a long, freezing cold stick up my hoo-ha, and the screen shows what seems to be my uterus. There's some fuzzy stuff, and she moves it all around to get a better view.

"There's baby," she announces, and I see what looks like a pinto bean with one side a little bigger than the other.

She uses a little dot on the screen as she talks. "There's the head," she says, and she moves the dot along the baby. "Body, arms, legs. I'm just going to take some quick measurements."

As I watch, I hear a whooshing sound on the monitor.

"What's that?" I ask.

"It's your baby's heartbeat."

Tears fill my eyes.

Holy shit.

It's real.

A little baby with a head and arms and legs and a *heartbeat* is growing inside me.

I listen to the whoosh-whoosh sound, and Juliette says, "Heartbeat is one-fifty-one, perfectly normal." She studies the screen some more, and then she says, "You're measuring right about nine weeks. Does that sound right?"

My mind is blank on what the date even is, let alone when nine weeks ago might have been.

"The week before Christmas," she clarifies.

Right. That's right around when I got over that awful virus and Cooper came over and ravaged me beneath the Christmas tree in my bedroom.

I open my mouth to say something, but instead of words, a soft little sob escapes. I force myself to pull it together. It's not on this poor ultrasound tech to comfort me.

But she does it anyway.

"It's an emotional time, being pregnant," she says quietly. "Between hormones and being a first-time mom, you'll feel everything more intensely than you normally would. It's totally normal." She offers a smile, and I feel a little better.

Maybe once I have the baby, the intense feelings I'm having about the end of Cooper and me won't feel so intense.

It's a nice sentiment to hold onto, but even I'm not naïve enough to believe it.

Chapter 9
Cooper

The last time I did this was over three years ago.

I was in a relationship back then with Stacy, but it was rocky at best even though we'd been together for several years by that point.

Still, I was a player without a care in the world, ready to tackle a new season with the same enthusiasm I had in my first.

Now I'm thirty-three. A little older, a little wearier, a little slower, and a whole lot more jaded.

We're practicing at a training field near the park, and the fields are open to the public. Pitchers and catchers typically report first, but being that this is our inaugural season, everyone on the team was ready to start practicing. We've had plenty of time on our home field as practices got underway, but this is different. This is the first attempt at putting together our team as we face our first real opponent. The first taste of what to expect this season. The first time we're all here and ready to put in the work.

Everyone else is having fun. Everyone else is laughing. Everyone else is enjoying their time as we stretch together, as we run sprints, as we warm up, as we throw balls and hit balls and field balls.

I'm not laughing. I'm not having fun.

Baseball used to be fun, but that was before my manager caught me kissing his daughter and decided to make my life a living hell.

"Thatcher, get on the mound," Troy yells from the dugout.

Thatcher?

We discussed Rush Ross pitching first, not Holden Thatcher.

It's practice, I remind myself. He's just seeing what everyone on the team has.

"Cade, take right," Troy yells next, and our starting right fielder—Duke—runs off the field and into the dugout.

What the hell is Troy doing?

My notes to him last night explicitly agreed with his practice plan to have the boys bringing up the back of our forty-man roster hit to the starters so we could practice our team dynamic.

Instead, he's changing everything up.

Does this mean he's changing up the starting roster?

I run toward the bench he's calling the shots from. "What's going on?" I ask.

He's wearing sunglasses, but I swear I still see him glare at me. "I don't need to explain myself to you."

"I didn't ask you to, Troy. I'd just like to know what your plan is."

"Get back on the field, player," he says snidely.

My brows dip together as I'm almost unsure whether I heard him correctly. I freeze for a beat, and then he repeats himself.

"I said get back on the field. I'm the manager, and I will manage. You get back to your spot on third unless you'd prefer a seat on the bench."

I blow out a breath as anger ices my veins, but I know better than to talk back to my manager.

Still…if that's how he's going to play it, I'm not sure I'll be sticking around to take the brunt of his anger.

A small crowd of maybe a hundred or so fans watches our practice, and I focus on making sure my elbow is ready to play. It feels good being out here, but I can't seem to walk out from the cloud that's pressing down on me.

I sign a few autographs as I walk off the field toward the team bus that will carry us to some classrooms at a local university where we'll have a team meeting. I sit and stare out the window on the way. I'm quiet as we make our way to a lecture hall. I listen during the meeting without opening my mouth even once despite the fact that Troy once expressed to me how I'm supposed to be the leader of this team.

And when it's all over, I spot Nick in the back of the room.

He's not a player.

He's not a coach.

He's a trainer. He's a neutral party who can listen to my concerns and potentially give me advice since he knows everyone involved.

It's either him or Mike, and if I go to Mike, I'm as good as gone.

I head over toward Nick and ask, "Can we talk?"

He nods once, and I follow him out of the room and to an empty classroom next to the lecture hall.

"What's going on?" He perches on a student desk.

I lean on one across the room from him and fold my arms across my chest. "I can't do this."

"Can't do what?" he asks.

"I can't act like everything's okay. I can't be degraded by my manager when he brought me here to lead this team. It's only been one practice and I'm already thinking about throwing in the towel. I want to go home to Gabby. I want to get her back. I want to beg her to be with me even after the way I ended things, but if I do that, I'm letting the entire organization down because her father made me choose. I don't know what to do, man." By the end of my rant, I'm tugging on the ends of my hair.

Nick is quiet a minute as he studies me, and then he asks, "Why'd you start playing ball?"

My brows draw together. I cut the open wound and bleed in front of him, and that's the question he asks?

I shrug as I let go of the strands of my hair. "My father," I answer honestly. "He always had a game on. He bled Cubbie blue, and I'd sit on his lap when I was little while he watched the game. As I got older, he'd explain things to me. He took me to my first game when I was five, and I still remember it. My brother, he didn't care as much. He liked going to the games but only because he got to eat all the snacks. But I...I fell in love with the game because it was something that my dad and I could share."

"What would he think about you walking away?" he asks.

My chest tightens. I wish he was here so I could ask him, but he isn't.

And so I have to go by instinct. I have to do what I think he'd want me to do, and I think he'd want me to play. But I also think he'd want me to be happy...and I'm not sure I can continue to play *and* be happy at the same time. Not without Gabby.

Do whatever will bring you the most joy.

She said those words to me the night we met when I was deciding whether to take Troy up on his offer.

I thought I made the right choice, but this for sure isn't it. There's no joy here.

The cut is fresh, and I know that. In time, it won't hurt so bad. But right now, I can't see a light at the end of the tunnel, and I can't imagine a time when I will.

Chapter 10
Gabby

Joanie didn't show up to the office today, but she wasn't expected to. I ran the marketing department as we had planned.

As if I'm not living through the single greatest heartbreak of my life.

As if I'm not carrying Cooper Noah's baby.

As if everything's normal when it might never be normal again.

I don't know when Joanie is planning to come back—or *if* she's planning to come back. All I know is I was in line to be her substitute while she's out, and I did the things she asked me to do. I even stayed late as I did some research on putting together fun runs for charity, and I emailed Kaylee with ideas for how to showcase both Tight Fit and StrongFitKids. Strong Tight Fit Kids?

But I'm just going through the motions. Work isn't serving as the distraction it might for most people post-break-up considering my ex has been in every room of this building.

My *ex*.

I'm not used to thinking of him like that. He isn't past-tense to me. Not yet. Not ever.

I don't want to be here. I don't want to see Cooper at every turn, and I don't want to act like I'm fine in front of Mackenzie. I want to break down and wallow.

It's as I'm driving back to my dad's place after a long day that my car announces, *Kaylee Olson calling. Accept call?*

I think about answering. She's grown to be one of my closest friends, but she was Cooper's friend first. Just the idea of what this conversation could turn into has me clicking the *no* button on the car display.

A minute later, my car lets me know I have a new voicemail. I click the button to play it.

"Hey babe, it's Kay. I got your info about the fun run and I love it. If you want to go ahead with the planning, let me know. If you don't, I'll need to find someone because I think it's a definite yes from both Ben and me. I also wanted to check on you since I know your boy is gone for the next month. When Ben has training camp he's only gone two weeks and I know how awful that is. I can't imagine a whole month. I'm here if you need me. Give me a call when you get a chance. Bye!"

It's sweet that she's thinking of me, but it's also clear she doesn't know that Cooper and I are over. She's in Montana right now, so it's not like I can meet her at Tight Fit in the morning.

I think about what to do as I navigate the short trip toward home, and I decide I'll send her a text once I'm in my pajamas with my dinner ordered, Ruby Sue has been fed and let out, and I'm settled on the couch with the latest from Netflix and a puppy on the cushion next to me.

Me: *Thanks for thinking of me.*

Send.

I don't want to talk on the phone right now. I don't want to tell her how Cooper and I are done. Saying the words is so much harder than spelling them out and hitting send. And at least if I text her, I can wallow by myself at home after I send it. I don't have to reply to any other messages. I don't even have to *read* any other messages.

Me: *PS Cooper broke up with me. Not ready to talk about it.*

I stare at the words without hitting send. The doorbell rings and I grab my food. I settle back on the couch and pick up my phone.

Send.

I draw in a deep breath and let it out slowly.

A reply comes through, but I'm just not ready to talk about it yet. Maybe tomorrow.

Maybe not.

It's not until morning when I read what she says.

Kaylee: *I had no idea. I'm here when you're ready, and Ben and I will be in Vegas for a charity soon. I'll be around if you want to meet for morning kickboxing or evening vodka. Or afternoon vodka. Love you.*

Welp, afternoon and evening vodka are both out.

And then there's morning kickboxing.

Can I even kickbox when I'm pregnant? I run a quick search before I write her back, and the consensus is it's probably dangerous but I should talk to my doctor.

Great.

I can't even work out all this aggression building up inside me.

I continue ignoring texts from my father.

I continue waiting to hear from Cooper. From Joanie. From Mia.

Still nothing.

I just got back from my Wednesday night marketing class and I'm eating dinner while scrolling my phone when I come across an Instagram post from the Vegas Heat.

It's from Dylan, obviously, since there are photos of the players. I scroll through the images and stop when I spot Cooper. He's lining up to catch a ball, and he looks…intense. Focused.

Maybe this is easier on him than it is on me. He got to walk away the day after he ended it, and I'm stuck in the same place. It's always harder on the person who has to stay. Now I'm living the same life I was living before, only the main key element is missing.

When I get to the office Thursday morning, I fire up Joanie's computer and do a quick check for Vegas Heat to see what sorts of social images are being posted across the web on our behalf.

And that's when I spot some photos I didn't see last night.

AJ Winters and Danny Brewer were spotted out on the town. They're chatting up some ladies, and just behind them sitting in a booth with Rush Ross sits Cooper Noah, sipping a beer with seemingly no cares in the world.

Has he already moved on?

Did he chat up a lady like AJ and Danny? Did he take one home?

It's not my prerogative to care anymore…yet I do.

Just the thought of him with another woman causes my stomach to twist.

I set a hand over my stomach. "It's okay, baby," I whisper.

That's the moment Joanie chooses to walk in. Her eyes zero in on my hand over my stomach, and then her wide eyes move to mine.

I slide my hand away and pretend like she didn't just catch me soothing the growth in my stomach.

"Oh my God, Joanie," I say softly. I rise to a stand, and I move across the office toward her. I wait for her to make the next move. Do we hug here?

I stare across the space at her. She's as gorgeous as ever, but she's wearing significantly less make-up than usual, and she's in joggers and a Heat tee rather than her usual business professional attire.

She presses her lips together as her eyes flick down to my stomach. "Hey," she says. She doesn't ask the question I'm sure she's thinking, but it's not like I'm going to tell her. I won't confess anything to her that I'm not ready to tell my father. I won't make her keep more of my secrets.

"How are you?" I ask.

"I've been better." She shrugs. "You?"

"I don't know if I've ever been worse," I admit, and I reach over to hug her.

"Cooper ended things?" she guesses.

I nod. "He wouldn't tell me what my dad said to him, but I think my dad made him choose and he chose the game. Speaking of which, have you spoken to my father?"

She shakes her head. "I've tried. He won't answer. He wouldn't allow me to travel with the team. Mike's heading up for a few days and promised he'd check in on him for me, but I hate not being there. I hate worrying. I hate not knowing where any of this stands."

I reach over and grab her hand in mine. "I hate it, too."

"Have you spoken to him?" she asks carefully.

"My dad?" I ask, and she nods. I shake my head. "No. He tried calling, but I can't find it in me to want to hear what he has to say."

"Oh, Gabby," she says softly. She hugs me again. "You need to talk to him."

"You're only saying that because you want me to check on him."

She shakes her head. "I'm only saying that because you center him, honey. You're his entire world, and while it's true we're all worried about his heart and his stress levels, you both went far too long without each other to let this come between you."

"If your father gave Troy an ultimatum that resulted in him dumping you, would you feel the same way?" I counter as I pull out of her embrace. I perch on the edge of her desk instead.

"It's hard to say since that isn't how things went down, but I know what I saw in you the night of his heart attack, and I know you shouldn't waste time being mad when we all know we're not guaranteed tomorrow." She lifts her chin a little, and I wish I could set the clock back to a few minutes before their wedding. I wish I could fix everything.

But I can't, so my only option is to make it through each day until things start looking up again.

"Where are you staying?" I ask.

She presses her lips together. "At a friend's house."

"Come back home," I say, practically begging. "I miss you. It's so lonely there."

"I miss you too, honey, but I can't. It's too hard." She glances around the office as her eyes start to get misty. "I don't even know if I can keep working here. He told me in no uncertain terms it's over, and I'm not sure how I move forward when every part of my life was so assimilated with his." She shakes her head. "I have family back in Wisconsin. I'm thinking about going there a while to figure things out."

My own eyes get a little misty at her words. "I get it. Believe me, if anyone understands not wanting to be here, it's me."

She nods. "I know you do. And I wish things could be different, Gabby. Really. I enjoyed getting to know you, and I really felt like we were becoming a family."

"So did I. And maybe there's still hope." I offer a shrug. My dad is upset at the lies, but maybe he can find a way to trust her again.

"For you, too," she says. She gives me another hug, and then she walks out as I try to rationalize why it's so easy to tell her there might be hope when I don't believe it for myself for even a second.

Chapter 11
Cooper

I don't think. I just react.

I leap to my left after I see the batter connect with the ball. It's coming at probably a hundred miles an hour, and the last time I attempted to catch one of these, I sat out for the next three years.

Today, though, I catch that fucking line drive. It slaps into my glove, and I grab it and hurl it across the field to Danny on first base to get the double play to end the fourth inning.

The starters sit after that, but we gave a good enough effort in the first four innings that the relievers just have to keep the Padres from scoring.

In the end, the Vegas Heat wins our first Cactus League Spring Training game with a score of four to one.

We have thirty-four games over the next month with three doubleheaders and a grand total of two days off before the season begins.

It's supposed to be fun. It's always been fun. But as hard as I try, I can't seem to find that feeling of fun in any of this.

I'm far from doing what brings me the most joy. Hell, at this point, I'm far from doing anything that brings me any joy at all anymore. And it makes no sense because this was always my *thing*. This has been my life for nearly thirty years. It's the thing that brings me closest to my father even now.

But after my talk with Nick, I can't help but wonder what my father would think of any of this. Nick was right—my father wouldn't want me to just walk away, but he also wouldn't want me to be this unhappy. He wouldn't want me to just simply fulfill a commitment I made if my heart wasn't in it.

But he was a man of his word, and he taught me to be one, too, in the few short years I had with him. The last thing I'd ever want is to do something he wouldn't be proud of, and letting down an entire organization after I agreed to be its leader feels like the wrong thing to do.

But does it feel more wrong than not having Gabby in my life?

It's the same argument I've had with myself a million times over the last few days. It's just not an apples to apples comparison and I think that's what's causing me to have such a hard time with it.

The next day is our first doubleheader, and we lose the first game but win the second. It's a split squad, so I only play in the second game, and it's as I'm coming off the field and heading toward the locker room that I hear it.

"Cooper!"

I turn at the sound of my name and spot a very pregnant Stacy Earnhardt smiling at me from the front row.

I don't know if she was here for the whole game, but my focus was on the field, not who was in the stands. I freeze for a beat before I turn back and walk over toward the first row.

"What are you doing here?" I try as hard as I can to keep the venom from my voice, but it's nearly impossible given the fact that I'm talking to Stacy of all people. She's not the person I want to be dealing with today—or any day.

But a lot of other people are around to witness this exchange, and so I need to remain civil.

"I came to see you, baby," she says.

Is she fucking high? "Well, you saw me. Thanks." I can't help when the sarcastic words drop from my mouth.

"Can we talk about the baby?" she asks.

Other people are listening. I know they are, and she's implying somehow that this baby is *mine* when that could not be further from the truth.

"I'm happy for you and your baby," I say. "But I have team responsibilities to get to. I'll catch you later."

I don't mean that. I will not be catching her later, but it's one of those things that's polite to say when you walk away from someone or when other people are around.

As I turn to walk away from her, I spot Dylan catching our exchange on his phone. I don't know if he's taking video or photos, but it doesn't matter. I already know what's going to happen here—as if I'm some sage who can predict the future.

I'm not sure what went down between Mia and Gabby and whether Dylan and the internship had something to do with it, but I do know that Dylan will use the footage to create a story where there isn't one.

It doesn't matter what I say here. It doesn't matter what I do. He's not the only one aiming a phone at me, and somehow, someway this will hit the internet and I'm certain Gabby will see it.

I don't want her to see it. I don't want her to be hurt or to jump to conclusions.

But maybe it's what she needs to see so she can press on.

I don't join the guys for beers at the bar since I'm exhausted after playing today combined with the mental strain from everything going on. Instead, I sit on the patio by myself, a fire roaring in the fire pit, and I try to figure out what the right thing to do is.

When I'm on the field for four innings every day over the next six days, my focus is there. I push everything else from my brain in an attempt to perform at the highest level. I'm supposed to be setting an example for the younger guys as the man tapped to be the face of this team, and I throw all my dedication into that because this is where I am right in this moment.

I go through the motions. I go out a few nights a week to drink beer with my buddies. I reject any advances coming my way. I try to stay out of trouble.

Mike drops into town during our second week of games. He spends a lot of time with Troy, but my interactions with my manager are limited to practice and game play. He doesn't ask for my input on strategy anymore, and part of me is even wondering if he's still considering me to be a starter. I've started every spring training game, but this is the month where baseball players need to prove themselves. This is a month where we will work to get noticed by our coaches so they can see what we are capable of.

For old guys like me, this month is meaningless. We're already assured our spot because of our big money contracts, and we don't need to prove ourselves since we've already done that in the past.

But I still study the game when I'm benched after the fourth inning. I watch the younger guys and see what the future of this team is going to look like. If I stick through my commitment and remain healthy, I don't know what's at the end of the line. I don't know what comes next for the Heat.

It might be one of these guys, or it might be somebody from another team, but part of what I'm doing here is building a legacy.

That means looking toward our next generation and who's going to carry this team forward once I retire.

And as much as I keep thinking all that and studying what everyone else is doing, the more I think I won't be here for all three years to figure it out.

Chapter 12
Gabby

"What the fuck?" I mutter. I stare at the photo and scroll to the video just below it. I watch it again for the hundredth time since it was posted.

I don't know the exact date it was taken, but I scan the article to try to find the information when my eye catches on the headline once more.

Cooper Noah spotted with pregnant ex! Is it his?

Right below the headline is a photo of a very pregnant Stacy.

Is it his?

Nine months ago was before he met me but he never mentioned going back to his ex for seconds after they broke up. In fact, I feel like I know him well enough to believe he'd never do that.

Still, it hurts to see the photo. It hurts to see him talking to her at all even though it shouldn't. He can talk to whoever he wants to, and that was true when we were together or now that we're apart. But it doesn't change the fact that my chest tightens and my stomach hurts looking at this photo.

She can give him everything he ever wanted.

But so can I.

He never wanted it with her.

I think he wanted it with me.

He left anyway.

"I'm so, so sorry," Mia says.

Yep, that's right. Mia. She showed up at my door with the photos when I got off work. She came over full of apologies and wanting to get our friendship back, and I guess she thought showing me my ex with another woman was the way to do that.

I don't even know how she knows Cooper is my ex other than the Dylan connection. I sure haven't spoken to her about it.

"How did you even know about this?" I ask.

"Dylan took the photos."

Of freaking course he did. "You can see yourself out." I spin and start to walk away, but her voice stops me.

"Are you kidding? I came here to try to fix things. Why are you being like this?"

"You came here to prove that your boyfriend has access to my ex that I don't have. You came to brag that he sold photos to some celebrity gossip site that I don't even give a fuck about. You did not come here to fix our friendship. You came here to one up me and to show me that he deserves the social media job more than I do. I don't even care about that job anymore. You know what? I'm withdrawing my name from the running for it. Please go."

She stares at me with her jaw slackened for a bit, and then she spins and walks out the front door, slamming it behind her.

I want to cry over it. I want to be upset over it. But it just feels like the hits keep coming, and I'm at a point where I'm starting to get numb to them.

She doesn't know I'm pregnant, and she's not the kind of friend that I'm going to tell that to anymore. She drew a line in the sand. She decided to choose her boyfriend over her best friend, so I guess that makes me her former best friend.

A text from Kaylee comes through.

Kaylee: *Back in Vegas. Tight Fit in the morning?*

She has been really good about not pressing me or asking questions about what happened between Cooper and me, though she has checked in on me every day via text. I think she wants me to talk about it, and I'm guessing this invitation for tomorrow is the vehicle she's going to use to get us there.

Me: *Sure. See you at 6:30.*

She responds with a party horn emoji expressing her excitement.

I make some dinner and settle into another movie with Ruby Sue, and I fall asleep on the couch.

I wake up at five in the morning and get a little work done before I head over to the gym. It's crowded as it always is at this time in the morning, but considering Kaylee is married to the owner, we tend to get preferential treatment here.

Kaylee is standing by the doorway when I walk in, and she squeezes me into a tight hug.

I can't help it. I burst into tears.

"Oh, friend," she consoles me softly. "I'm so, so sorry."

"Thanks," I manage. I draw in a deep breath as I force the sobs away before this gets real ugly in here. "I keep waiting for it to get easier, to stop hurting so much…but it's just not."

She lets me out of the hug and keeps her arm around my shoulders. "I've been there, and maybe there's still hope. I thought it was over with Ben, but we found our way back to each other. You know, once he got his head out of his ass."

I can't help a small laugh at that.

"But I have to tell you, I felt the same way you're feeling right now when it was over with him. It felt like there was a weight so heavy on my chest I couldn't breathe. You two will find your way back, too."

"I just don't see a way." I shake my head sadly. "He chose the game over me. He's had the game since he was five years old. He's only had me since August."

"Love makes men do crazy things, babe." She side squeezes me.

"Yeah," I whisper. "I just wish it was his love for me that made him do the crazy thing and not his love for the game."

"I have faith you two will figure this out," she says as we walk through the gym toward the classrooms at the back. "I know Cooper pretty well, and I've gotten to know you well, too. You two belong together, so keep your chin up and keep the faith. Now let's go sweat our asses off and make ourselves feel better."

I nod and follow her to the kickboxing room where a session is just about to get started.

"Oh," I stammer. "Can we, uh, do something else this morning?"

Her brows knit together. "No kickboxing? But that's, like, our *thing*."

I nod. "I know. I'm just feeling maybe treadmill or cycling today. I haven't done kickboxing in months and I'm out of shape." It's a feeble excuse.

She studies me for a beat, and my heart races. I feel like she can see right through me, but she doesn't say anything about my reasoning. Instead, she just nods. "Sure. Whatever you want, girlfriend."

We head over to the treadmills, and I can't help but think I just dodged a bullet.

But I don't know how long I'll be able to keep the baby from Kaylee, and once she finds out, I don't know how long I'll be able to keep it from Cooper, either.

Chapter 13
Cooper

When I walk out of the locker room and to the bus lot, a flurry of reporters waits. It's par for the course, but today, they're all yelling my name.

And there's more of them than usual.

And they're snapping my photograph and getting up in my face.

We just lost a game thanks to a catch I missed. I struck out at bat *twice*, and I never touched a base today. It was a shit game, and I'm sure they want to know why I played so poorly.

The last thing I feel like doing right now is answering questions about why I suck.

But nope. It has nothing to do with the game or the way I played. It has everything to do with my personal life.

"What can you tell us about Stacy Earnhardt?"

"Will you be there for the delivery of your child?"

"Are you back together with the mother?"

I stare at the reporters for a second like they've all grown two heads, and maybe they have.

"What?" I finally ask.

The questions come firing off at me again. I'm helpless as I stand there taking the bullets.

"Noah, get on the bus," Danny says from beside me as if ignoring any of this will make it go away.

I shake my head, and I look at the reporters. "Stacy is my ex. We broke up years ago and I have not been with her since the break-up. So if she's pregnant with my child, it's some sort of divine intervention. I am not back together with her nor will I be. Excuse me."

I'm proud of myself as I walk away.

A weaker man might've pointed out that the baby belongs to Alex Hamilton, who she cheated on me with. But I didn't say anything that wasn't true—even though I'm sure there will be headlines tomorrow telling the world I'm denying the child my ex is carrying.

Whatever.

I can't be moved enough to care.

Tonight's for drinking.

I head out with the crew to the bar we've been frequenting, and tonight, the bar is filled with players from the team. I spot Troy across the way, and Dylan the intern is hanging out with some of the guys from the minor league. And I even see GM Mike hanging out with some of the coaching staff.

Everybody's here, and for a second it just makes me want to crawl into the corner and hide.

With the big brass here along with the intern who's my only direct connection back to Gabby aside from Troy, I should be on my best behavior, right?

I'm not in the mood to be good tonight.

I'm not in the mood to be the team leader. I'm not in the mood to impress Troy or Mike.

I'm in the mood to get fucked up and to try to numb some of the constant ache in my chest.

And that's why I opt for tequila shots.

It's stupid. It's immature. It's ridiculous.

But it also works quickly, and that's what I'm going for right now.

After a shit game, shit headlines, and a shit love life, it's the least I can do. Except I know I'm not doing myself any favors. As I toss back the second shot and wince at the horrible taste, I know I'll play even worse tomorrow—if I can drag my ass out of bed to play.

But as it turns out, I *have* to drag my ass out of bed.

I hear loud knocking, and as I peel open my eyes, I'm not exactly sure where I am for a split second. Then I remember we're renting this house in Arizona, but I'm not exactly sure how I got into the bed in my bedroom.

I glance to my left.

At least the other side of the bed is empty.

The knocking won't subside.

"Dude, are you alive in there?" It's Danny's voice, and he's yelling. "Are you naked?"

I lift the covers to check. Nope, not naked. I slept in jeans, which I never do unless I pass out cold and I'm too wasted to take them off.

"Come in," I croak, and my mouth feels like I chewed on cotton balls all night.

"Dude, wake the fuck up! One, we have to leave for the field in an hour, but two…" He pauses, and he shakes his head. "No, you need to get up and showered before I hit you with two." He sets a cup of black coffee down on my nightstand, and I've never been more grateful to have his friendship.

I pick up the coffee and blow on it when I see the steam coming off the top, and then I take a gingerly sip. "Ahh," I say, and I'm reminded of my father.

He'd take that first sip of morning coffee and follow it up with an exaggerated *ahh* every time. And as I recall, it drove my mom nuts, so he'd do it after his second, third, and fourth sips as well. And beyond.

I can't help a small smile at the memory even though I feel like I got run over by a dump truck.

Or perhaps a tequila truck.

"What the fuck are you smiling at, man? Do you even realize what's going on?" Danny asks.

"I'm sort of enjoying the oblivion of *not* knowing what's up your ass, and I'd appreciate it if you could lower your voice about fifty decibels."

He shakes his head, and then he shoves his phone over to me.

I close my eyes for a beat before whatever this is hits me. I live in a moment of peaceful ignorance, and then I open my eyes to read the headline.

Cooper Noah out drinking as his child is born!

"You have got to be fucking kidding me," I mutter. I toss the phone back to him without bothering to read the article or look at the pictures. "So she had the baby?" I ask brightly.

Danny doesn't laugh as I expect him to. "What are you going to do?" he asks, his tone gravely serious.

"Noah!" a voice calls from another room.

But it doesn't just *call*. It yells. Angrily. And it's immediately recognizable.

"I told you to get up," Danny whispers.

"Thanks for the warning," I mutter dryly.

A second later, Troy Bodine appears in my doorway. "You want to tell me what the *fuck* is going on with you when you're supposedly so *in love* with my daughter?" he booms.

Jesus Christ. So I can't be with her, but I also can't be with anybody else?

I get that isn't the issue, but my personal life is literally none of his business. Back talk won't do me any favors right now, though, so I keep my trap shut.

"And a top of the morning to you, too, sir," I say. I take another sip of coffee, and I can't help another *ahh* out of habit.

Troy looks like he's about to bust a vein in his neck as he looks at me. "You're sitting here all relaxed without a care in the world while my daughter won't answer my fucking calls and you're knocking up your exes and galivanting around town like it's no big deal? I brought you in to be a leader, Noah, and you're acting like a clown." He shakes his head. "Don't bother coming to the field today."

As much as it pains me to get out of bed, I rise to my feet so I can stand the fuck up for myself. "There are two separate issues at play here. You gave me an ultimatum, sir. You told me you would not allow me to fuck up the team, and you gave me no choice. It's not my fault if your daughter doesn't like what you did and won't answer your calls. You made me choose the team, to adhere to the ninety million dollar commitment I signed off on to make you happy, to end things with Gabby, and here I am. I'm fucking up, and I'm heartbroken, and I'm a fucking *human* trying to move on."

He stares at me with that flinty look in his eyes again. He doesn't like me talking about his daughter, and that's why we haven't. But we're here to have it out, so let's fucking go.

"As for the second issue," I continue, "I haven't been with Stacy in years. That baby is not mine, and I told the press as much. She fucked Alex Hamilton, and he won't take responsibility for it, so she's hinting that I'm the father. I don't know if she's doing it to fuck up *my* life or if she's doing it because she knows I'm the type of guy who would help out. She has nothing to do with any of this, and how I handle her is not anybody's business but my own. Did I get fucked up last night? Yep, I sure did. Have I made all the wrong decisions lately? You bet your ass I have. But my father taught me to see my commitments through, and that's why I'm here. If you choose to bench me, you're doing exactly what you said you wouldn't do when I chose to play."

He's quiet a beat, and then he asks, "And the photos from last night?"

My brows draw together. "What photos?"

Danny, the silent witness to all this, nudges me.

"What photos?" I say a little louder.

"That's what I was trying to show you, man," Danny says. He hands me his phone again, and this time I scroll past the dirty headline.

I blow out a breath at what I see.

Normally I wouldn't care. People can say shit about me all they want and I just brush it off. But I never cared so much about somebody else before, and this is something that would hurt her to see.

It's me with my arm around another woman as we laugh together.

"Nothing happened," Danny assures me.

We're not kissing. We don't even look that close, but it's clear it was taken by an insider and sold to this gossip site.

And I can bet who the fuck took the photo.

"That fucking intern," I mutter.

Troy's eyebrows dip as he looks up at me. "The intern?"

I hiss out a breath. I didn't want to get into this with Troy, but here we are. "He's dating Gabby's friend Mia, and he doesn't like that Gabby's a shoe-in for the social media position. He thinks it's not because she's the best person for the job, but because she's related to you, and he and some of the other interns don't like it."

"Is that why I haven't seen Mia around lately?" he asks.

I shrug. "Could be. Or could be that you've been too busy to notice."

He glares at me a little, but I don't care.

"I don't want Gabby to see these," I mutter.

"They're everywhere, Cooper. I don't think she'll be able to avoid them," Troy counters. "But I'll take care of the intern, that little shit."

I think about asking what he's going to do, but that's when I realize...I don't care.

And as much as I wish I could get ahead of this, I can't. It's already out there for the world to draw their own conclusions, and my only option is to keep my head down and forge on ahead. "So am I getting ready to play or am I sitting out?"

"Get your uniform on," Troy says gruffly, and then he walks out without another word.

Chapter 14
Gabby

Me: *I'll finish out the month but once the team is back, I won't be able to continue working at the stadium. I'm also withdrawing my name from the interviews for the social media position. Thank you for everything you've done for me.*

I click send, and my message goes through the airwaves to land somewhere on Joanie's phone. I don't know where she is, and she wasn't in again today.

But those pictures were sure all over the damn place.

Cooper smiling. Cooper laughing. Cooper tossing his arm around some woman who's still pretty young but not quite so young as me.

It's too painful to be here even when he's not here moving on in front of my face. I can't imagine how hard it would be to witness it all in person.

Screw that. I'm out.

I text Kaylee next.

Me: I just gave Joanie my notice and I took my hat out of the ring for the SM position.

She told me to keep her updated, and here we are.

I head toward the bar next since that's where the other interns have gathered after a long day of work. We're prepping for the season now, which means we're open to the public and giving tours on a daily basis. Justin has led the majority of them, and for someone who claims to dislike baseball the way he does, he sure enjoys giving the stadium tours.

I collapse into the booth beside Justin, who's now squished in the middle between Brian and me. Brian may no longer be an intern, but he and Justin are still going strong. At least I think they are. I've been sort of wrapped up in my own drama to have really taken notice.

Chloe is across the table with Mackenzie beside her, and Mackenzie glares at me a little.

I glare back, and then I announce, "I withdrew my name from the social media manager interviews just now."

My announcement is met with silence.

"What?" Mackenzie asks at the same time Chloe breathes, "But why?"

"Let's get this girl drunk!" Justin says rather than asking.

I realize Mackenzie thinks Cooper and I broke up a while ago, so I'm careful with my answer. "It just wasn't the right fit for me."

I excuse myself to the restroom since the baby has decided to make my bladder her pillow today, and when I return to the table, I catch the tail end of what Mackenzie is saying.

"It's about damn time. She never deserved it."

I don't sit. I don't slide into the booth. Instead, I fold my arms over my chest. "What the fuck is your problem?" I spit at her.

"Excuse me?" she asks very innocently.

"You've never liked me, and that's fine. But to talk shit that I don't deserve it?" I shake my head. "That's just nasty."

"You don't. You only got the internship in the first place because of your father," she says. She picks up her drink, her hands nice and steady, and meanwhile I'm shaking like a leaf as this confrontation way too long in the making finally takes place.

"I'm damn good at my job. It doesn't matter how I got there. What matters is that I proved myself while I was there."

She rolls her eyes.

I look at Justin. "I'm sorry, but I'm out. I'm not dealing with this shit." I spin and walk away, and he chases after me with Brian hot on his trail.

Once I'm out front, I'm still shaking. "I fucking hate her."

"I know, baby girl," Justin says, his arms looping around me. Brian hugs me from the other side, and now I'm the meat in a Justin-Brian sandwich.

"She sucks," Brian agrees.

"But you told her off, and I've never been so proud of you." He kisses my forehead, and it feels good to be with my friends. He lets me go, and he glances at Brian. "Ready?"

Brian nods.

"Just before you got there, we decided we're telling my parents tonight. I want you to be there with me," Justin says, squeezing my hand.

"Me?" I ask, my hand moving to my chest.

"I'm not sure I can do it without you," he says.

"Then let's get the hell out of here before you lose your nerve," I suggest, and he laughs as we part ways to get into our own cars and head over to his place.

Three cars pull into Justin's driveway at the same time, and we all walk in together.

"Mom?" he yells. "Dad?"

His mom appears in the doorway with her brows drawn together, a kitchen towel in her hands, and his dad walks down the stairs a minute later with the same expression on his face.

Justin looks at Brian, and then he looks at me, and then he takes a deep breath. "Can you both sit down? I have something I need to say to you."

They sit, and I note that they don't sit close to one another. His mom takes the love seat, and his dad takes the couch. They don't bother looking at one another.

"What's going on, honey?" his mom asks. I've met Laura Larson a handful of times—more when Justin and I first became friends and I was trying to escape living in the bedroom next to Cooper.

I thought things were bad then. They had nothing on things now.

Justin draws in a deep breath. "I love you both, but I've been hiding something for a long time now. In fact, it's probably been a secret for ten years."

His dad's brows knit together further, and he leans forward on his knees and clasps his hands. "What is it, Justin?"

His parents are looking at him so earnestly, so lovingly, that I have a hard time believing they'll react the negative way he assumes they will.

"I, uh…I'm gay."

I brace for their reaction.

His dad blows out a breath, and his mom blinks at him for a few beats before she tilts her head and narrows her eyes.

His dad glances at his mom, and their eyes meet and lock for a beat.

"Finally," his dad says.

"We know, honey," his mom says. "We've been waiting for you to be ready to tell us." She stands, and she walks over to him and pulls him into a hug. "And I'm so proud of you for choosing today. For choosing honesty. For choosing to love yourself."

"Seriously?" Justin says. "You're not mad?"

"Why would we be mad?" his dad asks, walking over to hug his son next, and I can't help the tear that splashes onto my cheek.

"Because I'm not who you thought I'd become," Justin says sadly.

"You're everything we thought you'd become," his dad says.

"You're a hard worker, and you're smart, and you're kind," his mom adds. "That's what we wanted for you, but above all that, we want you to be happy. And if it's Gabby that makes you happy, great. If it's Brian, great. If it's being on your own, great. We're here to support you and love you through the ups and downs we all share in life."

Justin's brows dip in confusion. "Seriously? I waited ten years to tell you and there's not going to be an arguing match? There's no trying to convince me to be somebody I'm not? Just acceptance?"

"Just acceptance," his dad repeats, and he hugs his son again.

My heart swells for my friend. I know how hard it was for him to do that, and I'm so proud of him for finally confessing his biggest secret to his parents. For coming out. For putting his own happiness first.

I wish that I could find a way to do that, too.

I just don't think I can do it here in Vegas.

Chapter 15
Gabby

I start my Monday morning by meeting Kaylee at Tight Fit. It's the week the Heat comes back from Arizona, and I have not braced myself for it the way I should have. Instead, I'm a nervous wreck, and I'm hopeful some morning exercise will center me.

"Have you thought about my offer?" Kaylee asks as soon as I walk in.

I giggle. "I have, and working for SFK full time with you would be an awful lot of fun. But I don't know if I'm cut out for staying in Vegas."

She grabs my arm and pulls a little. "Oh come on," she says, drawing out the final word. "You *have* to stay. Don't be dramatic. Things will get better, and Vegas is the land of opportunity."

"Isn't *America* the land of opportunity?" I ask, my brows scrunching together in confusion.

She laughs. "Maybe in the old-timey days, but now it's Vegas, baby."

"When do you need an answer?" I ask.

"Yesterday."

I laugh again, but it feels a little forced. As much as I'd love to work with Kaylee, something keeps pulling me in another direction. I don't know if it's a good idea to continue being close to someone who is also close to Cooper. Still, I do think it would be a great opportunity since I pulled out of the social media position with the Heat. "Send me the contract terms and I'll look it over while I decide what to do."

"Fine, fine. Can I convince you over the rowing machine today?" she asks.

"I can't use the row," I say before I realize the words have fallen from my mouth. My eyes go wide as she narrows her eyes at me.

"Wait a minute. No kickboxing, no rowing…" She trails off as she puts the pieces together. "Sit-ups?"

I shake my head.

"How about some planks?" she asks.

"I shouldn't."

She sighs, and she glances down at my stomach. "Are you going to tell him?"

I'm both terrified and relieved at the same time that she knows…that I don't have to hold onto this secret by myself anymore. "I have to at some point, right?"

She pulls me into a hug. "He'd never, *never* let you go through this alone, Gabby. It's everything he's ever wanted with the one woman he's ever wanted it with."

"Except he's the one who ended things, remember?" I point out.

"I get that, but maybe this is what will bring you back together."

I shake my head. "I don't *want* a baby to be the thing that brings us back together. I want him to come back to me because he wants *me*, not because he wants some ideal picture of the perfect family. He already ruled me out of his future. He made his choice, and it was baseball. It was my father. It wasn't me."

She presses her lips together. "He hasn't been answering my calls. I've tried, but I know he's busy with spring training. But I know him, and I know his heart. I still have this gut feeling that somehow you two will find your way back to one another."

"I wish I had that same gut feeling," I say sadly. "Now let's hit the treadmills, okay? I don't want to talk about him. I'll tell him when the time is right."

"How far along are you?"

"Fourteen weeks," I admit.

"*Fourteen* weeks?" she screeches.

"Shh," I warn, glancing around.

She shakes her head in awe. "Girl, you can keep a *secret*. But listen, you don't have a whole lot of time before your body won't let you keep it anymore."

"I know. And speaking of which, I need to pee before we start our workout."

She giggles. "I remember those days well."

"Are you ready for number three?" I tease.

Her eyes widen in horror. "Oh God no," she blurts, and the act is all a little much.

I have a feeling she and Ben are probably already trying for number three. They seem like the type who can't keep their hands off each other.

I can't help but dwell on that for a beat. They have it so easy. They have ten years between them, and they ended up with their happy ending.

Why can't I?

I take a quick shower after our workout and head to the stadium for one of my final days of my internship. The team gets back Wednesday, and the first game of the season is Friday. Joanie asked me to stay until Thursday, and I agreed.

At our morning meeting, Joanie says, "The interviews will be tomorrow, and Justin, Mackenzie, and Chloe have all been selected for a spot." She glances up at me. "And I'd like you to interview, too, Gabby, just for the interviewing experience. It won't hurt to have the practice, and our team will be there anyway."

I nod. "Thank you."

"And of course you all know Dylan was never an option as his campaigns and work weren't quite on the level we're looking for, but with him being fired, he's out of contention," Joanie says.

"What exactly happened there?" Mackenzie asks, finally making herself useful for once since we're all wondering the same thing.

"He sold photos he took of some players to the highest bidder and made sure the gossip outlet would create a storyline to make things appear a certain way." She gives me a pointed look, and I immediately know it was the photos of Cooper that have been all over the internet.

"So why is she still here if she's not even going for the job?" Mackenzie asks, jutting a thumb in my direction.

"Not that it's any of your concern, but she's finishing out her internship." Joanie offers her a glare, and I've never loved her more than this moment. "And you best watch your tone if you want a serious consideration for the position." Okay, maybe I love her even a little more.

Mackenzie huffs a bit at that but does keep her mouth shut for the rest of the meeting. We're released for our morning duties, and I can't help but wander around a little. Soon the stadium will be filled with people waiting for tours before the season gets underway, but there's something peaceful about walking around before the chaos. I'll miss this place.

I walk by the StrongFitKids area on the Spade Level, and I can't help the tears that spring to my eyes. I stop in front of it, and I can picture children laughing as they run through the play structure and race their siblings and other kids at the game. I check out the circuits with the trampolines in between.

Cooper and I made this happen together.

I had less of a role in it, but I was still there for its inception. My dad is the manager of this team. It's not like I'll never come to a game even if Cooper Noah is playing third. Maybe someday our child will run around this area we built together.

The thought makes me sad. Our child won't have a sibling to run around with—much like I never did. I can't even fathom ever finding someone to love the way I loved Cooper. I don't want children with some other man even if it would give this baby the sibling he or she deserves.

I brush the tears away, and that's when I hear footsteps coming up behind me and a throat clearing.

"You okay?" Justin asks.

"No," I say with a shaky voice.

He pulls me into his embrace, and I feel safe here. Warm. Cared for.

But it's not the type of safe and warm I'm really craving right now.

Only one person could give me that.

But he chose to walk away.

Chapter 16
Cooper

The best part about the intern getting fired was that Troy did it in front of us all as we arrived at the stadium for the game.

"Intern!" he yelled, and Dylan scrambled over to him. "You used insider knowledge both to your advantage and to your profit, and that is not something this team stands for, nor is it acceptable," he said as he raised his voice at Dylan.

I have to say, it was far more satisfying watching someone else get yelled at than being the constant brunt of Troy's anger.

I was sure it would center back on me before long, and I couldn't help the tiny feeling of hope that took root in my chest. If Dylan was no longer working with us, would Troy call in another intern?

Would he call in Gabby?

My gut knew he wouldn't, and the hope dissipated pretty quickly. He didn't want me around her, and bringing her here would only have given us access to finding our way back to each other.

She had to be feeling it too. I knew she did.

Because I knew how I felt, and I knew how we were together. There's no way she just picked up and moved on.

And maybe *that* is what gave me a glimmer of hope.

But with her in Vegas and me Arizona, Troy had an entire month to widen the divide between us. It was always unlikely he'd choose her as Dylan's replacement, and she had a weekly class she needed to attend anyway.

And as it turned out, it isn't her. They didn't send a replacement, which means we didn't get the social media coverage we were expecting. Instead, we were told to share any images we take with a team email address. I opted out of that nonsense since I haven't exactly been in the photo-taking mood.

As the month went on, the ache in my chest seemed to be getting worse instead of better.

And as the month of spring training draws to a close with no more threats issued to me from Troy, the anticipation of heading home looms closer and closer.

I've been going through the motions as I battle the media frenzy surrounding Stacy and her insinuations, and through it all, I wonder what Gabby is thinking. What she's doing. How she's feeling. If she still loves me. If there's still a chance for us.

I could've picked up the phone a hundred times, but even when I get back, I know I won't. I can't.

Not when Troy drew a line in the sand. Not when I think about the real reasons why I chose to end it with her.

I won't come between her and her father. What they do now that I'm out of the picture is their decision.

But I also don't know that I can play for Troy. I'm starting to think I should cut my losses and move back to San Diego—maybe try to get my old job back at SFK.

As the bus rolls back into Vegas and the flashing lights of the Strip come into view once we pass over the hill in Henderson, I can't help but wonder whether Vegas was ever really the place for me.

"I miss Fun Cooper," Danny whines as he slides into the empty seat beside me.

"I miss peace and quiet," I mutter, and Danny laughs as he punches my shoulder.

"See? I knew your sense of humor was still in there somewhere," he muses.

"Who said I was joking?" I ask.

"We're going out to Honeys tonight if you're game," he says, mentioning the strip club frequented by players on the local athletic circuit.

"I'm out." I shake my head and hold up a hand. "I'm just glad to be back home, man. Besides, I'm sick of being around all you motherfuckers."

He laughs, but in truth I could use a few hours to myself. The only light that seems to be shining right now is on the fact that I get to go home to my big, silent house all by myself.

We only have one day off before opening day, and I don't want to spend it hungover or full of even more regrets than I already feel. Besides, I know the sentiment of *glad to be back home* won't last long. Our first two series of the season are at home, and then we're out of town for a week.

The bus drops us at the stadium, and we all scatter to our own cars and trucks. I patiently wait my turn to exit the parking lot while many of the others show off by peeling out, but that's never really been my style.

I head home, ready for that beacon of peace that's been just beyond the horizon for an entire month, and as I turn the corner onto my street, the hope for silence is gone in a flash.

A car sits in my driveway. It's not one I recognize, but it's a Lincoln SUV. I only know one person who rents Lincoln SUVs when he's away from home, and incidentally he also has access to a key to my house through our mother.

So Connor's here, and maybe his family, and maybe my mother, and while I'm grateful that we're close, grateful they came to visit, grateful to have such wonderful people in my life, it sort of feels like the wish and hope of peace and quiet flies right out the window of my truck as I pull into my driveway.

I walk in the front door, and it's sweet. Really.

Posterboards proclaiming *Welcome Home Cooper* and *Knock it out of the park* and *Twenty-One, He's my son* are hung in my foyer, and I hear music coming from the family room. I walk in that direction.

"Surprise!" my family yells at me, and sure enough, everyone made the trip—Connor, Marissa, Ethan, Jake, and my mother.

It's great they're here. I'm happy to see them.

But I also wanted a night off, and instead, I'm blindsided into the role of host.

They came out to attend opening day, and while I'm excited they'll be here for that, excited we can all be together, I just wish they would've given me a little notice instead of opting for the surprise visit.

And I really wish my mother didn't feel the need to confront me after everyone else went to bed.

"Have you talked to Gabby?" she asks. We're sitting on the couch in front of my fireplace and television, both of which are turned off right now. She's sitting with her legs tucked under her as she studies me while I'm collapsed back with my head resting on the back of the couch as I stare up at the ceiling.

Over the course of spring training, I talked to my mom a few times a week. Not daily like I usually do, but that's how it is during the season. Things get busy. But she knows I ended things with

Gabby, and she knows my heart is broken over it. That's the extent of what she knows.

I shake my head.

"Coop, talk to me, baby," she says softly. "You've been radio silent for the last month. You said you ended things, but you never said why, and I saw you two together. I know this is something special."

"*Was*, Mom. It *was* something special." My voice is soft but firm.

"What happened between you two?"

I feel her eyes on me, and as much as I'm not ready to revisit every detail of what went down, maybe she has some words of wisdom to help me figure out a way to move forward.

"Troy and Joanie decided to get married the night before we left for Arizona in a surprise wedding. I walked into the chapel to see if it was time for photos while Troy waited outside, and Gabby was in there. She was beautiful, Mom." I close my eyes at the memory of the absolute vision my girl was that day. "I kissed her, and Troy caught us. We had no choice but to come clean. Joanie admitted she knew, and he called off the wedding and stormed out. I found him at the club he owns, and he essentially told me I would not screw up the team over this and what I was doing was practically illegal. He told me I had to break it off with her before we left the next morning or he'd go to Mike and blow it up himself."

"So you chose the team over her?" my mom asks, and I keep my eyes closed but I can tell she's glaring and pursing her lips at me.

"It wasn't like that." I open my eyes and sit up a little to defend my choices. I know Gabby sees it that way, too, but that's not what happened. At least in my mind it isn't. "It wasn't about me at that point anymore. It was about her relationship with her father. It was about honoring the commitment I made to the team before I knew that this thing with her was going to become what it did. It was about protecting her from the fallout of all of this. From the judging eyes of the media and the fans and the general public."

"Honey, you can't protect her from those things. She has a famous father. She's in the spotlight whether she wants to be or not, and if anything, you there holding her hand might offer her a layer of protection," she points out, which is honestly something I hadn't thought of before.

Instead of thinking the two of us could get through this together by holding hands through it, my brain went the opposite direction to believe she's better off without me.

And now I'm left a little confused as to which answer is the right one.

"Even if that's true, what about Troy?" I ask. "I knew all along he'd never be okay with the idea of anybody with his daughter."

"Then why'd you stay with her as long as you did?" she asks.

"Because I love her." The answer seems so simple. "When we were hiding it from him, it was easy. It felt wrong, maybe, but we were flying under the radar."

"Love should never have to be hidden." She reaches over and grabs my hand. She squeezes it. "You're miserable, baby boy, and it makes my heart hurt for you. I want to fix it, but I don't know how."

"You can't fix the unfixable."

"Gosh, you sound so much like your father." She shakes her head as her words ping right into my heart. "He was so stubborn, and once he got an idea in his head, he had a hard time letting it go. It seems you have this idea in your head that you're the sole leader on that team. But you know what? The Dodgers survived when you got hurt. It's a *team* effort. I know you think you're doing the right thing by honoring the commitment you made to the team, but if it's at the expense of your happiness, then maybe it isn't the right thing after all."

My only response is to lean my head back onto the back of the couch and stare up at the ceiling again.

"What do I do, Mom?" I murmur, my voice edged with emotion.

"Only you can decide that." Her answer is predictable, but she's right.

"What would Dad have wanted?" I ask. "Wouldn't he have told me to honor my commitments?"

"He would have told you he loved you and he was proud of you no matter what you decided. And I think he'd tell you to consider whether you're doing what you *think* you're supposed to do or if you're doing what you *actually* want to do."

My chest aches that he's not here as part of this conversation—that he hasn't been here for any of these conversations for twenty-four years.

God, has it really been that long?

It's been just over a month since I ended things with Gabby—since Troy forced my hand.

I remember the sentiment back when I ended things with Gabby the first time, back when I found out her father was Troy and I was staying in the bedroom beside hers. Back then I thought about how time is a cruel bitch that steals things from us, and back then I felt like I had to wait out the clock until I could move out of Troy's place and get the season underway.

But now it feels like time is moving too fast. It feels like I've wasted the last month not being with her.

Things aren't the same with Troy, and I'm certain they never will be again. It's not like I chose his friendship over my relationship with Gabby. Either way I was going to lose him, I suppose. I always imagined I'd be able to shoot the shit with my father-in-law, that we'd be friendly with each other while he acted as the type of person I could go to for advice if I needed it. I always imagined the same thing about my manager. Instead, Troy has largely written me off when it comes to personal relationships, and instead his only focus is on coaching.

So I didn't just lose the woman I love. I also lost my best friend, and I haven't had the time to mourn either one of those relationships because I've been too busy with spring training.

But now I'm back, and I want my life back.

I want *her* back.

I can't keep living like this.

"How do I get her back?" I whisper. Heat presses behind my eyes, an unusual and scary feeling I wouldn't let out in front of anybody but my mom.

She grabs my arm and squeezes it in a hug. "You fight for her, baby. You chose the game when you ended things with her. So now you choose her. Whatever that means."

Whatever that means.

Even if it means walking away from baseball.

Chapter 17
Cooper

I tossed and turned all night after my mother's words.

Now you choose her. Whatever that means. Whatever that means. Whatever that means.

It echoed in my brain over and over, and it sparked a pretty drastic realization.

I only get one life, and it's a short one at that.

I can't spend it miserable.

If I have to choose between her and the game, I choose her. Of course I choose her.

I made excuses before. I was scared, and I was stupid.

I thought my commitment to Troy and the rest of the team was more important than my personal feelings, but as it turns out, I can't play my best if I'm heartbroken. I can't be a leader when I'm constantly wondering whether I made the right choice, or wondering what she's doing, or wondering how I can get out of this mess.

All I can do is fucking fix it, and if that means walking away from the Heat, then that's what it means. I walked away from the game once before, so I have an apples to apples comparison.

And the truth is that walking away from Gabby hurt far worse than walking away from the game.

I said it before, and I'll say it again. She is it for me. She is what I want for the rest of my life. I love baseball. I will always love it. But I don't love it in the way I love Gabby. It doesn't fulfill me the way Gabby does.

There is no guarantee that I'll get her back just because I walk away from baseball.

She's probably hurt and angry and upset. She probably feels rejected and abandoned, and she has every right to. I *did* reject her.

I *did* abandon her. She even said as much the night before I left—that I'm just like everybody else. So now I have to prove that I'm not, and I have to beg and plead and grovel to try to find a way to get her back.

But it's not something I've ever had to do before, so it's not something I know how to do.

Still, it starts with the first step, and that's talking to Mike today after the team meeting.

I've made my decision. I can't have both. Troy has made that clear.

And now, I choose her…if she'll have me.

I choose a life with her…if she wants a life with me.

I choose myself. I choose happiness.

It's the day before opening day. It's late to be pulling out. I'm going to be letting a lot of people down.

But I'd rather let the entire team down than continue letting the one person who means the most to me in the entire world down.

I arrive at the stadium minutes before the meeting. Most of the others have been there all morning shooting the shit or working out as they mentally prepare for what's to come tomorrow.

I slide into a seat next to Danny, the man who has become my best friend on the team, I suppose, and he glances over at me.

"Why are you so late?" he asks.

I nod toward the front of the room where Troy and Mike are exchanging words before they start the meeting. "I made it on time."

His brows dip. "Barely. What's going on? I thought you'd be here first pumping us all up with your witty platitudes."

I can't help a grimace at that. I should have been here, but when my heart's not in it anymore, how could I?

"Sorry," I mutter. I turn and glance at him, and I lower my voice so only he can hear. "I'm telling Troy and Mike after the meeting that I'm out."

His eyes widen. "What?"

"You heard me."

"You can't do that." His voice holds an air of finality.

I shrug. "Well, I am. I'm putting myself first for once."

"Selfish prick," he mutters, and I know he's joking. "Hey." I glance over at him. "We'll be fucked without you, but good for you, man. Get your girl."

I press my lips together. "I hope it's not too late."

The meeting starts. Troy speaks, and Mike speaks, and I'm guessing I was supposed to speak but I wasn't asked to. All I can do is think about how this is probably the last team meeting I'll ever sit in.

"It's all about the fundamentals, boys," Troy says as he ends what's supposed to be an inspirational speech. "Hitting, throwing, catching. We have something to prove here, and it all starts tomorrow. I want to see hustle. I want to see excitement. I want to see you bleed Heat red and blue. Let's fucking go!"

AJ starts an *LFG* chant, and soon all the players in the room are standing and pumping their fists in the air as we get ready to fucking go.

I do my best to blend in, but my heart's not in it. Not when I know I won't be on that field tomorrow.

Not when I know what's coming up next.

The team is dismissed, and most of the guys head out to go home. It's the last day of semi-peace before the season begins and life gets hectic for a while—for them, anyway. I guess not so much for me.

I wait until the room is mostly cleared out then make my way toward the front of the room, where Mike and Troy are still talking. I wait patiently until Mike looks over at me.

"Can I talk to you both?" I ask.

"I have things to do," Troy says flippantly.

"And I have a meeting to get to," Mike adds.

"It'll only take a minute," I beg.

Mike glances behind me. A few guys are still hanging around, and he nods meaningfully toward them. "Let's head up to my office," he suggests, and Troy begrudgingly follows.

We're quiet in the elevator ride up to the front offices from the conference room where we just held our team meeting. I suppose I could just get it out here in the elevator, and I open my mouth when the car skids to a stop to let someone on.

I close my mouth again. I'll just wait until we're in Mike's office.

We get up there, and my heart starts beating faster.

I'm really doing this.

I'm really giving up the dream I've had my entire life so I can pursue a dream twelve years younger than me.

Mike walks around his desk and takes a seat in the executive chair. Troy sits in a chair facing him. I remain standing. I grip the back of the chair beside Troy, the one I should be sitting in, but I can't sit right now. I'm too nervous.

"What's going on, Cooper?" Mike asks.

I draw in a shaky breath.

I wish I would've practiced this. I wish I knew how to begin.

I don't, and that's why I blurt my first words. "I've decided to walk away."

Troy sits back in his chair like I've issued a physical blow while Mike's jaw slackens. Neither man says a word. It's so quiet in here I could hear a pin drop.

"Troy, I'm in love with your daughter, and you made me choose between her and the game. I chose wrong." I shake my head. "I've already lost your friendship, clearly. But I refuse to lose Gabby, too. It may be too late, but I have to try to win her back. I'm not happy, and I'm not playing with my heart because it's in pieces held by your daughter. I'm incomplete, and I'm broken, and there is nothing I want more than to go find Gabby and tell her that I chose wrong. I never should have chosen the game, but your ultimatum made me feel like I didn't have a choice. I want to choose her. I will *always* choose her going forward if she'll have me, and maybe it's too late. Maybe I lost her forever. But life is too short to spend it miserable even if it means I'm walking away from the team, from a ninety million dollar contract, from this legacy we were meant to build together...from our friendship. Because I'm not meant to build anything at all if it isn't with Gabby by my side, and I need to go fight to get her back."

Troy stands, and his face is red and he's breathing heavily and for a split second, I'm worried I've given him another heart attack. I glance at Mike, and I expect him to be looking at Troy, too, but instead his eyes are wide and he's looking beyond both of us at the doorway.

I turn to see what he's looking at, and my broken heart starts to race.

Because there she stands, and I'm pretty sure she heard every word I just said.

Chapter 18
Gabby

My eyes are fixed on Cooper.

He's back.

He's the same Cooper who left me a month ago, but instead of complete and total dejection as he walks away from me, his shoulders are squared with something like hope.

And he's…quitting?

For me?

I heard a loud voice as I made my way down the hall, and I recognized it immediately. I heard my name when he said *I refuse to lose Gabby, too.*

And I heard everything else that came after that.

He already lost me when he pushed me away, and the anger and fear that he'll do it again won't just go away.

But overhearing those words as he spoke them to my father, to Mike…it's simply everything.

He's choosing me—or not even me, but the idea of me. He has no idea where I stand, but he'd rather fight to get us back even if he loses than play baseball without me in his life.

That is what will heal the hurt and the abandonment and the scars my mother drove deep into me. Being chosen every single day. Being first in his heart. Being *his.*

My dad turns around to see what Cooper and Mike are looking at, and I realize I also haven't seen my father since that same night.

He got back last night. I knew he was coming home, so I chose to stay the night at Justin's place.

"You…you'd quit for me? You can't do that," I say, breaking the awkward silence in the room.

"Gabby," Cooper murmurs.

"What are you doing here?" my father asks.

"I, uh…" Why *am* I here? My brows dip as I try to gather my thoughts. "I came for a meeting with Mr. Perry." I turn to look at my dad before I address anything with Cooper. I know what I want to do here, and I need him on board before I act. "Can we talk?"

His brows dip, and he glances at Mike.

"Go ahead," Mike says, and he doesn't look at Cooper as he turns to walk out of Mike's office.

I glance at Cooper and then at Mike. "I'll be back." I don't say *right back* or *soon* because I don't know how long this will take.

But something moves me to have this conversation before I have one with Cooper.

My dad closes the door behind us when we walk into his office. He moves to give me a hug, but I stand still.

"Gabriella, I missed you so much."

I press my lips together and nod. "I heard everything."

His brows pinch together. "I'm sorry. I had to do what was best." He turns and moves toward his desk, where he leans casually against the edge of it.

I, on the other hand, am anything but casual. I'm a freaking emotional mess, but I'm pulling it together for the sake of this conversation. I stay where I am beside the door. "I'm an adult. What you think is best for me is irrelevant. I'm sorry, Dad. I love you, but you manage a baseball team. You do not manage my life."

His mouth flaps open and shut like a fish for a beat like he's not sure what to say. I plow forward before he gets the chance to say anything at all.

"Cooper Noah is one of the best third basemen to ever play the game, and your ultimatum to him is absolutely ridiculous. I've never met a man like Cooper, and I'm so sorry you don't approve. But what he does in his personal time has nothing to do with how he plays the game."

"You deserve the world, Gabriella. I firmly believe you deserve more than a man who will be gone eight months out of the year. You deserve more than someone who will put his love of baseball first."

"You're right. I absolutely do." And Cooper just did that by telling my father and the general manager of this team that he wants to walk away so he could fight for me. Maybe my father will never see it that way, but that's how I see it.

Deep down my only wish was that he would choose me before he found out about the baby, and he just did.

"You can't let him walk away from the game, Dad. Think about the team. Think about what you want out of this franchise. Think about why you brought him here in the first place, about the legacy you want to build. I can't be the reason he walks from all that, and you're the only one forcing that hand."

"But he's way too old for you," he points out.

"Is age really the issue here? Would you approve of *anybody* I brought home to introduce to you?"

"Fair point." He sighs. "So you're going to get back with him and I'm just supposed to *accept this*?"

I shrug. "Yes. He was one of your closest friends before. That doesn't have to change just because he fell in love. My relationship with you doesn't have to change, either. It's unconventional, maybe, but we'll find a way to make it work."

He shakes his head as he stares down at the ground, and then he glances up at me. "Are you absolutely sure about this? You really love him? It's not just some fling?"

"I'm absolutely sure, Dad. We've been together since August, barring a few hiccups here and there, and I've never been with someone so kind, so thoughtful, so funny."

He nods as if he's starting to come around. "And you both have so many people supporting you. So many who kept your secret."

"We have a wonderful network of friends here. And there's one other thing."

His brows dip, and I draw in a deep breath.

"I'm pregnant."

He freezes for a beat as he stares across the small space separating us.

The silence is thick as I await his reaction.

"You're..." he trails off.

"Pregnant," I whisper, finishing his sentence.

"It's Cooper's?"

I nod.

"He doesn't know?"

I shake my head.

"I'm going to be a papa?" he asks softly—so softly that I can't figure out his emotional response to my news, but I have a feeling he can't quite make his voice work.

"Yes."

He moves across the small space toward me. He wraps his arms around me. "I never got to hold my own baby in my arms. I never got to give my father the gift of a grandchild. I'm sorry you've been going through this alone, baby. I'll be here. Cooper will be here. Joanie…" he trails off.

"Joanie?" I press.

He sighs as he pulls out of my arms. "I've been so stupid." He shakes his head as he moves back to lean on his desk.

"I know," I say lightly, though I can't help but brush a tear away at his admission.

He chuckles. "Life's too short for all this nonsense. We have a baby to celebrate, and we're going to fix all of this. And you're not quitting. I saw your exit papers on Mike's desk. You deserve that social media position, Gabriella."

"But I'm pregnant," I protest. "It's why Zelda left the position in the first place."

"Right, so she could be home with her husband and their newborn. If you want to be with the baby's father, then you'll need to be on the road with us."

Tears fill my eyes at his implication. "Really?"

He presses his lips together and nods. "Really. I never would've let Cooper walk away from the game even though I've been pretty hard on him over the last month. I was blinded by my own anger, but losing you and my best friend and my future wife all in the same day pushed me into a pretty dark place."

"Only you can fix this. Only you can get it all back," I say.

He shakes his head. "It was him. Cooper. He had the balls to stand up to Mike and me to tell us he chose you. And *that* is what I want for you. Now go get him."

I draw in a deep breath.

I guess it's time.

Chapter 19
Cooper

"He's not going to let you go without a fight, you know," Mike says.

"He doesn't have a choice," I say thickly. I'm sitting in the chair I was pacing behind after Troy walked out with Gabby, and I'm still not sure why she chose to talk to her father before me, but here we are. "I've made up my mind."

"And what if the best of both worlds was an option?" Mike steeples his fingertips underneath his jaw.

"I've been over it a thousand times in my mind." I shake my head. "Troy will never be okay with the idea of his daughter and me being together, and I can't play for a manager who treats me the way he did over spring training."

"I can't let you go without a fight, either. You signed a contract, Cooper. A hefty one at that. You can't just walk away."

The money is guaranteed, and it's a shitty thing to do to the team. But I don't want the money. I've never cared about the money. I just want Gabby. I just want to be happy. I just want a little sunshine back in my life after far too much darkness.

"Keep the money. I don't want it at the expense of everything important to me. I'm happy to remain close as a team consultant," I offer.

"What if it doesn't work out?" he asks. "What if you give up everything here, your dreams, the *team's* dreams, and you don't end up where you think you'll be?"

I'm quiet a beat as I consider that. "At least I'll know I tried."

Mike shakes his head. "God dammit, Cooper. How am I supposed to fight against that?"

"You can't. I've made up my mind. How do we proceed?" I ask.

"Why don't we wait for the two of them to return before we plow ahead," he suggests dryly.

I shrug. "Suit yourself."

He picks up the paperwork in front of him. "She put in her notice, you know. She was on her way up here for her exit interview."

My eyes dart to his. "Is that why you brought me up here?"

"In part. I also knew Troy hadn't seen her since the team left for Vegas. I figured she'd get through to one of the two of you. Fingers crossed it's both."

Fingers crossed.

But I'm not sure how much hope I have right now. It feels pretty bleak that she chose to speak to her father first.

Maybe I went too far. Maybe I crossed too many lines, hurt her too much.

Part of me wants to think maybe it's because she never felt the way I did, but I know that's not true. I know what we had, and it was explosive. Something that strong couldn't be anything less than mutual.

It feels like hours pass when Troy finally appears in the doorway, and I immediately stand and turn toward the doorway when I hear his light knock on the doorframe.

He looks...lighter.

Like the vein that has been bulging out of his neck for the last month has simmered down a little.

His face isn't pinched in anger like it has been, and it isn't as red, either.

Gabby appears behind him, and while she's biting her bottom lip and shaking out her hands as if to shake out her nerves, she's glowing.

Actually glowing.

She's even more beautiful than my dreams made her out to be, but I know her heart, and that's what causes the effervescent glow that seems to surround her.

My heart squeezes and my chest tightens. It's been far too long since I've seen her, or spoken to her, or held her, and as I see her walk into the office, I know beyond a shadow of a doubt that I'm making the right choice.

Baseball is a game, but Gabby is my life...if she'll have me.

She clears her throat nervously before her eyes dart to mine. "Can we talk?"

I practically leap across the room to get to her.

"You can use my office," Troy says to Gabby, and my brows dip as I look over at him. He offers a smile, and while I'm beyond confused given the last month, I take what I can get.

If I could be a fly in the wall in Mike's office right now…well, I'd still choose to follow Gabby to Troy's office to beg for a second chance.

She walks in, and I close the door behind me.

I lean against the door, and she wanders into her father's office. She finally stops and turns to face me.

"Hi," she says softly.

"Hey."

She clears her throat. "So you're um, quitting baseball?"

I lift a shoulder. "I meant what I said, Gabby. I choose you…if you still want this. I made the wrong choice the first time, but I thought I was doing the right thing. I thought I was acting in everybody's best interest, but I realized I was doing what I thought I was supposed to do rather than what I actually wanted to do." I push off the door and take a few steps toward her. "And so I'm here today ready to beg you for the chance to get you back in my life. I'm so, so sorry I didn't put these pieces together sooner, but I can't play ball with my heart when it's broken and in your hands, so I choose not to play at all. I choose you. I choose a life with you if that's what you want. I choose this incredible thing we've built, and I choose love and happiness and maybe most of all, I choose my sunshine."

She swipes at a tear that spills over onto her cheek. "I want all that too," she whispers, and I can't help it when I launch myself toward her and pull her into my arms.

My world has been out of alignment for the last month, but with her in my arms, it shifts back into the right place again. And then it shifts a few degrees brighter when she tilts her head back and my lips fall to hers.

It's a short kiss—way too short given what my body is telling me to do to her right now—but she pulls back. She isn't all the way out of my arms, but enough to break the kiss.

"We have a few things we need to work out first, though," she says softly.

"Anything," I breathe. "I'll do *anything* to get you back."

A soft smile plays at her lips, and she nips my mouth with hers. "You have me. You've always had me, Cooper. Since the very second I sat down at that blackjack table. When we ended things the first time because you found out who my father was, and when we ended things the night of the wedding...I always had hope in my heart we'd find our way back, and I thought maybe it was just my naivete speaking for me, that maybe it wasn't as special as I thought it was, but when I'm here in your arms, I know I'm home. Whether that's on the road after a game or at your place or here in my dad's office. This is home."

I glance down at her neck and spot the necklace I gave her for Christmas, and my entire chest warms. "You are home for me, too, Gabriella Rose Grant. You're not naïve. You're mature, and you're smart, and you're talented and incredible and sexy and kind and *patient*, which hopefully you won't have to continue exercising when it comes to me, and you are everything I've ever wanted in a partner." I tighten my arms around her, and she leans into me, resting her head on my chest for a beat.

God, this feels good. This feels *right*, and I'm not quite sure how we've spent the last month without it.

"I love you," I murmur into the top of her head as I breathe her in, and it's like the sort of breath of fresh air that clears my lungs and simultaneously clears the darkness.

"I love you, too," she says, and she tips her chin up for another kiss.

It's still too short, but she's right. We have business to take care of.

I have questions, but I need to start at the beginning.

"Can I ask you a question?" I pull back out of her arms for a beat.

She nods.

"What did you say to Troy?"

She raises a brow and lifts a shoulder at the same time. "Wouldn't you like to know?"

"Uh, yeah, I would. It's why I asked. He walked in with a smile on his face, and he hasn't smiled in over a month. One conversation with you and he's a different person. What gives?"

She chuckles, and I swear I spot a twinkle in her eye as she draws in a deep breath. "Oh, you know...I just told him he's going to be a grandfather."

It takes a second for her words to click.

He's going to be a grandfather?

Who's having a baby?

He only has one daughter...

Oh.

Oh.

"Oh my God, you're pregnant?" I murmur as hope lights a brand-new fire within me.

She drags her bottom lip between her teeth as she nods and looks up at me through lowered lashes. "Yes…Daddy."

Jesus Christ.

What that single word does to me in the seductive tone she uses should be fucking illegal.

I grab her back into my arms and swing her around as the feeling like we're going to have everything we ever wanted together washes over me. I went from dark bleakness to hopeful sunshine in a matter of the last fifteen minutes, and it's been a whirlwind of whiplash that appears to be culminating with being given all the things I've ever wanted at one time.

"We're going to have a baby?" Heat presses behind my eyes at my words.

She giggles as she braces herself with her palms on my biceps. She nods as I set her down, but I don't let her go. Her smile lights up the entire room. "We're going to have a baby. And, you know, hopefully two or three more after that."

This time when my mouth slams down to hers, I don't care about what other business we have to get to. This is a moment for celebration.

Chapter 20
Gabby

The way he kisses me is somehow both familiar and new. It's exciting and intoxicating. I never want it to end, but it has to. As much as we both want to spend the rest of the day making up right here in my dad's office, we have other things to attend to. There will be time to make up later.

And I plan on *really* making up.

He pulls back and leans his forehead to mine. "I can't believe it," he whispers.

"Can't believe what?"

"Somehow I'm ending up with the dream. All of it." His voice is quiet, but I can hear the wonder within it.

I feel his words square in my chest. Maybe I haven't had the dream as long as he has, but it's still the dream nonetheless. Things felt pretty bleak as little as ten minutes ago, and it's sort of incredible how quickly life changes.

It's a roller coaster, and there's no one I want to ride it with as we scream our lungs out and toss our joined hands up in the air than Cooper Michael Noah.

And then he kneels down. He presses his lips to my stomach where our baby is growing. "Hi little one," he says softly. "I'm your daddy." He presses his cheek there and holds me for a beat, and then he lifts to a stand. His gaze is hot when it finds mine. "And I'm your daddy, too," he rasps.

I giggle, but the truth is his words send a wave of need through my entire system that seems to land with a needy ache right between my legs. It'll have to wait, though.

When we arrive in Mike's office, he gives me a hug.

"Congratulations," Mike says.

I look over at my dad. "You told him?"

My dad laughs. "I'm excited, okay?"

"Okay, but let me make the announcements from here on out."

Cooper chuckles at the exchange between us and somehow it makes me feel like everything's going to be okay—even between the two of them. Maybe my dad didn't like the idea at first and that's okay. He doesn't have to like it. Maybe me standing up to him was what he needed to see I'm not just a little girl. I'm an adult capable of making my own decisions—and he got to watch as Cooper chose me, too. He can see for himself how right this is. How right we are together.

"When are you due?" Mike asks, and I can't help but find it sort of funny that he's the one who asks first...not the father or the grandfather.

"September ninth."

Cooper's jaw slackens at the realization.

"That's a month before the regular season ends, and then we'll have the postseason we're going to plow through," my dad says.

Cooper glances at him, but before he gets the chance to say a word, my father speaks first.

"I'm not letting you walk away, Noah," he says gruffly. "You're part of my daughter's life, and that means you'll be part of mine. I fucked up, you fucked up...we all fucked up. But this is where we make things right. We should probably sit down and set some ground rules for how this will shake out. Obviously we're not going to share our conquests the way we might once have..."

I wrinkle my nose at the thought, and my dad laughs.

"Sweetheart, if we're all adults here, don't make me point out that you're carrying his baby, so we all have a pretty good idea of how that happened." He holds up both hands as if he's just stating the obvious.

"Dad!" I screech, covering my blushing face with both hands.

"I believe it's safe to travel up to thirty-six weeks barring any complications," Mike says. "So if we hire you as our social media manager, we'll need a solution for what to do from August through the end of the year."

"Hire me?" I echo.

Mike nods. "You were head and shoulders above the rest and you weren't even fighting for the position. I knew I needed to find a way to get you to stay."

"I appreciate that more than I can say. And I can think of somebody who might have a good solution for the whole maternity leave thing," I say pointedly.

"Joanie?" Cooper suggests, his tone full of absurdity as if no one else considered that.

My dad draws in a deep breath and closes his eyes for a beat, and then he nods. "Let's go."

When the four of us show up in Joanie's doorway, she looks somewhere between surprised and shocked.

"What's going on?" she asks. She sits behind her desk, and her eyes move to my dad's. His are on hers, too. The tension in here is palpable.

Mike sits in a chair across from her desk. Cooper stands back, and he tosses his arm around my shoulders while my dad glances at me and offers the other chair facing her desk with a nod. I shake my head, so he makes his way onto the chair, and Joanie looks epically confused.

"I believe my daughter would like to throw her hat back into the ring for the social media management position," my dad says rather formally.

"I can speak for myself, Dad." I roll my eyes. "Joanie, I would love to be considered for the social media manager position."

Joanie's face breaks out into a wide smile. "That's why I had you interview, Gabby. I knew you were perfect for the position and I had to get you in the lineup just in case you changed your mind."

"You knew?" I ask. I walk over toward her and she stands so she can take my hands in hers.

"I had a feeling. I knew everything was going to work out the way it was supposed to, but it got hard to keep the faith for a while." Her eyes move toward my dad, and I'm certain the unfinished business between them is about to just be business again. She sits back down.

Mike picks up from his spot across from Joanie. "If Gabby is our final decision, which I want to confirm with the team before we officially announce, we're going to need coverage from August onward."

Joanie's brows draw together. "Coverage?"

I sigh. "I guess it's getting out. I'm pregnant, Cooper's the father, I'm due September ninth, and I know Zelda left this position because she was pregnant but her baby daddy isn't a player and this just seems to work out."

Joanie's jaw drops at my speech. "You're p...p...you're pregnant?"

I nod and smile, and Cooper tosses his arm around me to draw me in close again.

She presses her lips together and glances at my dad, and then she looks back at me. "So am I."

Four heads whip in her direction at the same time.

"You're..." my dad begins, and he stands.

Joanie nods.

"We're..." he tries again, and Joanie nods again.

"But how...well, I know *how*, but when..." My dad trails off his line of thinking.

"I just found out," Joanie says. "I'm not due until mid-November."

"The off-season," my dad says softly. He looks around in wonder, and then his eyes land back on Joanie. "Just like we planned." He walks around the desk and takes her in his arms.

"Just like we planned," she whispers, and he drops his mouth to hers.

"I'm sorry, kitten," he says softly, and he doesn't seem to care that the rest of us are watching.

"I'm sorry, too, boss," she says back.

Boss and kitten? I wrinkle my nose with a bit of disgust again.

"So let me get this straight," Cooper says, breaking into the sweet moment of reconnection. "My baby's aunt or uncle is going to be two months younger than he or she is?"

Everyone in the room laughs. "That sounds about right," my dad says, and he kisses Joanie once more before he moves back around the desk. "One big messed up but hopefully happy family."

She draws in a deep breath and turns all business again. "I have a solution to the replacement substitute for Gabby while she's on maternity leave."

We all glance over at her to hear her proposition. "The marketing department has seen the benefits of these interns, and I would like to propose an assistant social media manager who can step into that role. I'd also like to propose an additional content creator who can assist the assistant while Gabby is out."

Mike narrows his eyes at Joanie and steeples his fingers under his chin. He thinks it over, moving his two pointer fingers in front of his mouth for a beat, and then he nods. "I think it's fantastic. Justin and Chloe?"

Joanie nods. "Justin as the assistant. Chloe as the creator."

"Get the proposal on my desk and I'll sign off my approval."

I look back and forth between Joanie and Mike during this conversation like it's a tennis match. Mike's tone is professional as always, yet there's some merriment there as he makes this happen.

He's like another father figure in many ways, and I'm both ready and excited to work for him, and with my father and Cooper and Joanie, too. Permanently.

"Justin's going to be my assistant?" I ask.

"Spongebob?" Cooper asks, and I can't help but laugh at his nickname for the guy who has become one of my best friends.

Mike looks a little confused at Cooper's nickname, but he says, "As it turns out, Justin knocked his interview out of the park. He didn't want to follow in his father's footsteps, and he isn't. He's in a totally different division and he'll bring a fresh perspective to the marketing department. He has proven his talents over the course of this internship, and we're excited to bring the three of you on board."

"Does he know?" I ask.

Mike shakes his head. "We haven't made any of this official yet." He glances at Joanie, and she nods. "But I'd like to officially offer you the position of social media manager."

I put my hand to my chest and feign shock. "Me? This is such a surprise."

Everyone laughs. "It's a dream team," Mike says.

Cooper reaches over and grabs my hand, and I look at him and can't help but think *all of this* is just that.

A dream.

Chapter 21
Cooper

I'm still not quite over the whirlwind this day has been, and it's not even noon yet.

I got the girl, but I also get to play ball. It's the best of both worlds, and it's something I never imagined I'd get to have when this day began. And on top of it all, I've got my friend back...well, sort of.

Gabby had paperwork to complete to transition to her new position, and I asked Troy if I could speak privately with him afterward. While we both have things to do to prepare for tomorrow's home opener, this conversation seems somehow more important.

Getting back on the right track with my manager and my friend overrules whatever other plans I might've had today.

He sits behind his desk and folds his hands, and he's more relaxed than I've seen him in weeks—since before the wedding, really. I sit across from him, and while we've done some office hopping today, this feels like the right place to end up.

"I just want your friendship back, man," I begin.

Troy nods. "I know, and trust me when I say that's what I want, too. But I said earlier we need to set some ground rules, and I stand by that. Our relationship is different now. It *has* to be. Just because I'm her father doesn't mean we can't be friends, too. When I first found out about you two, I convinced myself it was casual. But after today, you've assured me there's longevity here, and if that's true, I want you to know you have my support."

"That means a lot to me, Troy," I say.

"But I want to make a few things very clear." His tone is pointed. "I don't want to know what goes on between the two of you when you're alone. Neither of you will ever put me or Joanie in the middle of anything between you. And if you need advice on something related to her, you go to someone else unless it's the sort of thing you'd ask of a father-in-law…if that's where you see this heading."

"It is," I say softly. "And to that end, I realize this is unconventional, but I want to marry her. I want to ask her to be my wife. I want to stand by her side for the rest of our lives, and I'd love to do that with your blessing and support."

He sighs and sits back in his chair, and I have a moment of panic where I feel like I've overstepped. I don't have a plan, but one starts to formulate as I await his response.

Eventually it comes.

He stands and makes his way around the desk, and he holds his hand out to me. I stand and grip his in mine.

"Of course, Cooper. I may not understand this, but if you make her happy, then I won't be the one to stand in the way of that. Well, not anymore."

I reach my free hand around to give him a one-armed bro-hug, and he gives it back.

"Thanks, man. I won't let you down."

"I don't care about myself," he says. "Just don't let *her* down."

I shake my head. "Never," I say.

"I'm holding you to that."

I chuckle, and then I change the subject. "My family is in town. I'd love for you to meet them, especially since it won't be long before our families are joining as one anyway. I'm planning to order in Desmonds if you and Joanie would like to join us."

"I'll check with her, but I think we'd probably love to. But between you and me, I'll be taking her to the club after that," he says, leaning in suggestively, and I laugh as I shake my head. So *he* can make the innuendoes, but I need to lay off them, I guess.

"Well I can guarantee you one thing. You won't catch your daughter and me at your club."

He laughs. "Thank God for that. I'll let you know about tonight. Joanie and I have some making up to do."

I refrain from telling him Gabby and I have the same thing to accomplish, and I wonder for a beat *where* we're going to make up. My family is at my place, and we can't do it at her dad's house…but Caesar's Palace is always an option.

It represents so many important moments in our relationship, so why not this one, too?

I make a reservation for tonight, and then I head to Joanie's office. "Is Gabby around?"

She nods. "She's in her office."

"She has an office?"

Joanie chuckles. "She sure does. Across the hall and two doors down. And dinner tonight is a yes, by the way. What time should we be there?"

I go for early to get it over with so I can have the night to go slowly with Gabby. "Come over at five. We'll eat around five-thirty."

She nods and winks. "Thanks for making it early. We'll see you then."

I head down the hall and find Gabby in her brand-new office. She's bending over her desk arranging something on it, and I can't help but walk over and take her hips in my hands, bumping my very hard dick against her backside.

"Congratulations on the new office," I murmur.

She straightens and whips around toward me, her eyes wide. "You heard what Joanie said! No shenanigans at the stadium!"

"That was before when nobody knew about us. Now, though?" I shrug, and she laughs.

"You will definitely be the first to christen this office, but maybe not on my first day in it. Or my first five minutes in it."

"I'll be the first? As if there will be...more than one?" I challenge, and she laughs.

"Only one." She sets her palms on my chest as those green eyes pierce into mine. "My number twenty-one."

"Damn right I'm yours. Remember when you were going to call me Snuggle T-rex?"

She giggles. "That was never an option. It was always going to be Hottie McHotFace or Captain."

"You were always Sunshine. And you always will be."

She leans forward and rests her head on my chest for a beat, and we both draw in a deep breath at the same time. We exhale as if we're letting out all the negative energy that has surrounded us for weeks, and just like that, we're back to where we were.

Only this time, it's with a baby on the way.

I still haven't reconciled that fact in my own mind.

"I need to get back to work," she says. "Justin and Chloe are getting called in with their offers, and Mackenzie is getting nothing, and I need to head over to Joanie's office to celebrate."

I nod. "I need to get home. I'm, uh, *entertaining*."

Her brows knit together. "Entertaining? Like a lady friend?"

I laugh. "You're my only lady friend." I shake my head. "No, nothing like that. My family decided to surprise me with a visit, so they're all over at my place."

"Everyone?"

"Everyone," I confirm. "They wanted to come to opening day and they're staying for all three games in the series."

"I want to see them!" she says.

"They'll want to see you, too. I invited your dad and Joanie for dinner tonight at five so the families can meet. I hope that's okay."

"It's perfect. But why five?"

"Well, your dad and Joanie have some making up to do, so I went for an early time slot."

She makes a face of disgust, and I laugh.

"We have some making up to do, too, in case you forgot. I have a surprise, so be sure to bring an overnight bag when you come over."

"A surprise?" she asks.

I just shrug mysteriously, and then I change the subject. "By the way, my mom was already on my case last night about you." I roll my eyes, and she laughs.

"What did she say?"

"She said I was miserable and needed to fix it. She said a lot of things, but walking away from that conversation made me think about how I'd rather walk away from the game than continue on this road without you."

Her eyes get misty at that. "I love her."

"She loves you, too. And just wait until we tell her that you're going to have her grandchild."

"Are we telling them tonight?" she asks.

I shrug. "Your dad knows. May as well make it official, right?"

She nods, and she leans on the edge of her desk.

"How have you been feeling?" I ask.

"Pretty good, all things considered. Not really any nausea, but sometimes I get headaches, and I'm always hungry. Like always. And I have to pee a lot."

"The baby is healthy?"

She nods. "Everything is growing just as it's supposed to."

"I know September ninth is the due date, but where does that put us now?"

"Fourteen weeks, four days. About the size of a kiwi."

"A kiwi?" I ask, bypassing the way *fourteen weeks* stabs into my heart. I've missed *fourteen weeks* of this. An entire trimester. I walked away, and I could've missed even more.

I will never forgive myself for that, and I will do everything in my power to make it up to her.

But even as I think it, I realize I'm not sure what that will look like. I physically won't be able to be there for every moment since I'll be on the road with the Heat for a good chunk of the year. But plenty of guys in the league make it work. I'm confident we will be another success story.

"I have this app that tells me how big the baby is and I chose the food comparison." She shrugs, and I chuckle.

"Do we know gender yet?"

She shakes her head. "Not for a few more weeks, but I'm convinced it's a girl."

"How do you know?" I ask.

She shrugs. "Just a guess. An instinct, maybe."

"Do you already have a name picked out?"

She shakes her head. "Haven't even thought of that."

"I'm sort of partial to Kiwi."

She giggles. "You would be. Maybe Sunshine Junior."

"Our little Sunny," I say with a wide grin.

She gasps a little, and her eyes widen.

"Sunny," we say at the same time.

"Oh my God, I love it," she murmurs as tears sparkle in her eyes, and she pushes to a full stand and moves toward me, wrapping her arms around my waist. I hold her tightly for a beat. I never want to let go, but I know I have to. She has a meeting to get to. I have guests to attend to. I have a season to get ready for.

And now we'll do all those things knowing that the other one is waiting just on the other side.

Chapter 22
Gabby

"I'm so excited to announce that effective immediately, given that the season opener is tomorrow, we have made our selection for the social media manager position." Joanie has the interns gathered in her office, and now that Dylan has been fired and Chase and Brian aren't interning anymore, it's just the four of us—Justin, Chloe, Mackenzie, and me.

Justin and Chloe have both been offered their positions, too, but as far as I know, they don't know anything aside from their own roles.

"Congratulations to our new social media manager, Gabby Grant!" Joanie says, and she smiles widely at me.

Justin lights up. "Shut up!" he yells with glee.

I can't help a small smile. "Oh, we have a lot to talk about, my friend."

Mackenzie's face is absolutely sour. "Wait a minute. I thought she pulled her name from the running. I thought the interviewing thing was just for practice."

"She was the unanimous top candidate from the entire team of interviewers," Joanie says, not really bothering to answer Mackenzie's question. "Mr. Perry also agreed to add two additional positions to the social media marketing team. I'd like to introduce our new social media manager assistant, Justin Larson." She smiles at Justin. "Congratulations."

Chloe claps her hands together.

"Two positions?" Mackenzie asks.

"The other position is a content creator, and a big congratulations goes to Chloe Carter." Joanie's smile is warm.

"Congratulations, Chloe," both Justin and I say to her, and she smiles.

"I can't wait to work with both of you!" she gushes.

I can't wait, either. We've had a blast as interns together, but I do realize my life is about to change. I'm not going to have the time to head to the bar after work a few nights a week. Instead I'll be home changing diapers, or I'll be on the road with the team. But Justin and Chloe have both become good friends over the course of the past few months, and I can't wait to have a permanent position where we get to work together and pool our talents and creativity...without someone like Mackenzie there to bring us all down.

And speaking of Mackenzie, she is *not* happy with Joanie's announcement. "Wait a minute. So there are four interns left, and three got full time jobs?"

Joanie presses her lips together and nods. "That sounds about right. And those three will be transitioning into their new positions today. We'll meet every morning and do an hour of internship, and the rest of the day will be getting to know your new job role. Except for you, Mackenzie. You'll be our lone intern left." Joanie smiles sweetly at her, but I sure don't miss the punch she packed with her words.

Mackenzie crosses her arms over her chest and huffs petulantly.

"Is there something you'd like to say, dear?" Joanie asks her.

She rolls her eyes and shakes her head. "Must be nice to just get everything handed to you."

"Not a single person in this room was handed anything," Joanie says firmly. "These decisions were based on talent, results, and attitude, and unfortunately, yours isn't in line with what the marketing team is looking for in a full-time employee. And let's not forget your professors need me to sign off on your internship, so I expect you to continue your work at a high level through the end of next month. Now let's get down to business." Joanie runs the rest of the meeting, and as soon as she excuses us, Justin follows me to my new office.

"Maybe I can get the office next door," he suggests. It's vacant and ready for him, and I laugh.

"We should cut a hole in the wall so we can just walk back and forth whenever we want."

"Adjoining offices," he chuckles. "I love it. You said there was a lot to tell me, so spill it, baby girl."

"Cooper and I are back together," I begin.

"I figured as much. You've got the back together glow, but I also knew you wouldn't have taken the position if things were up in the air with him."

I nod. "And also…I'm pregnant."

His jaw drops, and a little squeak comes out of the back of his throat. "You're pregnant?"

I smile and set a hand over the baby. "I'm fourteen weeks along, and I'm guessing I'll really only be able to work up until mid-August. So my assistant will need to cover for me while I'm on maternity leave. Know anyone who might be interested in a career option with independence, creativity, and travel?" I repeat the words he said to me when we first met—when he told me how he doesn't really even like baseball and wouldn't want to follow in his father's footsteps.

I guess things change as secrets are revealed. We come to terms with what we really want out of life, and right now…I feel like I have everything I could ever hope for.

And the way Justin is smiling at me tells me he feels the same way about his own lot right now, too.

I sit behind my desk, and he sits across from me.

"How are you going to decorate this office?" he asks, glancing around at the plain white walls.

"You know those life size wall decals? I'm thinking of getting one of Cooper to put right over there," I say nodding toward the wall.

"Oh, that's perfect. Maybe with no shirt?"

"Or pants." I lift a shoulder as I picture it.

Whew. Is it getting hot in here?

"I feel like I may be spending a lot of time in this office…" Justin winks at me, and we both laugh.

"I haven't even had time to think about decorating this place yet," I admit. "This is all so new. This morning I woke up in lonely darkness with a broken heart as I thought today would be my last day. And now…"

"Everything's coming up roses?" he guesses.

"Sunshine and roses," I agree.

Chapter 23
Cooper

As I recall, the last day before the season begins is always chaotic. It's packed full of too many things to do and not enough time to do it all. But the last time I had one of these days was when I was with Stacy, and she wanted me to prepare the house like I was leaving for the next year.

It was a lot to handle, and she wanted all my attention on top of it.

It felt like a relief when I had my first away series and could leave the house. That should've been a sign, but it was too easy and too comfortable to leave things as they were.

Things are different now.

I want to soak in every second I can with Gabby even though I know we'll still be around each other after the season officially begins.

But first, I have to share the news with my family.

I'm excited to tell them, but I want her here for it. She's not coming until a little before five, and I don't blame her for staying late at the office considering she was just hired today.

She's dedicated, and she's a hard worker, and those are among the many traits I love about her.

I'm bursting with happiness when I get home, ready to spill the news even though I promised myself I'd wait, but it's fairly anticlimactic as the Lincoln SUV isn't in the driveway.

The house is empty, so my family must've gone off somewhere while they're here in town on vacation. I guess it was silly of me to expect them to be waiting around for me when they had no idea when I'd be back.

I text my mom.

Me: *I'm home and I invited some friends for dinner. Can you all be back around five?*

Her answer comes a few minutes later.

Mom: *We're down on Fremont Street. We'll be back by five and we'll all be hungry.*

Me: *Great. I'm ordering in dinner and I have a surprise.*

Mom: *Can't wait to see what it is!*

I place an order at Desmonds, and then I wait.

The front door opens at four-thirty, and Gabby walks through it carrying an overnight bag on her shoulder. She holds up her key as if to say she thought it would be okay to let herself in, and a wave of emotion plows into me.

This is it.

This woman standing in front of me is my entire future, and I cannot wait to get started on it.

I leap across the room toward her. First I grab her bag and set it down, and then I pull her into my arms.

"I thought your family was visiting," she says, a minor protest in her tone that seems to melt away in my arms.

"They're out." I drop my lips to hers.

She gives into the kiss for a beat. "For how long?" Her words are smashed against my mouth, and I can't help but laugh.

"They'll be back by five."

"So could be now, or we could have a half hour to ourselves?" she asks suggestively.

"Want to risk it?"

She giggles. "No. I want you to take your time with me and not rush through it because we're worried someone's going to walk in."

"Oh, I'm not worried." I tighten my grip around her. "It's my house and I can do what I want."

She tips her lips to mine again, and she seems to soften a little as I jut my hips toward hers.

"Mm," she moans softly, and that right there is one of the noises I've missed most. That sweet little sound of pleasure that falls from her out of instinct, as if she has no idea she's even doing it.

"Fuck, I want you naked," I growl, and she moans again as I drag my lips along her neck. She pushes her chest into me like she wants me to grab her tits, and I run my hands along her sides, cupping her breasts when I get to them before sliding them back down to her hips.

"Oh, you'll have me naked," she promises. "Didn't you say you had some surprise for me?"

I kiss her again. "I do. And don't worry. I plan to take my time."

"I can't wait," she breathes.

Jesus. I can't, either. And neither can my cock.

We both hear the doorbell ring, and I lean my forehead down to hers for a beat when it rings again. And again. And again. It's my nephews, and I can't help a small chuckle. "Ready for this?"

She closes her eyes and draws in a breath. "Ready."

The front door opens a few seconds later, and that's when the chaos ensues.

Jacob and Ethan are arguing about the doorbell: "No, you got to ring it more times!" "No, you did!"

My mom and Marissa are talking about some cupcakes they saw, and my brother heads up the rear of the pack, closing the door and locking it behind him.

They all freeze when they see Gabby standing beside me.

The loud ruckus of their entry ceases, and silences falls over the foyer.

Finally, my mom breaks the silence as a wide grin breaks out across her lips. "Gabby!" She rushes over to give her a hug, and everyone else follows behind.

My mom hugs me next, and she whispers into my ear, "I don't know what you did, but it seems like it was the right thing."

I squeeze her tightly. "I know it was."

Once the excitement starts to quiet, my mom says, "So tell us everything."

I toss my arm around Gabby's shoulders. "I told Mike and Troy I was walking away. I said I was in love with Gabby, and I couldn't play with my heart when she held it in her hands."

"So you're not playing?" Connor asks, his forehead wrinkling with concern.

"There's more to the story, Bro. She overheard everything I said, about how I choose her over anything else and how I should have done that from the start, and I guess that was what she needed to see to take my dumb ass back."

"Haha, Uncle Coop said ass," Ethan says, causing Jacob to snicker.

Marissa's lips tighten as she offers me a little glare, and she turns to her boy. "He's an adult. You are not. Knock it off."

"It was also what her father needed to understand that this is real," I continue. "He saw me willing to give it all up for his daughter, and that's all he wanted for her."

Gabby looks over at me and leans into my side, and I tighten my grip around her shoulder as I look down at her. I give her a little nod.

"And we have some other news, too," she says.

"We do?" my mother asks.

"I'm pregnant," Gabby says.

Her announcement is followed by another beat of silence, and then just like before, the room breaks out into a frenzy of excitement all at once. My mother slaps a hand over her mouth as she squeals, and then she bursts into tears as she moves to hug Gabby first. Marissa hugs me, and then Connor's next.

"Congratulations, Bruh," he says to me.

I chuckle. "You know I'll be coming to you for all the new dad advice."

He slugs my shoulder a little. "I think you're gonna be just fine, little bro."

I have a feeling he's right.

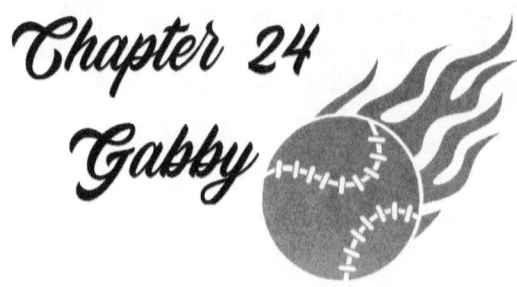

Chapter 24
Gabby

We bond over lemon chicken with cheesecake for dessert as my dad and Joanie get to know Cooper's family. Connor especially seems to find an easy bond with my dad, and I sit back for a beat to take a look around this table.

There's so much love here. So much joy. My dad has his arm around Joanie, and though they may have some things to work through, they're going to be okay. They have a baby on the way...I'll finally have a little brother or sister.

Cooper and I have some things to work through, too. It won't always be sunshine and roses. We'll bicker and argue, and we'll miss each other when we're apart, and we'll have a baby to raise together that will lead to sleepless nights and busier days, but we'll always end up right where we're supposed to be—by each other's side.

My dad and Joanie take off shortly after dinner, citing some business they have to attend to. I don't want to even think about what that might mean, but Cooper and I have some business of our own to attend to.

"I'll be back late morning for brunch," he says to his mom.

"Brunch?" I ask.

He nods. "Opening day brunch. It's a tradition."

"I'll take care of everything. You kids have a good time," his mom says, and I'm sure my face is as red as a tomato given that she *must* know what he has planned for tonight.

Well, he knocked me up. I guess I have to get used to people knowing what we do in our private time together.

We hop into his truck, both of us armed with our overnight bags, and he takes off toward the highway. I have a feeling I know where we're going, and my suspicions are right when we pull into the entry of Caesars Palace.

He glances over at me as he navigates toward the valet station. "We've spent so many important nights here, and I couldn't think of a better place where we could share some private time before the season gets underway."

I smile. "Don't you want to spend the last night before the season starts at home, though?"

He cuts the engine as he pulls in behind some fancy sports car. "I am." He shrugs. "I told you, Gabriella Rose Grant. *You* are my home."

Tears heat behind my eyes at the sweet sentiment, and then he gets out of the car and tosses his keys to the valet. He grabs our bags and meets me on the passenger side of the car, and then we walk in together and head toward the Augustus Tower.

"Penthouse?" I guess.

"Nothing but the best for my girl."

"When did you book this?"

"This afternoon. I had to bribe the woman on the phone to get it." He presses the button to call the elevator. "Worth it."

I laugh as I narrow my eyes at him. "You did not."

He shakes his head. "No, I didn't. I just got really lucky it was available."

We both laugh at that, and then we head up toward the penthouse. When he lets me in, I wander over toward the windows to take in the spectacular view.

"You said you didn't want me to rush through this," he says once the door is sealed shut behind us. He drops our bags by the entry, and he stalks toward me. He moves in behind me, aligning the front of his body with the back of mine. "And I want you to tell me exactly what you want."

"I want you," I murmur.

His lips fall to my neck. "What do you want me to do to you?"

"I want you to make me come harder than I've ever come in my entire life."

"How?" he presses. He moves his lips from my neck along my skin toward my shoulder, moving my shirt out of the way as he works.

"I want your mouth on me," I whisper.

"Don't be shy, baby. Ask me for whatever you want."

"I want your tongue on my clit, and then I want you to suck my nipples while you move inside me."

"What do you want me to put inside you?" His voice is low and raspy.

"You can start with your fingers and then once you see how wet I am for you, you can use your cock. What do you want me to do to you?" I ask.

"I want you to lie back and take it." This time his voice comes out as a growl, and as he says the words, he spins me around and lifts me into his arms.

He carries me over to the couch that looks out over the Strip, and he sets me down on my feet just in front of it. And then he strips *me*.

My clothes go flying off in every direction, and for a split second I feel nervous. This is the first time he's seeing my body in over a month, and it has started to change. My clothes are starting to get tighter, and I have a swell around my belly that wasn't there before. My boobs are getting heavier by the day, and I feel bloated all the time—which must be about the unsexiest feeling in the world.

But that thought only lasts a beat before it vanishes.

Cooper moves back a step after he strips me completely naked, and he just stares at me for a beat. He shakes his head with a little bit of wonder. "How did I get so goddamn lucky?"

The way he looks at me with all the love and adoration in the world is enough for me to know I have nothing to be worried about. He loves me for me, and I'm carrying a gift he's wanted for many, many years.

The pure, mutual love that passes between us in this moment is something different. It's unique and special, but it's also full of passion and desire and complete and total adoration.

My thighs clench together in anticipation as the ache that started earlier intensifies.

He rips his shirt over his head, and I can't help but tilt my head and stare. "Hi abs," I sing softly as I wave, and then I move toward him and run my fingertips along each beautiful ridge. "I missed you." I reach for the top of his jeans and tug on them pulling him toward me a little. Then I lower my hand and run it along his erection. "But I missed you even more."

He chuckles as he drives his hips toward my hand for a beat. "Oh, both the abs and the Captain missed you, too."

Then he grabs me up into his arms and sits me on the couch. He kneels between my legs, shoving them open a little wider to make room for himself, and he moves his face nice and close before he inhales.

He growls some low, throaty sound, and my fingers thread into his hair as my chest tightens at what we do to each other, at how turned on I am just by the sound he makes to tell me how turned on he is in this moment, too.

It's animalistic and carnal and *hot*.

So hot that it makes my pussy throb with need.

I nearly come when his tongue swipes through me, the feel of his stubble on my thighs raw and real, and I grip his hair a little tighter between my fingers as he moves toward my clit. He slows down once he's there, his tongue moving leisurely and magnificently, and it's enough to bring me right up against the edge. My thighs start to clench around his ears, but he doesn't allow it…not yet, anyway.

He backs away, moving his tongue off my clit and down inside me, and then he adds a finger while his mouth moves up toward my nipple. I cry out his name when he starts to suck, and it's an out of body experience for a beat as I imagine what the two of us look like, as if I'm standing above us looking down, watching his finger as it moves inside me and his head as it stops at my breast, watching his cheeks as they hollow at his sucking and watching my nipple as he pulls at it before letting it go and soothing it with his tongue.

He adds another finger and shoves it all the way in, and I ride his hand as my hips start to move along with him.

"Oh God, Cooper." My voice is breathy as my hands move out of his hair and to his back. I claw at him as I try to express what I need, but I can't seem to do it when this much pleasure pulses everywhere in my body.

I thrash in desperation. The need to come washes over me, and it's all I can think about. He shoves his fingers in and leaves them there, and I grind my hips around for some friction, feeling like I'm going to explode if I don't get it. I'm chasing my orgasm but he keeps moving the finish line.

He stops everything, pulling his fingers out of me. His mouth moves up to mine as I continue to thrash and claw at him, and I calm as I taste myself on his breath.

He kisses me slowly. Sensually, like we have forever when we don't—not really. We have responsibilities that come tomorrow, but tonight…tonight is just for us.

He pushes two fingers back inside me, and I gasp as the orgasm looms largely in front of me. I chase it, so close my body begins to convulse, and he drives those fingers into me harder and harder as I ride them faster and faster, his mouth hot on mine and my aching nipples dragging across his hard chest.

It's too much.

He pulls his fingers out to brush softly against my clit, and I fall apart. I shudder as the spasms rack my body, my thighs tightening against his hand and my tongue diving further into his mouth until I have to toss my head back and cry out in a song with the throbbing of my pussy.

He plunges his fingers back in as I ride out the wave, and I scream at the intrusion even as my hips move to fuck his hand.

"Yes, baby, just like that," he murmurs, and I know he's watching me and maybe I should feel awkward about that but *nothing* about this man ever makes me feel awkward. He makes me feel cherished and loved and maybe most of all...*wanted.*

Once my trembling starts to slow and my body moves from shuddering to warm tingling, I open my eyes and stare at him. "Damn," I say, drawing out the word.

He laughs. "Good one?"

"Uh, yeah. *Great* one." I lie back, my body feeling like jelly as I relish the bliss for a few hot beats, and then it's like I'm ready to go again.

"I need you to fuck me now," I say softly.

He drags me up into his arms. "Your wish is my command," he says, and then he sets me down on my feet, takes off his jeans, and sits on the couch. He grabs my hands and pulls me down on top of him, aligning his dick with my pussy as I slowly lower myself onto him.

He growls again as his body makes contact with mine, and I sit all the way down on him for a beat, the two of us losing ourselves in one moment of pure intimacy. His eyes are hot on mine, and he wraps his arms around me. My breasts are smashed against his chest, and I lean down to kiss him as I wrap my arms around his shoulders.

He deepens the kiss, keeping it slow and steady but raw and intense, and I mark this as the single most erotic moment of my life. Neither of us moves, yet I feel his cock as it twitches inside me. My pussy tightens at every twitch and my greedy nipples ache with need, but he just continues to kiss me as he gives our souls a moment to reconnect after too much time apart.

Eventually he starts to move, but his mouth never leaves mine. His hands move to my hips, and he controls our rhythm even though I'm on top. He drives into me, setting the pace slow and leisurely like our kiss at first, but as the need starts to build in us both, he starts to move faster.

I tighten my grip around him as I feel my body starting to coil tightly again, and he stops the kiss as he keeps moving. He trails his mouth down my neck as I lean back, and he buries his face between my breasts. He drops wet kisses along my chest until he gets to my nipple. He sucks it in, and he drops one hand and moves it between us to brush my clit.

"Fuck, baby, I'm going to come," he says against my breast, and then he lets out a few grunts followed by a roar. His mouth clamps back down on my nipple as he starts to come, and I yell out as I keep riding him. He comes hard, the warmth of his seed spilling into me, and it sends me flying into oblivion for the second time tonight.

I collapse over him, but he doesn't pull out of me right away as neither of us wants to break this intimate connection. Instead, I lean forward and he cradles me into a hug. I rest my head on his shoulder, my face toward him, and I kiss his neck.

He tightens his arms around me, and after a short while, I feel his cock twitch inside me again as if it's stirring back to life.

"Already?" I ask playfully, my breath hot on his neck, and he chuckles.

"I'm always ready when it's you," he murmurs.

He pulls out of me, and the sticky evidence of our sex drips out of my pussy.

"Fuck, that's hot," he says as he watches. His eyes move to mine. "You did that to me. I did that to you. There's something incredible about that and I just want to keep filling you up with more."

He's not kidding.

He makes me come twice more before the sun rises.

Chapter 25
Gabby

I wish we could lie here forever, but I know we can't. It's opening day, and I'm sure he has things to do and rituals to tend to.

It's in this moment as I lie naked in his arms that I realize I don't know what those rituals are. We know each other pretty damn well, but there are new sides to him that I'll learn as we move through this first season together, and then I'll learn new things about him when he becomes a daddy, just like we will learn new things about myself when I become a mom.

And each new detail I learn is like uncovering a new gift about him.

I turn in his arms to look at him, and he shifts a little before leaning down to kiss my forehead.

"Morning," he murmurs, his voice sleepy and raspy and oh-so-sexy.

"Morning." I lean forward and press a kiss to his chest.

"Move in with me," he murmurs.

"Okay."

He leans back and looks down at me in surprise. "Really?"

"Yeah. Really. I want to wake up like this every morning. Well, every morning that you're home."

He tilts his head down to indicate he wants to kiss me, so I press my lips to his.

"Me too," he says, and he tightens his grip around me.

"Plus I don't really want to be around when my dad and Joanie are making up." I make a face, and he laughs.

"They've got the club for that."

I wrinkle my nose. "Thanks for the reminder. And I'm not *totally* leaving my dad's place. I might need help at the beginning when you're out of town and I can't travel, so it'll be nice to have a place where we can go if we want to."

He nods as if he gets my meaning about who *we* is. "Joanie will be around, and you two will probably have plenty to talk about. And I'm sure my mom would come out to visit, too."

"I would love that." It's the truth. Really. I hit the jackpot with my potential future mother-in-law.

But Cooper can't say the same, and the thought makes me sad. I wish I had the type of relationship with my own mother where I'd want her to come stay with me to help with my newborn, but I don't. And that's okay.

"Hey," he says softly.

I glance up at him, and I love how he knows me so well. He doesn't have to ask me what's wrong because he already knows.

"You have a huge support team behind you, Sunshine. Whether that includes people society tells us it should include is irrelevant. We do us, and everyone else can fuck right off. But if you have a relationship you want to work on, then I'm behind you and holding your hand as we put in the work together."

Tears heat behind my eyes. "I love you."

"I love you more," he says playfully.

I lean my head on his chest with a small chuckle. "Happy opening day. Do you have any traditions or rituals you need to get to?"

"You know, I had some when I used to play, but as it turns out, they didn't really work. So I'm scrapping that idea, and my new tradition will be to get a kiss from my girl before every game and maybe take a quick run around the bases during warm-ups."

"What about when I can't be at the game?"

"Then we'll video chat before the game so I can kiss the camera."

I giggle as I imagine his lips moving toward the screen and kissing him back over a video chat. We'll do what we have to do, though. We both want to put in whatever it takes to make this work, and I'm confident we'll go the distance because of that.

"What if you have a game and the baby's on the way?" I ask.

"Then I take the day off." He shrugs as I get all teary-eyed at his sweet sentiment. "I call in sick. It's just a game, and some things are more important. Plus the collective bargaining agreement says I get three days of paternity leave."

I laugh as I smack him in the chest. "And here I thought you were just taking the day off for me."

"Even if there was no agreement, I'd still take the time to be there for you both." He reaches down and sets a hand on my stomach, and my chest warms with love.

So much love.

The kind of love I wasn't expecting but plowed straight into me anyway.

"So are you allowed to have sex on game day?" I ask.

He laughs. "You know, there's been a long standing myth in professional sports that you shouldn't have sex on game day, but the truth is that it can actually be beneficial. It might tire you out depending on the *type* of sex, but it could also reduce stress levels, which makes some guys play even better."

"Are you stressed?" I ask.

"Well it *is* opening day and I haven't played on a pro field since the day I was injured, so there's a little bit of nervous energy there."

I shift and start to move down his body until that beautiful cock of his comes into view. "Then allow me to reduce those stress levels, my friend."

I suck him into my mouth and give him the kind of blow job that leaves him panting, and after I swallow down his come, he just lies there with his eyes closed and a smile on his lips.

"Your mouth is magic and this is pure fucking heaven right now. Consider the stress reduced," he says.

I laugh, and then we shower together and get a start on our day.

Just before we're getting ready to leave, Cooper's phone starts to ring.

"It's Kaylee," he says. His eyes light up as we both realize she doesn't even know we're back together, and she's one of the ones who is most invested in us being back together. "You want to answer?"

I giggle and nod, and he swipes his phone.

"Hey Kay," I answer casually.

There's a pause on the other end as Kaylee presumably looks to see who she dialed.

"Gabby?" she asks.

"What's up?"

"I'm so sorry. I meant to call someone else..." she trails off awkwardly.

"Was it me?" Cooper asks.

We grin at each other.

"Cooper?" she asks, confusion still in her tone. "Are you two..."

"Back together?" I fill in. "We sure are. And he knows about the baby."

"He knows…" she trails off again.

"Wait, Kaylee knew?" Cooper asks. "And you didn't tell me?"

"I just found out like two days ago!" she protests.

I giggle. "We work out together a few times a week and it was kind of obvious when I didn't want to do kickboxing or rowing."

"I'm a smart cookie. I put two and two together," Kaylee says. "So how did this happen?"

"It's a long story, one Gabby can share with you later since I need to get home to do brunch with my family before heading to the stadium. But yes, we're back together, we're having a baby, and Gabby is moving in with me."

"And I'm keeping my room at my dad's place so I have somewhere to go when Coop's out of town and I've got the baby," I add. "Do you think Kate could help us add a nursery section to my bedroom?"

"I'm sure Kate would *love* to help," Kaylee says. "Wow! I am so, so happy for the two of you."

"We're pretty damn happy, too," Cooper says, reaching over to grab my hand.

"I love you guys. I just called to tell Coopster good luck on opening day. These football fans will be cheering loudly for you from home."

"Thanks, Kay," Cooper says. "And we love you, too."

He ends the call, kisses me like he needs my mouth to survive, and we head toward the car to join his family for brunch.

Chapter 26
Cooper

The game doesn't start until seven tonight, but the entire team has gathered in the clubhouse by one-thirty. Some guys got here earlier, but most of us showed up for the group stretches planned for two.

Getting here too much earlier than required usually means killing time or allowing nerves to kick in, though my poker buddies and I have a table set up in the clubhouse should the need arise for a quick card battle before game time since video games and poker are fairly traditional ways to pass the time before warm-ups.

We have batting practice where we each take turns hitting the ball or shagging in the outfield, but after spring training and the last several months, I'm ready for this. My body is ready for this. And, thanks to Gabby, my body and my mind are both relaxed.

We're all ready for this.

After batting practice, we have some time to kill. I play a few hands with Danny and Rush. Nick is busy making sure everybody is healthy and ready to play, so AJ takes his spot.

Since it's opening day and we're in Vegas, the marketing team decided to book some surprise guests for our fans. Even we don't know who they are—and I'm pretty sure Gabby doesn't know, either, or she would've spilled it to me. Troy let us know they'd be coming through the clubhouse on their arrival to hang out and chill before they take the stage for their performances.

A little after four as I'm deep into another hand of poker, the door to the clubhouse opens and a woman walks in. Behind her are the four members of the band Vail, all easily recognizable because they're international superstars. I'm fairly sure they have a residency here in Vegas now, but I've been a little busy since I moved here and haven't had the chance to check out the local entertainment. Maybe in eight months when the season is over, Gabby and I can check it out. Or maybe we'll just want to stay home, sit in front of the fireplace with a movie playing in the background, and stare at the little life we created.

Perhaps we'll find time for both, though I tend to think I'm going to want the latter above pretty much anything else. I set my cards down without finishing my hand and lift to a stand to introduce myself to the band.

"Cooper Noah," I say, and I walk up to the lead singer, Mark Ashton. I stick my hand out and he shakes mine.

"Cooper Noah," he echoes. "Man, I know who you are." He shakes his head. "Always beating up on my poor Cubbies back when you were a Dodger. You're here now?"

I nod. "First game in three years after an elbow injury."

"I remember that," he says. "Glad to see you're playing again. I'm Mark, by the way." He nods toward his bandmates. "Ethan, James, Steve, and that feisty lady is our manager, Vic. Everyone, this is Cooper and he's a beast on third."

I hold up a modest hand. "I don't know about that, but it's nice to meet you all." I nod at James. "And great to see you again." We played golf together not so long ago, and it makes sense that they're here given that James and Troy are colleagues.

"Haven't seen you by the club," James says quietly to me.

I chuckle. "Yeah, that's not likely." He looks offended for a beat before I follow it up with, "I'm with Troy's daughter."

He makes an exaggerated *O* with his mouth before he laughs. "Probably best to stay away."

I laugh, too, and then I get back to my poker game while the band members walk around the clubhouse as they introduce themselves to the players and wish us luck on our opening day. I wonder who else might show up to perform.

A short while later, the door opens, and a man walks through it. Standing just behind him is the triple threat Alexis Bodega—the woman Danny said would be his hall pass if he had the option to have one.

She's wearing a royal blue dress with a huge Vegas Heat logo stamped across the middle in shimmering red sequins, and she nervously flips her dark hair over her shoulders as she glances around the room.

I glance over at him, and his eyes are wide as they land on her.

The man with her slides his hand behind her and has her take the lead, but he still directs her where to go with his hand on the small of her back. Is he her bodyguard? Or her husband?

"Jesus Christ," Danny mutters beside me. "She's even hotter in person."

"Go introduce yourself," I prod teasingly, and he shakes his head.

"Nah. She'll come to me."

I laugh at the balls on this guy. "All the women in the world and the one you named as your ultimate fantasy just walked through the door."

"Shut the fuck up," he says, and I swear his cheeks redden just a little.

I stand and make my way over to her like I did with Vail. I hear Danny's faint protest behind me as I make my way over toward her, but I ignore him.

"Cooper Noah," I say, sticking my hand out toward her. She smiles at me, and she really is a gorgeous woman. She's got nothing on Gabby, though. "Are you here to sing?"

She nods. "I've been asked to do a song to open for Vail, and I'll also be singing the national anthem."

"Incredible. Thanks for being here to support us today."

"I'm so pleased the team asked. I'm happy to be here to cheer for the home team." She smiles, and it lights up the room.

"Are you local?" I ask.

She nods. "I grew up in Henderson and still have family here, though I'm based out of Los Angeles now. And sometimes New York."

"My buddy Danny is dying to meet you."

She chuckles, and the man with her doesn't react—which makes me think he's either used to it or he's not married to her. "I'd love to meet Danny."

I lead her over toward him, and he's clearly pretending to focus on the five cards he holds in his hands. "Brewer," I grunt out, and he turns to look at me. He sets his cards down and stands as his eyes edge over to the woman beside me. "I'd like to introduce you to Alexis Bodega."

Now I've known Danny Brewer a long time. I've seen the way he handles women. He's confident—as he should be. He's never had a problem with a single one of them falling over their own feet to get to him.

But something happens when Alexis Bodega's eyes fall to his.

I think Danny Brewer might be in a whole lot of trouble.

Chapter 27
Cooper

There was excitement and fanfare, and the loud roar of the crowd helped lead us to our very first victory…and our second.

And now we're in the clubhouse waiting to head out to the field to start our third game of the season. It could be a clean sweep of the Braves, something Duke is especially excited about since we're playing his former team.

Nobody ever believes in the expansion teams. The Vegas Heat, though? We're strong. We're fierce. We're fucking *ready*.

But today I'm a little extra nervous. It's not just the end of our opening series, but it's the end of our first home series.

We have tomorrow off, and then we're on the road for the next six games—six days in a row. We play three games against the White Sox followed by three games against the Padres. We'll be flying to Chicago and then straight to San Diego before returning home for one night off and then our next series will be at home against the Giants.

Gabby will be right by my side along for the ride as she takes footage and photos and creates captions to give our fans a behind the scenes look at what we do, but there are still team things she won't be a part of—plus she still has that last class to finish. She has a completely different perspective since she's not a player, and there will be moments that she can't be part of because of that.

But I'll have more of her than any of the other guys on the team will have with their women, and that makes me feel pretty damn lucky.

The nerves aren't just from closing out the first series and hitting the road, though.

No, I've got a plan for what's going to happen right after the game, and nothing would make that plan more special than clinching a victory.

Danny knows my plan, and he checks in with me an hour before the game. "You ready?"

I nod. "I've got this."

When it's thirty minutes before game time, we all head out to the field for our pregame routines. I take a lap around the bases. I swing by the first row and sign a few autographs. I glance around to locate my family, and I find them a few rows up near the third base line. Gabby sits beside my mother, and I grin at both of them from where I stand. My mom waves, and Gabby blows me a kiss. I pat my heart and wave back at them, and then I head over to the dugout to get my final stretches and routines in. I tug my sleeves down. I do some deep breathing exercises. I set my foot on the bench and lean over it to stretch out my calves.

And then it's go time.

The Braves bat first, and Rush strikes out our first batter. The second hits a pop fly to center, easily caught by Johnny Prater, and the third is a groundball fielded by AJ, who makes an easy out at first by hurling the ball over to Danny.

Troy has me at leadoff, so I hit first. The pitcher tosses me two balls, and when the third comes toward me, I knock it over to left field, easily getting on first.

Duke bats second and hits a grounder right to the short stop, and AJ is third. He hits a pop fly that's easily caught in left field, and then Danny's up at clean-up.

He knocks it all the way to the back fence right along the fair line in far right field, and I take off running. As I tag second and race toward third, I'm thankful for the training I did in the offseason. I'm grateful for Nick's program. I'm thankful I've gotten my speed back.

And, of course, I'm thankful for Gabby. I'm running as if I'm running toward her and our baby, and that's what pushes my legs into motion as I round third and head for home.

I check to my left to see the ball is coming in toward the pitcher, so I slide across the plate to the deafening roar of the crowd as I score the first run of this game.

I glance up at my family and offer a grin, and then I head toward the dugout where my boys slap me on the back and fist bump me as they cheer for my run.

Fuck yeah. It's good to be back.

We take the victory at three to two, a clean sweep of the Braves as Duke and Johnny score our other two runs.

After a quick celebration, the team clears the field and heads toward the clubhouse for food and rest. Some will hit the ice baths, others will get treatment from Nick, and most of us will head home.

But I head into the clubhouse, grab what I need, and head back toward the dugout as my heart races with nerves.

A moment later, Mike appears with a confused looking Gabby by his side.

"Thanks," I say to Mike, and he nods.

I grab her hand and pull her to me. I press a soft kiss to her lips.

"Good game, Captain," she murmurs, and I chuckle.

I pull her onto the field as the fireworks explode overhead, and I look at the jumbotron. She doesn't notice it yet, but it's there as "Love Story" by Taylor Swift fills the stadium.

"What are you doing?" she asks.

I smile down at her and offer a shrug as I turn her so she can't see the screen. "I fell in love with you the moment you sat beside me at a blackjack table, and every day since then you have completely stolen my heart. I want the world to know that you're mine and I'm yours. You are incredible, and you surprise me every day—from watching you turn from a girl who knew nothing about the game into this woman who manages the entire social media division of an MLB team to growing our baby with grace to patiently waiting for me to get my head out of my ass." She laughs, and that's the moment I choose to get down on my knee. Her wide eyes finally move to the jumbotron displaying a live feed of the two of us standing right here on the field next to the words *Say Yes!*

She lets out a soft gasp that comes just in between two loud cracks of fireworks as her hands move to cover her mouth in surprise.

I pinch the ring I plan to slide onto her finger between my pointer finger and my thumb. "I love you, Sunshine, and nothing would make me happier than spending the rest of my life with you. Will you marry me?"

She nods, and the entire place erupts into deafening cheers—maybe even louder than the ones I heard as I slid across home plate earlier.

I slide the ring onto her shaking hand, and then I push to a stand and grab her into my arms.

"Yes, yes, of course yes," she cries into my chest as she clings onto me, and then she tilts her head up and we kiss under the flashing shower of fireworks from above.

We only have a short beat to celebrate by ourselves before a huge group of people starts rushing toward us. Leading the pack is the man I thought would never get on board with this, but as Troy jogs toward us, he's smiling widely with Joanie just a few paces behind him. My mom and my brother and his family are just behind them, and I spot Kaylee and Ben behind them and my teammates coming out, too, but it's our families that get to us first.

We hug and we cry and we celebrate the joining of these two families, but we only have a few seconds to do it before I spot Danny and Rush. They each carry a bottle of champagne which they're currently shaking as they run toward us, and when they get close enough, I grab Gabby in my arms as they each unleash a spray of champagne over us.

I kiss her as our families and my teammates—my *brothers*—surround us, and as Taylor sings about the love story, I find my very own happy ending as it comes true.

I'm back in the game. I got the girl. We're having a baby. I have supportive friends, including my future father-in-law, who is one of my best friends. My brother is healthy, and my mom is here.

As it turns out, this life is pretty damn good.

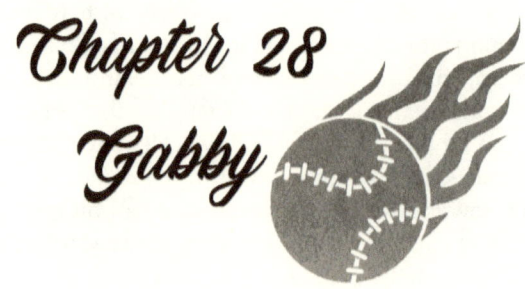

Chapter 28
Gabby

I meet Kaylee before the crack of dawn for a workout, and she takes me into a yoga room.

"We thought we'd try out some prenatal yoga, so we're interviewing a few different candidates," she tells me. "They're each here for a ten-minute segment with you today. Is that okay?"

"Of course."

"I'll be in there, too, but just to make it really, really clear, I'm in there for the interviews only. I am not pregnant."

"Right now," I tease.

"That I know of," she says with a shrug.

"Are you two trying?"

"He's trying every free moment he has, I'll tell you that much."

I giggle. Ben Olson is a former party animal tamed only by his sassy wife, but that doesn't mean he calmed down *all* the partying. He just parties with *her* now. Naked, apparently.

"I have some hot gossip, too, but I'm not supposed to talk about it."

"You can trust me," I say, goading her into telling me.

She giggles. "I know, and I also know you're a baseball girl now so you don't have a stake, but you know Travis Woods?"

I nod. "The wide receiver?"

"Yeah. I heard through the grapevine that he has some secret daughter nobody knows about. He's never even *met* her. Isn't that crazy?"

"Can you imagine having a child out there and not knowing?" I ask.

"I think it's a little different for women since we know when we give birth. I guess he slept with his mom's friend years and years ago and she and her husband couldn't have kids. Well she got preggo and nine months later out popped a girl with Travis's eyes."

My own eyes widen at the description.

"Kaylee?" a woman in a leotard and leggings asks as she walks up to us.

Kaylee's eyes widen as she pretends to zip her lips, and I nod my confirmation that I won't tell anyone the *hot gossip*.

The leotard lady is the first yoga instructor, so we get to our workouts as I help her decide which one to hire.

A few hours later, I'm back on the couch and I hold my hand out to stare at the ring again. The fire crackles in the fireplace as a movie plays on the television, and Cooper is snuggled in beside me with his hand on my thigh. I can't focus on anything but the gorgeous sparkle coming from the third finger of my left hand. It's a filigree vintage style halo ring with a round diamond, and I've never seen anything sparkle as brightly as it does…except, of course, for our love, as cheesy as that may be.

It's our one day off before we hit the road toward Chicago for our first away series, and I'm so ready for this. I'm excited to really dig into my job as I find my footing.

I know it will be chaos once we're on the road and it won't be like this, so I'm taking the time to soak in every second.

Until my phone rings.

I pick it up off the cushion next to me and my chest tightens as I flash the screen at Cooper. He pauses the movie.

"Are you going to answer it?" he asks.

"Do I have to?"

He shakes his head. "You don't have to do a damn thing you don't want to do."

"I have to face her eventually," I murmur, and with that, I pick up the call. "Hey Mom."

I don't get a hello back. I get a heavy sigh. "It's a sad, sad day when a mother discovers her daughter is engaged from a news story rather than from her daughter."

Yeah, it is sad. It's sad that she's the kind of person I don't bother sharing my news with anymore.

I don't say that. Instead, I say, "I'm so sorry. It's been a whirlwind and he did it in public so news broke fast."

It's not like I haven't had time to call her…but I honestly didn't think to. She was less than warm to him when she met him, and I'm not entirely sure I'm even inviting her to the wedding, whenever we decide to have it.

"Do you have any other news to share?" she asks.

"I got a job," I say proudly.

"At the stadium?"

"Yep. I'm the new social media manager for the Vegas Heat." My words are strong and proud as I sit up a little straighter.

"That's great. Did your dad get you that?"

I hear Cooper mutter a curse word beside me, but she's not the only person who will be wondering that same thing. "Nope. I got it all on my own, but thanks for the vote of confidence."

"It's not that. Don't be so dramatic. I'm sure you're perfectly capable. It's just that since he's the manager and part owner of the team, it would lead one to speculate—"

"Please don't finish that sentence," I say, interrupting her. "I worked hard to get where I am." I keep my tone even but firm.

"Of course you did. You know, when I was your age, I had to give up my career because I was pregnant with you." She sniffs a little, as if the damage of that still haunts her all these years later, and maybe it does. But you know what? It's not my fault, and it's not my problem.

"That's so interesting because the organization I work for actually hired me an assistant who can fill in for me when I'm on maternity leave, and then I can slide right back into my position once I'm ready and able. And I have lots of daycare options, too."

"Well, money will do that for anybody, I suppose," she mutters, and I wait a beat for her to connect the dots. "Wait a minute. Are you saying you're pregnant?"

And there it is.

"I am saying that," I confirm.

She's quiet on the other end of the line.

Imagine that.

My mother: speechless.

I never thought I'd see the day.

"Are you happy?" she asks softly.

"Happier than I ever imagined I could be," I say.

"Congratulations, then. I guess you turned out better than I ever could have hoped you would."

I'll take that as a win.

I hang up with her, and Cooper leans over and kisses my cheek. "What's that for?" I ask.

"Your volume is really loud. I heard every word you both said, and I just wanted to tell you that I love you, and I'm proud of you."

"Right back at you, Captain," I say with a grin.

He chuckles. "She may never say the things you want her to or be the type of mother you deserve, but that conversation seemed like a step in the right direction."

I nod. "I think it was," I murmur, and he kisses me again before putting the movie back on and I go back to staring at my ring.

That is, of course, until the phone rings again.

And this time it's Mia calling.

Just like a few minutes ago, Cooper reads the screen and pauses the movie.

"News must be out, huh?" he says, nodding at my screen. "Are you going to answer that one?"

"You know, I think I will." I shoot him a sugary sweet smile, and he gives me a warning look like I should probably play nice.

But maybe I don't want to play nice right now.

"Hi Mia," I answer.

"You got engaged?" Mia shrieks.

"I did, despite what your boyfriend did to try to tear us apart."

She clears her throat. "Ahem. My *ex*-boyfriend."

"You broke up with him?"

"Yeah. I've been such an asshole, Gabs. I'm so sorry. I stopped by your dad's house a few days ago but nobody answered, and I've been wanting to reach out and call but I couldn't work up the nerve. It had to have looked like I chose him over you, and it was never like that."

"It was exactly like that, Mia, and it hurts that you agreed with him. I got the full-time position, and I got it on my own merits. You can believe what you want to believe, but that's the truth."

"I know what a hard worker you are," she says softly. "I know you got it because you deserved it. As it turns out, I think Dylan might've been using me to try to get to Troy."

I sink back into the cushion at her words.

I never thought about how being the daughter of a celebrity could affect the people around me, and I'm sure the same can be said for being engaged to a different celebrity as well. Cooper reaches over and squeezes my hand as if he has the same thought at the same time I do.

"Oh, Mia. I'm so sorry."

"It's not your fault. I was stupid and I was blind, but I hope we can find a way to get our friendship back," she says. I can hear the emotion in her voice, and I have to admit...I miss her.

"It might take some time, but I think we can," I say, my own voice emotional, too.

We're both quiet a beat, and then she says, "So you're engaged?"

I giggle. "Yeah. And knocked up."

I think I shock her into silence for a beat, and then she squeals. "Holy shit! Congrats, girl!"

"Thank you," I say.

We chat another few minutes, and I do feel like eventually we can get our trust in each other back, though it might take some work on both ends—work that'll be hard with a job where I travel and eventually with a baby at home, but work I'm willing to put in if she is.

I feel like I have it all. A big circle of friends, a brand-new job, my father *and* my mother in my life along with a better group of future in-laws than I ever could've imagined, a baby on the way, and most importantly, the man sitting beside me currently lacing his fingers through mine.

When I sat down at that blackjack table on my twenty-first birthday, I never could've imagined the curveballs life was about to throw at me.

And I couldn't be happier.

Epilogue
Gabby

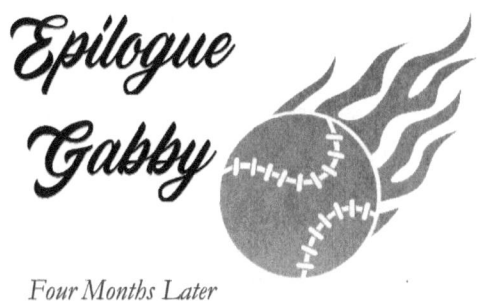

Four Months Later

My last day at work was August twentieth.

The week before that, Cooper and I celebrated our one-year anniversary on my twenty-second birthday. Three months before that, I graduated college with top honors.

All these celebrations have included lots and lots of sex with my future husband. Apparently seeing my pregnant body does unexpected things to Cooper, starting with the fact that he thinks it's ultra-hot that he put that baby in me.

It's been seventeen days since my last day at work, and I am already bored out of my mind...plus I miss Cooper. A lot.

Traveling with a professional baseball team has been quite the adventure. Most of the guys on the team have taken me under their wing. I'm like the team little sister to everyone except Cooper, who will call me *wife* at some point.

He put a ring on it, but we haven't set a date. We figure we'll hammer it out sometime in the off-season when we can both sit down and think and plan together.

We're grateful for the time we've had together through this first season. I've seen him more than I thought I would, but that all changed once I started my maternity leave.

And now I'm sitting at my dad's house with Joanie, watching him on television as I wait for him to text or call after the game. I've slept here all week just in case the baby decided to come early, and the room Cooper once stayed in has now been converted to a nursery thanks to the help of the incredibly talented Kate Dalton.

The Heat has had a series out of town since September first, but they return later tonight. They get one night off before playing the eighth through the thirteenth. This little one is due the ninth—

under a week away now—and I'm praying she gets here while he's home just to make things a little easier on us.

Yes, *she*. My instinct was right on.

Our team wins, and I get a text from Cooper shortly after the game.

Captain: *How are you feeling?*

Me: *Very large but okay. Good game.*

Uncomfortably large at this point. I think the baby dropped and now every time I walk, she's laying directly on my bladder and causing cramps.

Captain: *Hard to focus tonight. I'm thinking about you.*

Me: *Right back at you. Love you.*

Captain: *Right back at you too. Boarding plane soon, should be home by midnight.*

Me: *I'll make sure to keep this little one inside until then.*

He sends a laughing emoji, and that's when I feel it.

The first twinge.

Or, rather, the first rocket of pain as it shoots through my abdomen. "Oh shit," I murmur.

A seven-month pregnant Joanie glances over at me. "You okay?"

I shake my head as I wince. "I think I just had a contraction."

"Oh shit," Joanie echoes. "Does it hurt?"

I chuckle. "It sure as hell doesn't feel *good*."

"I'll call Cooper," she says, lifting to a stand.

I shake my head. "He's just getting on a plane. I don't want him flying worried when he can't make it go any faster. He'll be here soon, and I haven't timed these out yet."

"Right. Okay. Do your breathing, okay? I'll do it with you." She starts to pace as she sucks in loud breaths before exhaling like she's blowing out birthday candles. She's more panicked than I am, and I can't help a laugh.

"Does it feel better?" she asks, pausing in her pacing.

"A little, but honestly the entertainment here is top notch."

She tilts her head and glares a little at me. "Listen, you'd be freaked out if your future daughter-in-law was giving birth two months before you, too. First of all, I have to take care of you or your father will punish me. And second of all, I have to watch you go through this first. I get to see just exactly how painful it is to give myself two months to get even more worked up about it."

"Drama queen," I tease, and her glare deepens.

"I am not!"

I give her a *yeah, okay* sarcastic glance as I turn my attention back to the television, and she finally sits back down.

It's about ten minutes later when I wince as another one of those pains plows into me.

"That was twelve minutes," Joanie announces.

"Nothing to worry about until they're five minutes apart," I say.

"Right. But how bad does it suck?"

I work my way through it, and then I sit back and take some of those deep breaths. "I mean, if I have to wait through these overnight, I'm not sleeping, that's for damn sure."

"Let's do something, then. Want to go for a walk? Try to get things moving along?" she asks, standing up again.

"No!" I practically yell. "I want to slow things down so Cooper's here for the birth of his child."

"Slow down, slow down," she mutters as she grabs her phone and starts typing. "Okay, lay on your left side and drink a lot of water. Dehydration can cause contractions. Oh, and empty your bladder."

"So drink water but also have an empty bladder? Great advice, thanks." I roll my eyes, and she giggles.

"You do realize the two of us know nothing about babies, right?" she asks.

"Yes, I do realize that. I've read a couple books over the last few months, but I feel like nothing will prepare me more than actually being in the thick of it," I say. "Plus I have Cooper, who has nephews, so he has at least a little experience."

"Lucky. Troy has zero."

I shrug. "I know, with a big fat thanks to my mother."

"At least we get to watch you go through it first so I can get some pointers."

I laugh. This is what we have become. In a lot of ways, Joanie is more like a sister to me than a future stepmother. We work together, sometimes we live together, and we have fun together. We tease each other and we can laugh it off because we're family now.

"Oh God, here comes another one," I say.

"That time it was only nine minutes."

"Thank God one of us is timing these," I mutter.

"I'm here for you, girl. Lay on your left side. See if that slows things down."

It doesn't. They move to eight minutes and then seven, but they stick at seven for a little while.

It's a little after midnight when Cooper texts me.

Captain: *You still awake?*

Fuck yes I'm still awake! I'm freaking contracting!

Me: *Yep!*

Captain: *I'll be home soon. Can't wait to see you.*

I don't tell him to hurry because I just want him to get here safely. They'll take a bus back to the stadium and then he'll be home shortly after that.

Me: *I'm at my dad's.*

Captain: *Okay, I'll come there. See you soon.*

Joanie is still awake, too, and maybe a little traumatized by the fact that I'm going into labor, but that's why I'm here with her...so I don't have to go through it alone.

And I love her for being here with me.

Cooper and my father walk through the door at the same time. They're laughing at something they must have shared out on the front porch, and I'm wincing with another contraction as they walk in, my hand over my stomach as Joanie kneels beside me breathing with me.

Both Cooper and my dad freeze when they see the picture in front of them.

"Are you in labor?" Cooper asks.

"Her contractions just moved to five minutes apart," Joanie says, and I keep breathing because the pain seems to be getting stronger with each one.

"It's go time," Cooper says. "Is your hospital bag here?"

I nod. "In my truck." I open my notes app and read off what I need him to pack that isn't in my bag. "I need my toiletry bag in the bathroom upstairs and my phone charger. I think I have everything else."

He's as calm as ever as he heads upstairs to get the things I need, and he returns a beat later. "Snacks?" he asks, and I nod.

Joanie races over to the pantry and starts pulling things out, tossing them in a grocery bag.

"Calm down," Cooper says with a chuckle.

"I'm sorry if I'm not *calm*!" Joanie protests. "I've been dealing with her contractions for the last four hours while you all flew home!"

He sets his hand on her shoulder. "Thank you for taking care of her. I've got it from here."

And he does.

He tells Joanie and my father that he will let them know when he has any news at all, and he drives calmly to the hospital in my truck since that's where the car seat is already installed with my hospital bag snuggled into it.

And seven long hours later, at seven twenty-one in the morning, a beautiful baby girl with Cooper's blue eyes comes tumbling out of me.

I cry as the nurse places her on my chest. Cooper's eyes are misty as he kisses me and tells me how much he loves me, and we both stare down at the perfect little life we created together.

"Baby girl's name?" the nurse asks.

I nod at Cooper.

"Sunny Rose," Cooper says. The perfect name for our little one, made even more meaningful because we share a middle name.

He leans in toward me, a calming presence as always as he kisses my temple. "Good thing it's a girl," he says with a chuckle.

I glance over at him. "Why's that?"

"Because if we went with your nickname for me plus my middle name, the baby would've been named Captain Michael."

I giggle despite the exhaustion. "Captain Michael. Maybe for baby number two."

"Talking about baby number two already and baby number one isn't even an hour old yet?" the nurse asks. "You two must really be in love."

Cooper sits on the side of the bed. He sets his hand on the baby's back covered in blankets. With his other hand, he squeezes mine. "I thought I loved her as much as I could ever love anybody, and then she gave me this gift." He pats Sunny's back. "And just like that, I love her even more."

I smile up at him as the same sentiment seems to run through me.

We definitely played hardball to get here, but through all the curveballs life has thrown at me, Cooper Noah is my favorite.

The End

Hardball

Want more Cooper and Gabby? Scan this QR code for a bonus epilogue!

Acknowledgments

First as always, a big thank you to my husband who I couldn't do this without and also to my kids who are my reason for reaching high for my goals.

Thank you to the women who have become my team over the last decade that I've been publishing books: Autumn Gantz, Trenda London, Diane Holtry, and Renee McCleary. The release of this series wouldn't have happened without everything you've all done for me, and I could not appreciate you more. A huge thank you to my new beta reader, Billie DeSchalit, for your eyes on these books, too.

To my ARC Team, thank you for your enthusiasm and support in reading and reviewing all five books ahead of time and being prompt with your reviews. You are an amazing group of readers and I am forever grateful to have you. A special thank you to my Facebook reader group, Team LS, and the Vegas Aces and Heat Recovery Room for all your support and love of my books. I love you!

Thank you to the bloggers and influencers who read and review my books and to you, the reader, for giving Cooper a chance. I hope you loved his story, and I can't wait to bring you more VEGAS HEAT! Danny Brewer is up next, and he's got quite a story to tell. And I'm not done with football, so get ready for more VEGAS ACES coming your way!

Until next season, Happy Reading!

xoxo,

Lisa Suzanne

About the Author

Lisa Suzanne is a romance author who resides in Arizona with her husband and two kids. She's a former high school English teacher and college composition instructor. When she's not cuddling or chasing her kids, she can be found working on her latest book or watching reruns of *Friends*.

Also by Lisa Suzanne

SCORING POSITION
Vegas Heat: Bases Loaded
Book 1

DATING THE DEFENSIVE BACK
The Nash Brothers Book 1

www.ingramcontent.com/pod-product-compliance
Lightning Source LLC
Chambersburg PA
CBHW020604040726
47498CB00003B/624